IN THE WAKE OF OUR PAST

SCOTT P. TINLEY

MONTEZUMA PUBLISHING

SAN DIEGO, CALIFORNIA

Published by

Montezuma Publishing

Aztec Shops Ltd.

San Diego State University

San Diego, California 92182-1701

619-594-7552

www.montezumapublishing.com

ISBN: 978-1-7269-0273-1

Publishing Manager: Lia Dearborn

Cover Design: Angelica Lopez

Design and Layout: Angelica Lopez

Formatting: Angelica Lopez

Scott Tinley, a seventh generation Southern Californian, has been a university instructor and freelance writer for nearly twenty years. He has published five volumes of non-fiction, a collection of short fiction, and numerous texts in literary journals and mainstream publications. A former paramedic, sailing instructor, and professional triathlete, Tinley holds a Ph.D. in Cultural Studies from Claremont Graduate University, and counts the final end of the Selective Service draft for the Vietnam War as one of the happiest days of his life. His draft number was 13.

"Tinley has long been one of sport's deepest thinkers, an Ironman of words and wisdom. Here, in his sparkling debut novel, he combines powerful prose with a meditative journey. Like many of us who palpably felt the Vietnam War through its echoes, the author reminds us that its harbingers of waste are still haunting. Come along for the ride. You won't regret it."

– Armen Keteyian, 11-Time Emmy Winner, anchor for *The Athletic*

✳ ✳ ✳

"Tinley's characters personify the traumas of war and their profound effects on families and society as a whole. But in the end, there is hope that the Vietnam War and the evolution of the American South have taught us something about the resilience of the human condition; that even oppression can be repressed."

– Nico Marcolongo, CAF Operation Rebound Program Manager and Iraq War Veteran

✳ ✳ ✳

"Tinley's massive novel-cum-memoir is not only impressively knowledgeable and wide ranging, but both blessed and burdened with sentiment, the potent feelings of the heart."

– Harold Jaffe, Editor-In Chief, *Fiction International*, Author of *Terror-dot-Gov*, *False Positive*, and other volumes

iv

"Tinley writes, 'It's not so much the content that matters, but what it means to you.'" It is this theme that Tinley masterfully weaves into a compelling story. One that offers rare insight into the human experience of living through acts and events that betray our sense of self and the world. He rests the story on the overwhelming power that meaning has to deconstruct our beliefs about identity, purpose, and satisfaction. And, ultimately, the hope that renewed meaning can bring us back to a place of peace and understanding. A truly powerful and penetrating work."

– Nathaniel A. Brown, M.D., Psychiatrist and Combat Veteran

✳ ✳ ✳

"Scott Tinley daringly conjures spirits, channels voices, and raises the dead from a sprawling terra incognita. Time and distance are the measure and means by which the man has lived. Here he trades the bike for a tightrope. Audacious."

– Chris Carter, Creator of the *X-Files*

CONTENTS

The author would like to acknowledge the many people who have contributed directly and indirectly to this work: my Uncle Bill, who flew two tours with the USAF in the Vietnam War, a stand-up man/pilot who dropped bombs on the North from his F-4 and was never the same; Don Anderson, editor at the journal, *War, Literature, and the Arts,* who published an early version of one chapter signaling that themes of negotiating the effects of war were always and already resonant; Harold Jaffe, for challenging me to write that chapter more from the gut than the heart; the entire cadre of "Nam-lit" writers from Baker to Caputo to Didion to Greene to Halberstam to Heinemann to Herr to Ketwig to Kovic to O'Brien (especially to Tim O'Brien) to Maraniss to O'Nan to Stone to Steinman to Terry to Webb to Woods, and the many others in between—you all marched on point. And finally, to my amazing editor, Sandra Parsons, without whom this book, like the concept of war, would still haunt me from the dark corners of my writerly past.

BOOK 1

JOHNNY COBB

"Everybody might be just one big soul,

Well it looks that way to me

Everywhere that you look in the day or night

That's where I'm gonna be, ma

That's where I'm gonna be."

Woody Guthrie, *Ballad of Tom Joad*

PROLOGUE

A dying can do funny things to a person. Part of them can leave with the passing of another soul and another part might gain strength, as if the deceased gifted their final breath on the dying embers of some warming fire. And often, those who are closest to the death will not know how to interpret this newfound heat within their hearts as it pushes up against the steely cold pain caused by the loss. It's a fine line.

Here's a good riddle: What travels uphill faster than down? Fire, of course. If you can outrun the fire and jump off the other side of the mountain, consider yourself lucky. You will only fall though a hole in your life. It might be a space of soft clouds or clear air before you meet Mother Earth. Smack. Choose your poison or your perfume, for dying by fire will surely kill all of you. The brave ones though, they will wait at the top and hope the fires of pain will melt the snow near the peak, turn them into water that runs downhill. It's always a risk.

When Ruth died I felt the flames building alongside the winter of my heart, fire and ice eyeing each other precariously, the glacier her death caused holding fast. It was like my mind starting to work differently; sharper in the middle, but dull around the edges.

The words, too, they came out differently—thoughtful, strange, like a neighbor who'd lived next door for years knocking on the door to introduce himself.

This isn't Ruth's story. Or mine, or Harry's, or Phin's, or any one person who became a party to and a part of my life as it unfolded. And while it seems that this story is book-ended with tragedy, I like to think of its circularity as its truth; that it really did, really could happen this way. The lived life just ain't an easy thing to go through. But when you consider the alternatives—being mostly dead while you're alive, or never even being alive at all—I'll take what I was given.

Whether or not you think this is all made up or whether you take it as pure fact, it matters little. It's what I remember as far as I could separate the two. I done a lot of talking early on, mostly to try and make sense of it all. And then I let Phin tell his own piece. Probably for the same reason.

The other voice that fills in the blanks? Well, that's just a sound that made itself up, split down the middle of the page but joined together at the heart. Or maybe it's the reader's thoughts jumping out of their head and landing on the page.

Like I said, it's true, or at least ought to be. Because it's like those little silver charms shaped like half a heart-shaped puzzle—you can't buy them separately and you best be giving away the other half to the right person to complete the circle. I've done my best to keep my half. And I know that Phin and Harry and the others have done theirs. I'm beginning it and pray God if I don't get to, the right person will get it done. Or not. Ahab's whale showed us all that. White ain't always perfect and the best we can do is try and get some color and light to stick to the canvas along the way. Job talked about it in the Bible. So did Phin, in his own way.

It starts here with Ruth, the only one I knew who started out at both ends, looking skyward, and ended up in the middle, looking down.

My God, she was a woman.

CHAPTER 1

LUNCH IN PANAMA

It wasn't just a boat. It was the beginning of it all. That mahogany craft that'd feather across a shallow lake or inshore sound. Some place littoral. The little boat had transcended something that only floats time. Over the years, the eleven-foot skiff and everything that followed in its wake would melt the huge block of ice that had formed around my heart. How I'd sensed it at the time, I do not know. Many changes swept over me in those weeks and months after Ruth passed, reshaping and reordering the person who now speaks these words. My place in the world, how and where I'd plant my size-thirteen working boots, had been uprooted when she died. It was as if a great funnel of wind had ravaged an ancient oak whose roots had grown beyond the shadow of its leaves.

A dead wife and son and boat sharing a name; this is where my story begins.

✳ ✳ ✳

The *Ruth Henry David* belonged in a fisherman's hands, not mine. I'd come from the dark-red loam of the South. Only things fluid I was drawn to were ideas and draft beer. The boat wasn't mine, never was. It'd killed my wife, Ruth. I had a mind to burn the damn thing. But I was meant to give it away, to make it go away. It shoulda belonged to a man who made his living in the sea—a fisherman whose fate and reputation and identity rose with the tide and the day's catch.

The great oceans, the right and left coasts of the Atlantic and the Pacific, seemed too far away. The Middle South had a hold around me, not like a noose, but more like the thick arms of another Black man telling me that it would get better in years to come, that we deserved to be here, to stay the course, that we were part of this land, bound at first with chains, then with song, and now with bloodlines and will.

Of course, I'd fought the idea at first, taking a boat away instead of just letting the lake have it. Nobody knew its owner. And there was little chance they'd appear after someone had died in it. The boat had always been there, nestled between the sawgrass and the lake's murky edge. People had been using it to row around the lake since I could remember. But it belonged to me now on account of it was jinxed. I could burn the little boat or I could move it, seeing where its travels would take me.

At first, I resisted the trip I'd be taking to gift it properly. I'd have to go down to the Gulf, the closest ocean I knew of then. And to do it on the words of a White man whose name I didn't know? Who'd a thought it? But there was no denying the push from something near my head and the pull from another force at my feet: I had to go.

I'd lost a wife and our child-to-be, but something unidentifiable, a thing wonderfully tragic and mutated, and was growing out of me. It could never be a trade, but in the area between "whys" and "because so's," it was at least a bridge.

Ruth's Uncle Chuck hadn't returned after her drowning and the boat was just left there at the lake. Chuck, whose disposition had begun to oscillate between heavy weather and bluebird skies, seemed to be forever starring in his own movie. He wasn't so much conflicted as he was fragmented.

About the boat. I was told that one of the folks who kept a hunting shack near the lake had tied it to the dock the night Ruth left us. A few months after her dying one of the local Blacks sent me a message to please come and fetch it. He had tried to get word to Uncle Chuck through a mutual acquaintance, but Chuck wasn't ready to return to the site of Ruth's drowning; later, he would claim, for fear of lacerating self-doubt. Most people figured he'd just gone and checked himself out; put a lot of distance between him and what happened. But I was sensing it was something else. Some folk thought he'd gone away to off himself. I didn't believe that. Ruth's uncle never did anything easy. And I wasn't ready to go looking for a man who didn't want to be found. When he was ready, Chuck would find me.

In the meantime, I wrestled with my own absence that visited me each night as I lie alone without her, struggling with it all, thinking at first that no one, no one in the world, had any right to weep for her. No one 'cept me. Those were some hard moons to sleep under.

One night, early into the short, thin winter of '51, well over three hundred days since she'd died late last spring, my twenty-sixth year of breathing God's air, I left our bed and drove the farm truck out past the last row of alfalfa. Telling the dogs to stay in the truck, I walked alone into the wall of cypress and moss and earth so deep and unpredictable that you could fall into a bog, get stuck up to your armpits, and no man would find you until the turkey vultures had picked your upper torso clean down past the bone to suck even the marrow from your center. Before that night, I wouldn't go in that place beyond our property, even during the day with six men, five dogs, and three guns. Somehow, I wasn't afraid that night.

Darkness and aloneness, they deserved each other like I deserved them.

And there, past the wall of old growth that swayed and pumped in the wind creating moon shadows like a child's fingers on a bedroom wall, in the heart of it, was a hard-pack clay trail winding its way through the tall shrubs, sometimes straight and narrow, other times winding back on itself. It was paralleled by a thin, crisp stream with river rock supporting the banks where it might have eroded the path. At places, the waning gibbous moon would slice through the hanging limbs and I'd see footprints in the middle of the path.

I walked for hours, feeling closer to the world I had tried to separate myself from. The path never forked. Never was there a chasm so wide that I couldn't hurdle it. At some point the path made a small keyhole and turned back on itself. Any denial of Ruth's death would from then on simply be a fear of my own fear.

In the morning when the sun rose, I found myself asleep in the bed of the truck, warmed by dogs, leaves, and the beginning of acceptance. I turned the truck around and headed home, thinking that the young Black poet had said it right—*my soul had grown deep like the river*. Still, I wasn't ready to jump in or cross it. Just try and make some peace with it.

At first, I'd asked around if anybody in the area could use the boat. But people are funny about things like that. I'd heard a boat can take on a certain spirit, maybe its own personal history. The roots might be in Caribbean voodoo or they might be set in the tales laid down over the years from the great explorers and pirates alike, seaman from Portugal and Spain and England. All the locals knew this boat had originally been a White man's boat used on occasion by common Black people, a boat that had already killed a person. A lot of these folks were the type to keep one eye on their Southern Baptist dogma and the other on the color of a man's skin.

But they, too, believed that the most trustworthy of vessels is always named after a woman who had been the love of a seaman's life. The *Queen Mary* is as sound as the day she was rolled down the slipways in 1936. The *Arizona*, the *Titanic*, the *Indianapolis*—all bottom havens for fish and human skeletons, and the memories haunting those still on top who might've followed her down.

Uncle Chuck had stenciled in charcoal the words *"Foolish Pleasure"* across the transom just the day before the accident—some sort of thinly veiled reference to his penchant for cards, the game that had won him the next day's use of the boat when cash and violence were not options.

Weeks later when I finally went to pick it up, she was part sunk, banging against the old pier and half-filled with dirty lake water, rusty beer cans, and two unused life jackets that were already fading in the thin January sun. The stillness made me shiver and I fought the memories, almost deciding to abandon her. A voice came up behind me.

"You know there are people round these parts who say Negroes can't swim, that they weren't meant to be cleansed by water. This here section of the lake is one of the only places where the Black man is allowed to go in the water. Closer-to-town Black folks can't even go on the lakeshore."

Suffocating halfway between desperation and despair, the sound that joined me felt at first like two vocal hands around my throat. In the distance a dog barked and the sound carried out over the water. I lowered my eyes but did not turn around.

"This hate, it's a burden for the White man and the Negro alike." The voice softened a bit.

"The difference is that the Negro is constantly aware of it; it moves before and behind him, a two-sided shadow, a gray past, and a gray future. The Southern White man is the same, but different. Those, too, are chains, having to live inside the fear that someday the Negro might rise up and resist. And then what, I ask you? How many will suffer in the wake of this past ignorance carried down the years like a flesh-eating disease? I got a family. It's a good one. What will happen to them when the South burns?"

A long silence moved between us as the mirrored-lake reflected the absence of sound. Another dog bark, penetrating even the sun's brilliance, daring me to speak. The water was so smooth I would've been afraid to pick up a rock and skip it across for fear of cracking the surface.

I started to say, "Yassir," to move slowly to the left and face the voice. But then I heard a clicking metallic sound and gravel-crunching footsteps moving toward me. It sounded like chain and an air of musk-oil cologne mixed with day-old sweat seemed to envelop my head. A large hand came up on my shoulder and the voice spoke in the same even, factual baritone.

"I was here that day. I saw you pull her out. Saw her with child. Nothing a man can say to another 'bout that."

Out on the lake, a small carp jumped up and snagged a mosquito. They were rising early for such a mild day.

"Come on, son," the voice said. "I think if we can get this chain around a bulkhead we can winch her out with my truck. Got to be a man somewhere who's got better use for a nice little boat than letting her die a slow death by abandonment."

I turned slowly, gaining my senses and a feeling of hope released from indenture. Facing the large man, it was as if I was seeing a vision—part awe, part disbelief.

"Well," he continued, "had you picked out a name for the child yet?"

We stood on even ground, me well over six feet back then before gravity started pulling me down. But though I could say he looked thicker, he was no taller, and his skin, like any man's, was shaded by its location and his occupation: darker on the arms from working outside, redder around the neck from underexposure.

"Ruth had a feeling," I spoke slowly, clearing out the effigies that had snuck into my mind under the fear, "that it was going to be a boy, so we had mostly settled on Henry David."

"And so it is," he concluded. "After we load her up, you'll have a little boat called the *Ruth Henry David*, if you'd like."

I'd also heard that the only thing worse than misnaming a boat by gender was changing the name after she'd been owned. But I did not speak those words. Just reflected on Uncle Chuck's *Foolish Pleasure* and how it had all gone south.

Over the years I've found that when men are supposed to talk to each other, they clam up, and when they ought to respect the silence, they gaggle on like coyotes claiming a kill. When some men are full of bravado, maybe after their own form of kill, their balls swing like a clock pendulum, ticking away at the coward beneath. They will speak loud and sloppy on any subject that enters their mind. At times like these you can spot the better man by the language of his hands, his back, and the way he holds himself up against the sky and the angle of the earth that has just been pitched at him.

I never learned the man's name. He never offered, I never asked. We pulled the *Ruth Henry David* out with the chains and his truck and our backs. She was loaded in silence onto the back of my truck, tied down, and made ready to move. I wiped the sweat from my eyes with the back of my hand as the stranger returned with a can of black paint and a small brush.

"Go ahead, young man, it's not a tombstone."

I scrubbed away Uncle Chuck's *Foolish Pleasure* with sweat and intent and painted the new name, the letters almost child-like on account of my heart's pounding. And then I opened the door to the truck, pausing just long enough to push out my hand at the man coiling a length of rope and chain. He shook it tightly, motioned to the chains and said that one day neither of us will carry these. I nodded, said, "Yes sir, someday. Someday."

"I know of a man down in Panama City Beach on the Gulf," he spoke while tying off the rope, almost after the fact. "He fishes the outer bars for shrimp and bass and amber jack. Wife just had a boy. Reckon he might be in the market for a skiff like the *Ruth Henry*." He turned back to his rope, handed me a piece of paper with some writing on it, and said no more.

I turned the key in my truck. The motor started on the first try.

Heading south to the Gulf, more than just skirting the Mississippi/Alabama state line, across Mobile Bay, then east along the Florida Panhandle on Route 98 from Fort Walton and into Panama City Beach, there was time to think about how it had to be. Since the Ford would overheat if I drove it too long under any sun, the trip took me three days. Sleeping in the bed at night on dirt side roads, I chanced the daytime main roads, thinking that a Black man caught with a boat lacking proper ownership papers might prompt questions that had no acceptable answer.

Still, it wasn't an unpleasant time.

* * *

Back in that winter of '51, Panama City Beach seemed
a town trying its damndest to be one, but was falling short.
Its main road ran parallel to the coast, not but a hundred
yards from the water in places, and was slurry tarred over
a bed of gravel that had already leaked through the asphalt
at the intersections. There was a small gathering of shops: a
restaurant with a hand-painted sign in the window that said,
"No catfish on Friday;" a bakery that smelled like Sunday
mornings; and a bait and tackle store that advertised, "Our live
bait is guaranteed."

Across the empty streets was a filling station. Gas
was eighteen cents for a gallon, a penny more than up in
Mobile. The town was real quiet, and for me on that mid-week
afternoon in January 1951 it seemed hotter than it should be
for winter. There'd be no place to hide in this town if you were
looking to, especially for someone who was defined by his
wound—the loss of a good wife doesn't wash off with one bar of
soap. A Negro with a short fuse, regardless of fault, needed to
keep clear of White boys playing with matches.

I opted for the small family diner and pulled the truck
into the dirt lot. Entering the side door I removed my hat and
sat near the back in the *Negroes Only* section. The place was
quiet, well lit, and near empty. I couldn't recall which day of the
week it was, but it felt like a Wednesday, maybe a Thursday, but
definitely not a Friday or a Tuesday.

"Specials are there on the board. Soup's split pea today
and we're out of the chicken fried steak."

She wore her hair up in a high bun and the strands
running down her forehead were kept to the side by blowing
air through determined lips. The eyes and nose said Creole, the
name tag said *Winnie.* Her voice was mixed-up South and she
looked forty. But I would've bet cash money her date of birth
put her ten under that.

"We're out of menus and fixin' to shut the lunch specials
down in a few minutes so you best be thinkin' 'bout what you
gonna order right quick."

"That soup any good? I mean, did you try it for
yourself?"

Winnie looked around to see where the others were and lowered her voice.

"Reckon they're gonna scrape the pan and you'll end up with a bunch of burnt up black peas that ain't supposed to be black."

"I see. Well, that being the case, and you looking like a woman who knows her job, just bring me the bologna sandwich and a cup of black coffee if you don't mind."

Winnie seemed like the kind of woman who wasn't raised as much as she was jerked up by the world, a consequence of some bourbon and a lustful night. In her hybrid hostess world, she had to show covert kindness to the Negroes on the installment plan. I liked her straight away.

"You ain't from around here, are you?" She over-filled my coffee, spilling a little onto the counter, and letting it lie there.

"No, ma'am. I'm from north of Mobile, sort of 'tween Mt. Vernon and Chatom, off I-45.

"You down here to fish or something, 'cuz I seen that boat on your truck outside," and added absently, "Went to Gumbo Lake as a little girl...once."

The last part of her sentence trailed off as she spun around with an arm full of dirty plates, one eye on the manager who had an ear open to any conversation between the help and the customers. I sensed her dilemma and spoke to the two thin slices of Weber's bread that held the bologna and impotent lettuce in my hands. And thought of that watery grave called Gumbo Lake.

"No, ma'am. I'm not much for the water. Just down in these parts to deliver that boat to a man, a local by the name of Davis, Mr. Harry Davis." I pulled the slip of paper from my shirt pocket to prove it so. "He's a commercial fishing type, I hear. I'd be obliged if you might consider how I'd find this Mr. Davis."

The manager moved in our direction, a tall, thin White man except for the shelf near his waist that appeared as if he was hiding a basketball inside his shirt.

"Listen, boy, our gals is awfully busy here so if you're looking for conversation or information I suggest you join the other Coloreds in the back or go see the Chamber of Commerce."

He threw a look at Winnie, told the kitchen staff to shut down lunch orders, and moved back into a conversation with a couple sitting at the counter drinking well-iced Cokes. They reminded me of the audience I'd seen on the *Ed Sullivan Show* as I'd passed a downtown window in Mobile a few years earlier.

I got the bill from my waitress with an address on the back, paid it with a pocket full of quarters, and slipped the yellow paper in my jeans pocket. The manager looked over his shoulder to see me leave, but I turned and faced him for just enough time that it took for me to conjure up the right combination of strength and empathy. He must've seen it, though I doubt he felt it. He could match the idea of hate but not my empathy, and looked away in the pity of what I hoped but didn't think would be self-disgust. I'd made an enemy, but it was his world, not mine that would define the term.

I left a dollar on the counter and walked out into the heated ambiguity thinking I'd have myself a little quiet shade before I went looking for the man, Davis. I drove the beach road looking for a willowed spot close, but not too close, to the water. It was well-past noon and I could see men doing things here and there, but most of them doing nothing at all.

My mind wandering a bit, I'd see Uncle Chuck in the shadows of an old cypress, lying on his back, staring at the rays of the sun. Other times he'd appeared as a reflection in a puddle after a rain. Once he was right there in the rearview mirror and I turned around to see if he was sitting in the back seat. And then there was the time last week when he came to me in a dream, begging my forgiveness for the death of Ruth, like he had caused it, like I could forgive him. It'd be like forgiving someone for having a poor singing voice. There are some things that just is and the consequences, tough as they might seem, are just the cost of livin'.

Problem with Ruth and her uncle though, is that they were both a party to her dying: one doing it, one bearing witness. Like Jesus dragging his cross to Gethsemane. A lot of people saw and spent the rest of their lives wishing they'd done something more than nothing. But caused? Guilt will kill you like dying on a slow, self-erected crucifix. I wasn't taught that in Sunday School, but I seen a lot of it and didn't want it to kill me or Chuck.

I needed to keep moving until something grew up under me and kept me from drowning, too. I reckon Uncle Chuck must've known that as well. This little skiff with her new name on it had something to do with it; a connection I couldn't say but could feel like a faint pulse at the wrist.

My hardscrabble apprenticeship with dying was not a chosen profession. But neither was it a calling or a curse. Later on, I'd look back on it all indelibly, as if it had been written down and swore to by a Horseman of the Apocalypse. It just had to be.

I decided to skip the nap and stopped to have a better look at Winnie's directions. The '42 Ford Stepside truck that I'd cobbled together with old junkyard toss aways and sweat equity needed kid gloves. The truck's shell had been gunked-up and in need of parts, but it was running true. Most folks wanted their cars to go faster and built them around the accelerator. I always enjoyed the view from that tall cab and the confidence in knowing that if I stopped to have a look around, she'd start right back up, so I built her around the carburetor and the brakes. I'd find this guy Davis' house and drop the boat off, then decide my next move from there.

The beach was dotted with small cedar-wood-sided homes, mostly vacant and boarded up, standing sentinel to what families might've lost when their fathers went off to war and didn't come back. But there were other signs too—sights and smells of new blood, young families with extra money spending a few weeks in the mid-winter sun and warm Gulf waters, sunning themselves on the sugary sand of Panama City Beach before the winter felt winterish and they migrated back north to jobs and schools and resolutions to enjoy life more. Harry S. Truman was in the White House and he'd get us out of the Korean War any day now.

About a mile south along the coast road I spotted a long pier with large equipment and thick-armed men working toward the far end. I needed a bathroom break and knew that construction sites offered some of the best chances for a Black man to take a legal piss. I stopped the truck and figured I'd walk off that bologna sandwich, relieve myself, and look into the waters of the Gulf of Mexico from the safety of American steel.

Topping my tightly curled hair with a straw hat, I walked slowly out onto the pier and suddenly had this strange feeling of being lost and found at the same time. I'd lost a lot, even wondering if I could simply lose myself. But at the same time I felt like I was about to find something, or maybe I had and couldn't recognize it or name it, so it just sat there, waiting for me to open some door and let it in so it could introduce itself.

Suddenly, I was an fifteen-year-old kid again back in '36 rooting for Mr. Owens to win gold in Hitler's Berlin, living in a distant aunt's basement outside of Birmingham, working at the cabinet shop as clean-up boy while I watched carefully how the men handled the wood and respected the machines. There was that one night after I'd gotten off work and walked a different way home and the wind was blowing cold and stiff from the South. I'd looked in a window at the public library and saw rows of books and the faces of a few Black men peppered among the long tables, faces intent and serious, regarding their books like the men at the shop regarded a new plank of mahogany intended for a rich man's dining room table. And I'd walked in to a musky smell mixed with a hint of Pine-Sol. The checkered floor glistened under rows of single white bulbs. Nobody regarded my presence and though I had always enjoyed the few books I'd been exposed to as a child in the Negro schools, they were few. What attracted me to the library was it was simply a warm, well-lit place.

I asked the lady at the counter what it took to borrow the books, either to read at the long desks or at home. I remember her name badge. It was a black metal square with white letters spelling out the words, *Lillian, Head Librarian*. Her hair and voice matched the color of her name—airy, like high cirrus clouds.

"Well, now," she said, just above a whisper, her lips barely moving but her eyes unwavering. I had to lean my head in close to hear and bits of sawdust fell off my shoulders onto the counter.

"This is a public library and you are welcome to take any book from any shelf and sit to read it or look at the pictures. If you'd like to take a book home on loan, you'll need to fill out a form and show some identification, like an identification card or work permit."

I told her I had neither, but I had a job and a place of residence. I had a home.

"The library's policy is that we need some form of identification to issue you a card to be able to check out books." She was clear in her thin voice, but there was something like compassion in the way she moved her hands when she spoke.

"I suppose I could find someone to write something up to tell you I am who I claim to be and that if I find a book I'd like to ponder outside of when I might sit at one of these tables, I could borrow if from you, legally, that is. I wouldn't want to go against any regulations. I might just have a look around and see if there's anything here that interests me. Assuming that's okay with you, Miss."

I said it slowly again, careful to avoid any nod of malice or malcontent. "Maybe I'll just have a look around, if that's all right."

"Of course," Lillian said with the ends of her mouth moving up almost to what could be labeled a smile. "You'll find the titles categorized by subject matter, but if you tell me what you're interested in, I might be able to save you a lot of hunting." Something in Lillian seemed to be melting and I grinned back unknowingly.

"Well, Miss Lilibrarian," the words tripping over themselves, "I'm interested in lots of subjects, but have never had much of a chance to hunt them in books. I'd like to just look around, if I might."

"Of course, young man. You're quite welcome to explore." And she pushed her glasses back up her nose with a long thin finger and turned toward another man who had piled books and a library card on top of the counter; the books more than the card saying who he was.

✳ ✳ ✳

Those were my thoughts when I met Jed Riot. It was at the base of that fixed-steel pier, part construction zone, part permanent man-made metal. They were thoughts of self-identity rolling around my head and how so many of us had been fixed by labels of insignificant things like skin color and job and trousers and shirts. Old Jimmy Grayfalls, an Indian figure from my youth, used to say that a man was defined by his parents until he was old enough to hold his head up and test his eyes against the northern winds. After that, it wasn't where the wind carried him, but how the man shaped it with his thoughts and courage. But Jimmy said a lot of things that I never understood as a kid.

"Hey there, young feller. You here to apply for the job?"

Jed looked to be in his late thirties and was short and wide with a thick head of wavy red hair stuffed under a metal construction hat. His bare arms were sleeved with green ink tattoos displaying snakes and flags and women's legs that didn't seem real but looked real pretty. When he spoke, he looked up at me with hazel eyes, a look without judgment or malice. His smile was as open as a church. I wanted to like this man, needed to believe he was speaking the truth.

"Well, not really, sir. I was just having a look, maybe use your construction site's washroom if'n you got a Colored man's." He nodded to the left, said go right ahead, and I asked as I turned my body in that direction, just casual conversation if not respect for allowing a man a legal public pee, "You making this pier longer or something?"

"Nope, just putting back what Hurricanes Baker, Easy, and King stole when they blew through here last fall. Three bitches in six weeks, they were. Knocked down the last fifty-feet and the bait shop that old man Davis ran since they built this thing in '33."

"Davis?" I asked him. "Any relation to Harry?"

"Yep. Harry'd be Walter's only son, a local fisherman with a new boy of his own. Why you asking?" Jed took off his hat and scratched his head hard and fast like a dog will.

"The name's Cobb, Johnny Cobb." I stuck out my hand and said I was from outside Mobile and it was a long story but I had something to deliver to this Davis family, something that I needed to get rid of and was told they might be able to use.

"It's hard to explain, sir, but I'm kinda 'supposed' to deliver that little boat." I pointed in the direction of my Stepside.

"No need 'splaining things to me. Sounds like it could be personal or spiritual or both. That it, over yonder on the truck?" He cocked his head toward my truck that sat in the dirt lot where a few men from the job, White as well as Black, were sitting on a bench drinking from silver Thermos cups. "By the way, I'm Jed Riot. Sort of in charge of this little project." He shook my hand and I felt the thick calluses. I liked him straight away.

I said, yes, that's the boat, and I had directions to Harry Davis' house a few miles out of town and wanted to get it there before dark so as I could still find a place to sleep safely tonight.

"Listen, young Johnny Cobb, it's a ways back in the bush down some old dirt tracks. He's got pert near eighty acres and I doubt you'll find his place without a lot of wandering. And the Davis place ain't on no map."

I said I was much obliged, but I was going to have to try anyway, holding back the memory of the stares I had been thrown by half a dozen White folk in the half a day I'd been in his little town.

"Well, suit yourself, but even if'n you do find the house, I seen Harry puttering on his boat down in the harbor this morning. Men like that who make a living from the ocean don't punch no time clock. He could be back home now or not for a week. Told me he'd like to see his pa's old bait shop rebuilt a'fore summer tourists arrive in four or five months and I ought to be the one to do it. Only got three hands though."

I hadn't had a White man speak that many straight-up, honest words to me in one stretch since I attended the Pentecostal School for Boys one year and there'd been a young teacher who was color blind. I was momentarily caught, shocked, denied it, and then, finally, pleased. At first, I thought that Jed Riot was angling for something but decided, as he drew me a map on the back of a *Tommy's Diner* napkin and shook my hand again, that even though there might be some Negro-haters in that place, in one full morning I'd met two good folks. It was hard to know what to think and an ambiguous curiosity about the town opened in my mind. It would not be unmanageable. Parts of it could grow on a man—would have to—because Jed Riot's words to me were a universal thing, more than just a sound between a resigned silence, just two men talking, one helping the other.

Pride and hate, learned or innate, had held the South hostage for a hundred-and-fifty years. Now, this man's words hovered over me like a halo, like a blues song—just enough hope bleeding through the despair. I was naked to the sound, not because of its content, but its context. And the notes of the song reverberated deep inside me, stirring up some kinship along with an embarrassing shame that I even felt this way; that it should've been natural, should always be natural, but never would because there would always be hate and prejudice. I ought not even been noticing it; the world was doing its thing to me and the only choice I had was to hug my thin future like a mother's arms and then move out away from them and relish what good there was in the knowledge of what they'd taught me.

"Hey, Mr. Johnny Cobb." I was almost at my truck. "I clean forgot to ask. You know how to operate any machines?"

I stopped and lifted the brim of my hat to better judge the time and to guarantee the sincerity.

"Why you asking, Mr. Riot?"

"My crane operator got thrown in jail last night for beating up a kid in a bar fight. Reckon he might be there for while, seeing as it was...well, never mind. I need a replacement."

"Well, Mr. Riot, we drilled some pretty deep wells up on our farm and the mechanical workings of machinery have always come easy to me. I'll look at it if you need the help."

"Be appreciated. We're thin on nuts-and-bolts men around here. Most of them went on up North after the war to earn some real money. The rest got scripted to fight them Chinese North Koreans for God-knows-what? Cain't say I blame them or Uncle Sam. Things is complicated. Maybe in the morning, if you're still in these parts?"

"I've a feeling I will be," I told him and studied the napkin to Harry Davis' place.

"I got a feeling," I whispered to nobody, my delicate sensibility rising up for the air it demanded, and turned the key to the truck.

CHAPTER 2

THE EARLY WINTERS

TV's *Ozzie and Harriet* never visited the 1950's South. A lot of Black kids became adults as soon as they were old enough to guide a mule or drive a pickup or throw a ball or learn to catch life's shit. Still, choices were a luxury. Ruth Winters had been raised by her grandmother, Nadine, and her Uncle Chuck, the son of a father, Willis, who'd been with Nadine long enough for memory's chisel to effect harm. Ruth's own father, who'd been with Ruth's absent mother, Louella, only once, had become a thing—not a person—to forget. With only nine years separation between Ruth and Chuck, he had become a brother.

This was our South back in the summer of '46. Nadine was half-a-century old. Nobody knew where her daughter, Louella, had disappeared to after Ruth was born in '29, two days before the late October crash, and most hoped that Ruth's father was dead or in jail or both. Things weren't the same as up north. But they weren't that different. There was crucifixion for skin color and depth of tenderness for the same. The Winters made more than their due: they made something together, sculpted a life out of the issues.

As I came to know Nadine, Ruth, and Chuck, and watched them navigate their lives as best they could, "like watching the flying of a fly ball," as Nadine would say, "just hoping to get under it," I began to love them not only as people but as symbols of something larger, something between family and survival. Something that earned itself.

When I look back now at the few years I lived among them, it seems that the earth didn't deserve what they had. But it was the earth that swallowed them in the way it expands and contracts, as worlds will do. The last of the Winters' apparent lineage were living in a parallel way, but celebrating life in the most primal form—by breathing. In their early days as a family, Nadine would recall, it seemed they found it a joy simply to move air inside themselves and then let it out again. A day that wasn't a bad one was a great one. For Chuck, though, I think there were more bad ones.

Charles Samuel Winters never liked the name Chuck. But once it took to him, he was the kind of kid—then the kind of man—who was too discerning to correct everyone. Let them call him what they liked. He would've rather grown up into a Sam or even a Charlie. But somewhere along the way, he became Chuck and that was just the way it was going to be. Even if his stomach twisted just a little every time he heard the name that was not him. Every time the old Negroes noticed his distaste and regaled stories of how the Indians let their children pick their own names after they had an inkling of who they were relative to the animistic view and what path their lives might take.

"Chuck" Winters hadn't found his peace yet, let alone his spirit-animal; his life was more about being pointed in a direction and told to move. Sometimes he did because the options weren't good. And other times he didn't because they were. Lines in the dirt, fences in his head, times to do as he was told and, much later with others, to do the telling; his young life seemed an extended negotiation. And always, it seemed, just below the surface was something waiting. He'd know that time, he'd say to me when we were alone. He'd know that time.

"I'll know because I'm always looking," he'd say, his dark and darting eyes like a bird of prey. Chuck wasn't a hunter, but he gathered things and most of them were for protection of what family he had left.

His own daddy, Willis, he'd been told by neighbors, had worked the land and the livestock for the White boss until he got the fever and couldn't handle the fields. The boss was a decent man who paid him a wage, small though it was. His great-grandfather had also worked for a White boss, but had no choice—the scars on his back carving out that truth. His grandfather had been shot through the head by a Confederate soldier. The men in the Winters family seemed to be faring better with each generation. Still, Uncle Chuck had a volcanic core, unpredictable and angry.

Ruth's mother was called Louella. She hadn't wanted the child, had been sixteen. The father was momentary, the ancient lustful want of nameless men who deposit their seed and disappear into the forever-night. It couldn't be called a mistake—nobody really excused it—just temporary pleasure, forever result.

Louella's mother, Nadine, had convinced her to carry it full term. And when it came out, the grandmother took to raising it, called the baby Ruth after The Babe since Nadine loved all things baseball. Nadine, who taught herself to read at nine years-old and then never walked by a piece of text, glossy or newsprint, without reading it, deconstructed the White man's newspapers like a public scholar, often making excuses to hitch a ride into Mobile just to lurk innocently at the newsstand or, on her birthday, spend the whole day at the Central Library. She devoured George Ruth and the New York Yankees and was skeptical of anything that had to be plugged in, including, after her daughter's teen pregnancy, female sexuality in general. Nadine Winters might've been the only rural Black woman in the mid-nineteenth century South who'd not only read Freud, but understood him.

Besides Louella, Nadine had born only one other child by her husband, Willis, the farmer and farrier by trade. The son had been given the name Charles, for no particular reason and then was reduced to Chuck in the wake of his past. I called him Charlie at first on the account of it made us think of each other differently. At first, he didn't know what to think of me. But we shared the scars of the South and were bound to each other in ways that each had no idea how the present would shape the past. We both loved Ruth to the point of future pain.

Nadine used to say that Charlie had been a good kid at first, tall and straight, with a rebel soul held in check by the threads of his family ties, bonds that made him proud and angry in the same breath. She and Willis had gone six long years hoping and trying for more children after Louella and then were blessed with the boy. And then Willis went and died of the fever and nothing could ever be the same after that. The past had elapsed like small waves on the shore, but the ripples that passed through seemed to hit a wall and bounce, sometimes doubling in size, other times canceling each other out.

Nadine was a mother and a grandmother and a widow and was missing a child before her fortieth birthday. It wasn't a mistake.

"This is life," she'd say matter-of-factly. "Ya come on to terms with it or ya don't."

By the time I'd met and courted Ruth in '46, Nadine had grown that shell around her skin. But there were still openings to her heart, though it took a tire iron to get through. One day I'd told her that if she and Louella and Charlie would let me marry Ruth, I was going to take them to New York City and see Yankee Stadium.

"Oh, young Johnny Cobb," she chuckled. "You save up your money and make my granddaughter happy. I don't need to see no New York City. The Babe and the Iron Man Gehrig will be gone by then. Mantle's a good kid, but there's a lot of pressure on him. Reckon the Mick don't have the mettle— probably die like the Black men in these parts—from the pressure that brings the drink that kills the liver that kills the man." And then she busied herself in her little kitchen with the new propane gas oven she'd bought with money earned mending clothes, always finishing just this way, "Besides, I wouldn't want to be away if'n my other baby, Louella, come home."

Louella had been gone over sixteen years by the time I started courting Ruth, making her over thirty if she was alive. Nadine said that Louella had followed the heroin of a traveling blues musician. Never a word; the ghost daughter swallowed by the night horse. Charlie said she gone chasing things away, not following. And in a quiet moment out on the partly-screened porch one hot July night when Ruth and Nadine were busy in the kitchen, I asked Charlie if he'd ever consider going after Louella.

"I did." He considered me long and hard as if the question was more an investigation of him than his sister. "Found myself staring down a whole bunch of barrels. Some filled with whisky and others loaded with bullets. Not scared of the effects of booze, but the bullets are a different story." And then after considering the weight of his comments added, "Decided to save my response for another day."

That day in August of '46 when Ruth brought me home to meet her grandma and her uncle was one of those days when, even if you were to suffer from amnesia later in your life, you'd likely remember the details, not because of their significance at the time, but how you would set them carefully in your memory from then on, like family heirlooms to be brought and mused about when you thought being melancholic would do you some good.

The house was set back down a winding dirt road and was built of pine siding with the period cedar trim. It was small but clean and neat, and stood out from the other houses in the area for its tidy yard of gravel and seasonal flowers. The roof was tin and windows were framed in a deep shade of red. There was a mid-30s Buick in the driveway, but it seemed in need of attention.

"So, you're the young thing that Ruth's been swooning over last few months now," Nadine offered as I walked in with my hat in hand, looking me in the eye before returning to her chores. "But you ain't that young. Are you?"

"I'm almost twenty-two, born in the year of nineteen and twenty-five, ma'am, but that ol yellow orb has aged me a bit."

Ruth dropped a plate she was wiping dry and the crash split the air in the small kitchen. They all looked at the broken dish, said nothing, and then laughed and bent down to help.

"It's not the sun that does the aging, Mr. Cobb. It ain't even the work done out under it that can take the years away."

"Miss Nadine," I said, "you're talking about having to be under the man's thumb, aren't you?"

Ruth said she was gonna go on out and get just a few more berries and excused herself. When we heard the little tune she'd been humming reach the garden, I spoke.

"Well, I agree with you, Miss Nadine, "but lately I've been watching the way Ruth holds her head at certain angles, letting a few rays in when it suits her and then cocking her head in a new direction to fend them off when it doesn't. I don't see her under any man's thumb."

"What do you take of that, Mister Cobb?" Nadine turned and faced me full up. She seemed to grow several inches in that moment.

"Well, I know she's going to be as pretty as you when she ages up in the world," and added for effect, "if she ain't already."

"Look, Mister Johnny Cobb," Nadine put her thick hands on my shoulders and looked up in my eyes, momentarily paralyzing me. "I appreciate your politeness, but what I'd value even more is your honesty. Flattery is nice, but it don't sink in like it used to when Willis was around," and dropped her hands to more submissive stance.

Nadine began setting out the dinner dishes and grabbed an iron skillet in her large hands that became an extension of those biscuit-making arms. A long strand of thick, black hair had fallen out of her bun and she made no effort to replace it. She stopped, took a deep breath and looked at me with eyes hoping for something. Outside, I could hear Ruth and her uncle laughing as they chatted in the garden.

"Ruth is wise, Miss Winters, well beyond her seventeen years. She doesn't talk about her ma or pa with me. Reckon she looks at you and her Uncle Chuck as kin enough. She has a way of protecting her insides from getting hurt but encouraging others to put their own protection away." I took a sip of my water and looked out the small kitchen window. "I've learned from being around her these past months. Your granddaughter owns a collected view of what is and what ain't or, I mean, what is not."

"You speak'n in circles, Johnny Cobb," Nadine spoke with interest overriding a paper-thin cynicism, "but you come right to the point."

"Yes ma'am. My own family is beholden to the soil, as many of our color is, in one form or another. But the earth can only teach you so much. Ruth understands human folk. It's almost like she can…"

"Grandma, what are you doing to this man?" Ruth walked in the back door with a reed basket of berries, her face showing her disappointment. "He came over for a Sunday supper. I hope you weren't getting into him about politics and such now."

"No, Ruthie," Nadine pinched Ruth's cheek and pointed to her lower lip. "I could ride into town on that thing. I was checking up your man here. Put the lip away and help me with these here collard greens."

"Ah, Grandma, do you have to talk the heavy stuff now?" Ruthie shot me a concerned glance and then looked at Nadine. "Eventually we'll get onto an argument and the night won't ever be the same. In any case, if'n you were gonna get into the war thing again, Johnny was too young to enlist, weren't you?"

Ruthie's eyes morphed into a kind of fiery ice that you might also use to cool your brow on a hot August night and I couldn't break away from them. I remember thinking that every man deserves the love of a woman like this, if only for a few hours in his life. If you could bottle a *look* such as that, it would weigh more than the world it would make better when opened. But something always gets in the way, don't it? Free will or free won't—it's always something.

"Well, truth be known," my voice moving towards the women as they clipped greens on the wooden counter, face still fixed on Ruth. "I was sixteen in '41 and I reckon they'd taken me if'n I'd told them I was twenty-one. And in November of '42 when they lowered the draft age to eighteen I still could've cheated my way into patriotism. I was in line at the U.S. Army recruiter's office in Mobile and I got to thinking about having to aim a rifle at another person and I couldn't picture myself pulling the trigger at them without standing up and saying,

'Okay, your turn.' And a man in a pressed olive-green uniform with badges on the lapels walked by and said 'glad to have another nigger to clean the latrines,' so I stepped out of line and went back to the farm.

"I know what they did to the Jews and all, but America did kinda the same thing here to the Indians. I 'spose it's the glass houses and all. Heck, Miss Winters, soldiers are just boys dressed up in the same clothes, listening to men who can't get along as well as the boys do on their own. That's how I figure it, anyway."

I could see the sides of Nadine's mouth curl up like the edges of flowers at night as she stood at the sink and washed the greens.

"What about when you got on to twenty-one and such?"

It was Uncle Chuck who'd come in from outside, pulled up a chair, and sat at the table looking at a week-old newspaper. His jeans were clean, cuffed in the usual way, and his T-shirt pressed around the arms as if someone had ironed purposeful creases in it.

I'd only spoken to Ruth's uncle a few times before that day and he'd been cordial enough, but there was no denying that I was on trial, on judgment for loving Ruth. Nobody would ever be good enough for his niece and it was all I could do just to be myself and hope that was close enough. I'd of thought the same way and respected him for it.

"I wondered about why I never heard from the government and as the war in Europe wound down, I thought I'd be clear. But when it kept going in the South Pacific I finally got a letter requesting that I show up at the draft board up in Atlanta and take a physical."

Chuck turned his attention away from the paper and seemed to regard me in an entirely different light.

"So. what'd you do?" he asked.

"I went on up there, Chuck, and took that test," not meaning to add the silent drama that crept in as I paused to have a sip of the beer he'd just handed me.

"Lemme guess," Chuck stood up from the table and walked over to his mother who'd moved on to cutting okra into small pieces, and put his hands softly on her shoulders. She made a throat-clearing notice that was more signal that phlegm.

"The White government noticed that you already had a nice tan and decided they didn't need any more Negroes crawling around the jungles of Guam or the Philippines?"

"Charles Samuel Winters," Nadine spun around quickly but kept enough light in her voice to sound casual. I caught the weight though, it wasn't hard. "Don't you start in on *that*. Mister Cobb is here to have a nice dinner with us, like Ruthie said."

"You started it, Ma. I know you."

"That's okay, Miss Winters," the beer easing the words. "I have those same feelings at times, about living in America the Beautiful so long as you're White. But the war, Jesus, that was a difficult thing, unexplainable on so many levels," and added without expression: "Funny thing, after my physical exam they decided I was damaged goods—bowed legs or something with my rate of heartbeats; something like that. Just a man in a lab coat and a thin black tie telling me he's sorry. Couple weeks later there was a letter sent to the post office saying thanks but no thanks. Go figure.

"I would've gone, had they needed me. I really would've. But I doubt I'd have come back."

I asked Uncle Chuck if he went over and he said no because he was the last remaining Winters' male child and was needed to work the fields. Then he added it would've been different if'n he'd felt the country was in front of, as well as behind, him. Bullets are color blind, he said, and finished by saying that as far as he was concerned, the Civil War was still being fought in parts of Alabama. No reason to go fight another war when you still had one right here.

Nadine chirped in and said that they didn't know that for sure, you know, about being the last of the Winters name.

"Ma, you're the one who kindled that idea in me. What are you talking about?"

"We don't know *for sure.* Louella could come prancing in here at any moment with a passel of boys carrying our name."

An icy silence moved in and settled upon the kitchen air. Outside the crickets seemed to be laughing and the frogs down near the shallow creek that skirted the old field house took advantage of the retreat in human voices.

Chuck broke it as he went to the fridge and pulled out two more beers.

"Well...what'ja do after you failed the physical, Mr. Johnny Cobb?"

"Well, as I said, I failed it," the words rolling off easily and I watched the expressions change the way they do when questions of a man's abilities are held up for consideration. Then I told them a true story waked in my own past. It started slowly enough but like a bass run, built power with movement.

"When I was five years-old my daddy moved into the city to try and find work. The Crash in '29 had only taken a few months to spread like a rabid disease and affect the sharecroppers. We were getting by on what we could grow, but needed money for new seeds and supplies to keep the tractors running and the plants growing and to pay the White man's bank a percentage. He said he'd send money and come back on the full moon to help us during harvest. But something happened and the money stopped showing, which I understood. And something else happened and *he* stopped showing, which none of us ever did get an answer to. It was like Birmingham had just swallowed up this kindly, hard-working Black man with a wife and three young boys trying to work a poor, but rich-soiled ninety-plus acres."

Ruth, who'd caught bits of my past in the months we'd been dating, joined Uncle Chuck and me at the small kitchen table. But Nadine seemed suspended in her tiny kitchen as if she'd become a painting, a bowl of lettuce in one hand, the other set on the counter as if to steady herself while she listened.

"I'm sorry, I didn't mean for this answer to grow into a personal account of my history, a memoir the librarians call it. I guess I was taking the long route to get to your uncle's question."

"Whatever kind of memory your 'memwa is, you just go on telling it, Johnny." Ruth looked from her grandma to her uncle and they nodded at her, and then back at me saying yeah, Mister Cobb, you go tell it.

"Well, the shortened version is that our daddy disappeared and the cops never found out, and ma, she died a year later of heartache. As much as my brothers and I tried to replace our pa, heartache is more deadly than heart attack, the way I figure it.

"But right around '34, when I was nearly ten and my older brothers Earl and Ramsey had trained me well on the John Deere, we had a drought spring and we lost more'n half our crops. My daddy's brother—we called him Jacko because he was afraid of the dark and never went outside after sundown without an oil lantern—he'd been helping out, but the moonshine he'd grown too dependent on was getting the best of him. Old Jacko was like the village idiot boy, utterly without meanness or envy or desire to make his place in the world better. He was a tender man and had been taken advantage of all his life by those who built their own egos on the backs of those who had a hard time keeping up with life, let alone trying to improve it.

"He tried to apologize to Earl, the oldest at sixteen, but Ramsey, the fighter in the family and just ten months younger than Earl, had told Uncle Jacko that he'd have to choose between us and the land—which were inseparable—and the bottle, which always caused a distance. Ramsey said that Jacko ate more than he pulled out in weeds and work. But I told Ramsey he was daddy's brother and he best leave Jacko alone or when daddy got back he'd have his hide. It didn't end at that, but I'm getting' further and further from my answer."

I kept my story moving, pulsing between the way it came back into our present, folded into my story telling, and how it ended up as something for Ruth's family to chew on. I told about how things were between the drought and the drink, how things were bad for us Cobbs, how we started to quarrel amongst ourselves, and that struggle for meaning in each of us that had never been there. And our pa reminding us every morning of our youth when he'd wake us up before the sun and say, "Would you look at this, boys? All this good and great land, and all we have it to do is work our asses to the white bone, and keep paying the White boss and sharecrop a few more years and it's ours to keep and live on and live off of and enjoy until the good Lord comes down and plucks me right off'a my tractor. Then y'all can keep on living here...you so desire."

"Them's were hard times, Mister Cobb. We here to testify to that." Nadine felt the story going on and didn't want to get in its way, but she was the matriarch and this was in fact a Sunday supper, so she excused herself and got up to pull a meatloaf from the oven while Ruth set the table. Both did so in regarded silence while Uncle Chuck peeled the label from his beer and put out his hands as if to say, okay, then what?

"It was the most amazing thing."

I kind of looked into the brown glass of my beer bottle. I hadn't spoken of this in many years, and never to more than an audience of one. I told Chuck that things got real grim and the bank was threatening to take back all our land over the small payments to the government that'd become late. Then I spoke in a slightly different tone, of this old Indian, a Natchez elder as it turned out, who'd walked down our long driveway with a bridled mule in one hand and a hickory walking stick in the other.

"It was about sundown and I was making dinner while Earl and Ramsey were still out in the barn trying to jerry-rig a new exhaust for the John Deere out of some Folgers' cans. Jacko was looking out the window, sneaking sips from his flask and complaining about the lack of lamp oil that kept him a prisoner in the little plywood shack."

I stopped for a minute as if I was making sure I got it right.

"This Indian just stood straight and tall, looking west over our fields, like he was deciding something. My brothers had the tractor running now in the near-dark barn and hadn't seen him come up the path. I walked out in my overalls and bare feet, a cooking rag slung over my shoulder. The strange thing, Chuck, is that I was a nine-year-old kid in '34 and I'd heard all the stories about the Indians in the Old West, but I wasn't in the least bit afraid. He stood there, wearing thin denim pants, leather mocs, and some kind of necklace with claws under a big woolen frock coat. His face was dark like a Mexican's, with lines so deep you could fall in and never find your way out. But his hair...I'd never seen hair like that before— long and silvery white to his waist in one pony tail tied back with a piece of leather hide.

"I asked if I could help him, looking for any sign of weapons, but not finding any save for a big Jim Bowie knife sheathed to his calf.

"Good soil here. Good for crops. Flat, well-tended." His English was short and broken, but each word carried weight and meaning.

"Yes sir, we're sharecropping it and gonna get the homestead if'n we keep paying the taxes. You lost or something? We don't get many visitors."

"Looking for work," he said, finally moving his eyes onto me and off the dark horizon. "Name's Jimmy Grayfalls, Natchez Nation. Work hard, trade for food and a place no sun or rain will find my bed."

"Well, my brother Earl makes most of the big decisions round here and we ain't had much rain this past year. Things is looking pretty bleak. We got enough to eat, but not a lot extra for strangers."

"Jimmy no stranger after hard work. Rain's coming three days. You and the Earl need help planting. Good trade, just for food and roof over bed."

"But, aren't you kinda...old to work the fields, Mr. Gray... wall?"

"You have a name, little man with nice farm?"

"Sure. It's Johnny. We're all Cobbs here."

"Jimmy thinks it's too hot and dry to grow corn this far south this year."

Earl, who'd been listening from the edge of the barn as he wiped his greasy hands, started laughing. I jumped back, suddenly frightened in the new dark.

The Natchez turned his head slowly.

"You must be the brother, Earl. I like to trade work. Small Johnny and I talking of plan. He say you decide."

"Yep, little Johnny is correct.' Earl moved toward us. "His daddy woulda been right proud of him. I sure hope he ain't burning the supper somewhere."

✳ ✳ ✳

"And that's the way it started." I was trying to wrap it up. "Earl said Jimmy could stay a few days, it rained after three, just like Jimmy said, and he lived with us until about three years ago when Ramsey, who'd never really liked having Jimmy around, yelled at him for dropping a bushel of ripe tomatoes. Next morning he was gone. Eight years and he'd only lost half-a-step in his work 'tween '34 and '42. Earl used to say he'd out-live us all. Only thing left was a little note he'd left on my dresser written in Natchez. Some years later I found someone who spoke Natchez to translate it. It said he'd see me in the next life. It had been a good trade."

Nadine and Ruth had set out the food and after Nadine said the blessing, the bowls of fried okra, collard greens, boiled potatoes, and meatloaf in gravy were passed around in silence.

I could see Uncle Chuck thinking hard about my story and trying to make a connection that wasn't there yet. He'd nod his head, take a bite, smile, sneak a glance at me, like he was prodding, then go back to his food.

Finally, Nadine spoke up and said, "Jesus, Johnny, finish the damn story."

"Oh yeah" I was goofing with Chuck and suddenly he figured it out and said he knew how I failed the physical, but to go ahead and tell the girls as long as I had invested the whole night into it. "Well, the short version is..." I started in again.

"Christ, young man, y'all have to move in if'n I ever want the longer version." Nadine smiled and browned okra bits stuck to the spaces between her teeth.

"Sorry ma'am, I got carried away thinking about those days and Grayfalls and wonderin' where all the time went. But it's a simple story, really. Jimmy Grayfalls used to teach me how to control my breathing and my heart rate. He liked to hunt and even though I had no stomach or spirit for killing any creatures, I used to like to watch his movements through what forest Alabama has. I liked the way he slowed down time to a pace that allowed him to fall behind the present in which the animal lived; the way he thought as the animal would and for that moment, became it.

"And after he'd taken its life, thanked his Great Spirit and the animal itself for the offering, he would still respect it in death more than most people do in life. He used all of what he killed and my brothers and I were grateful for the rabbit and squirrel and venison he put on the table.

"That's when I learned it—the ability to alter your breathing and your heartbeat and the thing the U.S. Army was most concerned about even after flat feet—blood pressure."

Uncle Chuck was laughing now, not in disbelief, but in admiration. Nadine bowed her head and shook it like a pendulum with her heavy smile leading. And Ruthie was still waiting for the final details

"You're serious, aren't you, Cobb? Cuz' that's too good to make up." Chuck was incredulous. "You got out of having to go to war because an old Indian had taught you how to raise and lower your blood pressure at will."

"Well, he didn't really set out to teach me that. It was just a by-product of watching his purposeful simple-ness. The way the old guy moved among the elements, like he was the river in the water instead of the rock it split.

"When I asked him about it, he said that trees breathe all the time, but the White man can't measure it because they can't see it with White men's eyes. I learned how to be a tree and lower my blood pressure to nothing and then how to be the fire that could burn it and send my pulse into the sun's temperatures. When they gave me that physical for the Army in Mobile, I wasn't there—I was walking the forests with Jimmy Grayfalls, moving my breath through the trees as they slept and burnt and grew back in time. And when it was all done, the man with the clipboard and the lab coat with the pocket pen protector said he was awfully sorry, I had a serious heart condition and the U.S. Army couldn't use me. He really was sorry about it all."

When I was done with the story we ate berries for dessert and Ruthie said she was proud of what I done. Uncle Chuck said I'll be damned, and Nadine said she thought a young Roger Maris might be good enough to play in the Negro Leagues.

When Chuck got up to clear the table and clean the dishes, he slapped me on the back and said he'd be goddamned again, laughing as he said it.

It had been a good evening, one that was worth the pain of remembering.

CHAPTER 3
WAYS AND MEANS

In the beginning of that time after Ruth's death, I didn't know how to describe what it was that I was feeling. But I knew what she felt like, her cold feet on my bare legs at night, her high, disarming laugh in my ears. It was all familiar, evolving still, as if Ruth continued to exist in flesh among this world.

It would take years for me to unravel those months after she passed. And it seems that no sooner than the coffin was shut, I was being pointed somewhere. I trusted her to show me another life, as if it were her responsibility, as if she was as important to me dead as she was alive. We'd only been married for a little over two years after a long year of courting. I could never marry again.

And Ruth remained unvanquished.

In the years that followed her death I would often wonder if I should have grieved more; should've cried out "why" into those many dark nights I slept alone, worked the land and the rough wood in the shop alone, and rebuilt my life from the inside out—alone. As much as I loved her, as much as the pain of losing her tore at my soul, it was not hard to let her go. And that surprised me; confounds me still.

I went into that exiled state with the sincerity of a man on trial. Unknown as it was, that little mahogany and teak skiff tied in the back of my '42 Ford pickup existed as if it were the Dead Sea Scrolls, full of proverbial wisdom that was centered in the one woman I would love. Her with that sardonic insight bordering on the supernatural, her guiding me, her—no longer alive—appallingly human. Ruth's memory and the damn boat that killed her… life was strange.

I was about to reframe my alone-ness while the country of America boomed with post-war economic glee and 1951 was the year I met Phin Davis.

✳ ✳ ✳

Jed Riot had been correct, the Davis place was not signed or numbered, just hidden two, maybe three miles down a series of red clay roads that twisted and turned back on themselves as if designed to force the driver to slow their approach and have a good look around at the tall sugar pines, silver dollar eucalyptus, salt marsh grass, and low, low rolling hills. The sensuous horizon made the road wind and bent the time it took to drive from the corrugated tin mailbox on the main road to where the house might be. It was more a passage than a driveway. Even if memory is apt to be inventive, I was damn sure I hadn't been there before. Yet the familiarity crept in and stayed like a light spring rain on thirsty crops, each new moment welcomed and appreciated. This is how I came to meet the Davis Family when I took that little boat down to Panama City Beach in the winter of '51 with the intent of some sense of its role in Ruth's death. It sounds strange. But things were unfolding in the present that could not justify the past or foretell the future. It was just along for the ride.

Jed Riot had mentioned acreage, but there was no way to tell when I might find the residence of one *Harry, Grace, and Gillie Davis plus?* as the mailbox had said back at the road. The sun was flirting with the branches on a row of thin willows and a thought moved in that showing up right at suppertime might be impolite. I put the truck in low gear, slowing to a near halt, but it seemed that the trees and the light and the smell of yellow jessamine that had filled the cab were still streaming by on either side of me. My truck could've been dead in the water but still in motion, caught in the gravity of something unknown to me.

Just then four dogs came running out from behind a wild blackberry hedge and started yapping curiously. I couldn't make out the kind of dogs; maybe it was the fading light. More than likely their make and model were like this rural coast trying to be a town—indiscernible and rough around the edges. They surrounded my truck at a safe distance, guiding me in as fighter jet would a suspect plane, enjoying the run, their pink tongues hanging out, their paws gripping the moist ground and kicking up little clods of earth in their wake. I can't say for sure, but I'm pretty sure I smiled for the first time in months.

Round a wide arc of mature white cedar, the sun just nudging the western edge of the world, I came into a broad clearing. In the center was an oblong-shaped patch of St. Augustine grass grown tall, but trimmed around the edges of the gravel driveway crunching under my tires. There were several outbuildings in varying states of construction and repair, and in the dusky light there appeared a number of small to medium-sized marine craft nestled in and around the compound. Through the trees, along a short path, I could see a rather large garden, rowed, planted, and fenced. Plants I knew. This was a producing garden, the result of much work.

The whole scene—boats, small and tidy work shed, plants—spoke of care and effort not exceptionally organized, but aesthetic and nurtured in an involved way. Momentarily, I found myself thinking it would've been fun to grow up on a property such as this.

The dogs split off in pairs, two moving over to my truck parked off to the edge of the driveway near a slightly newer '48 Ford short-bed and a surplus Overland Motors Willys Jeep. The other dogs had stopped near a split in the tree line where the path to the home began. They had all stopped barking and appeared unthreatening. Odd for dogs on open land.

"Good boys." I put out my hand out the window for them to catch my scent. "Are your owners around?" I imagine I'd be a sight for them out of nowhere. "Maybe you better go let 'em know they got a visitor so as I don't scare 'em. Go on now."

I stepped out of the truck and one of the cylinders kept firing for a few seconds. I reached for a cigarette and then remembered I quit smoking two months ago. The crickets started in as if they were laughing at me.

That's when Harry Davis came into my life, with sound before sight.

"That's okay, Cain. You can stay. He's all right. You take Abel and the others and go on back up the house and check on the girls and Phin."

The voice was gravelly but smooth, as if the stones in his throat were small, polished pebbles. It was the voice of a judge who might've grown up on whiskey and cigarettes, secure and authoritative, but with an edge just under the surface. It was difficult to see his face, silhouetted by the last of the day's glow, and he carried no flashlight. I could tell he was tall though, well over six feet, and what he did carry was an unexpected calmness in light of the sudden appearance of a Negro man arriving at this White man's home unannounced.

"I like to give my dogs names from the Bible and talk to them like humans. Figures it gives them a chance of feeling like they belong here, know what I mean?"

"Personally, I hadn't considered that," I replied, "but then, it makes sense. Our dogs on the farm are also there for more than just keeping the varmints away from the crops. They do their job well enough, but I give 'em names like Rex and King—regular dog names."

I could make out the man's head nodding and the agreeable "uh-huhs."

"Listen, sir, ah, Mr. Davis, I don't mean to barge in on you with a surprise visit but..."

"You ain't a surprise. I knew you were looking for me since Winnie made that bologna sandwich for you. This town's got ears big as rabbits, 'specially when a stranger of color drives in asking for a local. I hear you've run across some polite and some not so cordial."

I leaned back against the truck, hearing this man's disarming words as an odd collection of down-home diction and downtown intelligence. I joined right in.

"We got folks up near Mobile so poor they can't afford to spend the night. Some are good, some not. I suppose that's the way of any town with people in it."

I saw his head nod in the silhouetting light.

"By the way, the name's Davis, Harry Davis. You want to come on in and tell me what's on your mind?"

I reached for his hand that wrapped itself around mine by one-and-a-half. My hands had grown rough and well-hewn from the years working the fields, but if my palms were sandpaper, this man's were steel wool. He squeezed it deftly and with respect, but there was no hiding the years of bait and hooks and salt. The graceful utility of his work on the sea must've found their way into his movements, but the power and force of the ocean onto his skin.

I followed him down the path, pausing once to apologize for failing to tell him my name. Harry laughed, said it was okay and asked if I was hungry.

"Well, Mr. Davis, I wasn't until you mentioned it and just caught that scent. Sure smells like some kinda stew, but I don't know if I can place the kind of meat."

Just then we stepped into the light from a hanging lantern fixed from the overhang of a wide, covered porch and I caught my first real glimpse of the face of Harry Davis when he slid up onto the landing first and turned to look at me. There was a broad grin across a deeply browned face with etches carved where you'd expect them to be if you'd spent a good part of your life smiling and squinting. His hair was thick and straight, sun-bleached a wheat color, and his eyes were hazel, unchallenging without any hint of suspect. He was thin, almost wiry, and walked with the light step of a boxer. I sensed he was older than he looked on the outside, but younger than others his age on the inside.

I'd turned twenty-five exactly ten days after Ruth passed last spring, but now felt that marking time had become more of an inconvenience than a celebration. Early in 1951 Harry could've been anywhere between thirty and forty-something; his face a kind of story, not ageless, but timeless.

"Well, Mr. Cobb," he spread his arms out like you would to say this is all I have, but there was much pride and virtue in his voice.

"Please, call me Johnny."

"All right there, Johnny. This here is our home, Grace and the kids and me. Some people like to call these mobile homes because they're ashamed, but sure as the sun's down, it's just a big trailer we hauled in on a flat bed thinking we'd get around to building a permanent one as soon as I had another couple of good years on the boat. But truth is, we spend most of our lives out doors and this little place has grown on us like a turtle shell. We like it."

He opened the solid wood-framed door with a small carving of a mermaid near the center, then the screen, and waved me inside.

"I did put this door on the house, though," Harry said. "I hate the sound of anything hollow."

"Darlin', we got comp'ny for dinner."

✳ ✳ ✳

"And I couldn't leave the cemetery that night; just stuck my body to the warm, moist earth with my ear on a small clump of crab grass...listening. They found me like that two days later. It was a maintenance guy who told me I'd have to dig a hole and climb in if I wanted to die."

The stew had been Paella, an exotic type of fish soup from Spain, and afterwards there'd been some small talk and home-made wine, but it was the seven-year-old girl, Gillie they called her, who'd gotten me started talking about Ruth.

She was tall and thin, like her daddy, but her fair skin, light hair, and quick, inquisitive eyes had come from her mother, Grace. Like her father, her spirit and mindfulness were disconnected to her age. I had to ask.

"Gillie, that's an interesting name. I bet you're about ten or eleven years old." I'd padded it as a child's compliment.

"Actually, I'm seven, Mr. Cobb. Gillie is from Gilman, a writer mama used to read stories from. She was a kind of, what do you call them, Mama? Activates?"

Grace smiled and adjusted the young boy on her breast. She allowed the time lag that seemed to exist in the small living room of the trailer in the quiet comfort of the space instead of the facelessness of time.

"Try again, honey."

"Actionist? Activist!" Gillie was proud she remembered the word. "That's it, Mr. Cobb. She tried to make the world better for women. All kinds, like married and not married. Are you married, Mr. Cobb?"

That's how it started. I looked at Harry, who sat on a small stool in the corner, fiddling with a piece of wood and a knife, allowing the bigger chairs for his girls and me. He might've known some of the story, no doubt, or guessed by the language of my hands, and I did what I could with a glance to get his blessing to tell a sad story to a happy child.

Harry nodded and I saw in his eyes for the first time in that softly lit corner with the three candles burning on the wooden kitchen table, a kind of rolling down of a thin hood over the filmy iris, like this was the way that Harry protected himself from the tragedies of life. I wondered if Harry was seeing himself in me, Grace in Ruth. Years later I would confirm it time after time, realizing that every human was always looking for himself in others, in work, in mirrors, in the sounds and smells of ordinary everyday life. But mostly in love; especially in love. A man finds himself in the love of another and he knows who he is, exactly. And even at that young moment, I knew that love, same as hurt, comes in through the eyes and moves out the heart. Harry'd just pulled down a thin shade for the telling.

Grace got up to lay the baby in his crib and put on some coffee and to give me some time to compose my thoughts. When she poured the dark liquid and sat back I spoke, lightly at first, but gaining momentum like a big train until I had to back off and let Grace give me a rest.

"Ruth never spoke much with her lips—words just seemed to move around her, like wind around an old oak. She could, though, speak with other parts of her body: Her eyes when she was hard-thinking, the way she waved her hands when she was excited, or reeled them in when all riled up. But the way I figured it, mostly it was her feet that allowed Ruth to communicate the things that mattered to her; that ought to matter to others.

"When she was happy she sprang like a jack-in-the-box, ignoring the gravity of the time that tried so hard to ground-hold our lives. Or deep in her work out in the garden, those feet of hers, rarely shoed, the red soil drawing half moons under her toe nails, would plant themselves, fixed and firm in the moment, but pliable as the tall, thin pines that rimmed the edge of our land north of Mobile.

"And on occasion, when things went bad for her, those feet would carry her deep into the cypress groves and sawgrass, the prevailing south-easterlies pushing her into the sheen. It was a place that I'd feared as a child, rarely going into that swampy, misted void. But she embraced those shadows, allowing them to swallow her dismay as if the boggy soil could soften her steps and push her back out into the light.

"Johnny, someone spit on me in town," she said once, as if mentioning that the sky looked like it might rain. And when I'd hear the screen door slam, footsteps on the creaky back porch, I'd know where she was going. It was the same place where I felt that my heart could move darker and deeper into my chest; it was that thick canopy of trees on the edge of the field. I reckon one person's lock can be another's key.

"My wife's feet counted time, marked the moments and the years as human metronomes, beating out an old Robert Johnson beat like when we heard his records leak out the broken window panes of a blues joint in town, or they'd note another passing season when a small crack bled from between her wintered toes. Volumes of text were crafted by those limbs. And I loved all of their sounds."

I took a long sip from the refilled cup I'd been handed, and then a longer breath before continuing. Gillie was looking at me like a seven-year-old psychiatrist, scratching her chin.

But her eyes were devouring my words. Harry put some branches on the fire and I looked at him for permission again to go on about dead wife when I'd only met him hours before.

"What Ruth wanted above all was for those feet and those limbs to carry her far away from the South, carry her to a place where she could learn to speak openly with all her voices, raise up a child with hope that its future would eclipse her own. She didn't know where that place was, only that she wanted to be on the move, skipping over those canyons that ruled her life, running if she had to, but unchained within the freedom of the road. She had that itch.

" 'Johnny,' she'd say from time to time, usually while she peeled the potatoes for a stew and I worked up a cooking fire. 'I been talking to some of the other Black folks down at the laundry mat and I been sneaking a peak at some of those books you've been bringin' from the library. Now, I know this here land belongs to you and your brothers. And more so, all of you to it. But there's better places to live, Johnny, and better people to live amongst.' "

"I knew she was right. And Ruth knew I was connected to the land that our family had earned through sharecropping and sweat, and one kind old White man, and dumb, blind luck. My brothers and I were bound in time and blood to these ninety acres of soil so rich that if you threw out one seed, sixteen things would grow back. We all knew that if we left it, we'd be vandalizing our past. And we knew that the people from town would find a way to wrestle it back, compensate us a portion of what it was worth, if that. It's rare for a Negro family to own that much good earth. And many were the nights when my brothers, Earl and Ramsey, and our friends would walk the crop perimeter road in small groups, torches bright, shotguns cradled in their thick arms with hounds baying at the night noises. Ruth knew that a great conflict nearly burnt a hole in me. I was identified in the red-brown soil that fed our family— that kept us alive. But our skin color was too close to that of the earth. And I hated guns.

"She'd never asked me to choose between her and that land. But near the end, the signs were coming at me, and I had taken up a mind to move us away. We'd use her feet as a compass and I'd pray that my two brothers, who were still connected to the land in name and employ, and that their patience with the work, wouldn't erode with the irrigation berms.

"I had begun dreaming that Ruth's legs had become stiff and straight timbered trunks that would never again light up a Friday night boogie or bounce from berm to berm along the creek side. It was time to leave.

"Land I could find again, up north maybe; Canada, the Alaskan Territories. But Ruth I wouldn't let go of. Her mother had made me swear on my own mama's grave that I wouldn't leave her, always do my best to keep her happy. Nadine needin' have had to ask, though. I would of anyway. Beside each other at night watching the candle burn down, our dreams were telling us the same thing for different reasons. I was going to tell her that next afternoon, out on the lake after supper.

"The day before I was going to tell her, she already knew. Ruth had this gift of knowing things ahead and I'd wondered about it. I'd made my decision and guessed that she knew. I'd seen her with a sense of rising awareness, the way dogs speak when they raise their ears. There was this lightness to her step that told me it was right, even before I told her we'd be going after the crops were pulled come fall. If it would all work out with Earl and Ramsey, I wasn't so sure.

"But time came and went, those dreams dying alongside the ceasing of her heart and the quieting of her feet as they returned to the earth for the final time. And I would return to our land without my wife and child to come. It wasn't the same land anymore though; a different moon shone upon it."

There were tears running down Grace's cheeks and she'd long since tried to blot 'em out while I told them the story of Ruth's drowning in the boat, the complete one, including the stranger who'd told me about Harry, Uncle Chuck's disappearance, and then this strange mission I'd felt compelled to complete. Grace had stopped me at various parts to clarify a point or to make sure she could see and feel the whole scene as if she was there. In a polite way, Grace was making me dredge up the essential roots of the experience. Within her facial expressions, she forced my game of solitaire, at once tasting the exile that came in the words and breathing new air into the space that was left in their absence.

"That's a really, really sad story, Mr. Cobb"

It was Gillie, who was lying on the carpet resting her head on her elbows, brushing her hair out of her eyes and squinting when I told of finding Ruth's body on the lake bottom and pulling it up. Her eyes starting to dry, giving away an uncanny insight to her resilient psyche. Of all of them, Gillie reminded me the most of Ruth.

"Do you talk to her now, Mr. Cobb?" Gillie asked, almost matter-of-factly. Harry started to interrupt, but Grace shot him a well-telegraphed glance allowing the inquiry. "I mean do you go visit her grave?'

"I talk to her, Miss Gillie. But not as much as I did, and right after it happened it was like she was talking to me all the time. As quiet as Ruth was, she was giving me all sorts of advice once she was gone." I took a sip of my coffee, thinking that if any child could grasp this thought, it would be her. I hadn't spoken openly to anybody of this. And then to be spillin' my guts to a family I just met? "But no, I don't visit her grave often. Not sure why...really."

There was a thick silence in the room. I was in it and had to move through it as far as I could.

"Is that strange?"

Grace said no, not really, compared to the fact that I was even sitting here. Gillie seemed to be trying to put some simple meaning to the tale, but it looked as if her mind was tumbling like the inside parts of a lock.

"I don't know if I've loved her anymore in hindsight because I don't know where her soul is or that she's become what I've dreamt about. I do figure I've moved closer to what I admired in her. And I'm sorry if I'm being vague, but sometimes I think and sometimes I feel and at a time like this when they both come together, things come out in tongues."

Harry, who'd been quiet the whole time, listening and whittlin' the wood into a bucket and nodding his head and looking at his family, two eyes at a time, finally spoke.

"The White man down on the lake who told you about me and my new boy…you never asked him his name or why he thought I'd be in the market for a new skiff?"

"No, sir. I felt like there was something moving through me and I was afraid to get in its way."

"Are you a religious man, Johnny?" Grace asked, "I mean do you ever consider what kind of thing that *force* might be?"

"Well, yes and no, Mrs. Davis. I believe that there is a God out there, and He gives me some point to my being, though I was well and damned, excuse me, darned confounded when Ruth died. I don't believe that stuff about her being called home, as the local preachers railed on with. But I can't believe that all of her is dead, that her soul went into the ground with her body. Sometimes I go to Sunday services because it seems pointless not to try. But there remains a curious split, a give-and-take, between the living and the dying. And that's where I get confused. I reckon that I have no call for the organized religion of people who follow a regular man no matter what he tells him to do or not do. But I believe heartedly in a Holy Spirit, whatever it may be." I was going to tell them of what I'd been taught by Grayfalls about the Great Spirit, but backed off. The story of Grayfalls was best told by a man's actions, the time and place as important as the lesson.

There was a silence that entered the room and seemed to sweep into each person's mind. But it must've settled somewhere deep and safe enough for the quiet was no trouble. The space between us was comfortable and no one felt the need to force their rhythm on the other.

There was a sound at the door, not quite a knock, but neither a scratch. Gillie got up and let the last two dogs in. Harry asked her if she'd make sure that Sarah and Micah had water before they lie down in the corner next to the other dogs. Looking at me, Harry shrugged his shoulders and said it took awhile for the Bible to even use female names.

I sensed the night winding down, heard Grace tell Gillie to get ready for bed, then get up to check on the baby who she'd laid in a crib next to the fire.

Gillie kissed her dad on the cheek, pressed out her hand to mine and said it was nice to meet me. Then just before leaving the single front room of the trailer, she turned gracefully as if it was scripted, reached for the door jam and spoke in a tone somewhere between question and statement.

"Mr. Cobb, you think a lot, don't you?"

"Yes, Miss Gillie. I do that. I reckon it's become who I am, this pondering."

"You know what I think, Mr. Cobb? I think dead people keep on thinking, too. Good night."

Harry stood up slowly from the stool, sheathed his knife and then stretched his arms and legs one at a time.

"If I was in your shoes, Johnny Cobb, after that telling, I'd be wanting a belt of my home brew that's been curing out in the shed. But seeing as you're too polite to ask, I'm going to insist on it. Besides, the moon ought to be up by now and I'd like to see what the weather's going to be doing in the morning."

We walked out into the thick Florida air that kept all things damp and clumpy most of the year. Harry stood looking at the sky, breathing, feeling, much like the farmers up north did around planting time. Only he was a fisherman; he did it by the hour without even noticing.

He led me to a narrow shed with a high ceiling hung with assorted nets and floats. There was a workbench covered in rows of reels and spools of line and hooks and, underneath, a metal cabinet with a heavy lid. Harry said he'd grown the wheat, barley, and hops himself and it'd been exactly thirty-one and one-half days; it should be perfect. He reached in and pulled out two large dark brown bottles and popped the lids on the edge of the bench. He handed me one of the bottles, held the other up to the single light bulb with half a dozen mosquitoes buzzing in concert, and checked the sediment.

"Liquid bread with a kick?" I asked.

"Something like that. To family, Mr. Cobb, past and present."

He raised the heavy bottle in my direction and put it to his lips, tasting the earth that had grown its ingredients, set the bottle on the work bench and wiped the back of his mouth with his shirt sleeve.

I took his look and drank and heard the crickets in the yard and wondered what breath had put me here. But I didn't have to know right then and drank hard, feeling the warm beer flowing into my stomach and its effect already taking place, not because of the alcohol, but something else, something that came from nowhere. And everywhere.

"Your new son," I finally asked as Harry was busy studying the mosquitoes and then reaching into the cabinet for another. "What's his name again?"

"Well, I'll be damned. You don't know?"

"Not properly introduced a'tall."

"Well, there aren't any official papers on him declaring to the world what he should be called. Grace delivered him in the back room of the trailer with a little help, right where I reckon you'll be sleeping tonight. I'm getting on in years, Mr. Cobb—not quite young, but a long way from old. But I figure he's about the best thing I got going in my life, right up there with Grace and Gillie. I don't plan on letting the world get a hold of him for a spell.

"That boy is heritage and I can't deny him that without denying the purpose of my own living. He's a gift from your God, Mr. Cobb, that spirit force you spoke of maybe. I ain't as eloquent a thinker as you, but the connection between your Ruth dying off and my boy getting birthed and you coming here...well, it's enough for a guy like me to start thinking he ought to do more thinking. I'm a slow learner, Mr. Cobb, but once something is set in my mind, it's like a gaff through the gills of a shark—it ain't coming loose."

"And his name, Mr. Davis? His name?"

"Oh, well, it's Phin, Johnny Cobb, it's Phin, after every living thing in the water. But a PH sound."

"Phin." I said the word out loud and the weight of it struck bottom, surprising me. "Not Phineas?" I asked.

"A few people have adopted that but, you know, it being an odd name and such, I don't much care. He's our son, at least for awhile. And then he's his own. I'm sure you understand that, Johnny Cobb."

"I'm not sure anybody understands something like that. But I reckon we sure can have a go at it."

"You go right ahead, Mr. Deep Thinker. Lemme know what you find out. I think I'll just try and raise up these kids best I can."

I was momentarily stalled in the icy hard thought that more'n likely I wouldn't have a child of my own and pulled another beer out of the case without asking, unashamed of my action.

"You worry about your kids getting hurt?" It was a simple question, obvious, but unfair.

There was a shift in Harry, a pulling down of more than the eyelids.

"Of course. But nothing's gonna happen to my kids if I have anything to do with it. And around here, I have a lot to do with who comes near them."

I believed Harry Davis as he said this—he believed he could protect them from all evil in the world. At least until they had a chance to protect themselves. And even then, he'd keep on trying.

"Sometimes I think it ain't gonna be like it was in '14 or '41. We have enough work keeping our own county at peace, let alone the rest of the damn mixed-up world. But that shit going on in Korea has me worried and, honestly, I don't know what I'd do if Uncle Sam came calling on me to go fight the Chinese, though I reckon I'm sort of excluded."

"Oh," I asked in passing, "Did you serve...over there? I mean, in the army?" Soon as they came out I wanted to take the words back.

"Serve? Worse word y'all used all night. I like you, Johnny. But don't ever ask me about my 'serving,' okay?"

"That's fair," I backpedaled and made a note to keep Harry and the subject of war in separate corners of the world.

"And before I forget," changing the subject quick as I could, "I wanted for you to have a look at this present I brought for Phin, which was a something like a gift to me and had to be passed on, if that makes any sense."

"Shit, Cobb," the momentary tension between us gone. "As salty as my head can be, I actually thought you were more sensible than my freshwater friends who went off to college and think they run this town. I know exactly what you're talking about." Harry's words had thickened with the night air and a third beer.

"Well, she's on the truck. The *Ruth Henry David*, a birthday present for the boy."

"Well, he was born during the same year as your wife's drowning."

Harry didn't apologize for the words and grabbed two more bottles as he led me out of the shed to my truck. "*Henry David*, eh? That a family name or from that nature rebel-type from up northeast?"

"Not bad Harry. You got potential."

"That's Grace, Johnny Cobb. She's the one who likes to read stories about people bucking the system. Something in her blood, same as anyone, eh?"

"Yeah, sure, Harry. It's either in your blood or it ain't."

"Gonna be nice tomorrow," Harry said, running his hands on the splitting teak rail caps of the boat, moving away from something else that was too close or too powerful or that he couldn't control. It was as if he could manage boats and weather and the future of his family, but not his own past.

"It'll be a good day to get an honest week's work in. If'n I were you, I'd be thinking about sticking around for a few weeks and getting to know the ocean a bit. We got lots of it right here. Maybe you could find a job right on top of it." He winked and traded an empty bottle for a backup full one.

"Besides, I've never owned a gifted boat with both male and female names. Might need you to fill in the gaps a bit; both in these split floorboards and the details you left out tonight. I take that boat off your hands, Cobb, I'll need some book learning to go along with it, some book ideas to fill in the seams." Harry put his hand on my shoulder. "Reckon the men in this family don't read enough," and added, "least not stuff between the covers."

We stood in front of the little boat as the moon did its best to show us her graceful lines beneath the weathered exterior, the sudden hints and playful jabs turning back to a comfortable silence.

"Yep, Cobb," Harry was admiring the moon as he might a lover, "It's gonna be a good day in the morning...a damn good day."

And as we walked back to the house, I thought how fortunate I was to have had a reason to be here. I wouldn't say comin' down this way with no reason woulda been akin to an innocent man sent to prison. But it would've been different.

CHAPTER 4

NOT QUITE A MORNING AFTER

I woke up early at the Davis house, the sun far from hitting the edge. Thinking I'd just get a glass of water and go back to sleep, I noticed a light on in the living room and poked my head in to see the child, Gillie, reading a book. It was a collection of poetry.

"You're up late or early, Miss Gillie."

"You like poems, Mister Cobb?" She set the book down. Emily Dickinson. Made sense.

"I like any words, written or spoken, that say a lot in a small space."

"You think she was in love, Mister Cobb? I mean, there's a lot of really gushy stuff that's hard to get from your 'magination."

Again I was having a hard time fitting the young girl with her older soul. "I'm sure of it, Miss Gillie. I think she was in love with a lot of things."

Gillie sensed that I wasn't going to expand at this hour, on this subject, so quite innocently, she came around to what she really wanted to know and I was caught with no way to politely maneuver my way out.

"How come you only told part of the story of your wife's dying? Why'd you hold all the other stuff back?"

"Reckon it just wouldn't be polite to dump a whole night's telling on a family I just barged in on. Besides, I don't know anything about you or your parents or your little brother. Seems to me a relationship should unfold slowly, on its own time."

Gillie squirmed a bit and seemed to search her young mind for any answer that would move her quicker toward adulthood and all that she perceived it would bring.

"What if you didn't own a lot of time, Mister Cobb? Pretty soon I'm gonna be seven and one-half and then eight and ten and sixteen and then all growed up and maybe married and what will I know about bein' a grown-up unless I ask grown-ups? I don't read fairly tale books like the other kids my age. They all lie. I seen—oops...*saw* your face last night when you were telling the story. That's the truth, Mister Cobb. I don't have time for make-believe. I liked your sad story."

"Okay, Miss Gillie, you want the stuff that got passed over, here it is. Now, you stop me if you don't understand a word because this is the part where I don't normally practice telling it to kids."

She seemed quite pleased with herself and sat back in the chair, closed the Dickinson text, and folded her little hands like she was praying. Only they were lower, right around her tummy.

"Now where did I leave off?"

"You never really started, but my daddy told me that your wife drowned when she fell off a boat. He told me that when he tucked me in and I told him back that I should say a prayer for her soul. Sometimes Daddy forgets to remind me to pray so I remind him to tell me so we both don't forget."

"Well, that makes some sense, I reckon, and your daddy is correct. She was out on a small boat, the very same one that's sitting out in your front yard, when she fell. Her uncle, a good man, though kinda wild sometimes, won day-rights to the boat in a card game. They weren't far from shore and she was standing up and slipped. I think Ruth hit her head or something, because she was a good swimmer. Chuck couldn't swim a lick to save himself."

I was working hard not to get emotional and mostly winning the battle. I could see that Gillie was doing her best to follow the tale, but at one point she stopped me and wanted to know what happens after people die. Like we all do.

"I don't know yet, Miss Gillie, but I'll send you a sign when I get there."

"What did you do then, Mister Cobb, after you brought them in from the lake? Did you take them to the hospital?"

"Sort of." I swallowed hard somehow realizing that I was speaking more to my repressed memory than to a young girl. Still, like music coming from the backyard of a neighbor, I was unable to change the volume or the content.

✳ ✳ ✳

Chuck was alive but not Ruth. There were lots of other Negroes around by then. The women sang and Chuck coughed up some lake water and insisted on driving me and Ruth and our child in her tummy to the hospital, and I held my past in my hands while my future bounced around the bed of our truck. The world spun and the truck sputtered, splitting the fog as it crept across the surrounding marsh. From the back, with Ruth's face cradled in my lap, her lips an off-color of blue in the fading light, I asked Chuck to turn on the transistor radio, to help drown the other-worldly voice from inside my head as it was coming too hard and too fast. And from that radio Woody sang that ballad of his, "This land is your land, this land is my land."

"Turn it off," I screamed into the mist with so much force that I thought I might wake Ruth. "Take it back, I don't want it! Now just leave me be. I didn't need what you let happen."

Uncle Chuck must've known that my conversation was not with him, but with something after life ends.

"But others might, Johnny Cobb. Others might,"

The strange voice drifted inside my own while the clouds crept in from the east and the wind seemed to die like a breath gone quiet. Chuck slowed the truck and pulled over on the dirt road. He left the motor running and he left Woody singing and he came around to the truck bed and put his big black hand on his niece's cold blue cheek. His eyes looked dead as well, to my thinking.

"I done killed your wife and child, Johnny. It ain't God you ought to be blaming, but me. I killed her, Johnny. And isn't nobody bringing her back. I'm a sorry sombitch Johnny, just a sorry Negro." And then Uncle Chuck bent down and kissed the wrinkled forehead of his dead niece, touched me on the shoulder, and walked off into the walled sheen of cypress and magnolia and sorrow.

I called out for Chuck, told him we didn't owe heaven nothing any more. We shouldn't pay it any mind a'tall. But he disappeared into the thick and left me alone with the spirits and the dogs and the dead.

"Chuck you get your ass back here right now. I done saved it once and I'm not gonna go havin' to do it again."

I tried to pry myself away from Ruth, but when I moved her chest to go after Chuck, a pale fluid came out of her mouth and the dogs whimpered and Woody sang and crickets began their calls and I heard His voice as if he was sitting in the cab leaning His head around the edge of the truck.

"Others might, Johnny, others might. I'll watch over Ruth. You watch over those who most certainly will come after."

I wedged Ruth's body between a spare tire and the two old shepherds, Isaac and Jeremiah, and thought about running off into the woods after Chuck. But when a man like Chuck, who'd grown up in the thick and denseness of nature and the way things were there, and when he didn't want to get found, you wouldn't find him. I spoke to my dead wife as if she was sleeping: "We'll be there in just a bit, Hon. You rest a bit now. "

I drove the last few miles to the hospital and parked around back. There the nurses took her for a period, but I don't remember how long. Later, I watched them load Ruth into the barn doors of the local Negro hearse as it swallowed her feet last; her heels reaching out from underneath the lake-stained sheet in the yellow glare of the streetlights reflecting off the wet pavement. Everything that I had ever felt about her or would come to feel in later years could not flush the lake from her lungs or our child from her belly. The last thing I saw were her feet and I thought again of her in the garden, pulling carrots or picking worms from tomato leaves. When I would see those tanned feet with the rough-hewn soles standing sentinel to the hungry crows passing high above, I knew that Ruth was sound yet evolving still, same as the earth that would envelop her.

A man in a hospital coat came up to me and asked if I had any plans on burying her.

"No sir, the thought of putting my wife in a box and letting the earth swallow her was not something I had thought often about."

Then I asked him if he was married and did he think about putting his wife or child in a grave. He called me an uppity nigger and walked away. I was young then, but that's no excuse, only a testimony to my naiveté.

"You want the Parrish to pay for her burial in the city cemetery or you want to come back for her in the morning?" A coroner-type had emerged from down some pair of opaque doors and I wondered why hospitals always have so many doors that you can't see through. He said he worked for the County and tried to conjure up some empathy from way down below where a coroner-type might store it.

My tongue had filled my throat and was cutting off any sound. I just nodded.

"Okay then," he was back to business. "We'll box her up and have her ready for you in the morning. You best go on home now."

I looked across the room at the girl in the growing light. "That's the most of it, Miss Gillie, that's the most."

Gillie sat there as if cast in wax, listening and doing something else I couldn't be sure.

"Wow," she finally said. I don't really understand some of the words, but I'd be sad if I lost my mom or dad or Phin. Thanks for telling me, Mr. Cobb." And as she slipped off to her room she turned once and said it must be nice to know that God himself made a point of talking to me.

I sat there in the first hint of the new day and thought about the other middle part, the meaning of the missing words worth more than the telling of the ones that'd come out.

The death of Ruth and the unborn was my fate. They could've lived forever because, in fact, in my life they already had. And what was forever anyway? Just a long continuous silence without interruption? I knew I'd make the best of a solitary life if I had to.

Passing over my lifeless family to the coroner that evening, cheap whiskey on his breath, a stale, city smell lurking near the loading zone behind the hospital, the sun refusing to set as if God was waiting for my answer, I put my long knife in its own cradle, but kept it sharp and close and threatening for many years. I think He understood and was patient with my apprenticeship.

CHAPTER 5
THE FIRST HOMECOMING

What I know about Uncle Chuck's actions during this spell is pieced together from long conversations with Nadine and others who happened to see him passing this way and that. I can't swear it, but it's the best I can do to keep my need to do the telling flowing when sometimes big holes in a story will mess up the smooth parts ahead.

The old Studebaker pulled away, Nadine remembered, kicking up dust and gravel, spewing dark gray smoke from the cracked muffler. Uncle Chuck heard the two cylinders that were in need of pistons and rings and another one likely needin' gaskets. He watched the car pull away and the old Black man who'd given him a ride all the way from Tallahassee lifted and waved his big hand out the window as he drove off. It was a man rich in grace driving a poor man's car, but given two full days and some factory fresh parts, Chuck thought he would be able to fix the car. The man was gone and he'd never caught his name.

It had been three months, three near arrests, and countless bottles of cheap whiskey—cheaper hotels—and the cheapest excuse for a human he could ever come up with for himself, all because he killed his niece on that sweet spring afternoon out on the lake.

And now Uncle Chuck had returned to the home of his youth, or at least part of it. He'd been running around the lower South since that afternoon when he'd stopped the truck with a grieving Johnny and his dead niece, Ruth, in the back. They all knew she was dead, though the accepting of it came slowly. There had been no dangerous rush to the hospital or the morgue or wherever Johnny was to drive them after he said his goodbyes and stroked her still-wet hair in the back of the truck with the dogs trying to lick the life back into her body. And even the warm April eve and the blanket the Black townsfolk had wrapped her in, couldn't keep his niece's body from moving toward a colder side of the world; at least the side that Chuck had now placed himself.

For three months he'd asked himself why he'd stopped and run out, just leaving the two of them there on the side of the road, abandoned, while he folded further into himself and the thick underbrush where he'd run from his nightmares, sometimes a step ahead, but mostly swallowed in their night throats. Chuck had never run from anything. Was it long, overdue guilt? Fear? A chaos in his mind unwrapping itself at a time when he should've been cinching down the straps of courage? He didn't think it was any of these. Chuck had always gained his strength in family; his ability to fight the good fight had always come from the women he'd raised and was raised by. Now, he'd committed the unconscionable. And it had reduced his power source by more than one-half.

After a month on the road he decided he had slipped into the skin of some animal he'd never met. After three months, he knew that he'd forfeited membership in anything called integrity. Just last week it had dawned on him that whatever conclusion he'd come to about that private transaction with himself, it would forever be an intangible and unreachable brass ring of understanding. He'd made a mistake. And he'd spend the rest of his days trying to somehow unmake it.

There were no thoughts about how he might've stayed closer to shore in that neat little mahogany and teak skiff; the one he'd acquired day-use of in a game of cards. Just think, he'd been bluffing, too, when the stranger had put up a Sunday's use to that neat-looking little eleven-foot boat in lieu of the C-note Chuck had raised and everybody else had folded and said he was nuts or had balls or was just plain stupid. The ones who knew him well would bet he didn't have more than five bucks in his pocket. Then again, Chuck had always been a wild card—uncaring, loose, but loyal in the way that his people were to each other.

What was this gambling thing anyway? Just another way to see how people would react when the stakes were raised? Just another way for him to look for himself in the face of others? This man they called Uncle Chuck had always known he'd be a damn good soldier if only he'd had a war that was his own, that was legal. He'd avoided the thing in Europe because after his daddy, Willis, died, there would be no more men to carry on the name. Then why should he go and fight for a country in which he still wasn't completely free? Let the White boys go follow Generals McArthur and Patton. He was waiting for another Washington Carver.

But Chuck knew that he was capable of killing. The oppression by the White boss was more noticeable to him than to his parents, Nadine and Willis. But not his sister, Louella, before she'd run off. He knew he had it in him and it sometimes scared him—not the killing itself, but the beating drum of its potential.

I imaged what might've been brewing around Chuck's mind as he negotiated the death of Ruth.

"C'mon, Chuck," he tried unsuccessfully to lie to himself, *"it was only five feet deep. Okay, maybe eight, but no more than ten."*

You couldn't have been more than twenty, okay, maybe fifty yards from shore. You didn't know your niece was going to bolt up in the bow and try to hold a ballerina pose while standing on the gunwale, screaming at her young husband, Johnny, up on the shore to look.

"See darlin', your baby still has those moves. Look at me J.C. Your little wife moves like a cat even with a kitten-to-be in her tummy."

You didn't know.

Chuck sustained the idea that some passing wake from a distant White man's powerboat had hit the port hull like the slightest tap on the arm from a sleeping lover that awakens her with a violent lurch and she sits upright, as if a thumping nightmare had grabbed and shook her. You forgot the subtlety of the waters; that narrow balance beam between good and evil.

But did you ever really know then, Chuckie boy? Did you cheat on the Cub Scout swim test that summer out on Lake Jordan northeast of Montgomery when your mama, Nadine, when offered a free spot, had sent you away for the summer after your daddy died and Louella had still not returned? Mama thought it good for you to live among other boys before you had to join the race of men. And was it a White Boy Scout with a sash covered in badges that'd told the scoutmaster about the little Negro boy hiding under the pier when everybody else was being sent a hundred yards around the anchored canoe and back to the beach?

Oh, Chuckie boy, you didn't kill her. She was like your sister, Louella, who had the baby Ruth at sixteen when you were barely nine and then left the baby for you and your mom to raise up because Daddy was sick by then and your sis had discovered jazz and that stuff they put in their arms with needles.

But you could swim, old Chuck, couldn't you? You'd fished on the banks of every stream and creek that fed Mobile Bay after Daddy had finally died and Mama had moved you and little Ruth down to Mt. Vernon, just north of Mobile, to live with her sisters, Mary and Loretta for a spell. You remember when your lure got stuck on a rock and you had to wade out to the waist-deep water to uncatch it. Sometimes even on hot summer days you would dunk your whole head under water and think, no problem, I could've swum around that canoe if that asshole with the blonde eyebrows and peely nose had given me a chance. I wasn't hiding, just getting my courage up. They shouldn't have sent me home. I didn't mean to hit him so hard and so many times. He shouldn't have said that Negroes can't swim.

You'd do it again, though, wouldn't you, Chuck?

Hell yes. I would've made sure he knew that the Winters boys didn't buy into that Negro-calling shit.

But in a roundabout kinda' tragedy, you killed your baby sister-niece, didn't you? And you're here to ask Mama to give you absolution? Oh, Chuck, what will you do with yourself?

The truth was, Chuck could never know which words would hold the badge of finality and which ones might open up his mental frontier to sodbusters. Chuck could surprise even himself. He could look in a store's glass window, make his light brown eyes deepen and his wide lips curl back against white teeth that chewed on the ends of his thick and nappy locks that had started to fall into tight spiraled curls snapping at the collar of the only jacket he had and the only shirt he'd run away with that afternoon on the lake. Then he'd put those lips into a secret unsayable challenge to speak only what was real at that moment. Even if it killed him later.

I could've made it around that canoe. I was just getting my courage up.

✷ ✷ ✷

Inside the three-room farmhouse that sat on the edge of forty-two acres of good soil that grew alfalfa and romaine and sometimes tobacco, Nadine Winters sat. After Ruth passed, Chuck had gone away and I had headed south with that little boat strapped to the back of my truck, Nadine had left her little house and moved back in with her sisters, Mary and Loretta, and their husbands. When Uncle Chuck returned that late fall of '50, all the husbands were still out in the growing fields picking crops for the man who owned the fields and paid them less than a dollar a bushel for harvesting the alfalfa and ten cents for each head of romaine. Nadine's husband was deep in another field, but she couldn't remember, didn't want to remember where. Dead is dead, she'd always say, the living ought to remember that more. She'd stopped going to funerals after Willis died some twenty years ago and, in many ways, just stopped remembering any pain. She had her son, Chuck, and her granddaughter, Ruth. She knew that Louella would return someday.

When I'd driven through the first full night after Ruth died to tell Nadine that the grandbaby she had raised and had come out right and proper as a person was dead, and that her only son who was a bit of a rambler. but respected as all of the Winters men were, had disappeared into the thick world of the South, Nadine had looked through me and could only say that she couldn't make any funeral because she had to stay home in case Louella stopped by.

✳ ✳ ✳

Now, with the dust of the old Studebaker finally settled, Uncle Chuck walked up to the house of women that fall of '50 with a small duffel over his shoulder and eighty-five cents in his pocket.

"You're home, Chuck," he tried to convince himself. "You're a survivor; time to start pulling it all together."

But when he walked up onto the narrow wooden porch with two planks missing and called out, "Mama, Loretta, Aunt Mary—it's Chuck," the little clapboard house with the thin white sheets for curtains felt like a foreign country, small and strange. He was ashamed for his mama and for all Blacks. And he was disgusted with himself.

He heard a piano playing inside. It was a hymn he remembered from his church-going youth when his folks would dress up him and Louella in their Sunday best each week and catch the bus down to the Union Springs Baptist Church for services. It was Nadine playing because she'd always change the tempo and gave it more of a folksy, blues feel to it with her chord substitutions and subtle pauses before sneaking in a blue note.

Chuck set his duffel down on the rickety swing and opened the screen door. It still squeaked, but not loud enough to announce his entry over Nadine's pedal stomping action on the ancient upright. He said "Mama" out loud again, but she didn't hear him. "It's Chuck, Ma."

He noticed that the old brown bun she used to wear up on her head had morphed into a mere spirit of gray and silver, thin and wispy, and only a hint of the great locks she once carried. Her skin was a mortician's color, pale and icy peach. But her hands moved around the keyboard in a natural way as if she was commanding the music from somewhere other than her fingers.

How long had it been? How much rain had fallen—or failed to fall—on the crops that supported his mother , her sisters, their husbands, and the memories of all their children who'd left to find a better life in Mobile or Montgomery or even Birmingham? How long had he been standing there admiring this great matriarch, wondering what she would say when she finally turned and saw him frozen in life, five steps behind him?

That's when everything went black.

"Jesus, Mary, and Joseph! Loretta, what in God's good name? Is that...? Oh, my Lord, what did you go and do? It's Chuck, you blind old bat! Go and get some cool rags and water. Go on now!"

"I's sorry, Nadie. I just seen't a big man a'standin' behin't you, thinkin' I was a'savin' yo life. I couldn't sees if'n it was Chuckie. Is he a'right? I hit 'em purty hard."

"Loretta, I tol' you go and get some rags and water. There's blood coming outta' my boy's head. Oh, Lord God, don't *You* mess with him. Now git!"

The truth was that Nadine's sister, Loretta, was nearly blind, had the diabetes and gout, and was acting on pure instinct. So, too, was Nadine in her warning tossed up to the God she worshipped. She had never threatened anyone before, let alone the one she prayed to. But she'd done it now and she meant it and the words out of her mouth were closer to demands than requests.

Loretta had hit Chuck with a three-feet section of two-by-four that was left in the corner for carrying the big iron cooking pot when it got too hot. And she'd hit him good and solid, right on the left temple, the worst place to hit a man on his head.

That night after Aunt Mary's husband had gone to fetch the doc from town and he'd stitched Chuck up and cleaned the wound, the doc told them to keep an eye on him because, "There wasn't much else they could do 'ceptin they wanted to take him to the hospital in Mobile, assuming they had some money to pay for it," which they didn't.

Nadine went back to her piano playing and said, "It's outta my hands now." Her sisters watched with disbelief as she turned her back on her only boy in that back bedroom and walked toward the front of the little house. They looked at each other, eyes full of questions and grief and more questions, while the husbands went outside to get the bottle and smoke, and try to forget.

Out in the living room and on the front porch, a fat, dark, sound played in a minor key; brooding, horrible music they'd never heard the likes of. It was beyond the sadness of blues, an evil vibration of the thick wires inside of that black box with white keys. Loretta's husband drank from a brown bottle, scratched his chin, and said to no one in particular that it was a devil's sound.

Loretta and Mary stroked Chuck's clammy brow, dabbing their eyes with the edge of a soiled rag left by the doc, adding red war paint to their dark, puffy cheeks. They listened to his now rhythmic breathing; a sound that comforted them and lie opposed to the disturbing and discordant keys that Nadine welled up from the deepest of places they didn't know hid such dark vibrations. And Loretta prayed.

"Oh, dear Lord, I's as sorry as I ever bin in ma' whole life. Take me Lord and leave this man and then if there's anything left in my account, please Lord, take that devil sound out of Nadine a'fore it attracts the real thing hisself."

And the men outside behind the house shook their heads and lowered their eyes, but still drank hard enough to say out loud and to each other that a lotta things jus' ain't right.

CHAPTER 6

DISSENTION

It happened on one of those rare nights in the early summer of southern climes, when the days are warmer than you'd expect and the nights are sweeter still in the way the land holds the heat like the way you'd resist a lover's goodbye.

✳ ✳ ✳

The repair on the pier was nearly complete. I'd had a couple of months of legitimate work, honest work with honest men, as most men go. And the stars in the sky seemed close enough to finger and the sound of the breaking waves as they gave themselves up against the sugary sands reminded me of the passing of all things. I was still young, but it felt like my soul was aging in dog years. The year and a month or so since Ruth had passed could've been a hundred years. What did I know of these things, except they'd happened? In my quarter-century-plus-one, I had seen things come and go, known them, felt them like a wound that refuses to close and heal until persuaded with the sweetest of care. But they had not settled in that place where meaning meets purpose and peace rolls in on the morning fog. Something was shifting inside of me. And it was tectonic.

It was to be my last day working the crane out on the newly refurbished pier and knowing that, I'd come in well before the sunrise to watch the stars set, imagining that Ruth set herself inside Orion's Belt to surround my center. I climbed the long ladder to the control booth as if going to visit her for breakfast and stopped in my chair, fingering the controls that'd lifted and set the new pilings to replace and extend what nature had destroyed once and could do again in one of God's long exhalations. It had only been a short time, but quietude was beginning to settle in my chest and the shadowy figures in the wake of my recent history had gone to rest for the time being. If it wasn't acceptance, it was moving in that direction.

I opened my thermos and sipped the hot coffee that Harry's wife, Grace, had packed for me. Tasting the hint of some Hispanic liqueur, I smiled at the thought of Harry, up even earlier than me, making his unique blends that differed with the day and his mood and what he could get in trade from his connections on the docks.

The coffee slid down my throat and I could see the first of the day's rays bending over the distant flatlands in the east, past the curve of the Gulf, past the beaches of western Florida, past the long sandy finger of itself and into the Atlantic, which came up against Africa and the beginning of everything.

I put the thermos back in the pail and noticed a small black and white photo of the boy set next to a fried fish sandwich. It was young Phin. He must've been nearly eight months old at the time, and though too young to show the traits of his lineage, something in the photo reminded me of what Harry said that first night out in the shed, that all he wanted was to keep his boy from getting hurt. That's all. That's all anyone really wants though, right? Or should want; to keep safe the ones they care most about.

I looked at the photo and could hear a few cars pulling up in the dirt lot way down below me. It was just a picture of a kid, a baby who couldn't talk yet, who couldn't defend himself or fight back. All he could do was feel and make noises to display his pleasure or discomfort.

But when a photo is set up against a lived life and the boy is a man with a past all his own to carry around his neck or in his back pocket or on his sleeve, it's not that hard to see it even if it's a lie—you can pretend that you knew way back then by the way they see you looking at them behind the photograph. Memories I thought, as I took another sip from the thermos, are like pictures of small children; they grow into themselves. I took the photo out of the pail and placed it in the pocket of my work shirt. We would've had kids like that, Ruth and me.

I could hear the ruffling banter of more men arriving as they pulled up or were dropped off, talking between staccato spurts of ribbing laughter, sometimes loud and glowing, then silent and reserved. I could see the pulsing lights of their cigarettes, realizing the fire and smoke and places it passed through their bodies, enjoyed for the feeling it gave them, along with addiction, disease, and then the crushing back into the earth from where the tobacco had been harvested. This sentimentality was new to me. And as good as the whimsy felt, it also felt like a risk.

"Hey, Cobb," it was Jed Riot who'd spotted me up on the crane in the pale, growing light and yelled. "What're ya'll doing up there? Training for your new job as the first Black prison guard in the South?"

I heard the light-hearted laughter of the men I'd shared racial jokes with while I'd been on the job. There was a disarming musicality that set free the tension when I called Jerry the welder, "A damn inbred, red-necked Klansman with a room temperature IQ," or when he looked at me during a lunch break and said, "Hey, Cobb, this here egg salad be needin' some pepper. Can you scratch some a yer skin on it?"

It was the song of men struggling to define themselves in the definition of others who were different. It was men who'd come back from a war in another country fighting a foreign tyranny, but wrestling with the memories of their grandfathers and their grandfather's fathers owning men for the sake of their strength in the fields—that American tyranny of prejudice. They were men who were happy to be where they called home, satisfied in the sweat of the red-necking sun. They weren't immortal, but they'd made it back alive and were happy to have the simple security of a place to stand without fear. Just gimme a place to stand, they said, and they could move the world in the right direction.

"C'mon down here, Johnny," Jed called out through a long megaphone he'd found in the trash behind the high school gym and used to practice vaudeville imitations on lunch breaks. "We gots to all have us a little snort to celebrate this pier I let you guys build for me. Git yer butt down before another hurricane comes along and rips this beauty apart."

"A'ight big White-trash boss man," I played along. "This valuable crane-riding dreamer is a comin'.'"

Three steps from the bottom of a ladder I'd climbed a hundred times, I missed an edge with my boot and caught my foot between two metal rungs, breaking my lower right leg in two places. That was the beginning of me learning how to fish. Dang, that hurt.

What surprised me first was the sound, the way a snapping bone or, in this case, two of them at once, truly do sound like brittle twigs held in each hand and snapped over a knee. The second thing was the unique reactions of the men who stood over me, who helped me, or didn't help me, but watched me. Much can be said of how a man responds to another man's pain.

The crane ladder had short, steep steps, rungs stacked almost on top of each other. It was steel with eighth-inch holes drilled through the steps to let the mud and water run through, but grip the soles of work boots as they pushed operators up to the small cabin. Not many people used the steps; they weren't allowed or they just didn't trust themselves in the knowledge that even if they were able to climb them well enough as they faced the ladder, and when they'd seen or done what they'd gone up for in the first place was complete, the return journey down when their back was to the world below held even more dangers.

I knew this and reminded myself each time I'd left my perch for lunch or to call it quits for the day. But on that day, that last day, maybe the last time I'd descend them at all, my mind was still in the cabin or the past or the heavens, I missed a step; just slipped a little on the third rung, on the third rock from the sun, three feet from dirt, and it sucked my leather boot into its grip. At first, I thought maybe I'd just fall through a bit and my other foot would catch or my hand would reach out and grab another step as it might a stuffed animal prize while riding a carnival ride. But one of those hands held my pail with the coffee and Grace's fish sandwich. The other seemed to be cocked in an upward right angle like the way a rodeo star loosens it for balance or the way a beauty queen waves at her admirers as she floats by in a parade. Either way, it didn't save me, and when the foot lodged and the body kept moving, the lower tibia and fibula snapped at that crisp, biting fulcrum. Damn it hurt, too. But not right away.

I hit the construction dirt with my shoulder and lay there in an odd, contorted way, almost comfortable looking I suppose, except for the fact that my lower leg was bent in a place not intended for bending and the sharp, jagged ends of two bones protruded from beneath the cuff of my jeans. The skin around the open wound had interesting edges that quivered and curled back on themselves, rolling up as the taut skin of the shin pulled the opening wider. There was little if any blood, the bone's bayoneted points having missed the major vessels of the leg.

In the morning's false dawn, with workers still arriving and getting their tools and plans together, nobody paid much close attention to me right away. A rough carpenter who had been finishing up the long handrails that ran the length of the pier, just some older guy from St. Pete named Johnson, was the first to say anything.

"Hey, Cobb. Nice dismount. You trying to make the Olympic team and get a free trip to Finland next year? I hear the local African labor is as dark as you."

A few others looked over and thought I was just playing it up, seeing as though it was the last day before they took the big crane away.

"Crane boy," called out a White kid from Fort Walton Beach who helped pour concrete. "You ain't gettin' any sympathy from us. We gots two more weeks of work. Your job is done, less'n you want to smooth 'crete with us ground folk."

Jed Riot, who had been speaking with an early morning inspector from the city, looked up from his fixed gaze on the table in front of the small trailer that served as an office.

"Jesus, Cobb," he started to walk with a worried purpose in my direction. "What the hell did you go and do?"

"Reckon I busted up my leg. And from the sight of those two white sticks creeping out of my boot top, I did a good job of it."

Jed called for the first aid kit from the office, which consisted of a rusty metal box filled with Band-Aids, some rubbing alcohol, and a triangle-shaped sling in a waxed paper bag. Billy Ray, the plumber, said go get a doc and someone else said holy shit, Cobb really fucked up good. But most of the men kind of stood around, not knowing how to act. There was well-hidden pity, there was disgust, embarrassment, disdain, there was sadness, and, if I was correct, in one or two there was a little bit of pleasure in seeing a Black man who'd happened onto an important job get just what the hell he must've deserved.

The hopeless thing, though, was the way most of the men felt the confusion. Some of these guys had been fighting in Europe and Africa and the South Pacific not even six or seven years ago. But to them, the task at hand had always been clear: in wartime the job was winning the war. Out in the field of battle where the rhetoric could never fly like the bullets, justified or not, the reason was of no concern like the concern for one's life and that of the men in his company. Stuff like skin color was put away for awhile. Now, that *awhile* was almost gone for some of them and what we might've shared in getting the job of building something special was slipping away as well.

But a soldier who'd been in the shit always knew what to do in the shit, I thought. Some of these men might not have served or served as a token but necessary accessory, loading ships and fixing airplanes. The only way to tell would've been to look in their eyes and wait for someone to make a move.

In front of them lay a man in need of help—me, for God's sake. And that man had tried to close the door on oppression by laughing about it, repressing it, ignoring the subtle barbs because they were outweighed by the "atta-boys." He had pulled on the door's handle, but forget to turn the lock and caulk under the edges. The man had tried to erase the pain of personal loss by changing the *Code of the Southern Man* one day and one well-done task at a time. But how could he hold back the tide? How could the man stop the leaky heritage of a hundred years? Dark water would find a way in, he thought.

"You let your guard down, Cobb," the voice was saying. *"You fell when you were so close. And now when you're no longer up top looking down, the delicate controls in your hands that held sixty-foot-long pilings in the claws of the great crane; you are just another Black man with a busted leg."*

The extrication was made complicated by the way in which my foot was embedded between the rungs of the steel ladder, the way in which I lay there calmly. I must've still been in a form of shock and though nobody wanted to think it, was that some of those same men had never seen the insides of a Black man's body before.

Just after the pain came on with a sudden gush and I began to tremble, a scruffy electrician they called Sparky who'd served Uncle Sam as an army medic, took charge and instructed the men to lift my body to an angle in line with the foot, hold straight traction on the boot, and slowly move me off the ladder and onto an old army stretcher someone had pulled from the back of a truck. Jed, for his part, stood as a kind of vigil, unsure of the technical stuff, but doing what he could to keep the situation as light as possible.

"Now, Cobb, don't think I'm going to pay you for a full day after this stunt."

"That's fair, Jed," I wheezed at him. "But I'm not paying for a new ladder if my bones bent those steps a'tall."

Someone said they was gonna need a map to put all those bones back together and I thought there were a lot of ways to mapping the body and its place in the world.

When they moved me, the bones slipped back under my skin as my leg straightened out and someone said, ""Geez, Cobb, what a way to start and end your day." All of our days.

I thought I heard a distant *stupid Negro,* but the pain in my leg was beginning to cloud my thoughts and all I wanted was to get the hell away from the place that I had grown so fond of.

"Here, this ought to ease it a bit." It was Sparky putting a needle in my left tricep and driving the warm fluid into my body with the plunger. "I brought home a case or two as a lovely parting gift from the army. It sure files down the edges on hurt. I keep them in my car along with a few other souvenirs from my duty in the Pacific Theatre, and that's not the one downtown either."

"Much obliged, Sparky. The pain's only coming in waves now but I reckon that'll change, huh?"

"Count on that. Hey, Cobb, you know anybody in this town good enough to call in a favor? T'would be better if a real bone doc got a look at that. You're too young to say it don't matter 'cuz you're too old."

"I know Jed pretty well and a few of the other Negroes from the job. And some of the other guys like you been cordial enough." I was wincing between words, feeling light headed and faint, the drug doing something, though I wasn't sure what.

"Ain't you staying out at the Davis place up in the brush aways?"

"Yeah, they been terribly good to me, makin' me feel like kin and all."

"Well, only way you gonna get this leg fixed up correct is for Harry Davis, a man who's owed a lot by people of this town and ones up and down the road, to take you into the hospital in Pensacola or St. Pete and tell them you his kin."

"Oh, they're gonna believe that one, for sure," I slurred through thickening lips. "I could just be his long-lost brother who fell asleep on the beach, got an awful dark sunburn, and was run over by some kid driving a jeep on the sand."

"This is not the real South, Cobb. This is a strange mixture of Southerners on vacation, military families, fisherman, snowbirds running away from Minnesota, and guys like yourself who end up here because it's at the bottom of the continent. Texas and the rest of Florida don't count 'cuz they just stick out there waiting to get knocked off by a strong country or a stronger hurricane. This here is the Redneck Riviera where the people who act like they have money but don't mix with those who'll never have it and could care less if'n they ever gain it. It's a strange collection, Cobb. I don't pretend to understand them and I'd never try and predict what they'd do. But I can tell you that loyalty is a big thing in this county, maybe the biggest. And damn, Cobb, the beaches sure are pretty to sit on and think while them bones knit up."

"Good night, Johnny," the voice said.

Whatever you say, 'cause you're in charge.

CHAPTER 7
LEARNING TO FISH

There is a German word, "Dasein," I read about in one of the books that Lillian-the-Librarian would eventually direct me to as we came to know each other in my nightly visits to her library. It loosely translates as the human way to be-in-the-world, or to know one's unique purpose and potential—and also to forfeit it through inauthenticity.

What I remember about the hospital room where I woke up was its cleanliness and quietude. My *Dasein* was working overtime. It felt like a library for sick people and the books were medicine. I liked the little room that I was sharing with Mr. Smith One Tree, the one-fourth Cherokee from Youngstown who'd had two vertebra fused and was having the government pay for it on account of he worked as a mechanic on the base in Pensacola when he was young enough to hold a wing in one hand and tighten or scratch a nut in the other. I liked the clean white sheets and the clean white smiles of the nurses who changed my dressings. And the docs who came in and said I was lucky the bones didn't hit any major vessels, and lucky that they were the best docs in the county and could get those bones to line up proper, and lucky that I was a *distant*

cousin of Harry Davis, while they laughed and winked deep and purposeful about how Harry could take anybody he cared about to the hospital on the air force base, even if he had the ways and means to do that as well on the outside.

It all felt odd, as if this, too, this first-class care, another positive after a tough break that followed some sacred hurt that came in on the heels of dark tragedy; a roller coaster of incidents and accidents that had bore down on me aggressively and nakedly as if I was in fate's crosshairs or a swift stream. It occurred to me that it mustn't have been planned. It was too chaotic and neat and wildly ordered to attach any sense to it. The best I could do was to put my feet up in the river and float without catching a shoe on a rock or, worse yet, getting swept into a side eddy where the river just rolled passed you like a soundless picture show and all you could do was try and read the actor's lips.

I lay there that night after they fixed my leg, feeling the cool breeze from the ceiling fan, lost in its revolution. Smith, the quarter-Indian in the bed next to me was talking in his sleep, something unintelligible to my ears, but not to him. My leg was bound and cast in a wide swath of white plaster and held aloft by a shiny stainless metal bar and chain. What power was willed and wielded, deals made or remade, debts paid or accrued, so that a civilian could get care like a war hero might? The fan and my questions had unsettled the antiseptic air and replaced the quietude with an impermanent stillness. My intelligence had come up against the gratitude of the moment. The room began to shrink and the air thickened.

"Let the river take you," the voice was saying. *"A man did something good for you. This is not, cannot be, and will never be, a game of quid pro quo."*

The broken leg throbbed.

"Never an eye for an eye."

I tried to get up from the bed, but found the metal chains to my cast screwed down.

"It ill never be about getting paid or paying back. Let the water soak in," it said. *"All the way down past your bones, past your soul, and past your past until it comes around to*

your future. And then you'll quench your thirst by passing the glass.

"She's gone. You can't make her ungone."

In the morning Harry came and picked me up. The attending nurse, Phyllis, I think, or Gladys, who got me ready to leave had teeth as bright as the Mississippi sunshine. And I let her or them warm me, let it take me, passing the smile back.

I sat in the wheelchair as Harry rolled me out a side exit to the waiting truck where Grace sat with Gillie and the baby Phin in the cab.

"I think you'll be more comfortable stretched out in the back with Cain and Abel," Harry spoke flatly with impassive eyes framing his mouth.

"It's not the first time."

"Nor the last."

"Harry, I want to..."

"Forget it. Grace is busy with the kids. I need some help baiting hooks. 'Bout time you learned to fish."

"But how did you arrange the hospital, the docs, the..."

"Later, okay? Let's just say that I have—to use some of your big words—a social contract with the community. You were the fine print."

Harry pulled away from the curb, the warm dogs splinting my leg in the truck's bed, and I looked in the dark gray pools that were the eyes of the Davis' dogs. They knew it was only the beginning. They knew. In those big and round dog-eyes I saw the shape of clouds reflecting a seamless horizon over which someone close to me or maybe me, if I was lucky, would sail away or toward. I sometimes wonder if I was being shown the future in that animal's iris, a dimension where life exists before it unfolds—the perfect vision of an imperfect world.

Just when I was finding some reason for Ruth's death, which was no reason at all, and just when I was tasting the sweet human transaction of equality, the gray eyes clouded over and the dogs laid their heads on my lap. But there would be many good years and much deep blue water would pass under me and through me. Things would grow and prosper and children would begin to find their place in the world of grown men and women.

Once more the dogs looked up at me and it was just Abel who yawned and shook and made a low sound that seemed to come from another era.

I put my feet up and floated.

✳ ✳ ✳

On a clear morning in late summer of '51, maybe three ponderous weeks after my fall, we left on Harrys' thirty-eight-foot boat. It was a twin-diesel-powered vessel with lines from a distance appearing long and thin and clean and a high bridge that looked like a secret tree fort. On closer inspection, there was a utilitarian essence to the way things were laid out, the way they might have been handled on the fly, off the cuff, moment by moment. While I knew machines and men and the way they interacted, I didn't know boats. But after living with the Davis family in an unbeleaguered domesticity for some months, I thought I knew a fair amount about Harry. And when he finally invited me aboard his boat, there was no question of coming along or not. The leg was boat-worthy; the time to enter a new geography was here.

"No more living in the margins, Cobb," Harry had claimed one evening after Gillie and I finished a game of chess. "Time to fish and you're cutting bait."

I had no idea that you could learn as much as you could about a man by the way he organized a boat deck. When I limped up the gangway on my cane and was immediately guided to the rigger's chair, I didn't have to ask questions; I already knew the drill. It was more of the gift, it was real. To deny it was to deny my *Dasein*, my authenticity. It wasn't the fish of the ocean that both frightened and enthralled me, nor was it the siren's song of old. It was the crew—just Harry, a couple of other local recruits that shared a love of the process of hunting fish, and to my surprise, a savvy eight, almost nine-year-old going out on her first extended trip. Unlike most commercial fishermen, this crew cared little if they brought back a full hold or limped in empty. They would be out to sea pitting themselves against the odds, jockeying skills with a natural resource, another one of God's creations, if you believe, doing God-like work. They kept what they needed to keep friends and foes alive, to sell or to eat, and threw back all the rest. At times, they put their lives at risk. It was a good trade.

But Gillie, the newly minted first mate, was following some childhood instinct, her own *Dasein*, her own purpose. She would always feel comfortable out on the sea, especially in later years when her younger brother would come along, when her father would say, "I'm going below to make some sandwiches. You take the helm, Gillie." And one of the older crewmen would kid her, spreading his arms out toward the edges of the boat and say, "One day all of this will be yours, Kiddo." But Gillie would say that it wasn't her dad's or anybody else's to give away. She would be referring to the boat and the seas and all that was connected between the two. And she knew the difference.

Watching the young girl then and the way she moved about the boat with grace and ease, and with strength and control as she grew into herself, I gained both a greater respect and, in some way, a renewed fear of water. Watching the way the crew moved, each with a duty, the total being greater then the sum of its parts, and especially how the young girl with the very old soul was skipping years in her steady march toward adulthood, I knew then that my life would never exist on a straight line, in a vacuum, or without purpose and complexity.

And along the way, I learned about fishing.

We stayed out ten days that trip, chased back into port by reports of an unseasonably late hurricane in the central Gulf. The hold was full of amberjack and bass and few bins of shrimp for good measure. I saw these men and Gillie's inherent vote for Eros over Thanatos, that they had the sea in them. But it did not find me in the same way.

A day after we off-loaded the catch I was on my way home to the farm up near Mobile.

BOOK 2
WAR

The ancient Greek dramatist Aeschylus wrote, 'The reward of suffering is experience.' Let this be the lasting legacy of Vietnam.'

–John McNamara, Secretary of Defense for the Johnson and Nixon Administrations and chief architect of the Vietnam War

CHAPTER 8

TWO-WAY MIRRORS

Shall I meet other wayfarers at night? Those who have gone before.

–*Up-hill*, Christina Rossetti

Much would happen in the ensuing years. Some of which I could say in the passing of a moment as we might meet on some unfamiliar street in an unfamiliar town. The baby, Phin, had become almost a man on the outside, but inside he was just another kid who was happy to be a kid, never rushing into grown-upness like a lot of kids in the big city. He started driving a pickup around town when he was fifteen. That was around '66, I think. But I don't recall him ever getting an official license, even when he was old enough to.

He knew of the Vietnam War, of the protests, then a few years later, the deaths of Janis Joplin and Jim Morrison and a young Bobby Kennedy. We talked a lot in 1968 as he questioned the talisman of social revolution that seeped slowly at first into small towns like Idaho Springs, Colorado and Portsmouth, New Hampsire—and Panama Beach City. I think he tried to understand it all, but he'd seen the deep divisions it had caused. And while he wanted to do something substantial to go with the depth of his feelings, '68 was a time when things ran so deep no one could ever do enough to keep up with their emotions. After awhile I think he decided the best thing he could do was to stay at home and be with his family, help out around the house when Harry and Gillie were off fishing, work on the boat when they weren't, and just be a good kid.

He never did take to being on the boat for very long as Gillie did. Maybe he knew that it was her place or that his Ma would be alone if he went off with them. Other men offered him work, but he seemed happy enough to play it close to home, read what he could get his hands on, and let the rest just be. If he was concerned about the world, he didn't march it out. And while that world unfolded in turmoil, it seems to me that Phin made his own regular protest by trying to be a regular kid. Maybe he knew it would come looking for him sooner or later.

Sometimes the wolf knocks at your door and instead of letting him trick you with words, you might offer to let him run alongside if he could. In that way, the wolf could pose the great question of identity: *Do you know yourself well enough so as to know who am I? And what I want?*

Nobody but Grace had seen Phin's wolf by then. For everyone but her, the wolf was just one of those things that snuck up on you, like watching the wind blow all your life, wondering where it came from and where it was going. And then one day it just hits you: it's just the thickness of the air trying to find some balance, a place where there's too much pressure looking for a place where there ain't enough.

I remember a long, hot day, August or July perhaps, not September, definitely not June. I'd come down from the farm to spend a week or so with the Davises and Harry had taken Gillie and the boat up to Pensacola for repairs. Phin was off messing around with his pals and I sat with Grace, the Davis matriarch, in the back yard. She wore a long-sleeved cotton frock with little blood stains she'd incurred tending to her roses in the upper field.

"Roses are dangerous," Grace winked when she noticed me looking at the tiny smears of red and pink, "but worth the toil." She asked me about the farm and I told her that the Cobbs had finally earned ownership through three generations of homesteading, but there were leftover feelings from some deeper history; things with Earl and Ramsey were not good though the crops were doing okay, and all I could commit to was part-time residency and effort. "They can have the farm," I choked out an answer to Grace, "I'll just cherry-pick the memories." Then I redirected the inquiry to the nature of the boy. "Is Phin, uh...okay in this tumultuous world of ours?"

"I just can't say. Some days I think he's solid as Gillie, steeled to the strangeness that creeps in on the back of radio and TV and news. Other days his tenderness scares me to death."

I looked at Grace and nodded. And this feeling came over me that like many mothers of that time, she'd eventually suffer the ignominy of losing a son to a worthless war. Her skin went a different color and I looked to see if an afternoon cloud had caused the ashen shift.

"You all right?" I asked. And Grace tried to stand up like a baby giraffe making her way into a new world.

"Oh, I'm fine, Johnny, just getting these extra thumps in the heart when the weight of it all comes calling. Think I'll go see a doctor when Harry comes back."

I tried to make her swear to a promise that I didn't know she'd keep. But Grace had held dear that iconography of the repressed women demanding independence from all things, including male doctors. I made a point to ask Jed about any female heart docs on the coast.

✳ ✳ ✳

In the beginning of that decade of education, maybe '62 or '63, Phin tried hard to keep life from becoming an imposition on us all, even when the wolf had its jaws around his throat. How that was, I would never know. Other times, in a moment's laughter, that hurt temporarily lifted by the sound of joy, you could see that he had this ability to close the white space between him and those he came in contact with. I suppose that's what saved him in the end. And maybe most of the rest of us along with him.

For my part, I'd stopped going out on Harry's boat so much—only when the weather was fine and he'd been short-handed and was too proud to ask, but I knew in any case. The sea just wasn't in me. Not yet. I'd help out around the farm up north, take a temporary job operating a machine, sometimes for Jed, and occasionally go on up to Mobile and check on Nadine and her sisters.

Life had not been great to Earl and Ramsey on the farm, but I'd made it clear to them that as much loyalty as I had to them and the history of our land, I wasn't ready to come back full- time. Not yet anyway. And then the months grew into years, and years into nearly one-and-a-half decades, and "yet" came and went. Each seemed to accept my decision but for different reasons. The guilt I felt for leaving them seemed to me a mutual détente with the anger of loosing Ruth. Both lie dormant, not really going away, but waiting for a third party to catalyze some long overdue conflict.

In the meantime, I'd found a kind of peace with the Davis family and my years traveling the South as it wrestled with its conscience of oppression. I was't unhappy.

But then Gillie died, the cancer taking her at twenty-six. I was pulled even closer to the boy and what he could do to rescue me from myself.

✳ ✳ ✳

There was that time, the day of Gillie's funeral in the spring of 1971 when the entire world was trying to cool off from too much of itself. Geez' he loved her. All these people came over to the house to offer their condolences, as is the case with funerals and such. Phin was a sad, gracious host, trying to stand tall in the image of his grieving parents, protecting them as best a twenty-year-old kid can, soaking up his own ache. But the pecking order had become mutated; he was no longer a teenager anymore, but the oldest and the only. You could tell by what came out of other people's eyes. Somebody, told him he looked liked a fine young man, his sister would be proud. But the words sounded too heavy and too real for him. That was the first time Phin fell through a hole in his life. And his childhood became a souvenir.

He told someone who'd paid him a compliment that Gillie deserved to grow young again. That's what she was aiming for, to knock the hourglass on its side and watch the sand leak out of the broken glass shards. They said he sounded like the old Black man he'd been around since birth. I was yet forty-six then and had long since smashed my own time-keeping glass. Phin put his arm around the family friend, pointed across the room in my direction, and asked the man how old he would be if he didn't know how old he was. The friend forced a nod, but anyone could tell that he didn't understand.

And as I watched him from the corner that day, still not old enough to buy a drink in some states, it was as if someone else had told him he had to jump the chasm from twelve to twenty, like something else was pried loose with Gillie's hourglass from her cold hands and thrust at him.

And the sand gushed down.

Gillie was the old soul, working toward an old salt. At twenty-six and with almost ten long seasons crewing full-time with their dad out on the boat, she might've lost some of the outward signs of her femininity, but inside grew the best from each of her parent's seed. The sun and salt played heck on a man's skin. It played hell on a woman's. She'd told me that she felt like Icarus at times, sailing too close to the sun, ignoring her father's pleas to wear floppy hats and long-sleeved shirts, taking those memories of her mother's stories about resilient women all the way to the end. She knew it, but was helpless to heed his wishes. The natural elements made her who she was. And in the end, what she no longer was. Grace knew it, too; might've seen it coming, but was equally helpless. Who can deny one's essence? Chalk it up as naiveté. Write it off as the ignorance of youth. Call it some burden of lineage—Gillie had found herself in her father's world, but was prepared to take it further, into deeper waters for bigger fish that could fight as well as she could.

Phin could not yet see that part out beyond the horizon and into the myth, and then the abyss. He'd taken his mother's dark Italian skin and would for years try and blame himself for getting the genes that Gillie needed more than him. Where she had grown into the hunter who needed only a thin shield to survive, he had become the soft-hearted, reluctant survivor who'd spend years chipping off the outside coating that might've saved his sister.

And how could I have ever known that he might be a product of all that had happened to me as well as his own family? In trying to prepare him for all that might come his way, the strangeness in my own past might've worn off more than a little, like standing under a tall pine to keep out of the rain—always a bit of the tree's scent will find its way onto your clothes.

How could I have known he'd fallen into my own heart? I only knew that after it started, I had to see it through. All the way through.

Gillie was gone; the Big C had come and swallowed her whole from the outside in. They all thought it was the first and last, a dark blip on life's radar. How could they know? I felt otherwise because death had touched me, enveloped me. And with it came the burden of *knowing*, the gift of the deceased. I was sent to the family to deliver a boat. Did I deliver some curse as well?

Harry and Grace had followed Gillie's wishes to have her ashes scattered: "Partly in Mom's garden, partly out on the Tuscaloosa shoals where I'd caught my first big tuna with Dad and the rest. Just toss downwind and get the hell out of the way." It wasn't in any written will, just mentioned after dinner when they'd first come back from the hospital in Mobile and the doctor had told them all she'd have to be tough; this kind of cancer was a known killer.

Harry said that Gillie had laughed, had asked the doctor what was really the difference between a known killer and an unknown killer? If the killer had killed before, somebody would know, even if they were dead. Harry told me that the way she approached the subject had surprised him. She'd always had that old soul; maybe she was born middle-aged and lived out her childhood as a wise woman with a will made strong by something that she'd experienced before she was born. She'd said she'd fight the good fight, but if it was apparent that she'd loose, she'd throw in the white towel from the corner and save those around her the pain of watching her suffer. In that way, Harry'd said she was stronger than Phin, stronger than all of them. She was born with the innate understanding of death's paradigm. The rest of us had to learn it.

That was a rock-hard time for Phin. For many years it was made even harder by his reaction to Gillie's death. But he shaped himself against that stone, shaping all of us with the same chisel.

Nobody could've guessed that the soft-hearted kid would avenge her memory by trying to harden his own heart—by going off to a war that they all agreed was wrong.

CHAPTER 9

FROM THIS DAY FORWARD

Phin's broken body came back from the war on March 15, 1973, about six weeks after a piece of paper was signed in Paris. The fighting kept on in South Vietnam—as it would for years in Southeast Asia—the final remnants of post-colonial conflict lurking in the dark, shapeless jungles.

Phin had re-upped after his first tour was over. He hated everything about the Nam but the heightened sense of existence that war brought with it. And the camaraderie. Which was everything to him. He'd become a non-com-corporal and had responsibility for other misinformed, misguided, or patriotic kids who found their way over there for every naïve reason that they were too smart to figure out. For soldiers from every era and every epoch, there has been reason enough to go, even when they could choose to stay. They weren't so much deciding the fate of their lives as allowing others to decide for them. So, Phin spent an extra ten months in Southeast Asia, or seventy if you count in dog-years—many times that in soldiers' lives.

On that March day when his living shell was rolled down the tail ramp of a C-130 to the tarmac at Cheyenne Mountain Air Base near Colorado Springs, people had mostly forgotten the anniversary of Julius Caesar's murder by Brutus, Cassius, and other Roman senators in 44 BC. It was a rainy Thursday.

Two days earlier, Phin's dad, Harry, had received a telegram from the State Department informing him that his son was being returned to the U.S. and that he was in need of "some medical attention to be provided at a Denver VA hospital," there was an article from the wire services printed in the *Lafayette Daily Advertiser* titled, "Reconstruction-aid Talks to Begin Between U.S. and North Vietnam."

Harry clipped it out. Maybe he knew that deceit is an early form of truth and crab grass can only be stopped by killing the whole lawn.

At the top of the pop charts stood War's album, *The World is a Ghetto.*

✳ ✳ ✳

Harry still hadn't been outside much since a stroke had put Grace in a long-term care facility; a "home" they called it, "for assisted living." Nothing made sense to Harry, especially the titles of places and spaces his family had gone. His daughter was in a better place while his wife was assigned to a "medical apartment" and his son had been fighting in a country they referred to—when you were there—as being "in-country." Harry had been gradually erasing things in his head, subtracting one after the other. What a waste among an infinitely vast world of waste, he thought. He'd never tried to make their memories fly away by throwing his to the wind. First, he remembered, it was at Gillie's funeral, where one of his children's ashes lay in a small grave next to the plot of earth that might be visited for a day or forever by another Davis. Then, he remembered his wife of thirty-one years who wasn't at home, making, as she liked to say, "a home a good home that's better than good."

And then the other child, he imagined, who might be dying slowly a day at a time fourteen thousand miles away. With his daughter gone and his wife fighting for her memory and her mind, his last remaining blood child became an ideal, something that moved from a black and white photo on the wall to a prayer he'd throw out for anyone to catch and pass on to the right God, to a dream and then back to the reality of faith that the blood might flow all the way back home with his son in its current. In Panama City Beach, Harry Davis had always been practical, logical, hard-working, hard-loving, and family-devoted…a secular man. He didn't suffer fools, zealots, or the lazy. If you collected unemployment and weren't in a wheelchair, Harry wouldn't look you in the eye.

When word came that Grace might be away for a while, that she needed long-term care, that the prognosis was "less than what we'd hoped for," and that Harry might want to get her affairs in order, Harry begun to erase their mutual friends, the garden, the dogs, and then, as it seemed, he moved south toward the sea, that great blue firebreak where even water could burn when properly oiled and ignited. Sometimes it seemed that if he could just turn himself upside down and shake—like a human *Etch-A-Sketch* with no remembrance of anything—he could start over. But for what or why?

For a period Harry had been trying to hold it together with his images of Grace, their land, his world of fishing, and thoughts of his boy coming home. They had their own force field—he would swallow that thought—but so did the nightmares where he heard her soundless cry for help out in the yard while he and her children were all somewhere else; a place other than where they could at least hold her hand while her heart broke and the blood stopped moving north to her mind, and the God she felt had created her was slowly calling her back, one body part at a time.

In her garden, in the fall. Dust to dust. But not yet, Big Guy. Not yet. Not all of her.

I never did ask Jed Riot about a woman's heart and blood doc for Grace. But I'd ask God about that later.

✳ ✳ ✳

Harry had been working the shoals off Fort Morgan, thirty-odd nautical miles due south of the entrance to Mobile Bay. He fished mostly alone since Gillie died, just a handful of poles baited for dorado and cavalla, each trip moving further south and west, following some siren call he couldn't identify or resist. And while he and I had grown closer after Gillie's passing, I think now that as hard as he tried not to, Harry held me responsible for letting Phin enlist, for allowing the world to find him before he was ready to do it carefully and on his own terms.

Everyone in town allowed Harry to grieve in his own way, to follow the concentric circles as they spread out from the rock that was dropped in the pond. So, I stuck pretty close to Panama City in '71 and '72, working odd jobs for Jed Riot, driving over to Pensacola to borrow books from the library at the college there, and helping Grace around their parcel of land before her own fateful episode. Grace had been uncharacteristically quiet for maybe a month after Phin shipped off, and then started talking and hadn't stopped. Grace would carry on great semi-coherent conversations with the dogs, her plants, herself, and me, if I was within any hearing distance. She spoke clearly and made great sense even as the ordering of her thoughts were often jumbled as if tossed into a bingo barrel and ideas pulled and called out for all the listening players to hear.

"Well, Johnny Cobb, I can see that my romaine will exceed all expectations this year. Must've been the extra mulch or the worm juice, though who can ever tell with the organic and the inorganic.

"Wrote another letter to Phin today. Must ask him about the worms. Gillie would know about worms. Harry never used worms for bait even when they were recommended. Worms aren't always welcome in gardens, you know, Johnny? Think about that big one in Eden. No good. But when they live in the compost and the juice comes out, boy oh boy, the plants sure are appreciative.

"Hey, do you know what kind of plants they don't have in Vietnam? I get sad when I think about leeches in the jungle. I wonder if they are in the worm family. But I still don't know why Harry refused to bait worms though I've asked him twenty-three-and-one-half times.

"Johnny, do you think Emily Dickenson could write a love poem about worms?"

Those images were written in the blood of her own loss, made indelible by the beauty that preceded the torment both hers and Harry's life was becoming. And the guilt that moved in for good on the tails of all that was now beyond the control that Harry had...or thought he had.

Harry and I were both aging in our own way: Harry, the uncomplicated patriarch working the sea, simply, and me, the questioning Black bard of this world and others beyond. I'd become the wandering poet, devouring books and elevated conversations like a man casting a wide net in search of understanding.

Harry was always amused by my intellect, more than once asking me why it was so important for me to know so much when what he had known—what made him happy, what put food on the table and a roof over their heads—was more than enough. We had grown to respect, even love each other for what we shared: an absolute engagement in life. Once again, though, we would share the great tragedy of loss.

I knew so much but so little about Grace Davis, less so than about her daughter, Gillie. Much of the written histories exclude the great women behind and in front of great men. What we can hope for is that by the time we are through our collective imaginations will know them enough. And we will know them through the love of those whom they leave behind.

I was headed to collect Harry for the drive up to Denver in the evening and had wrestled with revealing dreams the night before. When I arrived at the dock late that afternoon, I witnessed what might've become an extension of those telling night tales as they unfurled into something real. Maybe more than real.

✳ ✳ ✳

Harry sat near the bow of his boat, broken. He'd just cleaned her up as if he might not take her out for a long while, as if he might just give her away as I had given Phin the little *Ruth Henry David* so many years ago. It had been the first clear day after a strong sou'easter had moved in and swept away the lingering low-pressure cloud cover. Straddling the bridge stays, each leg hanging off the boat as human divining rods that might point him to fresh water, he must've felt the sea air and salt breath beckoning him in, challenging him to slip off the side of the boat and be swallowed by the orange rippling glass, lowering his place in the food chain on par with the fish he sought to sustain those who were now gone.

And so, Harry entered from the port side. I stood, paralyzed on the gangway.

His high boots filled with water, his yellow foul-weather overalls filled with water. The water seeped past the woolen sweater, the sweaty undershirt, hit his rough-hewn chest, the thick, curly black nest of hair...and then it stopped. The weight must've been enough to take any man down. And Harry began to sink slowly, the failing light only penetrating the surface a few feet.

Who can say what pushes and pulls a person close to the point where they enter their own history? For Gillie it was the sweet and malignant rays of the sun giving and taking her life. For Phin, it was a war where he was more concerned with keeping men alive by killing than killing for the sake of something that he had no immediate stake in. For me, and maybe for Grace, we were happy enough to try and hold the center, to keep things from falling apart. Grace by maintaining a family and a home, by maintaining constant buoyed spirits in light of all challenges. And me, by slowly, assuredly, allowing myself to become a part of that family as the one that I might've had, had it not disintegrated in another drowning five hundred miles and five thousand days away.

Harry must've thought of his wife out in her beloved garden, humming a rock-n-roll song that she'd slowed down into a quiet ballad. He must've seen his daughter, Gillie, working the nets, bantering with the men who'd always ask why she wasn't married and raising up kids or at least away at college getting an education so that she could make something of herself. And he must've seen the telegram from the government he'd tried so hard to keep out of his family's life.

"Your son is returning from Southeast Asia and is in need of some medical care."

Those words must've taken hold of his head and all the hate of war that Harry Davis had finally purged himself of in the nearly twenty-five years of plying the Gulf waters for more than just fish; all the hate that he'd brought back when he returned from his own war in the South Pacific "theater of operations" came back to him in anger. And the anger lodged itself right next to his heart. He wouldn't allow himself any more pity. Not now, not ever again. Harry Davis might have to kill someone to set his son free. Might have to do even worse to set his wife's mind free. He was not afraid of it. He had nothing to lose because if he lost Phin now, after facing the fear of watching Grace lose her mind as well, then he'd have nothing to live and die for. So, he might as well kill a few of whose hands were bloodied in the wake of what they'd taken from him.

But who? And why?

I stood on that gangway near his boat and watched Harry roll over on his back, pawing the sea with sculling mitts to stay afloat.

"No, I won't let you in," he spoke to the ocean's surface and some God he was re-configuring in its own spilling body. "That's far enough. Some day you might take me, but not today, not this way."

Still they might've tried, but couldn't hold him down. He rolled over onto his stomach and spit the ocean out of his mouth so he could speak to the dead and the diseased. "Where are your hearts now, because I can't hear them from here?"

He swam around to the transom and pulled himself up slowly, diligently, the sea draining from him with each shim up the stern line until he could flop his wet being on the afterdeck. The sun bent itself into the edge and must've been a god-awful sight.

Harry hated sunsets lately. The best ones were always so...red.

I watched all this unfold and said nothing. Did nothing.

Just that morning I had loaded the truck with gas, a chessboard, Patsy Cline and John Lee Hooker, and left for the Panhandle to get Harry after a visit to what used to be my home. I'd been up to see what was left of the farm. Indeed, things had not gone well. But at some point, I'd realized that I'd let my interest in the farm go, not in small increments over the years but in one swift and final excision the night Ruth had died. The years that'd come after and my cursory worry about holding onto to what I'd imagined might've been my future had been nothing but a Trojan Horse that I'd snuck into my mind. Harry and Phin and Grace needed my help. And so once again I was going east and south through Mobile and Jackson and then Biloxi, going back so I could go forward. It was hard to guess what might help Phin; he wouldn't be the same kid who'd been put on the bus over two years ago. Were there material objects to support a return to the world? Something to remember the past with, something to forget the past? Were they more than just things? I'd grabbed a handful of books, some pictures, a few medicinal plants that Phin and I'd studied on and grown together, things that Grayfalls had taught me about, that had made a difference at various times in my own life.

Driving through Panama City where Phin had grown up, where he had played third base for the Bay High School Flying Tigers; where, on a bet, he had once stolen a pack of gum from the Ben Franklin store and then took it back to the owner's house that night, his eleven-year-old tears making the blur of car headlights look like dancing angel stars; the hospital where he had watched his sister die; the house where his dad arose each morning and tried to scrub Gillie's memory off the deck of his mind; and the facility where the shell of his mom, Grace, fought for her center. I noticed a type of permanent stillness that seemed to freeze the little town, framed within an old watercolor you'd find in an aunt's basement. It was an uneasy feeling; not quite crippling, but heavy enough that you couldn't lift it without some strong-backed praying.

Before I went to the dock looking for Harry, I'd stopped by the Davis' place and found the gate to their land closed. Funny, I didn't remember there being a gate, or a fence for that matter, just a lot of juniper and spruce and willows standing guard over the big double-wide with the wax-free linoleum floors. The weeds had grown up around the boats and trucks in the yard in the eight weeks I'd been gone. You could often see decent working trucks with potential tombstoned in these parts. But not at the Davises. Now, even the skiffs he used to fish the inland waterways when weather kept him from his regular runs were no longer covered and clean and were missing the huge spruce oars that stuck out the transom where an outboard might be. I didn't see the *Ruth Henry David* at first and knew better than to pass judgment.

I'd left Harry at the dock and returned to their parcel to wait for him, not wanting his to know I'd witnessed his aquatic episode. When Harry arrived, he moved slower than I'd remembered, tottered over to one side when he walked, always to the north, his old *Johnson's Bait and Tackle* fishing cap like the point of a compass. I got a sense he was making the pain of his own life worth the pain of living it.

I should've stayed closer those months, I thought, and realized I'd done more harm to Harry by leaving than staying. I'd left my friend alone with the knowledge that Grace needed help. There was a part of me that figured Harry needed his space, his own place from which to negotiate. One dumb-fucking mistake. I'd thought it wasn't tough love, but more like survival love. And even now, the two of us back together with as much as I had to tell Harry, there were no words that could be shaped on the anvil that Harry carried in his chest. Later on, we'd talk. Yeah, when we were finally out on the highway and the wind was fresh and the dinner had been good and the tank was full and no cars before or behind us and Harry had shaved some iron from his bars. We'd talk.

But not until then.

I opened the truck's door and walked out into the yard. The only dogs that come running up were Saul and Daniel. Harry shuffled over and hugged his old Black friend who was still younger than him, but had aged faster than time, as he had. Harry pulled away and looked at me, a part of his lower lip trying in vain to rise up and smile. He must've tried.

I said let's go fetch your boy and Harry climbed in, his head automatically bending toward the metal dash upon which sat a compass that pointed magnetic, not true north. One of his eyes was bloodshot like a cartoon monster, the other as clear and clean as a three-year-old on his birthday. Beneath them both was pain leaking over into momentary relief and then coming back as uncertainty.

"I need my boy back, Johnny. I need 'em."

He closed his eyes and fingered the strap on his pack, clasping and unclasping the buckle. I put my hand on Harry's shoulder and started the truck.

Harry didn't breathe for nearly a minute. And then he said, "My boy's coming home."

"You need anything beside that little tote sack, Harry? There's a chance we aren't going to be picking up Phin like he was just away at school for the weekend."

Harry rolled down the window and gave out a low whistle. The two dogs came out from behind the trailer and jumped in the bed. They looked part-lab with bits of spaniel and a long collie nose. I called their names just to get Harry thinking. But Harry only said I know that you know. He didn't say anything else until we were half way across Texas.

As we skirted the northern edge of Fort Worth a light, pissy rain fell and I pulled over into a dry wash that swallowed the rain thirstily. We both got out and I grabbed a heavy blanket from the cab, tossed it to Harry who threw it into the bed where Saul and Daniel immediately made it their home.

Harry looked up across the bed of the truck at me. His lips moved a few seconds before words came out.

"The world's just whittlin' itself down, ain't it?"

"Yeah Harry, I wonder what it's gonna be when it's done."

"That old war had itself a sharp blade."

"Either that or a dull one with a strong, steady hand behind it. Always a hand behind the killing, eh, pal? Always a war to hone those blades on."

"Which one you referring about?"

"Does it matter? They both did wrong."

"You ever met a war that did someone right?"

"Not personally."

"Cobb, I asked you once not to bring it up; that other war."

"You brought it up, Harry. You just didn't see it on the screen."

"Forget it. Let's go before the despair turns to anger. Gillie wasn't the only one in this family that knows when something deserves killing."

From there to Abilene, we two men wondered in the road's silence and the motor's hum. We wondered about a lot of things; mostly we wondered if we were strong enough. When we stopped for gas, we drank coffee so black and deep that we were afraid of looking in the cup. And when we stopped to pee or let the dogs run their legs, we'd look up at a black-coffee-sky, listen to our piss hitting the sandy roadside, and keep on wondering.

In El Paso, somewhere between imagination and fact, we sought the disabling quiet of ignorance. Nobody saw this coming, we tried to convince ourselves. Nobody knew what the sun would do to Gillie or the blood pressure to Grace or the U.S. government to Phin. Soldiers and regular people alike aren't always born as fighters and men and women who end up at war or sick or dead are only labeled victims because that's the way it's always been. Vietnam and disease were not new...they just always were.

When we made the northern turn at Albuquerque, Harry told me to stop the truck. We pulled over in a choppy shoulder just north of town, watered the dogs, and lowered the tailgate where so many great questions had been addressed in my life. The sun was getting soaked up by the west and finally Harry's eyes sought purchase with something tangible.

"Phin ain't going to be the same," he was telling, not asking.

"Harry, kids go off to a war clean, for the most part. Doesn't matter why they go, whether they want to kill or Uncle Sam tells them to, they get dirty; some of them so covered in shit that it won't come off after years of scrubbing. Phin's likely gonna have to try and make some kinda sense of the world that's he's just coming from—which is about the worst kind you could think up—before he can start making sense of the one he'll be living in."

Harry shot me a look that went right through me, cutting me in half and then looping back around to heal the wound. But only part of it.

"Johnny, what the hell you know about war? You got outta going because you were smart and Black, or both. Trained by a red man, huh?"

It was only the second time I'd seen Harry loose control in the twenty-two years we'd been friends. It was the third if you counted the time he'd found out that Phin had gone and enlisted in the Army without telling him or Grace. That was right after Gillie died. Harry just got on the boat and left for a month by himself, more to silently implode than what I was bearing witness to right then.

"You ain't seen it, Cobb, not up close. You only lost a wife."

Harry was right and wrong, not his White against my Black, but still stuck flying through a cloud of necessary confusion, imperfectly clear from two paces away, but muddied thick in his own mind.

"You're right, Harry, all the dying on paper I've seen close to date is confined to Ruth and Gillie; Uncle Chuck if your counting MIAs. But the only son I'll ever have is the same one you got. He was your blood to start with, but something happened. Hard as you tried to keep him from the world, he became one of its inhabitants, one of its victims. I can't take the blame any more than you or the kids from North Vietnam. There is no sense in it, Harry, no sense at all."

And I kept on.

"You want to tell me about that mission in '45? You want to tell me about when you served in the U.S. Navy, like you've been avoiding telling me since I asked you the first night I met you? Like you told me again never to bring it up just a few hours ago? Maybe there's some reason in it. Maybe not. Personally, I don't give a damn about it any more, not like I used to. Nope, I haven't seen the Reaper up close like you, Harry. But lest you forget, you and Phin 'bout the only real kin I have left since...."

"Ah, fuck off, Cobb, you and your book-learnt ideas on living and dying." Harry had a small dribble of spittle on one side of his mouth and the blue vein on his forehead spoke in tongues.

"I ain't going back to '45 and ships splitting apart on the open sea and men swimming in a sea of fire trying to put the flames out with oil-water that was nothing more than more liquid fire; and dripping flesh, those men stabbing at their faces with stubs for hands and not even knowing that one of their legs was gone...and then the sharks comin' around. No man can make me, least of all you, Cobb, last of all you."

I had to plow ahead for fear that if he stopped, his heart would set a sea anchor and the ensuing silence would kill us both in the wake of a young soldier's history, which was the history of all soldiers and every war and was unsolvable until the species killed itself off or thought differently of resolving its differences. *That*, I didn't learn in a book.

"No, I can't make you, Harry. But don't tell me I've not seen death. I've seen plenty of it and most of it in living, breathing men and women—White folks killing me with their M-16 eyes every damn day of my life. And don't think a bit of me didn't die with Gillie, and now hopin' Grace comes all the way back, and Phin's enlisting. Don't you ever think I didn't love them with every bit of feeling that hadn't already been sucked out of me. Don't do that, Harry."

Harry regarded his old friend, one eye narrowing in the building of defenses, the other rounding in the ancient purchase of trust, knowing the problem had gone beyond discussion, and called for the dogs. There would be time for the telling later, after his boy and his wife were home and well and a regular kid and mom again.

The next day, when we pulled into the parking lot of the big VA Hospital just south of Denver, Harry spoke for the first time in seven hours and four pouches of driving tobacco.

"Don't figure I'll recognize it."

"You talking about which building where we'll find Phin?"

"Naw, the world when it's done whittlin' itself away."

"We have time, Harry, that's something, you know. We ain't broke for everything. We got time."

Phin's the one who'll know, I thought to myself, but not anytime soon. He'll know something when he's done. And so will Grace. Time will treat them on their own terms, same as it's been treating the Black man since he was brought here in chains. Then I looked for a spot to park where the dogs would be out of the rain.

Harry told the dogs to stay and asked me if I was coming, but I told Harry that I'd be along shortly and that he shouldn't let Phin be defined by any wound. So he best not define himself that way either. Harry nodded, realizing the honest truth in his old friend and moved off in search of his only boy, a morass of brick buildings spreading out before him, head bent down into the cold March rain, a compass dressed in Wranglers and a wool flannel shirt.

I let him go off on his own. And then I remembered.

When Phin was to report up at Ft. Tuscaloosa near Montgomery, it was raining. It had been raining for eight days straight in the wake of Hurricane Arlene. Harry and his two crewmen were still holed up in St. Pete, having followed reports of large schools of seabass farther east than normal. Now they had no choice but to wait for the bitch to pass. He'd make a killing if he was first to the shoals where the sweet bass had been spotted. Word would leak out to a few who shared those kinds of secrets, but by then he and the smart or lucky would be headed to port with their holds full and their futures temporarily topped off.

Harry fished differently now, with aggression and need. And some would say an unnecessary vengeance, like killing fish and giving them away would bring back his daughter that the cancer and its indiscretion had taken from him. If the ocean's quietude had healed him before, he'd take whatever he could get from it now on another tack. He used to owe it, but now it owed him as well. Where Harry was not the same, the ocean, too, had changed. It was rougher around the edges and in the middle, a young thing gone bitter and middle-aged.

It wasn't a battle but it wasn't peace either.

Grace had worried herself sick all that July month of '71 about Phin's enlisting. He'd tossed out a few hints about joining up after Gillie had caught the cancer and passed within a few short months. Harry had thrown himself to the sea and Phin had wrapped himself around with his grief. He didn't want to hurt others in revenge so much as he might want to even the score of self-suffering. In that sense, he and Harry were no different at all. And why should they be?

But in recent weeks, Grace was so worried she'd tried to get ahold of me half a dozen times, hoping that I could talk to the kid before he shipped out. As if he could just fall back into the shadows of non-existence. But I was dealing with my brothers and the farm and Nadine had only left one message about Chuck. It was a postcard sent general delivery to the Mobile post office with the words "Cobb Farm" and a little map drawn in pencil. On the back it said that he'd "stopped by for a spell but left without saying where he was headed." Finally, though, Grace had gotten word to Harry through another captain and Harry had dumped his entire catch of sweet seabass to make better time on the run back up the coast. Harry had never invested in a good radio. Said they were for pleasure boaters.

But by the time Harry made it home, Phin had just gone and done it. There was no reason or explanation that he cared to share. And his own mother was thinking that she might have to drive him up for induction and all she could feel was a blend of love and chaos and angst and hope. And when she allowed it, her own form of saintly hate with the secret desire to save her only remaining kid from wrecking his life. She would drive Phin to Mexico if that be the case. Park the car in the Oaxacan Desert and throw the key into the sand. Grace had lived quietly, painfully, compassionately with Harry's quieter memories of war. Still, nothing could make her allow the circle to go on unbroken. So, by and by, she did nothing.

Grace had always lived by the sound and meaning of her name. She knew what faith was and trusted in the one that had instilled it in her. The spirit within her was strong in ways that might help her in the life she believed would be next and would be perfect. Her gentleness in this one had exposed her to the rawness of the elements. Where Gillie had a thin veneer over a steely core, Grace had dropped her shell early on, allowing anything earthly to enter her soul. Her faith would filter out the bad stuff. But this one was had hit hard. If Phin went off to the war, pieces of her soul might be so torn that no surgeon or priest or shaman or holy man of any faith could stitch it back together.

Phin got a hold of me on a job site outside Mobile and said what he'd done, that he was just going to take a bus, save his mom the grief, and would I mind meeting him there a day early. He had run out of ways to deal with Gillie's dying. For him, it wasn't about 4S deferments, hardship cases, or conscientious objector applications being put on hold while the Supreme Court made its decision. Phin was running from the government of his mind, the United States of His Sister's Memory.

Ironically, Phin still wasn't even in the "system." Harry had successfully kept him off the government's radar screen—no birth certificate, no taxes, no driver's license, no ID card, no voting. He was just a happy kid going to a small school, playing in the waves with his older sister and his friends near the rebuilt pier. Washington didn't know Phin until he showed up at the Pensacola draft board saying he was a real person willing to join a real U.S. Army. They'd find him in the files sooner or later or just start a new one. Right now, they had the body. That was what they needed, what they coveted.

Harry had almost accomplished his goal. He protected Phin from the draft board coming after him, but not from something in his conscience that made him go looking for answers in places that only begged for questions.

There was no way to predict it and so there was no way to stop it. Whatever made him decide to go in was something that lived inside his own head and was not a party to the world that just now learned of his existence. Harry had never wanted to register the boy with the world until he was ready to take it on. In his father's mind, the world might think it ready to take his son as a "document" the second he'd left his mother's womb. But the world itself was too unstable for his only son. If Harry had anything to do with it, Phin was to be a man-child of the highest bearing without outside interference until he was ready, if ever. There would be time. They'd talk about it after they'd both gotten over Gillie, if ever.

✳ ✳ ✳

The war was changing. But American kids were still dying, in Nam and at home. It was July 4, 1971, exactly one year and two months after National Guardsmen had murdered four students on the Kent State campus—four dead in O-Hi-O. The tin soldiers and Nixon had come. President Nixon had been on the TV news the night before and told the American people that the incursion into Cambodia had begun and would be among the most successful of the Vietnam conflict. The next day the student protests at Kent State resulted in death. In his speech, Nixon had stressed that the troops would evacuate that country by June 30th. A year later they were still there.

I drove over to Montgomery to meet Phin on the day he was to go in. Just a year ago the war had seemed so far away, seemed like it might just burn itself out like the other residual strangeness that came with turbulent times. I remembered that June of 1970, before Gillie had gone, when Phin's softball team had made it to the league finals, when the fishing had been spectacular, and Grace's tomatoes near perfect. Now I was shaking hands with a tall kid whom I barely recognized after spending nineteen years with him.

A year ago, jury selection for the Charles Manson trial had yet to begin, ten months after the Tate-La Bianca murders. There were civil rights riots all over the south. Within twelve months, Janis Joplin, Jimmy Hendrix, and Jim Morrison would be dead. South Vietnamese troops would invade Laos and Lt. William Calley would finally be found guilty of killing twenty-two Vietnamese civilians in what was called the My Lai massacre of 1968.

How could Phin have known at nineteen-years-old that the same rain falls on the just and the unjust?

As I watched him disappear into a drab green door below the letters, "Welcome to the United States Army," another boy told his dad he'd make him proud. I just said to just make it.

The door shut, swallowing everything innocent. A captain with a Chesterfield wobbling between his fingers like an erect penis stared after me.

"A Black man sending a White boy with a redneck to fight the yellow. You gotta love this country, don't you, boy?"

I knew then that Phin wouldn't come home the same. I just wanted him to come back with a chance.

CHAPTER 10

HE HAS MET THE ENEMY

Harry was losing it. I'd caught up to him in the morning's hunt through the VA labyrinth. He'd been to three buildings, six floors, two wards, and four different rooms looking for his son. He'd even asked at the front desk for directions.

I sat Harry down on an olive-green vinyl bench in some endless corridor with black and white pictures of earth taken from outer space and overflowing ash trays. Handing Harry a newspaper from some clerk's desk, I told him I'd be back in ten minutes with the exact location of his son.

On the front page of the newspaper was a picture of a band of Oglala Sioux Indians flying an American flag upside down at the spot where cavalry guns massacred their ancestors in 1890. The caption read, "Day 47 at Wounded Knee and No End in Sight." I heard Harry grunt as I walked away.

My patience was wearing off, like Novocain.

I went to the main entrance and asked again how we might find Corporal Phin Davis who'd been brought in with a partial amputation a few days earlier. The clerk sat in front of a desk scattered with papers and forms and cigarette butts and one old black glove holding them from blowing away when the front door opened and a mountain breeze came in. He took off his glasses and set them down, rubbed his eyes and asked what was my relation to the deceased.

"Excuse me," I leaned in to the young clerk, "did you say deceased?"

"No, I meant to say diseased or maybe displeased. What did you say the soldier's name was again?" The clerk started shuffling some papers and bent a cynically triumphant grin.

"Davis, Corp. Phin Davis, U.S. Army, from Panama City, Florida."

"And you are next of kin?"

"Yes, besides his father and mother, I'm the next kin he has."

"Where is the father?" the clerk finally looked up at me.

"He's right there in the hallway." I pointed to Harry sitting on a bench, staring at the past.

The clerk tried to stifle a laugh, but couldn't hold it back. "You boys from the South have taken inbreeding to a new level."

At six-foot-three I was one-and-one-half the size of the clerk and I fought the urge to do something I would regret. An image of old Grayfalls came into my mind; the way he'd let things pass quietly as we'd gone into town when I was a boy and people would ask, "How, Chief. Shot any buffalo today?"

Grayfalls was gone, too, though, and only existed in my memory and sometimes my imagination alongside Ruth and Gillie and, please, Great Spirit, I thought, not Phin or Grace. I stared at the young clerk and began speaking in a Natchez chant, slowly, quietly, but building in power and volume. I picked up the one black glove holding the stack of papers down and placed it on my right hand. Then I walked over to the main entrance doors and opened them both wide.

The wind came in, appearing to accelerate with my native song, stirring and swirling papers from the desk, sending them down every hall and into windows and ducts and up against metal carts and brown walls, and some just floating in a circle, refusing to land.

I closed the doors, set the black glove down on the now empty desk and ceased my wailing call. And as I walked away from the ranting clerk and back to where Harry had stood up but still had not moved, he called out, "Just one glove to choose them all." Who could know how this phrase or its indifference had come to the lips of a fisherman.

A few more orderlies arrived along with two soldiers that looked like MPs. The clerk pointed and they moved down the hallway toward Harry and me. But then a wiry, youngish man in hospital scrubs and a cammie vest came up to the clerk, looked both ways, leaned in real close, butted the little clerk's forehead with his own, and then walked away calling after the MPs.

"Sirs, Blackie saw it all. The door flew open and Dilbert's papers scattered all over the place. Little twit can't do his job. Doesn't even think the MPs should be in the hospital. All true, oh, company cops. This man was helping Corporal Dil-twit pick up the mess the overpaid clerk made."

The MPs looked at each other, laughed, and walked on past Harry and me. The young kid in the mixed-outfit approached us a little nervously and then began speaking. He didn't stop for several months.

"Name's Blackie, but people around here just call me Blackie. It's not short for anything, and then again I'm not long for much else. Hey, that was a good trick out there, smooth, what's your real name, man, you played it real cool for a cool cat. Blackie does not care for that little paper-desk-man, no, not at all. Bad, bad, bad. Got the goods on him, plus he thinks I might poison his coffee cup with strychnine. Never do it though, non-violent, that's me. Just trying to keep a step ahead of the Man who already stepped on me once.

"Hey, are you a vet, I know you aren't, but I have to ask, part of the job. Darn that was a good one, have to remember it, sure had that nerd and his ego going. Did I tell you my name? It's Blackie, come on, I'll show you around, unencumbered as such, I been here since I lost my self over there and they shipped me back to the world, but this isn't the world...it's just another kind of battlefield. Where do you want to go? I know every crack of this hole, every paying customer, so they let me roam free 'cuz even though I'm not quite right yet, I'm a nice guy and I help out, you know, sort of like an official greeter or something, but I know when to keep my mouth shut and when to scoot the total schizos away from the inspector types, the media, and the greenie psychos that will just plain off the manic psychos if they get too close, plus I got the goods on some of the admin types as well—the power of the Polaroid! Whoopee, kinda gross but it gives me my hall pass, hey what's your name? Take that frown off so you can see how handsome Blackie is. Man, you look just like yourself...only older. So, welcome to Denver VA, where the war rages on for those who still rage in their war. We got it all here, Blackie the greeter says. Ah, the vicissitudes of war. The odds aren't good here because the goods are a bit odd. Hey what was your name again? Was that a Kiowa chant out there or Natchez? The wind thing tells me it's shaman. They're pretty close though, says this doctoral candidate from Duke, anthropology, class of '66, not like the route. Sounded Natchez. Pretty good too. Caught me by surprise, you did. What'd you say your name was? Didn't know whether to have you sainted or tested. Where'd you...."

"Blackie." I touched his shoulder softly. He flinched, but didn't back away. "Name's Cobb, Johnny Cobb. We need to find a boy who just got shipped in. Big Brother told us he was here but nothing else. His daddy's sitting right here. His name is Harry and he holds the record for the biggest seabass in all of Bay County, Florida. He isn't in a chatty mood and I reckon' you'd be doing us a big favor by finding his son for us."

"Well, why didn't you just say so, Mr. Johnny Cobb? You Southers are all so polite. But you don't sound like Deep South; I'd say Louisiana, northern part. Yeah Big Brother, he be keeping the goods from y'all if'n it ain't 'specting to be a purty sight. It's good you come on up here and take that boy home quick like. It'd be a hoot talking with yawl like this, but I 'specting once you seen't your way around here you'll realize it ain't the Mayo-fuckingClinic. I picked up a master's degree in linguistics on the way. How's my Southernese?"

"Blackie, his name is Phin Davis. He just came in from Cheyenne Mountain Air Field. Greet us, Blackie, greet us with news of just one man."

Blackie's eyes rolled in separate directions and he looked at us for a moment in a dull, absent, lock-tumbling silence.

"This way, Mr. Cobb."

Blackie led us through a small courtyard where men in wheelchairs sat wearing stained gowns and five-day beards. It was cold outside and the pissy rain fell on their old wool blankets, blankets that covered stumps and scars and holes and hate and guilt and feelings that there were not yet words for. Some were happy to be alive, others sad that they weren't dead. Most didn't know the difference. And they smoked in the rain.

We went up an outside elevator and Blackie pointed us to a long narrow room lined with single beds, most of them filled with human shapes and forms that were connected to glass bottles by plastic tubes. At first glance it looked like barracks from summer camp, only the children's chatter sounded like nightmares and the smell of pine trees became a mixture of Pine-Sol, feces, ammonia, and angst.

I looked at a nurse sitting and reading a chart. She was a big Black woman and I forced a smile. She grinned back, the edge of a single gold tooth peeking out, but the smile began to do weird things.

Harry was gathering strength from a place he knew he could. Days on the boat with Gillie and Phin in the Florida sunshine, pictures of his wife and daughter standing at the counter making dinner in their little trailer home. He moved ahead of me, slowly, tentatively, head straight and tall, seeking.

I fell back and looked at the names scribbled in chalk at the foot of the beds. I wanted so much to read *McNamara, Robert S., Pvt. Third Class, Sec. of the Defense, gunshot to the thorax.* Or, *Rusk, Dean, Sec. of State, Corporal, lower leg amputation.* Secretly, I might've given my own leg to move down that corridor with the steady drip-drip of overflowing urine on the floor, the sound of men gurgle-drowning in their own backed up fluids until someone finally noticed and strolled over with a suction machine; and then to see amongst this assembly line of mangled bodies and minds awaiting some deliverance that rarely came, a single twisted wreck off to the side awaiting not his own deliverance, but an overdue enema to clean out his impacted bowels. The name on the chalk board would be *President, Chief of the Armed Forces. Diagnosis: impacted bowls, systemic overflow, and reversal. Treatment: none recommended.*

In here, it seemed, Agent Orange had been a friendly spy and it was all in your head. There was peace, they told you, *peace with honor*; just so long as you honored the insanity of war.

Harry spotted Phin first and ran up to his bed. He was asleep, or at least he appeared so. His hair had grown longer and darker. His right foot was casted up to the knee and held in a gallows sling six inches off the bed. The foot seemed short without the appearance of toes poking out.

Harry picked up his son like a father picking up a three-year-old who had fallen in the driveway scrapping his knee, like a sick five-year-old at school, and squeezed him close. He stroked the back of greasy brown hair as he had done when Phin crashed his bike at twelve, his scooter at fourteen, and his car at seventeen.

Phin opened his eyes and tried to step out of the war and into his past. But some unknown enemy grabbed him by the back of his gown and slammed his head up against the full-metal headboard. Harry reached again for his boy, his lips moving up and down without words, and Phin opened his eyes. Harry turned and looked at me, as if to ask "who, why?"

Still, there was hope in Phin's eyes. But you had to look hard to see it, hard and deep. And it wasn't visible to all who looked.

I was moved back within my own past, my own healing and morphing wounds, and felt their jagged, lumpy scars. There was a small transistor radio playing in the background. It spoke of dark days of future passed and eves of destruction. They were just numbers, bits of current events that stayed with you like herpes; that and so much more. An anger welled up in me from some place I thought was locked and shut tight. And my own immediate war of patience and understanding versus the ignorance and greed that had put my best friend's boy, the son I couldn't have, here, in this place that seemed a semi-sterile jungle complete with an enemy who dressed in starched white instead of pajama black, was loosened upon the world. I stepped back from the bed and let my eyes stay with Harry, whose reddened eyes clawed their way into that place.

I thought of Old Grayfalls and how he had always taught me to wait for the right moment because the irrational always moved too quickly and without consideration. I thought of Sun Tzu's knowledge of strategy; that to overcome an army without fighting is the hardest skill to learn. But still I wanted revenge. Somebody had to pay. But who? Everyone was at fault, duplicitous in the fact that Phin laid here now, one among many.

I vowed to myself that I would stifle the anger even if Tzu had said it would kill the enemy of me. What I wanted was the enemy's goods, and that was motivated by reward.

"Elsewhere," the radio playing in the background said, *"The siege at Wounded Knee continues into its 47th day. Two men were killed in gunfire today, one an American Indian, the other a Vietnam veteran. And now, Roberta Flack's number one hit, "Killing Me Softly with His Song.' "*

❋ ❋ ❋

Seventeen hundred miles away, Grace Davis lifted her right arm to scratch her chin. The view of this starboard moving part surprised her, not for its previous absence but for the simple fact that she was able to cobble together an element of hope. They told me I'd never walk, she thought, might need help just breathing. They told me it would be years, if ever, when my feelings and memories and abilities to feed myself might return. She stared at that right hand and moved it as if it was the most malleable piece of human engineering that her God had ever created. She formed a V for victory and an OK for everything else. And then to the wall of some place she did not want to be, she flipped and raised both her middle fingers. Grace Davis would not be left alone in some mangy *home* with lime green wallpaper and lime green food and insolent attendants with bad teeth and untrimmed nose hairs while her husband went in search of her last living child. It took her the better part of the day, but Grace Davis dressed herself and moved down the long linoleum hallway with a dime in her pocket. The pay phone was next to the lobby bathroom and those beautiful fingers of that beautiful right hand that had picked countless tomatoes placed the coin and called the only person who could give her that chance at that moment.

"Jed-th." Grace struggled to transport her words from her mind to her mouth and into the lower part of the phone. "I, I, I don't know where-th Harry's gone to off to...gone. But please oh puleeze, get me the hell out of here."

And in some strange, cloudy everness, the rain still fell on the just and the unjust.

CHAPTER 11

ROUNDS

Sometimes I felt like my past was held prisoner, leveraged against a peaceful future, just hanging there in that gallowed sky.

–From Gerald's Diary

McReady slid his hands under the patient's back slowly, angled like twin spatulas. When his hands reached the far side of the hospital bed and he had the fulcrum he wanted, his thick arms went to work.

Changing bedpans, replacing catheters, checking bedsore bandages—those duties were never in his dreams. By the end of the day though, when he had finished his round of duties and made some acceptable peace with his present, Gerald R. McReady, senior orderly at Denver VA Hospital, could consider himself a healer.

Most days that was enough.

It was late winter outside the hospital and Harry and I had been watching McReady before he knew us. It took some time, but we began to know his story. And it mattered. The muddy snow outside suggested it might be an early spring. Inside, the seasons moved quicker, the ordinary days longer.

Time marked nothing but itself. Memories and medications said so.

In this place, Gerald R. McReady mattered.

At the moment McReady was only thinking of how he would keep this patient, this large man whose medical chart hung at the foot of the bed like a dark chapter in his life's story, from rolling back onto the full bedpan, the leaking catheter, and the festering bedsores. McReady's arms were Popeye'd, his forearms and biceps formidable. But he had only two of them. He'd done this thing himself many times, but today he was tired. He'd get it done, though. He didn't make mistakes on other people, only himself.

Just as orderly McReady was finishing his unenviable duty, a doctor walked in, acknowledged him curtly, and reached for the chart. The patient, almost a month back in the world, was paralyzed from his C-5 vertebrae down to the earth his feet no longer felt, courtesy of a well-thrown frag grenade. Nam had done its thing.

McReady had seen a dozen just like him, each with their own injury, their own story of cheerleaders they'd known, cars they'd hopped up, and plans that had been torn up in a moment's side-slip toward hell. They'd each had their private transaction with the war. And there wasn't much he could say to them in the currency of spoken words.

Still, hard as he might try, he couldn't always play the cool technician. Many times he felt bad for them; like he should be able to do more; like he did in his dreams—reconnect the severed nerves and vessels and ask one of the other less talented doctors to close, and then move on to somebody else who needed him. In his dreams, he made more of a difference.

During his own ordinary hours of life he had been a former captain of the track team at Oregon State, voted "most likely to succeed" in his yearbook. He was estranged from his wealthy family over "one big fucking mistake" because, as his father had said, "No McReady had ever set foot in a jail, let alone slept there." Gerald was also ineligible for the military on account that he was a convicted felon. Truth was, Gerald had been what he wanted to be. In the middle, life just got in the way.

As an intelligent, thirty-year-old, single, White, 1970s American male, odds should've placed him in a better position. McReady didn't believe in odds anymore. The system controlled the odds. His past read like some dime store novel in which the author couldn't decide whether to make his protagonist a success or a failure, so the writer simply wrote him as failing to succeed but not quite succeeding at failure. McReady had buried much of this reality, mostly by reminding himself of the good he was doing.

He hadn't been to Vietnam, not physically anyway, but in his mind he knew the place; or at least the place that was responsible for the boys who moved through his floor like defective, returned Christmas presents . He knew that place where they went when they'd lie in those little twin beds lined up like purgatory coffins and stare into a slow-moving ceiling fan as if it were a roulette wheel deciding their future against long odds. Around and around and around, but never stopping, just mixing up the ugly air and the septic smells and the screams; and worst of all, that suspended silence when parts of their past tried to do an end run on their present.

McReady couldn't explain why he knew. He just did.

"Why is the IV drip rate on this morphine not consistent with hospital protocol?" He had almost forgotten about the new doctor.

McReady ignored the whiny question from the fresh-faced young doctor as he gently rolled the big man back into place on the sheets, talking to the patient as he always had, telling them inconsequential things like sport scores and where to get a good deal on civilian shoes when they got out. Most of the time he just made things up, but there was always some kind of hope lining his words. Or at least some diversion from the present.

"Excuse me, orderly, I asked you a question about this patient," the doctor's voice waking up the other sleeping patients on either side of him.

McReady glared back and motioned to the end of the ward. He noticed how crisp and white the doc's lab coat was, how evenly his fingernails were trimmed. God, he thought to himself, why don't they skip the illusion of a residency away from here and just send these docs right into the mainstream of average medical care? *General Practice* was a good term, he thought. Or better yet, let them go back and practice medicine in the countries where they graduated from medical school. At least in Guadalajara or Canada they might learn compassion.

Gerald had his hair cropped close for ease of maintenance, his eyesight made acceptable by the thick lenses that doubly kept him out of Nam on a 4F. He didn't own a car, choosing city buses in the winter, a bicycle in the summer. He lived in the loft of an old friend's garment factory, liked to make clay pots, and had lunch once with Jacqueline Kennedy and a great aunt who'd known her well. That was almost eleven years ago. He'd written Jacquie a note when her husband was killed and she'd written back. His daily journal said so.

McReady was not a simple man and carried a complicated past that he vowed never to let influence the future of those whom he might affect. This vow was immutable, between him and his creator. It played no small part in Gerald the orderly. It defined Gerald the healer.

"To answer your question, doctor, the morphine drip was probably increased to 3mg per hour because the patient was in severe pain, most likely returning spinal shock. His vitals were stable and nothing contraindicated it."

"I trust you're not over-stepping your boundaries, orderly."

"I know my boundaries," Gerald said. But he knew his patients even better. And he'd never stopped studying medicine.

"As far as hospital protocol," Gerald tried to sound distant, "it exists, as you will learn if you stick around for more than six months, as a way to keep the authorities under the impression that there is order and control inside these walls. Truth is, we do what we can with what we are given. Some days we have just enough patience to go around, other times we run dangerously low on empathy, morphine, and clean sheets."

He walked away slowly while the doctor mumbled something derogatory, maybe even threatening. But it didn't matter. He had plenty of other kinds of pain to address.

The hallways inside Denver VA were long and straight and dead-ended. The building was shaped like a giant X that made it impossible to get anywhere without coming back to the center. Each arm of the X was lined with beds, filled with bodies, made up of skin and bone and heart and muscle and nerves and blood and, Gerald believed, a soul. Every body in every bed had a different part broken, but each came here with something wrong within their soul, Gerald thought, and while he could not be considered religious, he felt it useless to fix one broken part and not the other.

Before there was a hospital there had been twin, intersecting ridges covered in sage and wild prairie grass. The tops had been pushed off to fill the valleys and make the earth flat so that men could erect a structure. Before the valleys had gone dry, thin, crisp creeks wound through them, and in summer, native peoples came to drink and heal their high-plains thirst. They gathered the sage, too, to heal other things.

The hospital's residents now came from many states, most of them by way of one small country they couldn't find on a map when they had played army as kids in their neighborhoods. Kids, McReady thought, they were still kids, some barely nineteen or twenty. But as he moved down the long hallway, the lower right arm of the X, he figured that a soldier's age might be counted according to a different scale; something having to do with what the war did to them, like the war itself became its own timekeeper.

When Gerald was a kid he played army, but he was always the corpsman, never a hunter or a hunted. And so it was that when a patient screamed into the night, "Corpsman! Corpsman!" He was well-conditioned to know the sound, even if his only battle experience had come in the creek bed behind Tommy Louder's house.

He walked past the TV room where a group of men sat, some in wheelchairs, some on wooden chairs, playing cards. Cards were a serious thing at Denver VA. In fact, cards seemed to be a serious game for every soldier. He wasn't sure why. One kid from Omaha who'd come through last year with a toaster-sized hole in his ass, courtesy of friendly mortar fire, had told him that cards told others who you were—the way you held them, how you bet, what you kept, and what you threw away. Cards were a way of getting to know another soldier without having to say anything. You'd know a little about the guy, but weren't invested in him if he bought it. The soldiers who played alone often fought alone, died alone. And when they went back into the world, they stayed alone. Solitaire had always been a game for exiles.

These soldiers' playing cards now seemed to have a lot to say. And during the day when the meds, prescribed and otherwise, were working their magic and the cards were dealt well, they spoke loudly.

Loudly. *Louder*.

Whatever happened to Tommy Louder? Gerald stopped at the bed of a man who was ready for a bandage change. He had taken a bullet through the left thigh. The bullet had done this strange zigzag around the femoral artery, like it was afraid to hit it and shatter the large vessel that carried so much blood.

He had seen a lot of blood one time. At least he thought it was a lot of blood. Tommy Louder had been running low and swift through the dry creek bed behind his house. He ran quickly, dodging bushes and stumps and the dirt-clod bullets being thrown by the enemy. He ran like a ten-year-old, running from the Russian Army kids who lived up the block.

McReady pulled the bandage off and saw the red streaks around the edge of the exit wound. They weren't there yesterday, but infection, like Russians from up the block, can move in quickly and without warning.

"I'll have to irrigate this wound and set you up with an IV antibiotic drip," he told the patient. "No reason to tempt fate twice on this little scratch."

"Whatever, Doc." Everybody in a stained lab coat and stethoscope around his neck was called "Doc." McReady ignored the address and prepped an irrigation tray, smiling at the thought of how one or two of the old doctors here knew he was pushing meds, reading x-rays, and making notes on charts. He'd seen them check up on his work. They would've said something if he was screwing up.

Just *protocol,* that's all.

"How come one hole is bigger than the other?" the kid asked. "I mean, the fucking bullet was the same size around, right?"

"It's like this, soldier," McReady looked at the young man, tried to guess his age and wondered how he had beaten the odds. "When things are in your body that aren't suppose to be, they take along some kind of souvenir when they leave."

"Whatever, Doc. Hey, you got anything for the pain?"

He had asked Tommy Louder if it hurt when Tommy ran into the old rusty fence wire and cut his shoulder down to the bone. The slice was wide and deep and filleted open by the force of the impact on the smooth, taut skin of a ten-year-old. He was Gerry back then, and he could see little bits of flesh and muscle and a thin white shape that he took to be the shoulder blade of one Tommy Louder, escapee from a Russian prison up the block.

He thought that it looked like strawberry cottage cheese. That was before it bled. After that, everything turned dark red, then bright red, then dark red again. Gerry didn't think. He acted out of instinct—plug the hole, keep the blood in the body where it belongs, tell Tommy he was going to be okay and that the Dodgers had beaten the Giants in extra innings last night.

That's when he knew what he wanted to be. Not in some flash-of-light revelation, but in the way his friend Tommy Louder deferred to him, the way he let go and stopped crying when Gerald gently pressed his own wadded-up T-shirt into the wound and said that Mays had struck out, 0-3 in three at bats.

Someday, Gerry McReady would grow up to be a great doctor and make everybody's pain go away.

It was almost suppertime at Denver VA. He hadn't been out to the end of the X since mid-morning. That's where the real windows were, where you could find a view from behind a machine and see the Front Range off in the west, the gateway to the Rockies that had been formed when two great slabs of earth tried to occupy the same space at once. He made a point of getting out to the windows at the end at least twice a day, if only to remind himself that there was a greater force than war. And it, too, had made mistakes.

There had been no time for lunch today, but Blackie had scrounged a PB&J for him. And that was what powered him up the left arm of the X as the sick, sweet smells of hospital food rose up through the dusty vents and checkered linoleum floors.

He looked at his clipboard of patients to attend to. Some needed help in walking to the toilet, some needed help in swallowing their meds. Everybody needed help in swallowing their lives.

An older doctor by the name of Drake walked by and nodded. McReady liked Drake because he still cared. But his stern, unyielding eyes reminded Gerry of his father. His father had eyes like that.

Cleaning a soldier's infected wound on his left thigh, those eyes returned.

Gerald had gotten into three out of the four medical schools he'd applied to. The fourth wanted to see his family's tax records before deciding about the scholarship.

"I'm not showing anybody my tax records," his father had bellowed. "I'll just pay the damn tuition. But I still say you'll make way more money and a lot quicker working with your brother and me. Real estate, Gerry, look where it's got me."

He had done okay the first year, but the didactic element of medical training had not come easy. Practicing medicine was more than formula and protocol. The second year when they got to work with patients, he would show them all. He'd pay back all his fellow students for their help. He'd try to look into those gray eyes of his father and tell him that the world needed good doctors, maybe more than people who owned tall buildings.

He'd keep it light though. He hated being called "an idealist without an idea, without a clue."

But there were many days since when he figured maybe *he* hadn't had a clue. One lousy mistake, one mean cop, one week in jail, one conservative judge, a single letter from Stern Eyes refusing to let his lawyers try to get the charge reduced, weeks of pleading with his father, his court appointed attorney, the fellow student who he had delivered the package for, that kid's attorney's, the school authorities—anybody to please, please give him a chance. All he needed was a chance, just a statement or two from an appropriate authority explaining the details, helping to clear his name. He didn't know. His mistake was being naive. That's all. The punishment didn't seem appropriate. He'd make up for it, given the chance.

Right now what was appropriate for orderly McReady was a good meal, a hot bath, and two ice-cold beers. He finished rebandaging the thigh, wrote on the man's chart, and moved up the X, hoping to catch a peek of the sun before dark. That would be appropriate for everybody in this hell hole: one beautiful sunset, one good meal, one hot bath, two ice-cold beers, and one letter from an appropriate authority apologizing for putting them in here.

"We're so sorry," it would say. "What can we do to help you?"

That's all it would have to say. That's all.

Gerald McReady would get that meal and that bath and those beers. But not for awhile. There were bandages and bedpans and doctors' barely legible orders to read on charts that hung at the feet of good men, on the foot of poor beds.

He'd get to the end of the X, everybody does. Right now, though, Gerald the thinker, couldn't afford himself the luxury of thinking. Blackie had asked him to go see a young kid fresh in from the Nam.

"Kid's kind of a freak, freaking out, G-Man," Blackie had told him. "Came in couple of days ago, dazed ago, I said. But check it out, G; kid has like a big Black uncle who speaks native Natchez and a sad, sad dad who don't speak at all. The dad had to be put in restraints by some of your pals when he refused to leave his son after visiting hours were gone and gone for the day. Old Black man, name's Cobb like the corn, tried to bust it up, you know, make things right like when the trailer your're pullin' jack-fishes and knife-swerves and what you really need is to speed up, but most guys hit the brakes. Southern cats, oh shit. Blackie always knew that family was tighter than a... oops, sorry G. Been trying not to swear. But I saw it in-country. Boys from the South, speedin' up to slow it down, 'specially blood kin. Nobody tighter."

Gerald loved Blackie. He'd loved the kid from his first day he started working at the X three years ago. Everybody knew his story, how he came in as a psych patient after just four months in the Nam and had somehow never left; just became part of the chaotic landscape, helping out the orderlies, nurses, and any staff member who could see his big heart through his colorfully neurotic veneer. Not everybody agreed, but he was smart enough to stay below the radar. In fact, he was smarter than most of the MDs in residence. The war had scrambled his neurons and with his intelligence, he would have to rewrite the code to put them back in sequence.

"Okay Blackie, I'll go see him on your recommendation."

"Yeah, yeah cool Doc G. Name's Davis, forgot to bring home half his right foot. Even with the shit they got him on, he talks the same common, crazed, anarchical sense as you. Smart crazy G, like you and me."

So Gerald R. McReady went up the right arm of the X, to floor thirteen, cursing the odds, going to see some kid who'd reportedly lost half his foot and most likely the stability of soul.

Another one.

He shook his head as the cigarette cart moved past him and the words *Lucky Strike* jumped out. The doctor who had sewn up Tommy Louder's shoulder called him lucky, lucky for not slicing his throat on the fence, just his shoulder. And lucky for having a "corpsman" like Gerry to hold pressure on that battle wound.

McReady had a sudden urge to call Tommy Louder, to pick up any phone, dial information and find his boyhood catalyst. He'd tell him in a slow, pitiless voice how he hadn't been able to add those two letters after his name; how he'd made a mistake, an "error in judgment" he'd say, without pausing for effect. He would tell Tommy he'd been unlucky.

"Yeah, Tommy," he'd say, "I'm a lousy fucking orderly at the VA in Denver. It's all I could get with my record."

"Yeah, but Gerry, I'll bet you're the best orderly there."

"Tommy, I was so close."

"Gerry, my shoulder is fine. We'll win the Cold War with men like you."

But Gerald McReady would never call Tommy Louder and he could never call his father. He'd already had enough of tall buildings. He couldn't think about the view right now—only how far it would be to fall.

McReady could not talk about it and never would. Outside, the sun had gone down and with it the temperature. He scraped the pity off his mind and threw it out like a bad houseguest. Now, here he was at the very end of the high-right X, ward one, bed seven. Hmm, he thought, better odds.

The patient appeared to be sleeping, but so did the ones that died in the night. Gerald pulled the chart off the foot of the bed and started reading. Something caught his attention and he sat on the metal edge of a cold table. The patient had been sent to Denver with a temporary *Lisfranc avulsion-amputation* procedure. Three of his toes, from the middle to the smallest, had been blown off by a toe popper mine. But instead of amputating the entire foot below the ankle and preparing him for a prosthetic foot, the M*A*S*H* unit surgeons in-country had performed the delicate operation named after a French doctor by the name of Lisfranc, a surgeon who had come up with an operation to save more of the lower limbs of soldiers during WWI, many of whom had taken traumatic falls off of horses while the front end of their foot stayed in the stirrups. Lisfranc had guessed correctly that if you could successfully prevent infection, the patient would still retain that tripod support of ball, heel and outside of the foot to walk on instead of being subjected to the advanced debilitation of loosing the entire foot. It was risky because of the constant threat of infection, so they didn't see many of these type operations and closures back in the States; few surgeons in-country had the time, the skill, or the patience to do it right.

But here was one staring at McReady. And something shifted in him, some welling up of motive from his past. Tommy Louder, Phin Davis; their names even sounded familiar in his head.

"Phin Davis, I presume. Not bad. If I forget which name is first and which is last it won't matter, will it? So, Davis, looks like you left one of your fins for Charlie to make soup with. Was that some kind of lovely parting gift?"

"Hey, Doc," Phin tried to find some coherent words through the dark reigning silence, tried to diffuse the past ordinance with present humor.

"You're not gonna' like... ask me to dance, are you? And it's Phin, like the shark. Not Phineas." McReady liked him straight away, started to say something, but then the darkness from the war came out, smuggled back into the world inside the heart of a simple kid with a funny name.

"You let them cut off my foot and I'll hunt you down and kill you. And in twenty-two months in the Nam, I can't swear that I murdered anyone."

"Alright, Corp. Davis, you and I will treat this wound like it's the last foot you have. But you have to trust me, because I'm not real doctor. But I will do my very best."

Phin looked at McReady through the filmy coat of painkillers. It was the first honest thing he'd heard in months.

"Deal. Only two things I need."

"And those are...?"

"Cut the pain meds out and tell my dad the only way around it is through it."

McReady had seen the heroes come in and ask to be taken off the morphine and other masking agents. But most of them didn't have the right intent; wanting to suffer was never enough. You needed the right reason.

McReady had to ask. "This for you or someone you already lost?"

"It's for all of us, Doc, yourself included."

"This a spiritual thing, Davis?"

"It's a Nam thing, but they overlap."

CHAPTER 12

NIGHT VISION

There was a malicious lack of majority that manipulated the murder of millions.

–From McReady's M-Dream

Some days later, after Harry and I had set up camp inside and outside of the Denver VA waiting for a truthful dispensation on Phin, McReady began to trust me. Gradually, he began to spill his mutant thoughts and dreams about war, those feral and denizen images that make sense only to the dreamer. In a dark corner of the ward, god-awful coffee in our hands, Gerald offered this one.

He'd been feeling that if the smallest drop of blood was spilt, and was spilt in vain, his god would see it. Then a message would be sent, maybe in the form of a screeching parrot or in the way a twisted jungle vine could almost be taken for a letter from the alphabet. It wouldn't be an A or a Z. No, that would mean there was a beginning and an end. No, this letter-sign would be an M, an M because it's in the middle, stuck, squeezed, up and down'; down then up the line it goes; an M for madness, for Mary, for mayhem, for mother, for malaria, for morphine, for methods, for marching, for morals, for ministry, and for medic—yes, a winding, twisting, morphing vine in the shape of an M for medic. That would be his sign from his god that somewhere a man's blood had moved from inside his body to outside his world. God would see it as the little "g" was made a capital letter and he would know it and the vine would tell Gerald-the-medic. *It wasn't that hard.* The jungles were full of men spilling blood, full of M-shaped vines.

In Gerald's dream, there had been six men, now there were five, and none of them could tell if they were lucky or stupid. The two bookends in the front and back of the platoon were from the South, from poor families. The color of their skin said it. It said they didn't have a choice. The inside covers were older, hardened. At twenty-three and twenty-four, respectively, they had lived a hundred years in eleven months. They put Gerald in the middle, told him to stay alive, to watch for signs. They told him if he went and got hit, they'd fuckin' kill him.

It was quiet and they followed the river Son Tra Han downstream, each wondering if it could have gone differently, each stuck in his own world musing on what they could have done differently so that they would have been six, three pair, a straight flush with one card to hide in his sleeve for the next hand. One extra so that there would still be a barrier between what might happen and what already happened. They didn't lose a throwaway card; they had lost an even number. Odd numbers in war were bad juju. Everybody knew it. No grunt, no greenie, nor recon sniper-spook in his right mind would wear a gook ear necklace with three, five, or seven shriveled and dried apricot-shaped body parts around his neck.

They moved past a small *ville* and stayed in the thick, five ghosts with all their blood where it was supposed to be. Fields of rice paddies moved out from the edge, dropping slowly as the river fell, small checkerboard squares dotted with the litheness of small hunched-over frames clothed in black cotton and triangular straw hats. Planting, gathering, planting, gathering—in the rain and heat and shadows for centuries before the Chinese and French and now the Round Eyes.

The two in front and the two in back could smell the shit trench before the cooking fires and animal stalls and it reminded them that the term "Third World human waste" could mean many things. The lieutenant moved to point and felt the jungle begin to open up in front of them, tempting them with sunlight and air that could be unzipped and breathed freely, air that could not be cut and shaped or drown a man in its moisture. But he moved them back into the jungle, zipped them back in. In Gerald's dream over the previous month the platoon had lost two, maybe three to the duplicity of peaceful villages and North Vietnam Army cover. And once more he told Gerald, the monkey in the middle, to "fucking stay alive so you can at least keep the others from going dead." Gerald was shackled to the four by immaterial chains. He knew it, more than accepted it. He had never been more alive, more frightened, but calm at the same time. Right there, right then, he was immortal, as men often are in dreams. He was asleep and happy.

And so, Gerald McReady marched on into the present morning, looking for His signs.

✱ ✱ ✱

I stared into the black muddiness in my cup and asked Gerald if that was it. How did it end? But I knew it never did nor never would. I just wanted to hear this man talk for my own sanity in an insane place at an insane time. In that late night convergence in a quiet, darkened corner of the Denver VA, McReady's dream made more sense than the sights and sounds of the present.

"That last part," he continued while scanning the sights and sounds and smells of the ward. "When we had skirted the small *ville* and went back into the jungle—that was new. In my dream we had always gotten to where the Son Tra Han turned east toward the coast and stopped to fill our canteens before pushing southwest."

Gerald stopped and stirred his coffee with the eraser side of the pencil that lived behind his right ear.

"Ever since the dream began that night when the judge told me he would not give me the option of '*paying your debt to society by serving your country*' by allowing me to enlist instead of learning my lesson in jail, it had been mostly the same. The only difference was that we had lost multiple men for every year of the recurring dream. One man I could not save, one more man every month since I began my two-year sentence at Soledad, was released after eight months, then eighteen months in a vocational nursing school outside Albuquerque. That was seven months, three days, and eleven hours ago that I landed here. Never thought I'd get the job, you know, being a convicted felon and all, but I started my tenure here by cleaning up blood, pus, and feces. Not sure Uncle Sam could find enough qualified applicants so that part of my past sort of disappeared."

I looked at Gerald and pondered the pain that must've pulsed through his veins. Each time a man had died in his dream, I imagined, he had missed his god's sign. I nodded at him and touched his big, flat, helping hand gently. Then...

✳ ✳ ✳

"Now we were going back in after tasting just a ray of sun drop. We were moving away from the river to a place that would be unknown to me and the other men. Something had happened, or would happen. And me, Gerald R. McReady, was looking forward to it in my waking life and in my dream. That feeling of being needed, it's heady stuff; better than any drug I'd unknowingly transported back then or willingly carried and administered in my sleep or slipped to those who needed it most in my present work.

"I knew I couldn't die right in the middle of my dream. Too many had already slid away from my attempt to right every wrong, to keep my finger in the dam. Me and my suture kit and large compresses and morphine and splints; they weren't just in the middle anymore, now they were at the center. And me, Medic McReady, could move out like spokes from a hub if I had to. The men needed me. I knew it because of their threats. So, I stayed alive so I wouldn't get killed before I could save them. And save myself."

✳ ✳ ✳

It was dog-shit weather outside McReady's Denver loft where he lived, the snow on the lawns melting just enough to uncover the canine crap that had been frozen on the lawns since the first snow in early November. But the roads were clear and McReady decided to ride his bike to the hospital today. The dry, crisp air and the vigilance needed to avoid stubborn patches of black ice wedged into the shaded corners would do him good. He didn't want to think about the dream right now. When he ruminated on the dream in the everyday movement of his morning, the dream never became as dangerous as he wanted it to be, and he never knew how dangerous it really was. Better to let it settle on its own and move in with his pulse and his past. Better to go to the hospital and do what he could, because he could. Better to keep things moving, whether it be crumpled bedpans, crippled bodies, confused minds, or careless docs— he'd push them in the right direction before they were pulled over the edge.

So Gerald R. McReady pedaled his old three-speed bike that he'd purchased at a police auction for twenty-five dollars through the potholes of Cherry Street, dodging mud and shit and crazy drivers, so he could get to his job at the Denver VA and do pretty much the same thing.

✳ ✳ ✳

I was wide awake. Truth is, I hadn't slept much at all last night, just kept listening to Gerald and then talking to Harry until Harry could get some control of himself and fall asleep, not out of exhaustion or surrender, but because there wasn't a single damn thing he could do to make it better for Phin at that moment. Then sleep had come and I could stop telling him old fishing stories and stories about better times, and anything I could think of that had a hopeful theme. When I knew Harry was finally asleep inside the cold truck, the windows fogged over, I promised him that I would do everything in my possibility to get the boy home safe, God and the great bluesman Robert Johnson willing. But it was more the sense of commitment I was promising; I knew those kinds of things can only be sought after, hunted, but never assured. That's why I had evoked those two as partners.

I looked over at Harry, his head propped up against the side of the truck window with a pillow that Blackie had snuck out to us after we'd been physically thrown out of the hospital last night for refusing to leave Phin when visiting hours were over. There were bracelet-shaped, bluish-black marks on Harry's wrists from restraints the guards used, waning crescent moons under his eyes from the worry. I felt that Harry would pull out of it, but it would be tough; he'd always hid his own pain in front of Phin and would do it again. This time it would be different though. Unless Phin didn't make it all the way back.

So I let Harry sleep as the sun began to crawl its way out of the eastern Plains and craw its spidery veins of light up the sides of the Front Range. I'd watched Harry shift, trying to get comfortable, the way most people do when they sleep sitting up, and imagined how much pain he must have borne in his life—losing a daughter, perhaps the best part of a wife, half a dozen good dogs, and a boat or two to real weather. But I knew that he hadn't lost it all, only transferred what he could in spirit to his son when they'd shipped him off to the war. What lie in that hospital bed on the thirteenth floor, ward one, was his only son and something I couldn't explain in simple words. It was no wonder he had attacked the orderly who grabbed his arm to escort him out of the building last night.

I opened the truck door quietly, woke up the dog Saul, sleeping under an old tarp in the bed of the truck, and began to walk across the asphalt acreage.

"You want to stretch your legs, old boy? Yeah, I bet you do." Saul made that eerie dog-yawn sound that had always intrigued me. It almost sounded like Natchez, or maybe Lakota Sioux. The other dog, Daniel, coked his head from side-to-side as if to say, "I'm pretty happy sleeping here. But thanks for asking." So I pulled the fleece collar on my old big barn coat up against my neck and the early cold. And as we walked around the VA's perimeter lines, I retold the story of last night's scrape to Saul, stopping for effect or when Saul twisted his head and looked up at me, a sure sign, I'd always pretended, that Saul wanted further explanation of a detail. Or maybe Saul simply wanted me to keep talking to him. The words didn't matter as much as the talking.

"We ought to be in jail, old boy. We were that close," and I held up my gloved right hand, thumb and forefinger an inch apart. "Only thing saved us was Blackie's blackmail on the two heavy hitters who wanted to call the MPs when Harry jumped the first one."

Saul stopped and looked up at me.

"It's like this, boy; sometimes you gotta do bad things to people for good causes."

Saul didn't move and twisted his head further to the right.

"Sorry, boy," I stopped and watched a large plane fly overhead while digging into my deep pockets for my pipe. "You know how I forget that you're only a mutt sometimes and I have to 'splain things down for you." Saul made one of those long, low growling sounds that made me laugh and the pipe I was trying to light bounce up and down in my teeth like a springboard.

"Damn, it was a joke, Saul. All right, you know how you have to buy insurance for a shop in case a fire burns the whole damn place down? Well, apparently Blackie has been buying 'insurance' with his old Polaroid camera and tape recorder for some time. Last night he put in a claim and they let us go. Damn gallant thing of the kid. Seemed like he was a tenuous employee to begin with. Reckon we owe the boy. Best we go see him today and say a proper thank you and see how he's gettin' on."

The elephant in the room and in our talks, however, was the state of Grace. I hadn't broached the subject of Harry's wife for fear of sending him to a place that might require his own "medical apartment" at a half-way house between what was and what could be. Earlier that day I'd called Jed Riot. If anyone could get an accurate report on how Grace was doing after the stroke, it would be Jed. But the best return phone number that I could leave for Jed was a payphone on the edge of the VA's lobby, not trusting anything officially incoming to the Denver VA. Better to not take the war to multiple fronts, I decided. But I could've been wrong.

And so we walked into the morning, an old Black man, son of a farmer, graet-grandson of a sharecropper, great-grandson of a slave, talking to my friend's dog, son of a labrador and a collie, an unknown lineage that might've included cocker spaniel and wolf, domestic, wild and everything in between, into the new day we walked as an old married couple, both concerned, wondering, formulating plans in human and animal ways of thinking, thoughts of how to ease the cloak of pain as we crossed the short and shared distance. And each of us happy for the company.

✳ ✳ ✳

"Hey, G-Man, man, man, am I glad you're here."

Gerald had arrived for the day and as usual, sought out Blackie first for any reports on the previous night.

Blackie's eyes darted from side-to-side like the kids in psyche wards will do when they have advanced paranoia episodes, especially the premorbid ones. His pupils were tiny laser dots and he moved in close to McReady, his breath almost fogging the orderly's glasses.

"Whoa, Blackie, hey slow down. Geez, you look high-wired. What's up?"

"Okay, okay, okay, the Blackster's breathing in, breathing out, slowly now, slower, slower."

Blackie pulled McReady by the elbow into the corner of a side hallway where empty cloth bins on roll-around racks were lined up like early morning garbage trucks at the city service yard, just waiting to pick up the waste that came from humans in one form or another. Blackie wore the light green scrubs he was allowed to wear, "because the nut is harmless and it makes him feel important," they'd said, and there was sweat through the armpits and the chest in strange patterns that made his scrubs look like a medical version of cammie fatigues.

He'd never seen Blackie this way before and thought what a shame, what a big god-damned waste of a good mind. Blackie should have been an associate professor at some big eastern school by now. He should have been standing in front of freshman kids who'd be enamored of his intelligence and charisma, who lined up to see him during office hours and afterward at the school pub discussing the world's people as one race and many cultures.

At twenty-eight, Blackie was no kid anymore, but when his 4S deferments ran out at age twenty-four, midway through work on his master's thesis in anthropology with an eye on a doctoral program, all that dreaming of hard-earned letters after his name were reduced to three—PVT; all those letters that said he could be a scholar were replaced with ones that said he was a grunt. The man/child with the potential of molding young minds at one point, capable of pointing a gun soon thereafter, stripped of his future, robbed of his mind, living on the edge in a place that was supposed to keep those who were close from falling over. Now, it appeared, he was being pushed.

"Blackie's cool G, I'm cool now. Remember last night when I told you to go check out the kid fresh in, ward one, half-a-wheel, Black 'uncle,' mute pop? Well, that dadio went off on the goon orderlies, Roberts and Wilcox, when they told 'em to leave."

Gerald knew bits of the incident. After telling his dream-tale to me, he'd stayed for another hour rapping with Phin while Harry sat nearby. Just before the incident and after the close of visitor hours, a supervisor found him and sent him on some bullshit errand twenty minutes before his shift was over. Blackie kept talking.

"Well, this kid, Davis, his paparama went and tweaked Wilcox's arm pretty good. I don't like that Cox, naw, naw, naw. Blackie thinks he has a bad heart. Know what I mean G? One of those cats who went 4F and has been fightin' his own war in here 'cuz he never got a taste of the real shit.

"So, Wilcox is really pissed, rubbing his arm, and I hear him telling Roberts he's going to call security and get Papa Davis and the heavy-duty soul-chief uncle arrested for assault. Man, the pop, he knew he had gone temporary 5150, realized it, felt bad, even apologized to Roberts and Coxy Boy. But I saw Coxy calling in the security thugs to hold them up at the exit.

"So G-Man, I had to play one of my cards, a real high one."

"Ah, Blackie, you didn't. What'd I tell you 'bout getting involved in the politics of this place? You can't win."

Blackie's eyes squinted and his narrow jaw moved out to let the words flow. And then he spoke in clarity of realism, of a truth reserved for those who fight mental demons every day of their lives and, on occasion, can push them back from whence they came. Blackie took his momentary mental truce and spilt what truth he could.

"Gerald, I got involved when Pressie LBJ pulled me from Duke six months before I could be called a doctor, two months before I could scrounge enough money to hire a lawyer to get me out of it, and three weeks before I decided that Canada or a bullet for breakfast weren't the answer for me.

"You know damn well, G, that sometimes you get a chance to make a difference in here and you best be fucking making it. You know that I know you know it. Straight up know it. That Phin kid, he and his family have a chance to pass through the hell they've seen with only a few singes and a deep, deep tan. But they'll need some help and Blackie here told Wilcox he knew about the morphine he'd been skimming and had some cool records and pictures of meetings in the parking lot. Simple stuff like that, G. Insurance. Ace of spades. Even told the bluesman uncle, Mr. Cobb, all about it in case. Kind of a supplementary policy."

More employees and patients were moving down the morning hallway now and the fake rubber tree plants in the corner seemed to be bending toward them in their own attempt to know something of value.

"I'm involved, Orderly McReady," Blackie continued, "dog eat dog, man eat man, man need drug, kill or be killed. You see some light from a window, G, you gotta grab it. It's an old story, unless you've never heard it. And even this pseudo-schizo knows you know it."

McReady stood motionless at first, leaning into the light reflected on the linoleum a breath at a time, looking to ease his angle on the world just a bit. Whether or not he chose to credit the war for these snippets of unforsaken valor, even he could not say. It was bizarre, eccentric—but it was real and a small man had done a big thing.

"The tables have turned though, G-man. Wilcox has rallied his troops and is trying to get me committed to Bellevue. I heard he got his own pictures of me sneaking out some pillows and blankets to Phin's posse last night. There's kind of a poetic logic to it all, isn't there; the world doing its sickly-sweet best to make it all so relevant? Even the sad, lonely ones have to count their coups."

Blackie seemed eerily calm now, like an actor in a suicide watch training film. He turned and strolled away, leaving his friend to ponder the appalling drift of things to come.

McReady's first reaction was to go after Blackie, but he thought better of it, knew he couldn't undo what had been done. He had no leverage with Wilcox or Roberts or anybody on the orderly staff for that matter. He was his own threatening enigma. And no political animal. So McReady went about his duties with a coarse, quick manner, willing up faith from the creator of his dream, and went up the right arm of the X to ward one, bed seven.

Phin wasn't in his bed and McReady figured that the nurses had come to help him into a wheelchair for a trip to the head or; if his wound wasn't showing any sign of infection and he was feeling up to it, they'd park him in what was effectively known as the Gardens of Gethsemane, a small plot of dirt and snow-covered grass and a few blue spruce pines lining the perimeter. It was a place with its own twentieth century version of agony and arrest.

McReady looked at Corp. Phin Davis' chart and followed the treatment of Davis' injury from the day the medevac Huey had picked him up in a hot LZ after he had stepped on a land mine that blew the front of his left foot from the mid-tarsal forward, right back into the rich jungle earth outside of a small *ville* just south of the DMZ. There was nothing to collect or send along for the field surgeons or even the hospital in Saigon to try and sew back on. Dust to dust. Those little piggies went fucking bye-bye. Then an ambitious surgery in Saigon by one unknown and ambitious field surgeon to the rescue. Just so long as they could hold off the infection.

When McReady was talking to Phin just last night, the kid's mind clearing of the painkiller fog but honing in on the pain, neither spoke of the war or even the world. From Gerald's experience, that was either a very good sign or a very bad one. He was attracted to Phin for the way he could seemingly move in and out of his past and his present dependent on what they were talking about, gliding gently to some apex of innocence or dragging himself back into reality on the thin edge of a rusty blade. There was that constant, throbbing inner conflict of every returning soldier, but Phin Davis seemed to be playing some surrealistic game of survival chess with it, taunting the horror to come and get him, but then locking the door of his parents' bedroom and hiding under the sheets while it waited patiently outside for the man-child to formulate a next move.

Gerald sat on the edge of the bed, flipped through the chart some more and tried to recall some of the initial conversation that occurred only an hour before the confrontation that ensued with Davis' father, this large black "uncle," and his co-worker orderlies, Roberts and the asshole Wilcox. Man, he wished he had been around to defuse that before things started to swirl and Blackie became part of the swirl, and the swirl became a sucking whirlpool.

For the first time in many years, Gerald felt overly-involved, engaged. He had survived at the VA by doling out his compassion in strategically measured responses. He had titrated his care and governed his commitment with equal doses of reality, isolation, dream, and loyalty. This level of feeling could be dangerous.

Now something was welling up from a place long since repressed into some hole where Tommy Louder's bright red blood had spun and spurted and had gotten all over little Gerry's face, dripping into his mouth with a capitol M, and some place where letters to your father from prison come back "Return to sender."

Orderly McReady stood up from the bed, walked to the single window in the far corner of ward. If he walked any further up the high right X he would have had to smash the solid double-pane window and jump out into the same parking lot where an old Black man and his dog were returning to a younger truck and middle-aged man brushing his teeth in the mirror and rubbing his sore wrists. But Gerald would never consider that again; not after Blackie had told him if he ever killed himself he would personally go searching every inch of the Afterworld, find his sorry ass, and drag it back to earth to make him finish what he started.

"They all think I'm crazy, G," Blackie had told him that night when McReady leaked to him that sometimes he wished he was dead. "But I'm crazy smart, G, not like Picasso or Ulysses, but more like Don Juan, Krishna, or Coyote. Yeah, like Coyote. You ever 'off' yourself, I'll round up Solomon, Robin Hood, and Billy the Kidd and you'll have hell to pay with every former tormented soul that punched back through to your side of sanity! I'll reclaim my mind like the earth after a fire. And I'll find you."

✳ ✳ ✳

"Morning, Harry." Saul and I came up behind the truck, slowly. Daniel, the bigger of the two dogs, returned from roaming the parking lot by himself and began to lick Harry's bruised wrists.

"That it is, Johnny," Harry kneeled down to let Saul lick the toothpaste dribbling off his unshaven cheek. "That it is."

"Harry?" I stopped to relight my pipe and to gain Harry's full attention. But I knew Harry would be heaping the full measure of guilt on himself for letting the system get the best of him last night. And I knew that Harry wouldn't look me straight in the eyes for a few days until he had been able to compartmentalize the ordeal. So I spoke straight away.

"Don't know 'bout you, but I reckon we aren't too welcome 'round here. And I can think of a few far-better places for Phin to go and get himself healed up."

Then, after a long, not-so-uncomfortable look between us, added, "I called Jed and asked him to check on Grace."

Part of Harry, beginning with his eyebrows, started to rise up. But then the better part—call it a soul, call it regret, call it history—took control and he lowered his head just a bit, like a Japanese emperor might do toward a samurai who saved his life. And then Harry just said, "Okay, let's take the offensive and you tell me how, Mr. Cobb. You're the captain now."

Harry didn't know what Blackie had done for him and I wasn't going to burden him with it. But Harry, as distraught as he was, must've felt there was a pile of unfinished business here at this VA Hospital. It was business he couldn't fix but he couldn't run away from either. He had beat the thick chest of the world with his little fists and escaped with a scolding. For now.

The sun had reached the edge of the big parking lot and the glare off the pockets of snow clinging to the north face of every small hill was reminding me of how some things hang on well beyond when everybody thinks that they should be gone. And other things sense their presence would be unwelcome or somehow better served elsewhere before they even land in a spot. Harry must've known that he was under-gunned. We both needed clarity and time and coffee. And Harry needed his son, Phin, back. And his wife in whatever condition her God would allow.

And right now, I needed to take the point.

"I'm listening," Harry said while Daniel looked from man to man, his long ears flopping back and forth like pig tails at a tennis match.

"I'm listening."

✳ ✳ ✳

McReady had allowed himself enough rumination. There were bedpans and patients and there was the weighted task of Blackie's dilemma that would require all of his concentration. It would not be hard to keep things in motion today, for there was an eerie undercurrent of kinetic anticipation that hung from the low, dropped ceilings as he moved down the X, hoping to run into Corp. Davis before visiting hours. There was much to discuss.

And as he hit the center, Gerald felt something in his hand and noticed he had carried Phin Davis' chart with him, forgetting to leave it hanging on the foot of his bed. He turned around to go replace it and scanned the first page again where the initial details of the incident were logged. In the third paragraph were the map coordinates, but they had been crossed out; *security,* somebody would explain. Gerald knew the exact location was irrelevant, lost in time, lost to time. In the line below, he read the fading words "near the southwest bend of the river Son Tra Han, outside the village of...."

But those words, smudged out as they were, landed in his gut with a thud. It was a sign from Him. His dream had become fluid, crossing over and melding worlds.

Walking back up the X to Phin's ward he felt a sudden and heightened sensory perception, like he could have been a great tracker, only the sights and smells led him to injured and dying animals instead of Valhallic dreams of great game, golden cites, and lost cultures. And right then, Orderly Gerald R. McReady knew that his prey would be an eventual peace beyond the simple absence of conflict. And it would be a long and arduous hunt, one that would lead him out of the center, up the spoke.

CHAPTER 13

THE TRANSFER CASE

There are moments in a man's life that count. And there are moments that you might as well just throw away for they could never amount to anything other than wasted movement of a clock's hands, a tic, a toc, dropped over the round horizon. And as that moment unfolds, there should be no explainable way of knowing the difference.

Strange. An entire zone defining itself while the landscape of one's life passes from view; old photographs left as a book marker, grainy around the edges, clear in the middle. Memory is interpretable to most folks. The secret's in whether you believe the interpretation.

Those were the thoughts and images that gripped the mind of me, Johnny Cobb, as Harry and I stood over the body of Harry's son, Phin, crumpled under the thin, white sheets of bed seven, ward one of the Denver VA Hospital. Phin's sleeping figure formed a topographical map, his fetal torso rising like a shallow mountain of sorts, then falling such that the mountain was controlled by a silent anger, the weather of pain awakened then calmed. And as he heard the metallic click of the wall clock's hand, Cobb felt that Harry and Phin might be moving toward such a moment.

A single ceiling fan was throwing midday shadows around the ward, letting out a thin squeak with each revolution.

Orderlies were bringing pale, plastic trays of food to the patients: canned turkey on white bread, brown-tinged apple slices, and Jell-O...always Jell-O. The fan had the effect of stirring the food smells with the antiseptic odors with the cries for, "Doc, I need a fucking doc!"

All mixed with the surreal grayness.

We had been here since visiting hours began at 8:00 a.m. and I had not been able to get Harry to eat a bite or speak a word. The wall clock now read 12:03 p.m. and Phin started to roll from side-to-side, slowly at first, then quicker until his arms flung from edge to edge in violent thrusts and jabs.

"He's wrestling the devil again," I whispered.

Harry reached his arms around Phin and tried to calm him. But even with Phin's foot in a cast and wired to the steel-sided bed, his upper body was strong and the will to beat that evil which he fought in his dreams was empowering. He swung at the air and screamed out in foreign sing-song words.

Harry held his son, and then finally backed off, letting Phin swing and swat away. Then he spoke.

"That's the devil trying to get out, ain't it?"

"That's the war trying to get out, Harry."

"Devil. War. This cesspool. Look at my boy, Johnny, look at him."

It was the most words I'd heard from Harry in the three days we'd been standing sentinel at the hospital. And the first real sign that Harry knew just how deeply the war had embedded itself in his last remaining child, and the child in it; what Harry's dad used to call "quick sanded."

"Who did this to my boy? Who took out that simple kid we raised up correct and put back this man with enemies none of us can see?" Harry stroked Phin's stringy brown hair out of his sleeping eyes and then stood up to face me, his eyes narrowing and the lines in his face deepening like rain gutters draining anger. He looked at me for the longest of moments, holding his gaze, and then shook his head knowing that I had failed to answer the question of why men go to war, that he never could; he, the father, had seen it up close, but had buried it so deep that the only thing keeping the wild animals from digging up his dead body was all the rocks placed over the grave site. Or maybe it was just a rhetorical question prompted in angst, designed to keep the question alive so that one day a man or a god might be able to answer that which was is unanswerable.

"Who quick-sanded my boy?"

We had been friends for twenty-two years and barely an ill word had passed. I felt a white space opening up between me and Harry, impossible to enter or argue across. I could be the sponge for Harry's anger, I'd take it all, as Harry would do for me—had done for me in his own way.

I tried to calm him down, but felt something had broken free in him, a part that had been held in check since the day he'd found out Phin had gone and enlisted, when I had met his boy in Ft. Tuscaloosa with a black-and-white picture of Gillie in the back pocket of his favorite old jeans, the ones with the fishhook still embedded in the lower leg. For twenty-two months Harry had held it together.

When his only daughter and first mate, Gillie, had died of the cancer bitch, he had held it together.

When Grace, Harry's wife of thirty-one seasons, had been struck with the vagaries of bad plumbing, Harry held it together. And even now, as the cold-hearted realization that he'd left Grace alone and in the care of doctors he didn't know or had sold fish to, while he sought the soul of Phin, he'd held it together.

When he couldn't get the boat out of port in time and tropical storm Debbie had destroyed his livelihood in the fall of '57, he'd held it together.

With word that Phin had re-upped, Harry had stumbled, but he'd held it together.

When the letter with the plastic window came from the government telling him his son had been injured but was alive and a tribute to his country, *he'd be coming home soon,* Harry

Davis, the man who seemed to have been deflecting the notion of pain all his life, held it together.

And for the time he and I'd been at the hospital, watching his son, trying to connect the boy that left almost two years ago with the strange, confused, and struggling man that returned, other than one outburst, Harry had held it together.

I had thought that most men would not be able to hold themselves up against what the world had thrown at Harry. Now, Harry must've realized that his son, the beat of his own heart, would never be the rock he would allow himself to break against.

Harry looked at the erratic rise and fall of his son's chest, smelled the rehearsal of slow death from the hospital hallways, and picked up the glass IV bottle hanging off to the side of the bed. Suddenly, after unplugging the tubing that was heavily taped to Phin's forearm, he threw the bottle at the small view window, breaking the glass and landing seven floors down on the lawn that sat in the thin mid-morning shadows of the Front Range. Outside the hospital, no one noticed. Inside, the crashing noise seemed appropriate and a small applause came up from the ward. Fresh mountain air flew in. Somebody said "right fuckin' on." In that lag between space and time, Harry just might've broke and thrown himself out the window.

He'd cracked, but he hadn't broken.

And inside I smiled to myself. Well done, Harry, well done.

I allowed myself a grin because I knew that the final symptom of ultimate despair was a silence and a complete withdrawal. Harry's words and violence meant he'd hit bottom. But he'd survived and would now have something to push against.

I started to speak as I picked up the end of Phin's IV that was dripping blood in unique snowflake patterns on the linoleum floor and tied the tubing in a knot. Phin stirred but remained in a restless, drug-free sleep. Before I could get the words out, an orderly came running down the hall. Other patients in other beds with the common injury of war laughed, said, "Amen brother, break my window, would ya?" Harry sat on the edge of Phin's bed and watched his son's blood fill the plastic tube and try to run out, only to find my hasty knot and return to the body. Two more orderlies arrived along with a doctor who barley spoke English. The doctor smelled of ivory soap and fondled the ubiquitous stethoscope around his neck.

"Why me?" the young doctor muttered and told the orderlies to clean up the mess as he moved down the hallway with ambiguous steps.

"What the hell happened in here?" A short, wiry orderly looked at me as I stood like a dime store Indian: proud, silent, immovable. Two other patients moved in behind the orderly, one in a wheelchair with bandages leaking from the two stumps right below where his kneecaps had been; the other tall, with eyes like lumps of coal stuck into a clay mask.

"Man, it was a bird; a big, gray 'mutha fucker," the tall one spoke animatedly.

"Yeah," the chair-bound kid picked up the tale and ran with it. "Sombitch hit that window like a wrecking ball. Had a beak kinda like 'Tricky Dick,' only thinner." The vet in the chair wore a sleeveless fatigue jacket with captain's bars on the chest and picked the dirt from his fingernails as he spoke.

"Ever seen that kinda hole, medic? Ever seen a big animal slither his way through a small hole, a hole that isn't even a hole but an opening to a tunnel world that leads all over the country, invisible everywhere? But you can hear them gooks scurrying around like rats in the basement, knowing they could come out and bite your toe the second you fall asleep? Like *Alice in Wonderland*—only the white rabbit carries a pitch fork."

The orderlies cleaned up the mess and everything settled into the quiet chaos of life in the Denver VA in the spring of 1973.

I poked my head out the broken window and saw that I could now look east and see the beginning of the Great Plains, the edge of the heartland that had been the beginning and the end of so many dreams.

"I'm almost an old man, Harry, a weathered Negro not quite fifty years old who's seen enough shit to turn me into a damn priest. And you and I have been party to enough passing that it seems ridiculous we're even standing here."

Harry tossed a look back, a face that corkscrewed up his eyebrows but kept his chin firm and muted.

"I suspect your boy has seen more dying and suffering and heard enough good men yell out 'fuck me it hurts' and curse God, and shoot regular people on account of it, not knowing who's pulling the trigger."

Harry's face twisted on itself, the wind of my words spinning a dust devil before falling into the eye of every storm he remembered. The words came out thick and deep, moving past our ears like red mud. Something was about to be proposed.

He looked once more at his boy lying quiet and still for the moment, and imagined the firestorm that must be raging inside. He prayed to some indiscernible spirit that the boy hadn't gone rootless, that his essential ties to his childhood memories would hold him while he worked through his exile. Solitaire was not a game you wanted to get good at.

Then Harry looked back at me and the film that had coated his eyes since Gillie had passed and clouded further when Grace got sick, seem to bleed out in soapy tears.

"When the *Indianapolis* went down," Harry spoke in a whisper, staring into the glass jars on the shelves as if they were crystal balls, "we knew who'd hit us and what animal might finish the job. It was terror, but it wasn't the kind you could see and touch and feel. So at least you...you couldn't know. I don't know why my boy is here; I really don't."

"Harry?" my voice a raspy breath. "Someday we might, but right now you know what has to happen, don't you?"

For several days Harry's face had retained a constant and unwavering geometry. Now it was as if his own impregnable history had morphed into a facial biography, spilling out all that he'd felt onto the bloody floors. Harry wondered why the orderlies hadn't reconnected a new bottle of

IV fluid. Then, in some strange confluence of grip and release, Harry looked up at me from the other side of the bed, allowed himself the ends of his thin mouth to glide upward, just a notch. His sea-green eyes said they needed to take Phin home.

Harry needed to show Phin how to row the little skiff, *Ruth Henry David,* against a flooding tide. How to find an animal in the stars. There was a lot of undoing to be done.

My tobacco teeth must've reflected the dusty fluorescent light and I knew the ascent out of the one's psychic basement could take years and guaranteed nothing. But I knew that as Harry put himself back together, he'd be drawing on the strength of the one who, at the moment, had the least to offer— his twenty-two-year-old boy who lay naked, tired, and tied to the horror.

"Yeah, I know. Phin belongs somewhere other than here, some place where the war has begun to wear off. Matter of fact, after the way you busted up that orderly last night, I'm kinda surprised they even let us back in at all.

"But we only got us one truck now, do we. Just one truck and a couple of dogs."

"But we got ourselves, my son; we got Phin back."

Neither of us mentioned the toes that Phin left over there. We had the main body.

✳ ✳ ✳

For the first time since he'd come back from the war, Blackie recognized and labeled his feelings without empowering them. It was fear again. He knew his mind was crooked from being run over one too many times, but in here, this way-station purgatory where soldiers returned in various states of disrepair, he was at least doing something. When he was in the Nam getting his mind run over for the last time, something was always being done to him. Maybe Blackie hoped that someday it would all just go away, a bad night's sleep and he'd wake up in his classroom at the university, late for a lecture but knowing that his professors wouldn't abandon him. Now though, he'd taken his liberties too far. And he was scared shitless.

Frank Wilcox stood before him in a large empty supply closet on the fourth floor. The air was a mixture of Clorox and hydrogen peroxide and leftover cannabis from a clandestine toke on someone's break. Little beads of sweat had formed on Wilcox's brow, but they stayed in round buttons as if afraid to drip. And a small pool of spittle had formed on the lower corners of his mouth. Hot, white spit. Blackie sat on an old wooden chair and thought about Orderly Wilcox, the one he had blackmailed into dropping the assault charges against Harry when Wilcox had tried to get him to leave that first night before he was ready. Blackie thought he resembled a rabid bear.

"You know, little man, I've turned an eye for you to wander around here and do your, 'help a brother out' crap for a long time. Truth is, like everybody else, I know you're psycho. But I never thought you were stupid. And now you've become dangerous, a liability."

Blackie's brilliant, tweaked mind was kicking in now, just like it always had before league finals of the debate tournament at Duke. He was still afraid, but guys like Wilcox only have one good card to play and Blackie had seen it clearly in the opening salvo. Wilcox couldn't hold Blackie's stare and spoke to the five-gallon buckets of Clorox.

"Okay, so you know about the skimming and you say you've got photos. Big fucking deal. You know that half the staff here is pulling. The rest just get pushed until they fall off." Wilcox laughed at his cute phrase, as if surprised at the creativity.

"And you, my little psychotic imp, are *now* a prime suspect. Roberts saw you steal blankets and pillows the other night. And the way I see it, there must've been some heavy shit wrapped inside those blankets. Nobody steals just blankets."

Quid pro quo, thought Blackie, just as he'd guessed. Wilcox would try to turn the blackmail thing around, pull Blackie in, classic CIA tactics—admit nothing, deny everything, initiate counter-accusations. Maybe Wilcox would make a few threats about keeping his mouth shut or he'd pull some strings and get Blackie tossed out onto the streets where he'd have to fend for himself. Oddly, that didn't scare him. What had him worried was that Wilcox might just be in it too deep, might just be crazy enough to try and get Blackie committed to the psych ward at the old hospital downtown. He'd have to play along for another round and see.

"Frankie, Frank, slow down, hold your undies in a bunch, no, no, no orderly friend Frank. Blackie doesn't have the goods on you. No pics, black, white, or Technicolor. I was bluffing big boy, bluff, bluff, 'cuz that big Black fellow who hangs around the thin redneck pop of the kid who lost his piggies is bad news for Willi-Wilcox. I've seen their home on wheels out in the parking lot, Franco. Lots of guns stashed under that big tarp in the back of the truck; major firepower my man, all guarded by those hospital employee-eating dogs. They don't eat, Franco, unless it's roadkill. Them Southern boys have a serious dis-eating order. I was just doing the Gandhi thing. Blackie's on your side, big boy."

Wilcox folded his arms and shook his head. A bad sign.

"Frankie W., hear me well. If you and Roberts woulda put the big heat on the Davis cat, dollars for donuts they'd be shooting off your own legs. You know how them big Negroes from the South can burn cities down with a book of matches. Blackie's just looking out for the crew, like he always does."

"No dice crazy boy. I ain't buying it. And I got too much to lose if you do have the goods on us. It's just a shame for you that one of the chief admin cats here gets a little on the side from our 'entre-pruneer' skills. Looks as though you're going downtown day after tomorrow. And down there, nothing is true. So what you got just went *poof*."

Wilcox licked the saliva from his mouth and walked out of the room. For Blackie, who'd been fighting more demons on the inside than the outside, a certain hard-edged clarity started at his head and ran down. Like motor oil. It was the fear, he decided, that was messing him up all these years; the fear of not being tops in his class, the fear of dying alone in some country he'd studied about in grad school, fear of rejection as he began his duties as a young graduate teaching assistant, the fear of someone else labeling him nuts and then sitting off to the side while Blackie himself validated the label. At the root of his neuroses was fear. But James "Blackie" Black, budding anthropology grad student and patient/helper of the Denver

VA, recalled that he had joked with his colleagues: if you left on a trip traveling eastward, eventually you'd return from the west. Fear may have provided job security to the shrinks, but like most of the people he'd encountered in the army and the VA, they, too, had this deep-seated idea that the world was flat.

Fuck Democritus and Jefferson and Henry Dearborn and Himmler and McNamara. Fuck the men in the shadows who pulled the triggers from their polished oak desks and dirty ideals. He'd given his blood. He might not be the whiz kid he'd been, but the one thing that was keeping him down had made itself known. All he had to do was lose the fear, keep sailing until he came around again.

And poor Jim Black of upstate New York had no idea how to do that.

"Hey Wilcox," Blackie called out of as the heavyset orderly strutted down the hallway. "Whatever goes over a snake's back goes under his belly. The Black uncle says it's so and Blackie knows it's true." He locked the door to the supply room, sat on the stool in the dark, and wished he knew how to pray.

✳ ✳ ✳

Gerald McReady had the next day off. He had tried to make plans to do something different, maybe fire some of the clay pots he'd thrown in recent weeks, but his M-dream had hit him hard last night and he spent the sunrise trying to make sense of it. Most of it was the same. Each time, before their patrol had turned east at the Son Tra Han River, moving back into the jungle canopy that had become a lush poker hand: ambush or be ambushed, alive and famous, or dead and forgotten, give me two cards or three, blood-red or camo-green.

But in last night's version, they had stayed in the open, walked straight across the river with the lieutenant carrying on a conversation with himself, something he was doing more and more. He sent none of the other four soldiers remaining in the platoon to recon the flanks or look for a better place to cross. He just stayed out in the beautiful sun, pausing once mid-stream when the water was chest high and moving swift enough so that the men had to lean up stream to keep from getting swept down.

"McReady," he screamed when a patrol voice would've sufficed. "Get up here."

Gerald tried to wake himself at this point but something held his subconscious hostage and forced him to ride out the dream.

"You're from the South, ain't you, doc? I mean you're used to the hot sun aren't you, the way it feels on the side of your cheek after you've been stuck inside for too long?"

McReady knew the voice, but the dream wasn't letting him access all his senses. "Well, no sir," he said. "I'm from the Northwest. We can go for weeks without sun."

"Well then, you must be happy to be out here enjoying the sunshine and the feel of fresh water running through your dry rotted crotch."

"Sir, to be honest, I'm a little nervous about being exposed here in the wide open. I think I'd rather take our chances in the jungle, stay east of the river, and keep pushing south."

"You see, McReady. That's the difference. At some point you have to fold your hand, take your chips off the table, and hope you don't get mugged on the way to your car."

"I don't understand, sir. All I do is plug holes in people's bodies. I don't understand how they get here; at least not why."

All this was new terrain, a part of the dream that had snuck into those dark moments before the dawn. For this lieutenant, "no" was a word that the world had yet to say to him.

"You know, doc, like youth and money, this war is passing us by too quickly. We soldiers all start out at the middle and end up at the end. So, what's the point? Huh, McReady? You want to wake up in the next world and realize that this one was cursory? Just a damned practice? Justice makes a powerful demand on soldiers. You've seen enough men in this platoon die. Don't you want to kill back? It's only a dream, Gerald. A dream will let you heal and it will let you unheal. You've got the power, Gerald. Out here, you can do anything."

Gerald woke up at that point and began drinking coffee and looking at empty clay pots. They were empty pots, he thought; yes, these are lonely pots calling out for a plant or water or even some decorative sticks to fill them. At one point he pulled out an old LP and put it on the record player. It was *Cream.* He, too, found himself in the white room with no curtains at the station. How ironic. When he'd been in high school, the older kids were using derivatives of the drugs he administered today to invent a fictional world. Now, he worked with patients who were struggling to invent a new reality.

He had no clue what time it was, only that he wasn't supposed to work today. And something in the dream compelled him to go to the one place he didn't want to be—the Denver VA.

✳ ✳ ✳

I found Blackie out next to our truck. He was speaking with the dog, Daniel. And Daniel, for the first time since Harry had found him as a pup scrounging for food in a trash bin behind the Piggly Wiggly Mart nine years ago, was listening to another man besides Harry or me.

"Oh, Mr. Doggie, Blackie's in some deep stuff."

I stopped short of the truck and turned my head to listen.

"I'm hoping your pop can help me out. I don't really belong here, Mr. Dog, but I don't really belong locked up either. My world is easier imagined than described. But I don't imagine your kind would understand."

"You'd be surprised what Daniel understands, Blackie." I had come out to feed Saul and the younger mutt. "Daniel knows all about indentured souls. I read him most of the slave narratives while I was visiting the Davises. But hey, it was a long trip and I felt like reading.

"Blackie, we need a favor."

"Sure, Mr. Cobb, whatever Blackie can do for you in the last thirty-six hours of his employ here at the manor." Blackie told me the details of Wilcox's plan to have him committed downtown at the psych hospital.

I pulled down the tailgate and sat on the edge. I fiddled with my pipe, packing the dark tobacco into the bowl with my thick fingers, and then letting Saul lick the tips. Saul loved Prince Albert.

"Ever been to the Florida Panhandle?"

"With all due respect, Mr. Cobb, have you ever attended one of Graduate Teaching Assistant James Black's lectures on 'North American Regional Anthropology' seminars?"

I laughed long and hard, bits of pent-up worry falling away onto the asphalt parking lot.

"We need to remove Phin from this esteemed place of refuge. Or is it refuse? We want to take him home without stirring up the hive. And you need a hall pass for a few years until all this stuff gets lost in the files of some country's embarrassment. Seems to me we got ourselves a mutual paradigm of exit."

"Indeed, Mr. Cobb. Indeed. And I, behaviorally challenged Jimmy Black, some day to become Professor Blackie, know a man who thinks with keys."

Blackie found orderly Gerald McReady at his desk, feet up, still in his street clothes. His eyes were shut, but his mind was driving hard. He spoke as Blackie came up behind him.

"Something's happening here, Blackie. The rubber chasms are shifting. The X wants to become a Y. It's that kid from down South up in ward one, isn't it?"

"Bingo, G-Man. The two pops want to pop him right out. Seems they're pretty savvy to what's good for the kid. And you'll like this one, Mr. G-Mac. I'm going with them. Either that or suffer the slings and arrows of the wrath of Wilcox, spend a few years convincing some junior shrink that I won't cut my ear off."

"And all you need is my blessing, right, Blackie?"

"You are the smartest lab coat I've seen since Dr. Kildare went off the TV."

"Don't flatter me."

"Hey, Doc Gerald, I don't think it will be that hard. I already checked his file this morning while Fat Gladys was on her third donut. There's something funny with that toe-less Davis boy; lots of numbers missing from his forms, like he didn't even exist before the Army made him up. Maybe they did make him up, just invented a body and gave it a serial number and an M-16 and put it on a plane and said 'shoot anything without round eyes.'"

"So, you think we turn the thing around, Blackster; easy come, easy go? See how bad they want to go looking for a kid that's going to cost them money; that they made up in the first case because they couldn't pin enough numbers on him to make him real except when they needed a human shield? Is that it?"

Blackie smiled and said he knew that his graduate degrees would pay off sooner or later.

Gerald rubbed his eyes and then took off his jacket. He thought about his short conversation with the kid up in bed number seven. He thought about how Blackie had said he was, "smart-crazy, G, just like you and me." He thought about his father, old Stern Eyes, the rich developer who'd refused to help him when he'd been thrown out of medical school and into jail for delivering a fellow student's contraband. He thought about Tommy Louder, the kid whose life he probably saved when they were playing army as kids and he'd sliced his brachial artery on a rusty fence. He thought about how all he'd wanted to do was to get that feeling of contribution back, that feeling of making a difference. The schools wouldn't have him. His family wouldn't have him. The U.S. Army wouldn't have him, except in his M-dream. In here, in this mayhem mess called a hospital, the veterans validated the simple existence of Gerald R. McReady. In here, he mattered.

And now Blackie was asking that he do the paperwork to cover up a patient's disappearance. Including Blackie, the loss of one became two. Nothing ever made sense in here before, not on the floors or in the files. But Gerald was exposed already, watched for his indifference to the weaker docs; watched for his intuitive abilities with the men who rolled in and out of there. He was admired and feared. Loved and despised. Always somebody was watching him. Now let them watch this.

"Let me clean that wound again, pack a kit for you and then go home and put my pots in the kiln. Take the kid for a walk right before dinner. Then call me when you're on the road. But Blackie, you have to promise me that you'll watch the wound. It looks like he might be out of the woods, but I have a deal with him. And now I'm transferring that deal to you. This is our...this is your chance to make a difference."

"Got it, Doc McReady, benevolent soul. I'll look after the kid. Look after his big uncle and his dad and those dogs who listen to me like I'm not crazy."

"Blackie...the road is a good place for you. Yep, go on and get your ass outta here. I'll think of something. Just put yourself in a self-designed witness protection program and wait. I'd imagine there are a few people who would like to erase you from their future."

Later that night, with Phin Davis stretched across the laps of me and Harry Davis in a warm cab, and Saul and Daniel stretched across the lap of James Black in a truck bed made warm by a dozen woolen VA Hospital blankets, and a piece of half inch plywood forever nailed over the window above the empty bed on ward one, while Frank Wilcox and Bill Roberts laughed over their meal of chicken, powdered potatoes, and gravy about Blackie getting *committed*...Harry cradled what was left of his family and I hummed an Etta James tune.

So many great Black artists, I thought, had seemed to just fade away before their time was up. But to some folks, regardless of their color, after the artist was finally gone, dead, and buried, and the records were dusted off and set on the turntable, it seemed there was no lack of luster at all in the voice and passion. It ain't about martyrdom, Gerald must've known; it had to be the passion that couldn't be kilt.

The truck started on the first try.

IN THE WAKE OF OUR PAST

CHAPTER 14

A GRAIN OF SAND

The Panama City Beach Municipal Pier is rarely called that. More than likely the pier is referred to as the wharf, the docks, or simply, the pier. Of course, a tourist making his way on old Highway 98 from Apalachicola to Fort Walton Beach could easily confuse the odd collections of boat slips, rock jetties, and breakwaters with a pier.

The Municipal Pier is different though—it was never meant to protect boats or platform old men as they fished the end for cod and bass and the occasional amberjack. It was never built as a runway for lovers holding hands or kids on rusty bikes or lonely creative types looking for a muse.

"The truth is few people really know why the pier was built in the first place. Maybe it was that government work project funds were becoming more readily available as President Hoover struggled to lead the country out of the Depression—money was cheap, jobs were scarce, Europe was between wars and men were hungry to get their hands dirty."

The best explanation is told by Dickey Riot, who has owned and managed the Bait and Sandwich Shop on the pier's end since '71. The tale is confirmed by his father, Jed, who was the construction manager when the pier was built in '37 and rebuilt in '51. That was the early winter after Hurricane Easy came through in September of the previous' year and ripped off the last fifty-feet of the pier. Easy was only a Cat 3 hurricane, but she couldn't make up her mind where she wanted to spend her dying days and after she touched land at Cedar Key, she looped back into the Gulf and gathered strength for one dying effort as she landed again at Hernando Beach before Georgia and, finally, Arkansas buried her.

Jed, Harry, and any of the old guard who were hanging around Panama City Beach after the war will testify that the old pier was originally built because a couple of the local council members just plain wanted it. And a young Jed Riot found a way to get federal funds. That's what the boys on the council continue to argue. That's what they believe. Behind that, though, was a little town's search for an identity. A pier, yeah, one that was long and you could see from up and down the coast.

Over the years, the pier grew organically, one muscle crustacean upon another, as if it were the stayed bowsprit of some hand-built wooden boat, supported in three places, a trinity of physics with its parallel pilings and its cross-joists upon which people walked. The sea life that grew on the wooden pilings below, like the people who visited the top, added life to the pier. And in that life, was strength.

✳ ✳ ✳

There are twenty-six bones in the human foot. Including the calcaneus or heel, a foot is constructed with a series of tarsals, metatarsals, and phalanges or toes. At best, the simple act of walking upright is an exercise in the intricate delicacy and beauty of the human body. The foot itself works like a tripod, balanced evenly between the heels, the balls of the feet, and the outside toes. Take away any one of those and it's like having an ice skating blade for a shoe, like living your life on the thin edge of a dime.

Phin had erased his left phalanges, parts of his metatarsals, and a good portion of his tarsals on his third, fourth, and fifth toes in-country, in the Nam. It's an old story, I suppose—a soldier returning home with a war injury—but it's new to the afflicted. It's new every goddamn day for the rest of their lives. What Phin brought back was his heel, his big toe and the one next to it, and a collection of sixteen other bones in his right foot. He had that ice skating blade, but with rusty, tenuous training wheels welded to one side.

The surgeons in Saigon had filed off the rough edges of the bones that were left attached, pulled a big flap of skin up from the bottom, and sewed it to what they could find on top. They watched for infection and put him on a silver freedom bird back to the world.

You can imagine the scene: soldiers are coming in right and left, dusted off from a hot landing zone near a wicked firefight, and dropped at a M*A*S*H* unit for the surgeons to triage out the ones who had a reasonable chance, plug a few holes, and send them on to a bigger surgery near Saigon. The ones that didn't make the cut were handed over to the chaplains and the boys with the black bags. And one dog tag was removed.

Maybe the field surgeons were feeling like they'd done their best, but they'd seen things in the OR that turned their hearts inside out and their sense of right and wrong upside down. They knew that it would never go away unless they did something with it—this experience. Not everyone had the self-awareness to know they were a temporary healer, just the earthly fingers of something that exists on another plane: like being asked to play God for a year. They had to capture what they felt without attaching a label to it, without giving it a name. Otherwise they would just be waiting in this place, as the poet, Pete Brown had offered to the band, Cream's bassist, Jack Bruce, in '68, "Where the shadows run from themselves."

But then near the end of just another day, near the end of that cycle's killing when most of the men had been attended to and one last soldier comes in on a Christmas-colored stretcher as a nameless corpsman screams out, "Below ankle amputation, doc," and then busts out a bottle and grabs a few zees. One surgeon remembered the quick or the dread things he had done in the past hours for the sake of gaining a few more of both hours and lives. And he said no, "I'm not cutting this kid's foot off. Let's try a Lisfranc technique with a clean flap and load him up with antibiotics. Ship him stateside straightaway. This war is over anyway. If he's gonna lose that wheel, let the boys at a VA do it. I'm giving him a shot at keeping his foot."

But the rest of them said there's no time for glory surgery on this day, for this soldier. "Lop it off and put him on a Huey for Saigon. Grunts like this kid are always close to dead or plain dead."

The field hospital docs might have told themselves they were doing something, anything, but they knew better than most that in the end, war does nothing but jack up everything. The intestines spelled it out. The blood dotted the "I." The kid was alive. So what if he ended up losing his leg, he ought to be happy. Alive is happy. Dead is fucked up.

But the one surgeon glanced at the stack of stretchers in the corner, more red than green as the war wound down, and said, "No, you guys go ahead, get me a good nurse, the most sterile setup left, and get the fuck out of here. And find out his name." One corpsman, some hardscrabble kid from Detroit or the Southside of Chicago, says he'll stay and help. He scrubs in and hums the line, "Where the shadows run from themselves."

✳ ✳ ✳

Phin had been home nearly three weeks. But for a kid fresh back from the Nam, it could've been three minutes or three years; time was no longer a temporal thing, it took on its own form moving like men on a chessboard controlled by someone changing the rules. And even though Phin had grown up a giving sort, pain was greedy. There wasn't a whole lot left to give.

It was nearly three in the afternoon on his third week home and he hadn't risen from where his dad had laid him down on his old bed in his old room in the house on the eighty acres he had grown up in, four miles from the Gulf, and four minutes from the creek. In another hour it might be tomorrow. Or maybe yesterday. Men on the chessboard were telling him where to go and white knights were talking backwards.

He didn't remember much of the ride home from Denver. In Amarillo his foot had begun to swell and ooze.

By Wichita Falls the throbbing had begun and when they hit Shreveport, it was leading a Fourth of July parade down Main Street. But the sound had been muted by the war protests from the curbs.

Phin found himself welcoming the pain. For a while it reminded him that he wasn't a ghost or a figment of someone's imagination or letters on a headstone. He made it a character and cast his chances alongside it. And when Blackie had offered him something from the "traveler's kit" that Gerald had packed for them, "in case he changed his mind," he declined. He told Blackie that he didn't want to erase any more of his life than had already been marked over with a red pen.

"From where I'm at," he'd said, "morphine won't do nothing. Everything will always do nothing."

And then Phin fell back asleep, his foot propped up on the dash of the truck, me driving, Harry starring out at the changing landscape. Little Blackie was wedged between dogs and blankets in the truck's bed watching the three of us through the rear window, perhaps feeling empathy because he knew the kind of fear that ran through our veins.

We'd stop every hour so that Blackie could stretch his legs and put a damp cloth to the boy's head. And the dogs would lick Phin's stubbly chin.

"Got a fever, he has," Blackie said "One-zero-two, maybe three. Not four, but when the body gets that hot, a dialogue between parts begins."

I knew he was right. The trip had been hard on the kid and I imagined where his mind might be as we passed the border into Florida.

Mind: *There's something hurting down that way. Uh, we'd like to have that chemical you've been sending around the red highway since your little accident.*

Body: Yes, the bastard hurts, don't it? But so far, they haven't cut part of you off. You heard them talking about wanting to chop it off at the first sign of infection. Hey brain, how'd you like to end up in a dumpster out behind the hospital? Just so they could fit up a plastic version of me onto a ruddy stump left just below the ankle? Or maybe the knee if your "red highway" gets clogged up?

Mind: *We like that drug. Can't we have just a little more? You don't need to be awake. We don't want to actually think about where we've been? Would you? I mean, with a little help from your friends you can outrun whatever was defined as humanity.*

Body: There are too many of us coming back needing skill and attention we ain't gonna get in those hospitals. Better I'm awake while I sleep.

Mind: *Maybe just a few more of the pills? Or that long sweet needle with its warmth and tender point?*

Body: Deal with it. The living will take the dead with them when they die. I go, you go.

Phin had listened to this discourse and others like it for days now. It spoke across a hole in his chest where he thought maybe a soul ought to be, a body part he wasn't supposed to see, but he'd respect. But there was no sound from his chest other than the air being sucked in and blown out. In and out. That meant he was still alive. And Phin decided after a quick realization, for the moment, that was okay.

"Yeah, Mr. Soul, you own the world and the rest of us are just renting. But we all have a landlord somewhere, don't we, Mr. Soul? Don't we?"

But when the light left his bedroom window, he thought that maybe the war itself had just sucked it right out, left him with that hollow, impious feeling, a humanless form, like a rat or a fly.

He tried to get out of bed, beginning to realize that if he was ever to transform himself back into the person who bore his name, he would have to start by getting out of bed and taking a piss on his own. Simple as that. Piss the dark smoke from his innards and baptize himself in the healing waters of a toilet bowl. Phin looked at his bandaged foot and moved his head as close as was possible, trying to detect the faintest smell of sepsis that would indicate infection and the likely lopping off of it. Nothing. After twenty months of memorable smells he was glad to smell the sweetness of nothing.

Phin put one foot over the edge of the bed, then the other, placed his weight on the even balance of where he willed it to be. He spoke a four-letter line of courage and fell to the floor, hitting his head on the edge of the wooden dresser that Harry and he'd made in his high school wood shop. And the nightmares came again. They came back to him as he lay there, occasionally calling out for a mother who was in fact, a temporary ghost, a memory to be negotiated until their two damaged selves could meet again. He called out for his dad.

For the most part, Harry was trying to play the patriarchal role: the tireless, supportive figure, compassionate and quiet. But Phin, even in his own attempt at a return, thought that if Harry was trying to be as strong as the stands of old red maple, sycamore, and dogwood trees that rung the Davis property, he had chosen his trees well. For the cypresses, it was often thought that when exposed to wildfire, burnt from the inside out, the hard center core hot and crazy while the oil-textured bark could repel the flames, allowing tiny, burning embers to enter through cracks and toast its inner life. After the quickest and hottest of fires, Phin imagined, you could walk up to a thirty-foot cypress standing as if proud it had survived and push it over with one hand.

But when Harry found his boy on the floor, a small cut oozing red despair from above his right eye, he picked up the man-child as he had when Phin was ten-years-old and had fallen asleep on the couch reading *Moby Dick*. He picked Phin up with those same arms that he'd lifted his wife with when he'd found her out in the garden sleeping over a row of romaine after he'd returned from a three-day run up to Pensacola Sound chasing a rumor of large schools of squid. Harry Davis already had his insides burnt up. The world was doing its best to petrify him.

Not all history is lost to time and newly crafted stories. Most tourists will rarely question how a structure such as a cathedral or a statue or a pier is built, choosing instead to believe that, like sharks and roaches, they have always existed. The old timers like Jed and Dickey Riot have a connection to this pier as people have connections to photo albums or old pianos. And somewhere along their path, that connection becomes a conviction. They may move away, take a job in a big city five-hundred miles from the coast and forget how the pier smells on a Sunday afternoon in September, how burnt hamburgers are stirred with bait fish by the salt breeze, and the snapping of a good cast. The connection might be lost, but the conviction remains.

Phin had lost the connection to more than the pier he'd grown up around.

✳ ✳ ✳

Harry put a wet cloth and a dab of Bactine on Phin's cut. It wasn't that long since we'd rolled up the gravel driveway in my truck. He'd been so excited to have his boy home. Even more excited when the fever had broken and the local doc had said, "If'n he keeps that wound clean and takes that medicine, the infection would more'n likely stay away."

On the fourth week after I'd dropped them off, me and Blackie went over to Mobile to check on what was left of my own blood brothers and the family farm. Harry had left a message at the local pub and said Phin's pain had become so severe that he'd begged him to give him a shot of morphine from Gerald's preload. Harry knew that Phin didn't want any more blanks in his immediate and literal history; his story would have enough ellipses. But what father can stand to see his boy suffer? He shoved the needle in Phin's thigh. It was the war talking again, the pieces of Phin's foot left in-country calling out, trying to find their way home like a puppy lost in the woods. The phantom bone fragments screamed they'd been left behind and each toe had a message tied to it from a soldier left in a bamboo cage.

What had I told Harry after we'd carried the boy into the house from the truck?

"The boy must be dealt with as he is right now or not dealt with at all. The war will go on for Phin, as it will for anyone who got too close to it."

In this battle, the phantom screams grew louder and as Harry obliged, the drug taking his boy's mind into a world of comfortable numbness while Harry redressed the wound, checking closely for any red streaks running up from the suture marks like rivers drawn on a colored map. Phin stirred slightly as Harry put the new bandage over his foot. He stepped back from the bed and thought the foot looked just like a pedal version of Red Hamilton's hand when Red had cut three fingers off while trying to rip a two-by-six with a chainsaw and happy hour on his mind. Harry had taken his sweaty T-shirt off and applied it to Red's hand that day long before Phin was born. And he had put the fingers in the front pocket of his Wranglers and driven Red to the hospital. The doctors were able to sew them back on, but from then on Red could only play blues with a slide. And after awhile, the calluses on his fixed left-hand fingers were as thick and smooth as a glass tube. They all joked about it. But damn he could play.

The thought gave Harry hope. Hope. Something nice, something that he'd lost. It was a good thing, hope. Maybe the best thing. And I thought that might be a good line in a movie someday. Naw, faith was the better thing, but that was over some distant hill beyond too many valleys to count just yet.

Outside the house darkness crept over the low bogs and brought a Sou'wester with it, thirty knots at least. Harry knew this because the back of the trailer creaked at twenty-eight knots, the front at thirty. He watched the water in the glass on Phin's nightstand roll up the sides and back down. It'd blow forty tonight, he thought, better bring the dogs in.

Inside Phin's head the drug was filing down the edges of his pain but stirring up its own storm in the process. Images of an army of little toes ran after him, calling his name, their nails opening like the mouths of baby birds. Some were left behind. And they were cut down as a giant vulture scooped him from the trail.

In the fifth week, they spoke about Ma. Not real words, but something pretending to be. It was Phin who brought her up, exhumed her from his inventory of repressions in a moment of welcomed lucidity.

"Did she get any of my letters?"

Phin spoke as he wheeled himself in a borrowed chair toward the early morning dark of the kitchen where Harry sat thumbing through a stack of past-due bills. A sideways rain had fallen the night before and both men had not slept well in the trembling quietude of absence and remembering; the silent lull between gusts.

Harry ignored the boy's question.

"Well, look what the cat drug in. Get you some coffee, son? I ain't lost my touch in that department." Harry wiped his mouth and eyes with the back of his flannel shirt, trying to smooth over the worry and the despair.

"Pop...you got a few things left. Well, did she?"

Harry rose from the large spruce table that used to be the meeting place for the Davis family and went to the stove to get the porcelain coffee pot he'd always used to make "the best coffee this side of the red-neck Riviera." A single squeak came out of the third plank from the sink on the plywood that lay under the linoleum floor of the big, government surplus double-wide trailer that Harry'd anchored to a foundation and called home since he'd returned from the Pacific Theater in the fall of '45, sixty days after he'd come home, one of 316 survivors, nine months before Gillie was born. The earth and sea had been a confused place after the war. Britain was way worse. The U.S. Government sold land cheap on the backs of capitalism's finest hour. Harry added land to the little lot he'd inherited. And the fishing was legendary that fall.

"Yeah, she got 'em. For a while. But then the letters stopped coming." Harry spoke evenly, without emotion or thought.

Phin watched his pop pour him a big mug of steaming coffee and almost allowed himself a little bit of pleasure. Almost.

The mornings were the best in the Nam. The sauna heat and the humping of click after click and the leeches in their boots—that was the day after morning had passed. There was a lot of détente during the mornings, a lot of nothing but the simple inconveniences of war. During the mornings you could see the sky and the planes could see the ground. But they were nothing compared to the night. The night and the earth belonged to Charlie.

"I kept writing all the way to the end, Pop. I swear."

"I know you did. They came a few weeks ago, after her stroke, all bound up in string with lots of stamps with funny looking people on them. I got the letters there in the drawer. Still in the string and everything."

"Where is she, Dad, where's my mother?"

"Son, Dickey Riot was asking about you on the docks yesterday." Harry changed topics so fast it hurt his neck.

"Don't do this, Dad. Don't bury your head in the sand. Look at me, dammit! Where's your wife right now? Right now while we sit here at her fucking table and try to take one step at a time?"

Harry stood up, touched Phin's shoulder lightly, and walked out the big front door. Phin heard a dog bark and a truck start, the big wheels crunching gravel on the long thin driveway.

✳ ✳ ✳

Dickey Riot had grown up with Phin, the older brother he'd never had. Right now, though, his memories of catching crawdads down in the creek and selling them for fifty cents apiece as *petit lobsters* on a roadside stand were blurred along with the rest of their years together. Dickey and what he had meant to Phin worked in the past, but now it must have hid out somewhere out in the future—wandering, waiting.

Dickey had not gone to the war in Vietnam. He'd filled out a bunch of forms in '67 or '68, called himself a conscientious objector on account of he never liked to fight, which was true. Dickey had spent his tour driving four-wheel-drive Jeeps filled with colonels around the backroads of local army bases on account of he was lucky; that also was true.

As Harry walked out the door he had called back inside, "Dickey wants to come up to the house and see you. He asked me if you were, you know, crazy or something."

After Harry's exit, Phin could hear the first few birds waking up the world. He'd heard hundreds of birds in the jungles, sounds so strange and wonderful and exotic that he'd almost forgotten he wasn't in that strange and beautiful land. The birds were everywhere: long-beaked macaws, rainbow-colored parrots, sea birds miles from the ocean. Then the napalm came and the birds were silent. Except the vultures.

"Dad," Phin spoke to the absent hole that his father had just left, and maybe the birds. "I'll see Dickey and Jed and the others, but not here, not now. I got too many gopher holes in my mind. Tell him I ain't quite crazy, but I'm something."

Then, Phin, in some rehearsal of conversation he might have with his dad, took the voice of his father.

"Truth is, son," Phin tried to sound sure and convincing as he projected his father's voice, *"you ain't done much since you been home but read them books you asked me to get and stare at the ceiling."*

"You're trying to talk to me about the truth, Dad? You try to bring that illusion up at this table while you and I sit here, Sis dead gone, Mom in some medical facility you won't even acknowledge? Won't even name? Dad, in-country I dug shit holes one minute and then watched my friends fall into them with their guts shot out the next. You think I can't handle my truth? Let alone *our* truth?"

Phin paused and noticed one of the dogs, Saul he supposed, licking his hand and enjoying the salty tears as they fell without restraint.

"Pop," Phin spoke to Saul as if he was his own blood because he was the closest living thing within reason. "You're the beat of my own heart and I can't swear you were just sitting next to me at the table, right then, right now. That's what I know to be true." And Saul pawed gently at Phin's bandaged left foot.

Harry could not unfix his eyes from his wife and released in a sigh what he could not in a full breath. This closeness of death he'd seen move into Grace and Phin had brought a corresponding closeness of life. His wife was wrestling to recognize it. And this recapturing of mind, of memory, of life... he'd never be able to explain it. But he saw it at the bedside in a room overlooking the sea, a place of refuge that Jed Riot had made for Grace, a new morning as the sun crawled over the east ridge of the low hills toward Panama City, the storm clouds muting the sky to gray, Jed's own dogs stretching and shaking off the night. Harry always hated the color gray. It would be a long time in its purgatory shade, its Navy gray.

He got up to fill Grace's water cup and looked out the window. She was asleep as she'd been the last twenty-two times he'd secretly come to see her in these "homes," these, heretofore, half-way houses facilitated by intimate family and friends who had the means and maybe the madness to make Grace right again. But the smarter docs and do-gooders knew that neuroscience was the last frontier of modern medicine. Grace's brain had been deprived of oxygen during her stroke. And like a kid trying to swim the length of the pool under water, it was breathing hard to catch up.

Harry had always wanted to awaken his wife when he came to visit early after the incident. But something inside said let sleeping dogs lie. And those angry ones were his, not hers. So, when she began to stir or fidget or call out for someone, Harry wrestled with his own devil, held her hand for a second, and left the room. Harry let someone else who didn't or never could take that hand as well as he might and he walked out on his wife and his temporary truth.

But the last time she stirred, he stayed. And when she did not awaken, Harry stayed.

Harry remembered that as he continued the imaginary conversation with his very real son who he'd also just walked away from. Harry pretended that Phin was sitting there next to him, in that little refuge of Jed's overlooking the Gulf.

"Son," Harry looked out the window toward the southeast horizon and wondered how Jed had made that place happen for his wife when he couldn't hold her hand for more than a few minutes. And he spoke to Phin, not with his usual distance, but leaned in closely and pretended to take Phin's hand. But it was Grace's hand.

"When Dickey asked me about you, I told him that what a soldier is, the war knows. What a man is, history will someday tell. That's the best I got, boy. It's all I got."

"Bullshit, Pops!" Harry imagined how surprised he was at the strength of Phin's outburst.

"You know what a soldier is and what he ain't. I know all about the *Indianapolis*. Been reading about it for years. I know the names of the ones who went down, the guys floating right next to you waiting while the 'men in the gray suits' circled beneath. But you never talked about it, you never told me. Oh, Pops, you didn't owe that to me, just to yourself. Maybe it made you who you are or maybe it made you who you aren't. But I've come to think that the best you got ain't lying there beneath the burning waters and melting steel."

Harry stood up and remembered as his wife fought for consciousness and memory and connection and conviction. Grace had opened her eyes while Harry spoke to his son across the miles and said, "Harry, take me home." But at first Harry hadn't heard her. He'd shut the solid door of the little room overlooking the sea in a place that Jed had fought to get for her and for what was left of the Davis clan.

Looking east where the beginnings of all things are set, Harry froze.

"Harry?" Grace cried out again. "Harry, please, please. I want to go home. The tomatoes are ripe."

He returned to her bed and held her hand. Many years later, Harry would recall, he never cried. He might've sat there for five minutes or five years. And after that period, he opened the door on the rest of his life.

"Let's go home, Grace," Harry whispered, "Phin is waiting.

"I am waiting."

✻ ✻ ✻

On the sixth week Phin was back in the world, the special boots Harry had made for him were completed and there was a registered letter for "Mr. or Mrs. Harry L. Davis" at the post office. The return address was *United States Dept. of Defense.* Harry wrote "addressee unknown" on the envelope and gave it back to Postmaster Wilkes who looked over his shoulder, made the sign of the cross with worried eyes and blue stained fingers, and put it in the outgoing mail bin.

There was also my plain postcard with no return address that came home in Harry's pocket. It said, "Blackie and I well. Hello to Daniel, Saul, and the others. Have feelers out as to status of Gerald. Worried some. Will be down in a week or such. Oh yeah. I'm now in the woodworking business over in Shreveport. Took Blackie with me. Making frames for hippie beds that hold water-filled mattresses. It's good work, cutting and sawing and making people happy to sleep on water, though hell will freeze over before I'd do it myself." It was signed "JC (not Jesus Christ)"

Phin practiced walking with his new boot, his good foot, and one crutch. He fell. A lot.

That week, on the day that Harry brought Grace home, Phin's morphine supply ran out. His dreams turned violent again and Grace's recovering memory did a U-turn. In her own dreams she was asking Gillie to help her in the garden and reminding Phin to do his homework.

One afternoon, Harry went up to the edge of the parcel of his family's land and looked at the headstones—a body under one, a few good dogs' ashes under the other. When he returned, he got his twelve-gauge, shot out the only two windows in the storage shed, screamed out, "Father, Son, and mother-fucking Ghost," and then put the gun away in the closet and hid the bullets. He told Phin and Grace he was going to start fishing again. Maybe even soon. But first he was going to make sure his wife was well situated. Would Phin hobble around the parcel and collect some cut flowers for her today?

Phin thought about flowers and coming home and the deaths he'd seen of those who only came back in grainy black-and-white photographs and, if they were lucky, prayers. And then he thought of Lonnie, an old girlfriend, and wondered. How long had it been?

Lonnie.

The next afternoon, the weather turned nice and Grace sat on the porch quietly.

The seventh week after Phin returned, Harry rose early, put on coffee, left a note, and headed down to the docks. He could pretend to hide out in responsibility only for a while.

And returning a few hours later, seeing her rocking quietly on the porch, Phin pacing back and forth in the nearby yard practicing a cane-less limp, Harry stepped down from his truck, nodded to Phin as he walked to the porch, and scooped Grace up like a bride crossing the threshold. Harry saw her crooked smile un-droop and something intangible return to her mind. He turned and saw the ends of Phin's mouth turn north as well.

The next morning, Phin limped down the hall, past Gillie's old room, and put on his best Wranglers. Bracing himself against the bathroom wall he brushed his teeth and watched his spit coat the dog tags that hung from his neck and made a metallic sound as they bounced off the drain plug. He pulled on his custom boot and reached for his crutch. On a second thought, he reached instead for the bamboo cane that Johnny had borrowed from the hospital, shuffled into the kitchen. He poured himself a cup of Harry's darkest roast.

"Hey, Jeremiah," he woke up the oldest of the sleeping mutts. "Something's a-brewing. Get up. Go get Saul and the posse"

Jeremiah yawned and made that soft yowl sound that waking dogs make.

"You're right ole mutt. Ain't been a lot of signs that heaven's awaiting on me lately. Best I stick around until I know for sure."

Some months later, Phin would share a page from some notes he'd been keeping on that day. This one said:

For some, the hugeness of the ocean shrinks their arms and legs while empowering their fear. But a pier can allow the renewal that an ocean offers, a higher ground of timber lofted over a fluid rolling medium. To those who are bound by that fear, they can know that freedom of continual baptism without ever getting wet. Not all prostheses are attached to the body.

It sounded lush, awkward, gushing. But he knew that putting a pen to paper in that dark moment was better than letting his thoughts play three-flies-up in his head.

Phin, Jeremiah, Daniel, and Saul limped down the long gravel driveway to the paved road, each dog seeming to favor his left-rear foot. He stuck out his thumb and was picked up by the first pickup truck that passed. Two sedans had gone by before, the drivers working hard not to look at the man with two kinds of boots, a cane, and three large, ungainly dogs.

"You're the Davis boy, aren't you?" The pickup driver worked in the local market as a checker. Phin vaguely remembered him, but didn't ask his name until they had gone a mile or two. "Where can I drop you, son?" he asked and then added with a laugh that sent spittle onto the front window. "A shoe store that sells matching pairs?"

"The pier, Sir," Phin whispered while petting the dogs to calm his nerves. "I'd like to go to the old pier... if it's not out of your way."

"Anything for a man," and he winked with his right eye as his glass left eye followed the white line, "who gave his life to keep us free from the Commies."

CHAPTER 15

THE WORLD

The first step was supposed to be clear and absolutely certain. There should've been no pause or hesitancy in what Phin was doing; what had to be done. He was a big game hunter with his prey in the cross hairs, a Kamikaze pilot donning the scarf and downing the saki, a groom committed to the altar with purposeful steps. Turning around would've taken him further back down than the height he'd already rung of his own precarious climb back; back up from that hole, which was the hole in his life and had, to his mind, no bottom.

Standing still might've been worse. Movement, motion, yeah that's what he needed.

"C'mon kid," his inner voice was saying, *"use the cane and hobble if you have to. Don't choke on those old rotting planks that you know like the path from your bedroom to the kitchen table. You used to 'own' this pier, kid. Be the Phoenix, kill or be killed, fish or cut bait. Stillness will burn you alive. One step, kiddo. Seize any whim, any passion, and run with it; make it your own and follow it up and out of this shit-hole to the farthest reaches of nature itself. Go back in time. Start with Gillie or your memories of younger times; let those memories that haunt you now, guide you now. And your dad, Harry, look how he suffers, ponders his life; his strength that dangles an eighty-pound tuna on a twenty-pound test line. Watch the*

way he works that fish, letting it run and tire itself out while he rests and tries to put the situation in some perspective, knowing that at any moment he himself could be swallowed by the deepness in which you find yourself, swimming near the bottom but not on it, a hook in your mouth that was the war, but must someday work itself out on its own—a fish with no hands.

"What are going to do, Phin? You're smart. Look what the war taught you? All those good men dying there and bad men living here and Yin and Yang energies in every one of them and in everything you feel and touch. Go to the books Johnny recommended if you have to, find solace in all the great ones who pulled you back from simply imploding like that Black kid from Atlanta who simply stood up in that firefight near Hill 58 at the base of the Chu Pon Mountains, spread his arms, and bent his eyes toward the heavens. What did he say while that fifty-caliber tore his body into sections like a puzzle that would never go back together because the dogs had chewed the edges?—'Do not forgive them Father, they know exactly what they're doing.'*—Is that it, Phin? You wanna go down like that kid, only slower? Remember one of your favorites,* 'To snatch the eternal out of the ever fleeting…that is one of the greatest tricks of human existence?' *You're not the first to get knocked down, kid, nor the last."*

With that thought, Phin's voice moved off its plane where it had been gaining purchase and slipped. That must've surprised him. I had been kin; had shown him much of the world as he had come to know it. But the voice trying to reason with him now was only partly his. It was made up of a cast of characters; so many that he couldn't trust what he could, including me and Harry and Grace and Gillie's memory and Gerald and that kid, Blackie. Even Phin's high school flame, Lonnie, if she was still alive and able to love and be loved. And the great ones between the pages, people that I had introduced him to over the years and had spoken to him when he was in-country.

I wondered if he wished he was a convicted felon or a religious man or an elected official and could fold all of his fears into a cell a mass or a speech. But then he would be betraying all that I had taught him—to always think and be his own. Me, some Black man who was "sent." Those things that I had told him once and only once—the "things that had saved my life, Phin…when Ruth died on the water."

Phin must've thought outside the ears of his voice, but he would not betray his heritage. He'd just as soon stand up and get cut down with a fifty-cal, his pieces scattered over the ramp to the old pier, bits of flesh falling through the cracks between the boards, food for the crabs, and human blood for the workers to wash off with the fish guts. Grayfalls had told me that a man would know in his heart when it was time to die. Phin would have to trust what little he knew to be true.

Still, Phin was frozen; the only motion was backward in time, in his memory of this place as a child, a boy, a young man.

"And what are you now?" the voice taunted. *"Old, hurt, less a man because you have less flesh and bone to carry you? Wha'ja gonna do, kid?"*

The voice became many untrusted memories because nothing in his head was worthy of trust at this still moment of dripping stillness.

"Talk to me heart, quiet this voice."

"Yeah, holes are just space, kid. It's kinda tough to get a foot hold on air. Wha'ja gonna do? Fish or cut bait?"

Phin suddenly thought of the pictures he'd been shown at the first hospital in Saigon. There were all the same: him and a few buddies out in front of their hootch, slouching, smoking… pretending. He didn't collect the photographs because he didn't trust them, knew they were more than lying—they were failing to tell the truth. He'd seen some professional photos in *Life Magazine* and *Time* that got a lot closer because somehow they had hinted at the real Nam by allowing the screams and the smells to come along on the paper. But the photos that had made it back to the world with him, the ones of Phin and a few other non-coms in front of Madam Chong's in Saigon, or standing off to the edge of a safe LZ, relaxing (which was an oxymoron itself), they were fake because they denied what could never be said in a photograph. And the head docs in Saigon had shown him these photos to try and connect his memory with his feeling and thinking; something he knew instinctively that had to be done at some point in his life, but not now, and not by anyone connected to the immediate vessel of war or split off into the wake of his past by its own delirious cruise through his life.

So Phin stood at the base of the old pier, leaning on one bamboo cane, the same kind of bamboo he'd seen men impaled on, his foot throbbing, happy for the pain because it kept him just enough in the present so that the imagination and memory he didn't trust wouldn't leave him stuck on that pier as a ten-year-old boy instead of a twenty-two-year-old war veteran imagining he was ten again and the war had been playing army with his buddies. And courage was daring Dickey Riot to jump off the pier and swim all the way back in to shore because he knew secretly it bothered Dickey that he was the only boy in his class who hadn't done it yet.

"C'mon Dickey," he'd said. "I know you can do it. And then it's done. Simple as that. Feet first. Water is soft. You can't get hurt. I'll do it with you," the young Phin's voice, soft so others couldn't hear, feeling the fear of his boyhood friend and wanting it to go away before it became contagious. His "uncle" Johnny had told him that when he'd taught him to drive a tractor at seven years old.

"Fear is a funny thing, kid," I'd said. "It's kinda like the moon, the way it comes and goes in phases and even though we can be looking at the same moon, it affects everybody differently. I don't expect you to understand it 'cuz I certainly don't. Maybe your parents do. Some people are just afraid of different things. You're afraid of driving this tractor. But you can swim out past the breakers and laugh all the way to the end of the pier. I just plain will never be able to do that."

"You think being scared is only in your mind like some people say?" Phin had asked me as he gathered strength to start up the tractor.

"That's a good question, kid." I'd said it because I meant it. "I imagine fear moves around depending on what kind it is or where it comes from. Like a storm will do."

"You reckon it's contagious like a flu or something, Uncle Johnny?"

"Oh yeah, Phin. I know that for a fact. A little bit, we're born with. But the rest comes from living in the world and growing up and being exposed to fear germs and lettin' them get the best of you." The boy had noticed a change in the tone of my voice. It was the same as when I'd told him other things that had stuck in his mind from when he was a kid and they had come back to him out of nowhere when he was a man.

"I believe this, Phin. You don't want to be around a person who's afraid, no matter what part of the body it's hiding in, unless you have the courage to try and talk them out of it or soak up a little of it yourself to help them through."

✳ ✳ ✳

As Phin looked out from the landing toward the end of the pier, he wondered who'd given him this fear of walking out to the end of a place he'd skipped over, danced upon, and flew off of a thousand times in a thousand younger times. And he wished for someone to soak a little away.

"Hey buddy, you new around here?" An old man's voice came out of the stillness of the bright morning. He sat off to the side, near the steps that terraced down to the beach and the white, sugary sand below the structure that old Jed Riot had built around the time the old man was born.

"Looks like you're moving a little slow, what with that cane and funny shoe and such."

Phin, back in the present, spun to his right, using the cane as a supportive walking stick, just like he'd done humping click after click in-country. The voice was low and thick and gravelly. It come from the gray-whiskered mouth that was set in the weathered face of a timeless, tired body, one that appeared to have lived outside its entire life but likely had seen the inside of prison walls.

"Sorry," Phin tried to wrap his mind around the here and now. "I didn't hear what you said."

The old man narrowed his eyes for a second and squinted into the sun that now rose above the hotels and condos that were beginning to erase the low beachfront dunes of Phin's childhood. Then he let out a quick, sharp chuckle that grew to a roaring laugh. Phin watched the old man dispassionately at first, then with a growing curiosity. He looked vaguely familiar in his navy blue jumpsuit, which failed to cover the boney knees and dark curly leg hair. The hair framing the squared face was long and pulled back in a salty, gray-black pony tail and draped down from the edges of the standard-issue, green and yellow baseball cap; the uniform tractor logo that belonged to the Heartland and represented much about a man's ideals.

I said," the old man turned very serious, very quickly. "Are you new around here? Cuz' I ain't seent you around this pier and I been here damn near ever day the sun's out for coming on two years. You got wax in your ears? 'Cause I can't wait for my ship to come in awaitin' on your reply."

Phin studied the old fellow, rubbing his own whiskered chin, as he might look at a painting in a museum.

"No," Phin replied, barely audible. And then added. "I've been here before."

"Oh, a tourist. I see. Come down from up north to escape the pissy spring rains? Come down here to lay out in the sun? Cuz' we got plenty of it. No in-like-a-tiger, out-like-a-giraffe spring here. So, you stayin' in one of them fancy new condoms they building right there on the sand? What'd ya do to that one wheel a yours, anyway? Cat got your lips?"

"You ask a lot of questions."

"Well, you see, it's my job. Seeing as though I'm here a lot, the city has sort of contrapted me to keep an eye on things and answer questions on this here tourist attraction."

"Tourist attraction?" Phin's mind was trying to piece together what might've really happened to his town in the short time he'd been gone and what might be the ramblings of an old fisherman who seemed vaguely familiar but who he could not place.

"Oh, yeah. The pier is the happening place now. Bigger than Texas. Newer than New Jersey. Lots of snowbirds like yourself buying up those little apartments all clumped together like beehives with a view of the Golfo de Mehico. They like to come out here and let their curls down. Some of them even fish. But that's for show."

"Snowbird?"

"Yeah, that's what you is, right? Though you look awfully young to be able to afford one of them places. Hey, if your ship already come in or you got all your ducks in a row—hey, more power to you buddy. But maybe you're just renting a room someplace. You know what they say: if it floats or flies, rent it. And I'm dying if I'm lying about that."

Phin didn't know whether he enjoyed listening to this guy or not. He ignored his questions and after a minute sat down next to him on the only bench to rest, unable to decide if the smell of fish was coming from out on the pier or out of the man's body.

"You said you get paid for greeting people here?" Phin asked the man.

"Well, sort of. The guy who runs the bait and tackle shop out on the end here, kid named Dickey Riot—been around here since the earth was cooling—he's really fixed the place up since his old man retired last year. He keeps me fed and watered, you know, like a horse, and I keep the riffraff out. So, I'm kinda like a cop and a Shell answer man at the same time."

"What do you mean by 'riffraff'?'" Phin was becoming interested and it felt good to take his mind off his own troubles for awhile.

"Well, anybody who don't belong here, that's riffraff. Sometimes the Blacks come down from Mobile and they swim like rocks so I have to tell the lifeguards to go on and save them, and then sometimes the college kids will come down here over their spring recess and smoke marijuana. Then they get all lovey-dovey and start doing the wild thing right out on the dance floors. And once in a while the Hell's Angels roar into town with their bitches on the back seats, but that's just a bit beyond my statue of imitations. I have to call in the sheriff when they up and raise Cain out here."

Something was moving inside of Phin, some great block of ice or fire or long buried cataclysm that was log-jammed up near his throat. The old man's words were hatching a dead fetus that was lost inside the boy, turning inward on itself and asking questions with increasing volume.

"So," Phin tried his best to hold back the long-swollen river, "you sit here on this pier and greet people, but not all people, and Dickey keeps you around to keep those you don't think belong from hanging around."

The old guy's smile left quickly and his guard was up, his thin, dark eyes darting. "More or less. I decide who looks questionable. He mostly runs the bait shop. You sure you haven't been here before? What's your name anyway, cowboy?"

Phin brushed the question aside and felt the shift of the creature inside him. It wasn't all together unpleasant. Something was loosening and even if he'd wanted to stop it, it had a mind of its own.

"You don't like Black people? You don't like college kids? You don't like motorcycle clubs?" Phin was smiling in a disarming way while allowing the anger to build and the old man to take the bait.

And then added the hook of his profiling, "I know what you mean though, about Blacks. They seem to sink pretty quick. You know what I been seeing lately that pisses me off?" Phin asked while moving closer down on the bench next to the man. "Those crazy Vietnam vets. They come back thinking the world owes them something. Man, we got the GI bill, there are lots of jobs. They ought to just get over it."

"If that ain't the truth."

He'd taken the bait. "They getting free medical care and all; I see them on leave from the base over in Pensacola, coming down here and drinking and sitting in the corner of the bars in uniforms or not; you can tell the difference. Most of them ain't right, I tell you."

Phin stood up and walked over to the railing. Suddenly he was fourteen again, climbing the railing after Jed and the lifeguard had left to go home, taunting his friends: "C'mon you chickens, I'll save you if you drown."

"You're a strange one." The old man studied Phin and then stood up, stretching his back and groaning with the creaks of his bones and the boards under his feet. "What's your name again?"

"It's Phin. Hey, buddy, can you come over and tell me how deep you think it is right here?"

The thing inside Phin had shaped itself into a haunting tragedy, a travesty of heartache and heartbreak and red mist of outrage that had clouded his view then and maybe for a long time to come. But he didn't know it right then, and it would be some time before he could define its shape as well as any storm cloud that roared and growled and morphed its angry gasses.

"Phin? Hey, I heard Dickey talk about a guy with that name. Some kid from a long time ago."

"Oh yeah? Hey buddy, lookie here, over the edge."

The old man moved closer, suspicious maybe, but doing the job he'd fabricated in his mind. He leaned over the edge and asked Phin what he was looking at, not knowing the beast inside this kid from his employer's past was going to brace himself against the old wood rail, reach down as if to tie a shoe or pick up a dropped piece of bait, but instead the anger and witness to the killings and the soundless screams of women with long black hair pulled back under a wide straw hat and little kids playing in the paddies, same as he had done after a summer squall, just kids they were, being mowed down.

The old greeter in the faded jumpsuit said, "What the hell!" as the beast of Phin's war—which wasn't his war and shouldn't have been anyone's war—grabbed the old man's legs and lifted them, fulcrum-like, to throw the jumpsuit with the bony knees over the edge of that lovely tourist attraction.

And as an after-thought, without any such thing resembling thought at all, Phin climbed the rail and jumped over.

The warm saltwater leaked into his custom boot and past the stitches and into the blood and moved the fire that raged inside with the new bite of salt inside fresh flesh. The water felt good everywhere, especially in the edges of his foot where his toes used to be. It was a kind of specific, identifiable pain that you knew had only to do with the body and would go away at some point. He rolled over on his back for a moment and felt the waves massaging his mind, his hands drawing slow circles in the sea that kept him afloat while something else fought to pull him under but wasn't strong enough.

At some point he saw the old man clinging to a piling in three feet of water before passersby pulled him to shore. Phin's mind was momentarily and perfectly lucid, but he was dreaming while he treaded water; he'd been here before. He swore he had. It wasn't that long ago.

Then he heard the sirens and bullhorns. They woke the beast who'd gone quiet in the home waters where the boy was raised. He heard the voices of lifeguards coming closer and he knew he wasn't ready to go down, as easy as it would've been. He'd done it right there as a kid and gotten in trouble escaping from the lifeguards. He'd done it in the rivers in-country when he'd been separated from his platoon and the NVA were coming and he'd gotten his ass out of trouble because he could hold his breath. There was nothing to fear under the water. Ghosts couldn't go there. He was pelagic. The thought that he controlled the waters seemed to buoy his spirit and he smiled at the bright, burning, beautiful, blistering Florida sunshine.

The shouts got louder and closer and filled the air with staccato bursts of unnecessary lightning. But Phin didn't hear any of it—only the background of the Hueys from the base flying miles out to sea. Lonnie's dad used to fly those. Yeah, Phin thought he might see if his old love had survived the war in the states.

This wasn't a feeling of the darkness before the dawn, he thought, but the trust that there goddamn better be a dawn afterward, after all.

CHAPTER 16

LEAVING

These were the times of leaving. Nothing stayed the same and no one stayed in one place for very long, not because they weren't happy, but because, well...who can tell? The war was over. Sort of. Soldiers came home. Sort of. Fashion changed—Nehru jackets, faux-vinyl skirts, and false Afros-to-the-moon. And music—from folk and rock and blues to disco and electronica. Cars got smaller as gas became more expensive. Wars became smaller, too, but had more global significance. Universities began giving away degrees for playing football like candy. People began caring about the environment while feeding their suburban lawns with Monsanto and Dow's new "home improvement products."

Never mind our kid with the third eye. The Watergate Hotel became a linguistic icon. There was a push to get miniature golf in the Olympics. Snow-making became popular in Southern California's high desert hills. Landing on the moon had become passé. Interior designers were touting the benefits of indoor plants made of polyvinyl chlorides. Every late spring, dozens of people stood atop Mt. Everest, aided by oxygen and fee-based group leaders and Sherpas with a gentle hand-on-your-ass push up that tough section.

In the middle 1970s, the world felt false because in many ways...it had no claim to many things authentic or real to those who had written the old rules. At least that was the notion that Phin told me was driving him to leave.

He decided that he would get in a car and drive away because there was nowhere left to go. But before Phin left his home in search of his life, someone made sure he was "dead" because he liked the kid; respected the family. Always had.

It happened like this.

The lifeguards had done their job and saved the pier bum whose name turned out to be Willy, Willy Froman. He wasn't a bad man, as men go, but he wasn't a good one either. Dickey Riot had heard the sirens from the Jeep and came out of his office in the back of the bait shop, running, then leaning over the pier, wondering what the hell had happened. Who would jump this pier—my pier, my father's pier—in the middle of the afternoon without knowing they'd be spending the night in the Panama City Beach jail?

Phuckin' Phin.

"Phin!" he'd yelled over the side. "That you down there?"

Phin was drifting, knowing that Dickey had never jumped off the pier and made the thirty-foot fall, knowing that he'd spent the war in the states driving officers around the base. So, all Dickey could do was say dammit, Phin, what the hell, and run down the long steps at the base of the pier and onto the sand to take the harmless verbal wrath of Willy Froman while his boyhood friend and now vet drifted with the sun on his face.

But Dickey was smart; he'd always been smart.

Phin swam in and accepted the warming smile from Dickey as he waved off the lifeguards and cops with a wink and a knowing smile.

"Nice entrance, pal."

"Was it too big of a splash? We used to try and make a big splash, but I guess the professional divers like to glide in unnoticed, just let the water swallow them up without getting any of it on them."

"No, it was perfect. Besides, that boot might have prevented you from pointing your toes real straight."

"It's a good shoe; everything my pop builds is the best."

"I know that," Dickey said with empathy and truth. "And he's been working under tough conditions of late."

"Can't say the past few years have been kind to the Davis team. It's tough to get anything accomplished with your head in your hands and the sound of heavy breathing on your ears. Sure like to break that pattern."

"Not much is the same here or anyplace. Truth be known, I'm happy to keep out of the way, sell a few goods and sundries to the tourists, and live and let live."

Phin looked at his boyhood pal knowing that, yes, while much had changed in his world, little had moved for Dickey. He had a choice; choices Dickey had created for himself. And he always chose the safe ones, and he would always live a vicarious life. In some ways, he was the smarter of the two, but the fear that had always rested just behind Dickey's boyhood eyes had only lodged itself deeper. He would never go into a graveyard at night, even to watch his own funeral.

For just a second Phin wondered that if when he was young and had a choice to make, maybe the consequences were made impregnable by the action itself? Or did things just happen on some other, worldly schedule and there wasn't a damn thing you could do about it?

Dickey asked Phin if he wanted to go some place quiet and talk, you know, about the old days.

"Dickey," Phin choosing his words carefully, "what would we have to talk about?"

But Dickey wasn't hurt. That was something that he'd always admired in the kid—he knew his limitations.

"There something I can do for you then? Anything. It's a funny world, Phin; as little as I know about how things work. When we were just good kids, who'd ever think we'd turn into good ol' boys? The South runs by its own rules."

"Yeah," whispered Phin, "so did the Nam."

Phin knew that Dickey, for what he lacked or was fortunate enough not to possess—his "ignorance is bliss" ideals—just might've been his greatest asset. But he was as loyal as blood kin and that, too, forever endeared him to Phin.

"You know what I'd like is to disappear into the fold for a few years, to drop off everybody's radar but those whom I want to be seen by. I'd like the government that I represented in Vietnam, the system that tried to kill me, think that it did its job. I want to do what my dad wanted to do for me and I messed up."

Dickey's quick mind kicked in and he knew what Phin was asking.

"You want to wander around a bit without thinking about lights and tunnels and oncoming trains."

"You think you can help me jump the tracks? For a while, anyway?"

"I'll talk to Dad. He loves this kind of stuff. He'll take you off the payroll all together, if you know what I mean. We'll get it done, Phin; we'll kill you where a lot of others couldn't." Dickey was more excited than Phin.

When Phin told Harry he was going to be leaving, Harry nodded like a man agreeing to end a long feud with a neighbor, the compromise coming up hard against remembrance of the long fight, and the only thing worth noting was that it was all just a waste, an immutable garbage dump of memories to bury under the ground. And then a smile came over his face. Phin knew the smile. It was as knowing as a simple fisherman from Panama City Beach could have under the circumstances. So, he took in its pelagic grin.

There wouldn't be a plan, other than the erasing of him. How could there be? The boy was going fishing for himself. The only thing that'd guide him was memory. But even that was like a map where the parts you wanted to go to had coffee stains over the important parts. He'd skip the stain of the recent years and go back to the beginning of the end. And for Phin that was the hospital; that tale of his involvement in the war that was too vague, too strange, to serve as any foundation upon which to reconstruct a life.

But even as he remembered the physical pain in his foot and the mind-fire in his head that burnt during his short time there, he could recall something good about the place. Words maybe, a face, a hand—an orderly named Gerry or Gerald—and a frenetically likable imp called Blackish or Blackie.

It was the last thing he remembered in his life with substance and integrity. Later on, if he could look upon his home as the place he was raised, the coming back to it might seem nice. But for now, Phin Davis would start by going to Denver VA and looking for the origins of what little warmth still resided in his belly. Or maybe he'd come up to Lafayetter where I'd set up my new business making hippy beds. Maybe he'd go find his old high school girl friend, Lonnie. After only a few months back in Panama City Beach, Phin's spring break was over. It was time to go somewhere else.

But if he made it to the hospital, would he be a patient again? How could he? The day before he left town, the local news in the Panama City News Herald read:

"Corporal Phin T. Davis, U.S. Army, has unfortunately died just three months after returning home from the war in Vietnam and being released from the Denver Veteran's Hospital a few weeks ago. The native of Panama City Beach served nearly two years in the Vietnam War and was on medical leave pending his official discharge. The death certificate, signed by the local coroner from the County of Panama City, Florida, said he expired due to septic shock. His death was likely due to complications from a leg wound suffered while serving in the jungles of Southeast Asia, one of the last few men injured before the peace treaty went into effect in March. Corporal Davis is survived by his parents, Harry and Grace Davis, also of Panama City Beach."

There would be no service and the ashes were to be distributed by his father, "a well-loved and long-time local fisherman," a man of the sea who appeared resolute and stoic upon the news of his son's passing and had decided to move his boat down to Key West for awhile because, as the locals were saying, there were too many new things being built in Panama City Beach, Florida.

And while Harry and Phin stood in silence that early-summer evening, each wondering how all this could possibly play out, across town in a small office in downtown Panama City Beach, an older man remembered his son's longtime playmate, the son's generous father, the recently affected mother, the sister who'd died several years ago, the black "uncle" who'd helped him get his pier rebuilt on time and under budget. And, if the old man hadn't been laughing so hard and so deep at the great success he'd had in making a man dead to the world, then he would've been crying. No family ought to have all that pain in it. Just ain't right, he thought. And then he got stuck somewhere between laughing and crying as he thought how easy it had been to control pain, just like turning a spigot of hot and cold water. Jed Riot had never known deep pain. Had been born at a point where his age had kept him out of every 20th century war that America was involved in. Jed knew he was one of the lucky ones. When something like hurt or regret or sadness crept up on him, he'd simply do something good with the bad and the ugly and it went away. It seemed a simple concept, something he'd heard that holy men from the past had preached. But maybe it didn't work for everyone, or else they just hadn't tried hard enough. He didn't know, only that it worked for him. He'd lied, stolen, cheated, and bribed. All in the name of good.

And so, Jed kept giving parts of himself away, just living a good life by scratching others' itches. He was a happy man and he knew it. But he wasn't going to dwell on it. It was time for his daily walk down to his pier. He loved that old place ever since local civic leader, Walter Davis, Harry's father, had convinced the City Council that they needed it and Jed was the man to build it in '37 and the one to fix it in '51. And Jed convinced Uncle Sam to pay for both. Jed remembered getting that contract as a twenty-five-year-old and thinking how impressionable he'd been during the Great Depression. But how much fun it was to grow food and conserve and consign and recycle shoes with cardboard and rebuild Levis' with parts of grandma's torn curtains and to change Crisco Oil into fresh "butter" with a few drops of yellow food coloring. So when he was given the contract, he'd gone over to the councilman's home the day after the decision came down from the City Hall to take Walter Davis a bottle of the best twelve-year-old malt scotch he could get his hands on.

When he arrived at Councilman Davis' home they were all there—the teenaged Harry and a stepmother and her three older daughters. It was strange, he remembered, they weren't really crying, except the boy, and he was doing his best to fight it off. Walter had suffered a massive heart attack the night before and had died suddenly.

He left the bottle with the stepmother and waited for the funeral announcement that never came. Jed never saw the wife or the girls again. He didn't even know where the body was buried, though all sorts of rumors floated around for years. And while he knew better than to ask, the one he wanted to believe was that the teenage son, Harry, had stolen the body from the morgue, rowed his old man out to the Gulf in a small boat, and dumped it late at night. Harry never spoke of his parents, stepmother, or stepsisters. Back then, the town itself also knew better than to ask.

Jed finished his work and set the pen down. How sad, he thought, to grow up without grandparents, never exposed to that dimension. But he moved the sadness away and scribbled details of his latest plans on a piece of paper before memorizing them and burning the list.

Jed got up to go for his walk and smiled. He was a man born with a lot of luck that he'd planted and harvested. He'd do his best to give a good chunk away on this latest trick. As he passed through the dirt lot that separated his little office on the highway wedged between a miniature golf course and a shop that sold sea shells, he saw Harry walking toward him. He looked as if he'd aged with new lines running down his cheeks and a fresh grayness to the stubble that framed his chin.

Harry knew that Jed had stood more or less silently but powerfully over this little town for almost four decades. He'd made things good happen when few else could. Jed was a simple man with a complex mind born of hardship, struggle, and success; had never attended college, but when given the chance, he'd argue successfully that he was "an entirely self-actualized and meritocratic man." He read Emerson and Thoreau as deeply as the Sunday comics and architectural engineering plans. Widowed at twenty-five, he chose never to date again. At five foot two inches, Jed Riot, many thought, was the "tallest man in Panama City Beach, Florida." If you wanted something in town and deserved it, you asked Jed.

"Jed," Harry started in, "you and I go way back and I want to..."

Jed cut him off. "You and I will never negotiate or keep score. All good things and some bad things eventually get settled; they come out in the wash. Go take care of your wife, Harry."

Harry nodded, looked Jed in the eye longer than was comfortable for a guy like Jed, but not long enough for a guy like who Harry was becoming. And then Harry went back home to Grace.

BOOK 3

PHIN

It's making sense now, or might some day, that I can announce my protest by scaling this wall of words.

–Corporal Phin Davis, U.S. Army
(Scratched into the wood siding of
bathroom at the 18th Surgical Hospital,
Quang Tri, South Vietnam, Feb. 1973.)

CHAPTER 17

BETWEEN THE PAGES OF CREOLE AND RICE

During the early fall of 1973 it rained a lot. My dad, Harry, after sticking around all summer with mom and me, had gone to sea in late August, tempting the hurricanes that might try and sneak in before their season shut down for the year. Twenty days with little contact, then thirty. But there'd been sightings and bit reports coming back. One said he'd been chasing rumors of big shrimp sou'west toward Corpus Christi. The chasing part was true. But others had lied, as Dad told them to do, claiming he was in Key West holed up for the remainder of the season. He'd called once or twice, usually late at night, but hung up before I could hobble to the phone. Mom said, "Your pop will be all right; disappearing seems to run in our family, earthly and otherwise." And after she allowed her recovering speech to catch up with her sharpening acuities, added, "Besides, he knowingly lied to himself. Your pop might adjust to this new normal better on his own."

I'd been home in the world maybe six or seven months, but nothing seemed like home. Panama City Beach was my Libya Hill, I thought, after rereading Thomas Wolfe's *You Can't Go Home Again* while lying about the trees in our yard. "What's that like?" I remember asking Johnny when we read it together some years ago, "to have some of your best work edited, published, despised, and celebrated after you're dead?" Johnny said he had no need for considering a legacy and figured you did good while you were living or you didn't. When I wrote Johnny that I'd be leaving home for a while, I told him I figured I'd rather be traveling on to somewhere new than lost to somewhere familiar.

Mom was doing better each week, regaining parts of her memory and had been elected president of the Panama City Beach Garden Club.

"It does not mean anything," her speech measured out in 6/8 time, "but the ladies come over here each week and we babble on..." shifting to a more perky beat as her lips caught up to her brain, "...about nothing. Which is exactly what I need before I can relearn to talk about something."

If I'd stayed, I'd have to more or less confine myself to a sort of house arrest since the rest of the world, save the few I trusted, thought I was dead. So, I left the South sometime in the staleness of a late summer evening. Fall would be arriving soon, and the roads and the air would open up.

In the South, the air can put on a leather jacket and jean edge, but winter never really makes itself known to those who live south of the Mason Dixon line. It may hint at its potential, toss in the occasional frost just to mess with the cotton and the orange crops, but for the most part though, it just means a wool beanie instead of a green John Deere cap—the one with the sweat stains running up the brim like tree roots.

A '61 VW van had come into my possession that summer after a few locals had passed a hat down at Ray's Bar, a place where words spoken inside rarely migrated to the outside. They'd raised three hundred thirty-two dollars in cash money. But when the owner was presented with an offer for $300, he'd said, "Ah hell, my family has eaten that much in fish from Harry's hand. I'll give it to the boy," and then paused with a wink, "I mean...to his memory." I felt good about that, but not good enough to stay. The blink that man would take to his grave told me it was time to non-exist in this place of refuge. For a time, I'd need to "unbreak" the circle.

The van seemed to be running okay, not strong, but without betrayal. Patsy Cline belted it out through the blown speakers and for the moment, hope had come back to visit;

a gust of warm air and I welcomed it as I would Christmas, knowing it wouldn't stay, knowing it'd blow down Interstate 10 faster than I could drive, think, or pray.

It was at the beginning of the dog days that I left, well before Labor Day 1973. The Sixties were over. The war was over. There were no real winners and losers. Nothing was ever really a contest. I guess you had lost if the Nam fucked you up bad or you were born too late and missed the whole decade altogether.

It was something. The war and the decade were both something.

Before that, I'd spent the summer trying to make sense of the two. Among many parts of my life, thinking and feeling had split up and the way I figured it, I'd never make it all the way back from that landfill the war had tossed me in unless I could reconnect the two. I had no interest in simply adapting or "compartmentalizing," as the shrinks at the VA might've told me to aspire to. I'd take that goddamn war and everything in it and not in it, but related to it like a fourth-cousin, twice-removed might be, and I'd fucking own it. The good, the bad, the ugly, and the beautiful would be as close to me as the memories of home and mom's fish stew and Jed Riot telling us we couldn't jump off the pier, but following that up with a fat wink of his pterygium-covered left eye.

But somehow the war had leaked over into imagination, a kind worse than a nightmare because bad dreams go away when you're awake, or at least get the edges filed off. Imagination never goes away: it's part of who you are. Memory gets bad enough when it spreads over into imagination, like some psychological cancer, and it's not like you can cut out the bad parts. You got to talk 'em back into the box, relabel them, and just realize that they ain't ever going away. Compartmentalizing is putting your ninety-year-old grandma in a rest home. Relabeling is moving her into the back bedroom and feeding her and listening to her. Holding her paper-thin hand at night and listening to the same story you'd heard fourteen nights in a row.

That's what I tried to do all summer—chase the Nam out of my imagination and back into straight relabeled memory; it was never moving out of my house. If I had to, I'd put it in a back room so I could keep an eye on I, hold its rice-paper truths in my shaky hands. But since I was living in a place that held too many memories already, that place was filled. I'd have to leave and see if I could start new memories while I imagined a better future. I wasn't trying to trick my mind, just give it a chance to reset itself. I couldn't decide if the world was making more or less sense than it ever had. But I was bound to hang on by prying my fingers loose.

I'd sit out on the pier at night when no one was around, maybe go by and talk to Dickey a little bit about nothing. But mostly I just listened and waited for Jed to finalize my exit. He said he wanted to do it right, no loose ends, no chance of Uncle Sam ever second-guessing it. I was in limbo, the perfect purgatory for a man caught between heaven and hell.

Dad had gone fishing alone and late that summer. We hadn't heard from him, but some of his pals had told me he was in in Key West, drinking a lot of rum with some local writer. But he was safe. Ma was doing what she could, mostly present but sometimes gone past or gone future, and, Sis was gone deep. Johnny Cobb had gone to working up in Lafayette and then Shreveport. His letters said he'd opened his own shop building wooden frames for water beds, one of those ideas spawned in the '60s that flourished in the '70s. Most days my mind was all right, but at night like a bad neighborhood.

And then one evening in late August, the air thick and sultry, the beaches filled with bright-pink-skinned pre-teens, the roads jammed with pimple-faced high school football heroes in jacked up GTOs, Dickey came out to our house where I was sprawled on the porch watching the clouds go by, petting the dogs. He told me that it was all done. I didn't exist anymore. He said that his dad, in cahoots with the county coroner and the postmaster, and some friend of a friend in the JAG's office—whatever that was--had reinstated my non-status. They'd done with a few letters, a certificate, and some official looking stamps in a few weeks what the Nam couldn't do in twenty months. They'd killed me. Cause of death? *Septic shock as a result of a war-related wound.* It was to be announced in a few days; there was to be a little wake at Ray's Bar and everything.

"Such a shame," Dickey went on with the fabricated tale, obviously proud of his father's work and his supporting role.

"He was such a nice kid," they might say, "it seemed like he was healing up pretty good. Only that bad limp and his shell shock to deal with. It happened so quickly...one day he'd been down near the docks where his father's boat is kept and that night, good Lord, he's dead from an infection in his war wound. Maybe a few family types around, no services other than a drunken wake. Such a shame. One of our own. Pass the hat. I got the next round."

Soon, I was awarded the Purple Heart, posthumously. On paper, the war had both created me, took me away, and celebrated its success. All in the same breath—a thought as strange as the Nam itself. Like Wolfe, an editor had taken my best work and made something of it after I'd passed. A VA death benefit check arrived at our P.O. box. Nobody cashed it. It seemed that some of the Davis family had turned into ghosts, living and dead, memories and imagination, rooms filled with laughter and stories, and rooms barely filled with air.

At the moment there was little room for communal living. I asked mom about it and she said if I didn't leave now, she'd load dad's 12-guage and finish off my foot. She'd be okay. Send a note when you can.

"Phin, my sa-sa-son," my mom said, struggling to unslur herself. "It seems that we're all on our own for a spell—you, me, your pop. Leave now. Go!" And then added with a failed attempt at a disparate wink, "I have enough tomatoes to keep me busy."

✳ ✳ ✳

The three dogs that chose to come along, Elijah, Jeremiah, and Daniel, were fed and watered, and asleep in the back of the van. They were all mutts, pieces of other dogs from other places that made up a singular animal; no similar than what I was trying to accomplish in my connection with the road.

At that moment in time I couldn't imagine that there was any place else I'd rather be, like I had a choice anyway. The sound of rubber on road was real and in that scream of my life, any whisper or whine was a welcome respite.

Lobbing down that highway in the general direction of Lubbock, hometown of Charles Hardin "Buddy" Holley, on my way to Denver, Colorado, I had meandered a bit, had gone to see Johnny in Shreveport but had thought about opportunities to visit Greenwood and then Marshall on the edge of the great states of Louisiana, Oklahoma, and Texas. Fueled by this feeling that kept jumping out of my hands like a rainbow trout, it was good to be in motion again where my head and my heart might come together at that horizon.

I'd first gone up to see Johnny in Lafayette and came to find out he'd taken Blackie under his wing and was building those beds of water, was hiring vets, and earning money in spite of his high-risk choices. At night Blackie had been writing something he called his "Sanity Manifesto: Inside the Polemical Culture of Real-World Monopoly and Disparate Healing Narratives." Johnny had said that Blackie was talking to himself more than ever, but that the words had gone from "semi-sensical to mostly cogent to way too damn smart for me."

For the time being, Blackie had remained below the radar. He'd received a few letters back from Gerald and there had been an investigation resulting in the termination of Wilcox and Roberts, but the war had been officially declared "over" the spring of '73. People were in a hurry to forget about it. There were still soldiers in Southeast Asia and lots of them still died or got shot up and came to VA hospitals stateside. But the news left the front pages and frontal lobes. Only the smartest or the most affected knew that wars like this live on longer…and in too many forms. Others wars had definition, clarity, victory, and result. The Vietnam War only left a bad taste and bad smell and rough touch. As beautiful as the land and the people of Vietnam were, precious few soldiers thought fondly of their senses in the Nam.

I stayed in Lafayette a few days, a week maybe, doing odd jobs at Cobb's shop, trying to let the coils unwind, talking. I still don't know how he sold so many of those things the locals called "hippy beds." Some things never cease to amaze me. Johnny was kin, as loyal as bark to tree. And I promised I would make a point to put myself in his presence as necessary and as needed, if for no other reason than to remind me that there are good men left in this world, as far as men go.

Sometimes, when the war started to boil up to the surface and I'd get so mean I could hurt my own feelings, I'd call him from a phone at some cheap bar and we'd say nothing to each other, the silence of the wire's hum and his steady breath on the line enough.

Johnny had paid me for those few days or weeks' labor in the form of an old, reliable work-a-day bicycle, a bag of very decent dope, and a pristine copy of Twain's *Following the Equator*. In all the years he'd been close to our family, no money had ever changed hands. Even when he'd tried to work on dad's boat for a few weeks after he'd busted his leg on that crane working for Jed, his compensation came in the form of room, board, trucks, dogs, coffee, and conversation. Plus the odd home brew.

He never asked. Dad never offered.

It was a good trade. They both knew where the value lie.

Johnny and I would go out after work and dance our words around the edges of the war but only scratching its surface, only hinting at the death that defined it. I likened it to going on a first date with a girl you could easily end up bedding, but knew that it would be better in the long run to just have a few beers with her and talk, maybe hold hands, kiss her on the forehead. I knew its meaning so long as no one asked me to define it. I hoped that the wind of words would keep pushing me along and the broken white line would start to unravel the tangled knot inside my chest.

Johnny wouldn't swear to it—our talking as a way to make me right again—but he wouldn't swear against it neither. I wasn't so sure at first, but figured I'd go on living in the world as it was or not live in it at all. But that idea always seemed more bluff than threat.

That morning I'd lit out of Shreveport like a sick shark that drowns in its own stasis, moving to keep from drowning. Plain and simple, the dogs and me. It wasn't always that way. Hell, I used to think I'd never leave the sugary white sands of Panama City Beach, Florida. Nope. Those pâpier-maché miniature golf courses open eight weeks a year, the fabled Rednecked Riviera with its thick-aired carnival style and thick-necked cartoon character residents, well...those are my people. At least the local ones.

And the way sand squeaks under your toes on a warm July evening, Sis and me looking for grunion to put in Mama's fish stew. Yep, you weren't going to pry me loose from the Florida Panhandle with a tire iron from an eighteen-wheeler.

But then the cancer, and some God I thought I could trust, came and snatched Sis out from under us. One week we're laughing at daddy's stupid jokes while she and I help him clean up his boat, the next week she's in the hospital up in Mobile having a big chunk of her flesh taken out. Thirty-one-and-one-half days after that, gone—an angel, gold and shiny and clear, "working for God," the preacher at the funeral said.

And though at nineteen years and change, my worldliness could be held within a desktop globe, I sensed that the soul could not be deceived, that it held a truth that eats up our own. The result was a quick-slide descent into myself, a shrinking of my reach and trust, a circling of my wagons.

Gillie had first taught me to slow-bargain with myself. That one summer night when I was edging up on twelve years old and I'd asked her if she thought it wrong, us taking all those guppies, just them little fish from the sand, when they were laying their eggs. I had this image of some giant creature coming and grabbing Mama from the back bedroom just as the doc was about to yank me out from where I came.

But Sis just said that some decisions require a joining of the heart and the eyes and others things there isn't any chance of explaining in a rational way. It was futile, like trying to square a circle before God. That didn't make much sense to me then, but when that same God come for her seven years later, I understood most of what she had tried to tell me. Or had gained the sense to not even try.

When it comes to war though, whether in the heart or in the jungles, the only sense is senselessness.

That lesson began when I knee-jerked into joining up with the U.S. Army six weeks after Gillie's funeral. Reckon that was equal parts ignorance and rebellion. I was just stupid enough to make my protest against her death by joining a fight where I didn't even know what was being fought over. I didn't trust the news and I didn't trust the government. Hell, I was barely a nineteen-year-old kid from a small town on the Gulf of Mexico. I didn't trust the Easter Bunny or the bathroom mirror for any truth. But I couldn't stand the thought of a couple of men in dark suits coming up our long driveway in a white sedan with no hubcaps and taking me away in cuffs, like I'd seen in the papers.

I imagined Ma crying into her apron and Pop kicking the dirt and thinking about getting his rifle, and the dogs baying, and a salt air blowing through the tall pines. Dad never told me that wasn't likely, seeing as though I'd never been registered for anything. I should've guessed it when daddy rebuilt the sheriff's 350-short block in turn for a slip of paper authorizing my capability to drive a car in the county on a legal basis. The head of the school board lived a few miles away. Deals were made; simple agreements to accommodate. That was the South in the early '60s. That's the South every day.

That valorous indiscretion, however gunked-up and misfired, cost me plenty. And if it weren't for a few men over there, both dead and alive, it would've cost everything. Somehow, I made it back, all but for three toes and the front third of my right foot, which I let the North Vietnamese Army use as fertilizer for future crops. I didn't charge them anything. It was only body parts. Dust to dust.

Hell, they got all the dirt now anyway. Ashes included. And the suits in Washington who got out on 4-Fs due to acne, bone spurs, and enlarged bank accounts—well, I bet one day America will be trading with the Nam, maybe even put together tourists packages for vets to go back and "heal" themselves, to spend their disability checks on cheap drinks in a red vinyl bar outside Ho Chi Minh City with Duran Duran playing in the background, and the occasional blast of kids finding old land mines that my foot failed to unearth.

That ever happen, the roots will split the earth and wake every dead kid who came back in a black vinyl bag.

In some ways it was only yesterday that I was wheeled down the rear ramp, out the back of one of those big 'ol C-130s, just like it was shitting out used up soldiers, fragments of men, former kids down the block who ought to be going to college and working at restaurants and exercising their tendency toward violence by putting cherry bombs in old ladies' mailboxes.

What'd we know 'bout politics? Bunch of damn kids, cannon fodder kids thinking we were doing the right thing. Should've paid attention in history class, should've listened to the guys who'd been there, should've heard the music.

Four dead in O-hi-o? In one afternoon, no less. How about fifty-eight thou in ten years and a day? How about seventy-eight-K in a minute in Hiroshima? Six million in Germany? Eleven million in the Congo? Couple million Native Americans and their couple million buffalo? Where you wanna stop? Put your money on red or black. Spin the wheel. It's only a line item on the agenda, life for the fighting man and a little American flag on the antennae of John Q. Public's fancy Cadillac. *"Support our Troops."* the decal said. But what it meant was, *"Support my ideals about how this country ought to be run, how we, Mr. and Mrs. Caddie, became the new American bourgeoisie."*

What the hell do they know? American Gothic myops, all of them. Tired, brainwashed old men and women, fancy private school education or none at all, sitting around VFW halls and hallowed halls talking about how they crushed the Axis Power, the Evil Ones, how America won the "war to end all wars," and then the Big One. A lot of them flew a desk in some safe manufacturing parts' plant outside Chicago. And the ones who ate the horrors of war in Normandy and North Africa, who still had dried blood under their fingernails, or a kid from the Bronx who said that being a patriot erased the fact that his father was an immigrant, those men were not guilty by acts of commission; they were just unlucky bastards.

Still, this war was different. The sons should've been standing on the steps at UC Berkeley with Mario Savio, telling the world that "You've got to put your bodies upon the gears and upon the wheels." The old guys—kids who came back after a year or two at the ripe old age of twenty-one knew—they saw man after man, friend after friend, circle the drain, desperately clinging to the smooth porcelain walls covered in their own blood made slippery by the blood of thousands before them.

But there ain't no way to compare the Khe Sanh with the Bulge or Iwo Jima. It's like comparing fake tits with breast cancer surgery. Both serve a specific purpose but one keeps you alive and the other...ah, hell, I don't know what the other does.

The older men in the corners who'd seen it up close before in other wars and then sat quietly on their stools, sipping their gin and tonics as the "police action" of Vietnam became a killing field, some say they're as guilty as the businessman who misses a son's little league game because he's too busy screwing his secretary on top of his large maple desk. I don't know. They both claim to be patriots, acting for the cause, be it freedom from tyranny or freedom from responsibility. If you know the difference, and they should, you gotta get out and shout it.

"Oh, it's a different kind of war," they said. "But freedom is still worth fighting for."

"At least you had something plausible to aim at, old man. At least there was a...*consensus*."

We should've known, man. Vietnam was a war without aim; nobody cared where you pointed the gun.

We should've known.

But the van was running well and Patsy's voice was bright and brilliant. I reckon I owed it to someone to try and punch through.

CHAPTER 18

A KILLING TALE

People who are not buried in a field, they are buried in the heart.

–Anonymous Rwandan Adage

This is something I remembered about my life on the road those months after I returned. It happened in the beginning, but only cracked the block in my heart a little. But it piqued my interest, like reading the last few pages of a book, and drove me on when I didn't feel like driving. It's just a story. But it's a true one at that.

Johnny's eyes locked on mine, holding me, not down, not up, just holding me in one place; in effect, keeping me from changing the subject.

"How'd you feel after you shot her?" he asked, with enough *laissez-faire* in his voice to hide the underlying jolt I felt.

"How'd I feel?"

I was stalling. But I should have known the talk would eventually get around to something deeper than how many waterbeds he expects to sell this month.

More often than not, though, it got that way with Johnny and me, especially when he sensed that I might be thinking about leaving soon. After all the years of growing up with Johnny Cobb, all the times he'd come and gone with my Pa, I still couldn't figure out how he did it, how he might suggest a few burgers and suck me into an all-night conversation about stuff like the nature of our country's educational system or the difference between Maslow's theory of self-actualization, or Cooley's ideas as discussed in *The Looking-glass Self*. Oh, we might start off with how to stuff a 350ci straight block into a '65 Mustang, but somehow he'd loop it all around and when the five-syllable words flowed, the other guys 'round the place would look at us like they didn't know us and get up to shoot a little pool, maybe, leaving us "book freaks" to figure it all out, whatever it was we were figuring. Just some crazy old Black man and a redneck kid from down Panama City way.

When I first went to visit him I always felt like I was preparing for one of those game shows where the players just seem to know the damndest facts. Like, how the hell do you walk around knowing the average depth of Lake Erie, let alone whether the lake has gotten deeper or shallower in the past fifty years? Pa had his limits with this kind of conversation. But Johnny told him there were no limits to knowledge and that his boy might end up fishing for something that you couldn't sell when he grew up. Pa was okay with that; he and Johnny said the same thing in different languages.

This time was different though. This time I was on my own. Totally alone, my past stored away for the time being, a future tied to people I didn't know and a ribbon of asphalt. People who knew us both—Johnny and me—got to saying I'd taken on his language, said it must be on account we read the same books. Said I must've lived at some point with that old Indian he'd reference from time to time. But I disagreed. We both read deeply, but from different wells. I'd never met Jimmy Grayfalls.

Johnny had me speaking words I hadn't expected. I was talking about something that lived in some deeper level inside me, maybe the same as Lake Erie, just allowing the whole thing to come back up. Like when you know puking up too much whiskey is what's good for you, even with the understanding that you might wake up with your face in a pool of vomit.

We were in Lafayette that night for supper and I walked over to the corner of the parking lot out behind the restaurant-bar and sat on the tailgate of Johnny's truck. The red neon sign out front read *The Bar Non_,* the letter *"e"* on the end having burnt out years ago. Next door in the little strip mall was the Piggly Wiggly Market, and next to that the Slim-Me-Down Health Club. The stores deserved each other.

I found myself telling Johnny the whole damn story, or at least as much as I could reconstitute by unswallowing. It was the one he wanted more for me to tell than for him to know, sometimes using those words that hung and lingered just below the oily surface of some things in my life—my sister, my Ma, and war and books and dogs, and even some of my old friends from home that weren't family or dogs or books.

"You're trying to get me to talk about Lonnie, aren't you, Johnny?"

"Nope," he'd said. "I've heard that story sixteen ways to Sunday, kid. The way she broke your heart when she left town with her old man being transferred and such. Naw, I want to hear about the other women in your life."

"Ah, c'mon, Johnny. When have I had time for women? Besides, they all seem to up and die on me or move away."

Johnny set his beer down and looked at me, stroking his salt and pepper beard.

"Wha'ja mean by that?" he asked, seemingly uninterested.

"I was seventeen that summer," the first part leaked slowly at first. "I was a testosterone-fueled man-child testing anything and everything that I came in contact with. I would argue with a tree, maybe think about hacking it down if one of its branches scraped my arm as I walked by. I remember having this sense that, like every other human being, I had been born clean, but now I was getting dirty. My mind swirled and jumbled and black became white, and then suddenly *Alice in Wonderland* and the lyrics from Dylan's "Subterranean Homesick Blues" all made sense to me.

"The only living thing that wasn't a regular party to my rebellion was my older sister. Gillie'd known me better than all of them. She'd wiped my ass when she was seven and I only three months long in the world.

"One time I had come home from a party, a bit liquored up and on the north side of midnight. I knew daddy would still be out chasing fish up the Gulf towards Pensacola. Ma, who had worried some and waited up a spell, asked me why I hadn't called to let her know I was okay. I got a little belligerent and told Ma it was none of her business. Having to deal with my girlfriend Lonnie's dad, the colonel, was bad enough

"Well, Sis heard the confrontation from the tiny bedroom in the back of the trailer and came out in her big, fluffy, lime green bathrobe that made her look like an entrant in the Macy's Thanksgiving Day Parade. She asked me if I could come outside to look at her car for a moment, which seemed an odd request at one in the morning. But I went. And when we got some fifty feet from the trailer, she hit me.

"Not the kind of girl slap that surprises more than pains, she just nailed me with a balled fist, square in the jaw, knocking me back over the hood of the rusty Ford Falcon I had just tuned for her the day before.

"At first I wondered if she had learned to hit like that by working on Pa's boat with the guys. Then I remembered she was my sister and all. Then Gillie, she picked up a piece of rebar from the concrete block fence Pa had been working on since I was in sixth grade and held it over her head like a samurai. I lay back against the hood, rubbing my jaw, looking at a young woman I didn't know at that moment. I watched in awe as some foreign largeness drove the passion in her words. And then they came, softly, sweetly, with a razor's edge that was more foreboding than the four-foot sword of metal perched over my head like a guillotine."

Johnny kept saying, "Uh, huh, uh, huh," and handed me a beer from the ice chest in the back. "Go on kid, you're doing good."

"So, Gillie says to me, 'You're my brother, Phin, blood-fuckin' kin. Top of my head, caint' think of anything I love more. But you mouth-off to Ma or Pa one more time, I'll kill you. I swear to it. They don't deserve what it does to them now and you don't want what it will do to you later on.'

"Then she swung that big ol' piece of rebar down onto the windshield of that '61 Ford Falcon and exploded the world all around me, the sky raining chips and shards of glass like biting snowflakes that fell onto my face.

"I don't think I moved for some time, just slumped down on the ground, leaning into the right front tire, thinking that there was some aesthetic purity to her words, the way her tongue must have felt up against the truth. I think on the surrealism of that moment and believed truly that she could've killed me; not a doubt at all.

"In the morning, in those few ordinary hours of life while Gillie made us French toast like she always did on Sundays before church, I knew our private transaction had changed things. And right then, if I would have loved her any harder, I would have broken something inside me."

I got up from the tailgate of Johnny's truck and limped over to take a piss in the bushes. My foot was nearly healed; I just needed to relearn how to walk in the world. Johnny was sitting in the old wicker chair that he had screwed down to the bed of the truck, listening to the night and my tale of the killing began to unfold. The bushes reeked of a thousand drunken men who had pissed and puked in this crumbling, seedy parking lot. And I told myself that if I ever owned a bar, I would line the asphalt with a mote and fill it with Johnny Cat.

Feeling like the box was open I just let the words keep flowing at some mutually decided upon rate, an agreement between the heart and the mind to release the tale. But not all at once. That's how it is with some stories; they have a mind of their own, separate from the one who's telling it. Right spills over into wrong, love into hate, and back into love again. The stories objectify things, even if you have to make some shit up to help clarify what's real and what's not. Never coming when you expect them, they can be like a slow-thinking neighbor who stops by to show you his new tractor just when you're starting to get amorous with your girl. But you take the time to chat with the man because not too many people will, and even though you miss out on some lovin', you're glad you did because it's the right thing to do and you feel better for having taken the time.

Same goes for telling stories that need telling. I reckon that's why psychiatrists have people sitting in their waiting rooms—some tales don't take too kindly to being held in their box forever. They're not the ones you get up and tell to the polyestered Kiwanis Club or hard-lining Elk's Club members. It's not so much the content that matters, but what it means to you.

The worse thing you can do is keep that kind of story from getting told. Same as a bad staph boil that never gets cut open to let bleed the bad shit out. Sure it's gonna' leave an ugly scar on the outside, but what you need is things working well on the inside. Far as I'm concerned, it's hard to trust a person with smooth, pretty skin; it means they never had to deal with the stuff that teaches us the things that ain't a part of regular schooling.

I sure hadn't planned on going there that night with Johnny and talking about killing. We were just going to fetch a few beers to wash the sawdust down our throats. We are of the same mind that if wood chips from cutting hippy bed frames find their way into your body, they're best washed into your stomach for the night and dealt with in the morning instead of slowly absorbed into your lungs and dealt with over the rest of your life. Besides, of all the things that Johnny and I could talk about, killing was my least favorite.

I came back from the bushes and smiled as I thought about Johnny sitting up there in that big old wicker chair bolted to the bed of his new '73 Ford F-350. (Lafayette is a Ford County. Louisiana is split; some counties you drive Ford trucks, others, it's Chevys.) He was packing his pipe with a bowl of fresh tobacco.

"Johnny," I said, settling back into the spot on the steel tailgate my ass had already warmed up and fiddling with the edge of a *God Bless Elvis* bumper sticker. "Why do you want to hear the story about the killing again?"

Johnny pulled out the Zippo lighter I had brought back for him and lit his pipe, taking extra time to get the deeper tobacco ignited and to formulate his answer.

"First of all, get your damn honky hands off of my Elvis sticker; he's one of the only White men who deserved to be Black. Second, lot of things still ain't sitting right with you. I sensed it the day you pulled that oil-leaking VW bus of yours into my driveway—what, four weeks ago you got here? Most people wouldn't noticed, but I seen it in the way you spoke to your dogs and the way that edge was out of your voice. Hell, I know you got things on your mind. Problem is you don't think you're ready to go there yet. Funnier thing is, you been talking about it nonstop in other ways a man can't always say. Finish your story, Phin. Just get out of the way and let it tell itself."

I nodded his way because it was all I could do and picked up where I had left off.

"Like I said, I was seventeen that summer. And a few days after I had replaced the window on Gillie's Falcon I asked my Pa if I could go hunting with him and Uncle Larry. It was Friday and he was just getting home from the dock where he had been prepping the boat for the next week when he was taking her southwest past the ninetieth parallel to look for bonito and big sea bass. I knew we were short on cash money and Pa was hoping this last trip before hurricane season got too dangerous would give us an edge up before those gifts from the devil kept the entire fleet closer to home waters.

"As was usual for a Friday in April, Pa had stopped and picked wildflowers for Ma. He once told me that the look on her face when he came through that screen door on a Friday afternoon, her knowing he wouldn't fish on Saturday or Sunday, 'to give the city folks a fighting chance,' and him trying to hide the wildflowers behind his back inside that gnarled old sea mitt of a hand. Well...it was worth more to him than all that he owned, which materially speaking was the boat, the eighty acres, and a double-wide trailer with non-slip linoleum floors.

"You know how much he loved that land and that boat he had bought with money saved since he was a twelve-year-old with a paper route. The floors Pa and I had put in for Ma on their thirtieth wedding anniversary. Ah, hell, Johnny, you know all this. You were there part of the time."

He just nodded and tried to blow smoke rings in he dark.

"Anyways, I'd never shown any interest in hunting. Pa and Uncle Larry stopped asking me to go along a few years ago after something inside made me ask them if they ever felt bad about shooting deer and turkey and rabbit. And even though regular old bodily hunger had resolved me to being okay with eating the animals when Ma put them on a plate and set them in front of me, I still wrestled with the thought my being the cause of something no longer alive, something dying with its blood on my hands.

"Pa, he cocked his head from right to left and then back again like the motion would get him to the answer why his only son would ask to go along hunting with him after years of his being convinced that the boy's spiritual texture was more Buddhist than Baptist.

"Truth be known, I had a feeling that what was happening inside of me, all this rebellious confusion and disrespect for things that needed respecting, would one day have a reason, maybe get aimed at a target that could use some legitimate shaking up. I felt bad about the way I had treated Pa and damn if I didn't find myself missing the man, same as I did when I was eight years old and he would be out at sea for weeks at a time.

"I knew how much he loved to hunt, how tall and straight he walked when he came home with a twelve-point buck roped to the back of the truck. Hell, least I could do was to go along once before I went off to college in Mobile or got drafted or knocked up my girlfriend and had to get a job down on the docks working for Jed Riot. What harm could it do? I'd just carry along his old thirty-aught-six to this upstate forest, pretend to be interested, keep my mouth shut, and maybe fire off a round or two so I could trade lies with my uncle about the one that got away."

I paused for a second and looked at Johnny, whose two hundred twenty-pound frame had settled into a rocking motion in the chair, moving the entire truck just enough to squeak the leaf springs, reminding me of the time I had snuck Mary Lou Panicky into my bedroom and we were banging away on each other, but still trying to keep my noisy bedsprings from waking the family.

Johnny, big a man as he was, had grown an eighty-grit gentleness to him, smoothing with the years. He was closing in fast on fifty-years old that fall of '73. But he could've passed for sixty. Now he was more Santa Claus than Sasquatch. But even when he tried to get angry, most people who knew him, or maybe didn't know him, would smile and Johnny would end up saying something like, "Ah, shit. Just try and do a little better next time, would you?"

He slowed his rocking for a moment and looked down at me, speaking first as a second father, then as an uncle, and finally as a man who had felt and seen things so elemental and raw that they had yet to be named. As a Black man who grew up in the '30s South, he had earned his wisdom born of pain. He sometimes said he had premonitions, not déjà vu or clairvoyance, but more like reading a story before it happens and knowing that you are either in collision or sync with every thought you ever had. Said he got it from his only wife, Ruth.

"Reckon I'm going to be on social security before you finish your story, kid. That's okay though, just so long as you tell it right and tell it whole, which is to say mostly truthful as you need it to be. You don't want any trite bit of puffery. You need, no... you demand truth because without it you're nothing, not even human, which is to say you don't exist. That's why so many of your fellow vets have switched themselves into the off position. They already died 'cuz the truth of war has become too painful and the regular business of living seems like another lie. They reckon they're better off to the world dead, just stories in the living rooms of nieces and nephews who, when they get older, use those stories as lessons on how to live, but not how to die."

Johnny paused for a moment and the squeaking stopped. He put the pipe where his lips hid beneath that black and white beard. There was a mumble across the parking lot and the unmistakable sound of piss hitting the wheel well of an F-250.

"'Only the dead have seen the end of war.' An old dead White man said that. She was beautiful, wasn't she?" Johnny asked.

"Yeah, Johnny, she was the most wondrous living creature I'd ever seen. Tall, maybe six feet standing on her hindquarters, streaks of dark silver in her fur I imagined as the sun hit her, so rich you'd swear there were jewels woven in the fibers. And there was strength to her, the likes of which I'd never felt and doubt will ever again. Just an implacable godliness.

"Her teeth were white, just like the actors doing the toothpaste commercials, rows and rows of them that could rip a ten-pound trout in half or take an equal size chunk out of a man's shoulder. And the eyes—at first, they had a look of unknowing, not pretty exactly, more astonishing, slowly filling with a fluid of moral indifference, like she was telling me that we don't get to pick our own wars, like she was telling me that before man was, war waited for him.

"When I came around the sharp bend in the trail and saw her there off to the side, pawing at some type of berry bush, she only let out a low growl, like a dog will do if you pet it while it has its head in a feed bowl. And the sound had a sense of edgeless command to it, not a 'don't-fuck-with-me' scowl, but more like a friend who's playing hide and seek and warns you they'll count to ten and you'd *better* be out of their sight."

My voice was cracking now, but I didn't hear it. Johnny was rocking again and I sat there on the tailgate, swinging my boots in time with the rhythm of the truck and the night and the story.

"I froze, Johnny, fricking paralyzed by the awe and the beauty and my own fear. I opened my mouth to call to Pa and Uncle Larry, but no sound came out while they remained lost in their own Darwinian game of cat and mouse somewhere up the trail.

"But man, right after I failed to heed her warning sent in a voice understood by both man and beast, she rose up in all her splendor and I felt myself being sucked into the earth, unable to go forward or back.

"It was then, during one of those forever minutes, that I saw her cub come out of the green shadows, ambling along close to the ground, innocent, just a stuffed teddy bear with a heartbeat and a three hundred-pound black bear between it and me—this real live mama bear born and bred to protect that cub with her own life and then some.

"I tried to inch my way back slowly, averting her stare, just like I had read in a *Boy Scout Handbook* I had borrowed years ago to see what those badges some kids wore were all about. But in trying to go back I had gone forward, maybe by accident, maybe because I lacked experience in backing away from much of anything.

"In any case, that's when she came at me—a giant, black steam locomotive, slowly at first, but gaining momentum. She was one of God's splendid species of grace and power, a great moving monolith of flesh and bone and fur and innately unbridled defensive anger.

"My own horror took control of me and I acted no different than her—on pure stupid instinct. I raised my gun against some shadowy concept of ideals that had been run roughshod by survival and pointed the weapon in the general direction of the raging beauty bound on killing me. She was smart and knew of nothing more dangerous than a two-legged creature with a gun. I fell on my back, one eye shut, the other saucered, and slowly, painfully squeezed the trigger as a war waged inside my heart, a place it had no right to be, for she was fighting for the same thing: rightness of me and rightness of family. I deserved to live as did the bear and both our generations to come. I was raised up thinking there was no difference.

"And as the ground shook under her advancing charge, I pulled the trigger again and again. Aim, squeeze the trigger, shoot. Aim, squeeze the trigger, shoot. Just like Uncle Larry had said.

"After three shots went off, I saw her slowing, but coming still, the smell of her leading like the dust fronting a plow. I fired one more time as my feet come up under me and I began moving in retreat, picking up speed as I imagined her warm breath on the back of my neck, her sharp claws within inches of tearing deep gouges in my back all the way down to my soul.

"I had a funny thought of an old high school running coach who told me when you are leading a race and you look back, you're as good as dead.

"I never looked back.

"And after what seemed like a marathon, I stopped feeling her presence, rounded a corner and came up on Pa and Uncle Larry running toward me. I fell to the ground and mumbled something about when I was three years old and got lost at the beach while Ma had walked down to the sand to pick up a mortar,--I mean, a seashell—for me.

"Pa told Uncle Larry to stay with me and reloaded his and his brother's rifles, slinging one over his left shoulder while holding the right one out in front, pointed at the trail like a flashlight. He looked down at me and then moved in the direction of the shooting. I saw his eyes blink a few times. They were filled with something short of pity, closer to mercy than compassion."

I looked up at Johnny, his pipe long since gone out, but dangling still from the corner of his salt and pepper face. He was nodding his head, not quite smiling but showing enough curves in his lips to offer approval.

"And afterwards," he nearly whispered, "how'd you feel about it all?"

I had opened a vein on this story and, somehow, as hard as it was to tell, something dark had been unsoldered into the light. I didn't have to push because something was pulling me.

"Well, Uncle Larry, he sat down next to me, his plain hopea-wrapped belly straining against his overalls as he watched an old turkey vulture circle above like a Huey looking for a safe LZ."

"The world had just done its thing again, eh Phin?"

His words hung in the air for an instant, bold and crisp letters, then struck me right below the ear.

"After Pa came back and said she was nearly dead and he had to put her down with two more shots to the head, it was like I was watching a movie of myself."

I was done talking for the moment but, the story went on in my head as the film looped back on itself. I had just sat there in the shade of an old hopea tree, not even thinking about what would happen to the cub, and felt engulfed by a thick layer of ambiguity. My pores opened and closed, my body trying to let old air out and breath new at the same time. I longed for a former innocence, ached for the way my world was, but could never be again. Nope. Not hardly. Not even once.

I thought about how hard we try to grow up, speeding right past adolescence, bound for the hidden fruits of being grown up. And then in a single moment we slam the brakes on so hard and fast that we are thrown right through the front windshield, taking that same view we had of the world from the front seat onto the hood and then into the streets of our lives. Only now we are cut and bloodied and scarred and nothing again is ever as pure as when you are a kid. It's the same as when you go off to boot camp as a nineteen-year-old punk with a pimply face and after they put an M-16 in your hand and train you to kill, you never look at a swing set or a bicycle or a skateboard the same again.

"It was a year later," I was looking at Johnny now, trying to put down a period somewhere, "in one of those books you told me to read when I came upon a sentence that I have carried as a crucifix reminder—of what I'm not sure—but a reminder still: '*Some sins,*' the words said, '*are forever fresh and original.*'"

The big man nodded, a bit of his teeth leaking through and put his hand on my shoulder.

✳ ✳ ✳

That's where I ended my story that night. And as Johnny and I drove through the darkened back streets of Lafayette I recited the final part of the story in my head. It was the part that would come out another time, another night with Johnny.

Maybe in six months, maybe in six years. But come out it would and I would chase away the Trojan Horse that I had let into my mind. Like most good blues men will tell you, it's not the sound of the note played that gives the music, its feeling, it's the absence of noise between the fretted strings. I would tell Johnny everything—the truths he already knew, but which had not been validated and clarified by virtue of me speaking them in the plainness of real life. At the very end of the story, I would say that some final truth comes over you like a catalytic vapor and envelops and surrounds you and smothers you. And then, on a summer day, some years from now, when the sunflowers are in full bloom and the smell of jasmine is thick in the air, and your little girl's tiny soft hand is wrapped gently inside of your own...it lets you breathe again.

But you never know when the "killing" will return and knock you down and choke you like a serpent, or maybe like a malaria night sweat that creeps into your sleep after years of lying quietly.

Just before we pulled into Johnny's long dirt driveway, the sun stretching its first few fingers over the red dirt hills to the east, Johnny said it one more time, "She was beautiful, wasn't she?"

And I said, "Yes...with long, silky black hair pulled behind her in a pony tail tied with a piece of reed, dangling out from under one of those big triangular straw hats they all wore when working out in the rice fields."

"And the little girl?" Johnny asked while shutting the truck door quiet as the sky to keep from waking the dogs.

"I could feel her small brown eyes on me," I answered while moving away from the truck and toward what he had made me do. "They were...soft eyes, I imagined. Yes, thin, soft eyes."

The old VW started on the first try.

"Go on," he said. And I was gone.

CHAPTER 19

DRIVESHAFTS

It was dark and I had the head droops. The time was irrelevant and the bus's right headlight seemed trained to find snipers in the trees. I was hungry and pulled the vee-dub over at a truck stop and bought burgers for all of us—a couple of hungry dogs and me. The man at the counter asked me if I was feeding a commune or something.

"What do you mean by that," I asked?

"Lookie here, feller," his attempt at being cordial was failing. "We don't get too many long-hairs driving them hippy vans ordering ten burgers, six with cheese, four without, and one large cherry coke. I assumed you was taking them back to a camp or something."

"Well," I played along, "truth is, old-timer, I only been back from the war a few months. My hair grows fast and I don't like combs and I'm damn sick of people telling me how I got to look, asking who I might've kilt, and mostly I'm sick of MRE's and Asian delight. That's why my dogs and I decided on this fine dining establishment—because you don't sell noodles and there's no sign that says 'No crew cut, no service.' Hey, do you think I could get some extra ketchup?"

"Boy," the old man backpedaling, embarrassed but still proud, "you been in the war, your money's no good here."

"Well, I been out of it long enough for you to think differently at first, even if it's still in me. I don't want or need any handouts from society, just some extra ketchup," and then added extra teeth to my wide smile. "If it ain't too much trouble."

"Son," the old man trying to regain some of what he gave away but willing to leave some on the table as well. "I seen others like you. You're a piece of a puzzle that won't fit no matter which way you twist it. Likely it's you that changed and everybody else stayed the same. Here's your burgers with extra ketchup."

I picked up the bag, paid the man, and headed out the door.

"One more thing, kid, and I don't mean nothing by it. It ain't easy for those of us who didn't go over there to understand neither."

And as I stood there holding the bag, smelling the mostly-beef patties, wondering if I really knew the figure making my reflection in the glass exit door, he added, "And you're welcome to park that bus out behind the silver Peterbilt and roll over for the night."

"Much obliged," I told him without looking back, "and I didn't mean nothing by it either."

Curled up with the dogs in the back of the '61 van, the sound of big rigs coming and going all night, some strange détente between me and the owner, I hoped good dreams would come.

There was a dream that Mama was still her plain 'ol self and saw me as an eighteen-year-old kid headed off to a small college on the East Coast instead of a war vet, and she wanted to wash my clothes and fix me fish stew and, *by-the-way, How's Lonnie?*. How could I tell her that killing other humans changes a man in ways that aren't talked about 'round the dinner table?

Imagine that: *"Oh yeah, when the sergeant told me to cut off the gook's ears for his necklace, I realized that the Bowie knife Uncle Frank had given me before I shipped out coulda used a good sharpening. Pass the meatloaf, would 'ya, Mom?"*

I dreamt my pop, Harry, had at first wanted me to work with him on the boat. He said that the fishing was good and that the sea had healed him lots of times and he'd make me a special rubber boot for me with three toes. And Gillie woulda liked it.

It had been my pop who'd finally pushed me out the door and on the road. He just cornered me one day after I'd been sitting out in the back watching Ma try to tend to her garden while she spoke in the occasional riddle to herself, the tomatoes begging to be relieved of their weight on the vine. He'd been down on the docks working on his traps and lines, had come home for supper ,and as he walked up the driveway, the gravel crunching under his old Chuck Taylor's, the dogs nipping at his heels for attention, Pop looked at me with that combination of thought and intent, sorry and empathy. I limped out to greet Pop and noticed that the shadows weren't following him. It was late afternoon and just a few minutes ago, Ma had stood up in the shade of an elm to wave. Directly over my pop, it looked like a bright high noon, the sun's rays blurring the months I had been back in the world with the years I had grown up right there, right then. In the middle was my twenty months in the Nam. That part was in negotiation; turned into ellipses of a text. Even the clouds, it seemed, were sitting at the table.

"Phin," his words sounding thick and heavy, "it's time, son. Like Johnny said last time he was down here, your silence grows louder every day. I reckon that sanding and varnishing over your life won't fix the cracks. Best you go on and find the man whose name you own. It ain't like we're living with a person, boy. More like a shape. Your ma and me, struggling to get her right mind back as she is—we still got enough dead memories to negotiate."

In my dream I knew he was right. My troubles had made his even more real. And Pop was starting to talk like Johnny Cobb with all these allusions and inferences and such. Not sure how I felt about them speaking too much of the same language.

"The repetition 'round here is plain squashing you into a flat stranger. You're gettin' on pretty good with that cane now and I changed my mind 'bout you fishin' with me. Right now, kid, all you got is a hammer—an angry one that ain't got a claw or a hook on it. And the whole world has got to look like a damn bent nail."

I dreamt that Ma had been following the shadow of the elm as it moved one step at a time, taking it all in like any good mama would. Then she stepped out of the shadow and closed the deal, like every good mother will do.

"Phin, it's a bent nail at that. You best go out and collect some tools, boy. Your Pa and I ain't enough."

They were right. I knew it already, indelibly. But it didn't change my shape or remagnetize my compass. All it did was fuel the hope, which right then was as good as birthing me in the first place.

In my dream that night, with the smell of diesel big rigs passing by and satisfied dogs surrounding me in warmth, I think I started praying again. But I was mixing up God and Gillie. And I didn't care.

When the sun came up, my parents were still struggling.

✳ ✳ ✳

I heard a knocking on the window and had trouble opening my eyes since the sleep tears had dried my eyelids shut. The dogs started yipping and I saw the old shopkeeper standing there, kicking the dirt, looking around and holding a cup of real dark, original, gas station coffee.

"You best be moving on, kid. Regardless of what you done, Texas ain't no Berkeley and I don't want no trouble. Take this cup of mud and be on your way."

"What's your name, mister?"

"Ridgeway," he said.

"No," I said polite as I could, "Your Christian name?"

"It's Lawrence, Lawrence Willard. Why you asking?"

"It's just that I'm not used to learning people's full and proper names. I'm obliged for your help, Lawrence Willard Ridgeway."

"Yeah fine, kid. Now get outta here, would you?"

We drove until the thermostat rose above half-way and decided to turn off on Route 155 South and have a rest in Tyler. I could still make Abilene by dark. The van ran better after dark, but Texas nights in the fall can still carry the heat of Texas nights in summer. I'd look for a pay phone and try to call this guy, Mike Greer, in Lubbock, the one Johnny Cobb had told me was in C-Company; a mid-to-high ranking officer, but Johnny didn't specify. He'd offered me a job, sight unseen, working at his farm supply company.

"Did he offer it on account of you being one of his friends?" I asked Johnny.

"Nope."

"Is it 'cuz of my injury?"

"Nope."

"Is the job because I went to Nam, same as him?"

"Nope. It's because you came back, same as him."

When we got to Tyler near after sunset, I parked the van on a downtown street and let the dogs stretch their legs in a little grassy park rimmed with old bald cypress trees and a dark pond in the middle. Fishing in my pocket for a taste of the buds I'd been compensated by Johnny for that week-or-so of work, a voice came up behind me.

"Dogs have to be on a leash, sir." It was a young man about my age in a dark blue uniform, a badge on his chest, and a gun on his waist. "City law. Can't be having loose dogs running everywhere. You'll need to put them on a leash."

Déjà vu all over again.

"What's your business in Tyler, by the way?" He looked me up and down, but not into my eyes.

"I'm Phin Davis from Panama City Beach, Florida. On my way to Lubbock by way of Lafayette, Jackson, Biloxi,

Columbus, Khe Sanh, and the Quangtin Province. Got work at Mike Greer's shop there, sir. Only one problem." I looked at his name badge and he butted in.

"Listen buddy, I'm from Corpus Christi and don't know *every* city in Texas. You gonna have another problem if you don't leash them dogs."

"My problem, Officer Larimore, is that, 'them dogs' have never been on a leash."

"Then you best go find some rope in that rig of yours."

I called for the dogs. Elijah and Jeremiah snapping right to, Daniel taking a last sniff, looking up to access the need for hurry on my face. The three of them collected, likely wondering about the toy soldier standing there, I tied their three collars together with the dog tag chain I'd removed from my neck. Moving three steps back toward the van, I heard a muted remark leak out of Larimore.

I stopped, not turning, thinking that neither of us wanted it this way. But we were inside the slow motion everness of myopic thought, denying choices and empathy, coveting what each of us desired—more of the empty space that lie between us. Or less. Elijah and Jeremiah growled and pulled on the chain in the direction of their gauntlet. But Daniel held them strong, licked my hand, and moved us toward the van.

Another kid with a gun had filed the edges off my hopes. And behind the mirrored glasses, his eyes were dark and round; just a kid from Tyler, Texas.

"Sin lỗi, Larimore," I spoke to his edges while holding the dogs and rubbing the rank and serial-numbered tags with my thumb. "Sin lỗi. I'm sorry."

Back in the van, I gently pulled Patsy out of the cassette and let Johnny Cash have a turn. It was a moment for the man in black. When the bus hit sixty miles per, she backfired and the sound sent me *in-country*, in my van, in Texas...Texas, Vietnam.

✱ ✱ ✱

I saw myself lying in the blood-brown dirt of that country. It'd been thirty-one weeks and four days after I'd landed in-country at Tan Son Nhut and I was hardening like catalyzed resin. One afternoon, we were just setting there in our hooch after a three-day patrol that lasted six months; just me and another enlisted schmuck by the name of Sanders—never asked his first name on account I thought he'd get killed quickly and didn't want the extra baggage of knowing. A kid from the Northeast, talking and pulling leeches from our shins. But Sanders, who had earned the label "Worm" for his constant book reading, seemed to be within his thoughts. I figured he might be like the rest, flat and singular in the defense of their shrinking world in this land of mayhem and rice. The less we knew about each other, the less we cared when we carried their split bodies.

I brought up the subject of good fishing spots, not really caring if Sanders heard, just validating my existence with the sound of my own voice. But Worm stirred a bit and I took that as a sign of interest. Worm asked me about the book that rested over my own closed and colorless eyes. I didn't want to admit it at first, but I told him it was a book about the Buddha. One of the locals had translated a few parts for me after I'd tipped the village off before one of our patrols went in and made a general mess of things. I'd been in-country just over three months and had already done several things that'd get me court martialed. A lot of grunts didn't go that long.

Thirty-one weeks. Geez, it only took three to figure out this war had a serious identity crisis. The best soldiers were either really stoned, really good killers, or really dead. That's the way the sequence worked anyway.

"Worm," I answered as he rose from under his helmet like a turtle, "most of what I'm reading here doesn't make any sense. But a few points stuck in my head so hard they've become part of my Southern brain, especially the part about letting pain ride through you instead of putting up a backstop and watching it have a game of emotional ping-pong inside your heart."

"That's good, Davis. I like it." It was the first time I'd heard Worm laugh in a week of humping endless green curtains. "I'll have to keep my eye on you, bro. What else you read?"

That's how it started.

Worm's father had worked as a janitor at Duke University and had the key to the library. After high school he'd go help his dad for a few hours in the afternoon and then wander around this "tabernacle of literature," as he called it, just pulling books off the shelves at first, gradually working his way up to reading them, pondering them, and then questioning them. After awhile, he told me, the authors spoke to him, just like he was sitting in one on those big fancy classrooms. Only without the homework.

When he showed up in-country he had ten books with him, the most they'd let him bring, most of which I'd only heard of when referenced by Johnny Cobb. But gradually, between dodging sniper fire and the illusion of a real meal, Worm taught me about these books, introducing me to a whole world that existed between the pages. It seemed more accessible even than the insanity that waged around us.

Looking back on it now, Worm was way too smart for the war. And the more I read, the more I, too, realized the fatality of our presence; the way war bombs any bridges between intelligence and virtue.

I'd like to say we were just kids, but that's an old story. In the Nam we aged worse than dogs—seven years for every day. The kids that made it through their whole tour went home tired and ancient; twenty-year olds who'd lived for centuries. And it was between the pages these things became clear. A new world, more tangible than the present, unfolded with each chapter. I could dream of the Creole back home and eat rice while I read. I would never understand war, but I could study why some men embraced it and others protested in ways without limits. Every fictional character and philosophical thought held more truth than America's presence in Southeast Asia—was more real than the black shapes in the sights of our M-16s.

The books shed light on what preceded it. The bullets came after it, in the dark and for reasons that are still hidden in the men who sent us there. Worm had it figured out, though. He was just going to out-think the war, keep his virtue tethered to his mind. It was a brilliant concept, anyway. Hell, we should've bombed the North with Joyce and Kafka, carpeted Hanoi with Schopenhauer. At night I began to dream of meeting Henry Miller and telling him that to fail as a writer was *not* to fail as a man; he'd had it backwards. I dreamt of hiking with Thoreau, of getting shit-faced on seven-year rum in Havana with Hemmingway. I wanted to discuss plot with Hawthorne, characterization with Fitzgerald, argue religion with James and Donne.

I felt I could go round-for-round with McNamara. Kissinger I'd put down in two punches. One chance, I dreamed, just give me one chance at 'em.

A day arrived when Worm was short-timed and he looked at me perplexed, his head sunk low, wearing his worry like thick makeup.

"What's down, Worm?"

"Thinking I might re-up."

"Fuck you. You got thirty days and a wake up. You just got that 'last month scare.' Stay cool. We ain't supposed to go out on patrol until the new moon. You're the last grunt I know who'd re-up."

"Phin, their offering me a cush job at the rear doing research on North Vietnamese war tactics. I can read all day, file a few reports, and be on the veranda at the Continental by happy hour."

"Man, those days soaking up the bennies of French colonialism are done. You've seen the intel," and then added a question. "You trust them, Worm? Come on. NVA tactics? We own the day, they own the earth. We got the fire power, they got the staying power. Do the math. Even the pussy French figured that shit out. You don't want to be here when Ho's boys come over the wall."

"If I go home Phin, I'm looking at a two-bucks an hour job. I know it sounds weird, but this place is growing on me. Here I have the illusion of control. But at least it is a *kind* of control."

I couldn't talk Worm out of it. He had stopped trying to erase the three-letter beginning to *surreal*. He had beaten the war by out-thinking it, and in the process his mind had grown too strong for his virtue, imploding his own rationality. Six weeks later, he was killed as he sat in a booth at Jimmy Wong's by a Chinese-made grenade thrown by a thirteen-year-old Vietnamese girl on the back of an Italian scooter brought here by a Frenchman. So much for domino theory. A new form of globalization had begun. Worm had been reading the German philosopher, Nietzsche, sipping the local beer, Bin-Tang, which was made with hops grown in Laos and barley processed in Cambodia.

Worm, it seems, had out-thought his own humanity.

My literary supply line destroyed, I had to get creative. I'd been growing some real quality dope up in the hills outside the camp perimeter and began trading it for fake passes to Saigon. There, with some other forged docs, I could procure the texts I needed from the old French library near the Embassy. With Worm gone, I was mainstreaming the shit. I'd be the smartest redneck-motherfucker in-country.

You've got to love the free market system. It was Darwinism in disguise. You could see how the place could become a capitalist's dream market some day. Domino theory my ass.

When I finally got back to the world I understood most of Camus, a lot of von Clausewitz, and enough of Sun Tzu to know that I'd never really understand it. But I'd learned how the NVA tunnel system worked, how men in war learned to love each other in a way that there is no way to name—just a mutual transfer of heartbeats with the private goal of getting home, never winning. And that death always seeks to locate the freedom of the living that likely came home partially dead. That was the easy part. I knew how this daisy chain of contingencies and coercing had baptized our nation in some omnipotent pathos—it's one thing to discuss Conrad's *Heart of Darkness* in an air-conditioned humanities building and another all together to have a certain paragraph pour into your head while you pour your buddy's large intestines back into the hole where his stomach is supposed to be. It's not ivory or ideology. It's not oil or diamonds or water. It's just greed.

What I wished I could've learned, however, were the names and addresses of the shadow men who'd sent us there. When I got back, I knew it would be a long time before I was really back.

But I was moving and I had a goal, Lubbock, Texas, and a man named Mike Greer—another vet; an older one with a business in which I could be dutifully employed for a period. Fill up my tanks.

Right then I heard a loud bang-pop explosion noise and I nearly drove the van right into the ditch. But the old bus was headed for the ditch in any case, the victim of a thrown rod. I'm not really sure where this term with the sexual connotation came from and I doubted that I'd be able to find the parts to fix it at the closest place of business, *Big Al's Farm and Feed,* on the nearby corner of Route 284 and 33A. But the road is the road and the asphalt was the church pew in which I sat. I'd deal with it.

Outside, it was raining; a thick, loud rain, hard in noise but soft in touch. I stepped out of the van, let the dogs run in the wide openness of where I was, wherever I was, and watched the rain bounce off my shoulder-length dreadlocks. I was alive with material poverty, happy in the blunted point of renewed hope. It was a precise moment and I had no idea what the hell I'd do. I realized well and good for the second time that day that I was alive. Score a few for some God, I thought.

Then I smiled.

The vee dub had done me right and I was inclined to think—from a cocktail napkin map—that I was maybe sixty miles from Lubbock, a place I had never frequented but drew in my mind as a backdrop for *The Last Picture Show*: tumble weeds running through the empty parking lots of five-and-dime strip malls, ten-dollar Wranglers, and twenty-dollar hotel rooms run by people with names like Irv and Madge. And gun-racked Ford F-150s, lots of them. An honest place.

Most of what I owned I could carry on my back or strap to one of the tubes of the work-a-day bike Johnny had given me with some twine I'd found in a dumpster outside Lafayette last week. There were a few books to give away; what were books made for besides reading and giving away?

I pushed the van another few feet into her burial-ditch, took off the license plates, pried the serial numbers from the door wells with a rusty screw driver, and left a note for whomever found the van and might want to un-throw the rod. I carefully placed Patsy and Johnny in my shirt pocket and walked the quarter mile to *Big Al's Farm and Feed*.

"Hi. You Big Al?" He wore stained overalls, a perfectly sculpted ball-peen hammer gut, and the best collection of welcoming yellow teeth I'd ever seen.

"Yessir. Can I help you with anything other than a haircut? Those yer dogs? They're a nice-looking set, they are."

"Yessir back at you. If'n you had pruning shears with a diamond tip you might get through my mop, but I wouldn't trouble you so. Seems I've experienced a bit of car trouble and am pondering my situation and my options."

"Options, we got, young man. Troubles we don't allow. The name's Al Holmes. C'mon in and tell me."

Al and I worked out the details and after sizing him up a bit, I gave him a couple of Faulkner books, and a Louis L'Amour with a Quixotic image of man atop a huge white horse on the cover with the requisite ten-gallon hat shielding the Western sun from his crow-footed eyes. As an afterthought, I tossed in an ancient Zane Gray, the spine moldy and frayed, but intact and ready to read; quite similar to the way I was feeling right about then.

Worm had taught me well.

The books I gave as a present, knowing that a guy like Al would offer in return to watch my dogs for a few weeks, which he did, not out of empathy, but out of grace. Big Al joked about the dogs looking better kempt than me and wondered how I knew he was a Zane Gray fan. It was a good trade.

It's not overly difficult to size up a man when thinking about how he might treat your dogs. First, you look at his own dogs, and then you look at his wrists for dog bite scars. My mutts would be fine with Al, and he with them.

I borrowed Al's phone and called this Mike Greer in Lubbock to tell him I'd be in very late that night or tomorrow mid-morning, depending on how my legs and bike tires held up. He said I was welcome whenever, gave me an address, and said he'd leave the light on. Before I hung up, I reminded him that I wasn't too experienced in welding; the job I was supposed to be starting. He just said any man Johnny Cobb would drink and talk with could learn to weld. It's just fire and melted steel. I'd seen it before.

I figured so long as the full moon stayed bright enough, I'd be there before sun up. Then I paid my respects to my dogs, told them not to knock up any of Big Al's German Shepherds, shot-gunned a large mug of Al's day-old coffee, and climbed on my work-a-day bike carrying all my worldly possessions, including the Tolstoy anthology I had in mind for Greer. Then I rolled out into the wide Texas sky. I was heading south/southwest to weld alfalfa splitters. I'd make a point to visit Buddy Holley's grave at the city cemetery, maybe solve a few of the world's problems with this fellow Mike Greer.

Peddling that bike into the future, I laughed to myself about the possibility of my dreads getting caught in the spokes and tapped out a Blind Willie rift on the rusty handlebars. The flashlight that Big Al had duct taped to the frame was shining into the long-broken line of possibilities. And I hoped that the batteries would not fade away.

For the moment, there was a cease-fire. The hope was strong, the beast quiet, and I thought there was no place else I wanted to be.

CHAPTER 20

MUDSLIDE

I was getting to know Gerald McReady through the occasional letter that caught me up, through what Johnny would tell me, and through my long-affected memory of when I was a short-time patient in the Denver VA. Sometime later, I would know enough to understand his traits, talents, and talisman. And in return letters, discussions with Johnny, or notes in my journal, I was able to piece together this person called Gerald. You see, I was on the run. And so was the kid called Blackie. But we were separately remembering the details following mine and Blackie's exit from the Denver VA that past spring. These are the thoughts and images of how that period unfolded for Gerald.

–Phin

Gerald McReady watched the wheel go around and around longer than usual. The wooden plate was true, the circular arc without ellipse. And as he put his freshly washed hands into the rich, thick mud that lived in plastic bags, lifted out what felt like three pounds of earthen clay, he drew comfort in the steady hum of the electric motor. It was a good motor, attached to taut belts and it drove his clay without hesitation, even when he dug his heavy fingers into the early block before any life had been granted the object.

Gerald plopped the slab of good moist clay onto the wheel's center and sat back to think while the force of centricity settled what had come from the earth. He didn't think in terms of what to shape or how he'd get started or even what he'd do with the pot when it was done. Those things he knew: it was always a pot, and he always started by putting his hands on the fat lump and letting the wheel do the work.

He watched the lump go around and around with eyes that sank deeper into his head; bright, knowing eyes with pupils that acted as filters, screening out parts of the hellish world in which he lived and worked, in which he had choices but no choice, the place he hated so much that sometimes his Job-like patience failed him and he sent some of that hell back from where it started. And Gerald wasn't even surprised when it came back as love. Such was the curse of the healer, the curse and the blessed gift. Gerald never lied to himself; he simply had to remind himself.

His eyes were working especially hard this morning while a wicked north wind blew outside his Denver loft and a crisp mountain rain that had pretended to be snow last night pounded his windows. Two days ago the temperatures had reached the low seventies and people had said summer was here and put shorts on and bought seeds from the garden store. But when you live on the cusp of geography, as Denver is not really a mountain town nor a plains town—not even a rolling hills town, April and May are up for grabs. It was cold outside in the morning dark. And Gerald watched the wheel of clay go around. And he imagined what kind of pot that this earth would be sculpted into.

The eyes left the wheel for a moment and scanned the walls. There were so many pots: tall, fat, wildly painted and fired, simple red-gray, some with designs in the clay for the world to see, others with designs inside that only the creator would know about when more earth was put into the pots and seeds or plants set there to grow. But others never saw the designs, inside or out, and plants never grew in Gerald's pots. They weren't for sale. They were given away if he knew somebody that he wanted to have them. They were pugmarks of his creativity. They were signs of a hidden, unrequited passion.

They were a means of expression, a language. They were a connection to who he was. The dozens—maybe hundreds--of wondrous clay pots that cluttered and clamored about McReady's loft were a means to an end. But where, he had no idea.

Gerald's eyes moved back to the wheel and the clay and the moment. He was ready and moved his hands onto the lump, testing the density of the clay with the sensitivity of his fingertips.

There had been a girlfriend some years back, a nurse from Kansas City who'd invited herself over and, when she saw the pots, which were far fewer at the time, had asked to see Gerald throw one on the wheel. Gerald had mostly forgotten about her; too pushy he remembered. But he would not forget how she'd said that if he could make love to her like he did to that piece of clay, then he could have her any time he wanted. Too pushy, he thought again, and went back to the wheel that still spinning in perfect circles.

Something was wrong, though; he couldn't put himself into the clay, couldn't move his hands in and out and use his palms and his fingertips and his strength and his lightness of touch. Gerald McReady was in such trouble that this pot-to-be would never, could never, be anything but a reminder of the torment he felt when he shaped it. A pot built in this condition had no past and no future. It would only unhinge him to look at. He shut the motor off and watched the wheel slowly come to a halt, repressing the thought of what might happen if the Earth itself stopped spinning.

✳ ✳ ✳

It had started last week, not simply enough, with just a few questions by the hospital administrators. The incident had happened in the late spring. It was now early August. Timing around there had its own reasons that calendars never understood. This was the line of inquiry from the Denver VA administrators:

"Did you think this patient, Corporal Davis, was ready to be released?"

"It wasn't my decision, but I thought he was making good progress."

"Did you forward his release papers after they were signed by his attending doctor?"

"Yes, since I had the most contact with the patient, I made my notes, put them in the file, and sent them on to admin."

"Didn't you think it was odd that he was released before he was ready and the forms signed by a doctor who'd only seen him a few times?"

"Nothing surprises me around here."

"Orderly, please, this is a serious matter; please keep your personal opinions out of this inquiry."

"Fine. Yes, it seemed he could use some more time under observation, but we were understaffed as usual, and his father and...uh, uncle, were requesting that he be released into their care."

"Your comments about his condition as written in his file do not reflect your usual prudence and attention to detail, orderly. And don't you think it a bit odd that this seemingly rushed release coincided with the disappearance of the long-time resident patient known as, James Black or Blackie?"

"Gentleman, if you saw and did and felt what I do around here everyday, you would come to redefine your definition of odd. Yes, I wondered where Blackie went. Maybe you can shed some light on that as he was a fine helper and a friend."

"We have some interesting reports from other employees that put that friendship into question. And as for the early release of the Davis boy with the partially amputated foot, I must inform you that we received word from the U.S. Army base at Ft. Lewis where he was to be officially discharged upon verification of his wound, that he died of 'extended complications from his wound' three days ago.

Apparently, Mr. McReady, somebody let the kid go home too soon."

Gerald had held it together, he thought, never giving them anything to go on. No twitching of the eyes or tapping of the feet or blood rushing to his face. Acting was a part of good medicine. He had learned how to twist the truth into a kind of non-truth that came right up against being a lie. He knew how to tell the ones who only had a few days left to live just how great the rest of their life was going to be. He had been taught how to lie to men like Roberts and Wilcox simply by watching their mouths open and close. And pure survival had taught him that if he was to be able to tell any truth to the patients, he had to lie to the liars who ran the place. But he would never cross the indelibleness between him and who he was. That would make him just like the rest. And he would spin out of control.

With the word of Phin's death, Gerald had entered that white space where even the purposeful blurring of reality got lost in the shuffle. The "uncle" had been resourceful and Blackie was adept at manipulation, but McReady hadn't come up against anyone willing to take on the long-arm and the long-odds of the *system*. Oh, how he wanted to believe this small group from Florida was the first. Oh, how he wanted to know that Phin was alive and Blackie was safe, and that the Man had been duped as he had duped others. He was almost happy at the thought of somebody getting nailed at the VA for malpractice, a big fat civil suit by the family with names and dates and pictures and testimony and cameras and newsmen and a fat settlement. He'd indict himself if he could, just to drag a few down with him. He wouldn't lie since the truth would scream into the jury's ears and people would lose their jobs and that would be the means to an end he sought without really knowing. The world would keep on going.

Of course, it would never go down that way. But Gerald was proud that he'd help drown a few bad lifesavers. He had thrown himself on the grenade and could care less if Old Gray Eyes even came to his hanging, closed coffin and all.

He stood up and looked out the window. The rain had stopped and white cumulous rolled down the Front Range in shapes that children could lie on their backs and imagine were animals or ice cream cones. The wind had clocked around to the west. He put on some B.B. King and turned the wheel motor switch.

CHAPTER 21

YO, DOC

I got to know Blackie at first through the letters he'd sent to Gerald. Blackie had been working for Johnny at the waterbed factory in Lafayette, and thus came under his protection. And when Johnny would write me each week, forwarding those letters to a location that I thought I might roll by, I'd come to know the careful and intimate respect that Blackie and Gerald had for each other

—Phin

Hey Doc G:

Guess whoooo? Hey hey, my my, Doc Mac, it's Blackie the Black getting right back to you and your cloud. Not that you called because how could you, eh? I'm sitting here at this desk in the corner of Johnny "the Beautiful Corn" Cobb's sweet and delicious kitchen writing a letter to you, Gerald R. McReady, the profound order of orderlies in a house without order.

I'm tempering this communiqué to some degree, not knowing, check that—not trusting—the U.S. Govie to keep their damn paws outta your mail box. But there is much to say and, of course, I will do the words no justice within these short lines. But, man-who-should-be-doctor, you are as perceptive as a blind owl or the quiet, endearingly cute, eighth-grade girl who always sat in the back row—you will decode the message as it is meant to be.

I am safe. I am alive. Hot damn, G-Man, I'm on my way back to the real world, ready, willing, and able to willfully enable those who I can, ready to take on the slings that have been shot through our hearts. I will spare you the DSM-II definitions. When I was interred at the VA, I thought that *non-descript neuroses with psychotic tendencies* was a way of saying, "this guy needs help but we don't know how to give it to him." Now that I am younger-than and so much-saner than before, I know it can mean many things. I can say that essentially it is a *dishonest* way of saying that this guy needs help and we don't have a clue as to how to give it to him.

I know this sounds cylindrical, cyclical, and mostly cynical, but hey Ger, Houdini of my soul, I'm more than just a wee bit bitter. But that's enough about me. What about you, what do you think of me?

I imagine that you are still at the VA, the perfect plausible placidity that placates. And if I know you, even as you help pry loose those greasy souls, Wilcox and Roberts, who needed a greased exit—you—well, I'd bet G. Gordon Liddy's ego that your soul is still lost in the shuffle letting someone's else's body drive your own dream.

If you feel any heat from the J. Edgar types down the hall, across the way, far and away from the darkened night shapes of mangled men who've been manipulated, castrated of their mental state, and debilitated of late...let me know.

You know that Blackie always kept a hole card or two.

Mr. John W. Cobb offers his salutations from this unique locale in which he has ensconced his body and commercial enterprise. He says he owes you, but that something of a higher order will be paying his debt. The guy talks more riddle-ishly than I do, though in a willful contract with his will. But I've come to dig the cat. He's the real deal, G.

Now, I must say that the region here offers it own particular form of cultural studies. The intelligence pendulum we find here is swung more toward the bayou than the book, the essential than the ethereal. I like the folks because when you call them folks, the assignment fits. It's more generic, more folkloric, than specific. It is like, in a Pogoian way, meeting the real people, and they are us.

Johnny has me working in the factory where we make the wood frames for the waterbeds. He had me sleep on one for a week before he would hire me; just wanted me to be able to talk the talk, he said; to sleep the deep without a wakeful peep. But if I would've gotten seasick and regurgitated all over his spare room floor and the carpet he said was a gift from, "just a girl from India I met one day," I doubted I would've gotten the job. The factory reminds me of the hospital, in a diametric way, of course; certainly, it's staffed with enough vets. It's not an X but a Y. We ask each other why and words do the work of meds.

People talk of the war, but not the way they did in the hospital. We speak of it in the present because it is still in us. Nobody hides it under the bed, within the meds, or behind the medulla oblongata. It's not quite realism, as you might think, and metaphors are rarely used. It's somewhere between sorrow and acceptance, with a healthy dose of guilt added in. There is anger, yes, but its release is governed in fits and spurt, as is the revenge. I would say it's similar to having your little sister murdered by some thugs when you were too small to do anything about it, let alone act on the tragedy. And you grew up knowing and living that particular form of scar. People said *there goes the kid whose sister was kidnapped, shot in the head, and buried out in the woods off of Highway 66*. You adapted, did the best you could and thought about her when you weren't repressing the thought. In your braver and angrier moments, or maybe when the teacher yelled at you for something you didn't do, you imagined growing up and learning how to fight, how to defend yourself, maybe how to hurt someone. And then when your coach got mad at you for missing a short hopper at third base and it cost the team the win, you'd stand in the locker room shower, no one willing to talk to you, the hot water hitting the scruff of your tight shoulders and dripping down to the fresh new scruff of hair above your balls and the image of your little sister on Christmas morning with loud girlie *hee-hees* coming too close to the sound of what must have been *please, please, don't*, a deep haunting plead with her killers before they shot her...and the coach says, "McReady, let's go pretty boy. I want to get out of here and forget about this damn game." And you turn the water off but are confused by the handles and the water is scalding on your back and suddenly your thoughts are quick and precise and very, very clear—you must find and kill your sister's murderers. And a hardball of soap, high and fast, goes through the coach's window.

The point is, Doc Gerald, no matter where you go, people who did the war are never very far from doing it again, in forms that are socially acceptable and not. We are marked men, remarkably tainted; we are damaged goods that nobody wants to claim in their inventory. And most of what we have as a way out is each other. Someday the truth will come and people will ask, "How the hell did we let that hap-hap-happen?" Especially, when the groovy kids back home on college campuses were making other anti-war hap-hap-happenings.

Now, what about the Kid Phin? I refuse to believe he's gone back to the earth, which already took his piggy-wiggys. Don't call. I don't trust the lines. Besides, I'm not sure where the phone is located.

Some days I don't trust myself. But today is a good day. How are your days, old friend?

—Blackie here, gone now. Blacked out for now.

✳ ✳ ✳

Blackie:

Good to hear from you. Amazing, actually. I've been in the dark, the black about you, Blackie. I had a feeling Mr. Cobb would help set you free; and it's a long path, little brother, a path I assume Mr. Cobb has traversed. You are in good hands.

I'll get right to it. Things are hot here at the VA. I've been interrogated several times about the coincidences and accidents that had you and the patient, Phin Davis, disappear on the same day. I don't think the Man would go so far as to do a wire tap or steal mail over this; that's a bit of paranoia that you might be allowed. I don't think they mind "losing" a diagnosed schizophrenic—they'd say you just walked out the door one day and disappeared into the fold—unless there was pressure from family members wondering how that happened. But you seem to have covered that bit of your past well enough, or at least distorted it enough, that it would be too much work for admin to mess with.

However, there is pressure being brought to bear on Roberts and Wilcox. Admin found some of the thinly veiled clues you left for them regarding the "activities" of these two and R and W are none too happy with you. I am watching them closely, Blackie, but I'd keep an eye skinned. As you've seen all too well, when men are backed into corners they can be unpredictable. Rage and ignorance are double-edged swords, my little friend; when wielded, many are cut, most of them deep.

I must tell you that there were reports that the Davis boy died from septic shock or some such bullshit. But that ain't likely five months post injury. Well, what can I say? I can't seem to distinguish the map from the territory. Either way, he's gone, at least for awhile. When admin informed me of this, they provided a copy of the death certificate sent up from Ft. Lewis, perhaps to validate their inquiries, but more likely to see if it stirred a reaction in me. But it wasn't hard, future professor Blackie; I liked the kid and his kin, but I didn't know him that well. Death I can deal with. Dishonesty no, unless we are expropriating the expropriators.

Or maybe you were right about the kid's records having deep holes in them; like he didn't exist to begin with and when he showed up in their hospital as a real body with real dog tags and a real war wound, it confused them. So when he died and a real coroner from a town that is known to exist on most maps says the boy is dead, well, it was a relief to them. *"Close the file. Let's go get some coffee. Boy, when will this war really be over?"*

Now, if he did die of infection, I'd have to say something unpredictable happened to his wound, something profound and tragic and I would shoulder most of the blame. But I wouldn't take it personally. How could I, Blackie? How could I go on doing what good can be done with the access that I have if I took everything personally? I keep the deflector shield up all the time. Sometimes the thought of not giving a fuck mocks me. Suppose I was to really care? Then where would I be? There are enough Wilcox-type "wardens" around here who pretend, who embrace, the illusion of patient care. My distortion has meaning.

Geez, why am I telling you all this stuff? You're supposed to be the crazy one who can't seem to make anything out of the boney sinew tossed up by this world. I do think that we will see the Davis boy again, in this world or the one come after it. If I killed him by facilitating his early exit, I will know sooner or later and will pay the consequences...in this world or the one come after.

Good to hear from you. Regards to Mr. Cobb. Please keep me informed.

—Gerald

Hey Gerald,

Wow, I don't think I've ever called you that. I do hope the world of the sane won't make me a boring guy. Will you promise to tell me if I am boring, Gerald? So that I might try to throw a little sand into whatever psycho-social machine is lubricating my return and I can be gritty and goofy again? Swear to it now, cross your heart. Better yet...pinky swear.

I'm still here with the Big Black Uncle, screwing hippy beds together, doing research, and chipping away at my dissertation so that when and if I can re-enter the world in some way that is legal-worthy enough for the government and land that job bending and shaping the minds of America— covertly detailing my own saga in the process—then I will be armed with the scholarship to do so. Blackie is thinking about taking all his skills in manipulation gleaned from his tenure at the VA and reversing the pendulum. That's right young Doc G-McCree; I'm so damn smart and so damn smooth I'll have high six-figure grant money coming into whatever college that bids the highest for my highly sought-after skills. All before they figure out that I was crazy but not insane, not kilt all the way, as the cat on *Rawhide* says, but I rose up from the dead like a few other tormented geniuses have done. If I pull it off, I'm in good company. Won't even alter my ear lobe. Cuz I'm a "rollin', rollin', rollin'." Double pinky swear.

Art. I was thinking about your art after I heard from you last. That's right, I know about the pots. No way to keep a secret from the Blackster. I got you figured, Doc, the patient treating the physician. Okay, so you aren't the real MD or an RN or a PA, heck, GM—the only letters assigned to you are the those of your employer, the VA, where the patients are mostly a form of physical and mental POW. You tried to help someone out and the Man nailed your ass and now look at you, an orderly at some internment camp-come-hospital when you should have a nice private practice in some plush homogenous neighborhood like Newport Beach or Tampa Bay where you could pull down some long dough by treating a few coughs and the flu and dispensing medications that the patients don't need, but make money for the drug manufacturers, and they kick some back to you in the form of "consulting fees" and lecture gigs in Hawaii and Australia where your trophy wife with the big tits and 2.3 kids can soak up the sun and read trashy romance novels while working on her skin cancer so that some plastic surgeon can fix her face when she thinks that you've fallen for your lovely new secretary.

But that isn't you, now is it, Gerald?

No, you make clay pots that no one sees. Not even yourself. And you heal people, you make them feel better. You're a damn Captain Kangaroo for soldiers. No, Gerald, you might never have an MD after your name, but your function in life is to cheat death by creating a form of immortality. Your life is validated and contextually bound by how you perceive its value, your relative goals, the needs you fulfill, the way you talk to the men who come back from Vietnam sans a limb or two and who are angry and beg you to finish off what the Nam began for them—to fucking take them out. And what do you do, Orderly McCready, whose fat cat father fucked him over? You make people feel better. Sometimes it lasts, others times it doesn't. And then you go home to your lonely loft at night and put on Dizzy Gillespie and Charlie Bird and you shape clay pots on a wheel, pots in as many sizes and shapes as the men who you treat. The only difference is that while some of the men get better and some don't and too many to count are released and get swallowed up by the world but live forever with the jungle virus of having been in-country, your pots hide out in the darkness—damn lonely, empty pots—killing time, as Thoreau said, without injuring eternity.

But admit it G, you write me letters about the world after this one when you're hiding out inside dozens of clay pots molded by your own hand. Maybe those pots are the hands of time and each one marks something, which not even you can identify. Your humility and service to mankind has become its own virtue. And if you ask me, which no one ever will unless this whole thing goes upside down and I'm put under oath where Blackie can really turn the system on its collective, distrustful ear, I think it's killing you the same as the fear was killing me.

Listen carefully, Doc. I think you need to jump, jump, just jump inside those pots of yours for awhile and see what's inside. You may need to smash some and you may need to plant some with flowers and others with deadly nightshade. If you don't, slowly, but assuredly...well, you go ahead and sit before your only candle. And Johnny and I will come to your funeral when the wick falters. Because, Shaman Gerald, what you possess is the last true and honest currency of any human value—the love and pain between those in need and those who give relief.

You know, G, this Blackie is getting smarter every day, even surrounded by these beautiful, thick rednecks I'm coming to love. You won't look the same in that coffin, won't be as effective either. And you couldn't talk back to the worthless assholes at the VA. It would be a great funeral though. We'd cry and tell stories and drink too much at your expense.

I'd rather you went searching for genies in bottles. Johnny says hi.

—Blackie

P.S. Phin Davis isn't dead. More later.

✳ ✳ ✳

Blackie:

Well, well, I can hear a change in you, a shift of epic proportion. Like the gorilla who escaped from the zoo, put on a three-piece suit, and testified before the Senate subcommittee on animal rights before sneaking back in to unlock all the cages; you have indeed risen from someplace. I liked you when you were nuts. I have a feeling that we'll get along fine as you shed labels and evolve into whatever form of animal you are meant to be. Somehow, this Cobb character seems to be having an affect on you. Or maybe it's the hippy beds. Do you think they would cure me of the inadequacies you attest to in your last letter? You make me laugh, little brother; you make me laugh and then I cry.

And then I make pots.

Yesterday, I almost broke one; almost threw it against the wall. The anger has been building, Blackie. You know about that. There are two kinds of angry people: the ones in the post office line who are late for an appointment and there's only one counter open and they keep looking at their watch and, when it's their turn, they say something derogatory to the postman, buy a roll of stamps, walk away, and write a few letters to the right people. The other kind is the postman who has to take all these angry people's anger for ten years and smile and say they are understaffed and he agrees there should be more counters open, *you know, budget cuts and all*. But one day a very angry and very unlucky person vents on the postman and the postman reaches into his mail pouch and pulls out a Glock 9 and puts six bullets in the customer, sets the gun down, and calls out, "Next."

Blackie, you are the customer. I am the postman. And I don't like it one bit.

Wilcox was fired yesterday and Roberts was put on administrative leave pending further investigation. Your buddy Willie Wilcox cornered me and said I was involved in this and I said what the hell are you taking about, I'm too busy doing my job because people like you aren't. The guy wanted to hit me so bad it must've hurt, but the MPs were right there to escort him to the door and he said, "I'll get you and your little psycho friend," and I said,"Bring it on you worthless cheating asshole," which made even the stoic MPs laugh because Wilcox outweighs me by sixty pounds.

Blackie, later that day I was telling the story to a three-tour marine while I was pulling bits of shrapnel out of his ass as they rose to the surface over the last two weeks of trying. I had to vent somewhere; my pots weren't listening. He'd told me he'd help me out but he was somewhat indisposed at the moment. When I went to my locker before leaving last night, there was a little cardboard box wrapped up in medical tape with a note that said, "For that day...because metal rises out of assholes in different forms." The marine's name is DuPuis, Lorenzo Dupuis, and he says he's from Lafayette, same joint you're hanging out in. He's going home in a few weeks and I told him to look you up. I'm sure he will, Blackie. This guy is the type that would drive thirty miles back to a store if they gave him too much change for a Coke. He told me he killed four NVA one afternoon, not because he had to or wanted to, but because he had told a young kid who was short on time that he'd watch his ass so he could get home on the outside of a plastic bag. You know how we hear all these stories in this place? This one has teeth, little brother. And he thinks I'm Jesus of Nazareth because I pulled some lead from his ass.

That package he left for me...I opened it after I got home that night and had put on some Vince Guaraldi. Inside was a .45mm semi-automatic, army issue, serial number ground off. Blackie, I haven't been in a fight since fifth grade.

Like I said, I almost broke a pot against the wall. The postman in me riseth. And when I dreamt last night, I was carrying the gun on patrol. It was in my hand. It felt good, cold and hard against my palm; like it belonged there, like it had been there a long time. I was in the middle of the squad, as usual. We were still at the number five and just as we started to climb out of the jungle up a steep ridge where the sun would dry our fungus and firing pins and heat our jungled-spirits, we took fire and the column split into two halves with me forced to make a choice. The rear pair retreated for cover and regrouped before deciding their plan of attack. The guys in front, including the LT, hit the ground hard, but had their M-16s blasting over the low brush before they knew where they were aiming or what at. And me, I was all alone with my med kit and newly-manned malfeasance and that metal-gray .45mm molded to my hand, that lovely steel that had a mind of its own, a Ouiji Board weapon that danced and momentarily waved while bullets zipped by my head, and I froze in time and space, unable to decide because the decision wasn't mine to make.

Just before I woke up, the gun was pointed at my father's head, a head that was attached to my body. And we were having target practice on my clay pots.

You'll hear from the Dupuis kid.

Blackie, what news of the Davis kid? Am assuming the word came up from his father through Mr. Cobb. Beautiful thing it would be, to die and go on with the reification of your life. Only thing better than beating the Man is getting a second chance to beat him again. Yeah, second chances are good things.

—Gerald

CHAPTER 22

LUBBOCK, TEXAS, FALL 1973

I don't know how far I'm going to have to go, to see my own self or to hear my own voice.

—Woody Guthrie

Some things, I'm not good at. I'm not good at noon. I'm not good at lying. I've never been able to balance Pa's checkbook when he asks for help, and I'm not too likely to stick around bad people.

Other things, I can get the job done. I'm good at clouds, I'm good with words—my voice is frightening to some—but I'm not afraid to sing in front of a stranger; just belt it out. And I'm good at night. Yes, me and night, we're pals. I wasn't particularly fond of the Nam nights, but they didn't turn me inside out like they did to others.

My big sister, Gillie, she wasn't afraid of much a'tall. But sometimes she'd get frightened when we were young and the noises of the night would swirl and spin through the Florida pines around our trailer. I'd be lying there, still in my street clothes, just thinking on things of the day and I could tell she was awake, stirring around what might trouble her like a dog doing circles before it lies down.

"Hey, Gillie," I'd pretend I was cool but being much older as she was, she owned me. Still does, in a way. "You want me to go have a look around? I still have my school jeans on."

She'd say, "Nah, reckon it's just the wind coming off the Gulf, talkin' to the sky. Eh, Phin? Go to sleep. I'm all right."

But sometimes she wasn't and I'd get up like I was going to the bathroom and sneak out the back, take our big shepard we called Luke and our old mutt Caleb, that seemed to be equal parts wolf and poodle—but who would ever know—depending on what he had to eat that day, and I'd walk around hardly scared, reminding myself that nobody short of an escaped convict or one of Pa's drunken fishing buddies tossed out of their houses by a begrudged spouse would be coming around our parcel after dark.

I knew sis would be lying in there, listening to us ramble around the yard, relaxing finally, not because an eight-year-old boy would kick the shit out of the boogie man, but because he cared enough to go out and do so. She'd probably be asleep by the time I got back. So I'd let them dogs wander off into the brush and just be dogs doing dog things, and I'd sit down in the chair that Pa had made out of longleaf pines, just kinda melting into those smooth barkless limbs. Then I'd let the night have me for awhile. Even at eight years old, the night, it never shook me much. They used to say the VC owned the night, but I took exception to that. Parts of a day, even if it's dark, ain't meant to be owned. Still, even when I was a young'n trying to be the Great Protector of my older sister, I'd cross any man's fence to hunt down an intruder. I was supposed to be fighting black pajama-wearing kids from a country I couldn't pronounce and I kept thinking that what if my own kids, if'n I had them thirty years from now, were asked to fight kids from our commiserating countries like Iran and Iraq and Afghanistan?

That'd be like kissing and killing your own sister.

And that's how I earned respect in the Nam, simply because I had equal relationships with the moon and sun. And if I shot a few focused rounds in-country, I was never very sure which side was doing the sending and receiving of lead bullets. Other times, I think I was meaner as a kid with no hair on his balls than I was as an adult with deathly anger who'd held them same balls up as a shield against his own mortality.

When you reach that existential point, you can either swallow the tequila worm or go home to your mama. Isn't much difference when you think 'bout it.

One time I was lying out on the back grass, smelling the fresh dew on the mossy lawn mixed with newer resin from Pa's work shed, making up stories about the pictures I saw in the stars. It was stuff like, if one group of stars looked like a diamond and another looked like a shoe, I'd conjure up a tale about a girl who had so much money she covered the outside of her diamonds with old leather shoe soles. Counterintuitive kinda stuff that singers like Paul Simon might write a song about.

Well, one night it must've been coming up on ten or eleven o'clock, well past bedtime for a little guy on a school night, and Pa walked out to catch some of his own night and damn near tripped on me.

"Holy smoke, Phin! What in a good God's name you doing out here? I thought you were asleep. You best not let Ma catch you out here this time a'night."

I knew as long as I was honest, I wouldn't get in trouble. Pa had made that clear from the time my ears started to work.

"I was just thinking about the night, Pa; how most people are afraid of it 'cuz they don't understand it. It's really no different than the day, exceptin' you can't see as well with your eyes. But I been practicing a bit and I think you can learn to see with other things. You think there's any truth to that, Pa? I asked Dickey about it but he said the boogeyman don't come out during the day."

He looked at me for a second, did that little tic-toc with his head, and then he just laid down next to me, put his big hands under his head for a pillow and chuckled to himself.

Pa was quiet for a spell, though I could swear I heard his mind working, the gears meshing and grinding and spinning and finally spitting out a fitting answer. He reached over and pulled me to his chest and said, "Yeah, Phin, I think you're onto something, especially the part about seeing without eyes. For me though," he said, while looking over his shoulder to see if Ma was around, "the night is a woman, full of intrigue, mystery, sometimes beauty, sometimes danger, and just when you get too comfortable in it, the sun comes up and bites you on the ass. Someday that might make sense to you."

Well, I understood the part about intrigue and mystery (after I looked them up in the dictionary at school the next morning), but the "getting too comfortable" part seemed confusing.

"Pa," I asked him the next day, "Mama ever bite you on the ass?"

He laughed and said no because my mama is a beautiful sunset, with all the qualities of both day and night.

✳ ✳ ✳

That night was becoming brighter as I made my way on the bike along a route headed toward Lubbock, Texas. The moon climbed the sky like a ladder, taking center stage from the stars and sending them to rest while tossing light to night critters looking for food, for a place to sleep, or for the odd traveler like me moving through the countryside. It seemed that I was bent on and lured west for a thousand reasons, none of which I could think of at that moment.

Sometime after midnight well, actually I wasn't sure it was after midnight, not owning a watch and all, but I swear, true to all Texan stereotypes, that a county border sign signifying some invisible line where a different set of rules applied on either side stood as big as a highway billboard. It was full of shotgun holes, too, not that I ever remember seeing one that wasn't.

I got off my bike there and sat down, just leaning up against the signpost on the side of the road resting my legs, tossing a few rocks into the ditch, letting my mind roll forward into Lubbock. Riding a bike was different, slower; no one to talk to, but the field of vision was good. I wondered how Big Al was getting along with the dogs. But I was more worried about him than the dogs. They'd do just fine and I'd return for them when I could. And I hoped both Al and the dogs would forgive me for the absence.

I wondered if it would be like this—whenever I was about to open a new page in my travels forward, some inexplicable force would pull me back. I felt like I was going to be starting a series of jigsaw puzzles in a hundred rooms of my past. But none would ever be finished; some left with half a face, maybe one eye, or a tree that looked like the top was just shot off. Pieces were scattered on the table or worse yet, lost to some black hole that eats crucial corner pieces or the horizon line where earth and sky meet on a single, funny edged piece of cardboard.

There was this one piece of a *voice* that seemed to be pleading with me to come back and finish a few puzzles. But something in my gut told me they would all come together by going forward. Maybe that's why my pop had turned me loose and took off to fish. We weren't running away, just running so that we wouldn't get sucked backwards—like swimming upstream in a river just hard enough so that you stayed in one place, just a momentary eddy, constant enough to know that the water around you was never exactly the same. And never could be again. Same as it ever was.

So I kept moving, starting new puzzles in hope I'd find a piece in some new box that would replace a lost one from years ago. And much of the time I moved under the moon's blanket.

I had a thought in hindsight, a found piece maybe, while sitting under that road sign in the middle of the night, my whole material life tied with twine to a bicycle that was propped up on a split-rail fence because the kickstand, the only real thing on a work-a-day bike that was worth anything, didn't work...this sucks. And hell, the bike didn't even have a real light.

The VC never had lights. They slept late into the sultry morning when the moon was full. The night was more than their friend; it was their partner, their protective lover, their means, method, and *motus operandi*. And it was how they killed 58,220 (But who's counting?) boys who should have been home working in hardware stores, studying college biology, and making out with their girlfriends in a safer night where all you had to fear were bored cops and unwanted pregnancy. Someone told me a few months ago that nearly three quarters of the men who served in Vietnam were from middle and lower-income families. And he said that over one-half of those killed weren't even twenty-one years old. I believed his numbers because I lived with those numbers.

We were told that it was part of the Cold War. But everything in the Nam was hot, even when the nights were cold. There were times on night patrol when some of the guys were so scared they pissed their pants and didn't even know it; wouldn't believe it if you showed them. In time, with some kind of luck that no one could explain, they would've been rid of the war, back working on their Chevys in the yard, sneaking just enough of their pa's Jack Daniel so he wouldn't notice and, Lord willing, copping a feel on Saturday night. But lots just ended up stuck in that dusky fear that haunts the muddy fog between night and day.

The ones that shipped in already a little fucked up—an abusive father, a rough neighborhood, under five feet eight— they were the ones who adapted best; they were the ones who already had practice in feeling nothing. Charlie was not an enemy to them. He was nothing at all, just another thing to vent their hatred on. Bullies didn't do so well. But the bullied, at least they stood a chance.

Some of them were from impoverished houses and hoods that came alive after dark. An M-16 or M 50-charged firefight was just another daring, ugly game; sort of like running your trucks at each other down a single-lane dirt levy, the last one to chicken-out drives into the ditch. The difference was, though, after a day or a month in-country, they knew they could never make sense of it; never explain it to their folks, their girlfriends and their parole officers. It was like being in the witness protection program and not even being able to bare witness.

The intelligent, sensitive ones like Blackie were lucky if they came home only slightly neurotic. The smart ones, like Dickey, figured out how to keep away from the war altogether, but stay out of jail all the same. The really fucked up guys became heroes.

I'm not sure if my relationship with the dark had helped bring me home in mostly one piece, or if it had sent me there in the first place. I suppose it was Gillie...and me trying to protect her from the boogeyman. A man can do some strange things at eight or eighteen or twenty-eight years old that don't wash off with soap.

If I knew anything at all, it was the fact that I was sitting there under that county line sign, rubbing what was left of my right foot, my toes fertilizing some bamboo just below the DMZ courtesy of a "toe popper," a land mine that pops up like a child's jack-in-the-box and bites off a piece of flesh like a serpent or a skill saw.

My half of a foot, it worked okay most of the time, but it looked awfully strange. You would think that toes wouldn't make that much difference either in looks or performance. But they do. It reminded me of a foot on a G.I. Joe doll where the mold in which they are created isn't detailed enough to create toes that are separate—just little indents on top of the foot to denote where the toes would actually separate if they were real toes and this was a real fighting doll.

Sitting here, thinking about stupid things like the war and dolls, a hint of remorse swarming in, I did what I had always done when my mind started to race and splinter: I laid on my back and looked at the sky. And wondered. I was wondering if it was true that when people died they became stars in the sky. My toes wouldn't grow back like a bum fingernail does, but I was sure hoping all this traveling and thinking and reading and talking would reconnect me with the pieces of my soul that were floating around my head like an old dead catfish that can't decide to float to the surface or just stay on the mucky bottom, still plain dead.

And even if I was okay with the night, I always thought that my life would sort of just revolve around the sun. Get up with it. Work out under it. Watch it go down after supper. And get up with it the next day. There was a mutual order to that, like having a beer as partner when the sun left the sky each day, knowing she'd be back the next day. There was a thin layer of wild bramble grass not far from the road and I found a spot that looked thick enough, took off my jacket to use as a minor barrier against the odd scorpion wanting to warm himself by crawling up my sleeve, and stretched my body against that Texas earth. The night was warm, though, it being late summer and all, and I was quite comfortable. I figured I was intruding on the bug's home anyways.

Soon enough I forgot the war and Charlie and G.I. Joe feet and old puzzles left unfinished. I focused on the sky, imagining myself having a conversation with God, not a prayer where I was asking Him for something or saying thank you for the food on the table, but a real low-key, honest talk—just a couple of guys sitting at the bar yakking away. Only difference was, one of them was God and the other was me.

I fell asleep with that thought and dreamt about me and God buying each other cold draughts, figuring out the world's problems. But in my dream, I knew that God already knew all the answers. And he knew that I knew. But in typical God-fashion, he just let me go on proposing this and asking that, like we were buds coming from the same place, a couple of old dogs trying to make some sense of the craziness, and maybe the beauty in which we existed.

God was letting me do most of the talking, probably because I seemed to be answering my own questions. I think that's what He wanted though: me to figure it out with a few tools, a little subtle guidance on the count of His part. I reckon there's a heap of that "you got to figure it out" stuff in the Bible, along with some good tales, at least after you get through the part in the beginning where they make God out to be some hard-ass dude who'd zap you for eating the wrong fruit, stone you to death for being wired gay. The preachers and politicians and single-minded types who take that literally are reading stuff into the Bible instead of taking out its message, if you ask me.

"Why do we hurt sometimes? How come there are bad people? Why did you take my sister when she was so young? I think I have an idea, God, but I just wanted to run it by you. Hey you need another beer?"

In the end though, I didn't ask Him any of those youthful queries. Nope, only two requests. I asked God if He would take care of my Pa and Ma and Johnny Cobb as they aged on, and God said He would. Then, as an afterthought, I asked Him if he knew where I was supposed to be heading. Well, He looked at me for a long time and I felt a strange peace come over me, one that I hadn't known in many years. Then, while reaching into a leather pouch and pulling out an ancient-looking gold piece that he flipped to the bartender, who looked bewildered at first and then smiled and said, "Much obliged," God pushed his chair away from the bar and said that I was headed in the right direction; that I would know when I got there.

I tried to follow Him out the door, but the bartender had ahold of my hand and kept asking me if I was alive and was my name Phin Davis. Then I woke up and the bartender had morphed into a very tall, thin man with deep, deep crow's feet radiating out from each of his well-set brown eyes like rays from the sun. He wore a white cowboy hat, yellowed from the elements and stained from years of adjusting it with dirty earthen-coated fingers. His hair was jet-black, as thick as August straw and pulled back in a long pony tail behind his ears, which, on the right, hung one sliver earring in the shape of a howling coyote. He had one hand on my wrist, apparently checking for a pulse or something, and was gently shaking my shoulder with the other, asking me if I was alive and what my name was, as if the two were relevant to each other.

When sleep finally left me and my senses returned, I told this man that yes, I was alive but he could call me anything he thought fit for a guy whom he found thirty miles due east of Lubbock, asleep in a field, his life tied to a bike propped up against a wooden split-rail fence. This man sat back on his haunches and let out a laugh that shook the morning fog from my head.

"Well I'll be a clock with no hands. You're a card, ain't ya? Not much to look at it, but if you're a friend of Johnny Cobb's you can sleep in this field all day long and I'll tell the county to give you a wide birth when they trim the road's shoulder. Might suggest you tuck that field of hair coming out from your head up under a cap or something though. Looks like it could be harvested for profit." His voice was low and rough, like an old blues singer or a man who had smoked all his life.

"The name's Greer," he continued, "Mike Greer. Al from the feed store called last night, said I best keep an eye skinned for some honky with long, blonde, kinky hair that looked like a bottlebrush plant run amok. Said you'd be riding your bike on the highway. Wanted me to tell you that your dogs had been asking about you, too. Al is sort of a Dr. Doolittle type, if you know what I mean. Hey, you want a lift or you want to be a hero and ride that bike the rest of the way into town?"

I stood up, brushed some weeds from my jeans and stuck out my hand.

"Name's Phin. Friends call me Phin. Spoke to you yesterday from Al's."

Greer took my hand, shook it and leaned foreword, looking into my eyes. At first, I thought he was looking past me, but then I noticed that his eyes seem to work independently of each other, like he could focus on a subject and scan the horizon at the same time. A slow smile came over him, his teeth opening to the rising sun like a garage door, a half-dozen gold covered molars mirrored the glare in my face. It was not a reflection as much as it was a reminder. I was still here, alive, air going into my lungs and coming back out again, a heart beating somewhere inside my chest, a head, bloodied in the past, but unbowed.

Greer put my bike in the bed of his '56 Chevy Stepside truck, placed a well-worn but clean boot on the running board, and climbed into his side. I watched him as he motioned for me to follow, riding shotgun, liking this man as he inserted an old eight-track of José Feliciano in the dash. Still burning in the rusty ashtray was a thin, tightly rolled cigarette.

I got in, took his offer of a long hit on the smoke, realized it was *special blend,* and chased it with a can of ice-cold Lone Star beer that Greer shoved my way. I closed my eyes, searched what little was left of the darkness—the waning night for some element of security, some truth to my dream, some confirmation of my Man at the bar—while Greer sang back-up to José. The sun finally poked her head up over a sea of soybeans and I took another long drag on the joint, held it, and then blew the smoke out the cracked window, chiming in with Greer at the top of my lungs. The gears ground, the smell of alfalfa and soy and weed wafted through the cab of the old pickup, a half-blind man telling me I couldn't get much higher and me knowing it was all true. Yeah, I was in the right place.

The road rolled under us and things got quiet. I felt like saying something but couldn't think of anything. Or maybe my lips just weren't working at the moment. We seemed to be going very, very slow and I asked Mike what our speed was, hoping to blame the effect on the smoke. He didn't look at the speedometer; just drifted to the middle of the road, pulled back a piece of plywood that served as a floorboard, counted the white lines as they rushed by, and looked at the second hand on his old military styled watch. His brow furled as if mentally doing the math in his head.

"Reckon were doing close to fifty, depending on how much the county road workers had been drinking the last time they painted them lines."

"That true?" I asked

"Nah. But it sounds good, don't it?"

I nodded and could see why Johnny had put me in touch with Greer.

"Johnny Cobb tells me you read a bit".

"Books you mean? Reckon, when I find time."

Greer reached for his sunglasses in the glove box, relit the joint that had gone out, and replaced José with a Buddy Holly tape, steering the truck with his knees in the process.

"The farm equipment biz ain't exactly a license to print money these days. Takes a lot of my time. Shoulda bought me a liquor store like my dad told me to. People drink when times is bad. And people drink when times are good. Heard you're a bit of a consumer of words yourself."

Ah ha, I thought. He played his cards too early, slipped out of the vernacular too soon.

"Well, I've been on the road apiece so I've had the time, but I left what I had in my van and with Al, 'cepting for this Tolstoy anthology I brought for you."

"Amazing how many good words came out of old Russia. Ain't it?

"Did the first shift over there, huh?" I switched gears purposely on him, but he must've known I was referring to his early tour in Vietnam.

"Oh yeah," he said with no passion in his voice. "Almost forgot. And you worked the late innings."

"I do my best not to keep it front and center. But it's never very far."

"No doubt. Sometimes it's better to fill the heart with a struggle of any kind, so long as it is simple and productive. Yep," Greer mumbled while steering the truck with his knees and tapping to a Buddy tune, "one must believe that somewhere, Sisyphus is happy."

Oh shit, I thought. The bastard's read Camus. I needed to throw him off track with an original.

"You ever think that you don't have to know what the meaning of life is to know that life has meaning?"

Greer scratched his stubbly chin a bit, his mind searching fast and hard for the author, frustrated that it wasn't coming up quick. "What kinda New Age, hippy mumbo-jumbo is that shit?" He called me out but not all the way.

I tried to redirect quickly, feeling bad that I had unearthed something I had no right unearthing. "You married? Got a girlfriend?"

"Yep," both, since you asked. But not at the same time.

I laughed, smiling with a sense of relief as I looked out the window at the unpaved sky and thought of where I needed to be after Lubbock, about old loves, new friends, new loyalties, old commitments. About meaning.

It was quiet again, except for the music as the outskirts of Lubbock loomed up ahead. I was using my dreads as a pillow and was almost asleep when the voice came from across the wide bench seat through the smoky cab.

"You know, Phin, I knew Buddy when he was coming up. Nice kid. Couldn't see shit. Bad eyes. Big damn soul, though.

Kid could carry a note though five or six measures, lungs meant for singing and...."

Then the voice was gone as Greer ended his sentence right in the middle. Nothing but wheat, tobacco, and soy as far as the eye could see, like when you got to the end of the earth and began to fall over the side.

"You ain't getting sentimental on me are you," I joked. "You know, 'the day the music died' and all that shit? Because sentimentality is only sentiment that rubs you the wrong way".

"Oh please, Somerset. You think I'm as uneducated as I look?"

"You think I came to Lubbock to weld your cotton gins?

"I bow my head. Ashes to ashes."

"Dust to fucking dust. You got anymore of this stuff?

"Hey, you remember that old movie *'Reefer Madness?'* "

"Cult movies for two hundred, please," I said while pulling back that plywood floorboard to watch the white center lines point us into town.

CHAPTER 23

JESSICA

The girl looked up from her math book, arcing a gaze into Mike Greer's face, and returned to the problem, focused. His daughter's eyes then began to sweep circles from the page to her father's wrinkling brow as his lips moved in silent contemplation, across the room to me, and back to the page. Twirling one long braid of hair in her left hand, a pencil tapping out a tune in the right, she seemed to possess a built-in happiness. Just a kid, I thought, an eleven-year-old who could somehow see across the moment. But something wasn't clicking and I couldn't place the misfire.

I studied those brown eyes of hers, the ones that held her father's presence in their soft grip, the ones that projected some sort of hot-wired compassion. If Mike Greer felt it, he never let on—just burrowed further into the tattered textbook.

"Dang, Jessie, I was just starting to get the hang of this new math until they started using words like 'come-and-nominate her.' " He turned to me and winked.

"Dad, that's common denom..., oh shoots, you did it again."

Laughing, Greer seemed proud that he had deflected his confusion with humor, let the raw skin of the earth show as he leaned back in his chair and allowed his dry and cracked lips to show teeth that had been broken by fists and windshields and the clinch of hard life.

Melting my way into the old La-Z-Boy, struggling with the one rebellious spring intent on doing harm to my eighth vertebrae, I took stock in Jessica Greer. Not quite tall for her age, lanky, with braided pigtails bleached the color of rum and orange juice by the Texas sun.

Jessica got up from the table and walked to the little radio sitting on the windowsill, a coat hanger giving it reception "all the way to Houston City," she chirped proudly. Credence Clearwater's "Proud Mary" was playing and her pigtails swooping and swishing like a cow's tail. She asked me what kind of music I liked.

"Loud," I told her, trying a little too hard to impress.

"Well, we got both kinds of music here in Lubbock," she said off-handedly. "Country *and* western."

Mike wrinkled up his nose a bit. "That was weak, Jess. I'm sure our guest has heard the cliché. No points for that one." He walked to the fridge and pulled three beers, then added, "If you want Mr. Davis to play, you have to tell him the rules."

I wanted to have a look around the old ranch that was home to Mike and Jessica Greer and maybe someone else I hadn't heard nor seen yet, purposely or not. I wanted to look at the strange, engaging paintings that stood out against the knotty pine walls. I felt that inevitable pull to know a new place, to know if I was safe or if I should keep moving. I had this feeling that I hadn't so much as met these folks as inherited them.

But I hadn't been asked nor told.

Jessica looked at me, biting her fingernails, and asked how long I had known Johnny Cobb. I noticed her feet were bare and her voice seemed to have two people inside of it: an eleven-year-old girl and a full-grown woman.

"Hmm, lemme think," I told her, trying not to sound like the way I felt right then, dark fear and memory starting to well up again. "Over twenty years, I guess. Give or take a few holidays. Long enough to start talking like him, but not long enough to know if what I was saying had the same meaning."

She seemed to like my answer and fiddled with the one ring she wore on her left thumb. It was a nice-size diamond, real or not, sized to fit with black electrical tape.

Refocused on her dad and math homework, Jessica hummed that CCR tune while I brushed a piece of stuffing from the recliner off my cheek and asked where the head was.

" '*Left a great job in a city*'—down the hall, Mr. Phin—'*working just for the man*'...hold the handle down until the water's gone, okay?"

Lifting the seat, since I was a guest and all, standing there looking out the little window with a tiny spider web in the corner, I wished like hell I was still stoned. There was something lurking behind my eyes and I couldn't seem to open them wide enough to let it out. What could this young girl and her benevolent dad be thinking about a guy who had rolled into Texas with all his possessions tied to an old bicycle; sitting upright in the cab of their '56 Stepside as it kicked up dust and pebbles, lurching, pinging, and caroming over the long dirt driveway while the father laughed and sang along to the radio?

What the hell could I have been to them? Who could I have been to myself?

The relationship wouldn't make sense to her, with her dad finding me on the side of the road, an old friend of a friend, a few calls in advance, nothing else. But she must have sensed the mutual respect, the irregular but imbedded pasts we might have shared, we must've shared. We had both been *over there*. The war with the funny name had bonded her dad to me as it had to other men. She sensed that much to be true, an unbreakable code that she might better understand soon enough but never totally enough. When you live with a vet, you live with all that he brought back with him. It might be up to the soldier how much he wants to bring out of his footlocker, but what he lets those around him see up close—well, the viewer could not deny it without denying the man.

Greer seemed like he was doing okay; his daughter Jessica, no problem. But Greer had done his tour before the

Nam had gotten really hot, like going to the beach but only walking in the wet sand. That turned out to be the second mistake in thinking I'd made that night. I was on a roll, pushing the big ball uphill without even knowing it. Like too many things I'd figured too quickly and needed to go out and lie on the ground and look at the sky. I knew nothing of his tour but dates. Greer had come and gone before I really knew how to pronounce the word *Vietnam*. Maybe he'd been living with the images of having to put a bayonet in the gut of a kid no older than his own daughter. I washed my hands, looked in the mirror, and watched the slab of tragic memory slide over the lump in my throat. Someone was walking over my grave again. And she was a beautiful young girl with her whole life opening up in front of her.

Pull it together, Phin, damn it! Turn away from the mirror. Don't look at yourself.

No, don't turn away. Face him, return to him; become him once again. Quit lying. Stop the perfect murder of your psyche.

It's only a reflection, kid. It's not the real thing. It's just a nightmare caught red-handed. Hang your tears out to dry, kid. Bury them. Bury her. Leave this place now. It's too close. Forget Gillie and the killing tale—if it is a tale—forget Mike Greer and his precocious daughter. And forget Lonnie.

✳ ✳ ✳

I hadn't thought of Lonnie, at least not with a clear-head, since the flight back to the real world. Like every soldier in every war, I had taken a girl I knew back home, maybe a classmate, a neighbor, maybe just a girl I had gone out with a few times, and had morphed her into a combination of Mother Mary, Raquel Welch, and Helen of Troy. It was a soldier's right to do so. The perfect woman waited for him at home, thought about him every minute of the day, prayed to sweet Jesus for his safe return where she would be waiting for him to descend from the plane, ribbons on his chest, having slain the evil dragon, crushed the dirty Reds, and made the world a safer place in which to raise their kids and march in the Fourth of

July parade. A soldier's woman back home was as important as his M-16. You could lose a rifle and survive, but not a warm-skinned, life-raft-of-a-woman who would cry at your funeral and mean it.

My Helen's name was Lonnie. She was from Pensacola and her dad had flown B-5's in WWII. We went out our junior year of high school and had said "I love you" to each other after splitting a twenty-ounce King Cobra malt liquor. We were dangerously close to meaning it, or at least realizing that we couldn't deny our feelings any more than our naiveté, with or without the booze.

Lonnie's dad was a lieutenant colonel and accepted his last transfer to D.C. to fly a desk as a full bird. Lonnie and I wrote each other for that summer, but then she told me it just wouldn't work out and that we should see other people—the usual high school brush-off line. By Thanksgiving, she wouldn't answer my calls. I'd been turkey-dropped.

In-country, I created her as the "one-who-always-waits." That was the first tour. The second tour she went off the radar screen with most of what else reminded me of all things back home, all things clean and fresh and good. One or two letters had come from the quiet safety of her college dorm room that year, but I was too savvy by then to read them, too aware of how they would affect me. And then she reappeared on the flight home. I was in an army-issued wheel chair, my foot undecided as to stay or go at that time and held up in a makeshift sling, when a volunteer flight nurse came by to check on me. It could've been the meds; it could have been her name tag, *Lennie,* only a letter off; it could've been the little tattoo written in green ink on the inside of her tricep that only showed when she reached across the seat and propped me up with the steadiness in her voice.

"What's your tattoo say, Lonnie," I asked?

"It's Lennie, corporal. Can you read it?" She leaned into me close and her scent took me back to pep rallies and ditching class to go to the beach and wishing I had told Lonnie that I did love her, that it wasn't the beer talking, and wishing even more I hadn't carpet-bombed her memory by telling the guys she was there, at home, waiting, looking at houses and china and wedding dresses.

I paused and drank in all the magic Lennie had brought back. And I knew that I would never feel like that again.

"It says, Corporal Davis, '*Nothing in life is to be feared.*"

"Why didn't you finish it?" I asked, slowly, in a thick whisper. "Not enough room on your arm?"

She smiled a knowing smile and said she had others to look after as she moved down the aisle. I called out, " '*...only to be understood.*' Marie Curie, right? Lennie?"

Lennie stopped and her eyes did something smooth and mysterious. It wasn't quite a twinkle, more like a long slow dance under a mirror ball. I could swear that her pupils went suddenly round and deep blue with gold edges. It wasn't the most human look I'd seen in twenty months, but it was close. If I'd had but one swallow of King Cobra I would've told Lennie that I loved her. And I would've meant it, even with the booze.

"Skłodowska," I turned and called after Lennie, wanting her to look at me for one more second. "Marie was of Polish decent. Sklodowska was her maiden name."

✳ ✳ ✳

And it was obvious that Jessica loved her dad hard for all that he was. And all that he wasn't. I trusted Mike right away. Johnny must've seen it back then, must've known that I'd grow from meeting these two. He'd never mentioned the girl to me, though. That made sense. Mike had fathered his daughter at nineteen, eighteen months younger than the age I'd gone off to some war because I was pissed off at loosing a sister who could've passed for a grown-up Jessica.

There were no accidents. Thinking of Johnny, the feeling began to pass. I'd be fine here. For awhile, anyways.

"Dad, I understand fractions because you taught them to me," I heard Jessie say as I walked back into the room and the present. "You know, on your gas gauge, how it has that one-half marker right in the middle of the little cracked glass circle, even if the tank is full or empty?"

Mike Greer was still dead-man-deep into his daughter's homework. I thought about what my dad had said before I left: "You can always tell the character of a man by how he treats his dogs, his willingness to buy the first and last round, and his ability to focus on the immediate problem at hand."

"Yeah, it always says it's one-half full. I'm gonna fix that. Been wearing out broom handles checking my fuel. That truck's just a fraction of what she once was."

Greer laughed at himself as he ruffled up Jessica's hair with his big, calloused mitts, the girl making no effort to smooth her hair down, like she didn't want to wipe away her father's touch. It was a tired laugh, but an honest one and I didn't want to be standing there at that moment for fear I was taking away something that belonged only to them.

Mike walked to the fridge, pulled out two more cold beers, even though neither of us had touched the first ones, and limped back to where I was slumped over the kitchen counter cluttered with books and manuals and eight-track cassettes. I was trying to weigh the unyielding gravity of my options, but I felt like crawling off into some tall grass and pressing my body back into the hard Texas earth. I thought maybe I needed to be alone, but realized my humanness, that this mixed-blooded man, his daughter, and me were set together for reasons that would unfold in due time, or maybe not.

"Jessie," Mike hollered over to his daughter working at the big plywood table, "You know your old man never liked anything in life with subcategories, including women, transmissions, business plans, and math problems. Try to keep those homework questions above board, eh Mija?"

He winked at me, handed me both beers, and said I needed to catch up.

I took both and forced myself not to look at the long, keloid scar on the back of his hand.

"Hey dad," the girl fired back, "your friend kind of looks like you, only younger. You want me to make you old guys something to eat after I finish my homework?"

Greer smiled and shook his head, then looked over at me with a hard, straight face, his eyes searching mine for something, but giving back at the same time. I felt uncomfortable under his gaze and tried to turn away but couldn't. Then it passed and he smiled, walked toward the door, opened it, and faced the inside of the house.

"Ah, c'mon, Dad," Jessica groaned, "not Alberto's again."

It was the longest, loudest fart I'd ever heard. But there was no smell, no apology, and little break in the conversation.

Mike had brought me straight here from the road with only one stop—at Alberto's for a burrito. I didn't think I'd have to eat for a week, though. Alberto had added just a sample of his "gringo sauce" to that beast to keep things moving in the right direction. I'd understood their *"tacos de perro para gringo"* joke and smiled wide as a barn owl back at them, guacamole dripping out the sides of my mouth, little green chunky bits on my torn sweatshirt, before walking out the door mumbling, *"Vatos loco."*

Lubbock, Texas. It seemed a cross between Hastings, Nebraska, Kansas City, and El Paso. The prices were realistic, the people real. There was a college up on the northwest side, but most of the farming and farming-related businesses were down south of town where the long, straight roads were peppered with truck repair shops, junk yards of old cars disguised as "salvage depots," and topless bars with a big dirt lot out the back so the patrons could keep their tractor trailer rigs out of sight should they need a cold one and a quick look on the way home from work. But the wives all knew that. It was just a quirky little game of mutual respect: "I won't park in front so you don't have to listen to your nosey friends tattle on me and you don't have to ask me why I was a bit late coming home with a bucket of chicken so you don't have to cook."

It was mostly an honest town, big on football, family, and farming with earthy smells that seemed to follow you around like a hungry cat: soybeans, peat moss, the odd cattle operation. Hell of a lot of alfalfa, too.

Greer had mentioned briefly that Lubbock had lost several dozen kids in the war, but still felt that America had done the right thing in Southeast Asia. Not exactly a bastion of intellectual or critical thinking, but I was only passing through without plans to stay any longer than it took me to earn some cash and pick up a reliable car. Maybe I'd spend a few tequila-nights arguing the merits of great Russian literature with Greer. Maybe I'd ask him if he really believed we should've been there and what nation his great-grandfather was from.

Only other thing I knew I had to do was to go out to Buddy Holly's grave. Owed him that much. I knew I couldn't leave before digesting this nuclear burrito in any case. And I had this strange sense as if I'd been here before. That had been happening a lot. I had a young body but other parts had aged quickly and suddenly. I was alien to this town, but then again I was alien to a lot of the world; unfamiliar but with pangs of déjà vu; there, but not really here.

And here I was. In Lubbock-fukin'-Texas. Might as well have rode my VW bus and my bike to fukin' Mars.

But war—it wasn't alien to me; it was clear as the water in the old spring creek back home. In war there are good men and there are bad men. The gray gets folded into its own brand of ambiguity. And any man can flip like a light switch, establishing the demilitarization of morality. It wasn't predictable or contextual. It was just the Nam, trying its damndest to be a war. And failing every step of the way.

Some days I woke up feeling like I could extinguish my troubles by simply going back over. But where? I'd up and re-enlist, if they'd let me. Soldier of misfortune. There had to be a war somewhere on the globe. I hated war, hated the killing. But I hated how dead I'd felt when I came back even more. Bullets were real. Television and Jack Daniels and old men at the VFW halls were aberrations—bad dreams that got worse the more you woke up.

In the Nam there was no inclination toward right and wrong because they were the same, based upon who held the hill and who charged from the valley. The concept of patriotism had eroded with the dirt on the hillside, with each rainy season, rising tide, and rising body count.

But there was no ambiguity about the bonds between soldiers who fought together, the communion was as thick as with any lovers, maybe thicker. In the field, especially at night, you might've spoken about a love back home, but what you felt was a love right there. A lot of guys tried to move back inside themselves where they couldn't be touched. But the lucky ones had someone who'd reach down their throat and pull their heart back up where it was supposed to be. Hell, you'd do it for them.

Why? Because it's war. And war breeds intimacy as it breaths hate.

That afternoon in Lubbock, I wasn't sure what day of the week it was, though I guessed it was Friday from the overflow of cars parked out in front of the topless joints we had passed on the way in. Yeah, I'd bet a day's wages it was a Friday.

Mike said he had to go back into his factory to pass out paychecks, something about how it fostered loyalty, but added, as he walked out the door of the old farmhouse he and Jessica lived in, "I like to do a fair amount of the compensation in cash money, too."

As I stood on the front porch looking at the work-a-day bike I had ridden part-way into the great state of Texas last night, missing my dogs already, untying the few material possessions that belonged to me from the racks and the rusty handlebars, I heard a little voice sneak up from behind.

"How do you comb your hair when it's all knotted up in a bird's nest like that?"

"Well, Miss Greer, that's the point. You don't. It sort of stays in one place no matter what you do. Kinda like those Barbie dolls with the wire hair. You think Barbie sits around fixing her hair all day? Heck no. She's got plastic Corvettes to drive to Malibu with Ken and little pools that hold water to sit by and keep that California tan."

Jessica squinched up her nose a bit as she tried to read me.

"I don't have any Barbies because they're fake. I mean, how could any lady have boobs that big and a butt that small? I'm eleven years old, Mr. Davis. I know about those things.

"And, Mr. Davis, I have a .22 gauge rifle under my bed that daddy gave me for Christmas. Taught me how to shoot it, too. Told me to say 'identify yourself' loud and twice...and then start shooting, aiming right for the stomach. Said a couple of .22 caliber slugs in the gut ain't gonna to kill nobody, but sure as shit will slow 'em down so long as you keep 'em coming. Hey, wanna see it?"

"Nah," I said, "seen my share of guns. They make me as nervous as the thought of you trying to get a brush through my hair."

"Hey, how do you grow your hair like that anyways? You have to go to a special beauty parlor or something?"

"Well, Jessica, it just sort of happens for some people. One day I didn't have a comb and it got all tangled after swimming in the ocean and I just let it alone. Next day it was worse, still couldn't find a comb so I just let it go. Couple of months later my friends are calling me the only living Rednecked Rasta."

"You like red pasta, too? Hey, I could make you some. Dad showed me how to boil noodles after mom...after she went away."

Noodles. The thought yanked me back in-country, downtown Saigon, thousands of little black heads running down the sides of the round-pebbled roads, each one asking, *"Hey Joe, you want noodle? Mama san's best. I get for you. Quick like. Just for you, Joe. Best noodles Saigon town."*

"Hey, Mr. Phin. That was a joke. I know what Rasta is. I got a book about Jamaica that Uncle Johnny gave me for Christmas. A record, too. The back beat is opposite of country music though. Where'd you go, anyways, Mr. Davis?"

"What do you mean, Jessie? It is okay if I call you Jessie, isn't it?"

"Sure. You're the adult so you get to decide. But Mr. Phin, I was wondering where you went in your head when I asked you about noodles. Daddy does it sometimes. He just goes somewhere in his head without moving his body. I think you went somewhere after I made that red pasta noodle joke. Where'd you go?"

"Ah, I was just thinking about a bad place I was in some years ago. There were a lot of kids your age who...hey, never mind. Can you show me around the place a little bit? That is, if you're done with your homework."

"Sure, Mr. Phin." She took my hand and guided me off the porch. "You can leave your bike here, it's a safe neighborhood. We'll start where all my daddy's friends like to go first, everybody except Uncle Johnny. He goes right to the library to see if daddy has any new books. I'll show you the barn where all the cars live. My daddy's friends like to go in there and talk like a bunch of old women. The cars don't even run. Except the dark red one with no roof. Dad says that car belongs to the 'ages,' but I don't even know where they live, let alone if they have any dogs or kids my age."

Jessie turned and winked, then said she was only being *sarchastic* with me. Both her eyes blinked in unison. A simple kid-wink.

I told her the word is "sarcastic" but she said no, "sarchastic" is the gap, the chasm that exists between just being witty and not getting the harmless joke; told me her daddy had made it up just for her to use.

"But you don't have to pretend that you didn't go to that bad place, Mr. Phin. I know about the Vietnam place. Daddy and me talk about it all the time. He says I'm the best psycho-shrink he's ever seen because I'm a kid and I ask a lot of questions that he doesn't want to answer, but he has to go on talking because he and I have a deal that whenever the other one needs to talk, we stop everything and listen until we understand what they're trying to say, which is hard because I've never been to a war place and daddy has never been a little girl. But a deal is a deal, don't you think, Mr. Phin? Don't you think a deal is a deal, that people should keep their promises and do what they agree to and listen if somebody needs to talk and not walk away? Don't you think a deal is a deal?"

Her eyes got wide and filled with water, deep clear water. But no tears fell and no hands came up to damn the river. It was if the water around her eyes was only water, afraid to become tears and fall down her cheeks and mark her as the eleven-year-old she was.

She wore boy's Levis, regular fit, baggy, with holes behind the knees from, "hanging on the monkey bars too long" she said, and a red, sleeveless woman sized blouse that was tied in a knot on both sides to make it fit. Her boots were well worn but clean and newly heeled. When I complimented her on them, she said without looking down, a statement made in raw belief without pretension, "Daddy puts a new sole on them every full moon. He's funny like that. But he can fix anything that is manmade."

We walked past the empty horse corrals, weeds climbing up the treated 4x4 posts toward some aimless gallows' sky that seemed to be reaching down with a heavy hand, pulling them up from the cracked, dry ground only to heave them back into the earth. It was a lifecycle I was not unfamiliar with.

I walked behind her as we ambled out to the large covered barn, eyes linked to her boots, and couldn't help but make her out to be a young version of Lonnie.

"Well, Jessie," I answered after the long silent walk across the yard, "a deal should always be a deal, no matter what. But what gets in the way is the '*what.*' "

As we reached the tattered but tight barn she said, "They were mom's favorite boots to ride in," and I thought I caught a glimpse of the edges of her mouth fall as the sun, too, was being pulled down by the long, flat Texas plains.

"You like to fix things Mr. Phin? Hey, how come you're riding a bike and not driving a car? And why do you think Uncle Johnny told you about my dad? You know what they call him in town? My dad, who can fix anything? 'Rube Goldberg Greer,' after that old-time guy who could fix anything. I heard there was a TV show about his machines, but we don't have a TV. Dad says they just try and sell you stuff. Reckon apples are a just a chip off the old tree, eh, Mr. Phin? Hey, you think I'm tall for my size? My mother was tall. I saw some pictures. But when you're just a tiny squirt-kid, everybody's tall."

"Hmm." I eased into it. "I ain't the smartest tool in the shed, but I know a few things, know that I have much to learn, 'bout fractions and puttin' things behind me a decimal at a time. I suppose that's why I'm here. That make any sense?"

"Of course, I'm eleven. I know lots of things. But I'm not so sure you can take feeling problems and turn them into math homework."

"Yeah? Well tell me some things you know, beside fractions and long division." It was a risky question but worth asking.

"I know that you're never getting a comb through your hair 'less you cut it off with a pair of pruning shears. I know you and my daddy are kind of like the same. And I know that I'll be needing to leave Lubbock one day to see what else is out there. Oh yeah. I know that Jerry's Place down on 63rd Street has waitresses with no shirts and parking places in the back."

"Oh, come on, Jess. That's easy stuff," I goaded her as we walked into the biggest barn full of old cars I'd ever seen. There's just something about old barns that makes a person feel connected to the rest of life, makes you feel like existing if you didn't yet. This one was old but well-kept; that musty smell of damp hay, old fertilizer, and motor oil in the air. And alfalfa, always alfalfa.

Most of the cars were hidden under dusty covers. But removing a man's cover on his classic automobile without permission is like taking off his wife's shoes. You won't get punched or thrown in jail, but you won't be getting invited back anytime too soon.

One car was uncovered though, right near the door, begging to be ridden around in, pleading to get some sun on her tanned-leather bench seats.

Jessica opened the door to a maroon colored '63 Buick Skylark convertible, motioned me into the driver's seat like a valet, and then walked around to the other side and vaulted over the closed passenger door, just like in the movies. She pulled her knees to her chest and answered my question.

"I know that daddy makes the sign of the cross every time he turns the ignition in this car. And I know that the things *you* need fixing are probably inside your body, not outside like on some fence or sprinkler on a ranch somewhere. What are you smiling at, Mr. Phin?"

"Ah, well, I was just thinking on a woman in my past. You reminded me of her for a second."

"You loved her a bunch didn't you?"

"What makes you think that?"

"I may only be eleven, but I'll be twelve in three weeks. A woman just senses these things."

"Yeah, I loved her. As much as I could for a kid, which is sometimes more than adults, but doesn't do me any good right about now."

I didn't want to go there right then, in this barn, in this car that I sensed belonged to Jessie's absent mother, a fact that no doubt troubled both father and daughter.

"Hey, can you show me the den where all your dad's books are?"

"Sure, Mr. Phin. Dad told me you'd be staying in there on the couch for a bit, so we can carry all your stuff in there. You think I should call over to the Thomas place down the road and see if Mr. Leroy's teenage boys could come down and help unload your bike?"

"Nah," I got right back at her, "I thought we'd just go on into town tonight and I'd buy a new car, a fancy wardrobe, one of those new stereos that plays the smaller eight-track cassettes, and a couple of ballpoint pens. Never have enough pens, you know. Maybe get my hair washed if we see one of those do-it-yourself car wash places."

"All right Mr. Phin. Turning around is fair game. Eleven is almost a teenager."

"Heck, you're good as twelve to me." We shook on it, her hand feeling like a smaller, female version of her pa's hard-working hand.

Mike seemed a good man. A few years older, but close enough to speak the same language. I remembered Johnny saying I'd learn from him as he waved his hand, a sign that Johnny wouldn't expand on a subject even if you asked him. Greer had been in-country, the story went, before everything unraveled, working at the rear, flying a desk in Saigon. I didn't believe it though. There was something about him that spoke covert ops. Something behind his eyes buried under the healing stones of time. Mike had filed his edges off. But one might've seen if they knew how to look, there had been a razor in his past. No doubt in my mind—he'd been in the shit.

The rest I knew about Mike Greer was just tidbits that I had picked up from watching and listening. Mostly things about a man who is straight up and wouldn't tell you on the count of he wanted you to learn them yourself. I found myself wanting to know about his wife, Jessie's mom, probably because it was like a story in my recent sawed-off past, over and over, never a fucking ending.

"Hey, you have any dogs, Jessie?" I asked, fishing for something neutral and warm.

"Not any more. We had a small Brittany spaniel and an Australian sheepdog. 'Closest I'll ever to get to that land Down Under,' Daddy would always say. But I was out playing in the yard one summer night back when I was 'bout three or four, daddy in making dinner, Mom was in town, probably drunk at that bar like she was a lot then, and this pack of coyotes came into the yard. They were yelping and screaming and running and pacing with white, frothy goop coming out of the corners of their mouths. Daddy came sprinting out of the house with his thirty-aught-six and fired a round in the air.

"But my doggies had already torn into them coyotes. I ran into the house as daddy tried to pull them apart, shoot a few if he could. But there were just too many of them.

We buried them out on the edge of the property. Had a little funeral and everything. Worse thing though, Mr. Phin...

mom was hung over in the morning and couldn't get out of bed to come pay her respects, if she hadn't drank them away.

"You ever have anybody up and die on you, Mr. Phin?"

She knew. The little punk just knew.

"Never mind, Mr. Phin. You don't have to answer. You just had those kinda window eyes that seemed like they were trying to get pried open and breathe something out. My daddy says the soul needs airing out same as bedsheets and old rugs. Sometimes when Uncle Johnny Cobb comes to visit, he makes daddy sit out on the back porch swing until he starts talking, mostly about mom and the war. Once I heard him say something about me growing up right without any other mommies around. One time they spent a whole day and a half out there straight. I got worried when they didn't come in for dinner and called Alberto up on the phone. He seemed to know what was happening and brought over a big bucket of Mrs. Alberto's tamales and a gallon jug of that margaret-frittas drink that looks like lemonade. Daddy seemed a lot more aired out after Uncle Johnny left.

"Hey, want to watch the sunset upside down? C'mon, I'll show you."

She took me around back of the ranch house where the back veranda stretched out into the far-reaching fields of wheat, barley, and alfalfa to some distant horizon to the south that held another country, another set of rules, but where life was simpler. Harder maybe, but simple: *y simpatico*. If I wasn't headed north after Lubbock to see some old friends, I'd consider a left turn instead. Or maybe I was afraid that if I ended up down there, I'd retreat inside myself and no one would be around to reach their hand down my throat and pull my heart back up to where it belonged.

Eleven-year-old Jessica Greer, daughter of a single father who made farm equipment and could rebuild the carburetor of a '60 Ford Falcon, a young woman-child who could make French toast without burning the crust, daughter of a woman who drank too much and was nowhere to be seen and who had probably skipped out on them but was still loved all the same—this eleven-year-old hung by her knees from an old rusty bar drilled into two six-foot posts and watched the sun set upside down.

She hung there, swinging slightly as the sky ran through every color in a forty-eight pack of Crayola Crayons, humming a Patsy Cline tune.

"Looking at it upside down," she said as she brushed a single long hair from her flushed face, "it looks like the sun's just coming up, like a whole new day starting over again."

Right then I was feeling as raw as a December oak, solid but weary, strong but endangered. I headed toward the house to hide from myself, but as I stepped onto the porch, I felt an honest madness claw its way up from some rooted bowel to strangle the old pain and give birth to something else. Or at least hint at it.

I walked back out to the bar, climbed up beside Jessie, embracing my childhood and everything good about youth. And as I let go my hands and hung by my knees next to this eleven-year-old sage, my view cut off by two feet of swinging braids, I felt like I was dancing in wide circles on the tip of an ancient arrowhead, and for that very moment, happy enough, alive enough.

I pulled my hair into a big knot and said, "I've had a few people up and die on me. My big sister's death caused me to go off to that war your daddy was in. Lost a few buddies there. Then with my ma getting sick and my pa trying to get me back home from that war, I stepped on a mine and blew up my foot. Not on purpose or anything, but I'm sure it happened for a reason; you know how that works. That's how come I have this limp."

We hung like two bats in the silent dusk.

"One time when I was little, like a hundred years ago," she said, "I asked Uncle Johnny why my mom and dad were acting like two dogs peeing on the same pole and he said that dad had started a dirty little war on himself and mom made the mistake of thinking she was the enemy when he was too afraid to teach her how to say, 'medic.' That's when I asked him if he'd teach me to shoot a gun so I could always protect my dad when he was fighting with himself."

We swung upside down, looking at the world the way it was and it wasn't. Jessie was quiet; didn't say a word for the first time all afternoon.

"You know, Jess, I went to a lot of funerals, some lasting all day, others just a few words before the chopper took off. And the funny thing is that none of the dead looked the same in a casket or a bag, even though they hadn't changed. Other than they weren't really there any more, inside that body."

It was almost dark now and Jessie kicked her legs over the bar, tried to stand up but started to giggle, like regular eleven-year-olds will, and fell to the ground laughing.

"Uncle Johnny made me read these books about a ring when I was ten. They were good. But what I remember most is the author saying that all those who wander are not lost. I don't think you're lost, Mr. Phin."

"And you. Miss Jessica," I had to risk it, "do you ever feel lost?"

"Oh, yeah." Her voice softened, "At least you got to see where they put your mama when they put her in the hospital. At least you got a place where her soul might be hanging around until its well. Mine just didn't come home one night. Left milk in the fridge and everything. Even left that darn car daddy saved up to get for her. Daddy says she went to get help and would come back to us some day. But I know he's just making it up until I'm old enough to sit on the porch swing with him and Uncle Johnny and do my own airing out. Yep, Mr. Phin, my mommy's still burning herself up."

"It's tough being a kid, isn't it?"

"No tougher than being a grownup."

"I'm not sure I'm grown up yet, Jess," tears dripping upside down, off my forehead, disappearing into the sand below.

"Well, after I'm twelve or thirteen, I'm goin' right out to that porch when Uncle Johnny is here and stepping out to the plate.

"Hey, wanna' go for a ride in mom's topless car? Dad says I'm a good driver. I'll take you into town on the back roads and we can look for a fire hydrant to wash your hair?"

"Or we can ride my bike down to Jerry's Place and peek in the windows."

"You do like to square a circle, don't you, Mr. Phin?"

"Just two pods in a pea, Miss Jessica. Why don't you go get those pruning shears and give me an upside-down haircut? You know, so we can surprise your daddy when he gets home. Maybe tie the old hair off the back of the topless car and pretend it's a horse's tail."

And as Jessica Greer ran giggling toward the tool shed, the sound of her laugh washed over me, a dry brush rain, cleansing, lifting. For a moment in time, airing.

"Hey Mr. Phin," she called out as she reached the back porch. Do you get the feeling we've been friends before?"

CHAPTER 24

BLACK IS BLACK

Blackie held the broom in his thin, calloused hands, fingers wrapped around the thick, smooth handle. He moved it across the floor of Johnny Cobb's shop in neat and practical swipes, gathering small piles of sawdust. The air smelled of fresh-cut wood and freshly opened, end-of-the-day Lone Star, and the sweat of men who were proud to have created a product. It was a good broom, sturdy and with a wide straw head that made a rhythmic sound as it glided over the concrete floors. It was much better than the long, low, stealth dust mops that he'd used at the VA Hospital in Denver. The men, too; they were good men.

Blackie thought he was doing okay. Pretty damn good, in fact.

He only had trouble with the little things, the strange little things that normal people did every day: washing their clothes when they weren't really dirty, eating huge meals, driving their cars when they could walk or ride a bicycle. It wasn't the *how* but the *why*. James Samuel Black knew a lot of *hows* about people, but the *whys* stumped him. And most of them were small, seemingly inconsequential details of decision: little choices they made about living.

It hadn't always been that way. When he was Jim Black the scholar, the whiz kid in the anthropology department at

Duke, he knew people. He knew all about the people of the world, the whys included. The books told him so. His professors told him so. His research told him so.

Then, when his 4S draft deferment ran out and he was sent to the war, the two didn't correlate. People's motives were as shapeless and fluid as water, mixing and spinning as did the soldiers and the villagers and men in fatigues and kids with no shoes either swimming to the top or drowning in the constant ambiguity of choices that weren't really choices...they just happened. Senselessness had become a sixth sense.

Blackie hadn't fought his draft notice like others did with lawyers and cigarette lighters and 4Fs–or on a midnight run to Canada as a supposed conscientious objector. He had always been a thinking kid, a smart one who had out-thought everybody from his parents to his thesis committee members. The concept of war was of great interest to him; why, he wasn't quite sure. But mostly, when it came to trying to understand why people went to battle, he wasn't interested in the psychology of battle as much as the influence of cultures on people and how they faced the vagaries of killing other humans from other cultures.

So, Jim Black, right in the middle of finalizing his master's thesis plans, went to Vietnam because how wonderful an opportunity to see the clash of cultures up close, to smell it and breath it and touch it, unlike the older curmudgeons in the department who had not—too young for one war and too old for the next ones. And then to think about it, maybe even out-think it. Out think war itself.

Something happened though, something so strange and unpredictable and immeasurable that little Jim Black got his ass kicked in Vietnam. The harder he tried to understand it, the hotter the wiring in his head became. He felt like his father out in the garage working on a cheap lamp that flickered on and off and so he'd started taking things apart and reconnecting wires and sockets and trying different bulbs. Late into the night he tinkered, twisted, tore down, and reset. He even read the manual. But by then it was too late and the lamp never worked. But his father was not to be vanquished. He would set it aside and come back to it with a fresh mind some day and start over, step-by-step. Blackie's father, to his thinking, was smarter than any piece of electrical equipment or any concept of electrical current.

For the young Jim Black, the war beat him quick and it beat him hard. Things started to unravel almost immediately. His superiors disciplined him, threatened him, beat him, all of which added to the confusion. Within two months he was grasping for his sanity. After the twelfth week and a thorough evaluation, the doctors had committed him. This was no snow job. He'd never help the war effort, they'd said; ship this one home and bring us another. While he sat in the midst of it all, Blackie couldn't grasp that the war in Vietnam was smarter than he was. Or at least, he reasoned in his more lucid moments, the ambiguity of the conflict was just too ambiguous.

And now, gradually re-approaching the wiring in his head, slowly, a day at a time, under the guidance of Johnny Cobb's eclectic collection of vets, nearly homeless and once homeless employees at the waterbed shop, Blackie knew that he had found the enemy who nearly stole his razor-sharp mind. And he faced him every morning while shaving and brushing his teeth.

"Nope," he spoke to himself without shame or confusion one day, "I should have done less, thought less, gave up trying to make sense of that chaos of battlefield peculiarities, that sense of marching order, and clarity of established theory of war and concept of motive. I should have set the lamp down and walked away. No, the only good thing was that the trauma was quick and compressed, the damage to the exterior systems moderate, but the internal core was kept intact. I threw the lamp against the wall and then jumped in the swirl right after it. I should have been reading the *I Ching* instead of how-to manuals."

Blackie had temporarily lost purchase on his mind, but his will had been there, inside those long white hallways of the VA, propping up his dripping synapses that were finally letting go. He'd never understand it, never be able to stand up in front of a class and explain what happened in Southeast Asia, never be able to do anything but say it was a waste, a terrible waste. Oh, people might come along years later, soldiers and journalist most likely, and try to write about the war, mostly to reassemble the wiring in their own heads that had been cut and crossed out and confused by what they saw or didn't see, by what they felt or didn't feel, and mostly by what they had smelled. The Nam had that *smell.*

Some might come close, Blackie thought that afternoon as he cleaned up from the day at the shop, sweeping the pine sawdust into little piles, that he'd come back and pick up with a metal dust bin. Oh, for sure, years from now people would try and describe it because it was one of those things: like how does an animal find his way home when dropped off miles away? Like how is it that you have so much energy when you first fall in love? Like how do some rivers flow uphill? People want to understand, Blackie thought, that which cannot be explained.

Blackie reached down and ran his fingers through the soft wood shavings that only a few hours ago had been part of a nice long board that was once a tree. And he knew all this could be explained in laws of physics and force and even nature. And yes, some parts of war could be explained in principles of psychology and politics and human nature. But as Blackie slowly stood up and cautiously allowed his mind to come together on its own time and in its own way, dumping the pine sawdust into the dust shavings' bin, he knew that as long and as hard as men tried to explain the war in words and quiet mournful pleas and stumping, amplified rhetoric; and as long as a nation itself, far removed and spoon-fed only what it could swallow, tried to understand what happened so a label could be put on it, so that they would know which shelf to place the book—Blackie knew it was utterly fruitless. Men witnessed things in the Nam and could not tell you what they just saw. *You just had to be there* was a negligible comment.

A waste is what it came down to, one big fucking waste. Even the fine particles made by a saw blade could be mixed with glue and used to fill small holes in wood products.

"Hey Blackie," it was a fellow worker calling from the back of the shop where stacks of plywood reached up to meet the high ceiling. They called him Tom-Tom because he said he only had one name and White men couldn't pronounce it correctly. Tom-Tom, who had a changing percentage of

Cherokee blood, lived in his '64 Ford Econoline van parked out behind Cobb's shop. "We're going over to Auntie's for beers and gumbo. You comin'?"

"Nah." Blackie leaned into his broom and called back across the room full of machines he was learning how to use but still scared him some. "I don't think so. I have some things to do tonight."

"Ah, c'mon kid. You don't have a thing better to do than to gather with us. I'll even let you beat me at chess again, assuming we can find most of the pieces with crowns and horses."

Blackie laughed and felt the old social lubricant of good people with good intentions run down from the edges of his upturned mouth, coating the frayed parts of his past.

"Aw'ight then," he used his best fabricated drawl. "I aim to come over to Auntie's a bit later on and whoop up on y'all. Soon as I finish up what I gots to do."

✳ ✳ ✳

On the other side of the shop Johnny Cobb sat in his office, the wooden rocking chair that a few of his employees had made for him last Christmas creaking in time with his thoughts as the hand-cranked adding machine totaled another week's figures. Too many on the payroll, he thought, but dismissed it. Wages were higher than need be, but not as high as he'd like to offer. Forty-eight bodies, thirty good men, eighteen good women. Ninety-six good hands under this roof, ninety-six hands to feed. How many other mouths, he wondered, depended on the demand of people wanting to buy beds filled with water? It was risky. People said it was a fad. He only said sleeping comfortably would last forever. If this venture failed, he'd do something else, find another way to keep a crew and their families fed and watered. Hell, he didn't need much, a little cot in the corner someplace, a field for the dogs to run. Most people buy things for themselves so people will want to be around them. Old Jimmy Grayfalls had said that to him one day when his older brother Ramsey was complaining about the ugliness of the work truck. But if it's love they're after, they should be giving things away, not acquiring them.

Ah, Grayfalls, where is the old guy? Johnny leaned back in his chair and let the day settle. The spirit world for sure. Yes, through the Western Gate out in California, that place he spoke of, the jumping-off point for all Native Americans. He must've made it there and seen the great Pacific Ocean before he left for the spirit world.

It had been a day like that, full of ruminations and surprises. And news. Gerald McReady, from the Denver VA and one of Blackie's pals, had called. He wanted to know all about the Davis kid. "Straight up, Mr. Cobb," he'd asked in his quiet, serious tone. "I need to know about the kid, straight up."

Johnny had told him everything, not because he felt he owed the man something, but because he sensed a caring that screamed through the unbreakable silence and distance. Gerald was more than trust: he was a healer, asking for news from another healer. That was more than enough. So Cobb laid it all out there for Gerald and then listened to the misty relief in the sound of deep breaths over the phone. But like all things living and not living, there was a force to balance it all, a light in the dark, an evil to make the good stand out.

Gerald told Johnny of Wilcox's threats and the investigation that was closed when the official reports of Pvt. Davis' death came in; he told of Wilcox and Roberts losing out on their "sweet deal;" and he told of the .45mm automatic in the drawer. Mostly he spoke to Johnny about fear because Johnny was the only one he could think of to speak to about this.

So, Cobb, his mind dragging up old scenarios from past White men pushing him around when his mother sent him into town for supplies, and his father saying one day he'd hunt them down one-by-one and watch the fear in their eyes as he pressed his shotgun into their temples hard enough to make a red dent. Revenge, Johnny thought as he listened to McReady go on about something that may or may not come true. Revenge for embarrassment; revenge for oppression; revenge for letting your kid get away from you, your wife get away from you, your life too; something that became chased after; and revenge for daring to start a civil war in a place that sounded like it belonged next to a number on a Chinese food menu. Could revenge ever be justified? How about qualified? Were there degrees of rebuttal? What was its natural enemy? Snakes eat mice, frogs eat flies; everything had a biological opposite that helped balance the scales. What would the old Indian say?

Grayfalls had been with him once when they'd gone into town and three White teens had taken their money and spit in their faces. Johnny remembered he was nearly twelve and wanted to race home and tell Earl and Ramsey, but Grayfalls made him promise not to—that Ramsey would hunt the boys down and end up where their father was, which was never known after he went into town one day, likely to balance some scale and not carrying any weight as a Negro in the South.

"But we have to do something," he'd told Grayfalls, with hormones cascading like rocks off a steep hill. "We have to get our revenge."

"It will come for evil men like these, though the decision of fate is not ours to hand down. It is written in laws beyond our world."

Revenge, Johnny remembered as if suddenly remembering that he must die someday, could only be sorted out by virtue, its polar opposite. He'd figured that out on his own after Grayfalls had folded himself into another world.

So Cobb listened to McReady's fear and then told him again that the Davis boy was indeed alive to those who knew him well and that he was sorting himself out on the road.

"You may see Phin again," he told Gerald. "He is where he is supposed to be, as is Blackie."

He wished the orderly well, asked him if he thought he was where he was supposed to be, and hung up the phone without waiting or expecting an answer. Even though he knew less of the McReady kid than Phin or Harry or even Blackie, he had not dreamed well of his future.

But what did he know? His dreams and his only wife were buried under eight feet of water and six feet of clay. At a place he wasn't sure of.

As Johnny was cleaning up his desk to leave, one of his best craftsmen brought in the mail and set it on the desk. Hopper could operate a lathe, a table saw, band saw, and a drill press better than any man Cobb had ever known. He'd lost an arm during the Tet Offensive in '68 and used his prosthesis to push large pieces of hardwood through the planers without fear of getting a finger caught. Plastic fingers were easily replaced at the nearby PX.

"Here's the mail, chief. I'm off to Auntie's," Hopper said with his assuring voice. Then he turned to the picture of President Nixon that Cobb had hung on the wall with crosshairs drawn over it lining up on the President's nose. Hopper bent the malleable fingers of his plastic hand down: all except the middle one and raised it to the photograph.

"See you tomorrow, chief," he said and left humming a Byrds' tune.

Johnny tried not to laugh, tried not to dwell on the richness of his life, tried not to peel back the mask that he had made for himself with the even richer fabric of the people who wove his life. *Cobb,* he told himself, *it'll work out. Hasn't it always? In one way or another? I mean, look where Ruth's death took you? Look at your father's disappearance, how it led to Grayfall's sage advice which kept you out of the war which led to...*

To what? To watching men come back who had no choice and seeing if they could make the adjustment from the heightened sense of dangerous living to the safe deadness of a couch and a remote control and a bottle?

Ah, c'mon Cobb, face it. You lost her. She's gone. It's no one's fault. You want revenge on God for taking her? Virtue, old buddy, keep giving. It'll come back to you. And she'll bring it on the backs and in the minds of these men who lost as well. Set the mail down and go over to Auntie's and buy those boys the first round.

And that's what Johnny Cobb decided he would do. He'd go on over there and buy a round and shoot some pool with Tom-Tom and Hopper and Blackie, if he showed. And he'd ask Auntie if she had any bones for the dogs; and he'd try to convince himself that he was okay, that people depended on him, that it could be a hell of a lot worse; that Phin had a good shot of making it all the way back. He was a smart kid; he'd begin to structure new psychological guidelines that rose above the biological ones. Scales were for accountants, odds for gamblers. Survivors didn't do math.

Johnny allowed himself a smile and a moment of grace. He threw the mail on the desk and watched it splay out like cards being dealt. And as he turned around and reached for the light switch, the one synapse in his own mind connected: there was a letter with no return address. In the upper left corner were the words, "From Harry."

He put the letter in his coat pocket, turned the light out, and closed the door. It was nearly a minute before he realized he had not taken a breath.

CHAPTER 25

AMNIOTIC FLUID

Good things love water. Bad things always been dry.

–John Steinbeck, *The Red Pony*

Harry swung the davit out over the port side and lowered the braided and galvanized steel hook wound around the heavy electric winch. He watched it go down. The shrimp net was laid out over the glassy waters of the Gulf in overlapping concentric circles. As the net sank to the bottom it would unfold and flatten and become the bottom itself. Harry didn't always like to shrimp; it offered too much time to wait and think.

He heard the sound of the cables unwinding and it disconnectedly comforted him from the other sounds in his head—the ones that sounded like bone on bone, a somber, rounded-edge file on rock. He thought he knew where he was, but he couldn't be sure. It didn't matter. He had shut off all navigational devices when he left Panama City Beach over a month ago, stopping only once in Sarasota for food, fuel, and to mail a few letters. Harry had run into a slick modern fleet near Siesta Key and told them he was headed east to Key West and all his nav was down, so could they get a message to his home port in Panama City Beach? And then Harry turned back due west.

Unsure why he'd fabricated this tale, Harry thought that maybe he'd courted the risk for the sake of discovery. But what could he find out here? Alone on the Gulf of Mexico while his son was on the road, his first mate/daughter dead, and his wife at home recovering from what the docs called a "cerebral vascular accident?" So, Harry stopped thinking.

And he stopped counting as well. Except fish; only fish. Fish had been the yardstick against what he had measured himself all those years: fish were his livelihood, fish were what he bartered with for supplies he needed, fish were his gifts to anyone who knew enough to ask kindly. To him they were more than beads and trinkets, more than loaves and fishes. Fish were a fabric of his identity.

In the quieter moments when the lines were set or the nets cast and the crew--back when there was a crew—were below sleeping or playing cards, he was able to admit to himself that, yes, the fish were the essence, but the ocean was the real catch. Just being out there, feeling a part of it, reading it, talking to it, having it answer you in heavy squalls and twenty-foot seas, sunny days, and light, delicate winds that cleared the way so you could see well into your future. It was the hugeness of the ocean that forced humility, but offered the confidence of control. Some days he felt like a child walking across the desert and others he was Triton himself, unqualified for any other job and desiring nothing as well.

This trip was different than any other. He hadn't gone looking for a catch; he'd taken no crew, consciously hoping to get lost in the great gulf of his mind. And he'd fished out of habit to keep his mind working, to remember or forget—which one he couldn't be sure. And the fish had come.

Harry's forty-one-foot trawler had its hold filled with snapper and bass and shrimp. He'd seen other boats that'd not been as lucky and had offloaded all or parts of his catch, asking nothing, offering no explanation. "Take it," he'd told them, "I've got enough."

"You must have good crew," they'd said, wondering where they were. And Harry had said yes, but he didn't know where they were right then.

So, Harry watched the stars and the sun and altered his course to west by southwest. For his despair he fished for the smallest reconciliation of peace and quietude. For his sorrow he fished for relief. For his pain he fished for understanding. And for his sick wife and dead daughter, he fished because he couldn't think of what else to think about.

Harry put in for fuel at Port St. Joe and left without a call to anyone but Jed Riot who'd said Grace was making progress and understood why he'd left. "Well," Jed thought before hanging up, "at least there's someone who does."

The weather had been fine. Working with a sextant and decent charts, he put in at Tampico, Mexico some four or five days later. But the sun and moon shots existed mostly in his log. And time had been reduced to a necessary piece of deduced reckoning. In Tampico, the customs office refused to believe he was working alone and had so many fish in his refrigerated hold. When he off-loaded a good portion of the catch as gift to the officials, they believed him and said he was a great fisherman, that he should make port there anytime.

Harry spent a few days holed up there, allowing a tropical depression off of Belize to make up its mind. Above all else, he respected the ocean. He sat in small cantinas and drank *mezcal*, allowing the smooth fire to slide down his throat and bypass the hollowness in his chest unnoticed. Then one night he allowed it to get too close to the truth. Later on he'd blame it on Francisco. But that wasn't the truth either.

Francisco was the bartender where Harry had been taking his meals and his drinks. He'd seen many like Harry before—old men, young men, good ones, bad ones—all running from something or somebody, looking for something or somebody, each of them from somewhere else on his way to someplace—where, they had no idea.

"*Amigo, con permiso.* Can I sit with you *momentito*?"

"*Siete se, por favor.* Of course, sit."

"You are the man who fishes alone?"

"No, not really. I'm just a little short-handed this run." Harry smiled at the man.

"Your boat says *Ciudad de Panama*. You come through the canal?"

"No. Panama City in Florida, *Estas Unidos*."

"Oh, I see. You are a long way from home in such a boat with no crew. And maybe no plans, eh amigo?'

Harry had not had so many words spoken to him at once in some time. Words in a darkened cantina in a developing country, hanging over each other's head, vibrating, sometimes sympathetic, sometimes straight up like the booze, laced with compassion and understanding because each had known the other not as a person, but as a past. It was this kind of unprompted commiseration of lost souls and high grace and the lowest of humiliations and, above everything else, a brutally sweet honesty, that could bring men and women into dank and passionate watering holes like this It mattered little if they went home alone, talking to themselves and the bottled microphone. Words spoken in places with loud thumping foreign sounds were for men who were stuck. And the words pried them loose, shook something, pulled them from the mud if they needed pulling. Any change was good because it was movement. Direction was irrelevant. And so they spoke.

On the first night, Harry and Francisco spoke of boats and ports and places they'd seen. They were two dogs sizing each other up, not for a fight, but for the ability to speak the truth, or at least what they regarded as truth. On the second night, they moved a little closer and Francisco asked Harry about the storms he had seen. Then he told the gringo about his life in Tampico, his many children, some of whom had not survived the cholera when it came. On the third night, Francisco asked Harry about his woman because the question of family had to be approached with caution. Lonely men in far-away places could become irrational and, therefore, dangerous. But Harry spoke quietly, almost trance-like, about his wife of thirty-one years, the loneliness oozing like sap from the stem of a cut flower; his words unsticking and happy to seep because spreading lead to dissipation.

Just before midnight he told Francisco that he'd up and left Grace alone.

On the fourth night, Francisco asked about the kids. Harry spoke in a long, quivering report punched with teary pauses and slamming glass bottoms and reverberating sighs. Harry spoke all the words that would come up. And then he put his fingers in his throat and spoke some more. Francisco sat as if the wise psychiatrist, nodding, adding his own short replies and, when necessary, pouring *mezcal*.

"Amigo, did you know that *mezcal* comes from my home state of Oaxaca? Many people confuse it with tequila and think the only difference is the *gusano*, the worm. But there are many kinds of agave plants; regular tequila only uses the blue agave. *Mezcal* can be made from any of them. It is a much purer drink, not watered down like tequila. Never the same drink from batch to batch, year to year." Francisco seemed proud of this. Harry said there was a difference between being watered and watered down. Francisco said, "*Si*, I know this. *Es verdad.*"

They talked through the night and began drinking coffee and eating tortillas with the sun. And as Harry finally rose to leave, he extended a large hand and said he'd see Francisco later. They both knew it was a gesture, not a lie, a formality among men who had shared words like they had shared a liver.

"Francisco? Can I ask you something?"

"*Si*, amigo, anything."

"You've asked me many things, and I have told you more than most. I don't care how you were able to get me to talk, but I'm wondering why you cared to listen. Why did you sit here night after night while I poured out my past into the smoky air and on the sawdust floor? And I know so little about you?"

"I will tell you, Señor Harry. You are an interesting man, yes, but I am also struggling with things that happened many years ago. My great-grandfather was a war hero when our countries fought each other over land that once belonged to Mexico and your government needed to make room for all the people of the *Norte Americanos* to spread out. He killed many soldiers and even after we lost, he was given great honor in our country. I do not carry any guilt about it, *verdad*. But I did not know if I should feel proud about it. I wanted to understand this. I never had that chance. And that is why I asked you about your son and your relationship with him. That is why I sit here with you every night. And besides, it is no fun to drink alone or worse yet, with the others around who don't understand.

"Amigo, you taught me that we are no different, that we all share the same problems. For me, Señor Harry, you separated the war from the warrior."

That morning Harry sold the rest of his catch, left an envelope at the bar for Francisco Pancho Maravilla, and headed northeast. For now, the words ended like the way rain did. They just did.

And things felt a bit cleaner.

✳ ✳ ✳

Phin stood under the steamy water of the shower at the Greer's ranch. It was the first shower he'd had in a week, not counting the garden hoses he'd borrowed along the way from Lafayette. The water had a cleansing effect, the same as it always did, and he wondered how he could go so long without finding himself a body of water to float on, to swim across, to cool his hot skin, or warm his cool fingers: to wash away some of what needed to go down the drain.

In Vietnam he'd often lie down in the small streams and float, his back and butt dragging on the round pebbles, feeling the cool water that started in the sky as rain and fell on the thick canopy of green up in the high hills and made its way down into the paddies and, finally, the China Sea. Cpl. Davis would tell the others he'd be right back as they sat and waited for something to happen or made camp for the night, and he'd go off on his own, looking for a river, a stream—just a damn trickl—he could get his face into and cool his brain. The water was his escape pod, his electrical conduit that could take him back to the pier at Panama City Beach or two miles off the coast on his dad's boat and him betting his pop six bits that he could swim all the way to shore.

He'd seen tires floating near his head in the Nam; thirteen-inch Jeep rubber as he laid in the shallow streams; tires and whole cars and body parts; and once, when he thought he might be dreaming, he saw a whole water buffalo the size of a Volkswagen float right by him. The animal was bloated and bugs and birds rode atop of it, feeding, grazing lazily in the bright sun, picking at the softest tissue that had been marinated by the trip down stream.

Oddly, Phin was not affected by the animal. It had been during his second tour and near the end of the war and little if anything affected him. Except water. Even tainted with death, he knew that the water carried life on top of death and life under the surface that no one saw except those who knew water and had always known it. Near the end he couldn't trust his imagination. He couldn't trust his memory. But he could trust water because it had been there in the beginning and he believed it would be there in the end. He knew that good things loved water.

In water, in the war, the tree snags and rusted canteens would end up where the stream took them, sometimes logged along the twisted shore, other times making it all the way to the sea where they sank or were carried into longshore currents or eventually degraded into nothing; pieces of the earth gone in few days.

Phin turned the shower to cold and closed his eyes. In his mind, it was raining in the Nam like it could do for weeks at a time. A lot of the men didn't like the rain. They didn't see the reason, the purpose of it having to fall on them and make them cold and stiff and uncomfortable. Phin didn't mind it all. He'd made peace with it early on and knew that the rain, like the river, was something real and life-giving and cleansing. Water comes from heaven, he whispered to the men as they grumbled and humped through the red mud. Rain comes from a Great Spirit. It gets soaked up by the pores of the land and then sweat back out when the Mother Earth has had her fill. And they'd laugh and say, "You're doing that Indian guide thing again, Davis."

And he'd smile and say, "Yes, yes, I am," while letting the rain take his thoughts back to the stories of the old Indian called Grayfalls whom Johnny Cobb had spoken of. Rain was a good thing. He wished it would rain very, very hard for forty days and forty nights. He'd wished the rain would wash away the top three feet of that ancient and exotic land. Not because he despised the land, but because it had been scarred by evil. Something of this world, something made and dealt by the hands of man had come and killed the trees, turning the rain into fire that burnt everything it fell on and kept on killing and burning even after the men had gone away.

The rain would find the tunnels and fill them and thousands of small men dressed in black would scramble out looking like ants coming out of a dirt mound.

And then the rivers would swell until they filled the lowlands and buried many, many homes with mud and sludge because what is a war without the destruction of property anyway? The lowlands would become small lakes and then larger lakes and everything imaginable, and some things unimaginable, would be floating dead in the lakes. Tanks would fill up and soldiers would climb out to swim for a shore that gained in distance. Dark green trucks would float by with camouflaged canvas looking very much the like the murky waters. And smiling Vietnamese in pangas and river boats and small craft made of reed and red dirt caulking would paddle by and wave, making the unimaginable true because what is war without illusion anyway?

Phin would build his own boat, a boat just like the *Ruth Henry David*, only bigger. He'd scouted the logs he needed in high country jungles. He knew he could do it if had the time. But it would never be big enough to take back who he wanted to take back. And any size that would allow the pain to stowaway and follow him home was too large a vessel. So, Phin bent his head back, opened his mouth to the sky, and let the rain come. He had become nearly invulnerable because he had almost stopped caring. If he could only cut the final ties to his lingering chameleon philosophy, he might just fold himself into the widest river and let go. Because what is war without shifting philosophies?

But something deep, some steel umbilical cord, would not let him.

The rains stopped and the former Cpl. Davis stepped out onto the Mexican tile floor of the bathroom, drops falling off his body and getting soaked up in the red squares. Phin let his daydream roll on while he dried himself off. Cobb, he thought; now there was a man who understood water, but hated it all the same.

"Hey, Davis," it was Greer calling through the door. "You about ready to go into town and get some chow?"

"Sure, Mike. *Que hombre tengo.* Thirsty too. Be ready soon as I comb my hair."

✳ ✳ ✳

It was called *Manuela's,* but it could've been any small cantina in any poor Hispanic part of town in the southwest portion of America. But it wasn't because it was in Lubbock, Texas in 1973 and the county was essentially "dry," allowing very limited access to alcohol, deviance, and some parts of the New Testament. It wasn't so much the Bible thumpers as it was the echoing thump of the '60s in West Texas. New ideas on gender equality and race equality had fallen on unequal ears. But Manuela's was a membership joint and mostly legal to drink, particularly when the bootleggers delivered the harder, clearer stuff to the back door. Greer joked that this neighborhood on the outskirts of Lubbock could be a dangerous place for "whettos, thumpers, and mixed breeds like me after dark," but they were safe because he employed at least a dozen of the homeboys. He had more than just "some" native blood in him. And he paid in cash. They would be protected. The race war in Lubbock had become economically determined: "Well, I can look the other way if that envelope is thick enough."

What was so different about the civil war in Vietnam, Phin wondered, than the Civil War between the states? Why hadn't Phin thought about this before enlisting? Would it have mattered?

Phin and Greer walked in and sat down at the bar, the only place to begin such evenings. The bartender came up and tossed a dirty dish towel over his shoulder, smiled a wide, gold-tooth smile, and reached his brown hand out to Greer.

"*Que undo, Ese*? What's going there, Señor Greer?"

"*Nada,* Jose, just some *comida y bebidas con mi amigo,* Phin."

Jose shook hands with Phin and reached under the bar to a rarely-used cabinet and pulled out a long, thin, blue bottle. He poured two shot glasses of a clear liquid Phin knew was good and well-aged tequila, because what else could it be?

They sat in silence for many moments and sipped as Jose kept their glasses full. He brought out warm tortillas and fresh salsa and saw that their silence was irrevocable and as strong as the drink. Phin thought that the drink made from agave and the nutrients of sandy soil tasted like something indigenous, like a sweet medicine from another culture, which it was. He held the silence, listened to the waiters calling out orders to the cooks, calling them names in jest, insulting their *madres,* laughing, running, wiping the sweat from their brows and, if a drop or two fell on the food, oh well, salt is salt. Phin heard the music, too, that telling folklore of ancient tales told in the rhythm of nylon string guitars strummed Mariachi style.

It was a good feeling and tequila became water.

But they'd come to talk, not drink. The silence gave way to the words that would expunge the disease of itself, crumbling and crashing as war stories told between warriors overlap and intertwine and grow together like serpents entwined on a tattoo.

"How bad are you?" Greer asked as he wiped bits of tomato and green pepper from his chin. Phin had expected the man to come out quick and clean when he finally spoke.

"On the good days I can see all the way into next week; the bad ones, maybe tomorrow," Phin answered without emotion or cause.

"So, you on the road running to or from?" Greer asked.

"Bit of both, I reckon, depending on the view and the company."

"Did some road time when I first got back," Greer parried. "Alaska. Ended up working at a hunting lodge for rich fat cats from the lower forty-eight, helping them find elk and moose and such. Good job for a while." Greer paused and looked at a menu that had been placed in front of him, pushing it away and asking the bartender for a couple of beers in his broken Spanish.

"Got fired when I hit one of the clients with the butt of a rifle."

Phin looked over at the man as if to ask if the incident had anything to do with the war, but he said nothing, just stared.

"The guy saw a griz 'bout three hundred yards across a steep valley and decided he'd try and just 'wing her.' Stupid city boy. Grizzly is just about the most perfect killing machine, not counting the white shark. Great killers ought to be respected for their skill, not fucked around with."

Phin remembered his own bear, but said nothing.

"You think NVA were smart, Phin? You think they were smarter than us? Or were our hands tied? What do you think, kid? Locally or globally? I heard you had a choice—that you wanted to go."

Phin could see Mike was playing with him, seeing if he'd take the bait. So, he played back.

"You think I should've known, don't you? You think 'cuz I went in late I should've known it was bullshit. I don't recall Mark Rudd and the Weather Underground going door-to-door on the outskirts of Panama City Beach in early '71. Hell, there were only some seventy-five thousand of us still over there the week after Kent State. We could've all fit in the football stadium at once. Just one big collection of misanthropes."

Phin took a short sip from his tequila and a longer pull from a domestic beer that had risen from the table.

"NVA? Tenacious motherfuckers, good fighters for the most part, but just mostly conscripted kids like, well...like us. But the Montagnard of the Central Highlands—they are some people worth remembering. Strong, independent, spiritual. Even when the North reunites the country under communist rule, they won't submit. They're the Apache of Southeast Asia."

Greer turned his head slowly and faced Phin. He was nodding and his eyes became slightly hooded, almost black in the smoky air.

"Nah, I don't expect nobody to know nothing unless they see it. And even then you know as well as m, some of what was done over there was hard to process as real. I went in early '65, between what happened at Pleiku and the beginning of Rolling Thunder. But hell, there were guys coming back even then who knew. I should've known as well. Whoever knows? I was just wondering more about the reason you went in, that's all. Because I had no reason at all, at least not that's come back yet 'cept maybe youthful ignorance, which ain't ever comin' back."

Nobody had ever asked Phin directly why he'd enlisted. Not Harry, not Grace, not Johnny Cobb, not even Dickey Riot. He had barely asked himself, had mostly put it off as a reaction to Gillie's death; or something about having a perfect childhood and there being a cost for everything perfect, that you owed somebody something for all the good that you'd enjoyed. He didn't know. But what he suspected was that there would be a cost for him to find out the "great whys" of his recent years. There already had been. Bum foot, missing his ma's incident— what did the docs call it—a "cerebral vascular accident;" watching his Pa open up a new war on himself. Phin sometimes wondered why he was alive; usual stuff, he thought, for men returning from war.

But Phin Davis didn't feel like he'd been to a war. It was more like he'd been to a freak show, had spent nearly twenty-two months in a psychotic nightmare where nothing made sense, where somebody had stolen his sanity and was playing catch with it to the sound of an Iron Butterfly song—*Inna-Gadda-De-Vida, Honey*—those seventeen minutes and two seconds of perfect mayhem. Now, after the drum solo and the building organ riff, his sanity was his to find with only a few clues. Mike Greer was one of them.

They moved into a booth and ate rice and beans and enchiladas. They switched to Tecate beer when the tequila and Lone Star ran out—Mexican road flares—Greer called them, and squeezed fresh lime over everything. They spoke about their homes and fishing and dogs and trucks—steering clear of the Nam for the moment—and women.

But the blue agave had worked its magic and Phin couldn't help himself.

"What happened to Jessica's mother?" He slurred.

Greer didn't miss a beat and finished a corn tortilla, washed it down by sucking on a lime, and answered.

"Couldn't hang. I got out in mid '66 and came home to a twenty-six-year-old drunk being raised by a four-year old. Got her in rehab, the mother that is, and she was okay for a while. But I was wrestling the re-entry devils and took off north for a season. When I came back, I knew I'd make it and told my wife and Jessica that we were all better now, that this padre was 'ten-eight,' in service, and ready to put the pieces together. Three days later she up and leaves with a guy who sells shoes downtown. Something of an expert on arch support, I suppose. No note or nothing. Just has a friend tell me she needs time and space."

"Hell, it's been what, almost six years? How long you gonna wait?"

"Still working on that one. Closer to seven, maybe, and I think I'm just about done. It wasn't the time, so much as the space. And what it did to Jess." Greer ran his fingers through his long black hair and pulled it back into a pony tail. He slumped in his chair, pushed his plates away, and looked at Phin.

"And you? You leave anybody behind?"

"All of them, Mike," Phin looked up from his plate and started to cover his face with his napkin before setting it back down. "I left them to go over and I left them to come home. I left them to be sitting here right now."

There were tears in his eyes but they wouldn't fall as he moved the plates around the table like a model of the solar system.

"And the funny thing is that I could never tell when they wanted me to go and when they wanted me to stay."

Phin asked for a glass of water and drank it slowly, feeling the water spill down his chin, through his shirt and pants, and into his boots. The night would get better before it got worse.

"Jessica did a nice job on your haircut," Greer switched gears.

"She's done a nice job raising you back up." The words moved out of Phin a syllable at a time.

Greer raised his glass and said a man could consider himself blessed if he knew but one person who'd stick by him. Phin said he had at least three left and asked Greer if he liked to go for a swim.

CHAPTER 26

IF ONLYS

I shall be telling this with a sigh

Somewhere ages and ages hence:

Two roads diverged in a wood, and I—

I took the one less traveled by,

And that has made all the difference.

–From the "The Road Not Taken"
by Robert Frost

There were two Mike Greers: the one that was baiting and switching on Phin, trying to pull something out of him that would only come out on its own time; and there was the one that just sat and listened and understood because he'd been there, been here in that *place*, looking for a shadow of who Phin or himself might hang onto and use as a foundation to stack bricks of a self on top of, just one goddamn red clay brick after another without rebar or drugs or VA shrinks for support; just a couple of dead soldiers trying to claw their way six feet up where the air was clear enough to see into the next hour— assuming that shadows of light could hold the weight.

Two men, one past; both men with many futures and memories that had been cubed into a family tree with a large thick branch called war.

There were also two Greers because of the liquid (the Mexican truth serum) that had snuck up on him even when he knew it was sneaking, a kind of double-vision made kaleidoscopic when the tears covered his pupils.

They over-paid the bill by two and stumbled out of Manuela's.

"You think Jessie is all right at home by herself?" Phin asked as they looked around the parking lot for Mike's truck.

"Sheeeet, Davis. None of my friends will come close to the house if they know I'm not there because she'll fire one warning shot, one in the thigh, and the next between their eyes."

"That's not just your training, is it?" asked Phin.

Greer looked around the parking lot for his truck and began pissing in the bushes.

"Of course not. Every intruder, animal or human, is a chance for her to shoot out her anger at her mother for leaving. She was caught in that crossfire and knows the value of a well-placed bullet. She knows about misinformed choices and the lying veil of opportunity presented to those who feel they don't have a choice. She's old enough to know that her mother was lying to herself and to feel all the guilt that stays with those who couldn't pour enough truth into the afflicted to make them see what they ain't ready to see."

Phin remembered his idea for kitty litter rimming the outside of bar parking lots, smiled, and then recognized Greer's subtle inference to all the minorities who couldn't get out of the war on a student deferment or a phony 4F, or a well-funded lawsuit, or a well-placed phone call. "The minorities and the poor will fight this war," he'd heard Johnny Cobb tell his father when he was in school. And now he knew exactly what the man was saying.

Choices? How did he ever really come to think he could right the world's wrongs by doing something that could never be right?

Johnny had talked to him about choices when they spoke of Harry's long weeks away chasing fish or when somebody who didn't know Johnny came to town and uttered a racist comment just loud enough. All that was buried in the past.

But not very deep.

"So, if we go to Jerry's Place now, can we park in the front," Phin joked.

"I thought you didn't want to talk about girls," Greer shot back.

"What's a strip bar got to do with being lonely for female company?"

"Nothing, if you don't want it to. Not a goddamn thing a'tall."

"Can you drive?" Phin asked.

"Can you ride me on your handlebars? And don't forget we have to cross the Lubbock County line, have to leave the Bible thumpers, leave the sinners for the saints. We're going to Crosby County and a place called Jerry's"

✳ ✳ ✳

Jerry's was the kind of place that could've been anywhere beer was cheap and the music loud enough to drown out your thoughts, but not so loud that you couldn't pretend that people listened when you brought your troubles in and tried to pry them off your back with booze and the comfort of others doing the same. It was cool and dark inside and the vinyl booths were blood red. The floor was concrete with a sheen of Lysol leaking up to meet the cigarette smoke that hung from the dropped ceiling like a layer of cumulus nicotine. It was a good bar; Phin liked it straight away.

In the center of the bar was a low stage with the corners of the three quarter inch plywood chipping way below the flat black paint. And in the center of the stage was a chrome pole draped by a tall, scantily-clad brunette; the pole highly polished by the silk and satin and skin of Jerry's prime attractions.

Phin and Greer took the only open booth near the emergency exit door, sat down, and tried hard not to stare at the girl on the stage...but not that hard.

"Hey Mikey, when you gonna take me outta this dump so we can run away together?" She was a waitress, late-late thirties with eyelashes that might've kept the sun out of her eyes, bleached hair piled high enough that the ceiling fan might've cut the top layer off, and thighs so strong and thick they might've cut a man in half if she'd had the cause to.

"Ah, Lynette," Greer carried the playful joust on. "You know I like it near Lubbock, much as you are a sweet catch. It ain't Miami Beach, but when the wind ain't blowing and the temperature drops below ninety degrees it's downright livable. Besides, if I take you away, the hearts of half the men and a few of the women in this town would go and bust."

"Maybe next week then," Lynette winked at Phin.

"Yeah, maybe next week." Greer ordered beers, patted Lynette on the arm and turned to Phin. "I love West Texas. Everybody talking about trying to get out, but if given a wad of cash and a one-way ticket, they'd never leave."

Phin looked at Greer and said nothing. He knew this kind of place; the natural beauty worked behind counters and in fields and factories. There were few postcards of places like this, just colorful people who made you feel real; not always good or bad, but alive. Lubbock, Texas would never be on a TV show unless linked to a tornado, Buddy Holley, or a damn good football team. The beers came and Lynette stood at their table making small talk, eyes darting at Phin, flirting because it made her feel alive like a Sunday afternoon football game between men too old to play without limping home, tired, sore, a little drunk from the post-game beer, feeling something like...vital.

"So, you guys are war buddies?" she asked, knowing full and well that when men went off to war they came home with similarities both tragic and wonderful, if they came back. Lynette's husband hadn't—not his body or anything connected to it. She knew the full drill, her case slammed home when she saw those others whose bodies did...but not much else. Lynette Williamson would never be able to choose if she'd rather have her husband back in bits and pieces or not at all. Like so many, she put the war on the shelf until it fell off on its own.

"In a way," Mike introduced Phin properly and said they had a mutual friend down south, "One of Jessie's twelve godfathers," he put it.

Lynnette scooted away to another flock of men who watched the girl on stage gyrate to the thumping bass line of some band they might call "that damn rock music" in another setting. But for now it was just fine.

"Guess I should've figured there'd be twelve. You know, like the disciples." Phin spoke into his glass as if it was tempering his words. There was a pause in the music and a kind of hush came over the room. "Local Bible thumpers 'round here call this place, 'infectious human waste.' " Greer finally spoke with a serious tone. "Most of them haven't read the Book well, at least not the New Testament the way it can be read—as a tale of a good man's life, doing good things. Okay, maybe the man is the Son of God, but that's for each to figure out and not twist and turn into their own version of a historical story. Every reason they have for shutting this place down I can counter-argue, chapter and verse." Greer seemed proud of himself but then added, "It's kind of fun, but I ought not to rile them up. They can get to be an ornery bunch."

Phin liked how Mike could jump from topic to topic with only a thin thread of relevance. He made his own jump.

"How'd you come to meet Johnny Cobb, anyway?" Phin asked.

Greer heard the music come back on and watched a new girl step onto the stage. He pointed at her and said she was a real nice gal, that she worked at the five-and-dime store most days, and was engaged to a fireman in Amarillo.

"It was odd, really, in the beginning. I was working for my dad back in, oh, must've been '52 or '53. Reckon I wasn't quite eight or nine. Just doing some sweeping up and odd chores on the used car lot he was managing back then. I was saving nickels, thinking 'bout going out for the Pop Warner football team, building forts, not much else. When you're young and healthy and free, the rest of the world seems really far away. And you want like nothing else to get your hands on a slice of it.

"This guy wanders into town outta nowhere; Black man, nice looking except for this funny scar on the back of his head in the shape of a lightning bolt. Kept his hair short and nothing grew there. Kept his mouth shut too.

"So this guy drives up in a decent looking Ford pickup and asks my pop if he has any work. He must've been in his early thirties, but as a kid, adults all looked the same until they got to be really old. The car lot was rocking back then, middle of the Baby Boom. World War II vets trading in good used cars just to get something newer, bigger, shinier, with tail fins and round taillights. The ones who'd made a bit of money or came over from Dallas or wanted the rest of tiny Lubbock to think they had made it big, went for the convertibles. My pop asked the man if he was handy with a wrench and he said he'd work for free for a week if'n Pop wasn't satisfied.

"But the guy was a whiz, best I seen; could do a top end job on a straight-six in four hours start to finish. Quality work, too. Had a temper, though. Seemed like he was angry at every White man who come in, even the good ones who didn't pay no attention to skin color. But he was a Black man in a place that was lily White. I didn't think anything of it until I got older and the senselessness of it all made sense. Still, it seemed that this man had come to a part of Texas that was unwelcoming to Blacks. And he'd done it on purpose."

Greer stared off into the pipes and ducting that lined the ceiling of Jerry's.

"I liked the guy, looked up to him. He taught me a lot about things that go together and fall apart and need fixin'. Almost nine months he worked for Pop, living in a shed out the back for the first few, keeping pretty much to himself. I asked him if he had any kin, but he got edgy and dropped a 4mm end wrench on the floor and swore like no man I ever heard before or since, including buddies in the Nam. I didn't ask any more;

was too scared. But we became friends and he showed me more than a few things about growing up.

"Then one day around Christmas time this guy shows up—another Black man—and he walks onto the lot and asks if we'd seen a new guy in town, a man by the name of Chuck. I hadn't learnt to lie and told him there was a fellow working for us might be the one, but he'd have to see for himself. Then he asked me my name and talked to me straight up, like I was an equal adult with all the rights and privileges of an adult and said if I could tell this man that Johnny Cobb is in town and would like to see him, he'd be much obliged."

Phin was intrigued and sat up on the edge of his wobbly bar stool, straining to hear over the music, suddenly sober.

"Well...," he urged Greer to go on while Mike motioned to Lynette for another round.

"That's all to tell," Greed said trying to get to the point. "I told Chuck about this fellow Cobb the next afternoon on my way home from school and the strangest look came over him. It was a kind of sadness with bits of relief and calm layered over. At first I thought he might get real mad and throw a box wrench or a long Phillips driver, but then his voice got real soft and he asked me if I could do him a favor. I said, 'Anything, Chuck. Just name it.' Then he asked me if I could tell this man Cobb, if'n he came back, that he was okay, but he couldn't look into his eyes yet, so please don't try and find him.

"The next day when Mr. Cobb came back 'round, I told him the message. And Chuck was gone. Didn't even pick up his paycheck or say goodbye. To this day, Johnny never told me about it and I reckon it ain't my business to ask. But we stayed friends and when Pop died just before my eighteenth birthday. Johnny kind of made sure I was gonna be okay. That's the story."

Phin knew about Chuck; knew every detail because over the years they had leaked out of Johnny. And Phin had pieced them together like a quilt made of rags that you try and throw away but keeps showing up in your drawer.

Phin thought for a moment why Cobb hadn't told Greer the whole story and then on a gut reaction figured Johnny wouldn't mind if he did. Maybe that was just a part of him making the connection between the two. So Phin told Mike just enough, not every detail and image that he had carried in his memories of the man who had come to his family with a boat two-and-a-half decades ago. But enough so that Mike Greer would know about the man they called Chuck and taught him how to fix things.

All Greer could do was to shake his head and say, "I'll be damned," over and over.

Then after a silence that was now different between them, Greer spoke.

"A few years later, after my daddy got the ranch and before he got sick, he'd heard from some friends who worked in the DA's office that the mechanic named Chuck who had worked for him was in trouble with the law. They thought he had crossed the border and was living in Mexico. It was self-defense, they'd said, but he'd darn near killed a man up near Dimmit. Dad had tried to find him, wanted to clear his name, but also wanted a good ranch hand."

Phin had been watching the girl dance, allowing his mind to remember Lonnie, thinking that if he drank any more he might walk to the pay phone and look up her name, just as if she would be living in this place. But the words "ranch hand" had pulled him back hard and quick and turned his stomach.

Greer caught his own accidental reference as well and tried to bury it.

"If you're gonna be sick, please don't get any on my new boots."

Phin tightened his stomach muscles and then took a deep breath, the smoky air hurting his lungs. When he turned back to Greer his face had gone from brown to gray to green and now stood a pale yellow in the flashing lights.

"What do you know about Operation Ranch Hand?" Phin's voice had an edgy sorrow to it. And he wasn't sure why he was yanking Greer back into Indo China.

"They didn't call it that until after I was already back. But I knew chemicals. We had crops on the ranch, used herbicides, pesticides; I knew what accidental poisoning was before the C-123s dropped twelve million gallons of Orange, White and Blue on the Nam. And that ain't no accident."

Phin rubbed his chin and then lowered his head.

"You think that..." Phin started in but Greer jumped in hard.

"Do I think what? That the two buddies from my platoon that died of liver cancer, the other three that have kidney problems, and the fucking headaches that I have every mother-fucking-day are all accidents? Man, I went to the VA in Houston and told them I think my dick's gonna dry up and fall off like a hundred-year-old man, like the mangrove forests in-country because I was in that same shit for half my tour. You know what they did? They gave me an appointment with a shrink, wouldn't even test my blood." Greer's face had gone to bright pink now and his ears seemed to glow.

"You know how that shit works?" A little pile of spit built up around the corner of Greer's mouth. "It's a dioxin; it makes the cells grow and multiple at an accelerated rate, like growing into an old man in a matter of weeks or months. Jungles a hundred-years old withered away in the time it takes for a moon to get full enough to walk through them. Yeah, I think a lot of men who came back from a war that couldn't kill them with bullets and bombs will die at the hands of their own leaders who will never admit that deadly mistake—among many."

Greer forced himself a trite little laugh and said that one of the symptoms is loss of memory, but he seemed to remember even better now; he could still smell what was called 2,4,5-T. And it burnt the hairs of his nose when he thought of the sound of the C-123s coming in low and slow, pissing their agents.

"What do you care?" He asked Phin between the growing laugh, "It was over by the time you went in."

Something hit Phin and another piece of the puzzle slipped into place. It was like waking up in the morning and knowing the next step in a long-string calculus problem. He pushed his beer in front of Greer who was looking around for Lynette to refill his hand.

"You know the answer to that," he looked right into Greer's dark eyes. "I have to care same as you have to care. Ain't too many people 'round here or anyplace else doing the caring. And it's never over with or reified, just dealt with and plowed over."

A smile came over Greer's face, starting at the top of his head and dripping down like molasses, slow and thick and sweet.

"Not often I get a chance to hang with guys who use the words *ain't* and *reify* in the same sentence and seam them together like a scar he enjoys showing off. You gonna tell me about the girl?"

Phin eyes squinted as if he was trying to see something far away. "Maybe next time through, Mike; next week, next year, next time around when I have more to tell," Phin's voice trailing off. "Yeah, when I have a richer narrative with more chapters. Then I'll tell you."

Greer nodded and fished in his pocket for the truck keys while blowing a kiss to Lynette across the room.

"If only you had more time; if only you didn't have to leave in the morning."

Phin stopped, taken aback, "What are you talking about? I've been here less than twenty-four hours. I came to work for you, to weld things, just like Johnny said. I don't need to be rushing off. Where do I have to go?"

Greer stood up and ran his fingers through his long black hair again.

"Yeah, you have time, but what you need is space. You already know what to do; you just got to go do it. And you can't do it here in Lubbock."

Mike put his arm around Phin's shoulder and said he'd have to learn how to follow the signs better, because tonight was a sign, his haircut was a sign, Uncle Chuck's ghost was a sign. "Just make sure you say goodbye to Jessie in the morning. She was going to get your car ready for you tonight."

Phin was trying to put it together as they walked out of Jerry's into the warm West Texas night.

"We're just the middle soldiers in time, Phin, sentenced to a vacuum that was switched on by men who operated in the worst kind of evil, sucked in, then switched off and left to find our own way out of the bag in the dark."

Phin knew it was the evil of greed, the tragedy of ignorance. And it wasn't just a few men—it was a country. He found the door handle to the truck and climbed in. And as Mike Greer, the farm equipment manufacturer and single father who wouldn't live to see his daughter graduate from high school, the tumor in his lungs growing as they looked out the window toward the heavens; as the former soldier who had fought his way out of the bag with anger and patience and acceptance and hate and whatever love he could scrape from the walls of a life turned against him started to put the key in the ignition, the younger soldier with part of his body in the vacuum and part left in Vietnam and part swimming toward the light, put his hand on the keys.

"Let me ask you one thing before we go." Greer turned his head part way towards the younger man. "Why is it that when people think you are really dying they will listen to you instead of just watching your lips move and waiting for their turn? Why did I feel so alive in a place where so many people were dying?"

"This is your life now, kid. You come to terms with it or you don't. Look at me, I ain't perfect. I have a daughter with more wisdom than I'll ever find. I'm lonely as shit. My head hurts and lately I've had this crappy cough I can't shake. But I don't plan on dying again until I'm old. I know what it's like, so do you, whether or not you realize it. But some people listen to me on account of I know which ones to talk to. You need to learn which people to latch on to, which ones to run from, and which ones to hold at knife point. Now, if you'll let me start this here truck up I'd like to get home. I got some work to do."

The truck sputtered and belched a gray cloud of smoke. But it started and they drove away, Mike Greer feeling the bench seat for an eight-track tape, Phin Davis feeling so much that his ears started to ring. If only the ringing would stop.

If only he wasn't afraid of what the noise was covering up. If only...

Phin would leave in the morning. And for the second time in twenty-four hours he fell asleep in Greer's truck, this time wondering what Cobb was doing. He'd call soon. If only he could find a dime. Just ten cents.

BOOK 4

BEFORE THE DAWN:

JOHNNY COBB'S SECOND COMING

CHAPTER 27

THE GRID

'The world (war) breaks everyone," Hemingway writes, "but those that will not break, it kills. It kills the very good and the very gentle and the very brave impartially. If you are none of these you can be sure it will kill you too but there will be no special hurry."

—A Farewell to Arms, Ernest Hemingway

If only the rain would stop. That's what I remembered thinking that night. Rain meant water that could turn into floods. And things deep. Jesus, I would've thought, that I could come to grips with water. Harry was good with water. Phin was even better. Maybe if Ruth hadn't died within its confines I might've learned to appreciate its qualities, if not its dangers.

But I was making waterbeds, not learning to surf.

Lying in bed that night, I was trying hard to make a kind of peace with that hard-falling, soft southern rain, listening to Blackie bang away on his typewriter in the dining room. His high laughter was comforting as it punctuated his steady self-talk. The writing was curing the kid, it seemed, one key stroke, one thought, one re-ordered synapse at a time.

I had stopped listening carefully to his self-chatter, stopped trying to make sense of what he was saying, mostly because it reminded me of the senselessness that he and one-half million American others had gone through. Maybe a million plus North Vietnamese. But I was proud of this one; of how hard he'd worked to get back much of what had almost been lost forever.

"Blackie," I called out from my room, trying to keep my mind off the rain and the letter, "How long until Saigon falls?"

"Oh, Chief, thought you were sleeping. It's a good rain, is it not? You want me to start gathering two of every animal?" There was an unusual forced waver in the pitch of his voice.

"No, Professor Black, I would like your opinion on when we can expect the North Vietnamese to march into Saigon, now that we're out of the war."

"C'mon Chief, you know we're still there—at least enough spooks to keep an eye on the rats jumping off the sinking ship. But to answer your rather sudden but astute query: never. The NVA will never march into Saigon. You see, oh, Master Waterbed Builder, they will change the name of Saigon to honor one of their own, probably Ho Chi Min. And this man speaking and typing away, formerly known as Blackie, feels it will happen within eighteen months, two weeks, and three days. I'll need a few days if you want the exact hour."

I chuckled and let the subject go. Harry's letter was still on the dresser, unopened. I had tried to tap into the intuition left to me by Ruth, but nothing came up. Maybe the rain had jammed the radar. I got up, pulled on a pair of overalls, and put the letter in a pocket. Walking into the kitchen, I asked Blackie if he wanted a cup of coffee.

"Sure, chief, I'm gonna be up all night."

"You on a roll, are you?" I asked.

"Nope. First, I'm going to ask you to open up that letter from Phin's pop and read it, which is a lot to ask. And then I'm going to ask you if you have any ammunition for that old shotgun you have hidden under your bed, which, I suppose, you'll find an interesting question."

I looked at Blackie and realized that I'd missed it. His frenetic typing and wild cacophony were covering up a fresh fear, something that he'd not taken into Auntie's bar earlier that night.

"Fair enough, professor. Let's read the letter and then you can tell me who you'd like to see disposed of."

I made the coffee as we sat in the quiet of the kitchen hearing the rain pound the roof and noticing that it sounded just like a typewriter, the wind acting as fingers to control the dripping words and the story it told; the story that always began with "a dark and stormy night." I looked at the clock for some reason, forgetting that it had been broken for three years.

I poured the large mugs and set them at the table as Blackie's fingers drummed the top so hard it made the black liquid ripple in time with his nerves.

"It's the guys from the VA, isn't it?" I asked.

He nodded then folded his hands as if to pray but instead pointed to the crumpled white envelope in my breast pocket.

"You first," he said, and I opened it carefully and read aloud.

Johnny: The ocean is one big place. There are so many things out here, so much life, so much past and future. There's some kind of energy out here, a force that few land folk ever get to feel. It can pick you up and throw you from shore to shore or it can cradle you in its arms and warm you and feed you like a young'n. But you have to be comfortable out here, you can't fight it. You have to let it take you. I'm not so sure you ever got to feelin' that way when you were fishin' with me.

But it's taking me now, like that child, like a kid who's had the shit beaten out of him. It has taken me to places where there is no war; not now anyway. I only hope that the road is doing the same for my son. Hola to Blackie. Simpatico...Harry.

Blackie and I looked at each other and for just a moment, I believed that a shift in the tragic paradigm of days past was finally in motion. "What are you thinking?" I finally asked.

"*Pura vida*, chief. Your friend is making friends with the white whale."

"Do you think you'll ever make friends with yours, Blackie?"

"He's surfaced, Johnny. I saw him come into Auntie's tonight; saw him, saw it with my right eye. That's why I ducked out the back door."

"What does he look like, Blackie? And I don't mean Wilcox because I saw him, too. And he saw me."

Blackie's fingers stopped moving mid-beat and he regarded me in a way that I'd not seen before. We both knew he had the edge regarding straight-up intellect. But now it was as if he was sizing up our differences by the amount of shit life had flung at us; some kind of carnival game where you stand up against a wall and blobs of grime and gut are shot at you from a cannon you cannot see. Some you dodge, some you wipe off with a shirt sleeve, and others stay with you for years, maybe forever. He held my stare but his eyes seemed to move out to the side where he could expand his peripheral view, one eye to the past, the other to the future—whale eyes.

"Why didn't you say something, chief? There's only one reason he's here: revenge. Wilcox wants a piece of lil' ol' Blackie Black. I've been found out, Chief Cobb. They know. They'll hurt me and then they'll ruin my life. Blackie doesn't like this feeling. So, what about the gun?"

It happens that way with people on the mend. They make such progress and then a part of their past leaks out of the dark trying to find its own light because it knows that it's inextricably linked to the present. And it's not always bad. But it must be dealt with. I think Blackie expected his hasty exit from the VA Hospital and Wilcox to find their way back to him sooner or later, like an old loan that you owe or an operation you need to have—they're always there, lurking, waiting patiently, or tired of waiting and then they come hunting. But no matter when you meet the bill collectors and surgeons, you know it's going to hurt and it's going to change you in some way.

Blackie wasn't afraid of pain and he wasn't afraid of change. Like most of us, though, he wanted to be the one directing the metamorphosis. Not an Oz behind the curtain, but a sculptor without a deadline.

"What do you want to do, Mr. Black? Shoot him with my shotgun? You think a bullet will take away your fear? Least I remind you, it was bullets that catalyzed your decent."

"That was different." Blackie was highly agitated and paced the room. "They wanted me to shoot someone I didn't know, who never hurt me. They kept lying to me and saying that I'd go to the stockade unless I picked up that gun and shot it. I didn't hate those people, Johnny. I didn't want to kill anyone."

"You were in a war, kid. You didn't have a choice. There were thousands just like you who'd rather not be there, who didn't bring the propensity for murder with them from home. It was a...learned skill."

"Yeah, I saw it. But not too many of them were doing much about it. They didn't seem to fight it very hard. Most of them went for the distractions and coping mechanisms rather than choosing."

"But did you really make a choice, kid? Did you tell them to send you to prison?"

Blackie's powerful intellect was losing ground to his repressed emotions. He wanted to remember things differently than the way they were.

"I was too afraid of killing, of having to live with that weight. And I was too afraid of going to the stockade on some dishonorable discharge that would keep me from a good job. I was stuck in a fear tornado, a methadone of identity. And that's when I turned catatonic and they shipped me stateside to the VA. I read the file, Johnny. I was supposed to be treated and re-evaluated every three months until I was well, and then reassigned until I could serve out my stint with the U.S. Army."

He was breathing hard and his finger-drumming had turned into a crescendo.

"But you never were reassigned, were you? You served your whole tour of duty buzzing around the Denver VA, acting crazy, helping folks, pissing off a few others in the process. And you had no real plans to leave, did you, Blackie?" This would be the question he knew to be true, but he'd twisted and morphed and dodged so many times, he had all but decided it was the unanswerable question he needed answered. So he forgot about it.

"I suppose I'd have to go sometime." Blackie was measuring out his words with a painful force as if each were a kidney stone. "I was better, I mean, you saw me in my periods of lucidity. I was okay, for the most part. But I didn't know what would happen if I tried to leave; whether I could face what had happened to me over there."

"But you knew you *could* leave, *could* fall, right? That all you needed was an evaluation clearing you? You weren't a prisoner anymore."

"Oh, yes I was. My bars came in many forms. It was just that they let me out when I asked them to, the gated bars I mean. I knew I could fall out of the sky but not from grace. It was timing, I guess."

"Why then, Blackie? Why with us? Was it Wilcox's threat that you ran from? The fear that has come back to haunt you now, tonight, in my house?"

Blackie seemed to be steeling himself a bit, a cold, hard realization forged in the future.

"Partly, it was," he said, slowing his breath, speaking in measured tones. "But it was the others, too; the way you all watched each other's back. I used to go up to Phin's hospital bed after visiting hours and watch him try to sleep, watch him have these battles where his arms would fling about wildly trying to kill something bad and reach for something good. I imagined what he was going through because I had the same thing. I just had some time to modulate mine, to find some form of mutual détente where I, too, wanted all the weapons out of my body for good. Seeing that, I think, gave me the courage to ask Gerald to forge the documents to get you guys out."

"You don't know, do you?" I forced a calm into my words.

"Know what?"

"Your man Gerald McReady cleared you as well. Phin's release was a 'screw up' that was covered up when he was pronounced dead by the county coroner in Panama City. Gerald just got us out the door; the rest fell into place and Wilcox and Roberts took the fall when *someone* left the file of evidence you'd collected with the administrators." Blackie was looking at me incredulously and I noticed the rain had let up outside.

"What that orderly friend of yours had done, Blackie, was to play a few cards he had of his own; pulled in favors from a couple of docs around there whom you had failed to convince of your schizophrenia but knew well your buried intellect and obvious empathy, whom you had helped without asking for anything in return. Our orderly McReady had a full evaluation done on you, in his own words, on stolen forms. The docs signed off on them and you were officially released from the U.S. Army without penalty."

Crickets replaced the rain outside in noise and timing.

Blackie rubbed his eyes and shook his head. I got up from the table to refill our mugs.

"Why didn't I know," his eyes asked me? But I had no answer. Maybe Gerald figured that I'd tell him. Maybe he didn't want any evidence traveling through the U.S. mail. Maybe he had a reason, "that reason had yet to unveil." It was that kind of period in our history. Valor and deceit could get melded or lost in the smoky air.

I could only imagine what was going through Blackie's mind. He was out from under the thumb of Uncle Sam, the big hand pried loose by a strong, quiet man who liked to make clay pots, who had been dealt his own bad hand but remained inside the palm back in the VA hospital; the "X" he used to call it.

Blackie's head was bent over the table now, a pool of tears building on the surface until it began running toward the edge and then off, dripping on the wooden floors like the rain was dripping off the roof. I pulled my chair in close and put my arm around the kid. There was nothing to say, so I ran my fingers through the tears on the table and made lines that moved out from the center, like a pinwheel, like sunrays.

When the tears began to dry, leaving little rings of salt like stars on the table, I stood up.

"Go on to bed, kid," I told him. "If Wilcox steps into this house without my invitation, I'll shoot him in the gut. Ain't no big deal to me. I've been to a prison of my own making, too."

I'd do it, too, I said to myself, only slightly surprised at the commitment to killing a man. Blackie got up and walked to his room, a change in his gait that I couldn't label. And I went down into the basement to look for bullets that'd been in storage for many years. Outside, it began to rain again.

✳ ✳ ✳

I dreamt of Ruth that night. She was swimming around in the mud underneath Grace's garden looking for Gillie.

"I'll find her, Grace. She couldn't have run off too far. I'll look in the forest."

But up top on the earth's surface, Grace was clutching her chest and wondering how she was going to have dinner ready for her two men who weren't coming home. Dickey Riot, who had been visiting, couldn't get to her because he was afraid to climb the deer fence and his dad, Jed was telling the governor that he'd build him the best gazebo in the South if he could just talk to God and save this poor woman. In my dream, Harry had tied a stern line to his boat and held on to the end of it as the boat pulled him through the long wake. He was looking under water for something, but he couldn't tell his crew what it was because he didn't know. Inside the Davis' home, Winnie from the lunch counter was making sandwiches for everybody.

Phin wasn't in my dream when I woke up. But somebody else was trying to get in it. It was the creaks in the floor that I heard first; a long moment of deciding if they were real or dreamed. They were real, slow deliberate steps, light and cautious. My heart pounded and I remembered Blackie's words "of having to live with the weight of killing." I would pull the trigger on an intruder though. Any man comes into my house uninvited, unsponsored, or otherwise, he'll get one warning and then an ass full of buckshot. Probably won't die from it, but he'll have a lot of time to think about it as the tiny lead pellets work their way to the surface. Harder to trace, too. My brother Earl had taught me that. He'd said there were so many farmers firing buckshot into the air to keep the birds away from their crops that a Negro could be half-a-mile away minding his own business and suddenly find himself with a piece of lead in his scalp, less'n he be wearing a hat.

The steps came louder and I heard a deep, throaty whisper.

"Cobb, hey John Cobb."

I thought I knew the voice and with it came a turning in my stomach. I reached under the bed for the gun and prayed the old thing would fire. Funny thought, asking God to make sure the gun that you have pointed at another one of His creatures will go off so you can hurt him.

"In here, asshole," I said. And when the door to my room opened and the silhouette came at me I knew I could do it, that I had to do it, that I'd pay a price but it would be worth it to erase the fear in the kid's mind.

"That you, young Johnny Cobb?"

That voice. I knew it, but it brought no warmth. I saw the flash of light and took it for a firing mechanism. What kind of choice is that? That a man has to decide in a spliced moment whether to kill or be killed? How many things must the mind process in that cut-up second? Imagine a soldier having to do it day after day? I pointed the gun at the ceiling and pulled the trigger, the thought of the weight having won out. Let Wilcox kill me. Let the next life and somebody else decide my fate. I was tired of thinking about fate. I needed to let go as Harry was letting go.

The face was dark and hardened with lines right down from the skull. And in the glow of the match I could see that the eyes, too, were hardened, but they held the same sorrow I'd seen in them before they ran away so many years ago.

"Jesus, Johnny. That any way to welcome an in-law?"

"Uncle Chuck? Christ! Your re-entry is even more dramatic than your exit. What the hell you doing, sneaking around like that?"

"I was gonna wait until tomorrow, but I was getting all wet outside. I hate the rain. Next life I'm living in the desert."

"Me too, Chuck, get in here...dry up."

CHAPTER 28

KIN

...that those aren't busy being born are busy dying.

–Bob Dylan

It wasn't a reunion. It couldn't be called a *gathering* or a *meeting* or a *think- tank* or anything at all because it just happened the way most unplanned communions of people usually do—by unexplainable accident; some strange and wonderful convergence of eclectic mankind.

The gunshot had awoken the entire house where I'd offered room and board for my ragtag collection of hippy bed builders and Nam vets. First into the room were the dogs, yelping and baying and ready to tear into Uncle Chuck's shins with my slightest nod. But Chuck knew dogs as well and they in turn sensed that he was no enemy. They hadn't been raised as hunting dogs, but it was in their bloodlines, undeniable lineages, an extra sense beyond the capability of most within the human species: loyalty rarely ingrained amongst the two-legged kind.

The next person into the room was a man by the name of Snare. Snare was among the crew of Vietnam vets who came and went at my shop and my wayward home outside Lafayette. He'd only been a "resident" for a few weeks and was still unable to sleep under a roof since he'd been back in the world. Snare had been a force recon guy who'd spent most of his third tour in Laos and Cambodia. His government had denied he was ever there. But what kept his mind troubled was that they had, in ways that would count, denied he was still, now, here. Snare had been in and out of jobs, hospitals, trouble, and jail. He slept with a loaded semi-auto .45mm under his pillow—when he slept.

A fellow vet had put him onto me and the others at the shop had taken to working with him like old ranch hands might with a wild mare that refused to be broken. They'd never take all his spirit away, but they showed him how to live with others after having been away from the herd. They show him how to quiet the demons, at least until *that day* came. Everybody who'd been where Snare had been and seen what he'd seen would have a kind of "that day."

Snare had been sleeping under a tarp outside in the rain and within seconds of the gunfire and dogs barking, he was ready to jump Chuck from the rear, his long sharp blade in one hand, the .45 in the other. Snare seemed mildly, wickedly impressed that he was able to sleep while an intruder crept right by him. But I'd called him off just in time and now, after the full round of introductions and explanations, we all sat at the big kitchen table. I kept shaking my head at the irony. Blackie, who seemed pleased at Chuck's sudden appearance, wanted to know everything, and Snare sat quietly, his eyes fixed on Chuck's every move.

Chuck stood up from the table and went right for the cupboard above the fridge to remove a bottle.

"Never met 'nother nigga' that didn't keep a bottle above the fridge," Chuck mumbled to himself while looking for glasses to fill with Jack Daniels. "And speaking of names, first honkey here calls me Charlie gets a fistful. The name is Chuck."

This drew an odd look from Blackie, who sensed a good story behind it, maybe something he didn't understand about the Afro-American culture. Snare laughed out loud for the first time in weeks and said, "Okay, Charles, whatever you say." And I kept shaking my head, sensing that as hardened as Chuck might have become over the years, Snare could kill him with a piece of kite string if the tightly strung wires that held his mind together snapped.

"A name is an important thing. It defines the man, says much of his, uh... *being* without words. It is not a label, it's something that belongs to him and can't be taken away." It was Tom-Tom, whom I thought had not come home from Auntie's bar last night. He was standing in the doorway to the kitchen, his hands folded, his long hair pulled back into a dark ponytail, his face smooth where everybody else had shadows and scrub. Tom-Tom wore old fatigues cut off just above the knee and nothing else. His feet were wide and tan, the bottoms hardened like old leather. Sometimes down at Auntie's, he'd bet a new face five bucks that he could walk on broken glass. Tom-Tom was good with forms and he was patient. He'd convinced the government he was three-quarters Cherokee when he was barely one-eighth on a good day. It wasn't simply because he was Indian, a racial designation we'd gradually began to refer to as "Native American" because they were here before the rest of us, "natives" and according to the American Constitution, were American, but because his great-grandmother had been full blooded and there had been a "settlement" for the land-based mineral rights her tribe had owned. The U.S. government, in a long-negotiated form of partial mea culpa, agreed to compensate her Native American nation, even to their heirs, not for steeling land, but for a kind of economic manifest destiny: *"Sorry, you Indians, but we're building a country here. Here's a few bucks to ease the pain of us stealing your lands, inclusive of water, gold, silver, et al."*

The small checks that arrived each month brought the same comment from Tom-Tom—*expropriating the expropriators*. Tom-Tom liked to say that the next generation of Natives would begin to rise up on the greed of the Wasichu, the Sioux name for White man.

"For Christ's sake, Tom-no-last-name." I tried to sound surprised, but I'd seen him there moments before and had kept quiet, letting the one-something-ith Cherokee feel his heritage of silent approach. "We've had enough sudden entries to fill a CIA academy, man. C'mon in and meet my Uncle Charles."

We sat at the table. We were five, then six: me, Chuck, Blackie, Snare, Tom-Tom, and now Hopper, who'd stopped by to give Snare a ride to the shop. Alternating between black coffee and brown J.D., we debated the importance of a name. Tom-Tom, who Hopper sometimes called Shoeless, said he was allowed to pick his Indian name when he was seven years old and had begun to learn what he was about. Blackie, who had regained his quick wit, reminded Tom-Tom that he'd grown up in a poor section of Fargo (as if there was a rich part of town).

"Yeah, but the 'Res' was always in me, man," he defended himself, "and I was in it." I agreed that a name was important, but only if it fit the man and was allowed to be changed as the man changed. Hopper, originally from a traditional Midwest family outside of Chicago, "just a regular family," he liked to say, "with not enough money but enough of everything else," said that a name tied you to history and tradition.

"You saying the name Hopper has tradition?" Tom-Tom asked.

"No, not in the traditional sense." Hopper pushed out his lower lip and jokingly spoke with a high nasal whine. "It enables me a personal history, a particular story and moment in which the name was awarded me. It's nothing substantial, but it's a memory that can't be removed easily. For me, the name is worth keeping. Think of it as a cost/benefit analysis when you opt to accept a nickname."

Tom-Tom and the others could have easily gone on the offensive with Hopper, asking him why he was self-exiled with a group of vets who came from families where "means" meant a Goodwill store, macaroni and cheese, and the reliance on aunties and uncles to keep you from getting too beat up after school. But they knew he was smart enough to realize this wayward stop of my hippy-bed complex was the perfect rehab center for, as Roger Miller had referred in his 1964 hit, "King of the Road," for "men of means by no means." Someday, I thought, if Hopper ever felt the peace of psycho-stability and had control of his father's financial empire, he would send out cashier's checks to each of these brothers-without-arms. There would be no return address and they would have many zeros after them. He would deny sending them. But they would know and the peace of giving would flow through his veins like a drug.

But the others were thinking of nicknames and only Snare's had not been discussed and never would. When Chuck looked at him the table went deathly quiet. For each of them knew that Snare's name must also have come with an indelible memory and a cost, one that was substantial, that he would keep even if he threw it away. It went beyond Hopper's cultural economics. Snare's kind was the toughest to melt because it was his tensile strength that had both allowed him to survive quite easily in the deepest jungles of Indochina, and then struggle with the quietude of his willow-lined hometown streets outside Omaha. It would take a great force to break him; an even greater hearth to recast the metal of his being, and neither was assured. A man like Snare could hold a sister's newborn with the greatest of care and then excuse himself gently, hand the baby to his kin, climb a bell tower, and put a dozen rounds into the cops before he put one in his mouth. Snare, the Stradivarius of Vietnam vets, could also become a senator; much depended on the re-entry process.

Chuck, who had listened to the whole conversation with great interest, swirled the J.D. in his glass and spoke, his eyes mostly fixed on Snare, returning to the subject of names.

"It's about respect, that's all. You could call me Nigga' and I could call you all Baby Killers. And if'n we both found a way to do it out of respect then it would be okay. That's the way I see it. A name ain't much different than other sounds coming out of a guy's mouth, except it's a good way to show respect. History is history. None of us is changing it. But respect is right now, at this table, if it's anywhere. It is '*all things to all men.*' "

The breakfast liquor had loosened Chuck's and the others' tongues. Snare included, they knew he was onto something. And they caught the biblical phrase right away.

"You see, it's like this," Chuck continued. "I know who I am because I know what my purpose is. I came by that discovery by trying to erase myself all together on more than one occasion. I don't pretend to understand the *whys* of what I'm supposed to be doing. Hell, I'm not even so sure I know who

God is. But a long time ago there was an accident, a girl close to me, close to this man sitting here some of y'all call chief. She died young and I could've prevented it. My purpose ain't to fix that 'cuz I can't never raise her up. But I'm living with this guilt and it swallows me every day, only spitting me out long enough to let me see that it's already night. But I've come to respect this guilt. Oh, not because I like the feeling or nothing. Hell, my life is one damn imposition on itself. But like having a name, it defines me and unhinges enough feeling in me that I know I have to go and play out the whole deck. Otherwise Ruth woulda died for nothing.

"That's my purpose: to hang on until the end, the end of something. And I'll know it when I see it. That's who I am. I ain't a survivor; I'm just not a quitter unless it's that time. I'm comfortable enough with the pain. I respect the pain on account of it is part of the guilt of not saving my niece and the girl Johnny was gonna have a regular family with. Not that y'all ain't kin enough to him. But I got transferred into the person who bears my name just so I could keep on living; like I was born White and rich and then I lost a big hand and was the poor nigger I am. But it ain't a game, it's real. So fuck the name Chuck, and fuck your Charlie...it don't matter so long as I get respected for being who I am and I don't have to live in *'a house divided.'* "

Chuck skipped the glass and drank from the bottle. The table was quiet. The only sound was the heavy breathing of the dogs at Johnny's feet.

Nobody looked at their watch because nobody owned one. Blackie was wishing he had some notepaper. Tom-Tom was remembering when he was a kid. Hopper must've been thinking that was a good speech but only him, me, and maybe Blackie really knew what the guy was talking about. But to a one they were searching for the chapter and verse. It was a game they played, something that I had got them onto, partly for fun, partly to deflect the Bible-thumpers who would accost them on the street. They knew the Bible as story, as power in knowing, as a common and sometimes interpretable language. And they knew about the heroics acted out between the pages. To them, the Good Book didn't offer redemption so much as it talked about people who'd been redeemed. The guys would argue over whose turn it was to do the dishes and then Blackie or Tom-Tom would ask what is this, *"a house divided?"* And the first one to blurt out "Matthew 12:25, *'against itself cannot stand,'* " would be excused from duty.

I finally got up to find my pipe and tobacco.

"You know, Chuck," it was Snare who finally spoke, "A few of us knew another Charlie who could cause us some guilt. But unlike your niece, he's still there and we're all gone." The words wore a coat of finality and I finished it for the moment by saying it was time to go make us some beds.

"You're welcome to come on into the shop with us," I spoke in the direction of Chuck, but didn't expect an answer that never came. "We'll be at Auntie's afterwards, you want to come in. Blackie has some friends he wants you to meet. Or you can just stay here *'under the sun.'* "

"Ecclesiastes 1:9," shouted Hopper as if he was on a TV game show. " *'There's nothing new anywhere under the world.'* " And the rest of them groaned and punched Hopper on the shoulder as they rose to head off to work. It wasn't his biblical knowledge but is enthusiasm for the game; for having a chip in the process of rehabilitation through some form of literary reference.

The reminder of Frank Wilcox from the VA and his past sent a chill down Blackie's spine. "Blackie has some friends he wants you to meet at Auntie's," I'd told Chuck, perhaps setting the stage for a showdown that night if Wilcox and Roberts returned to Auntie's. Or at least reminding the others that Blackie might be called out to face his old enemies on some dusty street, a scene from a Western movie. They all saw his expression change, but only I fully knew the reason. "What's with the look of *'the horror?'* " I put my arm around this kid, this man-child just trying to make his way home after a heartlessly dark period. "Is it Conradian? Are you going back up the river in your head?"

"Nah," Blackie straightened his back and forced a smile, "Deuteronomy 32:10, *'in a place of horror and a waste of wilderness'*...I can't go back there, Johnny. I won't survive it."

They climbed into their trucks and headed into town. As I drove away, Blackie sitting shotgun, scribbling notes on a napkin he'd found in the glove box, I could see the silhouette of Uncle Chuck still sitting motionless at the kitchen table, swirling the brown liquid in his glass. I'd left one of the dogs on purpose, the other two yapping at the house from the bed of the truck.

"You have any friends that are healthy, happy, and well-adjusted?" Blackie asked, only half-joking.

"All of them, kid," I'd said with pipe smoke following the words. "They just don't know it yet."

✳ ✳ ✳

We were all there that night: me, Blackie, Tom-Tom, Hopper, Snare, and newcomer Leroy from Mississauga, who worked in shipping and receiving. Strider, a surfer from Newport Beach who did finish carpentry was there, and Hunter from Green Bay who was in charge of mattress fitting and installation. It was a Friday and they had shipped two hundred and twelve waterbeds to twenty-four accounts across the South that week. They'd worked hard. The smell of cut pine mixing with sweat and boiled shrimp and spilt beer and Pine-Sol and cheap perfume ran through Auntie's like a lifeline. Auntie herself, somewhere between fifty and sixty, to the best of her recollection, was there and was making her rounds from table to table with an aim toward our group that was spilling over with girls from town. They could never explain it to their friends, but the odd collection of disabled, of veterans, of men of every color and shape, was uniquely attractive to the women. And so they came most every weekend and sat and talked and drank. Sometimes more.

Like most people of substantial character, Auntie had earned the right to have only one name. She hadn't assigned it herself or been given it by a forgetful in-law—history had given her the name. She'd always been the aunt that a lot of folk never had, giving until she had no more to give. And then giving some more. In the three decades that I'd known her, Auntie had never raised her voice, her fist, or her blood pressure as far as I could see. She'd outlived three husbands and had proposed to me on at least four occasions, three of them while sober. Auntie was taller than many Black women, thin and strong. Some of the regulars said she could've passed for Wilt Chamberlain's twin. And while I loved her like a sister, I could feel something moving down the mountain toward her, not unlike what I'd felt about Phin. I didn't like the feeling and on most days, denied it. Auntie was real. How could she not be?

"Well, well, Mr. Cobb," Auntie spoke in her softest loud voice over the roar. "It appears that you've brung your entire hippy-bed posse in here tonight. The tab get to be high 'nuff, you be doing chores over at Auntie's place all night long."

I smiled and my rows of tobacco-stained teeth must've looked like the worn keys of ancient ivory. "And I'd plow that fertile earth like it was meant to grow giant beanstalks."

We laughed, winked, and knew that was as close as we'd ever come; my own Ruth suddenly surfacing, my refusal to let her slip down until it was her decision to fade away. And then there was that dark premonition. On a night when things seemed like they had made a turn for the better, I had a feeling, Ruth's feeling, that it would get worse before it got better.

Right then Uncle Chuck walked in and the noise level went down just a notch. I glanced over and saw Snare looking at Chuck who was looking everywhere. I made a face that broadcast caution and allowed myself a moment. I wanted to ask Chuck about Nadine and Louella, Aunt Mary and Loretta; I wanted to talk to him about White oppression and Mike Greer and disappearing into the woods. I wanted to tell him that it was no one's fault, that what was done could not be undone, that he was okay, that I spoke to Ruth in my dreams, sometimes hearing back. And she wanted me to tell Chuck, for Christ's sake it wasn't his fault—she was the one who was dancing on the rails. I wanted to tell Chuck that I'd liked what he'd seen in himself that morning, that I was proud of the man, that I loved him. Mostly I wanted to say that I respected him.

Something had shifted at the core of Uncle Chuck. It seemed his anger had a kinder, gentler nature to it; had been replaced by a deep-seated sense of mission; maybe a quest to make something of his life that would live on. Chuck had given up part of himself, had traded his guilted-pain for some linear march toward his own eventual demise. He had achieved a shallow détente by letting his stony heart become the cloudy compass and beat his way along a rocky crumbling path. But at least it was a path he believed in. I respected the march. It must've kept him alive.

If I could only spend some time with Chuck I might take him back to Lake Texoma and 1950. I might tell him that maybe there was a reason God sent him to find me first before searching for Ruth. I would say he had no idea, but just maybe there was a reason. If only I could take him back to the beginning, the same place he had to go on his way back to the surface so many years ago.

I would do it, I decided. We would talk of Nadine and the New York Yankees, we would hope that Louella had lived a long and happy life, we would laugh about the night Aunt Mary hit him over the head when he first came back to visit them. I would ask to see the lightening-shaped scar on his head, and we would have a toast to the three beautiful old ladies, who outlived their husbands, sitting in that rundown shack. We might cry when Chuck told me about the funeral and about thinking he saw Louella standing back amongst the willows, the long dripping leaves swallowing her as he went to check.

And we would toast Ruth, the one who brought us together but left so soon, and yet was here so often still. We would drink late into the night with Ruth on the rim of our glasses. I would toast Dr. King and see what kind of light or dark came into Chuck's eyes. Yes, I would do it soon before Chuck was pulled away on his journey like a sleepwalker who befriends his dream. Maybe over the weekend. Yes, the sooner the better. I drank from my coffee cup and made myself feel better.

✳ ✳ ✳

It was a scene from an old Western movie: the bad guys come in and take seats at the bar. They order whiskey. The good guys see them and know that trouble's here. They don't necessarily welcome it, but in some strange way they're glad it has finally arrived and that they won't have to go on carrying the forecast of it with them like a string tied around a finger that turned to wire. Some of the more astute regular crowd sensed something, but they weren't sure just what it was. A few of them had been caught in the crossfire before and got up to leave. Others looked to people like me and my company to see how we reacted to the two White men that nobody had seen before. They wanted to watch the body language of us all; they knew it to be a human barometer of impending change in the local pressure. The rest just didn't give a shit—the were so hardened or so drunk or have so little to lose, they can't pay strangers no mind at all.

I scan Blackie's eyes and see the fear. I get up from my chair and walk past the kid, patting him on the shoulder on my way to the long bar that isn't varnished oak from the Western theme, but Formica. And the bar keep isn't a crusty character actor with an apron and a dish towel in his hand, but a twenty-two-year-old coed from the local junior college working nights to pay for tuition and books.

I walk up behind the two strangers and many eyes are on me. The score of the music begins to crescendo and everybody thinks a big fight is about to ensue and the camera cuts to worried faces on pretty maidens and clinched fists of young locals.

But filmmakers learned how to suspend suspense along the way, and just then they cut away to another part of the movie to check in with another character.

All this was going through the classically-trained and quite logical mind of Hopper. Hopper, not unlike Phin's wartime friend Worm, had not so much "figured out" the war as he had analyzed it and rationalized the behavior along various personality trait lines. "The mayhem was quite predictable," he liked to say. "From Babylon to B.F. Skinner; very predictable behaviorism."

What Hopper could not quite get his arms around, though, was the unspoken, unquestionable bond that existed between these men, especially between the legacy of the Davis kid, the White son of a commercial fisherman, and me, Johnny Cobb, Black son of a sharecropper, grandson of a slave. He had tried to discuss it with Blackie, but Blackie had gotten increasingly frustrated with him.

"Hop-Hopper," he used to say, "you're a theorist, you try to put everything in a box so you can understand it, label it, and therefore control it. I was the same way and the box imploded, sending bits of psycho-shrapnel into my cerebral cortex. You certainly can explain parts of the war and parts of these folks. But what this war did was change the way that people fought wars, the way people thought of war, and the way people will remember war forever. We don't *really* know what happened in Indochina during the last ten years. And it will be years before we are even ready to fully explore your 'predictable behaviorism.'

"I'm just happy," Blackie continued while stroking the thin whiskers on his chin, "to be sane enough to begin my data collection, to walk around with my eyes and heart open to these people. Come talk to me when you drop Freud and Skinner and embrace Maslow, Kubler-Ross, and Schopenhauer."

But Hopper was thick-skinned and above all else he was a pragmatist. He'd survived his tour in the Nam by careful calculation. He knew these people were good for him and he knew that they allowed his form of analysis without judgment. He set his movie comparison aside and slid in close enough to his boss, me, to hear what was being said.

"Hey, aren't you two from the VA Hospital out in Denver City?" I asked innocently enough. "I think I recognize you from when I went out to see a friend's son who was a patient there before he…before he moved on to another world."

Frank Wilcox and his sidekick Will Roberts didn't expect this preemptive strike and just nodded, waiting for Cobb to keep the charade going.

"You must know that gentleman working for me, Jim Black." Cobb nodded his head toward the table. "I think he was known as Blackie while he was also…uh, involved with the VA out there. Look, there's Jim now, sitting with some of my employees." I pointed to the big table and Blackie gave a thin wave and forced smile to the two men.

"What are you boys doing in town? Hey, why don't you come over and meet some of the guys? They're all vets. I'm sure you know the type. C'mon and have a drink with us."

It was precisely at that moment when Hopper understood what Blackie had been trying to teach him: everything and everybody involved with the Nam was beyond counterintuitive. The only way to begin to understand was to forget what you knew and hang on for the ride.

I went back to the safety of my Western movie comparison and cut to thoughts of where some of the other key players might be at that moment.

The movie score shifted to a haunting flute melody with dissonant notes and no resolution. The transition was perfect; everything moving toward a final climatic finish on the dusty main street that was Auntie's.

Then I remembered Blackie's words.

"The war took us all, man. Even if we never in-country. And it's never over, only modulated, compartmentalized, and hopefully accepted. But that dark tunnel will never compact to solid ground."

360

CHAPTER 29

WAR GAMES

What did anyone expect? That Johnny's words to Roberts and Wilcox in the bar might rise up and jam the artillery? All he'd done was to hold a torch to the fuse when under a different sky and a different moon it might've fizzled before exploding.

He'd invited the enemy into their little hooch of a home there in the middle of Auntie's, well-below the mental DMZs of those men. Wilcox and Robert weren't really to blame for their actions in the VA; they were victims like the kid who robs a liquor store is a victim. It's ultra-liberal thinking, of course, but that's what Johnny had come to in his final and irresolvable quest to forgive himself for Ruth's death. Guilt and forgiveness: just an old couple who fell out of love decades ago, but seem to make a life together; an ancient willow that loses a branch or two in a storm, but the trunk remains solid. One begets the other—you forgive yourself to remove the guilt or ignite the guilt for being too forgiving.

The two men would have liked to go off and kill the enemy. Heaven knows they tried. Their enthusiasm for war wouldn't have necessarily made them good soldiers. Often it was just the opposite with the gung-ho types getting nailed, dead in the first thirty days. That's what Phin had told Johnny last time he was up this way. He'd said he thought he'd made it home mostly intact because he'd tried not to kill or be killed. He was good at not caring, he'd said, good at "either seeking out and embracing what good came out of war, or simply disappearing into his past while tracers and RPGs flew by his head."

Wilcox and Roberts felt guilt, but it was the kind that was hard to forgive. They brought their failure to kill North Vietnamese into their heads as something that was their fault, which it was. Roberts had failed a psychological profile—a difficult thing to do—even the U.S. Army knew he would cause them embarrassment. It was right when Lt. Calley's romp in My Lai was coming to light. The good PR men had put the pressure on the recruiters to keep any potential mass murderers at home where they belonged.

And Wilcox? Well, Frank Wilcox had been convicted of a felony, grand theft, auto. He was damaged goods. Eventually, he'd traded some info to the feds in return for a reduction of the charge, allowing him access to the VA hospital job. But he felt remorse that he hadn't ratted his old partners out earlier so that he could've put on those high, shiny boots and those crisp fatigues sooner.

All this information had come from Blackie who'd gotten it from personnel in trade for other small favors, everybody benefiting from it along the way but him. Blackie had always been at risk, had always run with more than a little fear. But the two fellow screwed-up orderlies were only a collection point, a receptacle for all that he had feared. Did it start in the Nam or was the mania always there? Simply pried loose by the sight of the unthinkable? There is a pattern to human behavior in various cultures. Blackie knew that as well as any young scholar might be expected to. On paper, people of a certain region could be expected to exercise certain behaviorisms, certain norms. Where his friend Hopper had used his logarithmic intelligence to shield him from most vagaries of war, Blackie's brand of critical and qualitative inquiry had fragged his mind before the bullets could've shredded his body. In that respect, Blackie knew he was lucky.

And when the fear had grown quiet and dormant and he'd found out that Gerald McReady had cleared his name, released him back into society in a complicated and manipulative coup, Blackie had let his hair down. He was relearning peace. That's when the twin harbingers of Wilcox and Roberts showed up in Lafayette. And why else would they be there? Wilcox had told Blackie he was going to get him. He'd told Gerald the same thing. There was history, there was motive, there was anger, and there was always guilt.

At the table sitting next to Blackie was Tom-Tom and a local girl who had refused to go out with "anybody who had been a soldier," but always came around and sat with the boys when they held court at Auntie's. Next to them was Leroy who was playing checkers with Hunter, the loser paying for the next pitcher. Leroy had been drafted in '68, right after the Tet Offensive, did one tour as a grunt, and finished out his duty stateside working in a Ft. Bragg warehouse. Leroy was in charge of shipping and receiving for Johnny and once or twice a month he would punch a hole in the drywall for no apparent reason. His right hand seemed to be in a cast more weeks than not. Hunter had been a corpsman and had been hit three times in two tours. They tried to send him home after the second bullet grazed his cheek but Hunter refused, citing the over-used cliché, "chicks dig scars." Next to them, his back to the bar, long blonde hair held together in a ponytail, entertaining two giggling young women who seemed enamored by the California man-child, was Strider. Strider was a surfer from Newport Beach, California who'd served his tour as a lifeguard at China Beach. "Luckiest mother fucker in the room," he was fond of saying, and then, "good work, if you can get it." Snare sat off to the side just a bit, back to wall, watching Hopper eavesdrop on Johnny's chat with the two strangers.

Truth be known, everybody but Strider saw the men at the bar, sensed trouble, and was ready to react if something went wrong. Johnny's invitation to the men might've thrown them off for a second, but each had spent time in bars around the country, around the world, that made Auntie's quite tame. But only Snare had his guard fully up; him and Blackie.

Ironically, Wilcox and Roberts followed Cobb back to the table and brief introductions were made. Heads were nodded but no hands were shaken. Blackie wanted to get up and leave, but something inside him held him down, told him to ride it out. Face his white whale.

"So," Cobb continued his questioning, "What was it you two said you were doing in these parts again?"

Blackie tried not to return Wilcox's stare but felt drawn in by those eyes he'd hated. He moved around in his seat and sipped from a water glass. Wilcox spoke first.

"Looking for jobs. Things got a little slow at the hospital after they gave up and brought the soldiers home. Besides," he winked at Blackie who forced himself not to shutter, "the old place isn't the same without this kid around. He was good, uh, entertainment. Does he still talk funny? I haven't heard him speak."

At this point, Tom-Tom stopped in the middle of his sentence to the local girl, Hunter's blood pressure rose a few points, Leroy's hand held the red checker out in front as he pondered the serrated edge, and they all watched Johnny's pupils narrow to pin size.

"Actually, Mr. Wilcox, I'm doing quite well. Thank you for asking." Blackie spoke slowly, eloquently, focusiing his gaze somewhere between the two men across from him at the big table.

"Yeah," Leroy chipped in. "My little man here's gonna be a big time college professor someday. Smartest little shit I know."

"What about Hopper?" It was Hunter who was weighing in, trying to keep the conversation light, or maybe to give them all some time to better judge these two men who were larger than any of them except Johnny. "I'd take Geometry 101 from him, assuming the other co-eds were as good looking as me."

"Well, that depends on what you call smart," Tom-Tom had turned away from the girl and joined the table. "These two kids, Blackie-black and Hop-hopper, now they been 'edumacated' in the high-brow fashion. They know all about numbers and what-if's and what-could-be's, based on those numbers and all those book covers they had their noses between since the rest of us had our noses between others things. But are those really the keys of wisdom?"

Hunter drank from the edge of his glass while half-swallowing a mouthful of beer, the rest spilling on his black sleeveless t-shirt as it dribbled from his mouth. "Matthew, 16:19, keys to wisdom," he continued, "the ways to unlock the doors to heaven." He'd won the round and the right to follow up with his thoughts while the others paid more than attention.

"It's not as simple as book-smarts and street-smarts. Take these two over-sized psuedo-healers here...what was yer' names again, Rilcox and Woberts? Something like that? Well, I would imagine you had to do some real schoolin' to get a job at a hospital. And I would bet cash money that you learned a bunch of things about making it in this world while working at that hospital that you didn't learn in nursing school, or whatever kinda school."

Hunter was on a roll and edging, no, pushing, toward precarious territory. But he'd been hit three times in the Nam and he bore the signs on the side of his face like a topographical map of the country that he still couldn't pronounce properly. All anybody knew was that he was from Green Bay, had spent twenty-four months in-country as a medic, had skin and keloid scars he was proud of, and had once claimed to have thrown a football with the fabled coach Vince Lombardi. When Leroy, who would offer up his life story to a bus driver between route stops, asked Hunter about his past, all he got was, "I lived six doors down from Lombardi. What else do you need to know?"

"But, I'm not saying that what these two newcomers might have in combo is bad." Hunter was asking for a fight. "I'm saying that learning only one way or another can be a two-edged sword."

"Hebrews!" shouted Strider, whose last name was Rickman and had found the conversation so full of potential that he'd given the two girls a twenty and sent them off for another round. "It's 4:12, I'm pretty sure, '*cuts both ways*'. Am I right, Johnny, do I win? You old silent sage, am I right?"

Johnny, who had been watching the banter with great interest, said, "Yes, Strider, you won yourself another free month's rent at Hotel Cobb."

Wilcox and Roberts seemed to be taking in the performance with equal parts aplomb, disgust, and hidden impatient anger. They'd come here for one reason and everybody at the table knew it, each having been a party to its unyielding grip before, each trying to deny that grip and pry themselves loose into a room where the reverb of revenge had no echo.

Snare, who'd barely spoken since this morning's breakfast conversation, took a sip of his iced tea and scooted his chair in close. Johnny shot him a look, but both knew it was useless. The games had begun.

"You all come here and quote the Bible for fun like it's a word game, like Parcheesi or Yahtzee. The Bible might be part fiction in some people's eyes, but too many have spit upwind of what its roots hold onto. And sometimes that saliva lands on my face. I'm not saying that's what occurred here tonight but what we have here, '*Oh ye of little faith,*' Matthew 8:26, are two men who sit with us as Judas sat with Jesus." Snare looked at Roberts, and Wilcox, who reached for a blade hidden in his boot. "You all think you can '*eat, drink, and be merry,*' Luke, 12:19, while this asshole from a so-called hospital reaches now for a knife in his cheap faux-leather boots?"

Wilcox and Roberts stood quickly, even violently, from their chairs, but just as quickly Leroy, Hunter, and Tom-Tom reached across the table and slammed them back down by collar, by tuff of hair, and by on-the-job training courtesy of Uncle Sam. Wilcox tried to say something, but Johnny held his finger up to his lips as he would to quiet a library patron talking in the corner. Snare was standing, twirling a common table fork between his fingers like a high school girl with a baton.

"Just what is it that you think you'll accomplish by hurting our little friend here? Most of us at this table were trained to track armies of nation states as they moved across foreign countries under a cloak of earth and darkest dark. You march in here, a couple of faggot nurse-types, trying to get even on a crime that you are guilty of."

Snare rubbed his eyes with his left hand and held out his right in question. "You make me ashamed to be a baby-killing, psycho, fucked up Vietnam vet. Couldn't you have been just the least bit creative here? I mean, how hard a target is little Jimmy Black-Black? I really don't want to sit at the same table as you assholes. I might've killed a few of the right people for the wrong reasons, or fewer still of the wrong people for the right reasons, but hell, what did I know? I was only a highly-trained military machine covered in flesh and skin. At least I'm getting on with my life. You pricks are stuck. And men who get stuck are dangerous."

Snare put his hand on Wilcox's shoulder and squeezed it just hard enough to empower his message.

"So unimaginative, you are. You have deceived even yourselves. And now your destiny is about to manifest itself right here, in plain view of your own conscience. You all can stay and drink with these half-men," Snare slapped Wilcox on the face loud enough so that other people heard it and looked up, "but, I can't seem to get my tongue to swallow with the smell of Pine-Sol and morphine and overflowing bed pans in the air."

Snare stood up to leave and all eyes watched him—a fatal flaw in the unfolding of the tragic drama that was playing out. Wilcox took a final sip of his beer and all the guilt rendered by his past influences within and without, healthy and diseased, started at some synapse within the cerebral cortex, and traveled down his arm into his large and powerful hand holding the long neck of the bottle. It was not without warning, but came as a surprise still because revenge knows its own time and punches a time clock beyond the confines of rational behavior. And the bottle came up hard and quick and smashed the side of the biggest, hardest, gentlest, sorriest, most-revered head in all of Auntie's: Johnny Cobb's head.

There was the slightest of pauses just before the battle-hardened group took action. And it was in that split moment that the ancient and elegant proprietor, Auntie, pulled the small bore handgun out from under her flowery dress, out from where she had always kept it wrapped in soft cloth, and tucked in the large elastic waistband of her panties. Tonight it had real bullets, not salt pellets. She'd only shot it a few times on Saturday mornings when she'd driven out to the backwater roads and loaded it up and got a feel for its trigger and the sound of the bang in her ear. But tonight when the two men came in, Auntie had gone up to her office and loaded the gun with real bullets and practiced aiming it at the wall. She was frightened but not scared, and she knew the difference between the two. Nobody would hurt her Johnny Cobb in her place.

The first shot stopped the initial melee, each man in the place taken back to another time and place where the sound of gunfire meant much more than an old woman barkeep pointing a small .22 caliber handgun at the ceiling and firing.

There was a silence as Snare and Tom-Tom held Wilcox in a chokehold and Leroy had put a long, shiny blade at Roberts' throat. Hunter and Strider tended to the bleeding and unconscious Cobb. Hopper put his hands up in the air and said, "Auntie, this isn't the Old West. Honey, put the gun down. We'll take care of this."

Auntie, having lost her husband Jackson to the war in a friendly-fire incident back in '65, kept the gun trained on the back of Wilcox's head.

"You know, boys, I been meaning to tell y'all that the only time I get any joy outta my ol' life is when y'all come in here and treat Auntie with respect. I've known this poor man bleeding on my floor for thirty-five years and he's one of the reasons I ain't put a bullet in my own head. And then these two honkeys come in here and hit this poor man upside the head with a bottle."

Auntie said for the bartender to call for an ambulance, but not the cops, and moved her head to tell Hunter and Strider to get her poor, dear Johnny up off the floor and put some napkins on his head.

"Auntie," Hopper pleaded, "just give me the gun and we'll take these men out of here, we'll take them to the cops."

Blackie was now helping Hunter with Johnny's wound and feeling a rage building up in him from some primal source.

"Cops?" Wilcox summoned what hubris might be left. "An old crazy nigger-lady pulls a gun on two White men? Go on back to Boston," Wilcox said. "You're livin' in a Black dream world."

Auntie walked up close to Wilcox who was trying to break away from Snare, who had squeezed Wilcox balls so tight he'd felt one actually split in half and said to himself, "Huh, didn't know they broke like that" when Wilcox let out a primal scream that split the air.

And Auntie all but whispered, "I wonder how many .22 caliber bullets a man like this could hold 'afore he up and broke?" Then she put the gun up against Wilcox's right thigh and pulled the trigger.

People jumped and then quietly started to slowly file out the back, but they were the kind who would go straight home—nobody had seen anything happen that night.

Hopper said, "Geez, Auntie, you're making a mess."

Johnny was still unconscious and the bleeding wouldn't stop. Roberts flinched just a little and Leroy opened a small laceration near his left ear. Snare had this strange smile on his mouth, but it stayed there, refusing to travel to any other part of his body. *When will the war end,* he thought. *When only the dead have eyes?*

Wilcox was still writhing in pain but tried to speak a few words. "You guys...are all fucked up. Man, we...we were only gonna scare the kid."

Blackie held Johnny's bleeding head in his hands and whispered, "You know what Willie-Wicox? I'm scared, but not for me. You hit this man well; the bottle sliced his temporal artery. Direct pressure isn't doing the job. I'm afraid for this man, Auntie." Blackie spoke slow and empathetic, like a parish priest.

"A man can take quite a few .22 caliber bullets before he dies. Just angle that gun down a bit so you don't hit his artery and he's fortunate to bleed out, not inside his body."

With those words, Auntie turned to look at Cobb's limp body, straining to hear the sounds of sirens in the distance, a sound she'd always hated.

And she put another bullet in the right thigh of Frank Wilcox.

Roberts saw her turn away at the sound of the bang and made a lunge for the gun in her hand. Did he forget about the knife at his throat? Or the background of the man holding it? Leroy might've been a crazed Vietnam vet in the eyes of those too quick to judge, the ease in their labeling giving some shape to those looking for a mold in which to pour their own guilt and confusion. The quiet kid from Tallahassee who was raised by a single grandparent because, well, just because cycles are hard to break. Leroy was only reinforcing the stereotype. Send him to jail? For what? Self-defense? Was there anybody in this place who would bear witness against him? Not likely. It would be an indictment of the system, yes, but more an indictment of self. Too many had already died in the wake of skin-born hate.

Leroy hadn't killed Roberts on purpose. He just held the knife in place and let Roberts jump into it in his attempt to take the gun away from Auntie. A crazy guy like that would have turned the gun on the place and then himself. Leroy was sort of a hero: he was just saving someone the trouble. It was nothing new; happened all the time in the Nam.

There was, of course, blood everywhere and the ambulance still wasn't there. People knew why. If you got hurt in Auntie's you probably deserved it and if the cops weren't called, well, it was safer to slow down a bit and let the patrons take care of their own. So that's what the ambulance would do.

Somebody said that the White nurse stranger was dead and Snare loosened his grip on Wilcox.

"War's over, man. Didn't anybody tell you guys that?" Snare spoke quietly into Wilcox's ear. "In fact, why don't you do that? Why don't you just get up and go on home. We'll send your friend's body on in a few days after the paperwork is complete. Government regs and all that."

Snare stood Wilcox up and moved him toward the door as he released the injured man. Someone handed him a napkin.

Someone else said they'd call a taxi. Wilcox turned around and must've thought that the strangeness that existed in the Denver VA had spread out like a disease. He would never get to the point of knowing that he was the carrier. He limped to the door and opened it as blood oozed from his small bullet wounds.

And as he did, he quite purposely shouldered a large dark man entering the doorway—a man also new to Auntie's—sending the surprised man to the ground. "Get out of the way, nigger," Wilcox spit blood out of his mouth onto the downed man. It wasn't the last fluid to come from an orifice.

After Uncle Chuck regained his feet, he saw Johnny lying in the crook of Blackie's arm. The ancient and immutable dice in his head tumbled and he said, "Goddamn, bring him out to my car and let's get him some help. I'll pull it up front," and he ran out the door into the night. Some of the patrons started to drag Roberts' body off to the side. Others breathed sighs of relief. One dead, one hurt was enough. They helped get Johnny out to the curb and waited just a minute or two, maybe a bit longer than they anticipated, for Uncle Chuck to wheel his Oldsmobile out from the dark parking lot.

And as Uncle Chuck skidded to a stop near the front door, there was a thump in the back trunk as Wilcox's lifeless body rolled up against the back seat.

"Let's go, let's go," Chuck screamed. "We gotta get Johnny some help!"

And as they drove away an ambulance and a police car slowly made their way through the narrow streets towards *Auntie's Family Style Grill.*

CHAPTER 30

FINDING A PULSE

Gerald McReady had never done an impulsive thing in his life—not as far as he was concerned. As hard as he'd tried, he could not shake the tendency toward orderly preparation that he'd taken from his father's stoic genes rooted in upward mobility. He could never shake those gray eyes, only shield them. Gerald had a plan but it had failed, not because of an impulse or radical behavior, but because even the innocent act of helping a fellow medical school student was within his canon of thoughtfully-controlled behavior. That, he swore to himself, originated within his own mindful eyes.

Gerald thought that he might've looked upon his assistance with Phin and Blackie's "removal" from the Denver VA as impulsive or hasty. But when he forged the papers and asked a few benevolent doctors to cooperate with Blackie's release, he felt no guilt. There had been a certain order to the chaos. Gerald might've succeeded in that strangest of hospitals because he'd taken a very pragmatic approach to all that made the place a poor choice if you were really hurt or in need of serious medical care. He helped the sick and the injured by creating his own set of rules. He knew it was dangerous, but Gerald had few options left; if he wanted to heal, he had to operate under his own plan.

McReady was, of course, overjoyed at the news that the Davis kid was alive and had laughed himself to sleep for the first time in many years as he thought about the careful preparation and order it must have taken to fake the death of the corporal from the Redneck Riviera with the U.S. Army HQ. He even admitted to himself that he was jealous of the operation and wished he had thought of it, wished that he had been involved in the planning.

It was just something that Blackie might've conjured up, but he knew the kid, even with his amateur, in-house blackmailing, was without the resources to pull off such a large feat. Phin Davis's dad must've had some pull in that little town and there was a rush of warm blood to Gerald's head when he pictured the fake funeral, a few people laughing under a cloak of loyal secrets, the other half wondering if it was really true because he hadn't seemed that sick, only lost part of a foot. They might've known as well, but were just as anxious to put the war behind them, regardless if the number of killed was off by one. The locals might've discussed it for a week and then moved on, placing the strange death of the Davis boy right up there with the local folklore of the highest degree. But they wouldn't forget because it wouldn't matter if he showed up a few years later. With the help of Haitian voodoo, corrected DOD records. and old-boy politics, people used to come back from the dead all the time...until the government outlawed it. The Southern states held on to a dying creed that the North would never, could never understand.

Gerald had stayed below the radar as well in recent weeks. He'd given his testimony and thoughts to the cursory investigation by hospital administrators, but mostly he just did his job. The war was over but still they came: vets who'd been back in the world for several years started showing up with every malady in the textbooks and some that weren't. Funding was cut, jobs were cut, supplies were less plentiful.

And still they came.

Wilcox and Roberts had not been seen since they were officially fired. This bothered McReady, but the fear was passing with the summer sun and he did his best to keep focused on the patients. An occasional letter arrived from

Blackie and he seemed to be making his way with the odd collection of assorted vets who hung around the home and place of business of the old Black uncle. He missed the kid, his creativity, his zany neuroses, the way he spoke in frenetic riddles, some of which were subtle pastiche, others illustrating the genius that lie below.

Mostly, what happened in the fall of 1973 after the incident with John Cobb, Harry and Phin Davis, Jim "Blackie" Black, and Wilcox and Roberts, was that Gerald McReady got lonely; at least that's how he was able to describe the feeling when he sat alone at night in his loft as the days shortened and the moon rose earlier and he spoke to the growing number of beautiful clay pots that had mostly taken over his living space. Gerald missed people, even bad ones.

"You clay pot folks are beginning to intrude on my space," he mumbled one night in mid-September as he shook off a raincoat and hung his bike on the rack in the tiny laundry room, surprised that he was speaking to inanimate objects. "I made a few of you to keep me company and now look what's gone and happened—you've multiplied like the loaves and fishes. I can barely get to the bathroom without tripping over your ornate roundness, your intricate detailing, your suture-like lines of cross-hatching and railroad ties." The words surprised him but he had no control over his actions.

Over the next five minutes, Gerald R. McReady systematically loaded and fired U.S. Marine Sgt. Lorenzo DuPuis'. 4mm automatic six times, each time taking careful aim at one of his beautiful clay pots and squeezing the trigger slowly, thoroughly, as Miles Davis blew his horn thorough the speakers and the sirens came closer and closer to his home.

"How does it feel now?" A much calmer McReady asked his clay pots. "What does it feel like to have someone you love create you with his own hands, set your future in motion with his touch, and then blow you apart with the gun from somebody else's turmoil? You're on your own, with no direction home." Gerald launched into the familiar verse, "A complete unknown, 'like a rolling stone.' "

He'd turned the stereo up so loud that he didn't hear the banging on the door at first.

"Open up! Denver Police!"

"Yeah, sorry, just a minute," Gerald was making his own order out of the chaos again as he dropped the gun into the last pot standing.

McReady turned down the stereo and let the police—their guns drawn—into his loft apartment.

"We had reports of gunfire and from the looks of this mess it appears as if they were accurate. We'll have to ask you to step over to the wall and spread your legs. Is there anyone else in the apartment with you?"

Something dark and visceral started to well up from the core of McReady, something that had been there a long time, a festering sore that all he could do was treat with the ointment of his actions, the medication of his own freewill to treat others. But was it really free? Did he have a choice? No, not really. It was his purpose in life; he knew that, knew that from the day he had stopped the red river of Tommy Louder's young life from running dry. He'd seen what damage could be done when allowed to vent one's anger in violent ways—kids at the hospital ripping IVs out of their arms and hurling bedpans at the wall; those were the minor outbursts.

Gerald quietly stood against the wall of his loft, his face staring at black and white photographs of his mother and older brother standing on a dock on some lake, a vacation many years ago; they looked almost happy back then, as one officer patted him down and the other searched his place.

Gerald then sat down and quietly tried to explain the disturbance.

"Gentlemen, I made a lot of noise here. I can see the RP, the reporting party, thinking it could be gunfire. When you throw those large clay pots onto the old hardwood floor they pop just like a handgun. There," McReady pointed to the last big deep pot where DuPuis' gun laid hidden on the bottom, blending in with the dark-gray interior, "Go ahead and smash that last one. You'll see."

The police officers looked at each other and one of them said quietly that they had a "10-96," a mental subject.

"It's ironic, isn't it, officers? For many years I've worked at the VA Hospital here, watching kids return from the war, helping to patch them up and get them back on their feet and back into the world. And sometimes they don't make it the first time, or the second time. You guys pick them up for something, tag a label on them, and drop them off at the psych ward at our hospital. And then we get to try all over again. Some of them will never be fully right and you'll know who they are and drive by them, saying, 'There's old what's-his-name, pushing the shopping cart, talking to himself. Let's have a little chat with him; let's hear some of his war stories again.' And you'll laugh and tell him to stay out of trouble and he'll do his best, but then again, unless something changes in this world, in this so-called 'advanced society,' it will always have a label for him. And he will carry that war on his back and in his cart and in his mind a long time."

The officers, who were very young and a little bit jumpy, looked at each other, trying to make sense of this man's diatribe. They asked for Gerald's ID and McReady carefully removed it from his backpack and handed it over.

"I didn't go to the war," Gerald continued, growing calmer with each word, "and I doubt you went unless you were drafted at twelve-years-old. So how are we to really know about these kids who come into my hospital, who go out into the streets with all that weight around their necks? How will we ever know? Huh, how? "And what about us, you guys and me?"

Gerald stood up and looked out the windows as the two officers placed their right hands on their holstered guns, just as they were trained to do.

"We have our own weight to shoulder and try and throw down. What do you guys do, lift weights? Jog? Go to the firing range and run through a few clips? Huh, what's your release valve?"

One officer spoke into his radio and nudged the other toward the door.

"I smashed my pots tonight, four-years-worth of work. And damn if it didn't feel good. I made a lot of noise. Tell me who the RP was and I'll go apologize or cite me for a noise violation. But don't stand there and call me a 10-96 mental case; we're all mental in this fucking Age of Aquarius. It's just a matter of degrees, mostly dependent on controlling that valve. Wouldn't you agree?" Gerald sat down slowly on the couch and held his head in his hands. He suddenly felt very tired.

"Mr. McReady," it was the one officer who looked more like a point guard for a high school basketball team than a man who wore a badge and carried a gun. He put his hands on his wide leather belt with the extra holes made for his thin waist and tried to talk beyond his capability to understand what he'd just witnessed.

"You can understand our situation here. Lots of things sound like gun shots. You made a lot of noise. We were just doing our job. There's nothing to apologize for, from our side anyway. Please try to keep it down. Have a nice evening." And then added, "A member of the medical community will be visiting you tomorrow."

And as they left, Gerald could hear laughter out on the street just before the sound of squad car doors slamming—a sound also not unlike gunfire. He sat on the couch for a very long time, trying to identify his feelings without putting a label on them. Was he guilty for lying about the gun? Was he sorry about the destruction? Was he angry for someone calling in the complaint? Was there any release in his impulsive action? Or was there more stress now as he surveyed the chunks of shattered and shiny clay about his loft? He'd done something totally irrational, but it had the feeling of planned order; at least there was comfort now in that what was done, was done. Gerald lay down on the floor, kicking a few scattered pieces of clay off to the side, and stared up at the ceiling. And what about this DuPuis character whom he couldn't quite get his big strong hands around? He closed his eyes and for the first time in many months, said a prayer. But when he was through he realized that he hadn't asked for anything and he didn't know which god to send it out to. There had to be only one absolute greater power. But in war, nothing is absolute—not the result, not the victor, not the vanquished, not even the gods.

He fell into a troubled sleep wondering where war began and God ended.

The next morning he returned the gun to Marine Sgt. Lorenzo DuPuis, who was scheduled for release within the week.

"Keep it, doc," DuPuis had tried to convince McReady. "You might need it, you know, for that day."

"I already did, kid. It worked fine, just fine." And McReady refused to elaborate as he examined the sergeant's ass and pulled a few more pieces of lead from his backside. "More of the smaller pieces will work their way to the surface over the next few months, sergeant. You'll be sitting down for dinner at your parents' house and have to excuse yourself to go into the bathroom to remove one more souvenir from the Nam from your ass. Treat these wounds with care, okay? The dinner can always be reheated. Infection will land you back in a VA hospital, probably worse than cold meatloaf."

There was a long period of silence as both men considered the future and things from the past rising to the surface. It was DuPuis who broke the silence and came up with the idea.

"Hey, doc. Didn't you say that you knew someone in Lafayette; some old guy, somebody's uncle who had a shop out that way? I'm outta this joint in five days. Got me a one-way bus ticket, a hundred sixty-three bucks, a ninety-day leave pass, and a hankerin' to get on with my life as a war hero any way I can. I'm goin' home with a Purple Heart, a sack full of semen, and the ability to put a man down with one hand whilst the other holds a cold Pabst. I figure that all the hotties been waiting for Sgt. DuPuis whilst he was keeping America free. Whyn't you come along with me? I'll introduce you as the doc who saved my ass."

Lorenzo DuPuis laughed at his joke and said he was serious. He never joked about those kinds of things. He told McReady that he could trust him with his life because he done trusted his with him.

"I'm a fuckin' hero," he kept telling Gerald. "You can ride along on my coattails for as long as you want. C'mon, doc, the war's over. It don't matter that we lost, 'cuz we kicked a lot of ass. We'll get them next time. There'll be other wars, mark my words. C'mon to Louisiana with me."

Gerald was trying to concentrate on his job with the tweezers and each time DuPuis got excited he tensed up his muscles and moved the spot Gerald had been working on. He liked this kid; he had a kind of naïve energy that was infectious, like all that was so bad with the war was beyond his control. He'd called it right: there'd be other wars, whether they were around for them or not. DuPuis was cocky and lacked that dark cynicism so prevalent in the vets he'd seen. What kind of power had he possessed to kill other men and then say, "Oh well, it was them or me. Wasn't me who put us in this shit. I'll do my time and go home and pick up where I left off. The hell with them hippy chicks and their protest signs and all that hair under their arms. You cain't take the South out of a real Southerner. They love their war heroes, even when we lose."

This kid, he was a fast learner. Under that naiveté were some real street smarts.

✱ ✱ ✱

When Gerald awoke the next morning another shift had occurred at his center. He wondered if the ongoing M-Dream was maneuvering to become the architect of his own existence. Or was it just some nocturnal malfeasance of the mind?

And in that perfect lucidity of his orderly delusion, he went into work and told DuPuis that he would go to Lafayette, Louisiana with him, that he'd take an extended leave of absence and buy a one-way bus ticket. But before he did, he tried to tell Lorenzo DuPuis one thing—that in the war he might've been a hero, but things in the world, maybe even in Lafayette, had likely changed.

"Ah, hell," boasted DuPuis, "I'll change them back. I killed more gooks than I can count and worse thing I got is some birdseed in my ass. I feel bad for their families and stuff, but I'm lying here, baby, still living and they got Pabst on ice for me back home while them NVA who tried to put me down are just as cold lying under the ground. It's just war, doc, same as it ever was. Same as it will always be. Someone got a complaint about it? Take it to the government they elected or take it upstairs to their God because I only work for them. I ain't in charge. I'm just doing what they tell me...until I get home and then I'm doing what I feel like. No changed world gonna trip me up. I got some plans."

Gerald R. McReady, for the first time in many years, had no plan. He took his leave, got on a bus in downtown Denver, and headed for Lafayette by way of Wichita, Oklahoma City, Dallas, and God knows where. Next to him sat the man who would always be Sgt. Lorenzo DuPuis, U.S. Marines.

The sergeant, who insisted on wearing his full dress uniform, spent a lot of time standing and pacing the aisle. Outside of Wichita, he slipped into a rest stop's men's room and returned, offering both clinched fists up for McReady to choose from.

"Go ahead, doc. Pick a hand, any hand. You can't lose because they both got little souvenirs from the war." Gerald forced a smile and watched the many faces in the rest stop wrestle with their feelings toward all that this happy kid who, to them, represented killing.

"Man, the chicks are gonna dig my scars. Hey, you like Pabst don't you, doc? It ain't no down-river beer."

After a long, arid stretch of land between Wichita and Oklahoma City, when little had been said, DuPuis had been able to stretch out on a bench seat and get some rest, Outside the sun had gone down below the western edge of the Great Plains. The bus was quiet except for two elderly ladies up front who had removed their hearing devices and now played gin rummy at a volume that equaled their age.

Gerald was unable to get a true bead on DuPuis, that was why he was attracted to him; that was one of the reasons he went along with him. Gerald drifted down into troubled sleep, thinking that he might've been purged of his holier-than-thou hubris by the occurrences in Southeast Asia if he had gone. But he also knew without question that he would've died there as well. And still he couldn't decide if he agreed with DuPuis or not, only that he, too, had a job and it might be the polar opposite of what DuPuis knew his was. Or it might be the same.

When he woke up they were pulling into the Oklahoma City bus depot and the sergeant was shaking his arm.

"Halfway home, doc. Let's get out and stretch our legs. This place is the safest big city in America. Besides, you're with a decorated soldier, a marine in uniform. This is our country, doc; not some gookville-paddyland where they're fighting people who look just like them. On our soil, nobody fucks with us. C'mon, I'll buy you a Pabst."

And as they walked toward the bar next door to the station, out of the corner of his eye Gerald saw a young kid in holey jeans and long hair stare at DuPuis, boring holes in the back of his now-rumpled dress uniform. The kid took a long drag from a hand-rolled cigarette, shook his greasy hair from his blue eyes, and then spit on the sidewalk. McReady could swear that the phlegm beat like a heart, or maybe a fetus, before falling into a crack in the concrete.

Gerald tried to stare at the kid, but he couldn't conjure up what didn't exist inside him. DuPuis, who did, in fact, have eyes in the back of his head and would tell anybody who listened that they had kept him alive when lots of other grunts had got their asses shot off, took Gerald's arm.

"Hey, doc, don't mind them counter-cultured, hippy types. Most of 'em just following a fad anyway. My whistle needs a wettin'."

They sat in the small bar and drank their Pabst Blue Ribbon beers. Gerald was conscious of the many and varied reactions that DuPuis's uniform brought out. What was it about an outfit, he thought, that could emote so much feeling; everything from admiration to disgust to hate to pride to envy and back to hate? The uniform of the United States Marine Corps, replete with medals and ribbons and a few creases from the long bus ride that seemed to be disappearing as the bottles lined up on the bar in front of them, was a symbol. Americans loved signs and symbols. They might not understand language and discourse; they could care less about their dreams; but without ever knowing it, they would react admiringly, hatefully, or passionately to symbols that stood for something. This was both an asset and a fault of people, Gerald decided.

Somebody walked up and bought his traveling partner another beer, patted him on the back, and said welcome home, thank you for your service. DuPuis shook the man's hand and introduced McReady as the guy who saved his ass by pulling the gook-lead out of it. The man asked Gerald what part of the country he had fought in and when McReady had said, "Denver," they all laughed and chugged their beers.

"You boys will get 'em in the next one," the old patron said and stumbled away. "Yep," he spoke to himself, "there'll be wars and the U-S-of-A will kick some ass. This was just our mulligan, just our throw-away war."

CHAPTER 31

THE FEW, THE SHROUD

DuPuis fell asleep on the way to Dallas. It was nearly three in the morning and the bus was quiet except for the snores and hacking coughs and general rustling that only people on a long bus trip could possibly make.

Gerald was confused, but happily so. There was something in the unknown, the tilting at windmills that was oddly appealing to him. The irony was undeniable; his presence here somewhere between interesting and profound. And the best part was that he wasn't digging in the sand for answers. He wasn't tilling his mind like earth, looking for good soil to plant. It was either there or it wasn't. Throw out the seeds, he told himself. See what grows.

DuPuis stirred and awoke.

"Gonna drain my dragon, doc." His voice was chipper even while half asleep. "Save my place." DuPuis reached up on the shelf for his dress cap and marched upright and correct to the rear of the bus. When he returned, Gerald paid close attention to the way he moved in his seat.

"Your butt hurting you, Lorenzo?" McReady asked.

"Sure. It don't bother me, though. I just let it go right through."

"What goes right through? The lead pellets still inside you?"

"No, doc, the suffering. I read a book about it in non-com school. The pain is manageable on account of it has meaning. Pain is only really bad when you pretend it don't exist. You let it go right through you and it doesn't have time to get a'hold of you. It's like taking a tragedy and making a triumph of it. That's what I'm doing."

DuPuis slouched in his seat and pulled his cap low over his eyes.

"The Nam was a cluster-fuck. We all know that now. But I ain't dwelling on it. I learned how to keep alive and how to maintain my sanity when a hell of a lot of my men got shot up or went wacko."

DuPuis turned to McReady and showed bits of the soldier he must've been. He lifted his cap in a deadly serious way and his eyes came at Gerald as lasers, unbending, unyielding.

"The guy I read in non-com was in a death camp in WWII, a Jewish doctor, watching all these people around him die. And he figured out how to stay alive until the war was over and then to help others by studying and writing about the experience."

"Who are you talking about, Lorenzo?" McReady, of course, had read Viktor Frankl in graduate school, but was intrigued by the soldier's take.

"The guy who wrote this book. He was a doc, just like you. So, what I'm saying is that my ass don't hurt because I don't pay it no mind. And after what I seen and what I been through, I'll never have a bad day again, long as I live. Nothing could be worse than what I've seen, what I've smelt."

"You think the world owes you something for going over there to fight, Lorenzo?'

"Hell no, doc. But I don't owe the world nothing neither."

"How about this writer who survived the camps? Why do you think he wrote the book?"

"Probably to make sense of it in his mind. But you see, I already done that by not doing it. This guy had to ponder why anybody would try so hard to kill an entire race of people. Think about that...*an entire race.* Compared to that, the Nam was easy. It was a damn civil war, just like we had. Just a country trying to reunify itself. I got my opinions of why the USA was there, but I won't go into them right about now. It was stupid, so I never even tried. I just did as I was told and did it right."

"But if you didn't believe in the war how could you kill someone else?"

"I believe in America, doc, with a capital A. Wasn't my job to be concerned with why we was fighting over there. I'm a marine, we do what we're told. We stick with America regardless what the reasons are. Hell, if I'm ever a congressman or the president, then I can be in charge of choosing who we fight. And right now, I got me ninety days medical leave until I get new orders. So, I doubt I'll have to kill anyone less'n they run out of Pabst."

"I don't understand you, Lorenzo. Sometimes you make perfect sense and other times you confuse me. Didn't America try to systematically kill off an entire race when we slaughtered the Indians?"

DuPuis leaned in close to McReady and spoke quietly, barely above a whisper.

"This country has fucked up more than once; there's no denying that. But I think we learn something every time. At least some people do. I feel sorry 'bout them Indians, I really do. But the only reason you and I are sitting here is that America is cocky. Always been that way, always will. Those colonial cats took on the whole British Empire, man. That's ballsy. We never lost a war before. It'll take a few years, but the lessons of Vietnam will keep us out of other people's business unless they're an obvious threat. I think we'll let these other little pissy countries fight their own wars, less'n they got nukes or come over and mess with us here. Don't you agree, doc?"

"I don't know. Look how long it took to get you all out of that mess even after everybody knew it was useless. You said it, Lorenzo, the government makes the decisions and then you just take the directions. You also said that there'll always be another war. What about a conscious? What if you don't believe in the cause?"

Lorenzo was nonplussed.

"I can't let my conscious get in the way, doc. I'm a U.S. Marine. Oo-fuckin-rah. They're my conscious. I do as I'm told when I'm on my watch and then I enjoy my life. The pain moves right through me like a good bowel movement. That's why all that lead shrapnel keeps coming up to surface of my ass—I just won't allow it to stay in there."

The two men sat back and listened to the whine of the big diesel motor and stared into the darkness of the restless, sleeping heads around them. Each had developed an empathy for the other, wondering, as it were, how they could have come to the ideals that possessed them like a child clinging to a mother's leg—someday you'll have to shed them, but on whose terms?

"Doc, you don't mind me saying, I think you're afraid of not knowing everything." Lorenzo spoke straight ahead for the first time that Gerald could remember.

"I seen the way you moved around that hospital. You were more in charge than the big cheese docs who acted like they knew it all. I read another book in-country during the Christmas ceasefire. It was a Chinese one and my CO kept calling me a Commie spy. It was called *Yo Ching* or something like that. Kind of confusing in parts, but one thing I remember is that it said the universe is forever outta control. I believe that shit, don't you? Man, just look around us. It's a wonder this planet don't spin right off its axis. That's why we gotta relax and have some fun. That's why, hard as you try, doc, you're not gonna' figure it all out...ever."

DuPuis sat back and put his hands behind his head.

"One other thing, doc. You never got enough respect, you ask me. People don't give it to you, then you just gotta take it. We get to Lafayette, I'm gonna pay you back by showing you how to have some fun and get respected. Best you get some shut-eye. You're gonna need the rest. Wake me in Dallas. I got me a number of some birds we can call who'll come and meet us."

"Geez, Lorenzo, I just don't get it," Gerald muttered.

"These birds will give it to you, doc. And you can take it or leave it. It's just people doing what comes natural to 'em."

And then McReady said one more thing that he regretted, but at least knew he'd regret it as the sound came from his mouth.

"You mean, like killing comes natural for a soldier?"

The disappointment on DuPuis's face told the story.

"You know, McReady, I'm just trying to help."

Gerald apologized and DuPuis said forget it, he knew that not everybody had soldiering in them.

"It's like this, doc. It's kind of a game for me; not the killing but the strategy, the hunt. Think about those rich businessmen who won't live long enough to spend all the money they have in their banks. But they work like dogs trying to make more and more and more. For them it's just a way of keeping score. I'm the same way for me. I don't get any particular pleasure in putting a bullet through another man's heart, but if'n they put one through mine first, then I lose." DuPuis undid the top button on his uniform for the first time and continued.

"I won't be in this game forever, but I signed up for the corps. That's like signing up to build a new highway—you don't stop when you get tired or run out of workers or asphalt or even road. You're done when them cars are whizzing by and you're sitting off to the side, a chest full of ice cold ones just calling your name, the beer itself talking to you, saying, 'that's a damn nice highway, DuPuis, a damn nice one. Have another.' I guess what I'm trying to say, doc, is that I watched you like I said. You build roads by rebuilding busted soldiers. But you got to realize that you can't win every time and sometimes the best way over the mountain is around it. You would've made a damn fine army guy, doc, a damn fine medic. But not a marine."

DuPuis closed his eyes and let a long breath come out in the shape of a sigh. "You ask me, doc, your problem is that you ain't never had anyone you respected tell you it's okay to be done with a road."

McReady wanted to say thanks, he wanted to say that he thought DuPuis was right, that he appreciated him saying all those nice things. He wanted to say he was trying to find that "something," that "someone" who *could* exist and turn it into some one thing that did. But when he opened his mouth, a wall of history came up and it looked like his father's beguiled smile, smelled like his father's greed, tasted like the words of someone else telling him that he'd lost the game because they'd made the rules, not him.

So, all he did was to look at his friend from the corps and offer up his hand, not to shake, but in an awkward salute.

"We got to work on that one, doc, but thanks, really. I know what it means."

CHAPTER 32

FLYING SOLO

Someone once asked where the wind comes from. It must've been a child or maybe a philosopher, their questions possessing the same degree of unfettered universality. The meteorologists will describe in much detail: the physics behind pressure variances and storm systems, themselves both the catalyst and recipient of the invisible movement of air molecules across surfaces of friction. Distilled down to the layman, they will say that wind is simply an area of high pressure trying to get even, to get equal with a low one.

"You can't see it folks, but you sure can feel it," and then a chuckle for the evening news.

Harry knew all this; his years on the sea had taught him much about the "breath of God," as Grace used to say, that filled the sails that piled the waves, creating both energy and havoc among those who were within His exhalation. Harry knew the weather of the Gulf of Mexico and respected it as he did some higher force.

And while he had never been a religious man, mostly having directed what spirituality he felt outward to his family and friends and inward to the way he'd felt about his relationship with the sea and the creatures that he pulled from it to make a living. Harry believed in God. But in what form of being he was not so sure. Harry had listened to Johnny

Cobb's own tales of hating and loving this God of his in the same breath. He'd seen Cobb cry at the mention of his dead and drowned Ruth and seen him laugh with joy when he spoke of seeing her again in heaven. But Harry wasn't sure if Johnny Cobb really knew how he felt. Like everyone, he, too, was evolving day by day. Johnny just had a head start.

Something had happened to Harry on his solo trip to Mexico. The shift that he'd felt after his time spent alone on the sea, alone in Corpus Christie, and then with Francisco in the Tampico bar, had knocked something loose. And then Belize and Cancun—*puerto* after *Puerto*—that had all been lost to his feelings of loss and then tossed back into the sea in the form of negotiated memory or bad tequila. Whatever had fallen off had shattered when it hit and moved the tectonic plates or the unnatural swells of his psyche. The aftershocks kept coming. But there was a slow release of pressure with each little jolt.

He couldn't call it acceptance of all things and people now gone from his present life. Harry could never accept the fact that his daughter had died before her twenty-seventh birthday; his wife, alone and waiting and healing in the garden with no family to hold her and tell her of the good she'd brought to the world; and now his only son, the sole remaining heir to the Davis name, returned from a place that had taken a part of his body and thrown his mind out to scatter in the winds of ambivalent turmoil. He was too proud to accept these occurrences as fate and too gentle a being to blame any other man or any god. When his family and friends had needed Harry the most...he'd run away.

But Harry was getting too old to fight and too wise to bury his guilt where it might resurface from time to time. A kind of mutual detente had settled over Harry Davis and it came first with the realization that he had a son left, a boy at home or on the road to wherever he had gone, when the two men, the father and the son, had left on separate quests for similar reasons. Harry knew that his peace lie in that of his seed, what he and Grace had created, what Gillie had mentored, what Johnny had seen and also loved in the boy for more years than Harry could count on the rings of high cumulus clouds that began to encircle his boat as he made his way home. And he knew that if he was to secure that fleeting peace, if he was to come to terms with his God, his self, and his past at that moment as the sky darkened in the west five hundred fifty nautical miles due south from New Orleans, Harry would have to realize that they were all cut and unfurling from the same canvas. He'd have to go home and start over. Harry would take what Phin had said about being an Etch A Sketch and turn himself upside down, shake his boarded-up soul loose, and start with a clean slate.

And he'd accept Grace in whatever condition she would evolve.

The peace would last, he thought, if he worked at it. But he'd also let it work on its own. Harry would sail home, tie off the *Gracey*, and go looking for Phin. He'd sent him away. He'd sent himself away. Now he'd bring the family back together under the same roof.

The wind began to freshen from twelve to twenty knots within a very short period. Harry thought about what he and Phin could do: fix up Grace's garden, revarnish the little *Ruth Henry*, and drive up to Johnny's place together and see that crew of vets he was always bragging about in the few letters that had caught up with him over the past months. They could start over. Everybody deserved a second chance.

But what had he learned? Harry thought as a gust blew his heavy coffee mug across the deck and he looked at where his wind gauge used to be before remembering that he'd removed all electronic instrumentation from his forty-one-foot, twin diesel-powered trawler before leaving on this trip. He'd learned both everything and nothing. He was happier, he was satisfied. For the time being, that was enough. And for the long run, he didn't know. If this was as good as it got, then he'd make the best of it.

Maybe Harry had used up all the good he was allowed in his life. Like some "cat's nine lives" thing? And what comes after the ninth one? He'd ask his wife. She believed in something else. Something beyond. But Grace might go on to that next life of hers before she could explain to Harry if it was some sort of eastern reincarnation thing or a Judeo-Christian "eternity in heaven" thing that she'd discovered. And the temptation of guilt and abandonment returned.

Harry wasn't one to hedge his bets; just a man who liked to have a say in this life here or any such one that comes after it. That's what he was thinking when the big stern davit broke and fell off the port side taking rigging and gear and his new-found peace and his freshly warmed coffee with it.

"Goddamn it," Harry swore as he scrambled out of the small wheelhouse and back to the stern deck where he'd hauled in more fish in the last three months than in the last six years, all of them given away or released back from where they came. "What is this shit?" He spoke to himself as he reached for the cutters and set free the lines and cables and rigging tangled as they were and would've caused further damage to the vessel.

"I'm an easy two-day passage from Panama City Beach harbor, I'm almost home. Who is fucking with me now?" He screamed as the last of the sun's light fell away over the west and the wind, to his estimate, was now a steady thirty knots with gusts to forty-five.

There is always that momentary second guessing that occurs at a time like this when a wanderer wonders if his possibilities exceed his preparations; if he might've subconsciously sabotaged himself or his journey in deep secret hopes that something substantial would happen and force his hand—make him stand up to his training and his past ideals and maybe his God. And for just that moment Harry Davis did, in fact, question his motives. But not once did remorse enter the equation. He'd done what he had thought was right at the moment, as he always had. Harry might now contemplate what fate had been dealt him, but not at this moment, or ever, would he allow his remorse to affect his ability to move forward. He'd made mistakes—who hadn't?

Harry cut the last of the rigging with the big cutters and scrambled back up to the wheelhouse and turned the *Gracey* directly into the wind and pushed the throttle levers forward one-third. His eye caught the empty sockets where the radios and navigational aids had been, but still no remorse would enter this man. The privacy, the self-reliance on a hand-held compass, charts, sextant, and basic math had been a part of some immutable search for something that he was pretty damn sure he'd found. Which he couldn't truly identify any more than he could a god.

But what his deeper training was telling him now was that he was on the front edge of a big low pressure system, a storm with teeth. He wouldn't admit it just yet, but it might be at hurricane level. Not many low pressure systems would have as hard an edge where one minute you're cruising along at fifteen knots in three-foot seas and sunny skies and then, off on the horizon you see it, but maybe you don't quite let yourself believe it, because, Jesus, it's almost October, awfully late in the season for a beast of this size.

The next hour the winds came. And they came in geometric increases: five, fifteen, thirty, sixty knots as the seas rose in equivalent size, turmoil, and confusion.

Three months in the Gulf hugging the coasts, risking it because he didn't care, driving on with a thoughtful quest if not experience, gut-level instinct, and plain dumb luck, all during the hurricane season. And now near the end when the first few rays of hope had peaked over the eastern sky...this.

Harry kept the bow pointed into the wind in the advancing storm because that was standard, calculated, marine seamanship. He'd been a prudent captain, always playing the safe odds when he had crew and holds full of fish to get home safely. It was different now, it was only him: no communications, no knowledge of the size and severity of the storm other than what he felt in his bones, and how the deepening low pressure made his joints hurt like he was an old man with arthritis.

"That's it, *Gracey*," he spoke to his boat and the spirit of his wife. "You can take this." But within twenty minutes he knew that he might not be able to. This was no minor, late-season tropical depression. This was the real deal. Hurricane-strength winds of seventy-plus knots pushed the swell size to twenty-foot faces, more if he was honest with himself. The *Grace,* her holds empty of fish and the weight that could aid in ballast and stability, bounced and pinged from crest to trough as Harry fought for control. Forty-one feet of length, thirty-eight at the waterline; she wasn't enough boat. He needed another twenty, thirty…would forty more feet of boat do it? And would a thousand pounds of ballast be enough?

"Okay, God," Harry began his first real direct conversation with the deity. "Is this it? You take my best friend's wife, my daughter, parts of my life partner's memory, pieces of my son, and now me? Is that what you do, oh great God that so many worship? What is this all about? You wanna tell me or should I just fly by the seat of my pants as I've been doing since my own father died, ever since the *Indianapolis* went down and I couldn't get to all those men who died? Jesus, you'd think they'd at least make sure the men knew how to swim before assigning them to a naval vessel during war time.

"What is this?" Harry continued his conversation with himself and with whom he was convincing himself, or being convinced, was something far greater than any ocean or any storm.

"Is this guilt?" The conversation went inward. "Are you lying down on me, man?" Harry didn't hear the words so much as he felt the thought. "Are you feeling bad because you couldn't get to those few, those dozen, those many, many screams in the night that called out because they were burnt and broken or bleeding from limbs lost to the horror of Jap torpedoes and shark bites? And the fact that they were just kids like Phin, conscripted, seduced, and misconstrued into the union's army to fight because a walnut-lined room full of pasty-skinned old men couldn't agree on something?" Harry's voice and reply became the same as it moved up from his heart, through his head and then out between his lips. The two joining where a deity might act as moderator.

"Ah, but Harry, are you confusing wars? Wasn't there a difference between the last Great War and Vietnam? Ho Chi Min was no Hitler."

"This is no time to debate ideologies of war. I'm having trouble keeping this vessel under control. It's getting worse by the minute. This is the worse I've been in. But then again, you should know that. You saw how that last wave rolled the entire length of the *Grace*. If this *is* God, and this ain't no illusion, with your permission I think I'll just concentrate on getting myself outta this shit. I gotta boy and a wife at home."

"Yes, you do, Harry. A fine lad who you rightly suggested to go and figure out his own shit. And now you've decided that you're ready to help yourself by helping him. I congratulate you, Harry. Oh, by the way, this is a category two hurricane you're trying to out-race. Now, what I'm suggesting is that since you brought up the topic of the USS Indianapolis, *and you decided that I just might have the potential of existing, we should finish the conversation. What do you think?"*

"Ah, hell, look at this wave." Harry turned the wheel hard to starboard and pushed the throttle full ahead to try and move the bow out of the breaking crest. He knew it was a mistake, that he should have run her straight into the wave and taken the beating he deserved for finding himself out here in this storm in the first place. *Grace* rolled hard to starboard and her gunwale lie awash under a fathom of dark green sea foam. Harry was pitched to the side of the cockpit and his arm smashed the thick glass of the wheelhouse, sending a crack through his clavicle and the window.

"No need to use profanity, Harry. Now about the men on the Indy..."

"Yeah, there were a lot of them, too many to count, too many hurt, dead or worse. What was I supposed to do? I got to as many as I could."

"Yes, you did, Harry. You did well. Nearly twelve hundred went in the water; three hundred and seventeen came out. How long did you wait with the men floating there? Almost four days as I recall."

"It was five." Harry stared straight ahead and listened to the *Grace* creak and moan as she bent under the pressure.

"And you had just delivered something, right Harry? Something important." The voice in his head was agonizingly soothing.

"You know what it was—the uranium for the bombs that changed the world...for the worse. But we didn't know that. We thought the war was all but over."

"But Harry, why then did you choose a life at sea, a life that often took you away from the family that you love so deeply? That brought you back out here?"

"Hey, you're supposed to be God; you answer that."

"I know why. I just want to hear it from you, Harry."

Another wave pitched the *Grace* over and Harry heard one of the engines sputter and go dead. He would need that power to keep the boat driving straight into the storm's eye.

"I wanted to save them all. That's why. They were just kids. I was older, I knew better. What did they know? Some of them weren't even eighteen years old, never been to college, never even been laid. I didn't blame the Japs. Hell, they were just kids themselves, doing what they were told. But I wanted to save all of them.

"When the other ship came and they started to pick us up and the sharks were still having their fill and the screams kept coming, the sailors made me get in the rescue raft. They were just kids, man, just kids. Nobody should die on the ocean like that. Nobody should die before their time."

"Do you think it's your time, I mean, right now? Whoa, look out for that one!" A huge wave engulfed the *Grace* and other windows broke, sending glass into the cockpit with the spitting wind and pounding rain.

Harry's shoulder hurt and he was blinded for the moment by the flying glass and rain drops that seemed to move in every direction. But an odd calm seemed to flow over him, starting at the top of his head and moving down like motor oil. And he decided that it mattered little if his conversation was real or imagined. Everything else was real enough. Harry knew what he had to do and turned the wheel hard over while in the trough between two large waves.

"Ah, you think you can out-run her, do you?" The voice would not go away. *"That's a ballsy, excuse me, a very risky tactic, Harry. Are you up to surfing a forty-one-foot trawler with one dead engine downhill for as long as it takes? If you bury the bow in the back of one wrong wave and another wave*

lands on your back, then I'll be seeing you at my house sooner than expected."

Harry said nothing for a long while. He knew it wasn't his time. Not now after he'd come clean, after he'd been tested. Harry had the skill. All he needed was a little luck, a little push. These things sometimes move slow. The *Grace,* even under one engine, was a good downhill boat. She'd run with the best of them. He was going home, this time for good.

As the night reigned in on Harry and the *Grace* and he had done all that he could, he knew he'd done his best, always had. Who was he to judge? Let the Voice do that. He'd been no good at carrying around guilt while he was alive. Why should he carry that stuff around while he was dead?

He kept the boat moving, dodging the deepest troughs and highest crests, glad for her smaller size and nimble handling. It was a race of attrition, he thought. He needed enough fuel, enough staying power. These storms could stall on themselves without the warm water that fueled them. Harry needed to get out of her grasp before she could pick up steam where the Gulf Stream made its turn off the eastern tip of Cuba.

"I could use a little help down here," the sound of his request surprising Harry. There was no answer.

Out of desperation, Harry tried the second engine one more time and it coughed and spit, but came to life. The only gauge he'd kept showed his fuel at one half. It would be close.

A fight was okay, though. Yes, to go down fighting would be acceptable. Phin would know that he hadn't given up. He would know; he was intuitive like that. Johnny would take care of everything else.

CHAPTER 33

DESERT DATES

Green sod above, lie light, lie light.

Good night, dear heart, good night.

–Mark Twain, verses on gravestone of
Susy, Elmira, New York, 1896

It felt odd, even queer to be back in the upper Southwest again; vaguely familiar, not comforting, but not troubling either. I felt myself torn between my desire to open the 4-barrel carburetor on the old Buick ragtop that Mike Greer had offered me, make some real time through this world of sand and open road, and then use the excuse to let her cool down so I could stop and meander around a bit.

Most guys, women, too, for that matter, put their cars and trucks into the male gender, and give them names like Bud or Sam. But a ragtop, a convertible where the sky and the clouds and the rain come right in and sit down next to you on that big, old, soft leather bench seat, well...a ragtop can only be a woman.

The '63 Buick Skylark was ten years old and had not been ridden hard or put away wet. She had a big motor and plenty of heart because Mike had changed her oil often and kept her as original as he could without making her into a show car. "Trailer queens," he used to call them. Some cars and some women are meant to be a part of your regular life, not an adornment. The Buick was born to be driven. Her body was straight, no rust, the paint a bit faded, but nothing a good rub-out couldn't bring back to life.

The car had belonged to Greer's wife, the one that he claimed he was finally letting go of. He made this statement when he and Jessica woke me a few days ago, early, with the first hint of fall showing in the steam off the coffee mugs. Jessica handed me the keys to the old Buick and said, "You take her. She's left us." I saw the courage in their finality and said I'd take care of it; that I'd give it the chance for new life if it did the same for me. Jessica had laughed and said it was only a car now, nothing more.

"Go find a girl and rename the car."

But like most soulful cars, the Buick had a mind of its own. Someday she was a little slow in the morning, needing a bit of a coax to hit her speed. You could never push her too quick or she would rebel by stalling or by pulling to the left over fifty miles per, even after you had just realigned her wheels and struts. But if you kept her well lubed, the fluids full, and the eight-track cassette playing old blues tunes, you could be rewarded with the sweetest ride one might imagine. There was no doubt she ran smoother when the blues combed her red and white leather interior.

Lonnie would have liked this car, I thought, and then wondered why my past flame had been creeping back into my present. Maybe it was the desert. Lonnie had talked about leaving the constant moisture, the boggy ground, and the thick, humid air of Panama City Beach for the desert. She read all about its arid and stark beauty, and had once gone with her dad on a trip to the air force base outside of Alamogordo, New Mexico.

"Phin," I remember her gushing when she came back, "you should see the wide-open spaces and how the sky just goes right off the page. Your clothes are always dry and there's no fog to block the stars at night. Someday, when I grow up, I'm gonna move from this little town and live out west where the people and the land are newer than here. I'm going to learn to paint beautiful landscapes with sunsets and steep cliffs of red and brown rock."

I wondered if Lonnie ever found her way west in search of gold as so many before her had done. I had no interest in tracking her down. I was the one who'd told her I was dead. And now, according to official sources, my war-time rant had become surreal. Was I now supposed to rise from the dead to find a girl I hadn't spoken to in well over five years? It was a high school romance, I tried to tell myself, long done and over. I had been heartbroken when she moved away. But she was the first, the first of many things. My heart was rebroken many times in that period of absence. I blamed the war for that on account the war couldn't talk back. But geez, was I wrong about that.

It might've been the war's version of anti-cupidism. As I drove the old Buick that cool, sunny fall day, I thought I should look her up just to thank her for doing it right the first time, for that nearly-ancient clean break that right about then, began to feel muddy. I drove and daydreamed while headed west-northwest on some empty stretch of non-descript asphalt. I thanked Lonnie's memory for giving me the practice of loss to deal with when my pals in-country got shot through the head. I should look up Lonnie, I dreamed, and thank her for giving me something to hang onto that first tour, for being my "girl back home," my Helen of Troy. I had leveraged our six months of going steady into the life-raft illusion of sixty years and six kids. The three-bedroom box of stucco at the end of the cul-de-sac. She would be there when I got back, I'd promised myself and lied to others. A simple dance at the senior prom, a few months of open-mouthed kisses near the dunes had turned into a rewindable film clip to be pulled out when latrine duty was assigned or the boredom of waiting outweighed the fear of a firefight.

The desert made me think. I ought to thank Lonnie, I ought to pull into a gas station in the middle of some tiny desert town, find her right there in the phone book under the L's for Lonnie, go right on over and take her for a ride in the Buick at night, look at the stars, and say thanks for the image, thanks for that dance. That's what a long drive in a ragtop will do to your thinking.

The desert can also be a harsh place, a place of hardship and death. Absent are the alpine colors associated with the vibrancy in nature's life-giving forces. You will not find tall green cypress trees hanging over the road, long green shady tunnels of cool moist air. You will not see forever-rolling fields of yellow mustard in the spring or crisp orange and red fruit hanging temptingly from trees in the fall like you may in more temperate climes. The desert can seem young in the morning, but so old by the end of the day.

But the desert can reward you like no other place can, if you allow it. It is not unlike your mind. There are parts of the desert and your brain that, if tapped into, can offer a whole new view of the world. But most people never go there for fear of what they might find. That part of the mind carries with it certain truths and fears that send many running for cover, what Johnny Cobb called, "racing the shadowy something." The desert lives by its own climate, if not its own carriage and posture. It sets its own rules on levels that only those who tempt its fundamental laws will ever know. In that respect, it is no different than the Nam. You learned to live by its rules or became part of the soil, swallowed by the earth where you stood for the sin of refusing to let it take you where it wanted to.

That's what happened to Bobby McCafferty.

We were out on night recon, way up near the Laotian border, late '72, Paris Peace talks in full swing. Just me, Will Bidman, another drafted man/child who had ran out of options, and a handful of greenies—Special Ops guys who barely spoke anymore, just pointed and communicated with their eyes, three and four tours into the war. We also had this new kid fresh out of OCS looking to get some action before Kissinger took away his chance. His name was Bobby McCafferty. I called him Mac. Nobody else called him at all.

Mac was from Philadelphia, the son of a dentist, and wanted in the worst way to "kill a gook." That's all I knew about him, all I needed to know. I didn't have a good feeling about his ability to live in the Nam.

Bidman and I had hit a Tai stick before heading out that night, same as we did most nights. For Will, I think it eased his fears, made him relax when we got in the shit. And for me, it gave me another sense. Or maybe it was nothing at all.

The five of us were moving low and dark through an area known to be hot. The greenies were up on point, the three of us tailing, spread out. I was on rear when we saw the tracers light up the sky not a half click in front of us. One of the greenies grunted and started toward the lights. Bidman was right behind them as I came up fast on McCafferty, who had dug in, just frozen to the edge of the trail.

"C'mon, c'mon Mac, we gotta' go. Move. Move!" I told him.

But McCafferty just laid there, mumbling about how we needed to hold our position, watch for enemy movement.

"No, man," I told him, "They're all around us, everywhere. We gotta go into the light man, 'cuz that's what they won't expect. Let's go. Let's go. Get the fuck up."

Then he fired.

Of course, that gave away our position and Charlie's bullets rained down on us from every point on the compass. I held my breath and tried to be like Charlie, tried to fold myself into the jungle, become invisible. I knew we were about to get overrun so I crawled over to where McCafferty was to find half of his face lying in his lap, one of the eyes still crossed, the left part of his mouth still smiling.

✻ ✻ ✻

I decided to stop the car, which I'd named Norma. There had been another Norma.

"C'mon Norma, you can make it up this hill after a little rest." I'd reclaimed my dogs from Al's Feed Shop on a quick backtrack and could see that they needed some water right about now. Spotting a small stand of jacaranda, it was a sure sign that there was at least the possibility of some small, vernal pool nearby. That's another thing about the desert—it hides its golden stuff really well. The dogs didn't bother to use the door, just bolted over the side of Norma as soon as she had slowed to 10 mph, and headed off in the direction of the trees and some fluids and a much-needed break from the relentless sun. If there was water, they'd find it.

And under a big Joshua tree between a nice stand of ocotillo and sage, I took off my boots and laid down. Closing my eyes, I thought about how similar the desert is to the Nam. Similar, but different. Nothing out here wafts or weaves. Nothing floats or nibbles like it does in the Nam. Out here, even when the summer heat gives way to an oddly quiet winter chill, things slither and slink, *exactly* like they do in Nam. They sneak up on you, like a prairie dog +that steals food from your backpack or a sunburn on the top of your ears.

The desert, like the Nam, has its own sense of timing too. Its patient elements can slowly peel away a man's sanity if he wanders around too long, even if he knows where he is and where he's going. Or its long fingers can reach out from the depths of some mythic lair spoken of only in whispered tones by local indigenous tribes and grab the passing motorists, hurling them like plastic model cars while they search for a radio station. It'd happened in the Ia Drang Valley in October of '65 when the NVA attacked the Special Forces camp at Plei Me. And it had happened in January and February of '68 during the multi-front Tet Offensive when the U.S. military industrial complex, as intelligent at it might've been, didn't seem smart enough. And a bunch of young kids from Seattle and Fargo and Miami and Pittsburg and Jackson and Kansas City were killed.

And then she was there again, in my road dreams while I rested my eyes under the shade of an ancient yucca, the dogs watered, sleeping under the cooling steel bumper of Norma the Buick Skylark.

Lonnie had worn her blonde hair to the middle of her back when she was young, but now, in my dream, it was cropped shorter, framing the beginnings of tiny little lines around her eyes—crow's feet in training—creeping out of her large green eyes. Lonnie was small, five foot nothing, barely a hundred pounds. I pictured her in her studio up in the hills above some place like Santa Fe or Montrose or especially

Durango, a pallet of paint in her left hand, a brush in the other, as well as one clinched in her teeth. She would be wearing an old wool sweater stained with oils and acrylics, crimson red on the sleeve, ultramarine blue on the chest, and yellow—lots of yellow—dripping down the front like candle wax. She would have the Grateful Dead lofting out of the stereo, singing along while she lost herself in the worlds she created on canvas. Damn, Lonnie loved yellow.

A part of me had died when she moved away. But how could I have known that then? I was seventeen. Who the hell knows anything at seventeen?

And as I slept under the long shadows of that fall desert sun, I dreamt of missed opportunities, of life's connections, of hanging on and letting go. I had loved Lonnie before I knew what it meant. And it dawned on me that she had existed like the other Norma, a kind of mythic, lustful, projection of desire. Norma was to Lonnie what the Southwest desert was to Vietnam: related predecessors not in geography, but in some sad misinterpretation of identity.

The other Norma had been a waitress who worked at the International House of Pancakes up in Knoxville, Tennessee. We would go there after work when I was helping one of my dad's brothers, Uncle Frank, build himself a real home, not the kind that can be picked up and flat-bedded away if you failed to make the payments and that attracted hurricanes and tornados with a "come-and-get-me-bitch" taunt. I was just sixteen that summer. And I imagined that this IHOP Norma and I could become an "us."

Norma May Jarrel. She was a big gal; "breeder hips," Uncle Frank used to say. But she was as kind of a person as I'd remember meeting, and though she outweighed me by twenty-five pounds, I'd considered asking her out to the movies, maybe a soda afterwards. Maybe more than that, but the attraction was less physical, more of what I imagined lay in her heart. I never did, though I can't say why.

Sometimes I think of Norma May, the image of her standing over us in the corner booth in her pink apron, breasts just straining against that cotton uniform they had to wear, the name tag two inches above where I imagined her left nipple might be, asking us how the concrete pour had gone or what type of electrical conduit we were fixin' to put in—just like she had built a half-dozen houses herself. She would take our order, never needing to write it down, always seeming to spend just a moment longer with her big round swimming-pool eyes on me. Then she would walk away and the guys would get back to taking about the job or the kids or the weekend—never her. But I would follow her trail all the way to the kitchen until I was interrupted by Frank slugging me in the arm saying "breeder hips."

Damn, I wish I would have gone out for a soda with Norma May.

✳ ✳ ✳

When I woke up it was still warm outside, hot enough to make you stick to the seats when you drove with your shirt off, and I imagined a glimmering oasis up on the horizon, a mirage where the black road and the unpaved sky came together as one. I'd read stories of desert travelers from both recent and modern times who had followed the ever-static distant illusion right to the very end. It was a Valhalla, I thought, a faith in a place that exists somewhere, but not in this life or on this earth. When we were kids, traveling with my Pa and Ma across the Great Plains, Pa would tell Gillie and me we were headed "just yonder that pond in the middle of the road," pointing to the shimmering heat that made the horizon look as if a lake was indeed right in our path. I think I believed him until I was twelve. If I ever have young'ns, I'll use that little joke every time I can. But when they get older I'll try to explain to them my real thoughts on why we're better off just believing, even when we know we'll never get there in a car or on foot.

Lonnie had fallen out of my dream that afternoon and as much as I fought it, I had a strange urge to find her trail in the world of the waking. It was as if somebody had come and picked me up like an old pair of jeans and shaken me upside down, hoping for coins and guitar picks to fall out of the pockets, but instead, out came a childhood romance that you had used as a shield against the war. But then the coins turned into pieces of gold and jewels.

I found the dogs sleeping in the shadow of a huge jacaranda and told them it was time to go. They had found water in a small crack of porous rock under a stand of small palm. I went to the car to look at a map, but the dogs were insistent on showing me their find and I followed them, praising each for their discovery. I loved these dogs: Elijah, Jeremiah, and Daniel. Ever since they were puppies they carried a sense of grace and nobility about them. Daniel, in particular, always letting the other puppies suckle their mama's teats first. I knew they deserved significant names and was glad my Pa had assigned them.

And after they'd shown me their find, I looked at the map and easily found the Four Corners, the only place in the Continental U.S. of A. where four different states butt up against each other, a sacred place among Native American tribes, one of the only places where the huge Navajo Nation had allowed Sioux and Crow and even Apache to pass through undisturbed. For these early inhabitants, the corners of New Mexico to the southeast, Utah to the northwest, Arizona to the southwest, and Colorado to the northeast represented the center of their known world, which in and of itself it was, small in one way, vast and stretching in others. These lands belonged to no man, they believed, but the Great Spirit had guided them to this area, same as He was pushing me in that direction even though it was several hundred miles past my turn up toward eastern Colorado.

Norma the Ragtop started up easily and the dogs jumped in the back, burrs stuck to their fur, tongues hanging, ready to feel the warm air on their faces do its magic. I drove for a while and wondered what I would do when I got to Durango, Colorado. Had the dream been a premonition? Had Lonnie ever mentioned the town in her childhood travel dreams? How would I feel if I actually stopped and searched for her name in a phone book? How would I feel if it was there? Or not there? What was the chance that she still had her family name? And what was that name again? Wickless? Wicker? Wilder? Wilted? Whiting! That was it, like clearing a pallet or cleansing a soul—Lonnie Whiting. Shame on me for forgetting it. Shame on me for even allowing my dream to morph into fantasy. But I remembered her number: 943-2179. Lonnie Whiting, granddaughter of an English playwright who was the son of a union labor leader, but more Irish that British. How much of her was real or imagined I wasn't sure any more. Lonnie's father had been a colonel in the U.S. Air Force and somehow I was still mad at him for being transferred and taking his seventeen-year-old daughter with him.

The car sputtered and I thought back to Greer's words, "You just go and take that Buick. She needs a good road trip to remember what she was made for, blow some carbon buildup from the pipes. Bring her on back when you're finished with your business up in Colorado if'n it suits you. And leave the top down, would you? I don't want the roof fabric exposed to the sun."

Displacing Lonnie for a moment, I recalled the last few days. I had come across Northern Texas from Greer's joint in Lubbock on Highway 84 to the 60 across the New Mexico line, as lonely a road as man has ever constructed. Before I left I had asked him how I might send him a letter or two. He just said, "Mike Greer, Farm Equipment, Southwest Lubbock, Texas. Maybe stick on the zip code, 79401. It'll get here." The simplicity of it all seemed appropriate for the man himself and I wondered if I would ever be able to come to terms with all the emotional complications, simplify my life right down to the very basics, whatever they might end up being, and that I might be able to write myself a postcard and address it to, "Phin Davis, Driving a Buick Ragtop or a '71 VW Bus, last seen headed in a Northwesterly direction." I wondered if I cleaned out my soul as well as I had the air filter on Norma in Santa Rosa last night, I might eventually pull up to a little bar in Albuquerque or Farmington, walk in and order a beer. The bartender would say, "Hi ya,' Phin. Hey, gotta letter for you here." And I would smile and drink my beer and ask his name.

The sun was starting to lose itself in the west, changing the face but not the underlying feel and current of the desert. I was both afraid and enthralled by the directionless possibilities—the maybes. Maybe Lonnie's old man woulda turned down the transfer, maybe Gillie would have had the flu instead of the Big C; a lot of would-of's and could-of's, and all I had right then was the right now.

I sure as hell hoped God was watching right then. Jesus, the sun was bright for so late in the day; too hot for such a time. Man, I sure hope she's happy these days; but I didn't know if the *she* was Norma the Waitress or the Lonnie of Troy I was thinking of.

And then not soon enough, the sun was just about yanked below the low surrounding mesas and finally the Chuska Mountains themselves. And a change occurred. There were times like this when the desert was at its best, the heat subsiding, the colors moving from Lonnie's yellow to orange to brown and finally to burnt sienna, my favorite color in the sixty-four pack of Crayola Crayons. But it was also the time of day when the desert was the most troublesome, the most deceiving. *Hora de peligrosa,* the locals of Gallup like to say, the "dangerous hour."

It's a time when the light is dim, bright sunlight having given way to long, thin shadows. A time when travelers push on to make the next town or grow weary after a full day behind the wheel or hiking in the hills. It's a time the wind can change, when a man's thirst switches from water to alcohol. The sounds and smells of the desert change, too, as the sun slips behind the distant peaks.

✳ ✳ ✳

Charlie was the same way. You never saw him during the day. He'd hole up in earthen tunnels and caves and lie sleeping under dense jungle canopies. The morning after McCafferty bought it, Bidman and the greenies and I went back to get his body. The VC had gone through his things, leaving only his pants, his crumpled body, and one dog tag. Everything else had become property of the North.

We carried him out to an LZ, called in for a dust-off, and helped load his body into the Huey while the pilot looked expressionless at Mac's faceless face. I wanted to feel something, sadness maybe or grief, *anything* at all that would remind me that I was still a human being with emotions and feelings. But I didn't because the Nam had taken them away in a part of some subconscious scheme, some protective symbolism.

The Vietnam War didn't just have a heart of darkness. Its whole body was black.

The sun was almost down now—not day, not night—as we rode Norma the Ragtop north along Route 550 in New Mexico from Rio Rancho to Bloomfield. I would gas up and spend the night in Cortez, Colorado before heading back east again into Durango the next day. It had taken me awhile to get used to the idea of going backward to go forward. Johnny used to say that life was a series of concentric circles that looped on top of themselves. I'm still not sure what that means, but I'll bet that's one of the reason's I found myself drawn here—at some point you just have to hop onto a different circle.

It was this exact time of day when McCafferty bought it. Stupid shit. Poor, stupid Lt. McCafferty. I kinda liked the guy. Dumb ass.

I was just outside of Farmington before the road to Shiprock and I remembered being conscious when Harry and Johnny came up to the Denver VA to fetch me. How was my mom? "Not quite yet just another star in the sky," she'd always say about old people dying off." Too many images like sticks and stones and bombs from the past coming at me again and again. The desert had control of my mind—*hora de peligrosa*.

But the moon wasn't up yet and I refused to give in to the land. The car seemed to develop a mind of its own and Norma the Waitress, good, sweet Norma, was throwing our dinner in the sink, trying to get me to drive into the ditch. And then the night sounds of the desert began emerging. They can be frightening sounds if you aren't used to them or if you refuse to accept them. You get a sense that at night, the Nam and the desert are big game hunters and you are the game.

Finally, the dark came less than an hour from Cortez. Something had passed like the Wicked Witch of the West—you just knew she wasn't dead until the movie was over. The dogs were asleep in the back, piled up on top of each other like a bunch of stuffed animals tossed in the corner. I was getting tired and figured I'd hole up in Cortez for the night before heading into Durango in the morning.

When I looked up at the sky, my eyes refused to adjust and I flashed upon the time I put myself into one of those black body bags, the kind they used to ship home dead soldiers or pieces of a dead soldier. I told my buddies I wanted to see what it felt like in there, just in case I was accidentally pronounced dead and zipped up like a sack of old clothes bound for the Goodwill Store and then left on the tarmac, waiting my turn to go back to the world. They laughed and said it wouldn't happen, but I reminded them of who was running the show over there and they stopped laughing and thought maybe, or more than maybe, the U.S. government could make such a mistake. Stranger things had occurred.

The region had caused a longing for beans and tortillas chased with *cervesas y tequila un poco.* Just outside of Cortez a little place with a handful of cars gathered in the parking lot caught my eye. It was not much more than a square-shaped stucco box with a couple of windows barely allowing a faded yellow light to shine through. Something about it was familiar, but so many places on the road look and feel the same.

Behind the cracked glass dark shapes moved in circular patterns. There was an old split rail fence running the length of the parking lot except for the places where it had fallen down or been hit by tequila drivers. Hanging from the porch roof by a rusty chain was a wooden sign with freehand painted letters—"Jose's Place, Sum Food & Some beer." It was familiar, but I wasn't putting any stock in familiarity at that point. Along with some rest, that was just what I needed. I let the dogs sleep, ambled into the modest establishment, and sat myself in a corner booth. Someone had scratched their names into the old wooden table next to the words, "Those who have traveled the tequila road can speak of the way and the weight of the load." A few eyes followed me in, but they were good eyes. There was a mixture of barbecue, cigarettes, mesquite, and stale perfume in the air. A four-piece band played a slow country song: "It's true that it's sad, but sadder that it's true."

The bass player had dark, leathery skin that looked brownish red under the single yellow bulb that swung hypnotically from a black extension cord plugged into a socket in the ceiling. He was old, small, and wore his hair in a long, gray pony tail tied with what looked like a piece of fence wire.

But the lead vocalist, man, she coulda been Norma May all over again: a young, dark-skinned Hispanic version with soft hips and softer, kinder eyes. And when she hit that high D sharp on the chorus from a new cover song, "Go on, man, be a hero, be an old black and white. Turn those pages that leave the night." Ah shit, between my pondering on Lonnie half the day, the long turn at the wheel along Route 550, and the half-pitcher of a damn fine Negro Modelo...well, I had had enough. I did what I'd done as a kid when the feelings get too much for me to take—I curled up into a little ball and went to sleep on the bench right then and there, not giving a shit, going back so I could go forward.

I lie there on the red leather booth while a few locals do-si-do'd on the dance floor and dreamed about Lonnie.

✳ ✳ ✳

I was being nudged on my arm. Someone was trying to wake me up. In my dream I was now lying on the dirt, trying to get up, but there was this tremendous force pulling me down into a sandy ditch on the side of the road. I thought I saw coyotes, but they were men in big red jackets with coyote faces and lights coming out of their hands and sirens became their haunting howls. And when I was able to break free from the ditch, I went looking for Lonnie and found her on the side of the road under a plastic yellow sheet. I pulled the sheet back and she looked at me, swallowing me with those big green eyes, the color you will never see in the desert. And then she said, "I'm going away for a while, but I'll be back. Don't go anywhere, Phin. We're going steady, remember?"

"No," I told her, "I'll stick around. The area is secure now. McCafferty brought in a group of Force Recon in Hueys. We'll get you to EVAC and you can put all your paintings up in your room. They'll be there when you come back."

But Lonnie started to cry and her tears were as black as a moonless night and she asked me to just hold her before she went. And I did for a very long time while I felt my own blood mix with hers and the sweat from my brow became leaking gasoline that smudged the map of our lives, robbing us of all direction and plans and time.

Finally, in my dream Lonnie asked me which was the earth and which was the sky and how far it was down the river to the sea. She was thirsty. The desert had been too dry a place for her. She wanted to go home to Panama City Beach, just for a while. And then she seemed to be holding her breath, waiting for an answer while I heard the howling across the highway and in my head. But I could not tell her that I knew the difference. I could never answer her question.

✳ ✳ ✳

"Sir, sir. Please you have to wake up. It's very late and I have to go home to get sleep."

It was Jose, owner of the bar. My sleep was wearing off slowly, like Novocain, and when I opened my eyes I was looking into the lined face of the bass player. He seemed even smaller up close and offered me *huevos rancheros* before he left.

Jose told me that he had fed the dogs and that I could sleep in the backroom tonight on the cot next to the kitchen, just like the last time I was there.

"Why are you helping me, Jose? I am just a passing traveler who fell asleep in your bar. What last time?"

"Oh, no, señor. I know you. You have the name of a fish part and used to come in here many years ago when my father ran this place, when I was just a young cook. Do you not remember? You used to come in with the tall Black man who smoked the pipe. You were a boy then, but the man, señor Cobb, I think, he stayed for a few days and fixed the stove. He taught my wife to cook some special dishes using a fish we take from the river near Cortez. This is a favorite now. These things we do not forget easily. Yes, and do you not remember when you were here as a teenage man?"

I was awake now, enlisting every brain cell, unlocking wondrous memories of times with Johnny on these trips when Harry was at sea and mom busy with the yard and Gillie.

That's when I looked up and saw the painting on the back wall. It was of the Panama City Beach Pier, no mistaking, with the high rails perfect for climbing over and lots of yellow in the background sky.

"Jose," I asked, bleary-eyed, pointing to the painting. "Where did you get that painting?" I asked. "Who painted it?

"Señor Cobb. He brought it for my wife some years ago when he came through this way. He was alone then. I do not know who is the artist, my young sleeping friend.

"I have to go now," Jose told me, "but my daughter, Lolita, will fix you something to eat and get your cot ready. Maybe I will see you tomorrow, sí?"

I heard Lolita humming to herself in the kitchen and realized that she was the singer from the band. I watched her at the sink as she chopped onions and tomatoes and thought again of Norma May and how I had let her go before I ever knew her, and I thought of Lonnie, how we did have each other in a time of youth that some say doesn't count for love. It counted for me though, long after she had moved away and love had broken the rules of engagement.

I'd never really had a girl in my life, only thoughts and hopes of one, illusions of what was and what could've been. My parents had twenty-two years together, Johnny had two with Ruth. Sure, I had six months with Lonnie in the real world, and nearly two tours with her illusion in-country, including the later months when I let her memory fade like the ending of an old movie: fade to black.

None of this seemed real anymore. It was like parts of my dream had become real and parts of my life had gone dream—they just swapped places. The dream where Lonnie was hurt was a mistake, a stupid mistake. I shouldn't have allowed it. I don't even remember why we swerved in the dream. Maybe an oncoming car came at us. Maybe I reached down to switch the channel on the radio. Maybe the wind blew us across the road and into the ditch. Maybe the desert reached up and pulled us into the ditch for no reason at all. *Hora de peligrosa.*

But there was no one to blame. Not the desert. Not the U.S. government. Not ourselves. And even if there was, what good would it do? I guess that we don't get to control dreams. I've never met anyone yet who could.

I went outside into the blackest night I had ever seen and sat down on the wooden steps. There was no moon, no stars, no cloud reflections, and no sign of man or nature anywhere. I felt like I was inside that black body bag.

But somehow, I knew I was alive, vitally alive, and a part of some grand experiment. I knew this because Johnny and I needed to speak about a painting, because Daniel woke up and came up to me and licked my hand. I could barely make out his four-legged shape in the dark void, but I could feel his love and warmth flow through his big, wet, red tongue.

Lolita turned on the porch light and brought out a big plate of *huevos*. I scooped a portion onto a paper plate Lolita had brought and handed her the fork. We shared what we had.

CHAPTER 34

NORTH BY NORTHEAST

When I awoke in the small single-bed bed at the rear of José's Café, my eyes had welded themselves shut. Some fluids had leaked. The dry air had taken the water and left the stick. I licked my fingers and pried them open, the taste of salt pulling me pack to where I was. I sat up and saw that Lolita was sleeping on a low cot in the corner, the edges of her long dress from the night before peeking out from the bottom of the short, rough blanket she had pulled in close. Somewhere during the night bits of my past had re-joined my present and I knew—I had indeed spent time here before. Johnny had taken me on a few of his spring "road trips to sundown" when I was maybe six or seven. How and why? These details were not presenting well as I awoke.

There were quick flashes of me as a young boy trying to speak to a young girl his own age. Her words were different, but they spoke anyway, kicking a worn ball across a sandy yard out back, thinking that we must've known then what I had just discovered—we were young friends growing older, growing up.

"Lolita, *tu eres dormida*?" I asked in my weak Spanglish. "Sí, Señor Phin, I am asleep." I said I'm sorry and got up to check on the dogs. They weren't in the old Buick so I walked around back and saw the yard, the cactus, and palms that had grown tall since the days when Johnny brought me here as a kid, and we had stayed a day or a week on one of the trips my mother had allowed, knowing that I would see and learn things not possible in our small insular town on the Gulf.

I called for the dogs and they came running out from the edges of the desert that was the backyard of José's place of food and family.

"Hey, boys, what do you think? You glad to have some open country to remind you that you are, in fact, dogs?" They barked a chorus of "amens" and licked my hand once before heading back out to chase cottontails and lizards.

"You remember coming here before, Señor Phin? As a boy?" It was Lolita. She stood leaning up against the edge of the building, her hair falling across her dark eyes, making no effort to pull it back. For a moment, there were three of her: the beautifully, unadorned woman standing in front of me; the haunting temptress who sang on stage last night; and the young girl from fifteen years ago who spoke another language, who had come up from the south with her father and mother, who could dribble a soccer ball around me in her bare feet and homemade dress.

"Yes," I said, slightly hesitant but with an uncatalyzed smile behind it. "There are images of this place, the food and laughter, the words I didn't know, the smell of cooking out in this yard that goes all the way up to Durango."

"And they please you; these memories?" She asked.

"Yes," I was warming up with the sun. "I think I must have had enjoyed my short stays here with Johnny and your family."

"You think? You mean you aren't sure of what you remember or how you felt?"

"Well, Lolita, some of my past I can't trust or at least don't wish to place much faith in."

"Father told me you had to go to the American war far away. He receives letters from Señor Cobb. And that is why you walk with a limp. Is that why you do not trust your days here at my father's restaurant?"

"Well, I am learning these things each day. It's good for me to see people whom I remember fondly. It's good to see you again, Lolita, even if I didn't remember at first."

"It is good to see you again, Señor Phin. You could not speak the language and you were not such a good soccer player, but I laughed much with you. Do you remember our laughing?"

"I do."

I wanted to say that being there, seeing her, feeling the warmth of such days past was something powerful. It was a tangible thing, a bar I could pull myself up on, one more rung. I wanted to say that I thought I might be evolving and shaping my new life out of the shapes and colors of others. But I didn't know how to say that and wasn't sure if Lolita would think it right of me to show up out of nowhere after all these years and dump my troubles on her and her father.

"And you, Lolita," I asked. "How are you faring these days? Are you married? Kids? Do you still think you can dribble a ball past me like you did when we were seven, eight years old?"

"Only one for three today. I am busy with the restaurant, and then there is my singing that I so enjoy, but no man in my life. My mother was caught in Durango by *la migra* without her card and shipped back to Colima three months ago. We are having trouble getting her back across. But sí, yes, my soccer, my *futbol* is still good—we play in Cortez every Sunday afternoon. You would not stand a chance, even if your foot was well and your Spanish *mas mejor*."

Lolita threw her head back and laughed hard, her white teeth with the one gold molar reflecting in the sun. It was only then that the remembrance of the laughing and the good times came back in full.

"Where will you go from here, Phin? Is there something you are looking for in your travels?"

"I am looking for everything and nothing. I was not always in a bad place while the war went on. And I was not always with bad people, but I saw many horrible things happen to people for no reasons that I have come up with yet. I want to give up looking for the reasons, but I would be happy if I discovered something along the trip—maybe how to give up the search."

I realized that I had probably confused her, but there was no way to explain without confusing her more.

"You talk in a funny riddle, Phin. You remind me of your uncle, Señor Cobb, only you seem to be *poco loco en corazon*, a little crazy in your heart. Even Señor Cobb, when he spoke funny to my father in broken Spanish, my father would nod his head with understanding. I only nod my head in small parts listening to you now."

Lolita looked out over the desert behind the restaurant and a silence enveloped the moment. It wasn't uncomfortable.

Where will this trip take you?" She asked.

"I'm heading in the direction of Denver to see some friends at a hospital where I was treated. Some of them think I'm no longer living. I'll stop in Durango as well..."

"To look for the girl?" Lolita interrupted.

"What do you know of this girl?" I asked, trying to sound as inoffensive as I could while masking the inquisitiveness I felt.

"I just know the stories from my father and the words you spoke in your dreams last night."

"Does this girl—her name is Lonnie—does she live in the town of Durango?"

"I am not sure, Phin. Señor Cobb brought the painting to my father and told him something about the lady who painted it being from the same town as you. That is all I know. It was some years ago. You must have loved her, Phin, because your eyes just opened up very wide for a second and your pupils spread like when the moon covers the sun."

"That was a long time ago, Lolita. I was very young and not so lost.

Lolita walked over to a thin wire strung between two galvanized metal poles and began pulling dry table cloths down from where they hung in the morning sun. After a long while, she turned with her hands wrapped around a large wicker basket.

"Señor Phin, you are not the only one who is growing older every day and does not know where they are."

✳ ✳ ✳

Durango, Colorado is not a hard place to find a person. The phone book is thin, the canyon narrow, the people unafraid of strangers. There was no Lonnie Whiting who the telephone operator had heard of, but the manager of the second art gallery I visited said he had one painting in the back by a Lonnie Barth, a local woman who lived up the road in Silverton. When he showed it to me I knew all my dreams had been both right and wrong.

The painting was a large seascape done in oil on canvas. It showed a small fishing boat heading out of a harbor into what looked like a large storm front. The man said that the artist had become somewhat known in the few years that she'd been here, but there wasn't a big demand for seascapes in the mountains. I looked closely at the stern of the boat to see if I could read the name, but the brushstrokes pulled the sea's reflection up onto the transom, obscuring the last few letters of the name.

"I have a magnifying glass if you'd like to have a closer look." The manager could sense a potential sale. "A few months ago another man, a tall black gentleman with a funny accent not from around here, had the same questions. All we could see were the G, the R and then what looks like an A. I offered the Black man the glass, but he declined and then bought another one by the artist. It was a pier of some sort as I recall. I don't know when we'll get another painting by her. I can make you a good deal, but I'd have to contact the artist and all I have is a post office box number."

"It's all right," I thanked him. I don't know where I'd put it to keep it safe right now. And as I started to walk out I thought of my mother, Grace. It had been less than seven months since I'd returned and I could count on two hands the times I had reconnected with my mon since I came home from the war. The reasons were unclear, but I swore I'd make it right when I returned to Florida. I walked back into the gallery and gave the man one hundred dollars as a deposit, just over half of what was in my pocket. He said that was enough to buy it outright and ship it somewhere.

"No, I'll be back to get it. And the boat's name is *Grace*—the last few letters are *C* and *E* and maybe a *Y*; a little sea, a little e, and a long why."

I had to go quick before something happened, before I lost her name, forgot her new one, fell asleep, dreamt something that would scare me away or something that would be so strong I'd blurt it right out and she'd know that the war had done something, maybe something horribly immutable, immutably horrible. I had to hold it together until I could see her.

There were no ifs, no accidents. Lonnie Barthinski Whiting, my Lonnie, my rabbit's foot, my Helen of Troy, the only girl I thought I ever loved, the one I had kissed and got kissed back by, the girl I had gone steady with for ten months and four days, but with whom I had woven a silky web of security around my chest through Da Nang and Cam Ranh Bay and the hills and valleys with numbers assigned to them that had no meaning. Lonnie was the one who came home and sat with me on the pier for three days and two nights after Gillie died. She never asked me to leave, brought me food I wouldn't eat, and only slept when I slept. Then I joined the army.

And then I re-upped.

And in my second tour there were the dozens, the hundreds, of letters that would catch up with me at some resupply depot or I-Corp or some outpost where you'd think would be just the perfect irony to receive a letter from the world. But I couldn't read them. Not then. And maybe not now. They held more power in my imagination of what they told me, what my lifeline was whispering into my ear. But I was going to see her right now and nothing could stop me. If she wasn't there, I'd wait. She'd said she'd wait, I think, in one of the early letters I'd opened. I must've believed her then, otherwise why would I have elevated what we had to what may or may not have ever been? She must've said she'd wait. She must've...

The small general store with the singular gas pump out front sat just south of the main street that made up Silverton, Colorado. It was getting late and it was empty. I looked around, cleared my throat, and then asked out loud if there was anyone here. An elderly man in crisp denim overalls and a neatly trimmed gray beard came out of the back with a straw broom in one hand and a dustpan in the other.

"Sorry, young man. Didn't hear you at first. Something I can help you with? We're all out of gasoline right now. Saudis threatening to dole it out like gold just to raise up the prices, you ask me. Might take us twenty years but at least my grandkids will be getting their energy from the sun and what not. Now, what is it that I can help you find?"

I liked this guy right away, not because of his comment about a foreign country deciding when and how far we can drive, but because of his directness, his overt hope, and his intuitive nature. He seemed like family or that he could've been. The Southwest had been good to me in this respect. I had once thought that I could move here after high school, maybe with Lonnie. I could fish the rivers, take a couple trips down to the Gulf each year and see my family. In the summer when it got so hot in southern Florida, we'd invite Johnny and Ma and Pa and Gillie up, if they wanted to come to the mountains where it was cooler and the thin air would give way each afternoon to thunderstorms that rolled in on schedule, cleansed the high valley, and then moved on. That was then.

"You okay young fella? You lost or something? Those your dogs out front? I got a hose, we could water them?"

"I'm, uh, I'm sorry. Well, yes those are my dogs and I'm not really lost. I was just daydreaming during the middle of the day I suppose."

"Ah, hell. I do that all the time. Sometimes it's nighttime before I realize where the day went. But I'm old. You got a story or just a cursory excuse?" The man started to laugh at his own wittiness, infecting and pulling me into his laughter. Then he stopped short and said, "You look a bit familiar, but I've never seen you around before, I could swear. But I've seen your face, I could almost swear to that, too."

"We all got stories, don't we," I said in the form of a statement, avoiding his question. "Old guys and travelers more than most. But I reckon it's a bit late for anything worth telling. I just need some directions, if I could ask you."

"Never too late, so long as the story's true, but I promised the missus I'd be home for supper tonight. That's the reason I'm sweeping when I ought to be stocking shelves. Where you need to go, young man? Only been here five or six years, not since before they shut down the bigger mines in the area. But I'm a map with two good feet. Even better in the air."

"Well, that's good 'cuz I'm not from around here and I only have one-and-one-half feet and that's a true story that I'd never tell when dinner is waiting. No sir, I'm just looking for an old friend who, I think, lives up this way; a gal 'bout my age, same kind of long history, a painter by trade, not houses, but the good stuff you hang on walls. Lonnie is her name, Lonnie Barth ...I mean Whiting."

The old man's eyes did something strange, something showing a kind of search about my intentions or motives. He was sniffing me like a dog, trying to decide in the next ten seconds if I was a good man; at least good enough to answer in truth or not.

He sat back on his broom, ran his fingers through his thin, gray hair and then walked over and began switching off a few lights. He set the broom against the wall and took his coat off the rack. He, too, seemed vaguely familiar, like I might've known him in a previous life. But that was impossible.

"None of my business why you want to go on up and see her." He looked disappointed, almost angry. "You were a soldier, weren't you?"

I nodded.

"And you knew her before you went over there, didn't you?"

I nodded again and tried to hold his stare.

"And you stayed over there when you didn't have to."

"Yes, sir."

"Well, 'spose you'll find out in any case. They live up the canyon road, last group of mailboxes on the right. Jason's black Chevy ought to be parked out front."

The meaning of the words began to seek and find their way into the hollow part of my bones where I thought marrow might be. He walked toward the door and fumbled with a big ring of keys, motioning me to leave first. It was more command than request. I turned toward him without saying anything, the hole in my mouth closing up tight followed by a squeezing that ran down my throat into my chest.

"One other thing, young fella, before you go. I drug my family away from our comfortable little town when they didn't want to leave. But I was a soldier and duty called. And then I came up here to the mountains after it seemed there wouldn't be any more real wars that needed guys like me. I was trying to find something new to help me forget what I was then and am now...just an old soldier. But nothin' was new, nothing had changed from where I come from, but the things I wanted to remain the same."

We were outside the little store now and the dogs were asleep in the back of the Buick. The key ring was shaking in the old man's hand and there was a little drip of spittle running from the side of his mouth. He turned and faced me, appearing to grow an inch or two taller as he took a short step in my direction.

"The world keeps going while soldiers go off and get killed or forgotten by the folks back here living in it. Not my place to lecture you, but I need to tell you that. If only for me to hear the words come out of my mouth and not fall flat on the ground." Then something broke in his rhetoric and his voice. "Ah, hell...you know that as well as me. Look at you, the soldier boy from over there in Panama City, the one Lonnie waited for. Look at you. Well, at least you aren't dead like the papers said. Can't imagine how you pulled that off, but I hope you can play that hand for a few more rounds."

And then there was just the respect between two survivors of war; age and generation falling away.

"Yeah, kid, you go on up there and see her if you need to. And I'm saying that from one soldier to another. But from the looks of you, it seems you're still opening doors to conflict rather than lettin' sleeping dogs lie."

I tried to hold his stare, but something broke and I walked around to the side of the store and threw up.

It wasn't so much that this man had been where I was now, but that I was still marching toward where he had passed through. I felt as though something strange and powerful was about take place within me. And I puked again.

The old man was driving away in a late '50s Stepside truck and rolled down his window.

"You make sure you hose that down, okay son? You clean it all up."

BOOK 5

SOME FIXINS'

CHAPTER 35

DEAR PHIN, OH MY

Someone once told me, maybe it was Worm in the Nam, that the goal in life wasn't to arrive safely in a well-preserved body, but rather to slide in head first, completely banged and bruised, no worse for the wear, and screaming out, "Goddamn, what a ride!"

I'd been on the double-dipper of roller coasters for almost a year and was torn, tattered, and ripped. What mattered was that as bad as it had been, I was beginning to feel better, more alive. And I didn't have to be in a war of someone else's making to get there. I 'spose that's why I re-upped after my first tour, why so many guys went back in when they could've gone on home and gotten on with their lives. But when I went back home and Dad was out on the boat and Mom was busy with her onions and her flowers and things that moms get busy with—but mostly with Gillie gone and all—it was boring in Panama City Beach. And with college kids and snow birds and retirees coming down from up north looking to find un-boredom, my town started to get uncomfortable. Strange at times; half-dead and not connected to family or friends or a sense of place...I was confused. Ah hell, at least I felt alive when back in-country. Even though I didn't really have to kill anybody if I didn't want to, there's something strangely attractive about being up real close to others when they do. Because they have to.

Is that sick? Had my pathos met my pathology? Probably, but I saw a lot of killing and came to think I was just a bit more normal than the ones who, according to the definition, were sicker than me. And everybody above and below me in rank and file signed off on it because where are you going to draw the line? Nothing in the Nam was straight, not even the path of the bullets. I saw more than a few M-16s go astray and kill people on our own side. At least they wore the same uniform. But the confusion was starting to make sense to me in that second tour. And that disambiguity is the precipice a soldier stares over and decides what the rest of his life—if he has one—will look like if he jumps or does an about face.

✳ ✳ ✳

It was easy to find the long, narrow driveway that wound up to Lonnie's house—Lonnie and Jason's house. As hard as I tried to imagine that he was her roommate, her distant cousin, or a wayward uncle I knew nothing about, the truth was undeniable. The old man at the convenience store had conveniently said it with the tone of his words and the lowered slant of his chin and the well-honed cutting edge of his narrowed eyes: Lonnie was married. She hadn't waited. She wasn't there on the platform when my train pulled in. She wasn't there at the house when my dad, Harry, and Johnny and Blackie had pulled the truck down our own long driveway and carried me to my room. But then neither was Ma or Gillie. And in a sense, neither was I.

If she had been there, standing on the porch in her long pink dress with the blue bow that she'd worn to the prom, would she have recognized me? Been repulsed? Run away? Would her right hand hold the pile of unopened and returned letters while her left hand bore the unmistakable gold band on her finger? I had died while my heart kept beating and no welcome home party would ever meet any expectations until I had risen from my self-made grave.

I might never know if Lonnie would've really waited if I'd asked her to in a state of honest sanity. Without ever being anywhere but in a campus dorm room, she had been there for me when I needed her, whether she knew it or not. And that, I was trying my damnedest to convince myself, had to be enough.

I parked the car in a small clearing and sat there looking up the hill toward where I knew "their" house must be. More of Worm's stolen quotes kept flooding me and filling the car with the same musty air of the old libraries he might've discovered them in. I looked in the rearview mirror at *"my sallied, sallied flesh,"* opened the door to walk up to the house and found myself in my own shadow, the place, "between the idea and the reality." There, as I stepped out of the last of the day's shadows where, as the poet inferred, "in the end, I might find my beginning," I wrote and recited my own."

It was an emerging concept of the obvious. Call it wisdom, call it realization—just call it something so that you could move past it. If it was any kind of birth then I was about to be hatched.

I stood at the edge of the driveway and looked up the hill. There was the light of a small cabin near the top and I thought I smelled a kind of stew. I couldn't be sure, but even up here, a thousand miles from any ocean, I sweared it smelled like it must've had fish in it. I started to walk up the hill but stopped a hundred feet from the house. Even in the dark I could see the outline of a large black truck and the light from the window reflecting off the outline of the chrome Chevy logo affixed to the front end. "Jason's black Chevy," the old man had said. He knew, Lonnie had told him. I was the soldier who never came home. I was the one from her childhood. The old man just knew. It would've been just like Lonnie to confide in a man like him.

She had waited. Maybe a long time. And she had suffered when the letters came back and she'd called Harry and he'd told her that, yes, I was still alive, that I'd signed up to stay on. Lonnie had waited. But not forever.

What good would it do for me to march on up there? What good, I asked myself? What would I say?

"Hi, Lonnie, I'm home. Sorry if you thought I might be dead. I was in a bit of a confused state over there. But I'm getting better all the time. Oh, this is your husband and your

little daughter? How cute. Listen, are you free tonight? We have a lot to catch up on."

The old man was right. The world goes on whether a soldier likes it or not. Maybe it's not always fair. But who said war was fair in the first place? Life for that matter? It just *is*.

I had much to learn. Worm and the books and Harry and Dickey and Jed and Gerald and Blackie and Jessica and Mike Greer, and mostly old Johnny...they had been good teachers, all of them. But there was something or someone else that needed to step in and show me the way. I couldn't be sure of what or who it was, only that he or she was out there, waiting.

I sat down in a small stand of pines off to the side of the driveway and watched the house for a very long time that night. At one point I thought I heard laughter, but it could've been the wind in the trees. At another point I thought I heard crying, but it could've been the sound of my own breath. And at one final point I was sure I saw a tall, thin shape move into the window, framed by the light, and looking out at the valley bellow. The shape closed the drapes and then I heard a door open and saw the shape move out to the porch where it raised its hands to the sky. My dogs raised their heads from the clearing next to me, but I stroked their hair, as I had stroked hers, and they went back to sleep.

A voice came out of the shape and it was vaguely familiar, but I couldn't be absolutely sure. The wind was stretching and twisting the sound as if it was moving through a wooden instrument.

"Phin," it called. And my heart leaped. "C'mon, Phin, old boy. Time to come home."

I stood and as I moved into the driveway, I heard the rattling chain and loving bark of a large dog running into the light. Just before the dog jumped onto the porch it stopped and looked out over its domain. Jeremiah stirred, but I held him tight and whispered to stay quiet.

"Whatja see, boy? Something out there?" The shape asked. "C'mon in Phin, you can go chase him in the morning. He'll always be out there for the chasing."

✳ ✳ ✳

In the morning he—*I*— would be on my way to Panama City Beach, Florida. There was a father to track down; a father whose world had also changed. And there were others. I only had one stop to make on the way.

And on that drive, one thought kept reinserting itself into the stiches that were reconnecting my mind with my soul: if you want to try something very, very hard in your life, consider willfully falling out of love with someone. You will have to do it for their sake. And you will understand Shakespearean "love lost."

And if in your next life you find her, well hallelujah. But still, there is this one that deserves the "Goddamn, what a ride."

CHAPTER 36
DOWNHILL, UPSTREAM

Everything is so dangerous that nothing is really frightening.

—Gertrude Stein

The Buick went into reverse quite easily. I guess I shouldn't have been surprised. Things well-cared for aren't subject to the same strafing of life's bullets as those left to fend for themselves. But what constitutes *well-cared for* anyway? Why was I shot at by bullets that never hit my body but impaled my mind? Was I left to fend for myself? Ah shit, who can ever answer that? I never felt alone when I had my buddies around me in-country, guys from every nook of this big 'ole land we call America, and someone from Worchester or Wilmington would say quite out loud, "Hey, guess what? Today is Christmas"—or Thanksgiving or Halloween or Labor Day or Fourth of July.

And we would all say in a kind of chorus, "Yeah, but it ain't never Veterans' Day."

That got me to thinking about what a veteran really is or isn't. Did you have to have fought in a war? Fought for your rights? Did you have to be a soldier in the U.S. Army, or a soldier of God, or a soldier of peace, or a soldier of the working man, or a soldier of the rights of the property owners? A soldier of fortune, a fortunate soldier...where would it ever stop?

I must've decided that where it stopped was where it began—at home with my family: extended, dead, alive, blood, neighbor, black, white, fucking purple skin…it didn't matter. Keeping things together was at the root of my neuroses, at the root of my healing, and it had been at the root of the war in Vietnam. There was a kind of letting go in knowing that what belonged together was moving together.

I can't say if North and South Vietnam belonged as one country. Time will tell if all the men who died over there left any legacy other than the stupidity and ignorance of their leaders. Maybe the rest of Indochina will fall to Communism and Johnson and McNamara's "Domino Theory" will set the world in a state of disorder. Maybe we'll wish we would've sacrificed another fifty thousand men in order to spread our brand of economic-based democracy. But what do I know? I'm the son of a fisherman from the Redneck Riviera section of the Florida Panhandle. I simply can't think about it anymore.

Shit…all this thinking was giving me a headache. The dogs and I had slept for more than a few hours in a dirt pullout beside the canyon road and I was happy to have their heavy fur and warm-bloodedness surround me on the reclined bench seat. It was still dark when we awoke and after peeing in the brush, it seemed like I couldn't get on with my new life fast enough. As the Buick left the canyon and entered the main road into and out of Durango, I decided to stop the car at a filling station to see if the attendant had any aspirin, maybe some jerky for the dogs. Out west, gas stations were morphing into tiny stores with convenient items besides quarts of Pennzoil and day-old coffee. It was only after I shut the motor off and let my eyes adjust to the first few rays of sunshine that I noticed I was at the same place I'd been last night before I went looking for Lonnie.

"Well, now," the old man was exercising some restraint, "that was either a short stay or a long time in deciding that any stay was no longer a good decision. You all right, son? Get you something?"

The old man scurried around in the morning dawn and flipped switches and turned knobs.

"Yes, sir. I was wondering if you might spare an aspirin or two. Maybe some water for the dogs." He looked at me and he knew. And something else from the past stirred. There was no question.

"No problem. I'll get you some that the missus keeps behind the counter for when I get on her nerves. You can water the dogs around the back."

Did I know this man just from last night or was he a gathering of all the old souls that had bent and shaped me? I took Daniel, Jeremiah, and Elijah around to where the hose was and cupped my hands for them to drink from. Their rough dry tongues moved across my palms under the cool mountain water streaming from the long hose. Daniel backed away and let his brother drink and looked up at me. He put his paws on my knees, his face near mine, and licked the side of my scratchy cheek. Tears began to fall and the salt must've tasted good to him.

Then it dawned on me that I puked right here, no more than ten yards away, less than eight hours ago.

"Got your aspirin here when you're ready," the old man came up behind and then left before we both had to deal with what Daniel was cleaning up.

I wiped my face with my shirt sleeve, turned the hose off and walked around to the front of the station. The old man was filling the car with gas and cleaning the windows.

"I don't know how much money I have left," I told him, embarrassed.

"Nobody plans these kinds of trips very well, now do they?"

"I thought I might stay awhile, get a job."

"It's your life, kid. Isn't it?"

"Yes, sir," I was finally believing it, "I reckon it is after all."

"Then I'll be seeing you again?" he asked, but knew the answer already.

"I doubt it, sir, much as I'd like to get a chance to pay you back."

"Yeah, well you do owe me, but you could've owed my daughter a hell of a lot more. Not that it matters. You did the right thing, not going up there last night."

"Colonel Barthinski?" I asked, incredulous, remembering that Lonnie's father had given his wife's last name of Whiting to his daughter so that she would never be scorned for being German.

"Maybe. Or just an old guy living out his life, quiet-like in a small mountain town."

"You certainly look a lot like..."

"I'm sure I do. Like I said, nothing changes and everything changes. You just have to find the spot where you can get back on the big wheel. And then hang on."

I stood there, wanting to run off into the woods liked an escaped convict, but instead, frozen, motionless, a mannequin to my past. Inside the bombs began to fall, but suddenly there was a hand over my head softly catching them. I put out my hand to this man and he shook it just like the colonel always did when I dropped Lonnie off at home, safe and on time. He motioned his head south, southwest and I knew what he meant. The Buick started right up.

I stopped in "downtown" Durango for breakfast and to pick up the painting. Over a breakfast of really bad *huevos rancheros* I read the newspaper that had been dropped into a forgotten basket in the corner. I couldn't tell how old it might be and was afraid to ask the waitress which month it was.

It was two days ago, but the paper could've been four or six or eight weeks old. Yesterday—the paper said it was the 20th of September—Jim Croce had died in a plane crash in Louisiana. It had to be another sign I needed to go home.

Driving across Route 160, the sky seemed to open up and swallow me. I slumped in the soft, sweet leather seats of the old car and imagined that the broken white lines in the middle of the road were ancient Dead Sea Scrolls carrying messages to each and every returning soldier.

I thought I might fall asleep and pulled over to close my eyes.

"Go on, boys," I told the dogs, "go blow some carbon out of those pipes." And they disappeared into the fold of sand and scrub brush and sage and the inviting horizon that had no lining as the walls of a whale's belly.

Sleep didn't come, but something else in between the conscious and the dream state. It seemed that I was fighting my way back to a desperate state of mind, a place that I didn't want to go, but had proven to be a place of discovery. Everything had been falling into place. Little by little I was reifying the collection of cells, bones, and sinewy tissue that carried my mind and my soul. The only thing missing was my sense of self—I was no longer a kid, a soldier, or a brother to a sister. Hell, according to official records, the U.S. Army and otherwise, I wasn't even alive.

Even my fabricated life with Lonnie had been some kind of life raft that was now left to sail on its own. I was swimming to the surface, but the fluid was tar. I had been acting in a strange play and now the scenes were all backwards and I couldn't remember my lines.

"Action or reaction?" A voice from inside my bones startled me.

I looked around and saw no one. Was it the muse? The fates? Premonition? Or scratchy noise from the AM radio broadcasted across miles of Southwest dirt?

"What do you mean? Do I know you?" I asked with my eyes scanning the horizon for a figure, a sign...uncomfortable hearing a voice and then openly replying as if there was a person sitting next to me.

"You're going home to see your father, but what do you know of his whereabouts? Your mother has suffered from a stroke, but what do you know of her mind? And your Johnny Cobb," the Voice slowed its rhetoric, *"what do you know of the health and well-being of your grand mentor?"*

I heard the dogs barking in the distance and called them back. Go away, Voice, I wanted to say. I tried to start the car but my fingers were trembling so hard I couldn't get the key into the hole.

Something replaced the voice in my bones and it was a feeling of panic and tragedy, something worse than anything that could happen to me because it had happened to someone close to me. Suddenly my own existential crisis was dwarfed by one of greater and immediate proportions.

My father could be lost at sea. My mother could be lost in the living room. And if Johnny wasn't right, that meant other things wouldn't be right as well.

I figured I'd just plow ahead, stretch my legs in Gallup and catch Route 666 south; then east on the 40 to Albuquerque, Amarillo, Oklahoma City; south on 35 to Dallas; east on the 20 to Shreveport; and then south on the 49 all the way into Lafayette. It was not the same route I came out on some months and half a lifetime ago, but while I was headed back, ah hell, I didn't even know where Johnny was or wasn't. Lafayette would be a good start.

I'd use a pay phone if I ever came across one. There was one at José's outside of Cortez. Yeah, I'd gas up and get some food for the dogs at José's. But that meant going west again before heading east.

CHAPTER 37

WHISPERS AND ROARS

The thing about big surf is that it's loud. Large waves and winds of consequence carry power such that if you could harness but one hour of eighty-knot winds and twenty-foot seas you could light a major city for a week. But when you're in the shit like Harry was with Tropical Storm Gilda chasing you, you see the waves and feel the wind, but the sound of many tons of water nipping at your heels is something else altogether. It might have the same sound as an avalanche landing on the tails of your skis, or the same feeling as if trying to outrun a line of giant stone dominos in some telling and terrifying dream—you can't afford to look back because the sight of it all would freeze you and then swallow you whole.

But Harry did look back and he saw that he might have a chance. He'd put some distance on the edge of this bitch and even in the moonless night could see the white mountains of water falling farther behind.

"Ah, Gracey." He allowed himself to relax and remember the times he and his wife had taken the boat out just to watch the sunset or the moonrise, never to fish. "You've done well, old girl." But the memories brought such deep and sudden sadness at the thought that even if he did make it to port, there might be no one there to meet him. Harry realized that as unpredictable the natural forces of the ocean could be, they were made acceptable with the dependability of having a family to come home to. He had a great fear that he might outlast his son, Phin, or his old friend, Johnny Cobb. And that he'd left his wife recovering from her stroke with only the help of a few friends. And he just might be coming home to an empty house until he no longer was able to leave it.

Not yet though.

Finding strength from some unfamiliar source, Harry suddenly realized that he hadn't lost it all. When you give up hope, some devilish source told him, you've lost it all.

"Don't you remember the last few men to finally give up hope that last night before help arrived, Harry? Don't you remember telling them that someone would come for you; they had to send somebody. And just hours before the morning light brought the distant shape of a large gray vessel they had said, 'No, I've lost all hope'. And then they'd let their heads fall to one side of the orange life jacket and allow life to leave them. And if they didn't believe," the devilish voice said, *"I could negotiate for their souls."*

Of course Harry remembered. He'd seen the panic in the eyes of the men, the oil as it danced its hot flames on the surface, and the bits and pieces of the ship and the men who'd come apart in the explosion. And he'd seen the black eyes of the sharks as they prowled the waters, attacking in some Russian roulette fashion.

But he'd also seen the eyes of other hopeful men who turned to him and bore right into his young heart, telling him that he was not to give up because too many already had. He was needed.

Harry Davis would always be needed. And so he refocused on the *Grace* and the ocean and the storm. There were patches of clear sky above and he could make out bits and pieces of constellations that told him he was within three or four hours of the coast. He needed the following sea. He needed the *Grace's* fuel supply to give him more range than what was left in her tanks.

Harry turned around and looked at the hurricane-in-training as it seemed to be taunting him, speaking to him in forked tongues through the wind.

"This is no fun, sailor-man."

Harry shook his head and tried to deny the taunt.

"Give me one more shot," it spoke in a high whine. *"If I can't catch you, I'll burn myself up and head east only to dump a few inches of rain on Tampa Bay. Perhaps I'll fuck with Cuba and run up the East Coast of Florida."*

"Ok, devil-bitch." Harry took the challenge, secretly knowing he'd have to shut down one of the engines to save fuel anyway. "Let's dance."

With the *Grace's* reduced hull speed the storm lost no time in making up ground. Soon it was cat and mouse with Gilda throwing waves at odd angles and alternating the direction and size of the swells. The wind, too, was less consistent, not as strong, but unreliable. Gilda was worried now. She was doing everything to confuse the sailor-man.

But they had entered Harry's home waters, the shoals and bars that ran like trip wires for many nautical miles off the coast of western Florida were playing havoc with the storm's ability to gain power from the deeper and warmer depths out in the Gulf.

"I can see what you are trying to do, sailor-man, but it's no use. You'll run out of fuel before you reach your beloved Panama City. And I will have my way with you. I will have your soul at the crossroads."

"You may be right, Gilda-bitch, and we are both playing for our lives. If you are so confident, shall we up the stakes?"

"Of course your flesh will die eventually, as all humans must. Your societies are made, in part, by how the weak live and the strong die. Let us offer up one of your loved ones as bait, one who, as we speak, is fighting to live because a weak one wanted his strength."

"I have already given you a chance at my own blood. I cannot offer any more of my family."

"I was not thinking of the one you call Phin, but the older one who has guided many among you. You call him Johnny Cobb."

With the thought that Cobb might be in trouble, Harry's multi-influenced mind went deep into the weeks and months and years of his past sailing and fishing out on the Gulf. He turned and saw the wake of his stern move out in v-shapes with the tops blown off, but calm in the middle. And he knew what to do. He wasn't exactly sure who this contest was against; he might've gone insane, or he might be as lucid and sharp as he ever was. Who talks to a storm?

Whatever power it held over him might somehow be connected to the health and well-being of Johnny Cobb. Harry believed in the interconnectivity of all things living. And while the details were fuzzy, his heart told him that Johnny was in trouble. Or at least could be.

"I can bargain with my own life but not with others. You do what you have to do and I'll do the same. I will not speak to the wind again." And with that Harry turned the *Grace* hard to starboard, turned on the second big diesel engine, and made a run for Cape St. George to the northeast.

"Okay sailor-man. Pleased to meet you, hope you guessed my name."

The hurricane, seeing that landfall and its inability to refuel itself was close, opened up and sent all that she could onto the shoals off Cape San Blas. Harry and the *Grace* took hit after hit, pitching and rolling with mountains of angry water and gusts of wind that drove right through Harry. But it was too late for Gilda. Harry's strategy had worked and he coaxed a beaten and battered *Grace* into the lee of St. Vincent Island and followed the coast a few miles east to the wide and safe port that lay between Apalachicola and Eastpoint, Florida. As he motored up into a deep and protected cove made deeper by the storm surge, the engines sputtered and finally died, her fuel having been just enough. Harry had no power to reverse the boat and she slid up onto a muddy bank, shoreline trees normally high and dry scraping the sides of the *Grace*. She nestled her bow in the soft, thick mud of the Florida shore.

"Well," the storm's voice was soft now, almost angelic. *"You've beaten me and we shall go our separate ways. I am no more for you and you are more than you've ever been. There will come others like me in your time. But you know that. I am off to mess with Cuba and the Bahamas."*

Harry knew it.

With that the winds eased to a steady and manageable thirty knots and with the rain moderate. Harry could see people coming out of boarded-up shops and storm-windowed homes like kids waking up from a long sleep in the car and wondering where they were. He saw people who had expected to have their little town destroyed by the great storm jumping up and down, laughing. He saw old men hugging each other and kids stepping in puddles of water and storm surge that could've been twelve feet but was six. He wanted to run up and join them because they might've died in each other's arms except for the unpredictable beauty that is nature. He wanted to hear the old men who'd lived through a dozen of these big ones scratch their heads and say they'd never seen one blow apart before landfall, let alone turn back out to sea like that. They wouldn't say it was mystical; they'd just throw up their hands and say, "That's nature for you; a beautiful and unpredictable bitch. And good luck to the next port in her path."

Harry smiled and then left the little wheelhouse of the boat to walk around her and inspect the damage. He'd get her pulled off the beach and slipped, temporary patches to the hull, gassed up, and be under way to Panama City before the week was over. There was much to do. He was happy.

✳ ✳ ✳

They admitted Johnny Cobb to the Lafayette General Hospital. Who'd have thought a smashed bottle could be so dangerous? The dead man in the trunk of Uncle Chuck's car had done a good job with a twelve-ounce long neck. When they had raced Johnny's large and limp body into the emergency room, the doctors had pulled Blackie's hand away from the side of Johnny's head and said, "Ah geez, another Negro beat up in a bar."

Sewing up the gash that let some of Cobb's blood leave his body was not that hard. But the docs were worried that there was intracranial swelling between the brain and the skull. "An epidural hematoma," one of them had said. "Victims of blunt trauma who are unconscious either come around in a few minutes or a few weeks. This is how people die," the docs had told Blackie and the others, assuming they were medically ignorant. "There's not enough room up there and the swelling around the brain can shut down the whole system. The only way to remove the swelling is to isolate it and drill a hole to allow the pressure to dissipate."

"You want to put a relief valve in his brain?" Hunter asked.

"Precisely," the doc replied. "But we have to isolate the region and it's risky at best. Anything having to do with the brain always is."

Hunter, the two-tour Vietnam War medic, spoke from the back of the waiting room where they had all converged. "Timing is crucial. You don't want to drill if you don't have to, but you can't risk it either. I'm worried that he hasn't regained consciousness. You guys have one of those new x-ray machines that look at the layers of tissue?"

The doc seemed surprised at Hunter's comments and said yes, he agreed about the timing and no, those machines were years away, even longer for Lafayette General. Maybe if they transferred him to New Orleans.

"Look, doc," Hunter's words seemed as if they belonged to a different body. The others in the waiting room deferred to him. "You know that's not protocol for an elderly Black man with no insurance whose survival potential is less than the standard fifty percent minimum for transfers. Let's cut to the chase and look at plausible options here. What were his pupils like when you left him?"

Blackie, who had been in and around hospitals enough to get a street education on emergency care chimed in. "They were PERL when we were asked to leave the ER and wait outside in this room, but sluggish in reaction time."

"You mean like shiny white dots?" Leroy asked.

"No," said Hunter. He had been watching the exchange with keen interest. "It's just an acronym for 'pupils are equal and reactive to light.' When they are, that's a good sign in blunt trauma to the head. What were the rest of his vitals? Was there any change in his LOC since we brought him in?" He turned to Leroy and explained quietly, quickly, "Level of consciousness."

"Wait a minute, gentlemen," the doctor put one hand up in the air and held his clipboard tight with the other. "I can see that some of you have had some experience and think you might know what's best for Mr. Cobb, but this is a hospital and we have qualified doctors who will do their best for your friend and..."

"I'm afraid that ain't gonna be good enough."

It was Auntie, who had come quietly into the now crowded waiting room after cleaning up and disposing of the mess at her place of business. She had been listening to the men go back and forth; each offering up the best he could in his own way. But it was Auntie who wanted to have the final say.

"Johnny got hurt on my watch, in my place, while I held the gun. I should've just gone ahead and put a bullet in that man's ear straight away. This hospital's best ain't going to be nothing I'd risk this man's life on. Now y'all are like sons to me and I think you likely seen more of a man's insides falling out over there in the war than they ever see in this here hospital, but I think we need to call in some outside help."

The doctor threw up his hands. "Listen, folks, there's a potentially sick man here. We'll know more when we get the x-rays back. We could get him up to the bigger hospital in Baton Rouge in under an hour. Now, there's a surgeon up there I know..."

"What do you mean, potentially sick?" It was Snare, who had a knack for getting to the point. "I don't hear him nor do I see his eyes in mother of pearl, hazel, or dirt brown. Is he sick or not?"

"The doc's right," Blackie turned and looked at the gnarled and scarred vet. "With the head, you just never know. Maybe we should let them run him up to Baton Rouge."

"No time," said Tom-Tom.

"If we were in Chicago we could get a helicopter to take him," said Hopper.

"But we ain't, are we?" said Hunter.

"If'n he was White they might have a good surgeon right here," said Leroy.

"But he ain't, last I checked," said Auntie. "I'm calling my friend from Haiti. She has experiences with alternative methods and she don't trust White people."

"Listen to you all," Chuck finally spoke up. "This ain't about color, man. It's about revenge and Johnny got caught in the crossfire. I thought you guys were trained killers. How'd you let a couple of faggot nurse-types come into your house and bus' this man up?"

"I didn't see you protecting the old guy," Leroy faced Chuck and stood up. "At least I got me one."

"And left a trail of bloody witnesses a mile long," Chuck stood up to face him.

Auntie, who knew of Chuck's past from late-night talks with Johnny, caught Leroy's eye and shook her head in disgust.

"Those people never saw a thing," Strider weighed in anxiously. "That part of town is tight. Those girls I was talking to, they..."

"Anger and guilt," Hunter interrupted. "Man, they just accumulate like dirt under your fingernails."

"Like sediment in the river bottom," added Hopper.

"Like maggots on a dead rat," added Snare who pulled out his knife and started to clean his fingernails.

"Aw, geez, fuck all you guys. It's nobody's fault." Tom-Tom spoke as if he was now in charge. "Chuck's right. Johnny just got caught in the crossfire. You gonna write a book about it or get the job done?"

Blackie had been wringing his hands and trying to control his mind from moving back into the hole he had pulled it out of. "It is somebody's fault," he started to say but then the tears came and no sound but sobs left his mouth. Auntie held him and stroked his curly hair like he was a child who'd gotten a bad grade on his report card and worried his father would beat him.

The doctor tried to show some authority but it was rhetorical by this point. "That's it. I have no time for this. There are other patients. Who is his next of kin?"

The room was silent and each knew as much as they loved the man, they weren't *the next*. They knew Johnny had no living relative that they were aware of, and only Harry Davis could make any claim to being a relative to Johnny Cobb, regardless of what color he was.

"Well, whoever he or she is," the doctor kept clicking his pen in and out, in and out, "they had better make some kind of deal with the hospital quick. We can't do anything without some kind of authorization and you folks can't seem to come to any consensus on what you want to do with the patient. I'm going to look for the x-rays now. I'll be back as soon as I can." And he was gone, the pen-clicking sound following his march out the door and down the hall.

After a long moment in which the only sound was Blackie's occasional gasp for air, the sound that comes after a good cry, Snare stood up and said he was doing no good here.

"I'm going looking for the nurse-dude with Auntie's lead in his legs. He's probably gone to one of the other hospitals."

"Here." Chuck held out his car keys. "Knock yourself out, secret agent man. Take my car. But leave my luggage near the back door would you? It's in the trunk."

CHAPTER 38

DETOURS TO HEAVEN

"Señor Phin, you want to take my daughter with you in this car with no roof? You want to take my only daughter—the best cook and most delightful singer of *José's Place*—away from here?" José tried to look taller than his five-foot-five-inch frame placed him in relation to the earth and others who inhabited it. He was also trying to look angry, but wasn't a good actor.

I felt such empathy that I almost said no. I didn't feel bad for the truth, the truth of wanting to ask Lolita if she would drive with me back to Panama City by way of Lafayette or wherever Johnny Cobb was by the time I arrived. No. I felt bad for José because he must've known that it would be good for her to see something of his adopted country, to expand her horizons beyond Cortez, New Mexico. And then José had to act like it was *such* an inconvenience, like, "How could you even ask me?" I knew the Hispanic machismo better than most gringos and embraced it as part and parcel of the culture. I knew this was hard for José.

"José, she can come back to you any time she wishes. I will give her bus fare; I will drive her in a car with a proper roof if that is what you wish. I am not stealing your daughter or your cook or your singer."

"Then why ask her to go and un-step the carted apples? Everything is fine here now." José was playing all the cards he knew in English.

"José, if you don't want me to ask her if she would go, just say it and I'll be on my way. You think about it for a minute. Can I use your phone?"

José acted a bit put out but he said of course, it's in the office, and went to see his daughter.

I dialed Auntie's place, the only number I knew I might reach a living body twenty-four hours a day. A waitress name Gwendolyn answered and told me what she knew.

"He down 'der at Lafayette Gen'ral and they don't really have the stuff to see if'n he be needin' the drillin' on his head. I don't get it Mister Phin. They be'an a hospital an all and not havin' the tools to fix busted peoples? You ever take your truck in to get new brakes and they tellin' you they don't have the calipers to decide if'n you even need 'em?"

"Gwen," I held my voice calm, "can you tell me what Blackie thinks?"

"Well that man, Chuck they called him, says..."

"No, Miss Gwendolyn, what did the little professor, Jimmy Blackie-Black say when you talked to him? 'Cuz I know you did. What did the one they call Blackie say about Johnny Cobb?"

The line went quiet for a minute and then Gwendolyn came back as poised as a twenty-year-old girl with two kids at home to support could be.

"Mister Phin, the Blackie kid said if'n you call to tell you that the center cain't hold up, things be fallin' apart. I think that's what he said. It scared me, Mister Phin, when he said those words."

I told Gwen I'd be there tomorrow night and to tell Blackie that he should try to get ahold of Jed Riot down in Panama City. Maybe he could pull a few strings. "Write that down now, Gwen, *Blackie to call Jed. Ask about surgeons.*"

José walked back into the small office that was basically a corner of the small kitchen with a small desk and a large stack of papers scattered on top.

"Señor Phin," José pulled his shoulders back and raised his chin an inch or two. "I've known you for more years than you've known me. And I've known your uncle, señor Cobb, for more years than that. I met *su padre*, your father, one time and even though he was quiet with his words, I found him with trustworthiness. Now, señor Phin, I have traveled a great deal inside this small town of Cortez since I came across the river and earned my papers so many years ago. But things have changed and Lolita may not be able to find her fish in the same stream as her father. I think it might be a good thing that she goes with you. May I first ask if you love her?"

I looked at the small Hispanic man who'd come across from Oaxaca with his young wife over two decades ago. He'd started a business, earned a living, raised a family, brought a lot of people joy. And now he stood in front of me, wringing his hands on his dirty cooking apron, waiting for the papers to come back from Immigration proving that his wife had been wrongly deported, testing the integrity of the man in front of him who'd take his daughter away. Where does such resolve come from, I wondered? I owed him an honest answer.

"José, that's a strange question. I don't know if I fully understand love right now. I only know that Lolita is a kind person and that we get along. We have a kind of history, if you can call it that. Even if it was broken up by a dozen years." José had stopped wringing his hands and folded them in front. He seemed taller than he had a few minutes ago.

"She has a kind of peace, an *abrazos*, about her, no different than this little cafe. I like your daughter. I can't say exactly why, but she makes me feel...uh, better. José, I'm not even sure I'd know if I loved her."

José dropped his hands and then placed one on his hip and the other in a pocket. His lips began moving first and then the sound came out.

"But you are sure that you like my Lolita enough to ask her if she will travel with you?"

"Yes. Of that, I'm sure." I put my arm on his shoulder. There was a smell of something burning on the stove behind him and he turned away.

"Then you may ask her. And if she says no, then you will not try and persuade her. You will walk away and not come back for many years."

"Agreed," I said, *"es verdad."*

✳ ✳ ✳

"Mister Phin, you want me to go with you?"

The flat, calm tone in Lolita's voice belied the wisdom beyond her years. She knew why. But she had to hear me say it.

"Yeah," I was surprised at my awkwardness. "I need a traveling companion, someone to help me with the dogs, someone to talk to."

"Is that all, Mister Phin, because Willie the bass player can do that?" Lolita was going to test me but not beyond boundaries of compassion.

"No, there's more. I just don't know how to label it."

There was a long interlude between us as we sat out on the back porch and felt the mid-day sun drying our skin. I began talking in diction that I must've known Lolita wouldn't understand, but was the only way I could make sense of my own thoughts.

"I've just come home from this far away war and I get real nervous about anything with subcategories," I rambled on in short hyperkinetic bursts while the girl looked into my eyes for meaning. "Off and on, it's been a new kind of war, a war of nerves and tired laughter and truth and failed promises that weren't really promises but just invented hopes. Lolita, some days I feel like myself, only older. Other times I am a stranger in the looking glass. But there are those days I can reinvent those hopes on the bridge to my endless options. I'm no saint, señorita, but I will not let my candle burn so low as it was. I will find the person who is me and I will be a good friend to you."

I turned and touched her knee very slightly and then let my hand drop to the ground. "Do you know what I am saying?"

"Yes, Mister Phin, I knew many years ago when we played in the yard. You are not supposed to be a hero. You are no more a warrior than I am a singing star. Your father catches the fish and my father feeds the people. That's not so hard to understand, *es verdad, si?* We go and see señor tio Cobb. He gets better and then you teach me to swim. It's okay?"

✳ ✳ ✳

Gerald McReady had only slept through one M-dream scene between Oklahoma City and Dallas. But he wasn't in the mood to go back to the war. DuPuis was right: McReady was a man trying his hardest to make himself unhappy. You couldn't call it self-martyrdom or obsessive compulsive disorder; you couldn't call it anything because that would give it a label and, therefore, the ability to hold some real estate in one's mind.

McReady was a smart guy; he might've self-analyzed, self-directed, self-insured, self-diagnosed, and self-healed. He might even have self-medicated his non-descript malady of the mind that had him misanthroped and misaligned with his new mate. But he refused to be myopic. Gerald McReady was nothing if he wasn't open-minded. He hated his M-dream, but he followed it like a Hegira—a Holy Grail-ish quest for understanding.

The bus stopped in Dallas and DuPuis was up and in line to exit, his uniform smoothed, before the rest of the passengers could find their coats.

"Okay, doc, let's go taste some of what this 'ole city has to offer."

"Hey, Lorenzo," Gerald stopped his young friend before they entered the terminal. "I'm sorry. I mean, I...,"

"Aw, shit, doc. Forget it. The clocks a'tickin."

"No, seriously, I need to say this."

"All right then, shoot."

"Well," Gerald moved his deft hands in circles as he searched for the right words. "You and I aren't that different. We both had the war move into us, but in different ways."

"Yeah, it moved into my ass when some asshole shot me."

"But you see, you went there out of duty to your country, your Corps, and maybe yourself. I would've gone for the same reasons. The only thing different was the definition of duty. Men like us, Lorenzo, when life is boiled down to its naked essential, some primal mode of surviving, we don't have a choice. We find ourselves on some line of the continuum, either having to kill to survive or having to heal to go on living."

DuPuis rubbed his chin and looked at his watch. He then took off his dress cap and smoothed back his short brush-cut hair before letting out a long, slow whistle.

"You're a smart man, doc, much smarter than me. Lot of people just as soon want to bury that war in the past when all they're doing is hiding it in the future. But you want to know it so that it won't live inside your present."

"Gerald could see that DuPuis was trying hard to meet him at some common ground, but they both knew as similar as they were or were not, their minds worked differently; like a wind-up clock or a battery-powered one, both needed energy to tell the time.

"The past is just a term for what happened before the present. That's different than history, doc. If I were you, I wouldn't make the mistake of blaming the Nam for all of our problems. If it wasn't this one, it would've been something else, another tragedy for people to hide behind. The irony of it all is that most of the world's real shit is manmade. Things like tornadoes and volcanoes and big storms and hell fires are just a part of nature doing its thing. I don't mind that so much as when people fuck up."

"But you still believe in following our leaders? Even when they mess up?"

"Someone's got to keep order. Until the perfect world and the perfect human comes along, then I figure it's my job as a member of the Corps to enforce a system that ain't perfect, but it's better than most of the others."

"And what about someone like me, Lorenzo? What job would you have a person like me who doesn't know how to fight, but is drawn to the trauma in another way? Where should a guy who can't really define failure properly place himself in a world that is destined to?"

DuPuis put his arm around McReady and walked him into the bus terminal. "You're already there, doc. You been there since you even knew you were there. Some folks are cutters and some are sewers. Always there will be people like me who don't have a problem blowing shit up. And Lord willing, there will be people like you willing to pick up the mess. Like you said, doc, no matter which one we are, men like us don't have much choice."

The two walked into the terminal, each carrying a bag over their shoulder, each carrying just a little bit less than when they started.

DuPuis excused himself and went to make his phone call. McReady checked the bus schedule and saw that he could skip the overnight stay in Dallas and catch another bus headed to Shreveport in forty-five minutes. He could be in Lafayette by noon the following day. DuPuis came back with a fresh gleam in his eye but Gerald opened first.

"I need to go see some old friends, Lorenzo. I can't stay here in Dallas." DuPuis tried to hide his disappointment, but it leaked right into his words.

"That's cool, doc. You gotta do what you gotta do. Same as me. Hey, I'll catch up with you in a few days, okay? How will I find you?"

"Johnny Cobb's Water Beds... in Lafayette. That's all I know. I'll leave word there."

"Hippy beds, huh? I like this guy already. He a soldier?"

"In a way, yeah, he's a soldier."

McReady boarded the Shreveport bus and took a seat near the rear. He laid his head up against the cool glass of the window and fell asleep before the big diesels were even started. He dreamt of his father that night, the first time in many years. His father's body was translucent, almost clear, and he was standing on the side of the road holding a sign that said, "Will work for skyscrapers." Gerald stopped and motioned for him to get in. And when he did, he offered his father a drink of water from a small clay pot. The water filled in the color of his clothes and his body. It was all green. Not olive green like the Army, but a light teal like the surgeons wore in hospitals.

"Drop me here," his father ordered him, but Gerald said that he was sorry, he needed his help with something. And when the father started to resist, Gerald passed him the clay cup and he fell asleep in the car with his head on the window.

When McReady woke up, the bus was pulling into Shreveport. He started to dissect his dream and glanced at the front of the bus. He saw Sgt. DuPuis picking tiny bits of lint from his dress uniform, preparing to get off the bus. He looked splendid as a soldier. He did not turn and face the rear of the bus.

On Gerald's lap was a note written on a beer label, the words melting down in the moist thin paper wrap. It said:

"This is not the beginning of the end, but the end of the beginning'—Churchill, not a bad leader, as far as Limeys go. I decided to go see about a girl(s) in Louisiana. Dallas women want to be wined and dined to the nines. I ain't got that much time. See you at the hippy-bed place.

—Sgt. DuPuis, USMC."

CHAPTER 39

TOO TRUE TO BE STRANGE

It was the last week of September 1973 and the world was very strange indeed. The presidency of the United States was unraveling as the details of the Watergate break-in and President Nixon's secret recordings were being uncovered. The big news in sports centered on former Wimbledon tennis champion Billy Jean King's defeat of a boastful male named Bobby Riggs. Thirty thousand people had come to the Houston Astrodome to witness the "Battle of the Sexes." In Vietnam and America, soldiers still died as a result of the war, neither gaining much notice in the evening news. The North Vietnamese were gaining ground on the South and the Khmer Rouge government in Cambodia was silently committing genocide of that country's people.

It was all very strange and, quite honestly, American citizens where tired of it all. They were tired of the war, tired of the protests, tired of the general feelings of unrest that had permeated the country for nearly a decade. Make it all go away, they thought, just give us some degree of normalcy.

And so even as the strange got stranger and Oregon sought to decriminalize the use of marijuana, basketball star Wilt Chamberlain left the NBA for a contract with the ABA's San Diego Conquistadors for a reported $1.8 million dollars, and oil spilled on the beaches of California, the American people threw up their hands and said enough—we're going to worry about ourselves.

But everywhere, it seemed, there were new battles to fight. There was unrest in the Middle East and oil prices were rising. Trouble in South America and rumors of CIA's involvement, talk of computers shrinking in size and price so that eventually every home would have one. There was confusion in the air when a country only wanted to breathe open space and predictability.

✳ ✳ ✳

Blackie had called Jed Riot and Jed had made a few calls. A surgeon from Mobile and one from New Orleans would be there in the morning.

"That's the best I can do, Mr. Riot," the doc from New Orleans had said. "But I'll call over there right away and ask a colleague of mine to have a look at him." Jed thanked him and listened carefully as the surgeon had said before hanging up, "Y'all must have some very influential friends because I've been practicing medicine for thirty-odd years and I have neva', I mean neva', had the governor's office call me directly and request that I go see a sick Black man on the other side of the state. This country is too strange to be true. But I'll do my best because in the field of neurosurgery, that's what I am."

"I am much obliged, doctor," Jed laid it on thick, "The governor and I are much obliged."

Jed's son Dickey had been sitting in his father's office listening and watching his father work his magic. He loved his father deeply, but to that day, could not figure out how he did what he did.

"Pop," he asked, shaking his head, "where do you get the nerve to ask like that? I mean, aren't you afraid of important people saying no and getting mad at you?"

"Son, are you're askin' me if I'm afraid of rejection, if I'm afraid of failure. That's what your askin' me, aren't you?"

Dickey, who sensed some kind of truth about to come out of his father's creative mind and expose his own fears nodded his head just enough to mean yes, that's what he meant.

"To answer you, son, no, I ain't afraid of failing or loosing or getting hurt or dying. Don't get me wrong, I ain't brave or heroic, and I couldn't be called intelligent in any formal type way. But the way I see it is that you work hard, you're honest to everybody, and most of all you treat folks fairly and with respect, then you might not get everything you want, but in the end you'll get most of what you deserve." Jed was writing something down on a pad of paper and then stopped and considered his only child for a long moment.

"I know you aren't the gutsy type, son, but that's all right. You as loyal as bark to a tree. I seen it from the time you and Phin were kids. You got nothing to feel inadequate about if that's what bothering you. I never pushed you because I knew that'd be like trying to get a hold of a greased pig. You're a good kid, Dickey-boy; you came out just fine."

Dickey smiled and tried to say something but knew he couldn't without choking up, so he just sat there and let his dad talk.

"Now, as far as asking these important people for favors, there ain't no magic in that. You just have to understand how the South works. The Lower Thirteen—the New Confederacy—still operates in its own dimension, son. Been that way since they was formed as states. Lots of reasons for it, some of which I don't totally understand, but I get the gist of it. The whole slavery thing, awful as it was, was more a symptom of the system than men trying to hold others down. The system had to be altered and the basic beliefs of the Southern Man reoriented to fix the problem, but even that didn't change the basic nature of the Southern Code."

"Dad, what is all this talk about 'systems' and 'codes?' How come you never told me about it before?"

"Well, some say it don't exist anymore, that the Southern Gentleman, as your great-grand-pappy knew it, is dead. So I figured I'd just let you decide on your own if it was true."

"If what was true?"

Jed folded his hands as if he was praying and looked out the window, trying to organize his words into something that was both true but malleable at the same time.

"I guess it's not really that complicated. There are people living and people dead who still think we ain't a part of the rest of the country. And it's not so much the political ideas and what not, it's that there are things people from the North would do that a Southerner would never consider, and vice and versa." Jed was trying his best not to have it come out the wrong way.

"It's like this: if'n a family owned a nice piece of land, the code would say that it must remain in the family until Jesus hisself come back to claim it. That's one example. If you take another man's wife without proper permission, both said and unsaid from man and wife, that's grounds for hanging. That's another.

"Now, if you were to save a man's life, make him look good in front of important people, or take care of his family when he needed it most, then that man is indebted to you for the rest of his life. If the deed is strong enough, the implied debt passes down a generation. He may never get a chance to pay you back and you may never ask. But the system is set up so that the others of the Lower Thirteen look after each other and never forget when a man or a woman does right by him. If they forget, the system is there to remind them. That's as easy as I can make it, son."

"And where do the Black folks fit in now? In this 'system?' "

"It's taken a long time but it's finally changing. Changing a people's ideologies ain't like changing tires or shoes or lawn mower blades. I wish it would happen quicker, but some of the older folks don't take too kindly to burning the landscape behind them. Their roots are wide and deep in the area and people from down here don't move around like they do in other parts of the country. That's part of the problem with the system—it can breed some single-minded thinking. But I never said it was perfect; only a part of the world we inhabit down here."

Dickey looked at his father, who was still looking out the window nodding his head like a doll on the dash of a car. He didn't know if he believed in this "code" that his father spoke of, but the explanation brought many things closer into focus; not so much a lifting of a fog as a change in the prescription to your eyeglasses. He would ponder the words and begin to come to some conclusions of his own. He would search his past and see what affect growing up under the powerful umbrella of the Southern Man connected to the rooted past, but needing to sprout elsewhere, had had on him.

There was so much of this code he could embrace—the loyalty, the pride in one's land, the commitment to family and honor—but there was also the myopic focus, the dark history of oppression. These things he could not live with or be proud of. Where Jed had ventured out into the landscape to work within the system, Dickey had been confused, caught by the hugeness of the culture and his father's projects, the command he had over the many people whom he associated with. All this simply made little Dickey Riot shrink into the cracks and go about his life.

But sitting here in the silent presence of his father, Dickey realized that what he feared most was normalcy. He wasn't his father, but he wasn't the man who lived in his skin either. If he didn't do something, normal would get worse. He reached across the desk and pulled a cigar out of a walnut box.

"What are these for, Pop? I've never seen you smoke a cigar."

"They're just props, son, just little parting gifts that make some people feel good about themselves."

Dickey smiled a warm smile at his father and thought he might be some kind of melding of Thomas Jefferson, P.T. Barnum, and Robin Hood.

"So, Pop, you did some good things for some important people and when you want the favor returned, you just ask?"

"More or less, more or less."

"What if they say no? What if you ask too much?'

"You never ask for more than you gave, and if they break the code, then everyone will know that they cannot be trusted—those kind of men end up moving to the North. Their choices are extinguished."

"Let me guess—and you never discuss what was done or why."

"Exactly, my boy, exactly."

✳ ✳ ✳

When Gerald McReady stepped off the bus in Lafayette, Louisiana, Sgt. Lorenzo DuPuis was nowhere to be found. Gerald was tired, but anxious to get over and see his old friend, Johnny Cobb. There hadn't been any answer at the shop when he called from Shreveport, but it had been early and they probably weren't in yet.

He'd only brought one bag and threw it over his shoulder as he walked out into the thick, oppressive heat of Lafayette. He'd never ventured into this part of the world and the density of the air as compared to the crisp, light quality of Denver air felt heavy and pressing to him. It was late September, he remembered, and wondered if the sky ever backed off its downward push. Within minutes, he was sweating through his jeans and undershirts.

McReady wondered why DuPuis hadn't waited, but couldn't get himself to spend much effort on the thought. He hailed a cab in front of the bus depot and a dark-skinned man with a thick accent said, "Yassir, where ya'll needin' to be?" The man seemed genuinely interested, different from some of the drivers he'd encountered in Denver.

"Well," Gerald began, "I'm looking for a friend's shop. He makes wooden frames for those mattresses that are filled with water. I don't know the name of the shop or the store, but his name is Johnny Cobb. He's an older Black man and I…"

"Mista' Cobb ain't there, sir. He got hurt last night, is what I hear. Kinda' bad, too, they be sayin' round the streets."

Gerald was taken aback, jerked from his growing sense of peace, and sent into a sudden turmoil. How could this taxi driver know of Johnny Cobb? Lafayette wasn't that small of town. And how could he be hurt? Cobb had been the rock; it was his friend and the son who'd shown signs of damage, inside and out, back at the VA.

But McReady was that quick-thinking soldier who DuPuis told him he was, his mind switching from his own state to the state of the other.

"What's your name?" he asked the driver.

"It's Jerome, sir, Jerome Walkins the Third."

"Jerome, can you take me to the biggest hospital that you have in town?"

"Of course, sir. On the way. But it ain't that big and it's up where most of the White people live. Pretty good cab fare, but I give ya' a break, okay, mista'?"

"Sure, Jerome, whatever is right. And how do you know of Mr. Cobb, anyway?'

"Oh, everybody knows Mista' Cobb. His shop right down in the middle of the worse part of town. He gives jobs to any man willing to work hard. He has a bunch of young soldiers working with him. That's a good group, Mista', different but good. They all go to a place called Auntie's darn near ever day after work. I heard there was trouble last night. Couple of strange honkies—I mean White men—from outta town. 'Nother cabbie told me one of them got hisself kilt, the other one gone disappear. Reckon that's how Mista' Cobb got hisself banged up. That's all I know, Mista'. But I'll know more by time I get off. Not too many secrets in this town."

McReady gave Jerome two twenties for a fifteen-dollar fare and said, "You're a good kid, Jerome. Don't let anybody tell you differently."

"I know that, sir. We just need us a few mo' Martin Luthers to remind the world." And Jerome sat up straight in his cab, smiled a row of white teeth at Gerald, and drove away.

McReady walked into Lafayette General and up to the information desk.

"Can you give me the room number of a Mr. John Cobb, please, Miss?" Gerald glanced at her nametag, looked at his watch while he fidgeted with his bag, and then said, "It's urgent, Miss Lomax."

"Just one minute here, sir," Miss Lomax searched her large book.

"Sir, that would be room seven-three-seven, but he's in the ICU and only immediate family is allowed to see him. Are you next of kin?"

Gerald flashed his VA Hospital ID quickly and said he'd been called in to consult by Dr. Black. The receptionist wasn't buying it, but wasn't rejecting it either. By the time she'd written down the words, B-L-A-C-K on her pad of paper with the drug company's logo on top, Gerald was walking away. Miss Lomax tore up the paper and went back to her daydream.

"Thank you, Miss Lomax," she heard the man say.

"Second hallway to the left, doctor, right at the top of the stairs," she heard herself reply before once again sliding her recent issue of *Glamour* out from underneath the patient log.

Gerald slipped into a staff restroom on the way and changed into the pale green scrubs that he kept packed in his bag at all times. The lightweight hospital attire was the pugmark of the Western healer; from x-ray tech to night nurse to chief surgeon, they all looked the same.

Gerald found a stethoscope on top of a locker, set his bag down, and walked into the ICU. He pulled a mask up over his face, offered a serious and shallow nod to the charge nurse sitting at her station monitoring patient vital signs stationed around her desk like she was the sun and all her patients the planets.

Gerald immediately spotted the large figure of Cobb in an adjacent room and tried not to feel the disdain for rampant incompetence that was so pervasive in his experience with the health care industry. The world of business and commerce where products were made and sold for a profit had a much better chance of being wel-run than the business of basic health, soldiering, and the business that was the result of soldiering.

He slipped into Cobb's room and looked up at the IV drip running into his arm. McReady suddenly felt at home, almost as if he missed this environment where sick and injured people lie in strange beds with wires and tubes attached to them, existing in some netherworld between life and death, between what they once were and what they would be if they survived. He looked around the room. It was all very clear to him: the monitors, the meds, the machines, the markings on the charts signed by the MDs.

A sadness fell over Gerald McReady, the simple orderly from another hospital far away. It wasn't his place. He wasn't in charge. He was never really in charge, officially. He just loved all things medical, all things that heal the body. And so in the anarchy and confusion of a place like Denver VA, a smart kid with experience and connections and no fear of doing what he thought was the best treatment for a patient, could *feel* as if he was in charge.

But here in this little community hospital with its antiquated equipment and volunteer receptionist, Gerald McReady came right up against the truth of it all. DuPuis was right, he fought to control things that would forever resist it. It mattered little what title other people gave him; he'd do his best to be "a guy who sewed people up," regardless if they kept coming in blown up, cut up, smashed up, with holes and sores and diseases and maladies not yet defined.

And if Gerald McReady didn't get the respect from people who should be giving it, well, so be it. There were always guys like DuPuis who would come along to remind him in so many ways that the world, as imperfect as it was, needed guys like him.

Gerald looked down at the unconscious body of Johnny Cobb and thought about all the people he must've healed in his own brand of fixin'. And then he went to work.

Gerald read the chart with all of Johnny's personal information and saw what they were concerned about—

intracranial bleeding. There were no specialists at this hospital and none of the talked-about equipment of the future that might tell them there were tiny arteries bleeding into the space between that brain and the boney skull plates. Even moving him was a risky thing. Gerald had seen this before at the VA and he'd watched the docs treat the patients right and treat them wrong. He had observed the good ones who rotated through the VA and the bad ones who got stuck there because no one else would have them.

Gerald sat down in a chair and tried to remember what the good ones had done. How had they dealt with their patients who'd suffered blunt trauma to the head? What had made a difference?

Gerald put his hand on Cobb's large face and lifted one eyelid. The pupils were normal in size and shrunk in reaction to light. Each eye did the same, but there was something more— they had questions in them. He'd seen these kinds of eyes many times before at the VA. They came in the conscious and the unconscious. They belonged more to the young than the old, the kids who came back hurt and didn't know why. Gerald had seen those eyes and had done his best to answer them. Sometimes it was a few words of encouragement. Other times it was a shot of morphine. And sometimes it was the brutal honesty of explaining that the leg was not there and it wouldn't grow back.

He closed Cobb's eyes, glanced over his shoulder to see that the ICU nurses were busy with other patients and then leaned his head in close to the unshaven and unconscious Johnny Cobb.

"Mr. Cobb, I can see you took a good swat on the right temple. And I don't blame you if you're mad. Now, I don't know how bad this is. The truth is, you're in a bit of a quandary here. The docs can't afford to wait and see and they don't want to move you. But what do they know, eh? So, I know this sounds a little rough, but you're kinda on your own right now, Johnny. It's more or less up to you. What I will tell you is what you already know—you have a certain responsibility to get well, to yourself and to others. You're like the rest of us who were somehow pulled into this war in ways nobody sane could even dream of."

Gerald sat back in the chair next to the bed and spoke openly, but more to himself than Cobb.

"It seems that some of us work really hard at being unhappy. And others, it just comes to naturally. But I've decided that we have a choice and that decision should not be forged in the decisions of others."

Gerald put his hand on the back of Johnny Cobb's big mitt and then wrapped his finders around to the wrist. The pulse was strong and steady with a rhythmic thump to it. Gerald squeezed the big man's hand and then gently placed it on his chest.

"Quite honestly, Johnny, I think you have a choice in the matter. Hell, we all do. I'll come back later and we'll talk some more."

And a guttural, almost primal sound was let loose by the big Black man in that small white-lined bed.

CHAPTER 40

A GRAND ACCIDENT

When Gerald returned to the hospital the next afternoon there was a new receptionist working the desk.

"Can I help you, sir?"

"I'm here to see a patient, ma'am. The name is Cobb, John Cobb. I believe he is in room seven-three-seven."

The woman, who appeared much more efficient than Miss Lomax, placed her reading glasses that hung around her neck up onto her long, thin nose and scanned the patient log.

"I'm sorry, sir. It appears that Mr. Cobb is no longer with us."

Gerald stopped breathing for a moment and when the air finally was allowed back into his lungs he asked if she had any information that she could share.

"No, I'm sorry, sir," the lady spoke without any hint of sorrow in her voice. "There's a security block on this patient's information. I can't release any information." And she turned her attention to the next person in line behind Gerald. "Can I help you, sir?"

Hurricane Gilda made a sudden and unexplained shift to the southeast before regaining strength and hitting Cuba and then the Bahamas. The weather forecasters were at a loss to explain it, and the thousands who had boarded-up their homes and stocked up on peanut butter and gotten in the gridlock evacuation routes simply turned around and went home to their lives, albeit with even less confidence in the National Weather Service's ability to predict what maybe even God hadn't decided to do with the weather.

Harry had his beloved *Grace* towed off the small muddy shore inside of Eastpoint Harbor and decided that she'd be better off dry-docked for repairs there than risking the short trip west to Panama City. As she was towed into the slip, he could imagine new creaks and moans in the old cedar hull. But they were real and the noise sounded more like the whimper of an injured lion than a bull elephant about to die. Harry wanted to curse the storm-bitch for what she'd down to his boat but knew that it would do no good. He'd grown stronger because of it and would offer thanks at some point in the future. Besides, he admired her fight and reveled in the struggle. It would've been a good day to die.

A U.S. Air Force lieutenant colonel on his way back to Ft. Walton offered to give Harry a ride back to Panama City Beach. Word had gotten around the small town of the man who had ridden out the hurricane at sea and the young colonel was happy to share the drive with his special access permits in exchange for the story. He was almost an engaging man, but his tone showed the stress and strain of having grown up to be a short man in a world that rewarded height. Harry didn't really want to tell the story because he hadn't made any sense of it yet, but he had to get home and this was a way.

"What were the conditions like out there?" The young man opened up as soon as Harry had clipped his seat belt.

"Angry, consequential, and not altogether unpredictable." Harry spoke straight ahead.

"Hmmm...sounds like women I've met." The officer laughed at his comparison.

Harry, who had known many military families from the bases near his home and had loved some and pitied others, didn't laugh.

"If you'll excuse me colonel, I've just come through something weighty and my sense of humor is a bit wigged."

"No problem, pal," the effable officer seemed nonplussed. "But you were scared out there? I mean, you had to have thought that was it."

Harry looked at the officer, at least ten years his junior, a man who must've seen action in Vietnam to rise to such a rank at such an age, and said no, he wasn't scared. He'd survived worse accidents at sea.

He could see that Harry was being honest and tried to keep the conversation light.

"Didn't learn your lesson the first time then, huh?" And chuckled to himself as he saluted a highway patrolman who allowed him onto a closed road.

"That's quite a good observation, colonel, but sometimes you just keep singing for the sake of the song, if you know what I mean."

"I'm not sure that I do, but I sense that if you wanted to tell me then you already would've by now."

The officer said something else, but Harry didn't hear it. He'd fallen asleep with his head up against the window, the rain pelting the outside and Harry's breath fogging the inside.

When he awoke the gray military sedan was parked in front of Harry's house up the long driveway. The officer opened the door for Harryand helped him into the house. Harry asked as he looked aghast upon his familiar home with its landmarks and colors. "But how did you..."

"I know who you are, Mr. Davis. You said many things in your sleep. And there aren't many secrets on the base. I'm sorry to hear about your son. The Armed Forces of America offers its condolences."

For the slightest moment Harry forgot that Phin had been re-erased from the "books."

"What would you call it, colonel? When a man finally comes to grips with war that ended some months or years ago, but comes home to a world that is doing its best to forget a war that just ended last week, if ever, and took his son with it?"

The colonel looked out the window of the military-issue gray car and beams of sunlight bounced off the ribbons on his chest as they fell through the pine trees of the Davis yard. "Mr. Davis, I'd call that an American occurrence." The young officer shook Harry's hand and handed him a card. "It's been an honor, sir," he told Harry, mostly meaning it, and left.

When Harry entered the trailer home he'd left so many months ago, the dogs absent and settled with temporary homes, and the smell of must in the thick air, he called out for Grace. And the silence told him. Where could his wife have gone? Harry had called their house and Jed's office from the Harbor, but got no answers.

He heard a ringing in another room and wondered what that could be. Harry followed the sound to its origin and picked up the phone. That's when Blackie told him what had happened in Lafayette; that Jed had found a surgeon from New Orleans and had called the governor who'd facilitated a physician-attended transfer to a larger hospital in Baton Rouge. Blackie said they were thinking of installing a "relief valve" in Johnny's head, which was risky but that he was doing much better.

"It's all very peculiar and profound, isn't it Harry? Something more than simple tragedy."

"Yeah, Blackie." Harry didn't bother giving him the details of his own adventure. "A regular American occurrence."

And when Blackie hung up without mentioning Phin, Harry knew that nobody had heard from him. He'd have to go find his wife and his boy.

Yes, it was an occurrence, but with a confluence of fate and humanity and good and evil and God and the devil; what the Chinese call "Joss." The way Johnny Cobb landed in not one but two hospitals was not uniquely American or uniquely Southern—it was uniquely life.

Joss.

Harry jump-started the old truck by rolling it down the hill out behind his converted trailer home and drove to his neighbors to retrieve the two remaining dogs in the pack and to inquire about Grace. As he pulled up, a large woman of mixed race and culture stepped into the dirt driveway and ran out to meet him. Lynelle had lived on the property for nearly forty years with her husband, Raymond. They had not been able to have children and worked odd jobs while they, as Raymond was fond of joking, "waited around to open social security checks and then die quietly in their sleep."

Lynelle gave Harry a big hug, pushed him away and said. "Be prepared, Grace ain't who she was." Then she led Harry into their living room where he found his wife of thirty-two years slumped over in a rocking chair he'd built for her when he came back from the war in '45. Her eyes lacked the light they'd always shown and a small drip of spittle fell from the right side of her mouth.

"She was getting better and better," Lynelle spoke in a hushed tone, "but after the place Jed set up got sold and another month went by and you wasn't coming home and still no word, well, Ray and I decided we needed to bring her here." Harry stared at Grace, who seemed to stir a bit and move her arms in Harry's direction. "The doc say she only needs more time and more love. Like we all do, Harry...like we all do."

Harry kissed Lynelle on the cheek, nodded his chin, said, "much obliged," and scooped Grace from the chair as it emptily rocked back and forth, back and forth. Harry carried Grace out and placed her on the truck's bench seat. He whistled for the dogs and they cradled her as they had since puppies. Harry shut the door, started the truck, and drove away.

They drove through the night from Panama City, Florida to Baton Rouge, Louisiana and arrived at the hospital just as the shift was changing from night to day. Harry had talked non-stop to Grace for five hours, beginning with stories of how they'd met as sophomores at Panama City High, their first date, when he was drafted into the Navy, when they'd delivered the bomb, when he returned and bought the land with a GI Bill loan, their wedding, moving into the trailer, finding the right boat, his years at sea, and finally, for the last three hours, he told her of his trip, ending up with his conversations with the devil himself. Grace made only small noises that served as her opinion on what story Harry was telling.

When the sun came up, Harry found a wheelchair in the parking lot and started to push Grace toward the hospital doors.

"Ha-ha-Harry?" Grace's voice was ghostly soft, almost a spirit of sound. "You-you. Go. On. I watch. Sun come up." So, Harry pointed her chair to the east and told the dogs to keep an eye. Then Harry bent down on one knee and started to offer some kind of apologia that was cut short by Grace's deliberate effort to push more words out her mouth. "Ja-ja-Johnny is the key. He's...uh, ah, always brought us'es to-together. Ga, ga, go find your brother." And Harry Davis went straight to the admissions desk and told them he was there to see his brother, Johnny Cobb.

"It seems your, uh...'brother,' is a right popular fellow. His nephew was just here, but I told him visiting hours weren't until nine o'clock. And he'd have to wait outside if'n he wanted to go smoke."

For the slightest of moments, Harry thought hard about Cobb having a nephew. He knew that both of Johnny's brothers, Earl and Ramsey, were dead; one from cancer, the other by his own will and a bullet for breakfast. It had happened that time after Cobb had stayed on the boat, letting Ruth drift away from the surface of his pain, healing his badly broken leg and heart. The farm had not done well. The back taxes had mounted, the rain had been sparse, the price of seed and fuel had risen, and in the wake of sporadic "uprisings by local colored folk," no banks would lend money to Negro landowners unless they held the entire deed to the property with no encumbrances and equity to cover the loan amount.

Ramsey had panicked, and against the near-violent urgings of his brother Earl, and had done just that—given the National Bank of Mobile the title to the entire ninety-four acres as collateral for a ten-thousand dollar loan. It was all very official the bank had said when Earl went in to tell them that his brother had forged his signature along with his other brother's, who was away on business.

"Your brother filled out all the documents correctly, boy," the man spoke from behind a big maple desk and kept scratching at his scaly arms. "We gave your family ten thousand of our bank's dollars, all due and payable in six months. Gave you boys a good interest rate, too." The man scratched his arm and flakes of dead white skin covered the dark maple wood like flakes of dirty snow.

"Did it on account of your long history in the county. But I'm sure you know that. You brother must've explained it all to you before you signed the papers. Son, if you're going to own land you'll have to be more responsible and work harder instead of coming in here with these crazy stories about forgery and what not. Yes, it's all very official. Have the file right here if you'd like to review it. You can read, can't you, son?"

That was how Earl had told the story to Johnny when he'd gone home the next spring and found his brother living in a rented motel room in town, the cancer having passed through his prostate and moved onto his lower intestines. The money was gone, the farm repossessed, and Ramsey recently interned in a pine box, six feet down at the county cemetery.

Johnny had moved Earl in with Nadine and her sisters, Loretta and Aunt Mary, trying to bring some relief to his dying older brother, the second father he'd lost in his life. Earl slept in Chuck's old bed and Johnny on the couch, just a few steps from where the tormented Nadine played her haunting piano most nights.

"Louella is a'coming, Lord, she's a'comin home soon," Nadine would sing night after night to the tune of a church melody she'd taught herself. And Johnny would tell himself that the Lord would have all his family soon enough, what with neither brother having married or fathered children. The Cobb name would be well-represented in the afterlife, but only he was left here on earth to keep it going, to marry again, and have more boys to try and buy some land and work it and keep it, and get some good dogs and work them and keep them, too. But Johnny would have to find another girl to love first. And that would never happen.

One night he went in to check on Earl and saw that his color was better and he was awake, reading *Life Magazine*.

There was a picture of Earth on the cover. It had been taken from outer space. The planet seemed small, inconsequential.

"My, my," Johnny gave his brother a soft punch on the skeleton-thin arm. "Looks like we'll be out planting this place together come May and June. Heaven knows I can't do it with just Loretta and Mary's men. 'Tween you and me, they're useless as teets on a bull."

Earl laughed and when he did he coughed up something large and dark that landed on the dirty sheets and seemed to pulsate like a dying insect scraped from the windshield. Johnny saw the bright red blood ooze from the corners of Earl's mouth and quickly wiped it away with a corner of the sheet.

"Thata boy," Johnny forced a smile. "You hack that bitch right out of you. You gonna be up and around in a few days, get you some fresh air, maybe go on into town and see what the new crop of women have to offer you." Earl kept coughing through the night, nodding his head in faithful agreement to his younger brother's suggestions of brighter days.

"Man, you're looking good, older brother," Johnny lied. "The other day the doc said he thinks those pills are doing the job." Johnny stayed with him until a rough, thin sleep finally came to Earl. He could see the first hint of another day through the thick, musty curtains. A day at a time, he told himself, one damn day at time.

Johnny thought he'd get up and make coffee for the house, but maybe he'd lie down on the floor and rest his eyes for just a minute. Sleep came instantly followed by instant waking. A farming magazine had fallen on his head and Earl's rasping pleas jerked him to his brother's side.

"Don't let them take the farm, Johnny," Earl forced the words into his brother's ear along with little red dots that stuck to his cheek. "Ramsey was just being hisself. Bitter to the end. I'd like to think he did if for the life insurance or some such notion. Don't be mad, Johnny. Don't be mad at us." Johnny felt the life slipping out of his brother's surprisingly strong grip.

"I won't let them take it, brother. I won't let 'em have it."

"I believe you, Johnny. You already lost enough. You already..."

Earl was gone and Johnny took his large rough hands and closed his brother's eyes. "You got them all, God," he said while Nadine began to play her same minor chords in the next room. "You got all the Cobbs 'cept me. I hope your hands are big enough."

✳ ✳ ✳

Harry's thoughts came back to the hospital. Johnny didn't have any living nephews that he was aware of.

"Sir, sir!" It was the admissions nurse calling out to the daydreaming Harry. "Mr. Davis, we don't take kindly to practical jokes at this hospital. The records show that the patient, one Mr. John Cobb, is of Negro decent. You say that you're his brother and that White soldier boy coming in the door behind you says he's his nephew. Either you're trying to play a bad joke on us or ya'll do some funny breeding where you from." The nurse's lips came together so tight that they became one thin red line of flesh.

Sgt. Lorenzo DuPuis, who had spent the previous day doing recon, using his military connections, his military training, and his military loyalty to find out all he could about the patient Cobb, the incident at Auntie's, and the other players involved, stepped up to the desk.

"Excuse me, sir," he smiled at a furious but restrained Harry, and removed his perfect dress uniform cap, placed it on the counter and leaned his large, freshly shaven face within inches of the nurse's.

"I think you'd better call your supervisor, the chief of staff, and security, madam," he spoke evenly but with a hypnotic force of power. "I think we have just a little discipline problem here."

The admissions nurse wasn't even a nurse; she just dressed like one. For her it was a job, a paycheck, and pretty good hours. The Marine outwardly represented everything that she despised: authority, diligence, order, and, inwardly, all things she wanted to hate even more. The soldier had probably gone to Vietnam and burned villages and shot local farmers who were suspected of helping the North. He probably had been with numerous prostitutes in Saigon and Da Nang and the Philippine Islands, had nice middle class parents, and went to a military academy. The lady imagined that DuPuis even liked himself and thought that the country needed people like him. And he enjoyed fighting in a war. And she would've been correct on all accounts except the last.

While the admissions lady fiddled nervously with the phone, DuPuis introduced himself to Harry.

"I caught the part about 'breeding' but what was all this about colored nephews and practical jokes?"

Harry was tired from the drive and sat down on the torn couch across from the big desk. He didn't want to tell any more stories; he didn't want to live any more drama. He had a sudden urge to lie down under a big sycamore or get in his truck and drive out west with Grace, maybe run into his son on the highway near Tucson or El Centro or Albuquerque. He even wondered how long it would take him to get the *Grace* seaworthy again.

DuPuis could see the strain in Harry's eyes, the heaviness in his step.

"I'm sorry, man. It's none of my business. It's just that I heard her mention something about the nephew of an older Negro. That's me, I'm the nephew."

Harry looked up at the kid and saw that he was picking tiny bits of lint off his uniform. He shook his head and mumbled to himself that all he'd come here to do was see his injured friend, Johnny.

"Johnny Cobb? The hippy-bed houser of vets? You know him?" DuPuis went on to tell Harry the entire tale of his time in the Denver VA and driving out with Gerald McReady and how he had went looking for the guys who did this to the old guy, Johnny, partly because he'd seen them at the VA and partly because he owed Doc Gerald.

"I would've took them out in the VA on principle alone, but I was indisposed at the time and there were lots of MPs cruising the place. Did you know this kid with the funny fish name that was a friend of Cobb's?'

"Phin is my son," Harry said it flatly, the conviction hidden beneath his mounting weariness.

"I'll be goddamned, you're the one who busted the window," the excitement in his voice causing the admissions lady to shoot a darting look as she spoke on the phone. "This is really something, meeting you here and all. Geez, they were telling stories about you on the floor."

And then DuPuis said he'd be goddamned again.

A regular American occurrence, thought Harry, complete with a new character every step of the way. This soldier seemed true enough. He was on a mission. I'm in history, Harry said to himself. A damned character in somebody's novel.

Three doctors and a hospital administrator approached Harry and Lorenzo. DuPuis' character changed in an instant. Suddenly he was tall and dangerous and very capable of killing the four men with dental floss or an ash tray.

"You boys have something for us?" DuPuis was on his feet and surrounding the others while Harry sat and watched the transformation.

"Well, yes. Mr. Davis?" The oldest man with a long patch of mousy brown hair he grew long in one spot and drooped over his bald head, spoke while looking at Harry and trying to move away from the Marine Corps figure who had moved into his personal space.

"Hmmm?" Harry's eyes had gone to half-mast in the wake of only a few hours of sleep in nearly three days. One of the men from the hospital was looking at a folder of notes and stroking his chin. He interrupted the others with an *I'll take care of this look* and motioned to Harry.

"You're Harry Davis from Panama City?" It was more telling than asking. Harry nodded, but only barely.

"Can you come with us? Mr. Cobb is asking for you."

"Go on up, Harry," Sgt. DuPuis said. "I'll be along in few minutes."

Harry followed the docs up to his old friend's room and when he walked in, Johnny Cobb had turned old. His short nappy hair had gone gray-white. The lines running out from his eyes had gained rays, deepened, and begun to connect with the ones coming up from the edges of his mouth. It hadn't been that long, thought Harry. The change was startling. And it scared him. But not that much because Johnny's eyes were still clear and bright.

CHAPTER 41

AN UNHINGING

Happiness isn't on the road to anything...happiness is the road.

–Bob Dylan

José stood on the old wooden porch of the restaurant and watched me try to wrestle the top up on the Bucik, silently asking Mike Greer for forgiveness. Lolita had put one small bag in the trunk and a large bag of fresh tortillas on the wide bench seat up front.

"Eh, Meester Phin," José wiped his hands again on the apron around his waist, the piece of cloth that had hung there for as long as anybody could remember. "Your car no want to wear a hat today," he laughed in an infectious tone. "What you worry about? Sunburn? Passing gas in front of my daughter? I never seen you so worry before." José's mood seemed to have changed directions, like a dog that knows he won't get another piece of steak from the barbecue, but is happy just to lie under the table and be with his family.

I knew he was right. Something had come over me and I found myself concerned about things that I either had no control over or shouldn't if I did. I'd told the dogs to stay when they had never run off before. I checked the tread on the tires, the sky for rain, even looked in the rearview mirror to see if I had any sleep left in the corners or my eyes.

"You kids go and let me get to work, eh?" José called out. "I need to learn how to cook good Mexican food by this afternoon. Or maybe I go into Gallup and look for a nice large waitress who can sing John Denver songs. Maybe I win the lottery and hire a gringo lawyer to bring my wife back across the river by nightfall."

José was trying to make me comfortable. It was working. I gave up on the top and went up to say whatever could or could not be said to a father as you take his daughter away for the first time.

"Eh, *Mijo*," José put out his arms. "I see you soon, eh? José is going to invest in a television set. Maybe next time you can show me how to use it."

I said that I couldn't do that. It would be like putting water in the beans to make then go farther. I'd bring him some good books instead. And then I pulled away from José and tried to tell him why I'd really asked Lolita to go with me. But José cut me short.

"Eh, *Mijo*, I know you now, otherwise I not let her go. This time I save you the confession because you already doing the penance." And then he reached up to hold my shoulders and spun me around. "Go fix señor Cobb. Go fix yourself. José be here when you come back."

✳ ✳ ✳

When we stopped in Albuquerque for gas I remembered I was broke and wondered where I could find a day's full labor. Lolita seemed nervous about all the traffic and red lights and many, many shops where people with money could buy things. I looked in the glove box for change and found an envelope. Inside was a stack of twenty-dollar bills and note from Mike Greer.

"For that day, kiddo. For that day."

"When I was young," the words came as if Lolita was still daydreaming, "I thought big cities meant that people felt alone living all by themselves and needed all this noise and things around them to feel comfortable. Now I am older and I know that cities can mean many things to many people. But mostly it means that people get lonely without other people and noise around them." I nodded my head but said nothing.

I drove with the dogs asleep in the back and Lolita asleep with her head on a rough Salvation Army blanket, leaned against the window, and the brilliant Southwestern sun pouring into the open car like fresh coffee on a cold morning. My mind drifted as the stark desert beauty rolled by. How was Johnny? What had happened to the men from the VA? And Blackie, how would this affect his own progress? Where was my dad? Why didn't he write?

These were things I would know soon enough; the beginning of the end or something like that. But about Lonnie I would never knew. I had the memories; I had her in my mind when I needed her. I had the painting in the trunk. That was more than I deserved. Could I ever repay her? What if she came looking for me some distant day in the spring when the water starts to warm and none of the tourists have arrived in town yet? What if she contacted the U.S. Army? They would tell her what they thought, what had come very close to being true, what I had told her in so many words or at least the absence of them—I was dead. How would she feel? Would she be relieved? Would she be sad? And what if the black truck no longer was parked in the driveway, the man at the gas station who was or was not Lonnie's dad having been just a weary flashback? What then, Phin Davis? Would you kill yourself to Lonnie a third time? Or would you die for her?

I looked over at Lolita asleep like a child who had simply decided she was tired and turned the switch off. It had been like that in the Nam at times; so tired that you'd fall asleep standing in the chow line, mid-sentence, with a tin plate in your hand. Your buddies would pick you up, carry you to your hootch, and set you in a bunk. They'd all been there at some point and might be again if they stayed in-country. That cliché, "dead tired," coming closer to dead than tired.

I patted her shoulder gently. Without raising an eyelid, she took my hand in hers and squeezed it gently, held it to her cheek, and then set it on her brown leg curled on the seat. My heart jumped and my foot pushed on the accelerator. How long had it been since a woman had touched me like that? Was it Lonnie? Did my mother's pre-war hugs count? And what of the love of men in battle? Was there any more unadulterated and raw feelings for another human, regardless of gender, when there was that something between men who marched into hell together knowing the chances were high that one would come back alive carrying the other on a stretcher. Others who knew this same thing never described as love, but existing more as love than what often happens in twentieth-century marriages between men and women. Didn't that count? If you held the lower intestines of the dying man from falling out of his torn gut and then off the side of the stretcher and getting tangled in the feet of the men who loved the dying man more than a brother ever could—did that make it okay? Tell me that's not love.

My foot began to hurt and I lowered my speed and heart rate the only way I could, by willing it away, by letting the pain, and maybe the feelings for Lolita, pass right through, unencumbered. There were some people I needed to say goodbye to before I could muster up enough courage to create some long-term hellos.

But what was the difference between saying goodbye and saying hello? There had been a letter that found its way to our home in Panama City that I barely acknowledged before I left on this trip. It was from a lady in Boston. She was writing because she found my name on a list that a fellow soldier had created and labeled "Just in case."

"Dear Corporal Davis," the pain drug withdrawal was making me laugh and cry at the words back then. "I am writing to inform you that our son, Dell Sanders, was killed during the final days of the war in Vietnam. He had mentioned you in his letters home. He had written quotes next to each fellow soldier he wanted contacted in case of his demise." *In case of his demise*, I laughed again. The moment that you boarded a plane for the Nam you were *demised*. Did I know a Sanders? The letter continued.

"Our son had this written next to your name and home address: '*I almost made it to the finish line because they allowed me to the starting line. In words and words alone will you find your Self. Because this is how feelings are created. On the other side, Your pal, Worm.*' "

Holy shit, I screamed into my pillow that day. They got the Worm as well.

The pain in my foot, or what was left of it, began to throb and I reached for the bottle in the glove box. Lolita's hand came up as some archangel and took my wrist and placed it back on the steering wheel. I went to touch her, but heard the complacency and quiet snoring and wondered if, in fact, I had hijacked one of God's lieutenants.

I glanced at the gas gage and wondered how far to Amarillo? Where was I, anyway? Purgatory, that's where, given a second chance at something called life, something disguised between the starting gun and the finisher's tape. I had been in a race, but what kind? A race to punish myself for the death of Gillie? For the fear of Dickey? For the blessed, youthful pleasures of our little town by the sea with our own private clubhouse called the Municipal Pier? Could I even have been trying to atone for Johnny Cobb's assigned blame on a God he was only now coming to know for taking the one woman he had the capacity to love? Or was it for leaving Lonnie?

The sign said "Amarillo 12 miles," and a pale thin crescent of moon was rising barely visible, like somebody's forgotten aunt.

A theme began to emerge and Elijah began to stir in the back. "What is it, boy? You hungry? We'll get you some answers...or food in twelve miles."

We rolled into town and the dogs were awake, ready to take on all comers. Lolita woke up and said that she'd had strange dreams, dreams of being stuck between the safety of the stage and the pressing crowd at her father's café on a crowded Saturday night.

"Are you okay?" I asked, wondering if she remembered our touch.

"You are funny sometimes, Mister Phin." She rubbed her eyes and for the first time I decided she was quite beautiful. Or at least now I could admit it. "You are so wise one minute and the next you are like a little boy. This is a great adventure for me. How could I not be any closer to fine?"

And then she asked if we should call the city we were driving toward and see if Mr. Cobb was getting okay himself. "Probably put some gas in the car as the girl is thirsty. I have some more money from my tip jar, from one girl to another, eh, Phin?"

"If you can walk the dogs, I'll make the call. Are you fine with that?" Lolita laughed and said she could be queen of Mexico if they just gave her a crown.

The hospital said he'd been moved to a larger one in Baton Rouge, but was still unconscious and that his brother and nephew were there now consulting with a crew of specialists who had been brought in. That would be Blackie, I guessed, who was behind the shenanigans, or more'n likely, Jed who'd gone and traded a few favors for smart MDs. But something deeper was bothering me. Jed's reach only went so far and Blackie was very careful to operate below the radar since Gerald McReady gave him the get-out-of-jail pass. Brothers and nephews? Ah, Gerald, maybe he was involved. That made me feel better and we nibbled on tortillas as we drove toward answers in Lafayette.

✳ ✳ ✳

The hulking bandaged figure of Johnny Cobb sat up square and straight. He'd been moved out of ICU and into a regular floor room with a view out the window of another gray building's air conditioning units. The tubes and wires still grew out of Cobb's arms, but there were less of them. He was conscious and speaking slowly but coherently.

"Save your strength," said one of the docs who'd driven up from New Orleans at the request of the governor's office. He turned to Harry and DuPuis.

"Your 'brother,' or whatever relation you wish to refer to our Mr. Cobb here, seems to have taken a sudden and dramatic turn for the better. The fact that he was unconscious for so long was not a good sign and I must say," the doctor paused and looked over his shoulder, "that there was a move in place to operate on this patient by staff surgeons as of last night before my colleague and I arrived and drilled the correct hole in the correct place."

Harry sat on the bed and looked at Cobb who rolled his eyes and shook his head slightly, dejectedly, from side to side.

"Now, I'm not saying that it would have gone all bad," the doctor was being honest but non-committal, "but anytime you go drilling in and around people's brains there are risks. And," lowering his voice and speaking directly toward Harry, "at a place like this they are substantial."

"So, he's out of the woods, doc?" DuPuis asked with an upbeat tone to his words.

"There are no outward signs of any internal bleeding and, of course, his regained consciousness is the key indicator, but I'd still like to move him down to our hospital in New Orleans. We're much better equipped to keep an eye on him for a few days while the period of danger passes."

Harry looked to Cobb for the okay and Johnny said that it must've been Jed who'd brought in the big guns.

"He came and saw me last night," Johnny's voice was still weak.

"Johnny," Harry was regaining his confidence to speak the words that needed to be said. "Likely it was a bunch of things. But I spoke with Jed yesterday. He's still back in Panama City."

"You were in the ICU yesterday, Mr. Cobb. No one but immediate family and other medical staff would've been able to see you. But your, ah, 'brother' here is correct. There had to have been many factors in your turnaround."

"I see." Johnny was fidgeting with the IV tube in his arm. His eyes seem to be moving around the room quicker now, soaking up the spirit of something good. "And why the military guard here?" He asked, nodding to DuPuis.

"Sgt. Lorenzo Dupuis, U.S. Marine Corps, sir." DuPuis threw him a salute, which Johnny Cobb had never been offered before, and Cobb in respect of respect itself, raised his weak, tube-laden arm up to his forehead. "Came out here with Dr. Gerald McReady who treated me at the Denver VA for lead in my ass. Met the infamous Harry Davis here on the way in and now I am honored to be in the presence of his brother and doctors on par with Doc Gerald. I'm at your service, Mr. Cobb; the Corps welcomes you back to the living."

"Well, thank you sergeant, for your faith that I'd be here when you made it out. And you say you came with McReady from the Denver VA?"

"Yes, sir. Man, saved my ass, so to speak. Had to pry him loose of that shit hole with a tire iron from a semi. He should be arriving anytime now, sir. We came in on the same bus yesterday about seventeen hundred hours."

Johnny laughed a tired but knowing laugh and then guardedly allowed himself the beginning feelings of tenderness. He drifted his words toward Harry, who was looking out the window, as if searching for the next reversal of tragedy before his luck ran out.

"You lose your faith; you lose your calling, eh Harry?"

Harry nodded and the two doctors in the room looked at each other. The one who'd spoken said in no uncertain terms that the patient had earned the faith of some high rollers, men in power who'd pulled them from their homes. The other doctor spoke for the first time, looking mostly at Sgt. DuPuis's shiny medals hanging from his chest, metal objects that seemed to have a strange relationship with all the other medical equipment in the room.

"Maybe there was another power involved," he hinted, "The aristocracy of fame, eh gentlemen?"

"How about the celebrity of respect?" Johnny forced through a gravelly voice.

Harry, who was listening and watching the conversation, his head moving from side to side as if on a string, felt a bridle snap. Forty-eight hours ago he was dueling with a magnificent force of nature, bantering with his would-be killer like he used to do with Johnny out on the boat years ago, before the light of something went out of him, switched off with too many lives ended too early. What Harry had to offer in verbal ammunition had been kidnapped and he was getting it back, demanding it because he'd paid the ransom.

"Nah," he turned away from the window and looked each man in the eye as his head swiveled and sailed cleanly, freely around the small room. "It ain't none of that. It's just people doin' right by each other." And then he added to the quietness, "It's extinguishing the flames that exist between people by setting back-fires in our own hearts first, if we have to." And then Harry added, "If ya'll will excuse me, my wife is somewhere down in that parking lot."

And so it was that Johnny Cobb was moved in a private ambulance from Baton Rouge to New Orleans, Harry and DuPuis in tow, to another hospital without fanfare and in the professionalism that comes with respect for another who you endorsed and defended with your life and your reputation because down here, they could be the same.

When Gerald showed up at the hospital that afternoon after having spent the entire morning in church for the first time since fourth grade, he was told that the patient, Cobb, was no longer there and that's all they could tell him. His VA badge did allow him the information that he'd been transferred, not expired. But somehow he knew that.

And Gerald remembered that he'd copied an address off of a file he'd perused in the ICU while visiting Cobb the night before. It was a habit, a just-in-case thing he'd taught himself a long time ago. He got in his rental car and went looking for that address.

Sitting out on the wide porch of Johnny's house were all the usual suspects: Leroy, the quick acting Black man whose knife poor, poor Roberts had fallen onto and died; Hopper, the numbers kid from Chicago who was as book-smart as they came, who'd "calculated" his way through the war; Snare, the badass, force-recon, natural born killer who said little, but said a lot when he did; Tom-Tom, the partial Native American grunt who carried more tracking experience than most Indians still left in America, and who was a wizard at working the systems that had committed genocide on a people that he carried some varying percentage of blood relation to; Hunter, the thrice-shot, analytical healer, a fast-acting medic from the cold, third coast of Green Bay who was as quick-witted as he was handy; Strider, the China Beach lifeguard, sometimes munitions expert, and surfer from Newport Beach, California who survived the war on dumb luck and maybe because he "just loved to blow shit up;" Auntie, the bar owner who'd lost a husband to the war, but loved Johnny Cobb more than she ever had the man who was dead; and Blackie, the recovering neurotic whose IQ had once been tested at one-sixty, but had let the war make him afraid of his own shadow.

Each of them had offered the Lafayette Police a corroborating statement. None were charged with a crime, though Leroy was asked to surrender his passport. When he said that he could not do that, the cops got angry.

"Guys," Leroy said, "while some guys were burning draft cards before the war, I burned my passport when I got back. Hell, I doubt I'll leave Louisiana."

These were hardscrabble people, their heads bloodied but unbowed. The lines on their faces had deepened with time, weather-beaten with tragedy. But somehow, in the unexplainable strength of the collective, the blood was leaving their eyes, the cracks were filled in with talk and each other and the passing of seasons. And even if the memories would suck them back, the government who'd sent them there ignoring their requests, as long as there were other vets and men like Cobb who had the capacity to understand, they had a chance to find a kind of peace in the future, a night where at least their dreams would be dead instead of filled with the deadly.

The only person missing was Uncle Chuck, Johnny's dead wife's brother and militant pro-Black Southern Man. Chuck was coming from a different kind of war; a battle that would only end when oppression ended; an unendable war.

They were talking among themselves, each fending off, making peace, or feeling guilty about how they'd handled the incident that left their employer and de facto leader lying unconscious in a small hospital up on the good side of town.

After a long, silent period it was Blackie who finally spoke.

"Would-of's, should-of's, could-of's...we're seducing ourselves to rewind the film and splice in John Wayne. It's only relevant if it carries weight. I'm tired of carrying the weight, tired of being a child walking across the desert. You all want to keep digging gopher holes in your hearts, go ahead. I'm not worried about Wilcox coming back. I wanna see Johnny get well."

Snare, who was wearing a change of clothes for the first time in several weeks, set his mug of coffee down and spoke as if commenting on the weather. "Wilcox is 10-7, kid, out of service, no *mas*, gone and gone. Folded into the mud from which he rose."

Leroy looked at Snare and started to say something but Snare cut him off. "Uncle Charlie opened the package; I just took out the trash. Amazing what can happen when a White man is rude to a Black man in these parts."

The scenario played out quickly in each man's mind as they processed the information and dismissed it. This was not the kind of weight that any of them would only temporarily allow into a pack that was mostly full and trying to lighten itself. For Blackie though, it was one more coin dropped into his slot. The dead can't speak for themselves, he thought, too bad. What bad tree had Wilcox and Roberts come from? What gnarled and hacked-at root had twisted and morphed them into something on the wrong side of meanness? They must've been revolting against something. That's all most of us were doing, Blackie thought, while looking around at this eclectic group of soldiers trying to keep the meanness at bay, the devilish embrace of things that war made you want to hold, things that before and maybe after would repulse you. The usual air of audacity had a wet blanket thrown over it.

Did Wilcox and Roberts deserve their fate? Did they ask for what they received? Or had the war simply followed them home as it had the others? They each wrestled with it, knowing that they had come back out of a dark nowhere and unless they fought it every hour of every day, like alcoholics who go to three AA meetings a week for the rest of their lives, they could fall right back into the vacuum of the vet.

That's when Gerald McReady drove up in the unmarked rental car he'd rented from a lot next door to the Lafayette bus station. The salesman had three gold teeth that reflected the afternoon sun when he apologized for the two missing hubcaps. "It's an undercover-car," he laughed, "if you want to blend into this part of town."

The group reacted quickly and spread out to the sides of the yard, some taking cover, others wondering if there were more Wilcox/Roberts types coming for one of them; all of them wishing the war would end. Only Blackie, who had crossed some thin bridge he'd been staring at for too long, remained planted in his fat deck chair.

McReady stopped the car and stepped into the bright afternoon sun.

Blackie sprung up like a jack-in-the-box.

"G-man! My Lord, what brings you to this neck of the nape, nape of the woods? Doc G-Mac, get yourself up here and feast your healing eyes on the Phoenix Child who's shed his beautiful neuroses!" Blackie ran down to a surprised McReady while speaking to the wiggling bushes around the car. And then he jumped onto Gerald's body like a puppy.

Minutes later he called to the others, "C'mon out, you spooks. This is the orderly-type doc from the VA I've been telling you about, the man who set Blackie free, the one filled with nobility and goodness and who makes clay pots. Get your soldierly butts out here and welcome my man among men."

They returned to the porch and after another full round of introductions, Gerald told them that Johnny was no longer at Lafayette General Hospital. He'd disappeared, transferred probably to another hospital. With any luck over in Baton Rouge. But he wasn't positive. They looked at each other, shaking their heads, making and unmaking the immediate history in their minds.

"It's too bad Johnny doesn't like phones," somebody said.

"Can you picture him sitting here at night talking on the phone?" somebody else asked. "He only answers the one at work when he knows he has to."

"Yeah, but it'd be nice to be able to make a few calls right now."

"At least one man, perhaps two were killed last here, in the last twenty-four hours. You gonna call the cops and tell them one of the men involved is missing and could you please help find him?"

"What we need is a plan."

"You ever have a plan in-country? You ever know exactly what you were supposed to do?"

"Good point."

Gerald, who had a strange feeling of confidence in these men, even though they looked beat up, haggard, and ghost-ridden, spoke up. Everyone looked at him like the new kid in class, which inside the new skin he'd been growing, he was.

"There will be a note at the shop. We should go there."

"What kind of 'note' and from whom?"

"A patient from the VA that I came out with, a Marine, a...well, a very resourceful and energetic man. Local kid, born and bred. If anybody knows anything about Johnny, it will be him. And the info will be at the shop."

They looked at McReady, each making up their own mind if this other guy from some VA hospital that had brought them two pieces of information—partly news, partly advice—was good enough to follow. Blackie was the first to say let's go. Then Snare stood up and walked past Gerald, touching his shoulder but only lightly.

"I'll get the keys to the truck," he said moving into the house. "Never met a man who could mold the earth into something good that I didn't trust. I'd like to learn how to throw clay sometime."

They moved in line like a company.

The truck started on the first try.

CHAPTER 42

FROM A LONG WAY DOWN

We are not survivors of a civil war.

We survive our love

Because we go on

Loving.

–June Jordan, "Grand Army Plaza"

Lolita and I arrived at Johnny's shop as the sun was going down over the low hills that peppered the world to the north. She'd asked me how I could possibly know where to go without mountains to use as reference and I said I wasn't sure, I just knew. Maybe I could smell my way around like the dogs.

We'd been to the hospital in Lafayette that Auntie had mentioned and were told that they could offer us no information, that too many people, the police included, had been there looking to talk to Mr. Cobb and he simply wasn't there. I'd stood in front of the receptionist, my mind reeling with possibilities, trying to control my rage, when Lolita came up from behind and put her tiny brown hand in mine. She spoke to me in Spanish, said please sit down and relax, she was going to look for a bathroom. "*Por favor, siéntese señor* Phin. *Voy a buscar un baño. Por favor, que todo va a estar bien.*" She would ask around.

The way she moved toward me, her eyes offering messages, the language choice, I sat down and closed my eyes, trying to piece together what-if's and could-be's as Lolita moved in the direction of a long hallway, quickly peeking in every room as she did.

In quieting my eyes, I must've fallen asleep because when I awoke fifteen minutes later, a small Mexican women in a soiled nurse's uniform stood before me with Lolita.

"Mr. Phin?" The spoke quietly so no one could hear. "The patient John Cobb has been moved to the big new hospital in Baton Rouge. Some famous surgeons came this morning along with a man who looked just like you, only older and smelling like fish. The hospital cannot say anything, sir. It comes from an important man in the government." The nurse winked, then giggled, and said we'd better go.

"Lolita!" I started to say as she put a finger to my lips and guided me to the door.

"How did you...?"

"The culture of Hispanic workers knows no silence when truth is necessary, my sleepy friend." And then she whispered a few other things in my ear that did not go unnoticed by my sleepy and surprised brain.

We fed the dogs and began to drive east on Interstate 10. As much as I wanted to find Johnny, news of the "famous surgeons" had buoyed my spirits; the "important man in the government" could only be Jed Riot. Would it be okay to detour, to stop for the night? Who would be at the hospital in Baton Rouge? I wondered. The people around Johnny must have come together for him, but they weren't the staying together type. These were good men, the ones I'd met when last at Johnny's place, but given a field of freshly fallen snow, they'd just as soon put on a pair of boots and walk across it than be content to look at the white-carpeted stillness.

Part of me was hell-bent for Baton Rouge, a place in which I'd always had a love/hate relationship. It seemed as if it was New Orleans-in-training; trying hard to attain the music, the gaiety, the unbridled craze of its northern cousin-city.

But the town attracted too many that'd leave their code, their integrity and their truth at the county line.

Lolita offered to drive and told me she drove her Papa's truck into town all the time to pick up groceries and mail. She even knew how to work the clutch and three-on-the-tree.

"You have a driver's license?" I asked.

"I am an American citizen, remember? I was born in Texas. I know how to drive and I feed the policeman of Cortez. Is that a license, Phin?"

"It ought to be," I told her, and then remembered that if I was to be pulled over and a background check done on me, I might show up as deceased, a warrior gone dead without fanfare, a morphing of the idea of an "unsung hero" into oxymoron. A frown came over my mouth and Lolita saw it.

"This disappoints you, Phin?"

"No, no," I apologized, "I was just thinking that there are costs for leaving the world, though I would still do it again." I tried to offer something in my eyes, but she wanted an explanation and there wasn't a way for me to tell the whole story right while I tried to keep the Buick between the white lines and my eyes from closing.

"I'll explain the whole thing when we can sit down and I can give it and you the attention they both deserve."

"It's okay with me. I wouldn't have come along if I knew you weren't a real person. I know you must have stories inside of stories and laughter inside of pain. There's no rush, Phin. There will be time if there is supposed to be time. It's dark now and you're tired and my license to drive is no good in this part of America. Do you think we should stop and rest or keep going to see Senor Cobb and your father in Baton Rouge?"

"My father!" The car drifted across the center line and I pulled the big wheel to get it straight again. "What makes you think my father is with Johnny?"

"The other cleaning ladies tell me that Senor Cobb left in an ambulance with the doctors from out of town and the man in the uniform and the older man looking like an older you but smelling of fish. I whispered these things to you when we left the hospital in such a hurry." She was not angry, just anxious to tell me her thoughts. "Who else can look like you and smell like fish?"

I tried not to let my voice get ahead of my thoughts but it was no use.

"These other ladies you spoke with, they saw me, or saw my father in me?"

"Of course, Phin, that is their hobby, their job, their right as citizens of two worlds but no country—to watch and hear and feel what happens in the hospital."

"Do you think they heard the man's name spoken, the fishy one?"

"Oh, Mister Phin, now you are testing me. It all happened very quickly."

Lolita furled her brow and pushed up her lips as if trying to push more blood to the brain and help her remember. "Okay, yes, here is something," she continued, very proud of her self. "One of them who was called the sergeant and the other one's name rhymed with Mary, like Jesus' mother. That is all I can be sure. I am sorry, Phin, but at least we know that Senor Cobb is likely awake now, eh? That has to be a good thing."

My mind reeled and spun, unable to crystallize on any one scenario. Famous surgeons, cops, soldiers, government offices; and quite possibly Harry was back and with Johnny. It had to be the Riots. Jed would've pulled in some key markers, but he was getting old. Did he have that many left?

No, Dickey had to be involved as well, making a few calls on behalf of his father, exercising The Code, ridding himself of his normalcy, shedding the cloak that covered and protected him since we were kids. The thought warmed my blood and I felt a kind of pride in my little town that had been absent since I'd come back from the war and seen all the new condominiums being built so close to the water that a full moon tide and strong southwester might push the ocean right into the living room.

And Lolita, she had surprised me, or maybe not. I was moving toward a feeling for her that scared me a bit. But not enough to run away from or deny. I was happily confused, satisfied to see that there was still a possibility of some kind of tenderness. Still, she both frightened and thrilled me.

The pieces were falling together like bits of rain collecting in a small pool that had room to grow into a lake big enough to dunk your head under.

"Lolita," I put my hand on her shoulder without even thinking about it, but then recoiled slightly embarrassed, but not enough to pull back. "If you are ever caught in a rip current, let it take you out and then swim parallel to the shore. Don't fight the water trying to swim straight in. The ocean will always win."

"Is that my first lesson in how to swim, Phin?"

"Your first, yes," And then I added, "I'm glad you came along."

"You should never swim alone, Senor Davis. Always take a friend."

We laughed, slightly unnerved in the quickly-growing comfort with each other and the dogs barked from the back seat, unaccustomed to the sound. I asked Lolita is she liked crawfish.

"Baby *langostino*? I have heard they are delicious."

It was decided then. I made a three-lane jump in the Buick toward the off ramp to Breaux Bridge, self-claimed "Crawfish Capitol of the World."

That's when I saw the flashing red lights in the rearview mirror.

I pulled over slowly and stayed in the car, searching my small wallet for some form of ID.

"License and registration, please," the cop said matter-of-factly.

I handed him my expired and fake driver's license, my expired and real military ID, and opened the glove box in hopes that Mike Greer had some proof of ownership in this old car. I found an envelope and took out what looked like a bunch of registration papers. From the corner of my eye I could see that

Lolita had pulled her blouse down low enough for the tops of her breasts to easily be seen by the officer.

The officer took the documents, looked past me, and smiled at my passenger. He'd said he'd be right back.

"We're fucked," I said under my breath and waited for the streak of good fortune to end.

"How long you been back, sir?" It was the cop.

"Excuse me?"

"How long have you been back in the world? Back from the war?"

"I, uh, geez, sorry, officer, you caught me by surprise. About eight months, I reckon, give or take a few nightmares."

"I came back in '66, served under Colonel Greer in the 101st. Small world, ain't it? T'would be just like him to register this old beauty to the U.S. Government. A rascal, he was."

"I'm sorry, officer. You're telling me this car is registered to a Colonel Mike Greer and it's a government vehicle?"

"Yes, sir, it is...the U.S. of Texas. There's a note right here on his stationary authorizing the use to one Corporal Phin Davis for official military duties, which," he nodded at Lolita and winked at me, then laughed long and loud, "you seem to be carrying out the colonel's orders in fine style."

"What are the chances that...," and my mouth kept moving but words no longer came out."

"Corporal, I'm not a particularly religious man, for a Texan or a cop, but I know Colonel Greer from Lubbock and I believe that you do as well. Seems to me we Vietnam vets oughta cover each other, less'n friendly fire kills us when the gooks couldn't."

The pool was filling quicker than I could count the rain drops.

"You ought to get that license renewed when ya'll get back to Panama City. But far as I'm concerned, you two have a good evening and keep on your side of the road if you can, sir."

I nodded, not knowing what to say, and the officer got in his squad car and drove away spitting gravel from the right rear tire, tossing a wave and, if I saw it correctly, a devilish smile.

"Lolita," I said, a little scared at my suggestion, "I think we should stop somewhere for the night."

"That's a good idea, Phin," she looked at me with those brown, swimming-pool eyes as she pulled her blouse back up, but only part of the way. "You need some rest, I think."

✳ ✳ ✳

Blackie and Gerald were the first to arrive at the shop. In the few days that it had been unattended, loads of pine, mostly 2x6s in lengths of eight and ten feet, were starting to stack up on the loading dock. And even though the shop was in the poor section of town, security was never a concern.

Taped to the front door was an envelope. It had "Doc G" written on the outside. Below the note was an old black women wrapped in a shawl, her head buried in the cave of her thick arms. Blackie and Gerald approached her and she threw off her coat in a violent swirl.

"I killed him, didn't I?"

Auntie spoke into the bottle, moving it to her lips like it was a microphone at a church meeting.

"I had me the gun in my hand and all I had to do was put one in his ear instead of his leg. Then my Johnny would be here, sitting at his desk, wearing those old ratty overalls he always did, smoking that pipe, laughing at my stupid jokes." Auntie took a long slow pull from the bottle and as an afterthought, offered it to the two men in front of her.

"They closed the café down, you know," she spoke in an almost wistful tone now, the two men bending down to help. "Damn cops put yellow tape all around it like someone was murdered. I don't understand it. After ya'll took my Johnny away they just kept coming, all sorts of men asking questions; most of them mean, too."

Blackie tried to interject, but Auntie kept on. "Only nice man I seen was a White boy in a fancy uniform who come around yesterday. Say he growed up here. I believe him, too. Say he gonna see what he can do about getting the place reopened. Ain't never be the same without my Johnny setting there, though." Her voice trailed off and her head retreated into her cave. "Nothing be the same."

"Auntie," Blackie put his arm on hers and peeled the thick woven shawl away and leaned his little head in close, the spiral of curly brown hair falling into his eyes. "This man is Gerald, Auntie, he works in a hospital. He went and saw Johnny last night and spoke to him. He's not dead. We're going to read this envelope right here on the door and then we're going to go in and call the hospital to see how he is. Do you understand me, Auntie?"

Gerald stood up and took the short letter out of the envelope and began to read it. Behind him, Snare pulled the truck up behind Gerald's car and the crew leaped out of the back along with a couple of dogs who'd been invited because Johnny's dogs were always invited. Hunter and Leroy were the first to get to Auntie and helped her up.

"Let's hear it, McReady," Tom-Tom gushed out the words they were all thinking.

Gerald, who had learned not to give anything away in his expressions, read it aloud:

Hey Doc G,

Sounds like we just missed quite a party at the pub. Cops are trying to put together how a White man died in a Black neighborhood and another one disappeared, but the only witness they could get says it was pure self-defense. No weapon, no motive, no trace. Sounds like a couple of guys from out of town didn't like the service and took it out on the waiter, eh Doc?

You all right? I'm worried about you, doc. You need a sponsor in this town. I hope you found that Blackie kid you were telling me about. Now, check this one out, doc—I met the famous Johnny Cobb. Turns out we have a whole passel full of mutual friends. He invited me to come work for him when I get out of the Corps. Said he needed a marketing guy, said he could sell a lot more beds if he had a guy with panache, whatever that shit is. Reckon I'll see if I can order some from the PX. Other thing he said, doc, was that I didn't have to wait until the Corps got out of me.

Here's the official skinny: Cobb's doing good. Couple of hot-shot docs were brought in on a called-in marker; part of the code I was fixing to explain to you on the bus. They're moving him out of this small town body shop over to the new hospital in New Orleans. We just stopped by to leave a note for you. Pass the word, eh, doc? And get your skinny ass down here. I'll show you some life worth living in the Orleans. Oh yeah, I met Johnny's 'brother,' Harry Davis. I believe you mentioned that his son also had the pleasure of being a guest at the VA under your watch.

Man, I thought I had some interesting friends. I can't keep track of the players without a scorecard. Harry don't talk a lot, but I'm getting him to open up. First thing I said was he smelled like fish.

Now get on over here. The Pabst is getting warm.

And maybe yawl ought to consider joining the 50's and get telephones.

Yours truly, Sgt. L.D, of the U.S.M.C.

Auntie was the first to speak. "Praise the Lord."

Blackie was grinning from ear to ear and for the first time in many years, he found no words at all.

Leroy was nodding softly to himself and fingering the long, thin blade in its sheath strapped to the inside of his right thigh.

Hopper said, "Ah man, I knew the old nigga' wouldn't die. It would ruin his reputation."

Strider said he could've handled the two dickheads all by himself. "You guys get all the fun. The next ones are mine."

Snare was casing the edges of the building and watching for cops. "You're right, surf-star, you're up to bat."

Hunter held onto Auntie and gently took the bottle away from her.

"You might as well take this, too," and she pressed the .22 caliber hand gun into the back pocket of the former medic.

Gerald, for his part, watched the intercourse of raw life unfolding in front of him. Blackie had been right. Gerald's pots and his patients had become his people, fulfilling everything that he'd asked of his family and all that they had denied him. His M dream had been showing him this for five years, Sgt. DuPuis for five days. McReady could not control the river, no matter if it was filled with champagne or blood.

And so he jumped right in and let it carry him.

BOOK 6

HIGHWAYS OF REDEMPTION

CHAPTER 43

SO CLOSE: IN PHIN'S WORDS

Everybody laughed at his misadventures, but nobody laughed at his intentions.

–Cervantes, speaking about Don Quixote

The concept of a motel seemed foreign to me. Unless the weather was bad and a man didn't have a blanket or a friend to call, there really was no reason to pay good cash money to sleep in a motel. But I was with a woman and something was shifting inside me, like tectonic plates. I wanted Lolita to be comfortable and even though she would've been just fine under the stars, the edges of the dogs providing enough warmth, there were emotions that were rising to the surface that I couldn't deny. They felt good. They felt right. And so, I embraced them.

We pulled over the old car that my curious new friend, the apparent Col. Mike Greer from the 101st Airborne, who'd registered the car to the government for reasons I didn't want to wrangle with just yet. Mike Greer a colonel; imagine that.

It must've been a part of something he was doing that was good, that was truthful to people who could fight their way up through the rhetoric and steer the manure, see things as they really were so that you could set about making them as they really ought to be. His illusiveness was making sense now as I began to drop my guard and float on the breeze, my mind moving back and forth between wanting to know his reasons and not caring because I had faith in his history, a belief in where he had come from.

I'd see him again; there would be a time if the shape of the future willed it. We'd drink tequila and he'd tell me about it and Lolita would laugh about the policeman and I'd tell the story about Jessica's haircut and all would be right with the world again—the shape of the future willing.

But it seemed I needed a space between what was and what could be before I could go back to what had been. I needed to be secure in my own shape to engage that time—that war— and then finish the puzzle before setting the kerosene and flame to it.

Nope, I was allowing warm and fuzzy stuff to return on the wings of a girl I'd met before I knew the difference between men and women.

But there was an odd kind of fear that came along with the shiny fluff of joy. What if she didn't have these same kinds of feelings? What if I disappoint her? Would the memory of Lonnie get in the way? Did I know how to be "with" a woman?

I was struck, blindsided by the realization that I was in my mid-twenties and I'd never even had a deep or lasting physical relationship with a woman. There was a handful of nights in Saigon, but I only remember the arrivals, not the exits. Nothing other than the stories I'd fabricated about my Lonnie for the men in my squad because that's what men in war have to do to escape the horrible reality of war.

I had taken other soldiers into thick dark jungles with sensuous-looking fruit waiting to be picked, with soft leaves and moist rain that became perfume when it danced on the flowers that grew in the highlands. I had gone looking for an enemy, not because I wanted to, not because I hated them, or because I was ordered to. No, it was because I wanted *my* life and those around me to go on. Simple Darwinism? Not quite. I was in the jungles of Vietnam because there were more reasons that put me there than had kept me away. And once I was there, more reasons to return fire than to run away. To be an *ongoing man.*

My hunt for the men who wanted to end my life was a form of procreation, an obscene metaphor for sex.

✳ ✳ ✳

I paid the man at the desk with the last of the wad of cash that Lonnie's dad had given me in Durango with help from Col. Greer's glove box envelope. "This will only get you a start, kid," they'd both said in different ways. "After it runs out, you're on your own."

The motel attendant counted the cash, slipped a five in his pocket, looked out the window at our car and said, "Nice Buick, but them dogs ain't allowed in the rooms." I told him they'd barely seen the inside of any building, they'd be okay out in the car. He told me they were expecting rain and I ought to get that top up, less'n I want to be driving a swimming pool in the morning.

I agreed and, with his help, we wrestled the thing up to the creak and groan of tired steel and rusty joints and Mike Greer's warning about driving with the top up. Lonnie and I took our one small bag each out of the back seat and put the key into the motel door. It opened into a single small room, one small desk, one single lamp, one sink in the corner, one door that opened to a tiny shower and bathroom, a little TV on a little chest of drawers with long rabbit ears that grew from the TV like a giant insect...and one double bed.

I suppose she could sense my discomfort in looking at that one bed and what it might signify and asked me if I wanted to rest, that she would go find us something to eat.

"Phin, you are driving. Your eyes are *muy cansado*, too tired. You rest and I'll come back with something for us. And I'll walk the dogs. They need *comida*; they need to eat some, too. It's okay?"

It was the way that she said that: It's okay? That's what got me. She was giving me permission to deal with my thoughts about all things, about her. There was no question about it—she was off to run her errand and I was to rest my eyes on the big double bed and think about what each of us might want or not want, where the transcendence of platonic friendship began and the ageless carnality between a man and a woman ended.

It's that wonderfully strange period at the beginning moments of a relationship, the palpable electricity when you look for things to say on your way to being completely comfortable in the silence of each other's presence. Most couples blast right through it on their way to something beyond, some carrot they think will be better when you know so much about each other that it hurts. But speed kills.

The best part is always the very first hours, that very first full and slow day. The best lovers, the longest lovers, know this.

Why *I* knew this, I wasn't sure. Johnny and Grayfalls had spoken to me of the women in my future, I'd read voraciously in the subject, (on accident), and I'd seen it in my folks. But I'd never really felt it until that exact moment when Lolita stepped out the hollow door of the tiny fifteen-dollar-per-night motel and turned her head in such a way, smiling in such a way. Then it all became very clear what they all had referred to in their long, rambling musings on how it feels between a man and a woman when it's right.

It could've happened with Lonnie, might've happened. But Lonnie, as much as she'd meant to me in youth, in dreams, in lies and in promises, was torched along with villages and the memories of men who died in violent ways because other men couldn't speak in non-violent tongues.

The firestorm that I had set when I drove away from my home, my friends, my mother, my pier, and my father—my foot still desiring the toes that it had left behind—was itself a strange fire, consumed with discretion, never quite erasing it all. I imagined a wall of flames moving up a canyon, fanned by hot, dry winds, the breath of the devil himself. It moved so fast that it barely had time to singe let alone destroy anything. It was like burning your morning toast because you went in to take a leak—you can't believe that short, white-hot heat could make something look so bad, but with the dark grains scraped away, it was a decent breakfast. Still, how many of us would throw it away out of convenience and ignorance and the want of perfect-looking bread if not a perfect memory of things gone down?

Lonnie was scraped away.

Lolita left for food and I fell asleep on the lumpy motel bed with the smell of stale sweat and mothballs and ancient perfume from a thousand liaisons hanging in the room. The last thing I remembered was someone untying my shoes. And then the memories came.

✳ ✳ ✳

We had marched down a long narrow canyon, the trail thinning as the walls closed in on us from either side. Up ahead the opening called, even beaconed us, as if some natural or unnatural force was pulling the men in my squad further down. The high walls were new to our diminished group. Most of our recon and engagement was done in thin, even wiry jungles, or open rice-paddy-lined fields. We knew this terrain existed. It was no secret. But few ops had been proven high enough *enemy killed* numbers to justify official maneuvers this far north, this far west.

We'd set out thirteen days ago, a final sweep of an area that intelligence had thought might contain a small camp of POWs, downed flyboys that the VC had moved out of sight, off the bargaining table. With the treaty set to be signed in Paris in six days, the combat information center—the CIC—wanted as much hard data on the POW issue as it could gather. It was one giant poker game, with human chips tossed into the pot as red, yellow, and white.

Our captain had known it, the sergeant, too...hell, all eight men in the squad knew what was at stake. And secretly, silently, we'd all replaced those images of prisoners' torn bodies and scarred minds with our own. It wasn't hard. Cut-and-paste shit. Tradable commodities. One man for one white chip, one soul for a blue.

So with six days left and eight men looking for any evidence, we descended into the valley on our own volition, believing the maps that said it was only four clicks long before opening up again. We did it knowing that some other force was at work. One of the men called it *Joss*, that universal Chinese term; one said it was God's work; one said he was marching to his demise; another said he'd be a hero, finally a hero. Four others said nothing, at least not that the others could hear.

We lost the captain in a hit-and-run ambush, the sergeant to a sniper. Two down, quick and dirty, and then a sweet silence coming in behind it. Or maybe just the distant white noise of the stream that ran down the valley, the hypnotizing flow of water as it moved from its origins in the cloudy heavens to the deepest part of the ocean where selected pieces of the molecules diverted to waiting fields that grew the rice that sustained life through the death of war.

Just one big damn circle, I dreamt, as I lay on that hotel bed—molecules of the men finding their way against heavy odds, finding those tilled and ready valley floors where the women of the village worked the fields with trowel in hand and egg in womb...waiting.

With the captain and the sergeant dead and hastily buried, I was in charge now, a simple corporal with no medals, no valor other than the shit made up by others who saw something that they wanted to see in themselves, but were afraid of what else might show up in the mirror. Unshackling visions can release all shades of contrast, especially white on white.

And so they followed me; we final six with six days left in the war, only four clicks to the mouth of the canyon, another two to the pick-up landing zone, for a total of six kilometers to walk. Not even four miles. Three sixes and a wake-up call. Home free. Back to the world. And so we marched deeper into my motel dream.

"Phin, wake up, you are having the bad dreams."

It was Lolita, back from the walk in the heavy rain.

"Phin, you are thrashing about this little bed like a fish on the dock. Here, wake up and have some of this sandwich I got for you."

No, I told her. I had to lead the men out of the valley. We had to know if there were others left behind, hidden from the views of the shadow men sitting at the long mahogany tables already sipping red wine from Bordeaux, fortunate fathers of fabricated 4-F sons.

Let me go back to sleep, I asked of her, something waits at the bottom of this valley lined with mossy trees like curly hairs.

✳ ✳ ✳

We moved down the valley as the sun followed us, knowing there would be no place to camp, no place to rest or rephrase our intent. Once you're in deep and moving at a steadily increasing decline, you cannot stop the momentum or the flow of gravity. The energy moves as if in concentric circles spinning closer and tighter into itself, into the center where something wonderful, something profound waits. But you don't know what it is. That would frighten you away. The anticipation is a childhood Santa Claus coming down the chimney: you might suspect that it's not what you think it is, but you stay with your image just the same.

There had been no resistance in the past two hours. No fire, no sound, no sight of anything indicating that any living soul had passed through these parts. There were noises, birds maybe, or tigers, or animals yet to be given a name, screeches and wails and howls and yaps that could only emanate from souls that existed in a world other than the one the six of us desperately clung to. The air was dense and musky; it had a personality all its own. And the smells were not of death, but of life in all its densely powerful nerve endings.

I sensed the end of that canyon and wanted to throw myself into its perfect, asymmetrical abyss; wanted to leave my mark on its walls, carve my name in the trunks of its trees, fire my seed into its fertile soil. But just when we could see the mouth and the flatlands opening up before us as free range, and two thousand meters to a called-in extrication we came upon a falling of the waters, the trail's end, the sixty-foot jump into depths unknown.

I wasn't ready to make the jump; couldn't lead my men into this pool without knowing the depths. Was there another way down? That's when I woke up.

I saw an image of a woman kneeling beside the bed, her head bent in prayer, silhouetted against the single light that shown outside the door to the single room with the single double bed. I heard the faint sounds of whispered and breathy requests: Dear God, please this, dear God, please that. So many dear Gods.

I'd heard these kinds of prayers before, mostly when we were taking heavy fire and men who'd boasted of previous conquests had the reality of Russian-made AK-47 bullets whizzing by their Ivy League ears and sloganed helmets.

"Just get me out of this shit, dear God, and I'll never smoke pot or sleep with a hooker again. I promise."

But the sound emanating from the edge of the bed was different; it had the tone not of fear, but of confidence, as if the voice knew it was possible, even likely; she just needed to make the request official.

"Lolita," I spoke into the darkness, "is that you?"

"It is all of us, Phin, we are here in this room: your dogs, your fears, my God, my prayers, your dreams, your men, my past, your past."

"What about our future?" I mumbled through the time lapse.

"We are strangers, Phin, who knew each other very well when we were very young. There is only one way down."

I felt for her hair and it was wet, like she had been walking under a waterfall for many years. I pulled her onto the bed and held her close to me, stroking her wet hair until she fell asleep.

My mind was drifting with the tide back to the Nam, as if the devil himself was willing it. But I fought him and beat him and stayed right where I was, right where I was folding myself into the body of another who cared, who wouldn't defy, deny, crucify, or put a bullet in my heart. I put my head into the crook of her neck and could smell the world she had come from: the muddy waters of the Rio Grande; the spring bloom on the desert flowers; the vats of vegetable oil that fried the beans in her father's *grande cocina*; the perfume that her padre, Jose, had brought back for her from his trips to Albuquerque; the stale residue of beer that coated the reclaimed microphone where she sang old Mexican ballads, and '60s songs of protest disguised as patriotism on Saturday nights when the place was packed with local ranchers and cowboys and tourists and passersby, because Jose's was the only place for miles…the best place for food and grog and camaraderie in the Four Corners.

All that was all in her wet hair.

And when my hand wandered down her shoulders that were covered by an old shirt of mine she had found in my bag, feeling the strength of her back through the cotton and mended tears, I could sense her slight shutters as my fingers moved from seam to seam.

Just before I slept, I placed my mouth on her neck and tasted the depth of her past, the commitment to all that she was. It was salt and dust and a clean, auburn world, a world with an ancient history beginning in Barcelona and existing now halfway between Alexandria and Lecompte, Louisiana. She tasted real. She was more alive in her slumber than any waking man I'd met before he was due to be shot in-country.

That was something.

Lolita pressed her body closer into mine until I couldn't tell where hers began and mine ended. Outside the rain fell even harder until it moved sideways, pelting the single-pane windows like tribal drums, ceremonial reverberations that thumbed and bent the glass when the biggest drops were driven by the wind.

I imagined her body was moving in time to the rain and I pressed into the sky until it seemed that I had gone through her, past her, into the parking lot, out onto the road, back on the C-130 transport, and was in the Nam again, the rain pelting us like salt pellets shot at kids when they raided a neighbor's garden.

The salt turned into lead and the stinging brought blood instead of welts. I reached for Lolita's hair again and felt that it was almost dry. It felt like soft, dependable rope, and I stroked it until I knew it would hold.

Then I found a long, sturdy vine and told the men it would hold. But I had to jump. I'd see them on the other side.

"C'mon men," I hailed the last of those who'd had faith in me, "We're almost home, the strands are thick and the water deep, the center will hold. We're so close, things will not fall apart. Anarchy is for the weak."

CHAPTER 44

MINING THE TRUTH

Intellectual disgrace

Stares from every human face

And the seas of pity lie

Locked frozen in the eye.

–W.H. Auden, *In Memory of W.B. Yeats*

Johnny got four days at the big hospital with all the well-heeled docs and sweet, South-talking nurses checking up on him. Harry got his scrubbed-in shower at the physical therapy center next door to the big hospital and checked into a small motel with Grace near the hospital. There was even an outdoor pool that he looked at for the longest time and then finally entered, opened his eyes under water, and realized that he might be closer to home. Grace appeared to be fighting the good fight back toward normalcy, her words and thoughts coalescing or conflicting by the hour. She would repeat herself, ask about Phin, look in the mirror, and wonder. Grace had been split in half by the stroke and the sides of the brain were not so much out of synch as they were unknown to each other. She would ask Harry to take her to see Johnny. Then she would remind her husband that Gillie was dead, Phin was MIA, and "You, Harry...

you ain't so well." Grace Davis had no time for one more sick person. And so Harry decided to take her home.

✳ ✳ ✳

Blackie and Gerald arrived at the hospital before the posse of veteran-worker devotees and sat with Cobb for an entire afternoon discussing deviant-opening chess moves and just who Woodward's "Deep Throat" character might be as he and Bernstein unraveled the evil duplicity of Richard Millhouse Nixon—and if Gerald Ford had any idea of who the Khmer Rouge was capable of killing. Johnny was anxious to leave the place, but he realized that he was a guest of the Southern Code and to simply get dressed and leave would affect Jed and Dickey Riot's ability to use it in the future—because always there would be someone who could benefit from a phone call, a marker called in, a favor requested. So, Johnny stayed and asked as many questions about the state of medical care as he could think of while Gerald ventured into Louisiana's capitol city for gumbo and "cultural de-volution," as Blackie called it, and wondered how the local university, LSU, could create the mascot name of an animal found more commonly in Southeast Asia than Southeast USA.

On that second afternoon Harry sensed that Cobb might want some quiet time and asked Blackie if he'd take the dogs for a walk with him before he fetched Grace and headed back to Panama City Beach. He could use a beer before finding Grace in the little hotel near the hospital. That left Johnny alone with the tall, intriguing nurse with the taller Afro that sat on her head like a brown globe of the world.

"Ya'll ask a lot of questions 'bout what goes where and who does this and if this medicine works the same as the other ones." She was the Black nurse from Mississippi that Johnny had befriended. And she answered most of his queries openly and honestly.

"Why do you need to know all this stuff? You planning of being a doctor someday?"

"Nah," Johnny played along with her, both using diction well-below their intellect. "Just interested in knowing what's going into my arm in this here tube and if'n it will make me sleepy, angry, horny, or happy."

"Truth is," the nurse spoke while reading a chart and propping up her patient with pillows, "most patients just sit there and take the treatment, never question the whys and how's."

"You think that's right," Johnny asked, "to want to know? Or should I just be happy that someone is looking after me?"

"What you think I'm gonna say to that?" She smiled and a wide row of white teeth reflected the afternoon light streaming in from the window.

"You're going to say that every patient has the right to know exactly what the treatment is, the illness they face, and the consequences associated with his or her malady." Johnny had put on his didactic face. There was little room for maneuvering when he wore it.

"You would be rather correct, Mr. Cobb, in your assumption of my reply. Now, would you like me to assess your current condition?"

"I'd be disappointed if you refused, Miss..."

"It's Dickinson, Nurse Randi Dickinson."

"Okay, Nurse Dickinson," Johnny had dropped his tone and was doing his best to keep the nurse from leaving. "Will I live?"

Randi Dickinson reached for the stethoscope around her neck, placed the ends into her ears, and set the small drum against Johnny Cobb's chest. She held it there for what seemed to Johnny, an extended period before his excitement got the best of him. As he opened his mouth he noticed a strange looking tattoo on the inside of Nurse Randi's forearm.

"Should I make funeral or wedding arrangements?" he blurted out, embarrassed after he'd said it.

"Both, Mr. Cobb," the nurse was dead serious. "Your heart has suffered much death, but it anticipates much life. The only real factor is the time before and after; but mostly the period in between."

Johnny regarded her as he had Ruth those first days they'd met so many years ago. "You can tell all this from listening to a man's heart?"

"Oh, no, Mr. Cobb. It's all things. I see the way you speak to your friends and the way you carry yourself and many other factors that I do not have time to explain at the moment." She gathered up her charts and brushed a few strands of hair behind her ears. "But I doubt we will have much of a chance to speak. I assume that you will be gone by tomorrow this time."

"But you said there is importance in the time before and after." Johnny knew she was right and refused to deny it.

"We shall see what falls in between, Mr. Cobb." And as she marched down the hall to carry on her duties she repeated just loud enough for him to hear, "We shall see how your heart handles the in-between."

On her heels in walked two men looking like two faces from a "before and after" picture advertisement. One looked his age, only older; the other could have been a teenager with facial hair of a thirty year-old with good skin. They were cut from the same something, the same past at least, but not the same future.

"Well, well," said the older man whose presence brought an immediate lifting of his spirits still hovering near the ceiling where Nurse Randi had left them. "This will be the first and last time I can rise above your Black ass."

"Aw geez, Jed," Johnny feigned hurt, "you really know how to keep a man down. I've been in this prison you sent me to for nearly thirty-six hours and have only met one woman I could fall in love with. Besides, even when I worked for you on the pier I could look down on your redneck, honky head from my crane."

Jed laughed and then moved his chair in close to the bed.

"How are you, Johnny? Really?"

"I'm good, Jed. Other than this thump on my noggin', I don't have anything to complain about." Johnny sat up and looked around the room at the starkness, the sterility, and then out the single window where he caught the edge of a tall sycamore tree in the distance. "I want to thank you," he stared first at Jed then Dickey, "and whomever else you pulled in to get me this solid medical treatment. I do appreciate it."

And then Johnny's eyes went back to the window and the tree. His eyes focused on the thin branches way up high and he could see them swaying back and forth in the wind as if they were waving at him, signaling him.

"Yep, I never would've imagined the way things have started coming back together after so many years of coming apart. There is something to it all that I haven't figured out. And I doubt I'll live long enough to put the pieces together." He was going to say he dreamt of Ruth last night, but changed his mind.

Jed, who was never comfortable in any of Cobb's pontifications, nodded his head, his mind already on something else. But Dickey, who'd known Johnny Cobb as a kind of mentor and older uncle to his boyhood pal, Phin, and had once asked Phin if he understood all the complicated things the old man was talking about, found himself strangely attracted to the words.

"Mr. Cobb," Dickey was surprised at his confidence. "Don't you think that sometimes the answers come easier when you just quit looking for them?"

Johnny hid his own surprise but his deep brown eyes that were sandwiched between the salt-and-pepper beard and the white bandages on his head, looked inquisitively at the younger man.

"I'd be inclined to agree with that, Dickey. Yes, I would. But I reckon I'm like one of those sharks that need to keep moving, maintaining the flow of water through its gills to stay alive. If I'm not looking for something, or considering the possibilities of something else, I'd likely just drown like the shark that falls asleep."

Jed stood up to look out the window, turned around and considered his careful son speaking in riddles with an older Black man he'd known for many years. Johnny could see that he wanted to say something meaningful, but might not know just how to do it.

"Say what's on your mind, Jed. Or at least tell me why you been so kind to me over the years; why you called in some heavy debts to get me this care."

"Well," Jed, stroked his chin and spoke to the pane of glass, his words reflected off the light and what he was thinking. "I'm glad you're gonna be alright. Be a shame if something as stupid as a beer bottle killed you, that and something, someone even dumber, wielding it."

Jed knew all the history of Cobb, all about Ruth and the *Ruth Henry*, his longstanding friendship with Harry and the boy, and the land that was lost. Jed didn't miss much of anything that occurred in and around Panama City Beach and its own essential and extended past.

"You're a good man, Cobb," Jed continued, moving back away from the window, "A hard worker; you done a lot for a lot of folk. And I been happy to call you a friend. Now, I can't say that you been treated fairly your whole life. And it ain't on account of anything you did or didn't do."

Dickey could sense his dad's awkwardness; something he was not accustomed to sensing. "Just say it pop, say what you feel."

Jed looked at his kid and a river went through his blood, mostly warm but with spots of tepidness he couldn't identify. "Well, truth is Johnny, I'm apologizing for the rest of the Lower Thirteen states, not for the fact that you're Black, and not that a lot of folk didn't like it when we were younger and your people were getting more rights, but what ain't right is that they don't like you much more now. And you still ain't got all the rights. So, maybe the fact could be that I've been trying to make it up to every Black man ever been held down by doing what I can to lift you up when I can, because I can."

Jed walked back to the window and didn't say anything more. And Johnny, for the first time in many years, couldn't think of what else might even be close to the right thing to say. And so he said nothing. But the quiet between the men was not uncomfortable. They knew it would pass, that things had to be said or unsaid.

"Pop," Dickey put his arm on his father. As much as he admired him, he couldn't recall the last time they had done anything more than shake hands. "Either you're saying it or I am. Johnny's gotta know."

"Son, I don't know what you're…"

"C'mon, Pop. I learned from the best. I made the calls, got the story. I learned from you. So, I know what you're gonna tell this man what he deserves to know."

Johnny, who was used to letting men have their say and work things out best they could, couldn't stand it anymore.

"I wish you'd both get the hell out outta the way and let the truth decorate this room with something real." And then he looked at Jed who seemed to be counting square tiles on the floor and to Dickey who began to speak slowly, without a pause.

"We were told that the Lafayette Police identified a Black man they'd shot and killed through his fingerprints. He'd been involved in the incident up at the place called *Auntie's*. His name was Charles Winters."

Johnny didn't ask any questions. His eyes just followed the tubes as they wove out of his veins and into the machines and bags and onto the racks and stands that sat waiting for another person who was sick or injured and who might come into the room and see the big sycamore or might see the white overhead light. Or after a spell, the pale horse.

Cobb put his hand on the cool sweating neck of Jed Riot and patted it as he would a tired dog, nodding. Dickey, sensing the inevitable, handed Johnny a sterile bandage from the table and told him to call if he needed anything.

Then, very calmly, Johnny removed all the needles and bandages from his arms, set them on the table, taped the smaller bandage in place, got dressed, and walked out into the sweet, moist night air of Baton Rouge. On his heels were the Riots; the three men moving purposely toward different directions on the compass as they passed through the hospital's exit.

Only Jed was thinking of how he could spin Johnny's premature exit in the direction of future ammunition.

There was the hint of rain in the air, but Johnny looked at the sky and sensed it wouldn't arrive for a few more hours. He heard the quiet of it all.

He thought of Old Grayfalls and what he'd said when he was going away to die in the low hills where he'd come from: "The wind will pass to places that I have been and the rain will fall on land you will walk. Keep a warm heart, young John," he'd said, "because behind it is an even warmer space."

It hadn't sounded like what his brother Ramsey had called "Injun speak." And it had stuck in the young Johnny's mind, soaked up like rain on the dry ground.

Johnny, looking for a vehicle, found Harry sitting at the cafe bar of the small motel he had checked into near the hospital. He was playing chess with Gerald and drinking coffee with tequila. They only seemed a little surprised to see him and didn't get up from their stools; just pulled one up for him.

Blackie was over in the corner near a small fireplace writing feverishly in his journal, making wide sweeps with his hands and wild gesticulations with his facial expressions when a certain thought or phrase came to mind. He didn't look up and probably wouldn't have recognized Cobb in any case, so deep into his work, he was.

Johnny said he needed to borrow the truck keys. And when Gerald said he'd take him anywhere he needed to go, that it would be better to have another person around him for a few more days, he declined. When he tried to insist, Harry put his hand on Gerald's knee and shook his head.

"Johnny, here's the keys. Just tell me where you're going."

"Lafayette. To bury a dead brother."

"I'm sorry, Johnny." Gerald had said it a thousand times before, always meaning the words.

"You want me to go with you?" Harry asked.

"No, you need to stay here and take your wife and boy home."

"What are you..."

"Phin's on his way here. And he's not alone."

Harry stood up, confused, excited, stunned.

"Did he call?"

"No, Ruth told me in a dream last night. She's speaking to me again."

Back at the hospital, Snare and Strider, Hunter and Hopper, Tom-Tom and Leroy, plus two girls they had picked up who'd been hitching just outside of Port Allen, had found their way to the Cobb-less room. They had missed the Riots by a few minutes and now sat tired and confused in the room that the front desk had told them would house their friend and boss, Johnny Cobb. Strider reached into his jacket pocket and found a warm beer, but a no-no-glance from Snare made him put it away.

Nurse Dickenson walked into the doorway and stopped when she saw the six men and two women lying about on the bed and the chair and the floor, speaking, wondering. Only Hunter was up and examining the IV needles and bandages removed by his friend.

"Johnny's not here anymore," Hunter finally said and turned around to explain just as the nurse walked in and immediately knew what had happened.

"Do you know where the patient, Mr. Cobb, has gone?" Hunter asked.

"It does seem," Dickenson said as she examined the discarded IV needles and bags from the trash, "that our Mr. Cobb had something on the landscape of his heart that wouldn't allow him anytime in between then and now."

Hopper, who'd taken a huge hit off the little pipe he'd found in the glove box of the truck, a nice chunk still in place, just before they entered the hospital, broke the odd silence.

"Whoa, am I in a time warp or has the patient had that big of an effect on you in less'n two days? He can make people talk like him, you know. You wouldn't be the first. Do you normally lose people that easily?"

"Did we get bad directions?" Asked Strider. "Is this the VA?" They all laughed but Hunter and Leroy, who looked at Strider and said, "No, asshole, this is the South and we got more shit to worry about than there being no big combers to surf on."

"Ah, c'mon," Hopper punched Leroy in the rips. "Maybe, Johnny's just gone down the hall to use the better bathroom. And it's waves, not combers."

"Well, we drove sixty-three minutes to find our main-man for these people to lose him in the jungle of hallways and rice-paddied dining rooms," someone said.

Nurse Dickenson smiled and set about cleaning up the mess. "Ya'll smoke that stuff, think it gives you a new sense of hope; now that's friendship if I've ever seen it." Then she walked over to Hopper, dropped the bandages, needle included, into his lap.

The two girls looked at each other and giggled, wishing they could sneak down for another toke. Tom-Tom buried his head in his hands, confused again, and wished he hadn't taken that last hit. Hunter picked the dirty bandages off of his friend and told the nurse that they'd all had enough bloody bandages for six of her hospitals. Leave it alone already.

"Mr. Cobb must've had a good reason to get up and leave. He's not out of the swamp by any means. My guess is that he went looking for someone just like the rest of you. Maybe you know. Because that trait doesn't take a brain surgeon to recognize. You're the one," the nurse said, looking at Strider, "who's lost." Her tone was even, non-threatening even with its knife-edged words. She walked over to the window and opened the shutters wide.

"And no, I barely knew the man. How well do you? Gentlemen, I'm not the kind of person to make room in my life for mistakes. Don't ever think Mr. Cobb's exit is a mistake."

Now the nurse turned up the volume but kept the level tone.

"I don't know him from Adam and I'm no damn Eve. But the way he up and left was no accident, no mistake. Now get the hell out of my hospital and go find him." And then the tone shifted to where Nurse Dickenson's eyes seemed to steal a hue of darkness and the hazel gave way to cold, gray stones.

"Goddamn you all and your holier-than-thou army shit."

She stayed in the room as if she was daring each to challenge her logic, her intuition, her years matriculating into an intelligent, single woman in the South, savvy beyond reproach, but suffering still because her skin was a shade of beautiful burnt sienna instead of a fleshy, peachy tan.

They all looked at Snare for support, each wondering if he would throw her against the wall or pretend she was air—nothing.

"The nurse is right; more'n right," he said while offering respect through the intent of his own eyes, hardened by death, softened by those who fought it.

"Get used to it. You can't act like you're over there when you're back here. What was the Nam, is still the Nam. Ya'all think we got away from it? Nah, it followed us home like a lost baby tiger. Raise it to be a lion or kill it. There are no zoos for what came home in our packs. This nurse didn't do no tour. Cobb didn't do no tour. But they been affected like cancer affects everyone who knew someone who been affected. Vietnam is cancer cells, man. It will mutate until they find a way to get cells to quit eatin' each other and start discussing how they can inhabit the same space. Which is fuckin' never."

It wasn't an afterthought; more like something he'd been saving up to say for as long as any of them had known the figure they called Snare.

"Getting' the shit beat outta you in the war is no different than getting the shit beat out of you at home. Only difference is," and Snare looked at Leroy with something close to compassion, "is that when you're Black and living in the South, you come to expect it. In the Nam, nothing could be expected. Far as I'm concerned, they're both equally insane. Guys like Leroy getting' fucked from both sides. Hell, VC, and the Klan both work at night. Only difference is one side trying to split a country apart and the other trying to put it together. Black silk and white cotton. Too bad they ain't like this nurse. Save a guy like me from having to kill."

Snare's eyes moved around the room like a camera, missing nothing. They stopped at the two girls and he asked them why the hell they weren't in school anyway.

"You know the funny thing?" He continued, methodically. "I'm not even a violent man. I never enjoyed killing Charlie. Charlie had balls. I did it because he killed my friends. An eye-for-an-eye thing."

Snare looked at Hunter who had been washing his hands at the sink for a long time. "Hey medic, you think that's how wars get started?" Hunter turned around and searched for something to dry his hands on before shaking them in the air, bits of water snowing around the room.

"Nope," he spoke to his speckled-reflection in the window. "But that's how they keep going."

"Hmm," Snare nodded and then added with enough conviction that everyone believed him. "Bet I'd get a rise outta hanging some fat old man running around with a pointy hat and a bed sheet. Yep, maybe just for a minute or two he'd dangle from a large magnolia tree while the moon hid in the branches and a cold spasm of his fear made him pee right through his wife's clean white sheet."

Snare got up to leave and put his hand out to shake with the nurse who took it without pause. And as he left the room, he said that cancer was just a genetic form of imperialism, oppression a social one. And that he wasn't even a violent man.

CHAPTER 45

LOVE IN A TIME OF CLOUDS

Many days passed, until not only the tongue was loosened, but something within oneself as well; then feeling suddenly broke through the strange fetters which had restrained it.

–Viktor Frankl, "Man's Search for Meaning"

When I opened my eyes in the morning, I wasn't sure where the world began and my dreams ended. I saw a fan on the ceiling with chipped paint, the ends curling up in tiny waves, and heard the thin click-click of the worn bearings as the fan spun around. It reminded me of the great Spanish and Portuguese explorers from the Fourteenth century who'd been convinced by the Roman and Anglican churches that the earth was the center of the universe and all planets rotated around it. And of course, the earth was as flat as the cracked and warped drywall ceiling.

But I wasn't at the center of that small motel universe, nor was the fan. It was the young woman lying next to me. She had the power to give life to me and to any propagation of the human species. It would've been easy for her. All she would've had to do at that point to accomplish both was to roll over and say, "Come to me, Phin."

She could deny both as well by getting out of bed, walking to the bathroom, locking the door, and getting dressed. It seemed almost too simple, this complete and total empowerment of one person over another; no different than when one soldier helped a prisoner with one hand, the other holding a .45mm pressed to his ear creating the imbalance. Was life and death that reduced? And if there were a myriad of other existential factors behind the obvious in any moment, what were they?

I watched the fan go around and around and with some effort, pulled my thoughts far inward, back from the ethereal to the here-and-now, the present real; back from Gillie's cancer; back from Dickey's fear that may have been a precursor of my own; back from Mom's last good days in the garden, tomatoes red and ripe and sweet; back from Dad's escapism with the sea; back from Worm's near-sexual relationship with the written word; back from the white-hot searing surprise, an afterthought explosion that left my toes in-country; back from the strange purgatory of the Denver VA and another kind of escape; back from Johnny Cobb's quiet wisdom; back from the road where people like Mike and Jessica Greer came together as one great spirit, offering a healing power that I'd never felt before and might never again—all those roads led to a single double bed with a mattress that pooled in the middle and Lolita and I were the two waterfalls that could not deny that water, when mixed with more water, is just a greater body of water.

The rain outside had stopped and the electricity in the hotel went with it, like they were connected by some electromagnetic force that could be easily explained in a physics class, but not so in philosophy or world religions or anthropology. It was still dark outside, but there was a faint glow edging up over the window sill as the fan stopped and the temperature rose. My inclination was to love this woman. And the more powerful the desire was, the further away the war became. I was surprised at how the two worked like opposing magnets and how the distance between where I'd been and where I wanted to be was far greater than the miles that physically separated the two. It was a new thing for me and I wondered how the bridge could be so challenging to cross.

Lolita was asleep, lying there in the big brown shirt of mine she'd borrowed and as far as I could tell, nothing else. Her scent surrounded me, like a cloud of cool mist that had come in from the ocean on a hot summer eve and worked its way up the swampy ground, belly-crawling until it found our home and we welcomed it.

I sat up on one elbow and stroked her hair. She made a low cooing sound and the ends of her lips rose in tiny amounts, but her eyes stayed shut. A crust of my shell was falling away and I began to feel some deep hush of peace, like that ocean mist, envelope the both of us.

I moved my hand down her back and felt each vertebra that held her strong shoulders in place and protected the heart inside. Was this what it was supposed to be like? I was as unfamiliar with love then, there, in that little room as I'd been with war when I climbed down the ramp of the C-130 in Saigon almost three years ago. Would it take me three years to understand what I was feeling? Because, though I'd never really known war, near the end of my second tour I'd begun to understand why men set about killing each other.

Lolita rolled over and opened her eyes. She smiled and took my hands in hers, spreading my arms so that our bodies became closer and closer until the small gold crucifix that hung on her neck was buried in the hair on my chest. When the awareness of the power that exists between a man and a woman becomes an irreproachable truth, there is nothing left. You don't have three years or three months or even three seconds to ponder its meaning. It is hard-wired into the deepest part of every human. I had but two seconds to figure that out. On the third, our lips came together.

By the third hour there was no difference between her body and mine. The waters had run together and we laughed and touched and exalted our way through the rest of the morning in that single double bed in that small motel, less than a mile from the Atchafalaya Basin Bridge.

And then the power returned and the fan creaked and groaned and we laughed some more.

As much as I wanted to stay in that bed with Lolita until the God I was beginning to trust again came and got us, I was also feeling the tug of family, the immense evocation of a father's gravity, of a need to find and fix a broken mother. We were less than an hour from where we expected to find Johnny and Blackie and maybe my pop and whomever else had made the trek from Lafayette to Baton Rouge or Panama City Beach. I had to know, had to find them. And Lolita sensed it, felt it, slipped from my grasp and stood at the foot of the bead, naked to the future and exposing me to all that we both had come from to reach that moment.

"Get out of bed, lover-boy. Let's go see the people who are waiting for you to come and see them."

I slid off the edge of the bed but didn't stand up. On my knees at the foot of the bed, the edge giving way to firm ground with smooth brown legs to help support it, I folded my hands as I'd done as a child and said a Hail Mary. It was the only prayer I could remember. The *hour of my death* seemed farther away than it'd been in three years. Someone was praying for my sins in that *now*.

✳ ✳ ✳

Lolita, the dogs, and I arrived at the hospital in Baton Rouge by early afternoon. When I inquired about the patient and was given side-to-side shakes of the head by the receptionist, I knew Johnny was not there. Lolita, squeezed my hand and stopped the trembling that was rising up again, trying to claw its way back into the position it once held.

I tried to reach the Riots on the phone, but there was no answer. The options were down to one: I was going home.

Lolita asked if we could get something to drink before we started the drive to Panama City Beach. There was a small hotel next to the hospital and it had a little café out front with a sign in the window that read, *"Creole Thursdays, every Thursday Night."*

I told her to go on in, handed her my wallet with less than twenty dollars in it, and went to check on the dogs. At the

Buick they seemed restless, agitated, like they knew something, but were frustrated that I couldn't see it. Jeremiah in particular was yapping away and could have easily jumped out of the car, but didn't because I'd told him not to earlier.

"What is it boy? What's got you so riled up? Listen, we don't have far to go. Just sit tight for a few more hours and I'll have you home by dinner, assuming no more motels get in the way."

But no amount of talking could quiet them down and even though I was anxious to get on the road and see if Pop and Johnny were home, I told them to get out, go find whatever it was that had them in a tizzy, bring it back if they had to, but just keep the noise down. This was a fancy hospital, after all.

They bolted for the little café that Lolita had slipped into.

Inside, she'd passed the red vinyl booths, the heavily varnished tables with nautical charts inlaid onto the tops, the sound of a jazz horn coming from a jukebox near the back, the thick smell of something—everything fried covering the café like a ground fog that refused to break up with the sunlight. Lolita made her way to the long bar where three men sat at the far end, backs to her, playing chess and drinking something dark.

Lolita felt at home in places like this; she'd grown up in one, cooking, taking orders, filling glasses, singing songs, always trying to make her father happy and proud and pay the bills that never stopped coming with their plastic windows and long Albuquerque addresses.

"Can I get two large iced teas, to go?" she asked the bartender, an older man with wavy gray hair and an eye for the younger women who came to visit sick mothers and fathers in the hospital. They were often grief stricken, in need of a stiff bourbon and some comfort. He would talk to them after he got off of work, help ease their pain, ease his want.

"I'll need to see some identification," the bartender was playing with Lolita, sizing up the potential while she played along knowing his tactics but not wanting to mix it up, innocently enough showed Phin's wallet ID with her thumb over the picture.

"That's a nice picture of your thumb, but what kind of name is Phin for a beautiful girl like you?"

Gerald's eyes moved down the bar.

Harry dropped a knife onto the floor.

Even Blackie pulled his pen from the paper.

"That's my friend's name. But he goes by Phin. I'm in a hurry, sir. Can I get those drinks? *Cuanto cuesta*, sorry, how much do I owe you?"

There are times in a person's life when they wish they might've made a different choice, not necessarily better, just different. And maybe everything would've been better off. But in that reflection, however fleeting or forever, there will also be times when you're glad that you made the choice, however painful the costs, bcause you saw a truth standing before you and you took it. Gerald would think of that in future years. He'd have plenty of time to think. He'd even have days when his life felt like grains of sand running through an hourglass, waiting for the strength to break the glass before the sand had filled in the bottom and covered up his view through the window. But his reaction in that café bar, on that day, was indicative of his advancement to health, not his decline. So he never regretted.

The bartender put his hand over Lolita's, covering the wallet, smothering Phin's picture, sending his intentions to someone who'd seen all these tricks and had fended off as many advances as the man behind the bar had made.

"I'm sorry," he said, a devilish cartoon-grin dripping spittle from the sides of his mouth. "This is a fake ID, I'll have to keep it and call the police...unless you can convince me you are who you say you are. Let me get you a real drink. You look troubled; tequila will do better than tea. All Mexicans enjoy good tequila. It's like mother's milk." And then he stared at her breasts and winked

It all happened very quickly, too quickly in fact, for Phin to stop. Lolita, somehow empowered by her night with a man who knew her history, who wanted her in his future, pulled her right hand away, lifted it to draw the bartender's eyes off her and with her left, threw the basket of dry roasted peanuts from the counter into his face. It was a scene from a B-rated movie, complete with the still-frame pauses when all the actors' faces are shown reacting in sequence.

Phin had walked in the front door, the dogs bolting past him to see their beloved Harry at the corner of the bar.

Phin, seeing the bartender wipe his eyes and calling the girl who was making a difference in his life, "a fucking bitch," and then throwing a full glass of iced tea in her face, stopped cold.

Harry, at the end of the bar, shocked and overjoyed to see his son alive and walking with only the slightest of limps, seeing the girl, knowing the girl but not being able to place her in the sudden confusion, stopped cold.

Gerald, who saw his father in the bartender, right down to the cold, calculating eyes and quick, aggressive reply, got very hot. Gerald was up and scrambling behind the bar. What anger that lingered after his epiphany had percolated to the surface like coffee grinds that just wouldn't dissolve? The bartender, regardless of his seemingly minor offense, was about to be crucified for every one of his past sins by a quiet, non-violent man. Who gets to rain justice? Because raindrops have no symmetry under any microscope.

Blackie, who was the only one who knew what dangerous dogs lie sleeping in his old friend's ear was jumping up from his seat, yelling don't do it Doc G, he's not worth it.

Phin, with his missing toes, was conflicted. Should he run full tilt at the bartender? Embrace his father? Pull Lolita to safety? Or try to stop McReady before he hurt the old man with the foul mouth? And so he did nothing, the rain of indecision clouding anything rational. He'd made enough decisions on the fly without radar. If only until he was grounded again, Phin decided to look before he jumped.

Nobody in the room was really thinking whether the man deserved what was happening to him. He was a dirty old barkeep, mostly ignored by the patrons who had other things of import on their minds. But Gerald had watched the whole thing unfold in slow motion while Harry pondered whether to move his knight out of harm's way. And what he saw was not an old man hitting on a nice-looking, young Hispanic female, but his own father preying on him, feeding him to the wolves, raping him by abandoning him. The years of quiet servitude at the VA had only been tempered by his patient care and his sacrifice and his clay pots. The dragon that was his father had been disabled by Gerald's acceptance of his life's work, but it had not been killed.

Gerald moved quicker than he ever had in any of his dreams. He was the savior, the healer, the man in the middle of the platoon who stepped out of the shadows and ran into the fire and the bullets and the malice and mayhem that paralyzed everyone else. He was still a sick man and now, more than ever, he realized it, swallowed it. Grabbing a pool cue stick on the way he was Sir Lancelot in a joust to save the queen's honor.

But it wasn't the queen's, it was his own.

Former orderly Gerald R. McReady might've hurt the bartender bad, might've killed him dead and then cut off his fingers and wore them around his neck on a string made of fishing line from the reel his father had given him on his tenth birthday before it all became so entangled. It was the dogs who saved the old man. When so much negative energy is directed at one man, any good dog, any dog brought up to know loyalty like the human loyalty that existed around them, would go after that man.

Daniel, thick and heavy from a steady diet of squirrel and left-overs, but still as quick and agile as a puppy, leapt over the bar, and knocked the bartender down just before McReady was ready to put the chalked-up lance cue through his stomach. Harry screamed at the dogs, "Down boys, don't hurt him," and there the three of them sat, perched atop the bartender, awaiting further commands.

Blackie grabbed Gerald's shoulders and held them, but not before he raised the rubber butt-end of the cue and pounded his patriarchal prey between the eyes, breaking his nose cleanly.

The climactic scene complete, the unfolding began.

Phin held Lolita. "Calm down, it's not your fault, no one's hurt."

Harry remembered the girl from José's and saw his son's future hopeful in the way he buried her face in his chest. "You boys get off this man," he told the dogs. And they did.

Blackie saw the great releasing catharsis roll off of Gerald's shoulders and smiled. He imagined clay pots filled with earth and growing flowers all over the Front Range.

The bartender stood up, confused, angry, his eyes already swelling shut, and started to say something, but it was the healer who quieted him down.

"I'm sorry sir. Are you alright? Let me have a look at that nose of yours. Hey, Blackie," McReady the healer asked, "Can you put some ice in a towel for this man? Those dogs didn't hurt you did they?"

Gerald knew what was in store for him. He was a conquering country ready to rebuild it. But there would be the U.N. to deal with; the rules of war had been broken. And there were witnesses. He'd be accused of assault. It was his second criminal offense. There would be mandatory time. Even Jed and Dickey couldn't get him off completely. He'd take the time, wanted the time. It was worth the explosion that had unclogged the flow. He was glad for the dogs, glad that he hadn't hurt the old man more. There was no assigning fault or reason or blame. What difference would that have made?

They were all better for it.

The cops came and took Gerald away, but he wasn't sad. Sitting in the back of the squad car while the police tried to make sense of the outrageous scene, Phin knelt next to Gerald on one knee, like he was posing for a picture with some high school team.

"You okay, doc?"

"Yeah, I'm good, Phin Davis, like the shark, from the high right X, ward seven, bed number one. I'm really good. And you?"

"Moving in the right direction, back to the center so I can see all the way to the sea."

"Good thing, kid, good thing." There was a squawk over the police radio and both of the men stayed right there in the present where they needed to be.

"A lot of people riding on your coming back, Phin."

"Yeah, I don't know what that is. I mean, what have I ever done compared to you and my pop and Johnny?"

Gerald, tried to brush a piece of hair out of his face, but his hands were handcuffed behind him and Phin said, here, let me get that.

"Thanks, kid." Gerald used the term of endearment even though he was only a few years older than Phin. You suffered, son."

"Yeah, but hell, we all got our asses kicked this go around. I know your story too, doc. It's been rough on all of us. I reckon our lives have been so hard to live these past few years because no one had done it before."

Gerald saw a cop coming up behind the kid. He knew what Phin was trying to say, but wanted to hear it again. "No one's done what, kid?"

"Live our lives." Phin smiled, patted Gerald on the shoulder ,and said he'd see him around. He didn't want to get mixed up with anything wearing a uniform. Then added as he walked away before the cop arrived, "I'm nothing special."

"Yeah, you are, kid. It's what you saw, over there. And what you represent now, over here."

"I don't know. doc," Phin stopped and seemed embarrassed by the words. "I'm no hero."

"Nobody's saying you are. But whether or not you like it, people pinned hope on your tail. Hope and future."

Phin looked up and could see Harry spreading his arms and saying something to the police about the dogs that were nowhere to be seen.

"I don't know, Gerald. We all have a platform of some kind, don't you think?"

"Yeah, but you've seen the best and the worst and when Johnny's gone, only you'll know it all."

"None of us know it all, doc, none of us want to know that much."

"I hear you kid. But you go trying to run from it, you're gonna end up in the same place as me, a place I already know; a place Blackie and Harry and you, in your own way, already graduated from."

"You know I went looking for you, don't you?" Phin's eyes were narrowed and his head was nodding subconsciously.

Gerald switched his tone to a Southern drawl. "I reckoned as much. Made a few detours tough, dint ya?"

"Reckon they were worth it though." Phin looked over at Blackie and Lolita who were sitting under a street lamp in deep conversation.

"Hey Phin, do me a couple of favors, would you?"

"Anything."

"Ask Johnny if he'll find a job for me down these parts when I get out of this little detour of my own."

"You think you can work with those crazy vets he's got up there?"

"Ah shucks, kid. It's a living."

"And what else?"

"Oh yeah," Gerald pretended it was an afterthought, but Phin knew he was unclinching still more parts of his heart. "If you run into a guy by the name of DuPuis, a soldier by trade, Marine Corps to the core, a parish priest in his ways, please tell him that I owe him a Pabst, a really tall, icy-cold Pabst."

✳ ✳ ✳

At the Lafayette County Coroner's office they peeled back the thin white sheet that covered the body of the last known Winter. Johnny Cobb looked at the dark, ashen face of Uncle Chuck Winters and nodded. It was him. The technician began to pull the sheet back over the face of the dead man, but Johnny put his hand on the young woman's wrist.

"Wait a second would you, please?" Johnny asked and then mumbled to himself, "The plowman homeward plods his weary way, and leaves the world to darkness and to me."

Johnny tried to decide if Chuck looked content but couldn't make up his mind.

"Lots of people offer poems and prayers and promises over their deceased," the technician asked. "But that one sounds smartly heavier than most. Maybe it's some churchyard elegy by a man named Gray, but it sounds old-world...you ask me."

"Guess so," Johnny said and then asked, "Do you have an uncle, young lady?" He nodded at the technician who pulled the sheet back up and pushed Charles George Winters's body back into the cold, dark drawer.

"Yeah, I have two of them. Why do you ask?"

"No reason. What's your name?"

The girl, pointed to her name tag. "It's *Doctor* Larsen." But she could see that the old Black man wasn't satisfied.

"Was this a relative?" She asked, looking at the bandages still worn on Johnny's head.

"Yes, doctor," he said with a forced formality. "It was my wife's brother."

A cautious look came over the young doctor and Cobb's intuition kicked into high gear. "What is it, doctor? Is there something you want to tell me?"

She hesitated, but then asked, "Did this man have any other family members pass away recently?"

"I wouldn't know. My wife has been dead for...ah hell, more than twenty-three years and I didn't have a chance to ask this man the things I needed to before he was murdered by the police."

"I see, because we had another person come through here with the same last name just a few weeks ago."

"Come through? You mean, like they came to visit or just to drop off their body while their soul kept traveling?" Johnny was trying to understand how a person could not be affected working in an environment like this every day.

The doctor just shrugged her shoulders and handed Johnny some forms to sign.

"Did he have a sister who was a sister?' She asked Cobb who set the pen down and lifted his hands as if to ask what she meant.

"The lady who died was approximately his age. She was a nun at Saint Catherine's School on the south side of town."

"Well, Winters is not an uncommon name." Johnny finished and got up to leave, wanting to get away and go see Auntie and then get back to Baton Rouge or maybe Panama City Beach where he might meet up with Harry and Phin.

"It's been, ah...enlightening, Miss Doctor." Johnny spoke, but the lady was gone.

The controlled doors began to close behind him then reopened suddenly. "Her name was Lou Anna, Mr. Cobb, Sister Lou Anna Winters."

Cobb, nodded, thanked her, and walked out into the night. He would now skip Auntie's in Lafayette, skip Baton Rouge. It was time to go back to that long, winding driveway in Panama City Beach. And for just a passing moment Johnny wondered if the doctor had said Louella, not Lou Anna.

The truck almost didn't start. He took off the air filter, choked it by hand, and then she ran great all the way home.

546

CHAPTER 46

A TESTAMENT

Who are these coming to the surface?

To what green alter, O mysterious priest...

–John Keats, *Ode on a Grecian Urn*

They drove along the big Interstate 10 freeway but decided to skirt over to coastal road number 90 at the Mississippi border and run down past Bay St. Loius and Gulfport. The moon hung one day past full, always a shade brighter the night before, like warmed over stew, and its reflection bounced and pinged between the islets in the Chandeleur Sound like an arcade game.

Harry loved the moon, always had. Loved it more than stars and hated the fact that man had landed on it. He tried hard to convince himself that the Apollo landing had taken place on a back lot in Hollywood just so the U.S. could convince the Russians that our system of government had a bigger penis than theirs. Harry knew it had happened, though, but more than any scientist at NASA, he admired the Polynesians who'd sailed all around the great Pacific Ocean in their big dugout canoes and their knowledge of the moving constellations.

Phin was driving, sitting behind the wheel of the big Buick, his still-healing foot splayed across the floorboards,

Lolita very close to him on the wide bench seat. Harry sat in the back with a quiet Grace, looking at the infinite lines of light on the gray-gray sea. It was as flat as if ironed. At Harry's feet was Daniel, looking proud for what he'd done, how he'd understood Harry when told to, "Go home, take the boys and leave quickly. We'll find you on the road."

Also in the back, Blackie was stretched out with Elijah and Jeremiah, the other canine perpetrators that had attacked the bartender and abandoned the scene of the crime. Nobody knew where the "rabid pack of mongrels" had come from, who they belonged to, or how they slipped away in the ensuing fracas. A distinctly Southern experience.

Blackie was smiling to himself with the knowledge that even though Gerald would plead guilty to attacking the bartender, the few witnesses in the café had only seen the bartender doing his same old thing, and then there were the dogs. Gerald would be assigned a young, aggressive defense attorney fresh out of LSU Law School wanting to make a name for himself. The Riots could arrange just that, maybe. Blackie would go over to the courthouse and testify because Harry would be back at sea, the Mexican gal, Lolita, could not be found and the kid with the limp came up as "deceased" on the records. You couldn't subpoena a dead man. Even in Baton Rouge.

Blackie lay on the thick red leather seat and stroked the thicker fur of the dogs. He stared up at the night stars and listened to Marvin Gaye ask, "What's goin' on?" on the radio. He pictured the trial in his head, how he'd get up there and tell them how the accused had saved the lives and sanities of many veterans returning from Vietnam. He'd tell the court, if it pleased, how he had suffered from Post Vietnam Syndrome—it had been called battle fatigue and shellshock in earlier wars— and that his daily consults with the accused man had saved him from hanging himself from a basement rafter with a crisp white bedsheet on more than one occasion. He would not be lying.

The court-appointed, impeccably-dressed attorney would ask Blackie if there was anything else he wanted to add and he'd say yes—he'd like to ask the jurors if they had ever been a close witness and party to so much horror brought back, like a terrible foreign disease? Did they think they would they be immune from one sudden, provoked act of aggression? Did this alleged act of violence against a man who had immoral intentions if not previous accusations of rape on poor innocent women erase all the good that the defendant had done in his life? He would look at the jurors, one by one, and ask them if they believed in the stereotype of the violent, addicted, psycho vet and the prosecuting attorney would object.

"The accused wasn't even a soldier," he'd scream.

Blackie would say, "My point exactly.

And then just after the judge bellowed, "Sustained," Blackie would focus his eyes on the two Black jurors and add, "Hasn't the South made enough wrongful assumptions in its colorful past?"

The judge would tell Blackie to stick to the questions asked, but the words had been spoken. And everyone in the courtroom would have to answer that question. Then he would pause, rub his eyes, maybe take a sip of water and remember the old Blackie who beat the system by knowing the system and turning it on itself, exposing the rends and cracks that existed both out on the edge and right down the middle.

Blackie looked up at the moon and wondered if the same amount of money American taxpayers had spent to put a couple of men up there collecting rocks and hitting golf balls was spent on understanding why men on earth still beat the crap out of each other at football games, would they still do it?

He closed his eyes and dreamed his closing statement.

Blackie would say that he had studied men and their interaction within elements of society for many years. He had learned much by his unplanned internship in a VA psych ward. It would be one of the truest things he could say. And then he would look right into the eyes of each and every one of the twelve jurors and ask them if it really made sense that a man who had been a proven healer all his life would hit a stranger with a pool cue and then immediately set about caring for him.

Blackie would pause one more time for effect and he'd look over at the former orderly and now defendant, Gerald R.

McReady, who would have his hands buried in his face, trying desperately not to laugh.

"Wasn't this man just trying to save the poor employee from the rabid dogs that are known to run in packs? This is, after all, East Baton Rouge Parish. Not everything can be explained, or should even try to be."

It would be one of his best, and though he couldn't swear to it, last great lies. Blackie fell asleep with a smile on his face and a long, thin, wet nose nuzzled in the crook of his neck. Next to him, Harry dabbed his shirt sleeve at the constant drip of spittle from Grace's mouth. He wondered how Johnny was faring in his '66 Stepside he'd loaned him.

CHAPTER 47

THE SPOILS OF LIGHT

Ever since I was a kid from Alabama, I've owned a truck. Earl and Ramsey and me inherited our daddy's farm vehicle after he went into the big city and never came back. He'd found most of it on the outskirts of Mobile one Sunday after church and it took a few years, but we found enough parts to make it go forward and on the good days, in reverse. And as I grew up and worked the homestead, always knowing that a man needs a dependable truck, my trucks became more dependable. Not only were they good for hauling tractor parts and bags of seed and people from the side of the road who needed a ride, but a truck bed will air-clean most any dog at 40 mph. Fleas and ticks and June bugs will just get blown off. A dog that's not happy in the back of a truck is a cat.

But trucks don't float.

So, if you're going to drive a car off of a causeway into a body of water, you should try to do it in a long sedan with a big rear seat full of basketballs intended for the local school. Because a '66 Ford Stepside is not a good car to take swimming. It's front-heavy. The bigger motor might be adequate protection for the driver on impact, but it sure makes the car go down quick on its nose.

That wasn't my first thought as I hit the low metal fence in the center-divide, corrected, fishtailed, swerved, jack-knifed, skidded, and finally jack-fished over the concrete wall and into the moonlit waters of the Gulf of Mexico. My initial mind wasn't even flung back to the inevitable why's.

It was this: "Ah geez, not again. C'mon, God. If it's you, well, I think I'm getting the point, whatever the point is. And if it isn't you, God, who do I need to go and see about the shit flung on me year after year?"

The second thing was, "Are my dogs in the back?" But fortunately not, though they may have saved me. The third thing that came into my mind was that Phin and Harry, ah hell, the whole lot of them, would have to deal with one more death. Thoughts of the day when Ruth died came back and filled what room I had left in my chest.

✳ ✳ ✳

It had been one of those thick sultry days in late July, a day that you prayed for thunderheads to make a quick stop on you and leave shiny drops on your hair, then run down your neck and into every wonderful little corner of your body before falling off your feet. There was no rain that day, but a rare, northerly wind came up early in the afternoon and stirred the lake into a chocolate with the stronger gusts building meringue whitecaps out away from the shore.

Ruth was out on the lake with her Uncle Chuck, a good man by most standards, as he showed her the new mahogany and teak skiff he'd won in a four-day poker game. I was up on the shore cutting some ribs, firing the coals, and happy not to be swimming. I could do it if I had to, but land was fine by me. Johnny Weismuller I wasn't.

It was a Sunday, and watching them push the little boat off the muddy shore and into the lake, Chuck acting like he was a tenured oarsman, Ruth's long crimped hair tied up in a bow and silhouetted against the afternoon sun, I had put the work world away. I was happy.

I 'spose the wonder in Ruth overshadowed her sensibility and she stood up in the boat, waved an oar, and yelled to me that she'd see me in the spring after sailing the great waters. Ruth slipped or the boat hit a mogul of chop or somebody who happened to be able to walk on water had come down and tapped her on the shoulder—it matters little. She hit her head on the gunwale, knocked herself out, capsized the boat, and sent all its contents into the mixing of something that would never be as good as the very moment before.

They couldn't have been more than thirty yards from shore. But what is distance anyway, when things like water and family relations are involved? Ruth went down quick and since Chuck could barely hold his head above water, by the time I got out there, it was all I could do to get him to the up-turned hull, keep an eye on where Ruth went in, and then dive again and again, feeling my way through the soft clay bottom covered in eel grass and duck shit, sweeping my hands across the bottom feeling for the body of my pregnant wife. That's all. Could of, should of.

I came up for air and saw other picnicking Negroes rushing over. And when I went down again, it was as if she was calling out for me in the language of the dead with her desires and her thin, dark body.

"Johnny, I'm over here. Please come quick, I can't see anything. It's getting darker Johnny. Please hurry." And I listened, trying to feel her presence, knowing that if the roles were reversed and she was saving me, her intuition would guide her.

"No, Johnny, not there. Over here, closer to the shore. Feel me, my man, don't leave me here. I'm getting cold and want to go home."

I came up and inhaled a sky full of air, trying to drown out the growing noise of the others wading out to help so that I could hear my Ruth.

"Oh Johnny, I see you've brought a light. Good, now you'll see me. Stay there and I'll swim to the light."

All I felt, though, was frustration, anger, guilt, and a growing sense that a part of me had left the lake. For just a second, I couldn't feel my legs and looked down to see that they were still attached. One time, I came up to the surface, vomited my disgust, and looked around. There was a collection of old Sunday fishermen, their wives, and teenage sons and daughters, most of them like Chuck, barely able to swim at all. They were wading out past their comfort zone, bobbing their heads into the thick lake water, breaking the surface with eyes wide, moving like spotlights, their straw hats floating away, screaming out, "Dear God, raise that young woman back up."

The burden of the task had encased me, kept pushing me deeper. It must've been written down in a past life, scripted in my grandfather's slave song. Every generation has their shackles, every man his own personal chains. At twenty-six years old, I was about to be handed mine.

I prayed to God for the first time since we were married two years earlier.

And He said to me just as plain as if He was sitting on my back steps, *"What would you do Johnny Cobb? How would it feel to lift your dead wife and unborn child up from some watery grave only to watch them lay her in the ground a few days later? Would you blame me? Would you, Johnny Cobb, son of a sharecropper, grandson of a slave, great-grandson of a tribal healer? Do you not think that they were children of mine, too?"*

I had no answer but felt my faith tested like a twenty-pound bass on a ten-pound line. I wanted to see my Ruth swim up from the depths right then, tell me her head hurt just a little, and could I take her in so she could rest for a while? Then maybe I would've sheathed my knife instead of holding the shiny blade above that ten-pound test line. The God I prayed to had put the question to me. This was my test. Would Moses kill his son if God asked him to? Would I blame Him if Ruth and our child were taken? I didn't know this God. Or, if I did, I was going looking for another.

Just before dark, I caught a glimpse of something soft and gray and pale. She looked like she was asleep, all cuddled up, only her eyes were open and dark and empty. And the current moved her lips as if she was trying to tell me something. Her skin was milky and beginning to sag, but her feet, the ones that failed her as they danced on a four-inch teak gunwale as it rocked and weaved and bucked, and she and her mother's little brother laughed less than two hundred feet away from me—her feet seemed to me brown and clean and perfect.

Did I feel betrayed? This God wanted to know how I felt. But I felt nothing, just the numbness of loss.

While the others who could swim helped me bring Ruth's body to shore, I had this strange thought of a poem by a young black poet I had just heard about. The words said, "I've known rivers ancient as the world and older than the flow of human blood in human veins." I was never so ancient as at that moment when we laid her body on the shore, with Uncle Chuck crying like a child, and the women in that crowd singing out, "Dear Lord, take this girl and her child." But He had come for her, leaving me in some luminous hole where the suffering of life lives.

There was no phone on that side of the lake and no regular ambulance would come for a Black woman anyway. So we put Ruth and our unborn in the bed of my truck and I climbed in next to them and the dogs that seemed to know something terrible had occurred in this world. Something I was not familiar with, a voice maybe, a radio frequency from another world, told me to ask Uncle Chuck to drive us into town slowly while I held Ruth's lifeless body in my hands, hearing again God's questions of faith riding on the backs of short, snapshot memories of Ruth. And as we left the dirt lot, the women who had been kneeling in prayer near the base of the dock began a hymn, the volume rising with each verse so that I might not hear the Devil himself sneaking around or believe his lies or the surrounding white noise I thought all life had become in that moment.

There was a bad feeling lofting out of the cab and I knew right then it had to do with her uncle, more voices, and feelings of things to come. My ability to feel and sense things ahead of me had come around in a way that startled me. It was as if another dimension had been added. I wondered if Ruth had passed her ability to know things ahead back to me when she left this world. Or was it some gift from God, a sign, an olive branch, something beyond my ability to know and understand until I had made it my own? Or just a weak radio signal?

At this moment though, the feeling had a message in the clouds. And like the clouds themselves, it could bring rain and shade, hide things or reveal the truth. As we drove away from the lake, I looked back at the moonlit surface and the whitecaps seemed to wave like sad handkerchiefs.

✳ ✳ ✳

About then I decided this wasn't the best time to be remembering that day Ruth left us. I wasn't going to die this evening. Maybe tomorrow if God willed it, but not here, not now, not this way. I'd figure out what'd happened at a later point, but right then I was a little busy.

"Okay, Ruth," I spoke into the leaking cab of the truck as it lay on its left side, pinning the driver's door against the muddy floor of the Gulf.

"What is it, Johnny? Are you here? Do you need something?"

Was I speaking to myself in some desperate attempt to gain confidence in an environment that had not always been friendly to me? Was it part of some reorganization of my brain function, courtesy of something very human and very ghostly at the same time? Or was I really having one of those rare but believable conversations with my wife who'd passed so many years ago? The voice came again as I noticed that the headlights of the truck had stayed on and shown through the murk, as if the truck was doing its damndest to be dependable.

"Johnny, it's not your choice. This is something that you don't get to decide."

"What do you mean? Whether I open the passenger door and swim up to the surface and then flag down a ride to Harry's place? Or just open my mouth and start swallowing?"

"Yes, my 'sometimes-thinks-too-much' husband. There is another essence that makes those decisions."

"Well, since you seem to be closer to Him or Her or It than I, can you explain the situation and see if you can pull a few strings?" The truck began to settle a bit and the mounting pressure difference between the air in the cab and the surrounding water, even though it couldn't have been more than ten or fifteen feet on the outgoing tide, was enabling leaks from vents and cracks that even I hadn't known existed on the old Ford.

"Ruthie, I'm kinda' rushed for time here, and as much as I want to see you again soon, there's some people left on earth I feel some responsibility toward."

"Ah, Johnny Cobb, you were always that way, even when you were looking for me on the bottom of that lake so many years ago. You were thinking about Uncle Chuck and the others who came searching for me, always wondering if they were all right. Would one drowning turn into two? It's always been that with you, hasn't it? Save at least one if you can. Don't let them have 'em all."

"So, is that it? Do I have to decide now, between them and you?"

"Of course not. It doesn't work that way. Like I said, it's not up to you. There are greater powers, powers beyond your imagination, that are at work in keeping this world of yours running smoothly."

"I wouldn't call the life I've lived since you've been gone, 'smooth.' "

"Johnny, it's not like you to complain. Especially when you have only a few minutes left on earth."

I sat there, slumped on my side, water reaching the bottom of the dashboard, wet and cool and murky, and I had to take this voice of my Ruth, my past and, with any luck, my future, and I had to give it credence or blow it off as the dimensions of an injured, cold, and tired old man. Considering how I was beset with the irony of my life, it was a job I was not qualified for.

The water rose alongside the words and questions, real or imagined. Had I identified myself so closely with the down-and-outers that I could never be comfortable as an up-and-comer? Had I mortgaged the untimely death of Ruthie in hopes that there would come a time when my peace and her peace, rolled in on a magic carpet wearing white robes and speaking in tongues? And now here I was, the passenger door jammed shut by the impact on the guard rail, trying to make sense of the after-life while struggling to roll down a window that never worked well up on land, let alone under water; and it seemed that all my dreams had morphed into some self-delusion; caught red-handed. Even if I could cry, where would I hang the tears out to dry?

"Ruthie," I cried out while lying back on the seat and kicking at the window with my size thirteen boots, "I don't want to seem cynical or unappreciative, but if I were to roll over and live and let die, I'd be prematurely disappointed in the future on this side." The water reached my chest and the window held.

"Now, you know God much better than I do; always did. But I reckon it's not my time yet so I'm going to see what I can do about learning how to swim well, right quick."

I remembered the tire iron under the seat that was clipped exactly where it was supposed to be in case of a flat. So for the second time since I'd gone searching for my drowned wife, I put my face under water, opened my eyes to the darkness, and felt around for the metal bar. It came out easilym and with the water at my neck, the iron in my hands, the options thinning quickly, a fluid peace came over me. It was thicker than water, more viscous than blood. I became invulnerable not because there was nothing left to hurt, but because I took on a partner in my struggle.

"Okay, Big Guy," I wasn't bargaining, just laying it out there. "Ruthie says it's your decision. I'll go with that. But I'm sure as hell not going to sit here and fucking drown when I have a chance. You fought them in the temple, smashed the golden calf, parted the Red Sea. You're a damn rebel, too, just like me.

"With your permission," the words were garbled as the water reached my lips, "I think I'll see if can find my way out. Besides, it's damn cold and dark down here." I smashed the window with the bar but nothing happened.

At least the headlights stayed on, reminding me how cold and dark it was outside.

✳ ✳ ✳

Phin held the big wheel of the Buick in his hands as he switched feet, the good one shifting back between pedals, the custom-booted half draped over Lolita's ankle. He entered the long causeway in silence, the radio signal low, his passengers snoozing away.

"Does it hurt?" It was Harry asking, quietly, hoping to let Grace and Blackie and the dogs sleep.

"Yeah, pop, sometimes it hurts a lot. But I don't let it bother me none. I kept the good parts."

"You know, son, lots of vets are having their injured parts cut off and then fitted with them new plastic feet and legs. Some of them say it's a lot easier, gives them something to balance on besides that weird stump of yours."

"I don't know. I kind of fancy keeping what parts of me I have left. I figure if I work at it and you can design a new boot, I'll be able to get around same as I ever did."

Harry looked out at the long, thin reflections of the moon, which were just reflections of the sun that hid around the corner. "Whatever you say, boy; I'll build you anything you need, just so long as it floats." And then Harry let his mind wander back to yesterday when all the craziness went down at the bar and, finally, he and Grace were reunited with Phin.

He'd offered a quick interview to the cops, said he hadn't seen much, didn't know the other patrons that well. Found the whole story about dogs attacking a bartender "distinctly voodoo-ish" and kindly excused himself. Phin, with his fabricated death and expired ID, had slipped out the back while Lolita, offering her testimony in the back of a squad car, gave the cops her permanent address as Jose's place in Cortez, Colorado. Wiping a tear, she handed Harry the keys to the Buick. Harry drove around the back, found his son in the ally talking with a homeless man, and drove the two blocks to fetch his wife. When Harry brought Grace out to the car, she looked at Phin, cried, screamed, and hugged him with one arm, the other dangling lifelessly off her starboard side. Her words came out in slurred staccato bursts followed by soundless syllables mouthed into the wind. Harry asked Phin to drive, said let's go get the others, and held Grace's head on his lap.

It wasn't the reunion he'd imagined. But it could've been worse.

✳ ✳ ✳

"You thinking I'm going to go jumping off the pier again?" Phin smiled at Harry.

"Not thinking, just countin' on it," and Harry looked at Lolita's head laid upon Phin's lap. "But I can see you you're 'bout ready to jump off something else as well."

"You like her, Dad? I mean," and Phin lowered his voice, leaning over Lolita towards Harry, "do you think she's right for me?"

"When I seen you two playing mumbly peg with that big cutting knife out the front of Jose's place before you were teenagers, laughing, taking extra care with each other's feelings and toes, I figured you'd do fine with her as well as anyone."

"Yeah, but I don't want just anyone. I been through too much. I need the right one."

"Ah hell, son. How does anyone know which one is right and which one is not right?"

"You did all right by yourself. Did you know Ma was the right one?"

"Of course I did. That's why I married her, why I think about her every day."

"So, how'd you know?"

"I just did." Phin slowed the car. He felt his pulse increase and his pupils open up. He looked out over the Gulf at the reflection of the lights and something—as beautiful as the night was with his new girl there and his dad and mom and Blackie and they were going home—something didn't sit right in the world.

"What is it, son? You having one of those flashback things you had when you first came back?

"No, I don't know what it was. Something in the way the lights were shinning on the water back a click or so. My stomach just turned."

"Maybe you're just hungry or anxious to get home. I felt the same way just when I knew I'd get the *Grace* in safe from that hurricane."

"You didn't tell me about that."

"I didn't tell you about a lot of things."

"Yeah, starting with the *Indianapolis.*"

"No, starting with how your ma and I never registered you at birth."

Phin slowed the car almost to a stop and Lolita woke up and asked if they were there.

"Not quite, but we're close."

"What is it, Phin? Why are you stopped in the middle of the road?" Lolita rubbed her eyes and then asked. "There are so many streaks of light on the water. How many moons do you have in this part of the country?"

✳ ✳ ✳

Johnny took one last swing at the back window with the tire iron and it broke. The Gulf came in on him hard and fast, pinning him against the driver's door while shards of glass lined the gush and cut his face and hands. The headlights that had gone out, and up through the water the light finally went dim and then to nothing at all.

He tried to move against the force but it was too strong and, as hopeless as he felt, he tried to keep his mind working. Then another voice came and he remembered it from many years ago. Only then he was sitting in the back of a truck with his wife's body in his arms cursing the thing behind the voice.

"Well, well, Mr. Cobb. Seems that once again you are in a life or death situation with water as your enemy. But you've come a long way, haven't you, Mr. Cobb."

It was indeed a different Johnny Cobb that faced the voice of God this time.

"It's not a matter of distance as it is of depth," he answered between gulps of water that reached his throat but he spit back out.

"Do you still blame me for the death of Ruth?"

"You know that I don't. I think I said that a long time ago."

"Well, it's hard to keep track, but I believe you."

Johnny took the iron bar and smashed at the sharp edges of what remained of the back window.

"What is it like, knowing that the next breath may be your last, Mr. Cobb?"

"This is an interesting time for a Socratic line of questioning. You should know that from when your Son died on the cross."

"Well, yes, I should, but you know how it is with young men; they don't want to talk about their own struggles, as much good as it will do them."

"I'm glad you brought that up," Johnny pushed his head up to the last small pocket of air that was left in the cab of the truck. He saw a small spider running for air and felt sorry for the loss to come soon. "You see, I'm okay with going now if that's what you want because as much as I'd like to stick around and help out a few young men who need to talk, I'm finding that there may be a certain immortality hidden in the calmness at which I will face this, uh, passing. So, I'm with Ruthie, Big Guy. It's your call"

There was no answer and Johnny knew that was his answer.

The cab was full of water now. No air. No oxygen. Just the cold and the dark and the quiet. The voice was gone and Johnny couldn't bring it back. All he could do was to embrace the calmness he knew he'd find if he just let go. Just swallowed the water and the cold and the dark. There would be another light for him on the other side. He knew that for sure now. Or at least he had enough trust in the voice.

Still, he could see a thin light above as it made its way through the muddy Gulf and into the watery grave of the truck's cab. It must be the moon, Johnny thought. All I have to do is go to the moon, but stop on earth for a while, just to hear a few people talk. Funerals were depressing. Uncle Chuck had taught him that. Old Grayfalls had refused to go to anyone's. He would disappear for a few days, take something of the dead with him, and return as if nothing had changed.

Johnny kicked the edges of the glass out from the back window and the voice came as his lungs began to ache and cry for air and his head was bursting with pain. But as had been the case before in the rippling curls of past experience, the pain opened another door he hadn't known existed. This one brought the voice back. But there was no playful chatter or lightness to it. It was real and heavy and thick as the water filled his cheeks and he began to swallow in small bits.

"Where will you be after you die, Mr. Cobb?" It asked.

"Right where I was before I was born." There was no question in Johnny's voice.

"Please, go on Mr. Cobb." Johnny's eyes fell back in his head and he wondered why he hadn't passed out yet.

"The meaning of my life will be found in the world *out there*, not in my own head as a man or even my heart as a carrier of the soul. It's in the collective of all peoples that I validate my existence and, I suppose, show my appreciation for being alive."

"Then go for that swim you've been avoiding for all these years."

✳ ✳ ✳

Phin didn't want to move his car, but a big rig had come up from behind him and there was no room to pass on the single-lane causeway. Blackie and the dogs were awake and everybody was concerned about Phin's concern. They didn't understand his feelings, but they all understood how it worked. And so they sat and waited and wondered.

"Something ain't right," Phin finally said. "Something just ain't right."

They drove on and the dogs stood up on the edge of the seat and howled at the waters and the moon as they left them behind.

Harry put his hand on Phin's shoulders. "You mother died from caring too much. You need to let things go. Nothing's perfect. We do the best we can and then move on down the line, make room for another person to take our spot, to take their own shot."

And then realizing that he was sounded a lot like his early self before and after he'd lost two of those perfect things in his life, Harry finished his words, but the conviction had gone out of them. "Life's pretty goddamned hard, but in a lot of ways it's pretty damn simple."

He looked back at Blackie, who nodded. Lolita was sticking with Phin, regardless if she understood him or not, and looked back over the Gulf as the big rig blew its horn and Phin pressed down on the gas pedal slowly, reluctantly. The loyalty had not gone unnoticed by Harry. Grace stirred and then fell back asleep and he took his own advice—he let it all go.

"Let's go home, son," Harry said as he tasted the salty tears in the side of his mouth. "I'll make ya'll a cup of coffee."

Phin drove the road he knew so well, his hands not quite relaxed on the big wheel. But he watched the moon and its reflection on the water in the rear view mirror for a long, long time.

CHAPTER 48

DEAD IN THE WINTER

Old habits of war die hard. Old warriors of habit die harder.

–Anonymous

It was dark when Phin pulled the long Buick up the longer driveway, her big round whitewalls crunching the old gravel made smooth, not by cars, but many booted feet walking and working and living amongst the white pebble-world of the Florida panhandle. The big moon had gone behind the tall trees and low, low hills. And the late fall air filled with a crisp edge of pine and salt breeze.

From around a stand of red maples ran three more dogs. They'd grown in his five-month absence, but their names currently escaped him and this scared him. He'd remembered names as if tattooed on his wrist.

"Hey, Dad," he called around to Harry who was helping Grace climb over the big car door that just wouldn't open. "I thought you left the other dogs with the neighbors."

Harry said that he had and figured that his old friends might've brought them back for the day and forgot to collect them again. But that didn't seem right, he offered, while helping Grace up the steps.

And then from out of the sultry shadows and the yellow porch light that had never been turned off walked a tall man dressed in crisp military fatigues, his hair cut high and tight, and his voice that of a game show host. The first thing Phin noticed was the reflection of the low moon that had just reappeared as if on cue. The light hit the man's glossy boots and seemed to stay there like it was happy to camp for the night.

"'Bout time y'all got here. I've had a decent meal prepared every night this week just in case. Ended up eating most of it all by my lonesome; seeing as the female population in these parts is an endangered species." The big man walked toward the car and Blackie subconsciously planned his escape route.

"Welcome home, Mr. Davis," Sgt. DuPuis's voice boomed across the quiet yard and bounced off the branches of the big trees before coming back.

"And of these fine folks, one must be your wife, Ms. Grace, and your son, Cpl. Phin Davis, and the young whiz kid from the Denver VA, James Black, who you spoke of." DuPuis shook Blackie's hand, saluted Phin, and then turned to Lolita.

"But I'm sorry, ma'am, I don't know your name."

The three men looked at each other, wondering how and why DuPuis had made himself at home in their place, each trying to keep from assigning a value judgment to his presence until they'd heard more.

"It's Lolita, Mister...?"

"Sgt. Lorenzo DuPuis, USMC, ma'am. Please, call me Lorenzo. Can I help y'all with any bags?"

Phin looked at his dad for endorsement and all Harry could do was smile awkwardly, the light from DuPuis's boots finally reflecting off of Harry's teeth. Phin liked him immediately. Gerald and Harry had endorsed him and that was good enough; Johnny would provide the details later. DuPuis had been a great help at the hospital with Cobb, he'd come to learn. That was more than enough. And Blackie took his cue from the Davis men. If this soldier was okay by them, he was, too. Lolita just liked everybody.

"Hope you don't mind me movin' in for a short spell. I was hoping to catch up with Doc Gerald and bag a few rays-o-sun before I get my new orders next month. But them hotels on the beach are outta my price range so I figured I'd camp out here in the yard and clean it up a bit fer' ma rent. Y'all have some deferred maintenance to tend to, but I think I took a nice bite out of her, anyway."

Phin processed this bit of information while Harry said he needed to help Grace use the facilities, looked around at the freshly cut lawns and trimmed shrubs, glanced at his father who seemed lost in thought, shook his head and tried to smile.

"Hey Lorenzo," Phin asked, trying to make sense of the thick conflict in the yard.

"Yes, sir?'

"Before I hand you these bags, Doc McReady requested that I buy you a cold Pabst. But seeing as though we are fresh out of Pabst, I'd like to offer you one of my father's best bottles of home brew."

"Yes, sir, Cpl. Davis. Doc knows I'm a Pabst man, but I seen them dark brown bottles in the old fridge when I was cleaning out that shed and you wouldn't have to twist this Marine's arm too hard to partake...assuming I'd have some company."

DuPuis was removing small traveling bags from the big car and spoke over the back of the trunk lid.

"Some things you don't do alone. And one of them is to drink another man's home brew without the pleasure of his company." They all nodded and watched the dogs reunite with the other dogs, nipping and dodging and taunting each other.

"By the way, sirs," DuPuis's voice had an edge of concern in it and Blackie knew what he was going to ask.

"DuPuis, that's French," Blackie interrupted. "A lot of DuPuis's up around Montreal. Any roots up north, sergeant?"

Lorenzo was taken slightly aback by the little man who'd seemed quiet at first.

"Father was from Toronto, mother from Brooklyn. I'm fluent in French, but favor Creole with an Appalachian twang."

"I see," Blackie walked up to the soldier who rose no less than ten inches above him.

"Gerald and Mr. Cobb are okay, you were going to ask? Mr. Cobb had some errands to run and Doc G, well…he's sort of indisposed as of the moment. But we have our best men on it. Not to worry. And I suppose Phin and Harry could use those numbers Mr. Jed provided."

"I see, well, yes, of course, sir." Dupuis repeated Blackie's words with a feigned vigor, but the concern hung in his brow and caused his eyes to squint like a protective shade.

They sat around the kitchen table, a big fire warming the little trailer that had served as home to the Davis Family for almost thirty years. Blackie was amazed at how quickly his core temperature had warmed from the top-down drive to the point to wanting to take off his shirt.

"It's all in the front door," Harry said, as he fiddled with different coffee beans collected from parts of South America, trying to decide what would go well together for this group, on this night. He felt like an artist and thought briefly about Francisco, the bartender in Tampico. "A good front door will take care of holes in other parts of the house," he told Blackie while deciding on a dark roast from Guatemala combined with a lighter coastal bean from southern Chile. He added in a few crushed vanilla beans from Costa Rica and some sugar cubes from Henry's Market in downtown Panama City, Florida.

"Hey Phin? You feel like grabbing a few bottles out of the fridge?"

"Sure, Pops," his voice trying to hide the reverberating uneasiness he'd felt on the causeway and how his father had avoided making the call to Jed. "You think the newer batch is any good yet?'

"You ever had a bad bottle of my home brew?" Harry asked.

"Only one, Dad, and it was on the night Gillie left us." And then Phin asked his dad to show him the good stuff in the shed while shooting him a look that suggested this was not a request. They met outside.

"Pop, whatever devil you're still wrestling with, it's not doing Mom any good."

And just before Phin continued his offensive, he spotted the reflected tear from his father's starboard eye. They'd shared a lot as father and son, but a tear from his dad was unexplored territory. Harry put his hand on his son's shoulder and walked him out into the thick dark yard as Moses and Jeremiah moved in synch, taking cue from the timber of voices.

"Phin, I've got more news about your mother's condition. It was before we went looking for you and Johnny in Lafayette and Baton Rouge. There was..." and the tear flowed south, finding a deep crease in Harry's face before landing on the earth where Moses touched the wet spot with his wet nose. "There was another stroke. The docs said it sometimes happens and she's not, well...on some days she doesn't know who I am. Hell, you saw it." And Harry said something he wished he could take back. "Or should have."

Phin sat with the idea of loss, again, for many long minutes while Harry moved to his knees to press his face into the crook of his dog's necks, a place he'd always found a kind of pure truth. Phin asked where his mother was, "right fukin' now?"

"I set her in the garden 'round back."

Across the yard, Blackie, not wanting to let the festive homecoming spirit die, jumped in with the conversation on beer. "Johnny Cobb loved his suds from a frosty mug that Auntie kept only for him in the back of the freezer box. She'd knock anybody upside the head who tried to use it."

They all thought of Johnny and his hasty exit from the hospital in Baton Rouge to go up to Lafayette and see his Uncle Chuck move down that line. There wouldn't be a ceremony or even a wake. The man died unquietly, purposely, with a hard edge of cynicism to the very end. Some thought he could've been saved and said so. But Johnny must've known he'd lived out his wick and flamed hot and bright at the end.

Grace was sitting in a wheelchair next to the garden that DuPuis had tended and tended well. She was talking to the plants, explaining why they needed to stay close to home. Phin watched from across the courtyard for several minutes before limping up from behind, placing his hands on her shoulders.

"Gillie," she burst out, "you're back. How was the catch? Phin will be home from school soon. Better wash up. You smell like your father."

✳ ✳ ✳

Phin returned to the house and took Lolita's hand. "C'mon, I'll show you the shed where all Pop's tools and home brew are kept."

They passed the solid door that Harry had built and Phin shut it tight behind him. Phin recognized the dog asleep on the porch as old Elijah. This made him happy. But as he stepped off the two landing stairs, Phin almost tripped, barely catching himself as Lolita reached for his arm.

"Is it the foot?" She asked.

"No." Phin knew it would be impossible to explain because he didn't understand it himself. "It's something else, some kind of force that's moving inside of me." He didn't mention the conversation with his mother.

"You think it's because you are finally back home?" Lolita asked, concerned, wanting to know, to help.

"I thought that it might've been it, but it started at the bridge, like someone else's body was trying to climb into my own."

"Maybe it was me," Lolita tried to cheer him up. "I was dreaming about us and there wasn't any space between the two bodies."

"I like that thought, but it's like I'm supposed to know things that I didn't see or haven't happened yet. I don't think I like it, Lolita. There's too much responsibility. I can barely take care of myself. How can I care for things that I can't control or even see or taste or touch? I don't understand this."

"Maybe you aren't supposed to, Phin. My grandmother had these same kinds of intuitions. She would say that the feeling always bore something...like fruit from a tree."

"Did she say that it tasted good, always?"

Lolita didn't answer. Phin knew that it was hard enough to get a tree to grow in the desert, let alone one that produced sweet fruit.

"Let's go then, let's go see."

Phin knew what she meant, knew where she meant. And he knew he had someone who finally understood him.

Phin went back inside, handed off the cold brown bottles, and told Harry and the others he was going for a short drive with Lolita. Harry knew there was more to it. So did Blackie. But neither mentioned it until they heard the rear trunk slam and the car drive away. Harry realized that Phin had not returned with enough beer and stood up to go outside. Just inside of that front door on the porch was a large flat box wrapped in brown paper. Written in Phin's neat handwriting on the outside were the words, "For her...and for you, Dad."

Harry opened the box and pulled out the picture of the *Grace* that Lonnie had painted so many lifetimes ago. He looked at it for a very long time, holding it on his lap as he sat in the big chair that his wife would sit in while reading books about famous Revolutionary people with Gillie. And then he returned to the garden, picked Grace up like a child and placed her in the old over-stuffed chair in the corner of the living room.

"Harry?" Grace was tugging at his sleeve. "Do you think Johnny is coming home from the war soon? Because I know Gillie went looking for them both in Southeast Asia."

And Harry, brushing a strand of long gray hair from Grace's eye and wiping a drop of spittle from the corner of her mouth, thought yes. Why not? But it was all Harry could do to smile and wonder why God was testing him beyond his ability to be godly.

Harry placed the painting back in the box, and disappeared into the kitchen. When he came out he said,

"Damn, DuPuis, don't you know where the home brew is by now?"

They sat by the fire and listened to a Miles Davis record while Grace pretended to knit. After one complete side where nothing was said, it was DuPuis who finally spoke. He turned to Harry and asked him if he thought that his son still had the war in him.

Harry didn't answer at first, just re-poured the beer and sipped it slowly, ceremoniously. There was an audible click each time the big black minute hand on the kitchen wall clock passed top-dead-center. Blackie heard six clicks all the way from the living room before Harry looked at DuPuis and asked him if he thought a soldier ever finally and forever rids himself of the killing.

DuPuis said, sure, it can happen. "But not a warrior. They carry the killing with them even before they're old enough to join up."

"You think Phin is a warrior, Lorenzo? He likes books and stories and interesting people, and he likes small places with water around him. Maybe like a moat around a castle. He joined up because he had to do *something* after his sister died."

"Maybe he's a different kind of warrior, Mr. Davis." Blackie was pacing around the room now, rubbing his chin, thinking. "A warrior isn't just about killing. It's about believing in a certain way of living your life and then living it that way regardless of the external circumstances that affect you."

Harry seemed agitated, upset that he didn't know exactly why his son had left after being home for twenty minutes, after being gone for five months.

"You think *I'm* a warrior, Blackie?" Harry looked hard into the kid. "How about Johnny or Gerald? Or Uncle Chuck? Or Sgt. DuPuis? Or my wife Grace, right here? You think they're unaffected by the dying they all seen?"

Blackie chose his words carefully, pausing to alternate sips of home brew with a cup of coffee that he'd brewed to "pinball my way to perfect thinking" he'd said, citing the upper/downer drug choice term from the '60s.

"I think you all have born witness, you all have spent time on the path; Johnny more or less than all us. Seeing all that death can send a man to the bottle, to church, to the bell tower, or inside himself. Sometimes the last is the worst. In the pathography of your life, the part that needs to be told the most is just ellipses—three dots saying it all." Blackie, paced the room in a counter-clockwise rotation. Now he reversed it. "But it's not about the killing or the dying," his steps measured out in numeric spoons of time. Then Blackie paused not for effect but because his excitement had advanced his interior metronome.

"Harry," a long deep sigh every three seconds. "It's about the living."

"Man, sometimes y'all talk in riddles." DuPuis looked at Harry and then Blackie and finally at Grace who held his stare to the point where this Marine was finally scared. Sgt. DuPuis spread his hands out to include those who weren't in attendance. "I seen a lot of dying, participated in more'n my share in the Nam. But I'm no warrior according to some definitions. I'm just doing my job, living my life in little chunks of time and place."

"Yeah, but that's what I'm saying, Lorenzo." Blackie ran his little hands through his thick curly hair and moved in close to the table. "You live by a personal standard, an integrity that rules all your decisions. Especially decisions about living and dying."

Harry sat at the head of the table pinballing his spoon around the edges of his beer and now his coffee in those twin mugs, watching the energy of the spoon make little wakes that ran up against the sides of the mugs and then died away. But at least they deflected some of that energy, he thought, back into the center of the fluid. Grace had stood up on her own accord and sat down next to him, the broken dice in her head tumbling.

The room went quiet again. The minute hand ticked. The fire began to die. The dogs that slept on the floor yawned or moved in some dog dream. Outside, the offshore wind began to fill as the inland valleys got colder and the ocean temperature stayed the same.

"I don't like labels," Harry said with a degree of conviction. "But if we're talking about warriors and soldiering for causes and living and dying and making right choices, then I'm gonna say that I don't buy it all, that all the warriors on my list are the ones who lie at the bottom of the Pacific off the coast of Guam. Nearly nine-hundred of them. And the one that lies in the ground up under that willow on the hill. They didn't die for the way they lived 'cuz they didn't get the chance. They didn't survive your 'external circumstances,' Blackie. They just died. And it wasn't anybody's fault. It just was. Calling someone a warrior is just another way of saying that they were, or are, or could be doing something good with their life. But they don't need the label to do good."

Harry, looking as if he wanted to wrap up the subject but not without coming to some conclusion, walked around the kitchen floor looking for the one board that squeaked when you stepped on it below the linoleum floor he and Phin had installed for Grace in what seemed like a lifetime ago.

"Jesus," he mumbled to himself while pressing his foot on each cut out square and listening. "I sound like Cobb again."

"Is that such a bad thing?" Blackie asked.

"I guess not, it's just that, well, I think I admired the guy because we were so different." And then Harry looked out the window as if he was expecting Phin to be back, which he knew wasn't the case, and instead he saw his reflection in the glass. "But we weren't, we aren't, are we, Blackie?"

"Does it matter, Harry?"

But before Harry could answer DuPuis chimed in.

"When's that old sage gonna be done with his errand. I wanna hang out with this cat and I don't have all day. I'm a soldier, remember? We go where we're told."

Lorenzo smiled to show that he was only partly kidding and then said he was going out to get some more home brew on account of Phin had split before adequately restocking their table. Harry took a jacket off the wall and stepped outside to lend a hand. The air had gathered its night edge and he put his hands in the pockets for warmth. One hand found a warm metal thing and pulled it out. His calloused thumb struck the flint of the old Zippo lighter and he saw his face reflected in the light, in the brushed aluminum with the letters H.D. engraved on the side. I know you, he muttered to himself.

✳ ✳ ✳

Phin and Lolita drove back out of town and onto the causeway. It was late now and the moon was getting lower in northern sky, tickling the tops of the taller eucalyptus trees that lined the inland edge of the water along the causeway. They drove in near silence with the top down and Lolita sitting close to Phin, her long thin fingers tucked under his old woolen jacket. She was humming an old Mexican folk song that brought back memories of the times he'd visited Jose's place when traveling as a kid with his parents and Gillie, but mostly the times he'd go off in summer with Johnny.

"Phin," she stopped her song and spoke into his neck, the top of his unshaven chin rubbing her forehead. "You have to be patient with me because sometimes I feel like I've known you for two lifetimes and other times I don't know you at all. Being around you and your big family of friends is like riding a tall roller coaster. It's exciting and scary, but in the back of your mind you can enjoy it because you know it won't last forever."

"Does it frighten you?"

"*Un poco*, Phin, a little. But I know that the ride will settle down and the hills won't be as high or the holes so deep. So, Phin...I have to tell you something, for me. Okay?"

Phin began to get a funny feeling in his stomach and realized he was nearing the middle of the long flat bridge over the still bayou.

"Sure," he tried to focus on the girl because he knew it was important to her.

"I want you to be patient with yourself, too."

Before the meaning of it sank in, before he could reply, before he could think about what she really wanted to say, almost before the words had left her mouth, he swerved the big Buick to the right in an effort to miss the large, dark object huddled against the low concrete wall.

The car jolted to the side, but Phin had slowed down in an effort to listen to Lolita's words and was able to regain control.

"Phin!" Lolita turned around and looked back while screaming. "You have to turn around. I think that's a body we almost ran over."

"I know," Phin's voice was clear, but the tone was cracking like old stereo speakers that are played too loud. "It's Johnny."

"How do you know that, Phin? How can this be Mr. Cobb way out here this time of night like a big rock on the side of the road?"

"I have no idea, but I know."

And Phin drove through the low wire fence that lined the center divider and went back to what they'd seen, hoping and praying that he was wrong, that even she was wrong, that it was a clump of old wet rags or a chair fallen off the back of a truck. But he knew he was right and said, "Lord Jesus, if I'm right, that man had better be okay. You owe me that."

But as they pulled up and Phin jumped out of the car, Lolita whispered that it doesn't work that way. That you have to be patient with Him as well.

CHAPTER 49

MATES FIRST

I knew what it was like to die. And it wasn't so bad.

There is something quite liberating about it all; about realizing that you can be both painfully mortal and blissfully immortal at the same time. It's magical is what it is, and it explains the unexplainable in ways that I could never explain. This is horribly cliché, but I guess you had to be there.

Of course, nobody else can, though. You have to go through it on your own, and survive, or go through it even more alone and die. Either way, you are not the same on the other side of life or the other side of death.

–Notes found in Harry's shed and signed by
Johnny Cobb

I'd made my way to the surface, to the nearest shore, to the road, and to a place I hoped where someone would notice me. I was following a kind of fading instinct and imagined myself as Pheidippides running across the Plains of Marathon or an aging carrier pigeon delivering the last tiny scroll attached to his withered leg. I just had to get there, wherever *there* was. After that, after my evening swim was complete, the world would take its due course and I'd either be in this one or, as I was coming to be convinced by the voice, another one.

And so when I had found my spot on the side of the road, a fat moon only one day past full lighting my path to just the right spot, I sat down and went to sleep. But no voice came to me, no inclination to wonder or worry about the men back in Lafayette or Phin and Harry just up the road. Not even Ruth came to my slumber. It was as if I had cleared my mind of all worldly things for the time being; I had no attachments and, therefore, no suffering. I'm not sure if I really enjoyed it because I felt as a ship sailing in front of a trailing sea and fresh winds reaching me across an ocean deep and pure.

But rudderless.

I had not made peace with water.

I had no destination, no purpose, no direction home.

And then a car began to approach and I awoke realizing that I was no wanderer, no alien, no immigrant with Neptunian tendencies. Phin was the flow; Harry the outcomer. I could be happy, safe, and dry behind the concrete dam. I had faith in hope, but no hope in faith; conviction was my fix. And quite honestly, I never really wanted Ruth's gift of premonition. It just came and, yes, I used it. But as often as it came true, I'm sure I wasn't fully invested in it.

And so I gave it up in that no-man's land between the perfect struggle of life and the imperfect journey of death. God knows where it went.

✳ ✳ ✳

We were back in the big living room of the trailer that had been the beginnings of the Davis home. The fireplace that Harry had tacked on was filled with white-hot eucalyptus logs, and the icy-cold home brew that Harry had pressed into my hand tasted just as it had the first time I visited them. I'd removed my wet clothes and Phin, in some quirky, joking testimony to fate, loaned me a set of clean U.S. Army fatigues he'd brought home from the war. I put them on and huddled close to the fire, trying to get my core temperature up while holding the cold beer bottle against the still-swelling lump on my head.

"Hey, Johnny," Phin poked his head from out of the kitchen, "That bottle fits better there now, doesn't it?"

Harry laughed and said he just couldn't get over the fact that I had climbed out of a '66 Ford truck with "half the damn Gulf trying to get in. Those trucks don't float well, do they?"

Blackie kept kidding me, saying that I was an Italian cat which had twelve lives instead of nine, and obviously I hadn't used up all of them.

Lorenzo DuPuis just kept staring at me as if I was some war hero, wanting to know every detail of my self-extrication because, "What if that shit happens to me? I need to know what to do."

Lolita was busy in the kitchen with Phin trying to put together a presentable Mexican meal on the limited stores the house had in stock.

At one point Phin came out of the kitchen wearing one of his mother's old flowery aprons and holding a plate full of fresh limes, salt, and a bottle of ageless tequila he'd found hidden away in some dark recess of a cabinet. He set the plate on the floor in front of me and started to walk back into the kitchen.

"Hey, kid," I called to him as I finally began to heat up and then to break a sweat in his camouflage jacket that had seen unsightly things. "I kinda like this army stuff. Can I borrow your dress uniform some time?"

"Sorry, Private Cobb," Phin tried to be serious. "It doesn't fit you well and you don't do it justice, not like the government who pays me to stay dead thinks a uniform should. And besides that, I was buried in that outfit. Don't you remember? There may be worms in the pockets."

"Oh, yeah," I replied, and then had to explain to Lolita in greater detail about Phin's fabricated death. She said that you would never have to go to such trouble to accomplish the same thing in Mexico, and to DuPuis, who said it was brilliant and pushed Blackie and Phin for the nuances.

"After I'm done doing what I'm supposed to do," Lorenzo sounded firm, like a drill sergeant, "I'm gonna do everything that feels right. Having the government that I fought for support the back nine of my life feels like the right thing to strive for." DuPuis had proven to be the ultimate positivist, happy in his own unknown future, whether real or imagined, manmade or manufactured.

"I'm gonna go wherever the wind blows the ashes of an old four by four. Just like y'all been talking 'bout."

Blackie said he write up a plan, but Lorenzo said he thought the plan was not to have one. And Blackie said he had a way to plan that as well.

Lolita asked, "Why not just move to Mexico? People die and go on living happily all the time."

"Be careful what you wish for," Harry said.

Grace opened her mouth and moved her lips. But the only sound was a kind of throaty gravel. Harry stood to rub her neck and said, "We know what you mean, hon. We know."

And Phin, trying to smile through it all, as peaceful as I'd seen him in years, turned to me before walking back into the kitchen to check on the beans.

"Johnny," his voice was soft, but had a twist of authority I'd not noticed in recent years. "Do you remember telling me of all the great winds of the world—the Mistral, the Trades, the Santana, the Sirocco, the Roaring Forties, the Screaming Sixties, the Chinook, the Horse Latitudes, and the Canterbury Northwester?"

I said yes, but I couldn't remember all the rest, but I did remember the Diablo and the Doldrums particularly well. I asked him what was the point of the question and he said nothing, really. Just thinking about wind. "Just thinking about how we were all scattered." And I could see he wasn't ready to offer more; just looked at his mom in the corner staring deep into the flames, an old knitted blanket on her lap, Harry massaging her temples. And Phin shook his head slowly from side to side.

Blackie was engaged in deep conversation about plot-making systems and manipulation with DuPuis and, as I looked over my shoulder at Harry, I saw his big wide back moving out through the solid oak door. He'd kissed Grace on the head, looked at me, and I stood up and followed the man outside into the night.

Harry sat on the porch, one hand rubbing the old hound, Moses's neck and the other trying to dab away the trail of tears on his cheek with his sleeve.

"You created immortality, didn't you, Cobb? You cheated death when Gillie and lots of guys in Vietnam were cheated by it." There was no anger or blame in his voice. It was a simple observation, like talking about the changing weather.

"You ever think that life is just one big exercise in loss, Johnny? That if we're not careful we'll just lie down and drown in our own past? You ever think that those great dreams are only found on other streets and other towns and that for men like us, our hopes are kidnapped and held hostage until the captors are finally dead?

"I think it every day," I told him. "I think it all, every day. But then I see the goodness of people coming back from the dead, like those boys sitting in there, and back at Auntie's, and in VFW halls and massage parlors and job-training programs and night school and every shitty honky-tonk, both sides of the Mason Dixon line. And I think that some humans are larger than human life."

I sat down next to the man and lit my pipe.

"We all lost a lot of flesh these past few years. But what we got, Harry, is the last true currency of any lasting value—we got history together. It ain't all been good, but it's something, eh? It's something.

"I'm sorry about Grace, Harry. I truly am. And Gillie. And Ruth and Louella and Chuck and Mike Greer and Buddy Holly and Earl and Ramsey and JFK and thalidomide and all that rain at Woodstock and the break-up of the Beatles."

We sat in silence, Harry's tears falling off his cheek and landing in the thick dog fur. But they didn't stop there; just rolled off and hit the wood deck and pooled and slid down a crack between the boards and then into the same earth where his daughter was buried close enough to hear.

I blew smoke rings that rose up and then joined the clouds and we listened to the wind sing through the tall pines until another song—that of a woman's—breathed a different sound through the thin walls, around the big door, right into the heart of each of us.

Phin opened the door and said supper was ready, if'n we two old men had enough strength left to come to the table, and went back inside. But not before Harry asked me.

"Were you scared, Johnny? I mean, staring at the end down there, in the dark...were you scared?"

"Hell, yeah," I told him and then asked. "Weren't you? After the *Indy* went down?'

"I've seen worse. It's just wind and water and sea creatures," his voice moving out across the yard behind his gaze. "Nothing a good boat and some large hooks can't handle."

"Harry," I stopped him before we went back in. "I'd like to try my hand at this fishing thing again. You plan on going out anytime soon?"

"First light, old man, first light after we get both Graces back in shape." Another kind of light came into Harry's eyes; the distant possibility that restoring his wife and his boat-that shared her name would help everyone connected. And I thought it would be the kind of light to flicker for months, maybe years to come.

"I hear there are snook the size of small coyotes," he said, feeling the warmth move out from the house, "and they're just southwest, 'bout three days sail. Right now, I think I'll get some rest."

"Done," I said, meaning it in ways I could never hope to imagine.

We ate mostly in silence except for this raspy cough I couldn't shake. After dinner I went outside to smoke my pipe, thinking the smoke would heat up my lungs and scare whatever was in there away. "I need to rid myself of all that water that seeped in through the holes in my body," I told Harry. "A good pipe full, a long piss, I'm as good as new.

"Good night," I said and stood up, but then sat down again to catch my breath.

"You okay, Cobb. You don't look so good, not that you ever have." Harry tried to hide his concern.

"I'm fine. Go on in, I'll be right there." And Harry said okay he was going to make up some bedrolls for the folks and went back inside. But the cough got worse and the color of things coming out of me began to blacken as the moon moved across the southern sky and sent shadows running from anything in its wake. Phin came out, sat down and handed me a handkerchief.

"You swallow much water out there?" he asked.

"Regular amount, I reckon. I ain't thirsty, if that's what you're asking."

"I've a mind to run you over to the hospital in Fort Walton Beach; get you an x-ray of your lungs."

"Nice try, kid. You're supposed to be dead, remember? And I ain't about to bother Harry or the others. Been in enough hospitals the past week or so."

"That's okay. I'll have DuPuis and Blackie take you. They have experience in these kinds of matters."

"Aw, c'mon, Phin, I'm all right, just need to hack up some saltwater that's sloshing around inside."

"You aren't better in an hour, they're running you over to the clinic at least. Deal?"

"Yeah, fine." I brushed it off and we sat in the rendered silence of uncertainty. After a long while, Phin asked if I ever thought about how it all came to be, you know, the way it was now compared to what it was back then? Sure I told him, it started with a boat.

"Uncle Chuck's new mahogany and teak skiff, a boat made of wood grown in Southeast Asia, India, and Thailand from trees rarely found in this country anymore. It all started with the boat—the ending and the beginning of things. I used to dream of the parable of Jesus walking on water, of calming His scared disciples in the storm as they fished and the boat began to sink. It made me think the Man was trying to offer me something—some capacity to engage in the world around me, some courage to follow Ruth and Chuck into that thick grove of overgrown and unknown. Maybe He was sorry about Ruth, but wives and daughters and brothers die and it's not their death, but what you do with it that matters; the obligation of the affected, you might say. I might've figured that out as I grew older, but He was offering to help then, to give me the capacity to feel more and see just around the corner enough when somebody might be needing what little I could offer. But I'm not sure I ever come to a deal with Him well enough. Until tonight." Phin nodded and his eyes watched my chest move up and down, deliberately.

What did I have to offer anyway? I thought in silence then wondered out loud.

"I don't have much anymore, Phin. But I reckon I've gained much more than I lost even if I can't say it plain and straight during regular daylight hours."

Phin, who was still watching me, still starring at the rise and fall of my chest as much as my eyes, said I done good, that he was obliged, said I was going to heaven whether or not I liked it. There was a change in the sound of his voice, not the tone or content of what was coming out but more like the *why* of his words. I didn't mention it, said I was tired and got up to go off and sleep in Gillie's old room. I stopped and put my hand on his shoulder, kept my eyes fixed ahead at the big oak door. Phin put his hand on top of mine, said good night, said he'd check on me in half an hour and I went in. I could feel his eyes following me closely, nervously. I was afraid and excited. Tired as I was, I didn't expect a good sleep. And as I crossed that big threshold I turned and said, "Kid, it can't be easy for you. Your dad will be fine. After a spell. So, I were you, I'd invest some time in your mom. She ain't long for the world.

"See you in the morning, kid," I coughed and hacked between puffs. "We'll talk some more."

CHAPTER 50

A COAT OF MANY COLORS

And in the end is my beginning.

—Mary, Queen of Scots

But neither *Grace* was going to be ready soon. Too much had happened in too quickly of time, like taking an incredible action picture, but the shutter speed was just too slow to capture it with any degree of clarity. Harry had thought he wanted to get back on the ocean quickly, but had come to the conclusion that he'd been doing that all his life—using the saltwater to heal open wounds when all it did was to keep them clean while they took longer to scab over. Always leaving a scar.

Johnny had risen before the sun, thinking he'd be the first one up in the old trailer. He'd not slept well if at all, and had heard Phin come in and check on him as he coughed and finally said damn, kid, just sleep on the floor. And he did.

Johnny had gone outside to feed the dogs. His cough seemed a little better, but he was still a bit short of air. He heard a strange raspy noise humming from the shed where all the old boat parts were kept. There was a glowing light peeking out from under the door and between the smooth, rhythmic grinding was an even courser sound—that of a man singing out of key, off key, like a key was stuck in his throat. It had to be Harry.

Cobb went to the window and watched for a while before going in. Harry had the *Ruth Henry David* up on sawhorses and was planing down the warped floorboards by hand, occasionally stopping to change the length and depth of the blade. Johnny had seen the boat tucked under an old part of the yard, its gunwales lying in the rich red dirt soaking up moisture, mixing earth with sea and rotting the wooden medium in the slow but assured process. He hadn't said anything to Harry or Phin about it, thinking that was like calling a man's wife fat. Nobody spoke openly about the condition of the *Ruth Henry*, but it existed somewhere in each man's head.

"Someday," they might be telling themselves, individually, collectively, "When the time is right—when it can get no worse or maybe no better—someday the time will be right and that little boat will get pulled out and set upon strong saw horses and worked upon by stronger hands."

That someday had come. And in the realization, Johnny knew it had been Harry whom it had come to.

Johnny watched Harry work and saw how comfortable he was alone, again. And then it struck him that he'd always been that way, even as the devoted husband and father, Harry Davis was the solitary wanderer. He was fine with others, but he'd shone brightest when there were no spotlights, no witnesses, and the consequences were all his own. Grace had been a presence, but she was a wanderer in her own way, never venturing too far from home or homeport. It was their autonomy that brought them together. And they loved each other for that.

Johnny watched him through the glass, heard his awful voice sing a song that nobody could recognize, but the glow in his eyes was as bright as the sun that was coming up over the eastern lip, pulling the edges of Harry's smiling mouth with it.

The boat was but a shell of its once perfect form with dark mold growing out of the mahogany ribs, and split and splintered gunwale caps. There was one small area, though, near the top of the transom, just above the tarnished, bronzed letters that spelled out the name of the boat—the gender combination of a farmer's wife, their unborn son, and her favorite author. Cobb remembered how it all came to be out on that lake so many years ago. And his eyes went to the one spot on the boat that seemed unaffected by time and weather and the beating that each can provide. The varnish was still clear and thick over the dark woody veins of growth standing sentinel, appearing to take on a life of its own that said, *If I can come through that, you can come back from it.*

Cobb let Harry alone and walked across the yard to go in and start the coffee. For the moment, all was right with his friend. And that made things all right with him. That's when he coughed long and hard, sat on the ground, saw the sun just come over the horizon, and laid his head down in the dirt and pine needles of the Davis's long driveway.

It was the dogs that found him, trying to lick his life back into him with their long red tongues, baying at the sweet, thick clouds rolling in off the gulf.

They buried Johnny Cobb out under the tall cypress on the edge of the property. Next to him were the bones and memories and future passed that belonged to Gillie and a space for those who remained to stand sentinel.

The wake lasted over a week and was only interrupted when the dog, Moses, dug six feet of dirt away and scratched at Johnny's teak and mahogany coffin, howling and baying all the way down. They all said it was the damndest thing they'd ever seen. They all felt like they ought to be doing the same.

CHAPTER 51

WIND SEEDS

With loss of Eden, till one greater Man restore us, and regain the blissful seat.

–from Milton's, *Paradise Lost: Book I,*
The Invocation

There would be no plea bargain. This was show time. Blackie testified at the trial of one Gerald R. McReady. Those in the courtroom were so moved by the words of the young academic, the former mental patient who'd been medically and honorably discharged from a short stint in *that* war, they wept for the accused. Blackie tried to convince himself that indeed, this might've been his best performance yet, but he wasn't really acting. Just coming clean with the help of some well-developed delivery tools.

Sgt. Lorenzo DuPuis was also subpoenaed to testify and, as the new Head of Recruitment, Southeastern Sector, his superior officer was happy to give him a few days off to, "show the world what a U.S. Marine looks like when asked to bear witness on the supporters of the Corps."

When called to the stand and asked about his dealings with the accused, Sgt. DuPuis produced a small bag of lead pieces that was poured out onto the judge's pulpit and offered up as material evidence. When questioned about the relevance of the bullet fragments by the prosecuting attorney, DuPuis said that the Communists had infiltrated his ass but Orderly McReady had done what the U.S. Government had failed to do and removed them from a place they shouldn't be.

The prosecution objected. The jury laughed. But everyone knew the soldier was right.

The strange pack of rabid dogs that had attacked the bartender was never located despite the largest dog hunt ever conducted in Baton Rouge Parrish. One of the witnesses testified that it was McReady who'd attacked the bartender first and it was the dogs who were trying to save him from this man from Colorado. The accuser's attorney mumbled out loud that maybe the dog hunt should be resumed since there appeared to be a rampant, valorous gene that might be bred among the city's population, both animal and human.

The other witnesses, including the young woman and her male friends, were never located and the information provided to the reporting police was false. Mr. McReady had only seen the boy once when he was a patient in the VA hospital he had worked at. He'd testified under oath that he'd been told that the corporal had died from his injuries after leaving the hospital. The records confirmed this, and after only three days of entertaining testimony, the judge threw the case out of court and ordered the bartender to seek professional counseling.

For the record, it had all been true, only the facts were misinterpreted; reality washed by illusion and hung back out to dry as truth.

✳ ✳ ✳

McReady moved to Lafayette and took over the helm at Johnny Cobb's shop. The men respected him.

Blackie returned to the East Coast and was immediately offered two separate postions as doctoral student and graduate teaching assistant at Ivy League schools, partly because he was qualified and partly because he'd already secured multiple seven-figure research grants from various public and private funding sources. His classes were always full.

Auntie never fully remembered the details of those days when the center could not hold at her little café or in her own normally resilient self. She told the cops little because they didn't really want to know and she couldn't really say. Things returned to normal, nothing really fell apart. She imagined that Johnny would've showed her compassion, but there had been a paradigm shift inside Auntie as well. Where Johnny would've looked older on the outside, Auntie took on the dark vicissitudes of age inside. After she learned of Johnny's passing she was still Auntie to the crew from the shop, but she was just a waitress to world. And sometimes an old aunt who tried to remember birthdays and anniversaries, but never anything more or less than that.

Most of the guys stayed on at the waterbed shop for a while, until the platforms they had been building came together, and then they moved out, into the rest of their live, differen, very different than before they had gone in, before they had gone in-country, before they had gone back into the world.

Gerald likened Hopper to a well-read book from the library that had nicely-added annotations in the margins. Tom-Tom was an old guitar that sounded better as the wood aged and was better able pick up the vibrations caused by the strings when they were plucked. Strider was freedom on two feet, the Golden Dream, interrupted, but embodied. Leroy was the guy voted "least likely to succeed" in his high school yearbook, and at his ten-year reunion he showed up in the same cheap thrift-store suit he'd used to graduate in. What he never told anyone was that he'd taken the novel idea of charging money for stressed executives to come to an out-of-the-way canyon and fire a rifle for fifty bucks an hour and turned it into a six-figure income.

War was strange like that. Every once in a great while you could take inductive reasoning and create these wonderful generalizations. You could take a few particulars and create the illusion of acceptable generalization. War has its place, they might say. It makes men strong, rids the world of tyrants. Hell, look at how we kicked Hitler's ass, eh? They'd say. But they were fallacies, Gerald thought. The world was not built on an either/or platform.

Gerald sat in Johnny's maple chair behind the big oak desk with his small feet propped on the edge. His boots set off to the side, he noticed holes in his socks worn through on each side where his ankles met his leather boots. How long had it been since he bought new socks for himself? Or had a woman buy a pair for him?

It was nearing Christmas and the shop was quiet; only a few of the new guys, most of them vets still wrestling tattered souls, puttered around the place filling last-minute orders. The Nam was dying, finally. But it still was being fought.

War. Yeah, well, people had made a case for it since long before there were people as he knew them and would continue to do so until war itself had altered people as the future would come to know them. Or maybe not know them at all.

It was still a fallacy.

But what about the profound brotherhood that exists between men in war? Was that a fleeting fallacy? A subjective memory? Or even a generalization? A dream projected in reverse, something that almost existed, but reviewed in the cold bright light of later years was only a wishful hope that it could've been that way? No, I won't allow that in my shop, in my crew, or in my mind. There have to be options to finding the truth. And when we find it, we deal with it. Even if it kills us. Uncle Chuck waltzed his way into just such an option because, for him, it was down to less than zero...which isn't going in the hole of debt, but simply none.

Gerald tried to organize a few files so that he could have an easier time running this growing concern. But he wasn't worried. The world would always need good craftsmen, men and women who could work with their hands and build things for a fair price.

What *price*? Gerald had a picture in his mind of Leroy marching into a fancy bank downtown, asking to see the manager because he wanted to set up a business account. But the manager would look up from his thin glasses and view a young Black man wearing fatigue pants and sporting a clean but threatening Afro haircut. He'd tell his secretary to "handle it," but she would say that the amount he wished to deposit was beyond her authorization to do. And so the manger would speak with Leroy about the sizeable account, wonder about the origins of the cash, but he'd take the man's money into his bank. Leroy would ignore the distain on the man's face, politely hand him a business card with the name of the popular shooting range he owned and ran outside of town. And then Leroy would get up to leave, put out his hand to shake, praying all the long that someday there would be no *price* of being born Black.

McReady organized a few more small items and thought of Hunter. He was the favorite, the embodiment of Johnny; of what he'd heard of Old Grayfalls, the quiet healer, the shaman who healed until he could do no more good and then quietly set off into the woods to die, alone. But Hunter had plenty of spirit left in him. Of all of them, he was the least affected by the Nam because, as a medic, he was exactly where he was supposed to be at that point in his life. Upon return and graduation from *Johnny Cobb's School of Re-entry, Rehab, and Recoiling Mattresses*, Hunter suffered through the didactic elements of med-school and promised to go to work as an emergency room physician at the worst hospital in the south part of Boston.

A few years later, Gerald imagined he'd hear from Strider, who'd sent a Christmas card every year from his boat anchored near a perfect point-break wave in southern Chile near the Patagonia border. Strider would say that Hunter will move to Chicago because the trauma cases in Boston aren't challenging enough.

What was a guy like Strider doing in Vietnam anyway? Many people had predicted correctly that the poor, the Hispanic, the Blacks, the regular under-represented of the country would fight more in Vietnam. And die more in Vietnam.

But there were many who'd gone and fought, and they weren't poor or ethnic or underprivileged. They went because they believed in their country, they believed in their leaders. They went because they were curious or because they thought they just might as well. They went because if they didn't, their lives wouldn't have been the same. But they could not have known the truth or the consequences of this realization. They went because they were drafted and their options, when considered as what truth an eighteen-year-old kid might possess, put Vietnam on a higher order than prison or Canada or a life on the lam or a life of perceived disgrace. It was their truth, Gerald thought, and they had all been deceived.

Maybe a case could be made for war, he tried to convince himself. Johnny had been a legally free man in the South because of war. That was something. Still, Gerald wanted to know if war was contextual, as the great theorist had argued. He'd have to put some time into considering that. But deception? Where would he begin? Self-deception was bad enough. That took work to fix, but it could be fixed. But malicious and purposeful deception of others, both overt and covert—that was criminal, worthy of prosecution.

But hadn't Blackie and himself deceived the courts then? Was it a clear-cut case of muddied waters? Situational ethics? Double standards? Stunt doubles? He didn't really know, only that some ultimate truth should be a goal of every man. Maybe he'd start with himself. He might not live long enough to find out but, geez, Gerald, what a way to try and live out the rest of your years?

Gerald got up to leave and took one last look around the office. Snare walked in. He had a big green rucksack slung over his shoulder.

"You look like Santa." McReady was glad to see him.

"I was watching you, McReady." Snare's eyes looked softer than the sound of his voice. "You were deep-thinking again."

"Yeah," Gerald sat back down and motioned Snare to a chair where he set his pack down and leaned into the back of it, rocking slightly from foot to foot.

"Let me ask you this, Snare. You ever think there'll be a war tribunal for Vietnam like there was in Nuremburg?"

Snare started laughing and the sound caught them both by surprise. Neither was sure that they'd ever heard the other laugh as completely as they were doing now.

"I know you're serious, McReady, so I won't even ask you if you are. But, c'mon? Think about that for a second. Who are you going to put on trial? Where would you start? With the French? With Kennedy? Johnson? McNamara? Diem? Westmoreland? Chairman Mao? Ho Chi Minh? With every person who really bought the idea of the Domino Theory? With the organized protestors who ran their own form of war here at home? The Panthers, the students, the Underground? With Lt. Calley? With the majority of the elected officials of the most powerful country on earth? With every small-minded barber and salesperson in every small town who really *believed* we were right to go there? Maybe Jane Fonda or Bob Dylan or Pete Seeger or Joan Baez?

"How about the dead, Gerry? Are they grateful or guilty for not choosing another option? And how about the shadow men in the corporations who profited? You going to put Bell Helicopters and Dow Chemical on trial? Every contractor that made a buck off of some piece of gear that was supposed to protect 'our boys over there?' That would be like putting capitalism on trial. Where are you going to start and stop, my good friend and most gracious small boss? Because you might as well start with me. I'm guilty of every crime committed by every person on that list...and many, many more."

Gerald knew that Snare was right. So he just shook his head from side to side and then up and down and blew a lung full of air out through his pursed lips. Then he asked him about the people, "You know, the South Vietnamese?"

"What can I say?" Snare put his hands up in the air and then behind him with his head hung low. He stood and walked in circles like a man sentenced to a Turkish prison.

"We were supposed to help them. Way I figure it, though, by the time we get used to the Commie-backed North running Saigon, the good 'ole U-S-of-A. will be disavowing and distancing itself faster than some college kid caught with his hand up her pants. First we get as many of our men as possible out alive, then we cut the economic aid, make a show of looking for the unaccounted, embrace a few movies that support that bullshit, then we wait twenty years and open up 'talks' with the bastards 'cuz the world's getting smaller. Ain't it,doc?"

Gerald thought that Snare might've been drawing a tighter circle on each lap of the office's worn pinewood floor.

"And the people from the South, like you asked about, they're basically good. They'll survive. But the country will never be the same as if we'd won the fuckin' war. I suspect lots will die before some stability comes to the area." Snare stopped suddenly in his tracks when they'd basically tightened into a motion of him spinning circles on himself.

"I suspect the U.S. will remember Vietnam as more of a war than a country. A united Vietnam will go on in the last decade of the twentieth century just like a reunited America went on in the last part of the nineteenth. In the case of South Vietnam, that ain't right because in the history of a war you can gradually erase the warriors. It's something else altogether when a country gets erased."

"So, what are you gonna do, Snare?" Gerald finally asked.

"Goin' back over. Got a job with the 'government.' " Snare made quote marks in the air and smiled. "To hang around Saigon, quietly, and 'advise.' " Snare made a funny movement with his eyebrows, like he couldn't decide on the best type of body language. "I was alive over there, Gerry. I know it's fucked up. I know the North is going to march right into Saigon within a year or so. Hell, Gerry, before you and I are dead I bet we'll be able to go back over there on vacation. It really is a beautiful country, especially up north in the mountains, where the napalm and orange didn't visit. Oh, and the Mekong Delta on a June afternoon."

Gerald rifled through his drawers looking for a distraction. "Do you think there is a difference between the guy who goes back into the minefields so he can come to grips with his fear, with where the dangers lie, and the guy who thrives on dancing cheek to cheek with his own demise because he fears having to go back to go forward, and so he waltzes in the minefield for fun?"

"Sure." Snare slowed his words, thoughtfully, intelligently. "Going back in is a means to ultimately moving forward and then, with any luck, through it. But someone who walks repeatedly though the mines just for the sake of being in the mines, you see, they don't really want to move forward. The addiction becomes the feeling of being there. To move out away into a safe zone would be a deprivation of sorts."

"But I think what you're referring to is the difference between addiction and a cry for help."

"Aren't they the same?"

"For a lot of those guys who don't have or aren't given the tools, they can't tell the difference. It's all muddied up like three clean, clear rivers—when they merge they become a murky shade of muck."

McReady was going to ask Snare if he knew the difference, but he knew that he knew.

"I'm okay here, McReady, but over there was just... something about skulking on the cutting edge. I loved it and hated it to death. So, I'm going to take Uncle Sam's money and go play in the minefields for a while longer. It's not for fun, it's because for now...it's who I am. And I'm defenseless to change him."

Gerald nodded; knowing that the honesty he'd been shown was a gift that Snare shared with few.

"What about you, McReady? You seem ready for some new scenery. This place allow you to do your healer schtick well enough?"

"Oh, I don't know. These guys need someone right now. Might take a few decades, but the war will slowly leave them. After a while, I might learn to fish or reapply to med school."

"McReady, you're a good man. Woulda made a good field medic. It don't matter, though; some fish aren't supposed to be caught."

Snare shook Gerald's hand, picked up his big duffel bag, and walked out the door.

Gerald mumbled softly to himself and everything that Snare stood for: "I'll remember that. Yes, I will."

There was something else though.

"Hey, Snare, one more thing before you go," Gerald had tried to resist, but he had to ask.

"If it's about money, buy a round at Auntie's for me. And I won't tell you my real name, even if I could remember it."

Gerald stifled a laugh because he was truly interested.

"Would you want to know how'll you die?"

Snare looked pleased with the question. It was the right one to end this conversation with.

"I already know, Doctor McReady. I've always known." Snare offered a gesture with his free hand; it was half-salute, half-friendly wave.

He shut the door behind him and the gust blew a few papers off Cobb's old desk.

CHAPTER 52

AN UNEARTHING

When Harry walked through the back door into the kitchen, Phin was frying bacon and Lolita was scrambling a combination of eggs, cheese, onions, tomatoes, chilies, avocadoes, cilantro, garlic, black beans, and few things that even Johnny, a man who was raised trying to coax things out of the earth, wouldn't recognize.

It'd been nine weeks since Johnny Cobb was laid to rest, and six since Grace had passed quietly in the Davis' back yard, huddled in Harry's arms while Lolita plucked a hand-me-down guitar that Phin had found in a tiny closet next to where Gillie had slept. Funny, Phin thought, it'd been a long time since this house heard music. Phin had even pretended to pick worms from Grace's pretend tomatoes—anything they could do to keep Grace in a real world. She had slipped further and further into some alternative reality after Johnny passed and Harry had not left her side in those last weeks, refusing to leave unless he needed to, as suggested, "shave, piss, or negotiate with God."

And just before Grace's final gasp in that late fall of 1973, the sugar maple leaves falling, Phin heard her efforts at clear speech, saw her eyes draw Harry into a place he could not escape.

"Do, do, do not you run away from all this, Ha, Harry. Don't you leave."

Things were shifting toward something other than what was happening for them now, which was a slow steady simmer, a burning off of leftover life. A twinge of nervousness was creeping around the edges of Harry and Phin, no different than the eggs. Lolita knew it and kept her bag half-packed, wondering if she'd bet on the wrong horse.

Phin poured two big mugs of coffee and asked his dad if he'd come out front and sit on the porch. And so they sat.

"You think it's over, Pop? The bad stuff, I mean."

"Ain't sure," he said, as Harry adjusted the belt on his old jeans and packed Johnny's old pipe. He wouldn't smoke it, but the smell of fresh tobacco brought a smile. "Pain kind of lives inside its own dimension. Reckon we don't get to choose."

"So, how do you deal with that, knowing that it could come around at any moment like some old jazz record that skips on a dissonant note waiting to be resolved, but it doesn't until you get up and push the needle over?"

"It's like this, kid," Harry fiddled with the unlit pipe, some of that old swagger back in his voice, the thing that had gone away with Gillie and then Johnny. And then Grace. "You look at the future and see two points converging on the horizon. There could be nothing there, out at that point of perspective, or there could be the promise of prospect, or gold, or..."

"Or just another point on another horizon."

"You got it, kid, just leap-frogging toward immortality."

The two sat there sipping the hot coffee, waiting for nothing, just sitting; a father and a son and a mutual memory of those who had shaped them both unequally. Inside they heard Lolita singing, "it's coming on Christmas, they're cuttin' down tress, putting up reindeer, singing songs of joy and peace."

Harry put Johnny's old pipe in his mouth and mumbled, "well there is always that—joy and peace."

"It's a song about a failed relationship, Dad. I listened to Joni's music in Vietnam. There's a line in that song, 'I wish I had a river so long I would teach my feet to fly'."

"And where would you go, Son?"

"Another point on another horizon."

"So," Harry asked finally, "Have you decided where you'll land this time around?"

It was a patented question, but one that had to be asked.

"Of course. Right where those two points meet."

"East or west?" Harry asked, tending toward the revolutions of the earth, forgetting about the sun and moon.

"South," Phin said with a kind of assurance in his voice that startled Harry. "Where time moves as slow as it will take you to grow old, to skate warm rivers like kids. Where nobody needs camo-fatigues and it's hard to tell where the earth ends and the oceans begin, where I can walk around barefoot and nobody will stare at the space where toes are supposed to be. And where *you* can sail right into my front yard."

Harry looked intently at his son who had a kind of deep smile that started at his lips and went right on into his soul. Phin looked back and asked.

"Where do you see yourself, Pop?"

Harry stood up from where he'd been sitting on the top step of the front deck, arched his back and then sat back down.

"I'm already closer to one hundred than zero. Never told you this but I was only less than a quarter-century old when the *Indy* went down. Some days I feel thrice that, others one-third. In the past year—you and me—well, we may have lived ten, or at least earned credit for it. I don't know about you, kid, but I think I'm gonna rest up for a bit and then go back to a point in my life that held some good times."

"You really think you got the energy to refurnish the *Grace* and take her out again?"

"What makes you think that's what I'm gonna do?"

"I don't know; I just have this sense about things now. Can't say where it comes from."

Harry smiled to himself and nodded as he watched the morning spread on his land. "This place is a good one to start out at and end up. But it's out there that keeps me honest." He spread his arms and Phin noticed that his reach hadn't lessened from what he remembered it as a kid.

"Yep," Harry continued, "it's a home, here. It's where you'll spread me out when I'm done and watch the wind carry me back if'n the breeze tries to move me. But I ain't ready to lie down. Nope. Ain't ready."

Phin thought of losing his dad, that last firebreak between saving the town and his own demise. It was a new thought, though. Even since he was a child he'd thought Harry would live forever, that *he'd* be the one to go first, to mutate the pecking order. His pop was immortal. Even more than other dads. Losing Gillie, Grace, and Johnny—it was just something he never considered. And so Phin resigned himself to know, not think, his dad, Harry was in fact...immortal.

Phin let the quiet hold the morning and thought of Johnny. He started laughing at the thought of it all, the irony maybe, or the plain old laughability of an aging Black farmer from Alabama making and selling wooden frames for mattresses that were filled with water, sold and shipped as fast as they could turn them out, to places like Oregon and California. It just plain hit him square. His laugh began somewhere deep and gathered steam. The sound coming from his mouth was not new, but he didn't remember it well—like the war had held it hostage. It gathered momentum and force, continuing to build as an avalanche or an earthquake or any orgiastic force of nature that desperately, undeniably needed to be released.

Phin rolled back on his shoulders and kicked his feet in the air. A laugh moved out from the core and down his legs and into his arms carrying with it bits and pieces of people who he'd watched die and others that he'd become as close to as any people could, even as hard as they tried not to. Phin looked over at Harry who couldn't see the grand humor in it all and sat amused by Phin's actions. Each time Phin tried to gain control of his laugh, he'd look up at Harry who was just smiling now, watching his last child let go and give up control of something. And then Phin would start again, somehow laughing harder, with conviction and clarity and a profound purpose of which he had no idea. At one point, Phin caught himself enough to blurt out: "And here's a good one, Pop. Think about this. Once, when I was in-country I had a captain tell me that we would have to do a lot of evil before we could do good. How's that?"

And, of course, that empowered *The Laugh* and now Phin was losing control; The Laugh had him by the hand, by the tail, by the balls.

"You know what I told him, Dad?" Phin wasn't even looking at Harry anymore but speaking to the sky when The Laugh would allow words to come out, carrying still more shit from Phin's past. "I said, hey, Cappy, you remind me of what Tacitus said about the Roman conquests: 'they create a desert and call it peace.' Oh, Pops, the captain didn't like that one and put me on point; probably hoping I'd take one in the temple.

"But I liked it up there, Pop. Fucking crazy, huh?" And when Harry looked at Phin, the tears were jumping out of the corners of Phin's eyes as if squeezed between two thumbs. But he was still laughing.

"Yep, old Dad, if you're not the lead dog, the view never changes. No chatter up there, no distractions, no fear because if you take one in the temple there ain't any time to think about dying, right? Am I right, Pop? Aren't I right, I mean, it's better to go quick than to have to sit around for minutes or days or months and think about it. Right? Am I right?"

And Phin called Harry, "Daddy."

Harry, slowing being sucked into The Laugh said there was dignity and illusion in both dying quick and dying long. But you never knew when and where the bullet was coming from, so you might as well cling to both and be prepared—say your prayers at night, treat other people and dogs right.

The Laugh had subsided for the time being and left Phin gasping for breath, exhausted. But all it had really done was to open some long-blocked channel, a logjam between the heart and the world around him. It was quiet for a moment and Harry put his arm around his boy whose breath had slowed to something regular but strong.

"You know, Phin, when I was growing up, most of my kind didn't get to keep our parents around us much and youth was just a period that you passed through on your way to growing up. But now, what with all the kids wanting to be Peter Pan and living in what they call communes, what we call a farm, staying young is everything. But when you lose family or go to war, you get tapped on the shoulder and Father Time pushes the fast-forward button on the tape machine. The way I figure it, you and I have gained about a quarter of a century of experiences in the past few years. And we learned most of them the hard way: one drop of blood, one hurricane, one mistake, one day at a time. But we done it with dignity, denying the illusion that it wasn't real. I'd say we're ready if anybody taps us on the shoulder."

Phin said he was right, he had no cause to disagree with that line of reasoning, that he didn't mean to knock anyone off their high horse of sentiment.

"But if you distill it down, that don't change the fact that you own a history of denial and fear and guilt—same as me."

That's when The Laugh returned, this time coming from Harry, coming on so hard that Phin simply submitted to it. And this time the purity of it all, the immutable and satirical burlesque, found its way into Harry's past when he let Gillie fish without a floppy hat, when he wasn't there when Grace got sick. Where Harry was just plane gone

Both of them, shackled by the force of release, the implosive unfurling, rolling around there on the early morning porch while the dogs, sensing something playful in it all, joined in, nipping and tucking at the kid who suddenly wasn't a kid and the older man who wasn't even old, just in dog years, tragic years.

The dam busted and out flowed Gillie's cancer; then the image of some kid named Glover spread thin like jelly by an RPG on the road to Dak to take back Hill 875. And there was poor Worm, who'd given him the gift of words, he was next. Then the thoughts of Harry treading water for five days after the *Indy* went down while the men in the gray suits and sharp teeth had their way with them. There were flashes of Lonnie, safe but not his, never really his; flashes of Jose, safe, but missing his daughter; flashes of Gerald, safe, but under some temporary lock and key; flashes of Dickey Riot, sardonically shedding his skin of normalcy like a snake; and out slithered the saintly, gallant-though-sinful, Uncle Chuck, marching in time to his own gallowed-hymn. And there was a future image of a grown-up Jessica from Lubbock with no one to walk her down the aisle since the cancer could always return and take her pop-the-colonel. And the image of the sea taking her Uncle Johnny just like the bottle had taken her mom...two slowly, the other quick, both from the inside out.

But then the explosion flashed in front of and behind and all around Phin; the one that only took part of his foot and not all, wounded but not dead, wounded to where they said it would be easier to walk if "we just cut the rest of you apart;" wounded in places that you couldn't fix with medicine and morphine and scalpels and surgery.

Phin Davis knew well what the wound meant. And now he was laughing it away.

"You know what I think is really funny?" Harry was breathing hard. "Your ugly foot that you hide in that boot I made for you. Now, that's something to scoff at."

Phin, pretending to act offended, removed the shoe and the sock. He began to inspect it carefully while Moses licked the bottom. Harry stopped laughing and began to apologize.

"Don't. I agree," Phin was acting well. "It's hideous to look at. But where I'm going, I'll walk in warm sand all day and sooner or later I'll forget about it and my body will compensate and all it will be is both a mockery of the government who killed me on paper and sends checks to an account that never cashes them. So, screw you, Pops. I like this lump." But Phin, hard as he tried, could not hold the straight face.

Then it was Harry's turn to act hurt. But he was doing what he'd been trying to do for so many months and had not succeeded. And truth be known, it was no act.

"You think you know the intimate and subtle joys of misery, do you? Okay, so you lost Gillie and you went and joined up. Well, we *all* lost Gillie, mostly me and your ma, and then we almost lost you. What kind of stupid fucking move was that? But alright, you up and did it. And then you think it's more peaceful to patrol click after click, as you put it, riding shotgun, humping point, because you can't decipher your own mea culpa from some ill-conceived guilt over the will of some God you don't fucking know from Adam. I won't even go into what it must've been like for your mother to lose half her mind, me out to sea, her daughter out to pasture, her son out of his mind. She wasn't clutching the warm hand of her family or a Bible; it was a tomato, Phin, a damn red, ripe tomato that blew up in her hand exactly like the vessels that blew up inside her brain.

"Well, that's just fine, my young son. All I had to do was lose most of my family. 'Ceptin' your ass. So, fuck you, too. Because at least in my old-man misery I've learned to put it all on the table and let the world and that God and everything in between decide my fate while you sit there with the comfort of a father who'd cut out his own liver and hand it to you if you asked him, and a girlfriend who is well on her way to doing the same."

Harry was not laughing, the words having taken on a power of their own that he had not anticipated. And Phin, who'd correctly guessed that it might've started as a gentle father/son banter, escalated to an acting exercise next, but he could not have seen nor predicted the depth and scope of what was to follow because the wind of Harry's words took hold and flew of their own accord. So, Phin sat and said nothing. But the feelings were still whipping and swirling. And while they stung Phin in swarms of tiny choppers, he couldn't deny them. He'd never denied the truth or his father. They were the same. He wouldn't start now.

"Dad," Phin's voice was soft, almost lacy in its texture. But it was sharp as well; the fabric cutting itself on the razor's edge. "Did you see them, out there on the water? I mean, did you hear their voices?"

That would have been just like the kid, Harry thought, to take it right on the chin and then parry with not a blow, but a kiss.

"Yeah, but we have some kind of agreement and I've let them go, for the time being."

"How can you just let someone go like that? After all they...and she was to you?"

But Phin knew he was asking himself the same question and both he and Harry knew the answer. So neither of them answered at first.

"Dad, long as you're cutting a vein can I ask you about grandpa? I mean you didn't really bury him at sea, did you?"

Harry looked at his son as he had his wife when she passed. And he said no, Gramps is where he asked to be—holding up a piling down at the pier.

"Can I ask *you* a question now?" Harry's voice had gone deep and scratchy, bluesy.

"Last one, Pops. Can't keep our cook waiting."

"Do you ever think about *her*? About the killing?"

Phin knew that Harry wasn't referring to Ruth or Lonnie or Grace or Jessica or Nadine or Louella or Auntie or any of the others who'd rode in and around the wake of his past life. Harry wanted to know if Phin had come to grips with the Vietnamese woman he'd shot. It wasn't about excuses or mistakes or justifications or provocations. It was about things that happen during a war that defy and deny explanation. Between the time when the shooting starts and when it stops. But after the last canon or bullet or grenade or rocket is fired, they live on in every cell of the person who pulled the trigger. They take the form of dreams and guilt and violence and other life forms like wolves and bears and always tigers. And you can never kill them. You only make peace with them.

It's not about apologizing, it's about acknowledging. It's very simple and very hard. Most men carry it with them to their graves, shackled with feelings that are buried and glossed and reinterpreted. But they are always there. Waiting.

Phin was lucky he'd had Cobb and now Harry to push the arrows through because they were barbed. And then to pull them-and her-back out. To remember because you never forget. Only make peace with it.

"She was beautiful, wasn't she?"

And Phin said, "Yes...with long, silky black hair pulled behind her in a ponytail tied with a piece of reed, dangling out from under one of those big triangular straw hats they all wore when working out in the rice paddies. And her fingers were long and thin and white, like a piano player's, each one clutching brown fruit she had picked from a nearby tree, the sweet fruit she would offer to the hungry soldiers who'd come to save them.

"But there were no trees next to the paddies, were there, Phin?"

"No trees, just rice."

"And she was going to throw the fruit to the soldiers, wasn't she?

"Yes, but I didn't let her."

"No, you didn't let her kill your friends with that fruit, did you?'

"No, the little girl working the paddies said not to."

"And that little girl, do you remember her?" Harry asked while standing up to answer the breakfast call.

"I could feel her small brown eyes on me," Phin answered while remaining deathly still, "Even behind the tiny, slit openings. They were, telling...soft eyes, I remember. Yes, soft brown eyes."

In the background the crickets stopped chirping. Phin was going to say, did you hear that, Dad? Instead he looked over at his father and asked one more question.

"You miss him?"

Harry stood up and reached a hand down to help his son stand on his one good foot.

"Johnny knew he was leaving. That last night while you were sleeping on his floor, he came into my room and told me if I ever got to the edge of reason again, I should stick around the rim for a while on account of the view. Asked if I had an extra blanket to cover you on account it seemed like fall had finally set in Panama City Beach, Florida.

"I miss 'em all, kid. Don't matter though. I can wrap myself around the truth of them being gone today. Tomorrow's another story. And that Phin, that's something."

"Yep," Phin choked out his words, "'tis something."

EPILOGUE

The true voyage is not in seeking new landscapes but in having new eyes.

–Proust

Papayas are always sweeter in the afternoon; something about the way they hang in the tropical sun all morning, its rays pulling the nutrients up from the dark-blood earth through the trunk as it sways in the trade winds, pumping and lifting the sugars through the plant branches, out toward the thick, fiery fruit.

There's only one day at a time down here. And you don't have to worry about being somebody different tomorrow than you are today.

Lolita will never pick papayas before the sun has passed its zenith. And even then, she will sometimes wait an extra hour or so; wait until we are just about ready to have our afternoon meal. She'll reach for her reed basket and tell me, *"Voy para papaya,"* adding coyly, "the ones shaped like *ojos de Naranjo, orange eyes."* And when I see her return with that woven basket perched atop her long black hair, dancing toward me on the trail in her blue and yellow sarong, the afternoon rain moving in on cue to cool the mid-day heat as the earth soaks up the sky like the soft part of a brain soaks up memory, one hand on the basket, the other lifting a plumeria to her nose—well...I don't think of what I risked to get here or how much I had to let go. Only of what I've found.

It is a strangely comfortable thought to look at a place and feel that maybe, just maybe, you have enough good fortune left in your life to die there; that you've earned the right to do so. But earning has little to do with anything. At least it hasn't in my life.

For many years I never figured there was any logical sense to it, unless you count random senselessness, which, I suppose is a kind of order in and of itself.

Some days I think of Lonnie, living up that hill with a good man to keep her out of the tragic ditches of my dreams I'd put her in. I don't regret not going up to the door, seeing her in real time, just some illogical fallacy that began as a childhood wish. She has a new life. And so do I.

And all those months on the road, looking to make sense of what my life was and had been so that I could allow it to go forward. There was no obvious order there, either; just a wandering—a walkabout—an unfolding, and unmasking of the hope in life itself that was trying to make itself known to me. Maybe hope is an illusion after all because it takes you out of the eternal *now*. But I like faith better. It lets you move between *then* and *now* without getting your feelings hurt. Think of hope as a starter kit; maybe when you get scared and hope you don't get shot. Then you develop the beginning of faith because even if you do catch one in the chest, you believe you have a good chance at living in another world, on this planet or some place in your dreams, a place that you have faith exists.

It's like sawing soft wood—the blade goes through easy, but you're still sawing. And you need a straight line.

It's been a few years now, but back then I could never find anything beautiful or uplifting about dying and returning to our maker. I'd heard of immortality. Johnny would touch upon it from time to time, but I'd never seen it in the Nam or at a funeral or in a dead body, even when I went looking for it.

What I learned about dying I learned through living—through getting close to the ones who left me. Death on its own taught me nothing. But the process and the feelings and the unbridled richness of life bubbles right to the surface when you know that your time, or the time of one whom you've gotten close to, is close. Holding your hands inside a buddy's guts ripped open by a frag grenade; pinching off a spurting artery and talking to him just like you were speaking over the backyard fence with your garden hose bent in half to stop the water while you chat about the game or the new boat he was looking at; and lying to him that it was just a flesh wound, that he'd be getting a month in Tokyo for recovery, lucky son of a bitch; and about this one place that you knew of where the girls were soft and went down as smooth as the sake; and to hang in there because "it was nothing the docs couldn't fix" and medics were on the way, "and they'll give you some morphine and you'll feel better. Now close your eyes and get some rest, but before you do, look at me, now. *Look at me, goddamn it, don't you fucking go and die on my ass 'cuz we got stuff to do back in the world; look in my eyes...you hear me, motherfucker? You hang in there!"*

You keep lying to him until the soft sounds of heart's footsteps don't echo in synch with the thump-thump of the Huey and he won't keep his eyes open and your criteria for falsity and truth is further cultivated by the schizophrenia you embrace like a three-year-old fondling a dead sparrow.

You'll be all right, you say again, and then you hold him like you held your mamma when you got lost in the big store. And he holds you back and whispers words unnamed and unknowable.

Then the son of a bitch goes and dies.

And for a brief moment you forget his name but remember his kid's birthdate and the color he planned on painting his Chevy Camaro when he got back.

You go on living, knowing more about life because when he looked into you with those young, scared eyes, he passed along all that he knew and felt and had learnt in-country as a kind of gift that would open on its own accord, on its own time, anyplace but there.

All this he did for you because he could, because you would've done the same for him. All this happened right before that long, deep sigh.

And if perchance he screamed and called out in some language of the lost that you couldn't respond to, you chased that sound away with every ghost that came back and you purposely, palpably exorcised on the outskirts of towns like Nogales or Houston or Boston or Laramie or Durango. Like a rabid dog, you could either shoot the sounds dead or shoo them into the next town. But no more guns, please.

And so you bargained and closed your eyes and hoped for the best. Never sure. Cognitive dissonance, they call it. And you've lived with it like a forever rash until one day that three-year-old girl opened her hand to offer you the dead sparrow, only it was a yellow and white daisy.

If war is hell, then what's below that? Can you punch through and come out on the other side? On top?

❋ ❋ ❋

Things are good here. What happens from day to day still can't be called order so much as rhythm, a natural ebb and flow, a simple existence on this island off the west coast of Mexico.

An island. Ironic, but not really.

Before I left, I'd gone by the old pier. I wanted to say good bye to Dickey Riot and to say something else, though I wasn't sure just what it was. He was working in his tiny office in the back of the bait shop, talking on the phone, a thing I'd never really gained any appreciation for. There were pictures on the walls of he and I as kids: skinny, brown-skinned little boys with peeling noses and sunny hair. In one image, we were holding up our prized catch of the day—two 8-inch perch dangling from the poles dad had made us out of bamboo. In another we were older, sitting up on the rail of the pier, looking defiant, purposely bored, in cut-off Wranglers and our hair falling across our eyes. There was another with just Gillie and me on the beach; no towels or radios or umbrellas. We never took any of that stuff down there, always figured if we needed something we'd come across it.

I stood up and studied the pictures, realized how much Gillie looked like our mother, how my life could've been so different. Right then I was wishing the past would come back and hold me on its knee. A second later I was hoping that this other past would pass quicker. Something chronic was trying to pry its way back inside my head. I looked at a picture of all of us: Gillie, Dickey, me, a couple other kids whose names I could remember, and when I opened up just a little, a fresh breeze came in through Dickey's widow and blew my fears out the other side. There weren't even any footsteps on the floor. I felt airy, like the good witch Glenda from the *Wizard of Oz*.

"Dickey," I said after he'd hung up and told me I was risking things by showing myself in public around this town.

"You aren't really in these photos, still being dead and all."

"Sure I am. Look there and there."

He pointed to where a few parts of me stood off to the side or in the background, just a half of a smile or baby teeth trying to peek out behind lips.

"No, you're not really *in* the pictures."

"Yeah, well, we were kids." I let it go; he knew what I meant.

"Seriously, Phin," the undeniable pragmatism returning. "People read your obit, they cried. You're dead, my old friend. You can't just come home and go about your old life after we've burnt the landscape behind you."

I looked out the window. There was an odd collection of characters moving in and around the end of the pier. They could've come out of a Hemingway novel or a play written by Coleridge. They were dried-up men fishing and drinking warmed-over coffee, young mothers walking their kids while their husbands were off working at jobs that made ends meet, but just barely. There were tourists from the big new condo projects, second-home owners from Mobile and Knoxville and Houston. Some were unaccountable-looking creatures that held no purchase on me, even if I tried to imagine their lives beyond what they'd shown to me. But a few seemed as if I could strike up a conversation with them and pass the morning pleasantly. I recognized exactly none of them. And I would imagine they wouldn't recognize me. I was dead. The Man said so. I only looked like the kid who used to spend time down this way. Just a ghost. A sad, funny resemblance whose grandfather helped build this pier and supports it still.

"I'm leaving in the morning with Lolita."

"Figured as much. Being dead is an occupation in itself, I suppose. Yep, this place has changed so much you can't even tell that it's different."

Dickey was trying to say something, but it wasn't coming out. I tried to pry it loose by projecting my own thoughts into the form that Dickey was trying to shape.

"Yeah, well, privacy is something you can buy, but you can't sell it back. Dickey, I been changing my opinion of life like tires and light bulbs. But somehow, I've kept my own form of certainty intact. Or it's kept me intact. And that sureness means that I have to keep going deeper, further into the light."

"Going south then?"

"As close to the equator as we can. Gonna rid myself of that malignant influence for good. Let the sun bake it right out of me. Least I'm gonna try because a dragon lives forever. What about you? You gonna sit here and sell smelt and cigarettes the rest of your life?"

Dickey knew it was neither challenge nor attack; just a prompt.

"But not so little boys" Dickey followed the song reference with the next line and then asked, "You got a minute?"

"Yeah, sure. Do you have a hat and sunglasses I can hide under?" I asked, only half joking.

We walked out onto the pier and into the private struggles of those who'd come out onto this wooden appendage to lose their troubles for a while.

"Phin, I've lost my own sympathy for the devil these past few years. Been walking that tightrope between the conspiracy of fear that lodged itself inside me when those pictures were taken and the great wide-open of doing right by the right people. But where there's no place far enough away for you, and no place is as good and close for me as this spot where we stand."

Dickey looked at me and I could swear he was taller than I remembered. Then he took his wallet out of his back pocket and handed it to me. He removed his shoes and set them on a bench next to the peeling paint and seagull shit.

Dickey Riot smiled at me for longer than seemed appropriate and set one foot on the rail and then the other. Then he jumped. Barely made a splash at all.

I waited for him to come up. People around pointed and spoke in hushed tones and one lady said, "Oh my good God." Seconds passed and then more seconds and I started to take off my boots and climb the rail.

A voice came from around the side of the pier where I wasn't looking; where none of the witnesses were. The head bobbed and weaved in the surf like a fighter, comfortable and with timing.

"Hey, little Jackie Paper," Dickey called up to me. "You ain't the only one been opening doors on themselves. Go find yourself on the great blue firebreak scattered with green dots, land yourself an island with a barrier reef; there's places I ain't looked under my pillow."

✳ ✳ ✳

Fighting for your sanity is a different war all together, a sustained, protracted jungle warfare that somehow seems at peace within the vines and branched synapses of your brain. But it's not like you can go to safety behind your own lines for R&R: you carry it around with you, like dog tags or dreams. There is no "peace with honor," just one more form of mutual détente.

I've concluded that it was all irrevocably predetermined. Maybe not genuine in my reflection of the moment, but truthful in the end because at some point, and I don't know exactly when, I stopped looking for answers. I stopped fighting and won—let the devil's germs and guns and concerns move in the front door and on out the back. *More Buddha, less Beowulf*, as Gerald loved to say.

Those ideas live in me like an ageless lap dog, forever loyal and available. Life down here is one long poem where I can bring up the ghosts one at a time and write them a shape, shake hands, and then wait for the trades to blow them away. Like Dad and Gerald and Blackie and DuPuis and the others, they still visit, but they don't stay.

There was one day in particular in my second tour. A wispy layer of clouds hovering above our post that seemed to be letting in only enough light to make you wish for hot sun or cold rain. I was short-timed, just thirty days and a wake up. The radio kept chattering on that the treaty in Paris was close enough to be signed and broken. And a letter from my dad finally reached me; it was a rare thing, mostly because he wasn't a great letter guy.

In his scratchy pencil he spoke of my mother lying in the garden, sick from a broken heart and the vessels it fed and, I thought maybe I would be happier as well, if plain dead. As the letters melted off the page, I didn't seem to exist anymore; my sense of self had evaporated into thin air, cigarette smoke rings blown haphazardly.

I fingered the .45mm at my side.

But somewhere from out of that smoky air came a tangible ideal, a rope to pull me up or hang myself with. It came up from that soft part of my brain and from a childhood conversation with Johnny Cobb and a long stretch of desert highway I'd wanted to explore: our life is all one human, whole, and if we are to have any real knowledge of it, we must see it as such. I'd read that during the war, believe it still.

And I holstered my gun, put it away, and immersed myself in reality, dark as it was. Life, if we cut it up, dies in the process, killing those around us, too, plain as day. War taught me that.

Still, some nights when I lie in our hammock listening to the jungle sounds and smells, at least I know which questions might come looking for me. They're the questions that will never be answered. And with that, oddly, there is some comfort.

And so I close my eyes, weave my arms and legs through Lolita like all those vines of my past, and let my mind take me where it will.

Fear turns men into coyotes, poisons their hearts. I guess that whomever lit my flame certainly had the right to blow it out.

The dream that reflects my life ends not so much in my memory's past, but in the wake of my experience, the footprints that led me to this place.

I've come to believe that the best stories always begin at the end, or at least you trust the teller because if something should happen while they're telling it, at least you'll know how it turns out and you won't have to wander around for years looking for the unquestionable answers in the middle.

And my dad, Harry? I must believe that he was swept in a warm, earthy tide, creating its own fire. And it thawed the sea he had frozen around his heart.

I dream that Johnny is pleased.

I hope that God is too.